Ruth Rendell

INSPECTOR WEXFORD

Ruth Rendell

INSPECTOR WEXFORD

A New Lease of Death

The Speaker of Mandarin

Wolf to the Slaughter

Put On By Cunning

CRESSET EDITIONS

This edition first published in 1997 by Cresset Editions,
an imprint of Random House UK Ltd,
20 Vauxhall Bridge Road, London SW1V 2SA

© Kingsmarkham Enterprises Ltd 1997

A New Lease of Death copyright © Ruth Rendell 1969
The Speaker of Mandarin copyright © Kingsmarkham
Enterprises Ltd 1983
Wolf to the Slaughter copyright © Ruth Rendell 1967
Put on by Cunning copyright © Kingsmarkham
Enterprises Ltd 1981

First published by Hutchinson Ltd.

0 7529 9906 0

Printed and bound in Great Britain by
Mackays of Chatham

CONTENTS

A New Lease
of Death

For my Father and Simon

CHAPTER ONE

The laws of the Realm may punish Christian men with death for heinous and grievous offences.

The Thirty-nine Articles

It was five in the morning. Inspector Burden had seen more dawns than most men, but he had never quite become jaundiced by them, especially summer dawns. He liked the stillness, the sight of the little country towns in a depopulated state, the hard blue light that was of the same shade and intensity as the light at dusk but without dusk's melancholy.

The two men they had been questioning about last night's fight in one of Kingsmarkham's cafés had confessed separately and almost simultaneously just a quarter of an hour before. Now they were locked into two stark white cells on the ground floor of this incongruously modern police station. Burden stood by the window in Wexford's office, looking at the sky which had the peculiar greenish tint of aquamarine. A flock of birds flying in dense formation crossed it. They reminded Burden of his childhood when, as at dawn, everything had seemed bigger, clearer and of more significance than it did today. Tired and a little sickened, he opened the window to get rid of cigarette smoke and the sweaty smell of youths who wore leather jackets in the height of summer.

Outside in the corridor he could hear Wexford saying good night — or good morning — to Colonel Griswold, the Chief Constable. Burden wondered if Griswold had guessed when he arrived just before ten with a long spiel about stamping out hooliganism that he was in for an all-night session. That, he thought unfairly, was where meddling got you.

The heavy front door clanged and Griswold's car started. Burden watched it move off the forecourt, past the great stone urns filled with pink geraniums and into Kingsmarkham High

Street. The Chief Constable was driving himself. Burden saw with approval and grudging amusement that Griswold drove at just about twenty-eight miles per hour until he reached the black and white derestriction sign. Then the car gathered speed and flashed away out of sight along the empty country road that led to Pomfret.

He turned round when he heard Wexford come in. The Chief Inspector's heavy grey face was a little greyer than usual, but he showed no other sign of tiredness and his eyes, dark and hard as basalt, showed a gleam of triumph. He was a big man with big features and a big intimidating voice. His grey suit — one of a series of low fastening, double-breasted affairs — appeared more shabby and wrinkled than ever today. But it suited Wexford, being not unlike an extension of his furrowed pachydermatous skin.

'Another job jobbed,' he said, 'as the old woman said when she jobbed the old man's eye out.'

Burden bore with such vulgarisms stoically. He knew that they were meant to horrify him; they always succeeded. He made his thin lips crease into a tight smile. Wexford handed him a blue envelope and he was glad of the diversion to hide his slight embarrassment.

'Griswold's just given me this,' Wexford said. 'At five in the morning. No sense of timing.'

Burden glanced at the Essex postmark.

'Is that the man he was on about earlier, sir?'

'Well, I don't have fanmail from beautiful olde worlde Thringford as a general rule, do I, Mike? This is the Rev. Mr Archery all right, taking advantage of the Old Pals' Act.' He lowered himself into one of the rather flimsy chairs and it gave the usual protesting creak. Wexford had what his junior called a love-hate relationship with those chairs and indeed with all the aggressively modern furnishings of his office. The glossy black floor, the square of nylon carpet, the chairs with their sleek chrome legs, the primrose venetian blinds — all these in Wexford's estimation were not 'serviceable', they were dust-traps and they were 'chi-chi'. At the same time he took in them an enormous half-secret pride. They had their effect. They served to impress visiting strangers such as the writer of this letter Wexford was now taking from its envelope.

It too was written on rather thick blue paper. In a painfully authentic upper-class accent, the Chief Inspector said affectedly, 'May as well get on to the Chief Constable of Mid-Sussex, my dear. We were up at Oxford together, don't you know?' He squeezed his face into a kind of snarling grin. 'All among the bloody dreaming spires,' he said. 'I hate that sort of thing.'

'Were they?'

'Were they what?'

'At Oxford together?'

'I don't know. Something like that. It may have been the playing fields of Eton. All Griswold said was, "Now we've got those villains wrapped up, I'd like you to have a look at a letter from a very good friend of mine called Archery. Excellent fellow, one of the best. This enclosure's for you. I'd like you to give him all the help you can. I've a notion it's got something to do with that scoundrel Painter." '

'Who's Painter?'

'Villain who got the chop about fifteen or sixteen years ago,' said Wexford laconically. 'Let's see what the parson has to say, shall we?'

Burden looked over his shoulder. The letter was headed St Columba's Vicarage, Thringford, Essex. The greek e's awakened in him a small hostility. Wexford read it aloud.

' "Dear sir, I hope you will forgive me for taking up your valuable time . . ." Don't have much choice, do I? ". . . but I regard this matter as being of some urgency. Col. Griswold, the Chief Constable of blah blah and so on, has very kindly told me you are the gentleman who may be able to assist me in this problem so I am taking the liberty, having first consulted him, of writing to you." ' He cleared his throat and loosened his crumpled grey tie. 'Takes a hell of a time coming to the point, I must say. Ah, here we go. "You will remember the case of Herbert Arthur Painter . . ." I *will*. "I understand you were in charge of it. I therefore supposed I should come to you before pursuing certain enquiries which, much against my will, I am compelled to make." '

'Compelled?'

'That's what the man says. Doesn't say why. The rest's a load of compliments and can he come and see me tomorrow —

3

no, today. He's going to phone this morning, but he "anticipates my willingness to meet him".' He glanced at the window to see where the sun was coming up over York Street and with one of his distorted quotations, said, 'I suppose he's sleeping in Elysium at this moment, crammed with distressful cold mutton or whatever parsons go to bed on.'

'What's it all about?'

'O God, Mike, it's obvious, isn't it? You don't want to take any notice of this "being compelled" and "against his will" stuff. I don't suppose his stipend amounts to much. He probably writes true crime stories in between early Communion and the Mothers' Meeting. He must be getting desperate if he reckons on titillating the mass appetite by resurrecting Painter.'

Burden said thoughtfully, 'I seem to remember the case. I'd just left school . . .'

'And it inspired your choice of a career, did it?' Wexford mocked. ' "What are you going to be, son?" "I'm going to be a detective, Dad." '

In his five years as Wexford's right-hand man, Burden had grown immune to his teasing. He knew he was a kind of safety valve, the stooge perhaps on whom Wexford could vent his violent and sometimes shocking sense of humour. The people of this little town, indiscriminately referred to by Wexford as 'our customers', had, unless suspected of felony, to be spared. Burden was there to take the overflow of his chief's rage, ridicule and satire. Now he was cast as the sponge to soak up the scorn that was rightly the due of Griswold and Griswold's friend.

He looked shrewdly at Wexford. After a trying, frustrating day and night, this letter was the last straw. Wexford was suddenly tense with irritation, his skin more deeply wrinkled than usual, his whole body flexed with the anger that would not suffer fools gladly. That tension must find release.

'This Painter thing,' Burden said slyly, slipping into his role of therapist, 'a bit run of the mill, wasn't it? I followed it in the papers because it was the big local sensation. I don't remember it was remarkable in any other way.'

Wexford slipped the letter back into its envelope and put it in a drawer. His movements were precise and under a tight control. One wrong word, Burden thought, and he'd have torn

4

it up, chucked the pieces on the floor and left them to the mercy of the cleaner. His words had apparently been as right as possible under the circumstances for Wexford said in a sharp cool voice, 'It was remarkable to me.'

'Because you handled it?'

'Because it was the first murder case I ever handled on my own. It was remarkable to Painter because it hanged him and to his widow, I daresay. I suppose it shook her a bit as far as anything could shake that girl.'

Rather nervously Burden watched him observe the cigarette burn one of the men they had been interviewing had made in the lemon-coloured leather of a chair seat. He waited for the explosion. Instead Wexford said indifferently:

'Haven't you got a home to go to?'

'Too late now,' said Burden, stifling a yawn that threatened. 'Besides, my wife's away at the seaside.'

A strongly uxorious man, he found his bungalow like a morgue when Jean and the children were absent. This was a side of his character that afforded Wexford many opportunities for quips and snide remarks, this coupled with his comparative youth, his solid stick-in-the-mud nature and a certain primness of outlook. But all Wexford said was, 'I forgot.'

He was good at his job. The big ugly man respected him for that. Although he might deride, Wexford appreciated the advantage of having a deputy whose grave good looks were attractive to women. Seated opposite that ascetic face, warmed by a compassion Wexford called 'softness', they were more inclined to open their hearts than to a majestic fifty-five-year-old heavyweight. His personality, however, was not strong and his superior effaced him. Now, in order to channel off that sharp-edged vitality, he was going to have to risk a rebuke for stupidity.

He risked it. 'If you're going to have to argue the toss with this Archery, wouldn't it be a good idea if we had a re-cap of the facts?'

'We?'

'Well, you then, sir. You must be a bit rusty yourself on the case after so long.'

The outburst came with an undercurrent of laughter. 'God

Almighty! D'you think I can't see your brain working? When I want a psychiatrist I'll hire a professional.' He paused and the laughter became a wry grin. 'O.K., it might help me . . .' But Burden had made the mistake of relaxing too soon. 'To get the facts straight for Mr Bloody Archery, I mean,' Wexford snapped. 'But there's no mystery, you know, no cunning little red herrings. Painter did it all right.' He pointed eastwards out of the window. The broad Sussex sky was becoming suffused with rose and gold, bands of soft creamy pink like strokes from a water-colour brush. 'That's as sure as the sun's rising now,' he said. 'There never was any doubt. Herbert Arthur Painter killed his ninety-year-old employer by hitting her over the head with an axe and he did it for two hundred pounds. He was a brutal savage moron. I read in the paper the other day that the Russians call anti-social people 'unpersons' and that just about describes him. Funny sort of character for a parson to champion.'

'If he's championing him.'

'We shall see,' said Wexford.

They stood in front of the map that was attached to the yellow 'cracked ice' wallpaper.

'She was killed in her own home, wasn't she?' Burden asked. 'One of those big houses off the Stowerton road?'

The map showed the whole of this rather sleepy country district. Kingsmarkham, a market town of some twelve thousand inhabitants, lay in the centre, its streets coloured in brown and white, its pastoral environs green with the blotches of dark veridian that denoted woodland. Roads ran from it as from the meshy heart of a spider's web, one leading to Pomfret in the south, another to Sewingbury in the north-east. The scattered villages, Flagford, Clusterwell and Forby, were tiny flies on this web.

'The house is called Victor's Piece,' said Wexford. 'Funny sort of name. Some general built it for himself after the Ashanti Wars.'

'And it's just about here.' Burden put his finger on a vertical strand of the web that led from Kingsmarkham to Stowerton, lying due north. He pondered and light dawned. 'I

6

think I know it,' he said. 'Hideous dump with a lot of green woodwork all over it. It was an old people's home up until last year. I suppose they'll pull it down.'

'I daresay. There are a couple of acres of land to it. If you've got the picture we may as well sit down.'

Burden had moved his chair to the window. There was something consoling and at the same time rejuvenating in watching the unfolding of what was going to be a lovely day. On the fields tree shadows lay long and densely blue and bright new light glinted on the slate roofs of ancient houses. Pity he hadn't been able to get away with Jean. The sunlight and the fresh heady air turned his thoughts towards holidays and prevented him from recalling details of this case that had long ago shocked Kingsmarkham. He searched his memory and found to his shame that he could not even remember the murdered woman's name.

'What was she called?' he asked Wexford. 'A foreign name, wasn't it? Porto or Primo something?'

'Primero. Rose Isabel Primero. That was her married name. Far from being foreign, she'd been brought up at Forby Hall. Her people were by way of being squires of Forby.'

Burden knew Forby well. What tourists there were in this agricultural country with neither seaside nor downs, castles nor cathedrals, made a point of going to Forby. The guide books listed it absurdly as the fifth prettiest village in England. Every local newsagent's contained postcards of its church. Burden himself regarded it with a certain affection because its inhabitants had shown themselves almost totally devoid of criminal tendencies.

'This Archery could be a relative,' he suggested. 'Maybe he wants some gen for his family archives.'

'I doubt it,' Wexford said, basking in the sun like a huge grey cat. 'The only relatives she had were her three grandchildren. Roger Primero, the grandson, lives at Forby Hall now. Didn't inherit it, had to buy it. I don't know the details.'

'There used to be a family called Kynaston at Forby Hall, or so Jean's mother says. Mind you, that was years and years ago.'

'That's right,' Wexford said with a hint of impatience in his

7

rumbling bass voice. 'Mrs Primero was born a Kynaston and she was going on for forty when she married Dr Ralph Primero. I imagine her people looked on it a bit askance — this was at the turn of the century, remember.'

'What was he, a G.P.?'

'Some sort of specialist, I think. It was when he retired that they came to live at Victor's Piece. They weren't all that well-off, you know. When the doctor died in the thirties Mrs Primero was left with about ten thousand pounds to live on. There was one child of the marriage, a son, but he'd died soon after his father.'

'D'you mean she was living alone in that great place? At her age?'

Wexford pursed his lips, reminiscing. Burden knew his chief's almost supernatural memory. When he was sufficiently interested he had the nearest thing to total recall. 'She had one maid,' Wexford said. 'Her name was — is, she's still alive — her name was Alice Flower. She was a good bit younger than her employer, seventy odd, and she'd been with Mrs Primero for about fifty years. A real ancient retainer of the old school. Living like that, you might think they'd have become friends rather than mistress and servant, but Alice kept to her place and they were 'Madam' and 'Alice' to each other till the day Mrs Primero died. I knew Alice by sight. She was quite a local character when she came into town to do their shopping, particularly when Painter started bringing her in in Mrs Primero's Daimler. D'you remember how nursemaids used to look? No, you wouldn't. You're too young. Well, Alice always wore a long navy coat and what's called a 'decent' navy felt hat. She and Painter were both servants, but Alice put herself miles above him. She'd pull her rank on him and give him his orders just like Mrs Primero herself. He was Bert to his wife and his cronies but Alice called him 'Beast'. Not to his face, mind. She wouldn't have quite dared that.'

'You mean she was frightened of him?'

'In a way. She hated him and resented his being there. I wonder if I've still got that cutting.' Wexford opened the bottom drawer of his desk, the one where he kept personal, semi-official things, grotesqueries that had interested him. He hadn't much

8

hope of finding what he sought. At the time of Mrs Primero's murder Kingsmarkham police had been housed in an old yellow brick building in the centre of town. That had been pulled down four or five years ago and replaced by this block of startling modernity on the outskirts. The cutting had very probably got lost in the move from the high pitch pine desk to this one of lacquered rosewood. He leafed through notes, letters, odd little souvenirs, finally surfacing with a grin of triumph.

'There you are, the "unperson" himself. Good-looking if you like the type. Herbert Arthur Painter, late of the Fourteenth Army in Burma. Twenty-five years old, engaged by Mrs Primero as chauffeur, gardener and odd-job man.'

The cutting was from the *Sunday Planet,* several columns of type surrounding a double-column block. It was a clear photograph and Painter's eyes were staring straight at the camera.

'Funny, that,' said Wexford. 'He always looked you straight in the eye. Supposed to denote honesty, if you've ever heard such a load of rubbish.'

Burden must have seen the picture before, but he had entirely forgotten it. It was a large well-made face with a straight though fleshy nose, spread at the nostrils. Painter had the thick curved lips that on a man are a coarse parody of a woman's mouth, a flat high brow and short tightly waving hair. The waves were so tightly crimped that they looked as if they must have pulled the skin and pained the scalp.

'He was tall and well-built,' Wexford went on. 'Face like a handsome overgrown pug, don't you think? He'd been in the Far East during the war, but if the heat and the privation had taken it out of him it didn't show by then. He had a sort of glistening good health about him like a shire horse. Sorry to use all these animal metaphors, but Painter was like an animal.'

'How did Mrs Primero come to take him on?'

Wexford took the cutting from him, looked at it for a moment and folded it up.

'From the time the doctor died,' he said, 'until 1947 Mrs Primero and Alice Flower struggled to keep the place going, pulling up a few weeds here and there, getting a man in when they wanted a shelf fixed. You can imagine the kind of thing.

They had a succession of women up from Kingsmarkham to help with the housework but sooner or later they all left to go into the factories. The place started going to rack and ruin. Not surprising when you think that by the end of the war Mrs Primero was in her middle eighties and Alice nearly seventy. Besides, leaving her age out of it, Mrs Primero never touched the place as far as housework went. She hadn't been brought up to it and she wouldn't have known a duster from an antimacassar.'

'Bit of a tartar, was she?'

'She was what God and her background had made her,' Wexford said gravely but with the faintest suspicion of irony in his voice. 'I never saw her till she was dead. She was stubborn, a bit mean, what nowadays is called "reactionary", inclined to be an autocrat and very much monarch of all she surveyed. I'll give you a couple of examples. When her son died he left his wife and kids very badly off. I don't know the ins and outs of it, but Mrs Primero was quite willing to help financially provided it was on her terms. The family was to come and live with her and so on. Still, I daresay she couldn't afford to keep up two establishments. The other thing was that she'd been a very keen churchwoman. When she got too old to go she insisted on Alice going in her place. Like a sort of whipping boy. But she had her affections. She adored the grandson, Roger, and she had one close friend. We'll come to that later.

'As you know, there was an acute housing shortage after the war and a hell of a servant problem too. Mrs Primero was an intelligent old woman and she got to thinking how she could use one to solve the other. In the grounds of Victor's Piece was a coach house with a sort of loft over the top of it. The place for the coach was used to house the aforesaid Daimler. No one had driven it since the doctor died — Mrs Primero couldn't drive and, needless to say, Alice couldn't either. There was precious little petrol about but you could get your ration, enough to do the shopping and take a couple of old dears for a weekly jaunt around the lanes.'

'So Alice was that much of a friend?' Burden put in.

Wexford said solemnly, 'A lady can be accompanied by her maid when she goes driving. Anyway, Mrs Primero put an advert in the *Kingsmarkham Chronicle* for a young able-bodied man, willing to do the garden, perform odd jobs, maintain and drive the car in exchange for a flat and three pounds a week.'

'*Three pounds?*' Burden was a non-smoker and no lover of extravagant living, but he knew from doing his wife's weekend shopping what a little way three pounds went.

'Well, it was worth a good bit more in those days, Mike,' Wexford said almost apologetically. 'Mrs Primero had the loft painted up, divided into three rooms and piped for water. It wasn't Dolphin Square but, God, people were glad of one room back in 1947! She got a lot of answers but for some reason — God knows *what* reason — she picked Painter. At the trial Alice said she thought the fact that he had a wife and a baby daughter would keep him steady. Depends what you mean by steady, doesn't it?'

Burden shifted his chair out of the sun. 'Was the wife employed by Mrs Primero too?'

'No, just Painter. She'd got this little kid, you see. She was only about two when they came. If she'd worked up at the house she'd have had to bring the child with her. Mrs Primero would never have stood for that. As far as she was concerned between her and the Painters there was a great gulf fixed. I gathered she'd hardly exchanged more than a couple of words with Mrs Painter all the time Painter was there and as for the little girl — her name was Theresa, I think — she barely knew of her existence.'

'She doesn't sound a very nice sort of woman,' Burden said doubtfully.

'She was typical of her age and class,' Wexford said tolerantly. 'Don't forget she was a daughter of the lord of the manor when lords of the manor still counted for something. To her Mrs Painter was comparable to a tenant's wife. I've no doubt that if Mrs Painter had been ill she'd have sent old Alice over with a bowl of soup and some blankets. Besides, Mrs Painter kept herself to herself. She was very pretty, very quiet and with a sort of deadly respectability about her. She was a bit scared of Painter which wasn't hard to understand, she being so small and Painter such a great hulking brute. When I talked to her after the murder I noticed she'd got bruises on her arm, too many bruises for her just to have got them through the usual kitchen accidents, and I wouldn't mind betting her husband used to knock her about.'

'So, in fact,' Burden said, 'they were two completely separate units. Mrs Primero and her maid living alone at Victor's Piece, the Painter family in their own home at the bottom of the garden.'

'I don't know about "bottom of the garden". The coach house was about a hundred feet from the back door of the big house. Painter only went up there to carry in the coal and receive his instructions.'

'Ah,' said Burden, 'there was some complicated business about coal, I seem to remember. Wasn't it more or less the crux of the whole thing?'

'Painter was supposed to chop wood and carry coal,' Wexford continued. 'Alice was past carrying coal and Painter was supposed to bring a scuttleful at mid-day — they never lit a fire before that — and another one at six-thirty. Now, he never objected to the gardening or the car maintenance, but for some reason he drew the line at the coal. He did it — apart from frequent lapses — but he was always grumbling about it. The mid-day duty cut across his dinner time, he said, and he didn't like turning out on winter evenings. Couldn't he bring two scuttles at eleven? But Mrs Primero wouldn't have that. She said she wasn't going to have her drawing room turned into a railway yard.'

Burden smiled. His tiredness had almost worn off. Given breakfast, a shave and a shower down, he would be a new man. He glanced at his watch, then across the High Street to where the blinds were going up on the Carousel Café.

'I could do with a cup of coffee,' he said.

'Two minds with but a single thought. Root someone out and send them over.'

Wexford stood up and stretched, tightened his tie and smoothed back the hair that was too sparse to become untidy. The coffee arrived in wax cups with plastic spoons and little cubes of wrapped sugar.

'That's better,' said Wexford. 'D'you want me to go on?' Burden nodded.

'By September 1950 Painter had been working for Mrs Primero for three years. The arrangement appeared to work pretty well apart from the difficulties Painter made about the coal. He never brought it in without complaining and he was always asking for a rise.'

'I suppose he thought she was rolling in money?'

'Of course, he couldn't have known what she'd got in the bank or in shares or whatever it was. On the other hand it was an open secret she kept money in the house.'

'In a safe, d'you mean?'

'Not on your life. You know these old girls. Some of it was in drawers stuffed into paper bags, some of it in old handbags.'

With a feat of memory Burden said suddenly, 'And one of those handbags contained *the* two hundred pounds?'

'It did,' Wexford said grimly. 'Whatever she might have been able to afford, Mrs Primero refused to raise Painter's wages. If he didn't like the set-up he could go, but that would mean giving up the flat.

'Being a very old woman, Mrs Primero felt the cold and she liked to start fires in September. Painter thought this unnecessary and he made the usual fuss about it . . .'

He stopped as the telephone rang and he took the receiver himself. Burden had no idea from Wexford's reiterated, 'Yes, yes . . . all right,' who it could be. He finished his coffee with some distaste. The rim of the wax cup had become soggy. Wexford dropped the phone.

'My wife,' he said. 'Am I dead? Have I forgotten I've got a home of my own? She's run out of housekeeping and she can't find the cheque book.' He chuckled, felt in his pocket and produced it. 'No wonder. I'll have to nip back.' He added with sudden kindness, 'Go home and have a bit of shut-eye, why don't you?'

'I don't like being left in the air,' Burden grumbled. 'Now I know how my kids feel when I break off in the middle of a bedtime story.'

Wexford began bundling things into his briefcase.

'Leaving out all the circumstantial stuff,' he said, 'there isn't much more. I told you it was straightforward. It was the evening of September 24th it happened, a cold wet Sunday. Mrs

13

Primero had sent Alice off to church. She went at about a quarter past six, Painter being due to bring the coal at half past. He brought it all right and departed two hundred pounds to the good.'

'I'd like to hear the circumstantial stuff,' Burden said.

Wexford was at the door now.

'To be continued in our next,' he grinned. 'You can't say I'm leaving you in suspense.' The grin faded and his face hardened. 'Mrs Primero was found at seven. She was in the drawing room lying on the floor by the fireplace in a great pool of blood. There was blood on the walls and on her armchair, and in the hearth was a blood-stained wood chopper.'

CHAPTER TWO

When sentence is given upon him let him be condemned ...
let his children be fatherless and his wife a widow.

Psalm 109, appointed for the 22nd Day

The nap Wexford had prescribed for him would have been
attractive on a dull day, but not this morning when the sky was
blue and cloudless and the sun promised tropical heat by midday.
Moreover, Burden remembered that he had not made his bed for
three days. Better have that shower and that shave instead.

After a canteen breakfast of two eggs and a couple of
rashers of the greenback he liked, he had made up his mind
what he was going to do. An hour could easily be spared. He
drove northwards along the High Street with all the car
windows down, past the shops, over the Kingsbrook Bridge,
past the Olive and Dove and out on to the Stowerton road.
Apart from a new house here and there, a supermarket on the
site of the old police station, and aggressive road signs all over
the place, things had not changed much in sixteen years. The
meadows, the tall trees burdened with the heavy foliage of July,
the little weatherboard cottages were much the same as when
Alice Flower had seen them on her shopping trips in the
Daimler. There would have been less traffic then, he thought.
He braked, pulled in and raised his eyebrows at the youth on a
motor-bike who, overtaking the oncoming stream, had missed
him by inches.

The lane where Victor's Piece was must be somewhere
about here. Those circumstantial details Wexford had been so
tantalising about were coming back to him from his own
memory. Surely he had read about a bus stop and a telephone
box at the end of the lane? Would these be the meadows he
remembered reading that Painter had crossed, desperate to
conceal a bundle of bloodstained clothing?

15

Here was the phone box now. He indicated left and turned slowly into the lane. For a short way its surface was metalled, then it petered out into a track ending in a gate. There were only three houses: a white-plastered semi-detached pair and opposite them the late Victorian pile he had described as 'a hideous dump'.

He had never been as near to it as this before, but he saw nothing to make him change his opinion. The roof of grey slates had been constructed — tortured almost — into a number of steep gables. Two of these dominated the front of the house, but there was a third on the right hand side and out of it grew another smaller one that apparently overlooked the back. Each gable was criss-crossed with timbering, some of it inexpertly carved into chevrons and all painted a dull bottle green. In places the plaster between the wood had fallen away, exposing rough pinkish brickwork. Ivy, the same shade of green, spread its flat leaves and its rope-like grey tendrils from the foot of the downstairs windows to the highest gable where a lattice flapped open. There it had crept and burrowed into the mealy wall, prising the window frame away from the bricks.

Burden observed the garden with a countryman's eye. Never had he seen such a fine selection of weeds. The fertile black soil, cultivated and tended for many years, now nourished docks with leaves as thick and glossy as rubber plants, puce-headed thistles, nettles four feet tall. The gravel paths were choked with grass and mildewed groundsel. Only the clarity of the air and the soft brilliance of sunlight prevented the place from being actually sinister.

The front door was locked. No doubt this window beside it belonged to the drawing room. Burden could not help wondering with a certain wry humour what insensitive administrator had decreed that this scene of an old woman's murder should be for years the home — indeed the last refuge — of other old women. But they were gone now. The place looked as if it had been empty for years.

Through the window he could see a large shadowy room. In the grate of the amber-coloured marble fireplace someone had prudently placed crumpled newspaper to catch the drifts of soot. Wexford had said there had been blood all over that

16

fireplace. There, just in front of the copper kerb, was where the body must have lain.

He made his way round the side, pushing through a shrubbery where elders and strong little birches were threatening to oust the lilac. The panes in the kitchen casement were blurred with dirt and there was no kitchen door, only a back door that apparently opened off the end of the central passage. The Victorians, he reflected, were not too hot on design. Two doors with a straight passage between them! The draught would be appalling.

By now he was in the back garden but he literally could not see the wood for the trees. Nature had gone berserk at Victor's Piece and the coach house itself was almost totally obscured by creeper. He strolled across the shady flagged yard, made cool by the jutting walls of the house, and found himself skirting a conservatory, attached apparently to a kind of morning or breakfast room. It housed a vine, long dead and quite leafless.

So that was Victor's Piece. Pity he couldn't get inside, but he would, in any case, have to get back. Out of long habit — and partly to set a good example — he had closed all the windows of his car and locked the doors. Inside it was like an oven. He drove out of the broken gateway, into the lane and joined the traffic stream on the Stowerton road.

A greater contrast between the building he had left and the building he entered could hardly have been found. Fine weather suited Kingsmarkham Police Station. Wexford sometimes said that the architect of this new building must have designed it while holidaying in the South of France. It was white, boxy, unnecessarily vast and ornamented here and there with frescoes that owed something to the Elgin marbles.

On this July morning its whiteness glared and glistened. But if its façade seemed to welcome and bask in the sun its occupants did not. There was far too much glass. All right, said Wexford, for hothouse plants or tropical fish, but a mixed blessing for an elderly Anglo-Saxon policeman with high blood pressure and a low resistance to heat. The telephone receiver slid about in his large hand and when he had finished talking to Henry Archery he pulled down the venetian blinds.

'Heat wave's coming,' he said to Burden. 'I reckon your wife's picked a good week.'

Burden looked up from the statement he had begun to read. Lean as a greyhound, his face thin and acute, he often had the hound's instinct for scenting the unusual, coupled with a man's eager imagination.

'Things always seem to happen in a heat wave,' he said. 'Our sort of things, I mean.'

'Get away,' said Wexford. 'Things are always happening around here.' He raised his spiky toothbrush brows. 'What's happening today,' he said, 'is Archery. He's coming at two.'

'Did he say what it's all about?'

'He's leaving that for this afternoon. Very la-di-da manner he's got with him. All part of the mystique of how to be a gentleman on nothing a year. One thing, he's got a transcript of the trial so I shan't have to go through the whole thing again.'

'That'll have cost him something. He must be keen.'

Wexford looked at his watch and rose. 'Got to get over to the court,' he said. 'Polish off those villains who lost me my night's sleep. Look, Mike, I reckon we deserve a bit of gracious living and I don't fancy the Carousel's steak pie for my lunch. What about popping into the Olive and booking a table for one sharp?'

Burden smiled. It suited him well enough. Once in a blue moon Wexford would insist on their lunching or even dining in comparative style.

'It shall be done,' he said.

The Olive and Dove is the best hostelry in Kingsmarkham that can properly be called an hotel. By a stretch of the imagination the Queen's Head might be described as an inn, but the Dragon and the Crusader cannot claim to be more than pubs. The Olive, as locals invariably call it, is situated in the High Street at the Stowerton end of Kingsmarkham, facing the exquisite Georgian residence of Mr Missal, the Stowerton car dealer. It is partly Georgian itself, but it is a hybrid structure with lingering relics of Tudor and a wing that claims to be pre-Tudor. In every respect it conforms to what nice middle-class people mean when they talk about a 'nice' hotel. There are always three waiters, the chambermaids are staid and often elderly, the bath water is hot, the food as well as can be expected and the A.A. Guide has given it two stars.

Burden had booked his table by phone. When he walked into the dining room just before one he saw to his satisfaction that he had been placed by the High Street window. Here it was just out of the sun and the geraniums in the window box looked fresh and even dewy. Girls waiting on the other side of the street for the Pomfret bus wore cotton frocks and sandals.

Wexford marched in at five past. 'I don't know why he can't get up at half twelve like they do in Sewingbury,' he grumbled. 'He', Burden knew, meant the chairman of the Kingsmarkham bench. 'God, it was hot in court. What are we going to eat?'

'Roast duck,' said Burden firmly.

'All right, if you twist my arm. As long as they don't mix a lot of rubbish up with it. You know what I mean, sweet corn and bananas.' He took the menu, scowling. 'Look at that, Polynesian chicken. What do they think we are, aborigines?'

'I went and had a look at Victor's Piece this morning,' said Burden while they waited for the duck to come.

'Did you now? I see it's up for sale. There's a card in the agent's window with a highly misleading photograph. They're asking six thousand. Bit steep when you think Roger Primero got less than two for it in 1951.'

'I suppose it's changed hands several times since then?'

'Once or twice before the old folks moved in. Thanks,' he said to the waiter. 'No we don't want any wine. Two halves of bitter.' He spread his napkin over his capacious lap and to Burden's controlled distaste sprinkled wing and orange sauce liberally with pepper.

'Was Roger Primero the heir?'

'One of the heirs. Mrs Primero died intestate. Remember I told you she'd only got ten thousand to leave and that was divided equally between Roger and his two younger sisters. He's a rich man now, but however he got his money it wasn't from his grandmother. All kinds of pies he's got his finger in — oil, property development, shipping — he's a real tycoon.'

'I've seen him around, I think.'

'You must have. He's very conscious of his status as a landowner since he bought Forby Hall. Goes out with the Pomfret hounds and all that.'

'How old is he?' Burden asked.

'Well, he was twenty-two when his grandmother was killed. That makes him about thirty-eight now. The sisters were much younger. Angela was ten and Isabel nine.'

'I seem to remember he gave evidence at the trial.'

Wexford pushed his plate away, signalled rather imperiously to the waiter and ordered two portions of apple pie. Burden knew that his chief's notion of gracious living was somewhat limited.

'Roger Primero had been visiting his grandmother that Sunday,' Wexford said. 'He was working in a solicitor's office in Sewingbury at the time and he used to make quite a habit of having Sunday tea at Victor's Piece. Maybe he had his eye on a share of the loot when Mrs Primero went — God knows he hadn't a bean in those days — but he seemed genuinely fond of her. It's certainly a fact that after we'd seen the body and sent for him from Sewingbury as next of kin, we had to restrain him forcibly from going over to the coach house and laying violent hands on Painter. I daresay his grandmother and Alice made a lot of him, you know, buttered him up and waited on him. I told you Mrs Primero had her affections. There'd been a family quarrel but apparently it didn't extend to the grandchildren. Once or twice Roger had taken his little sisters down to Victor's Piece and they'd all got on very well together.'

'Old people usually do get on well with kids,' said Burden.

'They had to be the right kind of children, Mike. Angela and Isabel, yes, and she had a very soft spot for young Liz Crilling.'

Burden put down his spoon and stared at the Chief Inspector.

'I thought you said you'd read all this up at the time?' Wexford said suspiciously. 'Don't say it was a long time ago. My customers are always saying that to me and it makes me see red. If you read the account of that trial you must remember that Elizabeth Crilling, aged precisely five at the time, found Mrs Primero's body.'

20

'I assure you I can't remember, sir.' That must have been the day he'd missed, the day he hadn't bothered with the papers because he'd been nervous about an interview. 'She didn't appear at the trial, surely?'

'Not at that age — there are limits. Besides, although she was actually the first to go into the drawing room and come upon the body, her mother was with her.'

'Digressing a little,' Burden said, 'I don't quite get this stuff about the right kind of children. Mrs Crilling lives over there in Glebe Road.' He turned to the window and waved his hand in the direction of the least attractive part of Kingsmarkham where long streets of small terraced brown houses had sprung up between the wars. 'She and the girl live in half a house, they haven't a penny to bless themselves with . . .'

'They've come down a lot,' said Wexford. 'In September 1950 Crilling himself was still alive — he died of T.B. soon after — and they lived opposite Victor's Piece.'

'In one of those white semi-detached places?'

'That's right. A Mrs White and her son lived next door. Mrs Crilling was about thirty at the time, little bit over thirty.'

'You're joking,' said Burden derisively. 'That makes her only in her late forties now.'

'Look, Mike, people can say what they like about hard work and childbearing and all that. I tell you there's nothing like mental illness to make a woman look old before her time. And you know as well as I do Mrs Crilling's been in and out of mental hospitals for years.' He paused as their coffee came and pursed his lips censoriously at the anaemic brown liquid.

'You did say black, sir?' the waiter asked.

Wexford gave a sort of grunt. The church clock struck the last quarter. As the reverberation died away, he said to Burden: 'Shall I keep the parson waiting ten minutes?'

Burden said neutrally, 'That's up to you, sir. You were going to tell me how Mrs Primero and the Crilling woman became friends. I suppose they were friends?'

'Not a doubt of it. Mrs Crilling was ladylike enough in those days and she had a way with her, sycophantic, sucking up, *you* know. Besides, Crilling had been an accountant or something, just enough of a professional man, anyway, in Mrs

21

Primero's eyes to make his wife a lady. Mrs Crilling was always popping over to Victor's Piece and she always took the child with her. God knows, they must have been pretty close. Elizabeth called Mrs Primero "Granny Rose" just as Roger and his sisters did.'

'So she "popped over" that Sunday night and found Granny Rose dead?' Burden hazarded.

'It wasn't as simple as that. Mrs Crilling had been making the kid a party frock. She finished it by about six, dressed Elizabeth up and wanted to take her over and show her off to Mrs Primero. Mind you, she and Alice Flower were always at loggerheads. There was a good bit of jealousy there, spheres of influence and so on. So Mrs Crilling waited until Alice had gone off to church and went over alone, intending to go back and fetch the child if Mrs Primero was awake. She dozed a good bit, you see, being so old.

'That first time — it was about twenty past six — Mrs Primero *was* asleep and Mrs Crilling didn't go in. She just tapped on the drawing room window. When the old woman didn't stir she went back and returned again later. By the way, she saw the empty scuttle through the window so she knew Painter hadn't yet been in with the coal.'

'You mean that Painter came in and did the deed between Mrs Crilling's visits?' Burden asked.

'She didn't go back again till seven. The back door had to be left unlocked for Painter, so she and the child went in, called out "yoo-hoo" or some damn' thing, and marched into the drawing room when they didn't get an answer. Elizabeth went first — more's the pity — and Bob's your uncle!'

'Blimey,' said Burden, 'that poor kid!'

'Yes,' Wexford murmured, 'yes . . . Well, much as I should like to while away the rest of the afternoon, reminiscing over the coffee cups, I do have to see this clerical bloke.'

They both got up. Wexford paid the bill, leaving a rather obviously exact ten per cent for a tip.

'I can't see where the parson comes into it at all,' Burden said when they were in the car.

'He can't be an abolitionist because they've done away with the death penalty. As I say, he's writing a book, expects to make a big thing out of it and that's why he's laid out good money on a transcript.'

'Or he's a prospective buyer of Victor's Piece. He's a haunted house merchant and he thinks he's got another Borley Rectory.'

An unfamiliar car stood on the forecourt of the police station. The numberplate was not local and beside it was a little metal label that bore the name Essex with the county coat of arms of three scimitars on a red field.

'We shall soon know,' said Wexford.

CHAPTER THREE

There are false witnesses risen up against me and such as speak wrong.

Psalm 27, appointed for the 5th Day

In general Wexford disliked the clergy. To him the dog collar was like a slipped halo, indicating a false saintliness, probable hypocrisy and massive self-regard. As he saw it vicars were not vicarious enough. Most of them expected you to worship God in them.

He did not associate them with good looks and charm. Henry Archery, therefore, caused him slight surprise. He was possibly not much younger than Wexford himself, but he was still slim and exceedingly good-looking, and he was wearing an ordinary rather light-coloured suit and an ordinary collar and tie. His hair was thick enough and fair enough for the grey not to show much, his skin was tanned and his features had a pure evenly cut regularity.

During the first preliminary small-talk remarks Wexford had noticed the beauty of his voice. You felt it would be a pleasure to hear him read aloud. As he showed him to a chair and sat down opposite him, Wexford chuckled to himself. He was picturing a group of tired ageing female parishioners working their fingers to the bone for the pitiful reward of this man's smile. Archery was not smiling now and he looked anything but relaxed.

'I'm familiar with the case, Chief Inspector,' he began. 'I've read the official transcript of the trial and I've discussed the whole thing with Colonel Griswold.'

'What exactly do you want to know, then?' Wexford asked in his blunt way.

Archery took a deep breath and said rather too quickly:

'I want you to tell me that somewhere in your mind there

24

is just the faintest doubt, the shadow of a doubt, of Painter's guilt.'

So that was it, or part of it. Burden with his theories that the parson was a Primero relative or seeking to buy the Primero house couldn't have been more wrong. This man, whatever axe he might be grinding, was bent on whitewashing Painter.

Wexford frowned and after a moment said, 'Can't be done. Painter did it all right.' He set his jaw stubbornly. 'If you want to quote me in your book you're quite welcome. You can say that after sixteen years Wexford still maintains that Painter was guilty beyond the shadow of a doubt.'

'What book is this?' Archery inclined his handsome head courteously. His eyes were brown and now they looked bewildered. Then he laughed. It was a nice laugh and it was the first time Wexford had heard it. 'I don't write books,' he said. 'Well, I did once contribute a chapter to a work on Abyssinian cats but that hardly . . .'

Abyssinian cats. Bloody great red cats, thought Wexford. Whatever next? 'Why are you interested in Painter, Mr Archery?'

Archery hesitated. The sun showed up lines on his face that Wexford had not realised were there. Funny, he thought ruefully, how dark women age slower than fair ones but the reverse was true of men.

'My reasons are very personal, Chief Inspector. I can't suppose that they would interest you. But I can assure you that there's no possibility of my publishing anything you tell me.'

Well, he had promised Griswold — as to that, he didn't have much choice. Hadn't he, in any case, already resigned himself to giving up most of the afternoon to this clergyman? Weariness was at last beginning to gain a hold on him. He might be equal to reminiscing, going over past familiar words and scenes; on this hot afternoon he was quite unequal to anything more exacting. Probably the personal reasons — and he confessed mentally to an almost childish curiosity about them — would emerge in due course. There was something frank and boyish in his visitor's face which made Wexford think he would not be particularly discreet.

'What d'you want me to tell you?' he asked.

'Why you are so determined Painter was guilty. Of course I don't know any more about this sort of thing than the average layman, but it seems to me there were a good many gaps in the evidence. There were other people involved, people who had quite definite interests in Mrs Primero's death.'

Wexford said coldly, 'I'm fully prepared to go over any points with you, sir.'

'Now?'

'Certainly now. Have you got that transcript with you?'

Archery produced it from a very battered leather briefcase. His hands were long and thin but not womanish. They reminded Wexford of saints' hands in what he called "churchy" paintings. For five minutes or so he scanned the papers in silence, refreshing his memory on tiny points. Then he put them down and raised his eyes to Archery's face.

'We have to go back to Saturday, September 23rd,' he said, 'the day before the murder. Painter didn't appear with the coal at all that evening. The two old women waited until nearly eight o'clock when the fire was almost out, and Mrs Primero said she would go to bed. Alice Flower was incensed at this and went out to get what she called "a few lumps".'

'That was when she hurt her leg,' Archery said eagerly.

'It wasn't a serious injury but it made Mrs Primero angry and she blamed Painter. At about ten on the following morning she sent Alice down to the coach house to tell Painter she wanted to see him at eleven-thirty sharp. He came up ten minutes late, Alice showed him into the drawing room and afterwards she heard him and Mrs Primero quarrelling.'

'This brings me to the first point I want to raise,' Archery said. He flipped through the transcript and, putting his finger at the beginning of a paragraph, passed it to Wexford. 'This, as you know, is part of Painter's own evidence. He doesn't deny the quarrel. He admits that Mrs Primero threatened him with dismissal. He also says here that Mrs Primero finally came round to see his point of view. She refused to give him a rise because she said that would put ideas into his head and he would only ask for another increase in a few months' time. Instead she'd give him what she understood was called a bonus.'

'I remember all that well,' Wexford said impatiently. 'He

said she told him to go upstairs and into her bedroom where he'd find a handbag in her wardrobe. He was to bring that handbag down to her and this, he said, he did. There was about two hundred pounds in the handbag and this he could have, take it away in the handbag and look upon it as a bonus on condition he was absolutely circumspect about bringing the coal at the required times.' He coughed. 'I never believed a word of it and neither did the jury.'

'Why not?' Archery asked quietly.

God, thought Wexford, this was going to be a long session.

'Firstly, because the stairs at Victor's Piece run up between the drawing room and the kitchen. Alice Flower was in the kitchen cooking the lunch. She had remarkably good hearing for her age, but she never heard Painter go up those stairs. And, believe me, he was a big heavy lout if ever there was one.' Archery winced faintly at this but Wexford went on, 'Secondly, Mrs Primero would never have sent the gardener upstairs to poke about in her bedroom. Not unless I'm very mistaken in her character. She would have got Alice to have fetched the money on some pretext or other.'

'She might not have wanted Alice to know about it.'

'That's for sure,' Wexford retorted sharply. 'She wouldn't have. I said on some pretext or other.' That made the parson draw in his horns. Wexford said very confidently, 'In the third place Mrs Primero had a reputation for being rather mean. Alice had been with her for half a century but she'd never given Alice anything bar her wages and an extra pound at Christmas.' He jabbed at the page. 'Look, she says so here in black and white. We know Painter wanted money. The night before when he hadn't brought the coal he'd been drinking up at the Dragon with a pal of his from Stowerton. The pal had a motor-bike to sell and he'd offered it to Painter for a bit less than two hundred pounds. Apparently Painter hadn't a hope of getting the money but he asked his friend to hold on to the bike for a couple of days and he'd contact him the minute anything came up. You're saying he got the money before noon on Sunday. I say he stole it after he brutally murdered his employer in the evening. If you're right, why didn't he get in touch with his friend on Sunday afternoon? There's a phone box at the bottom of the

27

lane. We checked with the pal, he didn't move out of his house all day and the phone never rang.'

It was a very tempest of fact and Archery yielded, or appeared to yield, before it. He said only:

'You're saying, I think, that Painter went to the wardrobe after he'd killed Mrs Primero in the evening. There was no blood on the inside of the wardrobe.'

'For one thing he wore rubber gloves to do the deed. Anyway, the prosecution's case was that he stunned her with the flat side of the axe blade, took the money, and when he came downstairs, finished her off in a panic.'

Archery gave a slight shiver. 'Doesn't that strike you as odd,' he then said, 'that if Painter did it he should have been so transparent about it?'

'Some are. They're stupid, you see.' Wexford said it derisively, his mouth curling. He still had no notion what Archery's interest in Painter might be, but that he was pro-Painter was apparent. 'Stupid,' he said again, intent on flicking the clergyman on the raw. Another wince from Archery rewarded him. 'They think you'll believe them. All they've got to say is it must have been a tramp or a burglar and you'll go away satisfied. Painter was one of those. That old tramp thing,' he said. 'When did you last *see* a tramp? More than sixteen years ago, I'll bet.'

'Let's come to the murder itself,' Archery said quietly.

'By all means.' Again Wexford took the transcript, gathering with a quick glance the information he needed. 'Now, then,' he began, 'Painter said he went over to fetch the coal at half past six. He remembered the time — twenty-five past six when he left the coach house — because his wife said five minutes to go before the child's bedtime. The time's not all that important, anyway. We know it was between twenty past six and seven o'clock that she was killed. Painter went over, chopped some wood and cut his finger. Or so he said. He certainly did cut his finger — cut it deliberately.'

Archery ignored this last. 'He and Mrs Primero belonged to the same blood group,' he said.

'They were both Group O. They weren't quite so accurate about the minute grouping of blood sixteen years ago as they are now. It was handy for Painter, that. But it didn't do him any real good.'

The clergyman crossed his legs and leaned back. Wexford could see he was trying to appear relaxed and making a poor job of it. 'I believe you personally went to interview Painter after the crime was discovered?'

'We were round at the coach house by a quarter to eight. Painter was out. I asked Mrs Painter where he was and she said he'd come back from the big house some time after six-thirty, washed his hands and gone straight out again. He'd told her he was going to Stowerton to see his friend. We'd only been there about ten minutes when he came in. His story didn't stand up, there was far too much blood around to have come from a cut finger and — well, you know the rest. It's all down there. I charged him on the spot.'

The transcript fluttered a little in Archery's hand. He could not keep his fingers quite steady. 'In evidence,' he said, speaking slowly and evenly, 'Painter said he hadn't been to Stowerton. "I waited at the bus stop at the end of the lane, but the bus never came. I saw the police cars turn into the lane and I wondered what was up. Presently I felt a bit faint on account of my finger bleeding a lot. I came back to my flat. I thought my wife might know what it was all about." ' After a pause, he added with a kind of pleading eagerness, 'That doesn't sound like the evidence of the complete moron you make him out to be.'

Wexford answered him patiently as if he were talking to a precocious teenager. 'They edit these things, Mr Archery. They condense them, make them sound coherent. Believe me. You weren't in court and I was. As to the truth of that statement, I was in one of those police cars and I was keeping my eyes open. We overtook the Stowerton bus and turned left into the lane. There wasn't anyone waiting at the bus stop.'

'I imagine you mean that while he said he was at the bus stop he was in fact hiding some clothes.'

'Of course he was hiding the clothes! When he was working he habitually wore a raincoat. You'll see that in Mrs Crilling's evidence and in Alice's. Sometimes it hung in the coach house and sometimes on a hook behind the back door of Victor's Piece. Painter said he had worn it that evening and had left it hanging on the back door. The raincoat couldn't be found. Both Alice and Roger Primero said they remembered having seen it on the back door that afternoon, but Mrs Crilling was certain it wasn't there when she brought Elizabeth in at seven.'

'You finally found the raincoat rolled up in a ball under a hedge two fields away from the bus stop.'

'The raincoat plus a pullover,' Wexford retorted, 'and a pair of rubber gloves. The lot was sodden with blood.'

'But anyone could have worn the raincoat and you couldn't identify the pullover.'

'Alice Flower went so far as to say it looked like one Painter sometimes wore.'

Archery gave a deep sigh. For a time he had been firing questions and statements briskly at Wexford, but suddenly he had fallen silent. Little more than indecision showed on his face. Wexford waited. At last, he thought, Archery had reached a point where it was going to become necessary to reveal those 'personal reasons'. A struggle was going on within him and he said in an artificial tone:

'What about Painter's wife?'

'A wife cannot be compelled to give evidence against her husband. As you know, she didn't appear at the trial. She and the child went off somewhere and a couple of years later I heard she married again.'

He stared at Archery, raising his eyebrows. Something he had said had made the clergyman's mind up for him. A slight flush coloured Archery's even tan. The brown eyes were very bright as he leaned forward, tense again.

'That child . . .'

'What of her? She was asleep in her cot when we searched Painter's bedroom and that's the only time I saw her. She was four or five.'

Archery said jerkily, 'She's twenty-one now and she's a very beautiful young woman.'

'I'm not surprised. Painter was a nice enough looking fellow if you like the type, and Mrs Painter was pretty.' Wexford stopped. Archery was a clergyman. Had Painter's daughter taken after her father and somehow come into his care as a result of her transgressions? Archery could be a prison visitor.

It was right up his street, Wexford thought nastily. Anger rose in his throat as he wondered if all this sparring discussion had been engineered merely because Archery wanted his help in getting the right psychological approach to a convicted thief or confidence woman. 'What about her?' he snapped. Griswold could go to hell! 'Now come on, sir, you'd better tell me and have done.'

'I have a son, Chief Inspector, an only child. He also is twenty-one . . .'

'Well?'

Obviously the clergyman had difficulty in framing the words. He hesitated and pressed his long hands together. At last he said diffidently and in a low voice, 'He wishes to marry Miss Painter.' When Wexford started and stared at him, he added, 'Or Miss Kershaw, as her legal name now is.'

Wexford was all at sea. He was astonished, a rare thing for him, and he felt a sharp-edged excitement. But he had shown all the surprise he thought consistent with policy and now he spoke soberly.

'You must excuse me, Mr Archery, but I can't see how your son, the son of an Anglican clergyman, came to meet a girl in Miss Painter's — er, Miss Kershaw's — position.'

'They met at Oxford,' Archery said easily.

'At the *university*?'

'That is so. Miss Kershaw is quite an intelligent young woman.' Archery gave a slight smile. 'She's reading Modern Greats. Tipped for a First, I'm told.'

CHAPTER FOUR

If any of you know cause or just impediment why these two persons should not be joined together in holy matrimony, ye are to declare it.

The Banns of Marriage

If he had been asked to predict the future of such a one as Theresa Painter, what would he have foreseen for her? Children like her, Wexford reflected as he recovered from his second shock, children like Painter's little girl started life with a liability and a stain. The surviving parent, well-meaning relatives and cruel schoolfellows often made matters worse. He had hardly thought about the fate of the child until today. Now, thinking quickly, he supposed he would have counted her lucky to have become an anonymous manual worker with perhaps already a couple of petty convictions.

Instead to Theresa Painter had apparently come the greatest blessings of civilised life: brains, advanced education, beauty, friendship with people like this vicar, an engagement to this vicar's son.

Wexford cast his mind back to the first of only three encounters with Mrs Painter. A quarter to eight it had been on that Sunday in September. He and the sergeant with him had knocked on the door at the foot of the coach house stairs and Mrs Painter had come down to let them in. Whatever might have been fashionable in London at that time, the young women of Kingsmarkham were still doing their hair in a big pile on the forehead with tight curls falling to the shoulders. Mrs Painter was no exception. Hers was naturally fair, her face was powdered and her mouth painted diffidently red. Respectable provincial matrons did not go in for eye make-up in 1950 and Mrs Painter was of all things respectable. There seemed to be very little else to her. On her dry fine skin lines had already begun to form, little indentations which marked a regular prudish pursing of the lips, a setting of the chin that accompanied an outraged flounce.

She had the same attitude to the police as others might have to bugs or mice. When they came upstairs she alternated her replies to their questions with reiterated remarks that it was a disgrace to have them in the house. She had the blankest, most obtuse blue eyes he had ever seen on anyone. At no time, even when they were about to take Painter away, did she show the least pity or the least horror, only this fixated dread of what people would think if they found the police had been questioning her husband.

Perhaps she had not been so stupid as he had thought. Somewhere in that pretty respectable mouse and that great hunk of sub-humanity, her husband, must have been the spring from which their daughter drew her intelligence. 'Quite an intelligent girl,' Archery had said casually. Good God, thought Wexford, remembering how he had boasted when his own daughter got eight O Level passes. Good God! What were Modern Greats, anyway? Were they the same as Mods and did that mean Modern Languages? He had a vague idea that this might be the esoteric and deliberately deceptive name given to Philosophy and Political Economy! He almost whistled. Painter's daughter reading — yes, that was the term, reading — philosophy! It made you think all right. Why, it made you doubt . . .

'Mr Archery,' he said, 'you're quite sure this *is* Herbert Arthur Painter's girl?'

'Of course I'm sure, Chief Inspector. She told me.' He looked almost defiantly at Wexford. Perhaps he thought the policeman would laugh at his next words. 'She is as good as she is beautiful,' he said. Wexford's expression remained unaltered. 'She came to stay with us at Whitsun. It was the first time we'd seen her, though naturally our son had written and told us about her. We took to her at once.

'Chief Inspector, times have changed since I was at college. I had to face the possibility that my son would meet some girl at Oxford, perhaps want to marry her at an age when I'd thought of myself as still a boy and when Orders were a lifetime

33

away. I'd see my friends' children marry at twenty-one and I was prepared to try and manage something for him, give him something to start life on. All I hoped was that the girl would be someone we could like and understand.

'Miss Kershaw — I'll use that name if you don't mind — is just what I would have chosen for him myself, beautiful, graceful, well-mannered, easy to talk to. Oh, she does her best to hide her looks in the uniform they all wear nowadays, long shaggy hair, trousers, great black duffel coat — you know the kind of thing. But they all dress like that. The point is she can't hide them.

'My wife is a little impulsive. She was hinting about the wedding before Theresa had been with us for twenty-four hours. I found it hard to understand why the young people were so diffident about it. Charles's letters had been paeans of praise and I could see they were deeply in love. Then she told us. She came out with it quite baldly. She said — I remember the very words — 'I think you ought to know something about me, Mrs Archery. My father's name was Painter and he was hanged for killing an old woman.'

'At first my wife didn't believe it. She thought it was some sort of game. Charles said, "It's true. It doesn't matter. People are what they are, not what their parents did." Then Theresa — we call her Tess — said, "It wouldn't matter if he had done it, only he didn't. I told you *why* he was hanged. I didn't mean he'd done it." Then she began to cry.'

'Why does she call herself Kershaw?'

'It's her stepfather's name. He must be a very remarkable man, Chief Inspector. He's an electrical engineer, but . . .' You needn't come that rude mechanicals stuff with me, thought Wexford crossly. '. . . but he must be a most intelligent, perceptive and kind person. The Kershaws have two children of their own, but as far as I can gather, Mr Kershaw has treated Tess with no less affection than his own son and daughter. She says it was his love that helped her to bear — well, what I can only call the stigma of her father's crime when she learnt about it at the age of twelve. He followed her progress at school, encouraged her in every way and fostered her wish to get a County Major Scholarship.'

'You mentioned "the stigma of her father's crime". I thought you said she thinks he didn't do it?'

'My dear Chief Inspector, she *knows he didn't do it.*'

Wexford said slowly, 'Mr Archery, I'm sure I don't have to tell a man like yourself that when we talk of somebody *knowing* something we mean that what they know is a fact, something that's true beyond a reasonable doubt. We mean that the majority of other people *know* it too. In other words, it's history, it's written down in the books, it's common knowledge.' He paused. 'Now I and the Law Lords and the official records and what your son means when he talks about the Establishment, know beyond any reasonable doubt, that Painter did kill Mrs Rose Primero.'

'Her mother told her so,' said Archery. 'She told her that she had absolute irrefutable personal knowledge that Tess's father did not kill Mrs Primero.'

Wexford shrugged and smiled. 'People believe what they want to believe. The mother thought it was the best thing for her daughter. If I'd been in her shoes I daresay I'd have said the same.'

'I don't think it was like that,' Archery said stubbornly. 'Tess says her mother is a very unemotional woman. She never talks about Painter, never discusses him at all. She just says quite calmly, "Your father never killed anybody" and beyond that she won't say any more.'

'Because she can't say any more. Look, sir, I think you're taking a rather romantic view of this. You're visualising the Painters as a devoted couple, kind of merry peasants, love in a cottage and all that. It wasn't like that. Believe me, Painter was no loss to her. I'm certain in my own mind he was in the habit of striking her just when the fancy took him. As far as he was concerned, she was just his woman, someone to cook his meals, wash his clothes and — well,' he added brutally, 'someone to go to bed with.'

Archery said stiffly, 'I don't see that any of that's material.'

'Don't you? You're picturing some sort of declaration of innocence plus incontrovertible proof made to the one person he loved and whom he knew would believe in him. Forgive me, but that's a load of rubbish. Apart from the few minutes when he came back to the coach house to wash his hands — and incidentally hide the money — he was never alone with her. And he couldn't have told her then. He wasn't supposed to know about it. D'you understand me? He could have told her he had done it, he couldn't have told her he had *not*.

'Then we came. We found blood flecks in the sink and faint blood marks on the kitchen wall where he'd stripped off that pullover. As soon as he came back he took the bandage off his hand to show us the cut and he handed the bandage to his wife. But he didn't speak to her, didn't even appeal to her for support. He made just one reference to her . . .'

'Yes?'

'We found the handbag with the money in it under the mattress in their double bed. Why hadn't Painter told his wife if he'd been given that money in the morning? Here it is, find it in your transcript. "I knew the wife would want to get her hooks on it. She was always nagging me to buy things for the flat." That's all he said and he didn't even look at her. We charged him and he said, "O.K., but you're making a big mistake. It was a tramp done it." He came straight down the stairs with us. He didn't kiss his wife and he didn't ask to go in and see his child.'

'She must have seen him in prison?'

'With a prison officer present. Look, sir, you appear to be satisfied and so do all the parties concerned. Surely that's the main thing. You must forgive me if I can't agree with you.'

Silently Archery took a snapshot from his wallet and laid it on the desk. Wexford picked it up. Presumably it had been taken in the vicarage garden. There was a great magnolia tree in the background, a tree as tall as the house it partly concealed. It was covered with waxen cup flowers. Under its branches stood a boy and a girl, their arms round each other. The boy was tall and fair. He was smiling and he was plainly Archery's son. Wexford wasn't particularly interested in him.

The girl's face was in sad repose. She was looking into the camera with large steady eyes. Light-coloured hair fell over her forehead in a fringe and down to the shoulders of a typical undergraduate's shirtwaister, faded, tightly belted and with a crumpled skirt. Her waist was tiny, her bust full. Wexford saw the mother again, only this girl was holding a boy's hand instead of a bloody rag.

'Very charming,' he said dryly. 'I hope she'll make your son happy.' He handed the photograph back. 'No reason why she shouldn't.'

A mixture of emotions, anger, pain, resentment, flared in the clergyman's eyes. Interestedly, Wexford watched him.

'I do not know what or whom to believe,' Archery said unhappily, 'and while I'm in this state of uncertainty, Chief Inspector, I'm not in favour of the marriage. No, that's putting it too coolly.' He shook his head vehemently. 'I'm bitterly, bitterly against it,' he said.

'And the girl, Painter's daughter?'

'She believed — perhaps accepts is the better word — in her father's innocence, but she realises others may not. When it comes to it, I don't think she would marry my son while his mother and I feel as we do.'

'What are you afraid of, Mr Archery?'

'Heredity.'

'A very chancy thing, heredity.'

'Have you children, Chief Inspector?'

'I've got two girls.'

'Are they married?'

'One is.'

'And who is her father-in-law?'

For the first time Wexford felt superior to this clergyman. A kind of *Schadenfreude* possessed him. 'He's an architect, as a matter of fact, Tory councillor for the North Ward here.'

'I see.' Archery bowed his head. 'And do your grandchildren already build palaces with wooden bricks, Mr Wexford?' Wexford said nothing. The only sign of his first grandchild's existence was so far evinced in its mother's morning sickness. 'I shall watch mine from their cradle, waiting to see them drawn towards objects with sharp edges.'

'You said if you objected she wouldn't marry him.'

'They're in love with each other. I can't . . .'

'Who's going to know? Palm Kershaw off as her father.'

'I shall know,' said Archery. 'Already I can see Painter when I look at her. Instead of her mouth and her eyes I can see

37

his thick lips and bloodlust. It's the same blood, Chief Inspector, the blood that mingled with Mrs Primero's, on the floor, on the clothes, down the water pipes. That blood will be in my grandchild.' He seemed to realise that he had allowed himself to be carried away, for he stopped suddenly, blushed, and shut his eyes briefly as if wincing at the sight he had described.

Wexford said gently, 'I wish I could help you, Mr Archery, but the case is closed, over, finished. There is nothing more I can do.'

Archery shrugged and quoted softly, almost as if he could not stop himself, ' "He took water and washed his hands before the multitude, saying, I am innocent of the blood of this just person . . ." ' Then he jumped up, his expression suddenly contrite. 'Forgive me, Chief Inspector. That was an appalling thing to say. May I tell you what I intend to do?'

'Pontius Pilate, that's me,' said Wexford. 'So see you show more respect in future.'

Burden grinned. 'What exactly did he want, sir?'

'Firstly for me to tell him Painter may have been unjustly executed, which I can't. Damn it all, it would be tantamount to saying I didn't know my job. It was my first murder case, Mike, and it was fortunate for me it was so straightforward. Archery's going to do a spot of enquiry on his own. Hopeless after sixteen years but it's useless telling him. Secondly, he wanted my permission to go round hunting up all the witnesses. Wanted my support if they came round here, complaining and foaming at the mouth.'

'And all he's got to go on,' said Burden thoughtfully, 'is Mrs Painter's sentimental belief in her husband's innocence?'

'Aah, that's nothing! That's a load of hooey. If you got the chop, wouldn't Jean tell John and Pat you were innocent? Wouldn't my wife tell the girls? It's natural. Painter didn't make any last-minute confessions — you know what the prison authorities are like for watching out for things like that. No, she dreamed it up and convinced herself.'

'Has Archery ever met her?'

'Not yet, but he's making a day of it. She and her second husband live in Purley and he's got himself an invite for tea.'

'You say the girl told him at Whitsun. Why has he waited so long? It must be a couple of months.'

'I asked him that. He said that for the first couple of weeks he and his wife just let it ride. They thought the son might see reason. But he wouldn't. He got his father to get hold of a transcript of the trial, nagged him into working on Griswold. Of course he's an only child and as spoilt as they come. The upshot was that Archery promised to start poking his nose into it as soon as he got his fortnight's holiday.'

'So he'll be back?'

'That will depend on Mrs Painter,' said Wexford.

CHAPTER FIVE

... That they may see their children christianly and virtuously brought up.

The Solemnisation of Matrimony

The Kershaws' house was about a mile from the town centre, separated from shops, station, cinema and churches by thousands of other large suburban villas. For number 20 Craig Hill was large, half-heartedly Georgian and built of raspberry red brick. The garden was planted with annuals, the lawn was clover-free and the dead heads had been nipped off the standard rose bushes. On the concrete drive a boy of about twelve was washing down a large white Ford.

Archery parked his car at the kerb. Unlike Wexford he had not yet seen the coach house at Victor's Piece, but he had read about it and it seemed to him that Mrs Kershaw had climbed high. Sweat started on his forehead and his upper lip as he got out of the car. He told himself that it was unusually hot and that he had always been prone to feel the heat.

'This is Mr Kershaw's house, isn't it?' he asked the boy.

'That's right.' He was very like Tess, but his hair was fairer and his nose was freckled. 'The front door's open. Shall I give him a shout?'

'My name is Archery,' said the clergyman and he held out his hand.

The boy wiped his hands on his jeans. 'Hallo,' he said.

By now a little wrinkled man had come down the porch steps. The bright hot air seemed to hang between them. Archery tried not to feel disappointment. What had he expected? Certainly not someone so small, so unfinished looking and so wizened as this scrawny creature in old flannels and tieless knitted shirt. Then Kershaw smiled and the years fell from him. His eyes were a bright sparkling blue and his uneven teeth white and clean.

'How do you do?'

'Good afternoon, Mr Archery. I'm very happy to meet you. As a matter of fact I've been sitting in the window, looking out for you.'

In this man's presence it was impossible not to feel hope, cheerfulness almost. Archery detected at once a rare quality in him, a quality he had come upon perhaps only half a dozen times in his life. This was a man who was interested in all things. Energy and enthusiasm radiated from him. On a winter's day he would warm the air. Today, in this heat, his vitality was overwhelming.

'Come inside and meet my wife.' His voice was a hot breeze, a cockney voice that suggested fish and chips, eels and mash and East End pubs. Following him into the square panelled hall, Archery wondered how old he was. Perhaps no more than forty-five. Drive, the fire of life, lack of sleep because sleep wasted time, could prematurely have burnt away his youth. 'We're in the lounge,' he said, pushing open a reeded glass door. 'That's what I like about a day like this. When I get home from work I like to sit by the french windows for ten minutes and look at the garden. Makes you feel all that slogging in the winter was worthwhile.'

'To sit in the shade and look upon verdure?' After the words were out Archery was sorry he had spoken. He didn't want to put this suburban engineer in a false position.

Kershaw gave him a quick glance. Then he smiled and said easily, 'Miss Austen certainly knew what she was talking about, didn't she?' Archery was overcome. He went into the room and held out his hand to the woman who had got up from an armchair.

'My wife. This is Mr Archery, Rene.'

'How do you do?'

Irene Kershaw said nothing, but holding out her hand, smiled a tight bright smile. Her face was Tess's face as it would be when time had hardened it and finished it. In her youth she had been blonde. Now her hair, evidently set that day and perhaps in his honour, was dyed a dull leaf-brown and arranged in unreal feathery wisps about her forehead and ears.

'Sit down, Mr Archery,' said Kershaw. 'We won't keep you a minute for your tea. Kettle's on, isn't it, Rene?'

Archery sat in an armchair by the window. Kershaw's garden was full of experimental rose pergolas, eruptions of rockery and stone sporting geraniums. He gave the room a quick glance, noting at once its cleanliness and the enormous mass of things which had to be kept clean. Books abounded, Readers' Digests, encyclopaedias, dictionaries, works on astronomy, deep sea fishing, European history. There was a tank of tropical fish on a corner table, several model aircraft on the mantelpiece; stacks of sheet music covered the grand piano, and on an easel was a half-finished, rather charming, portrait in oils of a young girl. It was a large room, conventionally furnished with Wilton carpet and chintz covers, but it expressed the personality of the master of the house.

'We've had the pleasure of meeting your Charlie,' said Kershaw. 'A nice unassuming boy. I liked him.' Charlie! Archery sat very still, trying not to feel affronted. Charles's eligibility, after all, was not in question.

Quite suddenly Rene Kershaw spoke. 'We all like him,' she said. Her accent was just the same as Wexford's. 'But I'm sure I don't know how they plan to manage, what with everything being such an awful price — the cost of living, you know — and Charles not having a job in line . . .' Archery felt amazement. Was she really concerned with this trivia? He began to wonder how he would broach the subject that had brought him to Purley. 'I mean where will they live?' Mrs Kershaw asked primly. 'They're just babies really. I mean, you've got to have a home of your own, haven't you? You've got to get a mortgage and . . .'

'I think I can hear the kettle, Rene,' said her husband.

She got up, holding her skirt modestly to cover her knees. It was a very suburban skirt of some permanently pleated material banded in muted blue and heather pink and of dead sexless respectability. With it she wore a short-sleeved pink jumper and around her neck a single string of cultured pearls. If cultured meant tended and nurtured, Archery thought he had never seen such obviously cultured pearls. Each night, he was sure, they were wrapped in tissue and put away in the dark. Mrs Kershaw smelt of talcum powder, some of which lingered in the lines of her neck.

'I don't think we've got to the mortgage stage yet,' said Kershaw when she had gone. Archery gave a wry smile. 'Believe me, Mr Archery, I know you haven't come here just for an inlaws' get-together over the tea cups.'

'I'm finding it more awkward than I thought possible.'

Kershaw chuckled. 'I daresay. I can't tell you anything about Tess's father that isn't common knowledge, that wasn't in the papers at the time. You know that?'

'But her mother?'

'You can try. At times like this women see things through a cloud of orange blossom. She's never been very keen on Tess being an educated woman. She wants to see her married and she'll do her best to see nothing stands in her way.'

'And you, what do you want?'

'Me? Oh, I want to see her happy. Happiness doesn't necessarily begin at the altar.' Suddenly he was brisk and forthright. 'Frankly, Mr Archery, I'm not sure if she can be happy with a man who suspects her of homicidal tendencies before she's even engaged to him.'

'It isn't like that!' Archery hadn't expected the other man to put him on the defensive. 'Your stepdaughter is perfect in my son's eyes. I'm making the enquiries, Mr Kershaw. My son knows that, he wants it for Tess's sake, but he doesn't even know I'm here. Put yourself in my position . . .'

'But I *was* in your position. Tess was only six when I married her mother.' He looked quickly at the door, then leaned closer to Archery. 'D'you think I don't watch her, look out for the disturbance to show itself? When my own daughter was born Tess was very jealous. She resented the baby and one day I found her leaning over Jill's pram striking her on the head with a celluloid toy. Luckily, it *was* a celluloid toy.'

'But, good heavens . . . !' Archery felt the pallor drawing at his face muscles.

'What could I do? I had to go to work and leave the children. I had to trust my wife. Then we had a son — I think you bumped into him outside cleaning the car — and Jill resented him in just the same way and with just the same violence. All children behave like this, that's the point.'

'You never saw any more — any more of these tendencies?'

'Tendencies? A personality isn't made by heredity, Mr Archery, but by environment. I wanted Tess to have the best sort of environment and I think I can say, with all due modesty, that she has.'

The garden shimmered in the heat haze. Archery saw things he hadn't noticed at first, chalk lines on the lawn, where, regardless of herbaceous borders, the glass had been marked out for a tennis court; a shambles of rabbit hutches attached to the garage wall; an ancient swing. Behind him on the mantelpiece he saw propped against ornaments two party invitations. A framed photograph above it showed three children in shirts and jeans sprawled on a haystack. Yes, this had been the best of all possible environments for the murderer's orphan.

The door was pushed open and the girl in the portrait came in pushing a tea trolley. Archery, who was too hot and troubled to feel hungry, saw with dismay that it was laden with home-baked pastries, strawberries in glass dishes, fairy cakes in paper cases. The girl looked about fourteen. She was not so beautiful as Tess and she wore a bunchy school tunic, but her father's vitality illuminated her face.

'This is my daughter Jill.'

Jill sprawled in a chair, showing a lot of long leg.

'Now, sit nicely, dear,' said Mrs Kershaw sharply. She gave the girl a repressive look and began to pour tea, holding the pot with curled fingers. 'They don't realise they're young women at thirteen these days, Mr Archery.' Archery was embarrassed but the girl didn't seem to care. 'You must have one of these cakes. Jill made them.' Unwillingly he took a pastry. 'That's right. I've always said to both my girls, schooling is all very well in its way, but algebra won't cook the Sunday dinner. Tess and Jill are both good plain cooks . . .'

'Mummy! I'm not plain and Tess certainly isn't.'

'You know what I mean. Now don't take me up on everything. When they get married their husbands won't be ashamed to have anybody for a meal.'

'This is my managing director, darling,' said Jill pertly. 'Just cut a slice off him and put it under the grill, will you?'

Kershaw roared with laughter. Then he took his wife's hand. 'You leave Mummy alone.' All this jollity and family

44

intimacy was making Archery nervous. He forced a smile and knew it looked forced.

'What I really mean is, Mr Archery,' said Mrs Kershaw earnestly, 'is that even if your Charlie and my Tessie have their ups and downs at first, Tess hasn't been brought up to be an idle wife. She'll put a happy home before luxuries.'

'I'm sure she will.' Archery looked helplessly at the lounging girl, firmly entrenched in her chair and devouring strawberries and cream. It was now or never. 'Mrs Kershaw, I don't doubt Theresa's suitability as a wife . . .' No, that wasn't right. That was just what he did doubt. He floundered. 'I wanted to talk to you about . . .' Surely Kershaw would help him? Jill's brows drew together in a small frown and her grey eyes stared steadily at him. Desperately he said, 'I wanted to speak to you alone.'

Irene Kershaw seemed to shrink. She put down her cup, laid her knife delicately across her plate and, folding her hands in her lap, looked down at them. They were poor hands, stubby and worn, and she wore just one ring, her second wedding ring.

'Haven't you got any homework to do, Jill?' she asked in a whisper. Kershaw got up, wiping his mouth.

'I can do it in the train,' said Jill.

Archery had begun to dislike Kershaw, but he could not help admiring him. 'Jill, you know all about Tess,' Kershaw said, 'what happened when she was little. Mummy has to discuss it with Mr Archery. Just by themselves. We have to go because, although we're involved, it's not quite our business. Not like it is theirs. O.K.?'

'O.K.,' said Jill. Her father put his arm round her and took her into the garden.

He had to begin, but he was hot and stiff with awkwardness. Outside the window Jill had found a tennis racquet and was practising shots against the garage wall. Mrs Kershaw picked up a napkin and dabbed at the corners of her mouth. She looked at him, their eyes met, and she looked away. Archery felt suddenly that they were not alone, that their thoughts concentrated on the past had summoned from its prison grave a presence of brute strength that stood behind their chairs, laying a bloody hand on their shoulders and listening for judgement.

'Tess says you have something to tell me,' he said quietly. 'About your first husband.' She was rolling the napkin now, squashing it, until it was like a golf-ball. 'Mrs Kershaw, I think you ought to tell me.'

The paper ball was tipped soundlessly on to an empty plate. She put her hand up to her pearls.

'I never speak of him, Mr Archery. I prefer to let the past be the past.'

'I know it's painful — it must be. But if we could discuss it just once and get it over, I promise I'll never raise the subject again.' He realised that he was speaking as if they would meet again and often, as if they were already connected by marriage. He was also speaking as if he had confidence in her word. 'I've been to Kingsmarkham today and . . .'

She clutched at the straw. 'I suppose they've built it all up and spoiled it.'

'Not really,' he said. Please God, don't let her digress!

'I was born near there,' she said. He tried to stifle a sigh. 'A funny little sleepy place it was, my village. I reckon I thought I'd live and die there. You can't tell what life will bring forth, can you?'

'Tell me about Tess's father.'

She dropped her hands from fidgeting with the pearls and rested them in her respectable blue lap. When she turned to him her face was dignified, almost ridiculously prim and shuttered. She might have been a mayoress, taking the chair at some parochial function, clearing her throat preparatory to addressing the Townswomen's Guild. 'Madam chairman, ladies . . .' she should have begun. Instead she said:

'The past is the past, Mr Archery.' He knew then that it was hopeless. 'I appreciate your difficulty, but I really can't speak of it. He was no murderer, you'll have to take my word. He was a good kind man who wouldn't have harmed a fly.' It was curious, he thought, how she jumbled together old village phrases with platform jargon. He waited, then burst out:

'But how do you know? How *can* you know? Mrs Kershaw, did you see something or hear something . . . ?'

The pearls had gone up to her mouth and her teeth closed over the string. As it snapped pearls sprayed off in all directions, into her lap, across the tea things, on to the carpet. She gave a small refined laugh, petulant and apologetic. 'Look what I've done now!' In an instant she was on her knees, retrieving the scattered beads and dropping them into a saucer.

'I'm very keen on a white wedding.' Her face bounced up from behind the tea trolley. Politeness demanded that he too should get on his knees and help in the hunt. 'Get your wife to back me up, will you? Oh, thanks so much. Look, there's another one, just by your left foot.' He scrambled round after her on all fours. Her eyes met his under the overhanging cloth. 'My Tess is quite capable of getting married in jeans if the fancy takes her. And would you mind if we had the reception here? It's such a nice big room.'

Archery got up and handed her three more pearls. When the tennis ball struck the window he jumped. The sound had been like a pistol shot.

'Now, that's quite enough, Jill,' said Mrs Kershaw sharply. Still holding the saucer full of pearls, she opened the window. 'If I've told you once, I've told you fifty times, I don't want any more breakages.'

Archery looked at her. She was annoyed, affronted, even slightly outraged. He wondered suddenly if this was how she had looked on that Sunday night long ago when the police had invaded her domain at the coach house. Was she capable of any emotion greater than this, of mere irritation at disturbance of her personal peace?

'You just can't settle to a quiet discussion with children about, can you?' she said.

Within an instant, as if at a cue, the whole family was upon them, Jill truculent and protesting, the boy he had en-countered on the drive now demanding tea, and Kershaw himself, vibrant as ever, his little lined face showing a certain dry acuteness.

'Now, you're to come straight out and give me a hand with these dishes, Jill.' The saucer was transferred to the mantelpiece and stuck between an Oxfam collecting box and a card inviting Mrs Kershaw to a coffee morning in aid of Cancer Relief. 'I'll say good-bye now, Mr Archery.' She held out her hand. 'You've such a long way to go, I know you'll want to be on your way.'

It was almost rude, yet it was queenly. 'If we don't meet again before the great day — well, I'll see you in church.'

The door closed. Archery remained standing.

'What am I to do?' he said simply.

'What did you expect?' Kershaw countered. 'Some sort of incontrovertible evidence, an alibi that only she can prove?'

'Do *you* believe her?' Archery countered.

'Ah, that's another matter. I don't care, you see. I don't care one way or the other. It's so easy *not* to ask, Mr Archery, just to do nothing and accept.'

'But I care,' said Archery. 'If Charles goes ahead and marries your stepdaughter, I shall have to leave the church. I don't think you realise the sort of place I live in, the sort of people . . .'

'Aah!' Kershaw wrinkled up his mouth and spread his hands angrily fanwise. 'I've no patience with that sort of out-dated rubbish. Who's to know? Everybody round here thinks she's my kid.'

'I shall know.'

'Why the hell did she have to tell you? Why couldn't she keep her mouth shut?'

'Are you condemning her for her honesty, Kershaw?'

'Yes, by God I am!' Archery winced at the oath and shut his eyes against the light. He saw a red haze. It was only eyelid membrane, but to him it seemed like a lake of blood. 'It's discretion, not honesty, that's the best policy. What are you worrying about, anyway? You know damn well she won't marry him if you don't want it.'

Archery snapped back, 'And what sort of relationship should I have with my son after that?' He controlled himself, softened his voice and his expression. 'I shall have to try to find a way. Your wife is so sure?'

'She's never weakened.'

'Then I shall go back to Kingsmarkham. It's rather a forlorn hope, isn't it?' He added with an absurdity he realised after the words had come, 'Thanks for trying to help and — and for an excellent tea.'

CHAPTER SIX

Yet, forasmuch as in all appearance the time of his dissolution draweth near, so fit and prepare him . . . against the hour of death.

The Visitation of the Sick

The man lay on his back in the middle of the zebra crossing. Inspector Burden, getting out of the police car, had no need to ask where he was or to be taken to the scene of the accident. It was all there before his eyes like a horrible still from a Ministry of Transport warning film, the kind of thing that makes women shudder and turn quickly to the other channel.

An ambulance was waiting, but nobody was making any attempt to move the man. Inexorably and with a kind of indifference the twin yellow beacons went on winking rhythmically. Up-ended, with its blunt nose poking into the crushed head of a bollard, was a white Mini.

'Can't you get him away?' asked Burden.

The doctor was laconic. 'He's had it.' He knelt down, felt the left wrist and got up again, wiping blood from his fingers. 'I'd hazard a guess the spine's gone and he's ruptured his liver. The thing is he's still more or less conscious and it'd be hell's own agony to shift him.'

'Poor devil. What happened? Did anybody see it?'

His eye roved across the knot of middle-aged women in cotton dresses, late homegoing commuters and courting couples on their evening stroll. The last of the sun smiled gently on their faces and on the blood that gilded the black and white crossing. Burden knew that Mini. He knew the stupid sign in the rear window that showed a skull and the words: *You have been Mini-ed.* It had never been funny and now it was outrageous, cruel in the way it mocked the man in the road.

A girl lay sprawled over the steering wheel. Her hair was

short, black and spiky, and she had thrust her fingers through it in despair or remorse. The long red nails stuck out like bright feathers.

'Don't worry about her,' said the doctor contemptuously. 'She's not hurt.'

'You, madam . . .' Burden picked out the calmest and least excited looking of the bystanders. 'Did you happen to see the accident?'

'Ooh, it was awful! Like a beast she was, the little bitch. Must have been doing a hundred miles an hour.'

Picked a right one there, thought Burden. He turned to a white-faced man holding a sealyham on a lead.

'Perhaps you can help me, sir?'

The lead was jerked and the sealyham sat down at the kerb.

'That gentleman . . .' Blanching afresh, he pointed towards the crumpled thing lying on the stripes. 'He looked right and left like you're supposed to. But there was nothing coming. You can't see all that well on account of the bridge.'

'Yes, yes. I get the picture.'

'Well, he started to cross to the island like, when that white car came up out of nowhere. Going like a mad thing she was. Well, not a hundred, but sixty, I reckon. Those Minis can go at a terrible lick when they've had their engines hotted up. He sort of hesitated and then he tried to go back. You know, it was all in a flash. I can't rightly go into details.'

'You're doing very well.'

'Then the car got him. Oh, the driver slammed on her brakes for all she was worth. I'll never forget the noise to my dying day, what with the brakes screaming and him screaming too, and sort of throwing up his arms and going down like a ninepin.'

Burden set a constable to take names and addresses, turned away and took a step in the direction of the white car. A woman touched his arm.

'Here,' she said, 'he wants a priest or something. He kept on asking before you came. Get me Father Chiverton, he says, like he knew he was going.'

'That right?' said Burden sharply to Dr Crocker.

Crocker nodded. The dying man was covered now, a folded

50

mac under his head, two policemen's jackets across his body. 'Father Chiverton is what he said. Frankly, I was more concerned for his physical than his spiritual welfare.'

'R.C. then, is he?'

'God, no. Bunch of atheists, you cops are. Chiverton's the new vicar here. Don't you ever read the local rag?'

'Father?'

'He's very high. Genuflecting and Sung Eucharist and all that jazz.' The doctor coughed. 'I'm a Congregationalist myself.'

Burden walked over to the crossing. The man's face was blanched a yellowish ivory, but his eyes were open and they stared back. With a little shock Burden realised he was young, perhaps no more than twenty.

'Anything you want, old chap?' He knew the doctor had given him a pain-killing injection. With his own bent body he shielded him from the watchers. 'We'll get you away from here in a minute,' he lied. 'Anything we can get you?'

'Father Chiverton . . .' It was a toneless whisper, as detached and inhuman as a puff of wind. 'Father Chiverton . . .' A spasm crossed the waning face. 'Confess . . . atone . . . spare Thou them which are penitent.'

'Bloody religion,' said the doctor. 'Can't even let a man die in peace.'

'You must be an asset to the Congregationalists,' Burden snapped. He got up, sighing. 'He obviously wants to confess. I suppose they do have confession in the Church of England?'

'You can have it if you want it but you needn't if you don't fancy it. That's the beauty of the C of E.' When Burden looked murderous, he added. 'Don't get in a tiz with me. We've been on to Chiverton, but he and his curate are off at some conference.'

'Constable Gates!' Burden beckoned impatiently to the man noting down the addresses. 'Nip into Stowerton and fetch me a — a vicar.'

'We've tried Stowerton, sir.'

'O God,' said Burden quietly.

'Excuse me, sir, but there's a clergyman got an appointment with the Chief Inspector now. I could get on to the station and . . .'

Burden raised his eyebrows. Kingsmarkham police station had apparently become the battleground of the Church Militant.

'You do that, and quick . . .'

He murmured something useless to the boy, and moved towards the girl who had begun to sob.

She was not crying because of what she had done, but because of what she had seen two hours before. It was two or three years now since she had what she called a waking nightmare — though at one time they were more real than reality — and she was crying because the nightmares were going to begin again and the remedy she had tried had not erased the picture from her mind.

She had seen it in the estate agent's window when she was coming home from work. It was a photograph of a house, but not as it was now, dirty and weathered, set in a tangled wilderness. The estate agents deceived you, they meant you to think it was like it had once been long ago . . . You? As soon as she found she was addressing herself as 'You' she knew it was beginning again, the re-telling of the nightmare. So she had got into the Mini and driven to Flagford, away from associations and memories and the hateful You voice, to drink and drink and try to send it away.

But it would not go away and you were back in the big house, listening to the voices that went on coaxing, cajoling, arguing until you were bored, so bored until you went out into the garden and met the little girl.

You went up to her and said, 'Do you like my dress?'

'It's pretty,' she said, and she didn't seem to mind that it was much nicer than her own.

She was playing with a heap of sand, making pies in an old cup without a handle. You stayed and played and after that you came to the sand every day, down there out of sight of the big windows. The sand was warm and nice and you could understand it. You could understand the little girl too, even though she was the only little girl you had ever known. You knew a lot of grown-ups, but you could not understand them, nor the ugly words and the funny wheedling way the talk was always about money, so that you seemed to see coins dropping out of wriggling lips and sliding dirtily through twitching fingers.

The little girl had some magic about her, for she lived in a tree. Of course it was not really a tree but a house inside a kind of bush all shivering with leaves.

The sand was not dry like the desert you lived in now, but warm and moist, like beach sand washed by a tepid sea. It was dirty too and you were afraid of what would happen if you got it on your dress . . .

You cried and stamped your foot, but you never cried as you were crying now as the good-looking inspector came up to the car, his eyes full of anger.

Did he seriously imagine he was going to find anything new after so long? Archery considered Wexford's question. It was, he decided, more a matter of faith than of any real belief in Painter's innocence. But faith in what? Not, surely, in Mrs Kershaw. Perhaps it was just a childlike certainty that such things could not happen to anyone connected with him, Archery. The child of a murderer could not be as Tess was, Kershaw would not have loved her, Charles would not want to marry her.

'It can't do any harm to see Alice Flower,' he said. He felt he was pleading, and pleading weakly. 'I'd like to talk to the Primero grandchildren, particularly the grandson.'

For a moment Wexford said nothing. He had heard of faith moving mountains, but this was simply absurd. To him it was almost as ridiculous as if some crank had come to him with the suggestion that Dr Crippen was the innocent victim of circumstances. From bitter experience he knew how difficult it was to hunt a killer when only a week had elapsed between a murder and the beginning of an investigation. Archery was proposing to open an enquiry a decade and a half too late and Archery had no experience at all.

'I ought to put you off,' he said at last. 'You don't know what you're attempting.' It's pathetic, he thought, it's laughable. Aloud he said, 'Alice Flower's in the geriatric ward at Stowerton Infirmary. She's paralysed. I don't even know if she could make herself understood.'

It occurred to him that Archery must be totally ignorant of

53

the geography of the place. He got up and lumbered over to the wall map.

'Stowerton's there,' he said, pointing with the sheathed tip of a ballpoint pen, 'and Victor's Piece is about here, between Stowerton and Kingsmarkham.'

'Where can I find Mrs Crilling?'

Wexford made a wry face. 'In Glebe Road. I can't recall the number off-hand, but I'll get it looked up or you could find it on the electoral register.' He turned round ponderously and fixed Archery with a grey glare. 'You're wasting your time, of course. I'm sure I don't have to tell you to be very careful when it comes to throwing out a lot of unfounded accusations.'

Under those cold eyes it was difficult for Archery not to drop his own. 'Chief Inspector, I don't want to find someone else guilty, just prove that Painter was innocent.'

Wexford said briskly, 'I'm afraid you may find the former consequent upon the latter. It would be a wrong conclusion, of course — I don't want trouble.' At a knock on the door he spun round testily. 'Yes, what is it?'

Sergeant Martin's bland face appeared. 'That fatal on the zebra in the High Street, sir?'

'What of it? It's hardly my province.'

'Gates has just been on, sir. A white Mini, LMB 12M, that we've had our eye on — it was in collision with a pedestrian. It appears they want a clergyman and Gates recalled that Mr Archery was . . .'

Wexford's lips twitched. Archery was in for a surprise. In the courtly manner he sometimes assumed, he said to the vicar of Thringford, 'It looks as if the secular arm needs some spiritual assistance, sir. Would you be so good . . . ?'

'Of course I will.' Archery looked at the sergeant. 'Someone has been knocked down and is — is *dying*?'

'Unfortunately, yes, sir,' said Martin grimly.

'I think I'll come with you,' said Wexford.

As a priest of the Anglican Church Archery was obliged to hear confession if a confessor was needed. Until now, however, his only experience of this mystery concerned a Miss Bayliss, an elderly female parishioner of his who, having been (according to Mrs Archery) for many years in love with him, demanded that he should listen to a small spate of domestic sins mumbled out each Friday morning. Hers was a masochistic, self-abasing need, very different from the yearning of the boy who lay in the road.

Wexford shepherded him across the black and white lines to the island. Diversion notices had been placed in the road, directing the traffic around Queen Street, and the crowd had been induced to go home. There were several policemen buzzing and pacing. For the first time in his life Archery realised the aptness of the term 'bluebottles'. He glanced at the Mini and averted his eyes hastily from the bright bumper with its ribbon of blood.

The boy looked at him doubtfully. He had perhaps five minutes to live. Archery dropped to his knees and put his ear to the white lips. At first he felt only fluttering breath, then out of the soft sighing vibration came something that sounded like 'Holy orders . . .', with the second word rising on a high note of enquiry. He bent closer as the confession began to flow out, jerky, toneless, spasmodic, like the gulping of a sluggish stream. It was something about a girl, but it was utterly incoherent. He could make nothing of it. We fly unto Thee for succour, he thought, in behalf of this Thy servant, here lying under Thy hand in great weakness of body . . .

The Anglican Church provides no order quite comparable to that of Extreme Unction. Archery found himself saying urgently over and over again, 'It will be all right, it will be all right.' The boy's throat rattled and a stream of blood welled out of his mouth, splashing Archery's folded hands. 'We humbly commend the soul of this Thy servant, our dear brother, into Thy hands . . .' He was tired and his voice broke with compassion and with horror. 'Most humbly beseeching Thee that it may be precious in Thy sight . . .'

It was the doctor's hand that appeared, mopping with a handkerchief at Archery's fingers, then feeling a still heart and an inert pulse. Wexford looked at the doctor, gave an infinitesimal shrug. Nobody spoke. Across the silence came the sound of brakes, a horn braying and an oath as a car, taking the diversion too late, veered into Queen Street. Wexford pulled the coat up over the dead face.

Archery was shattered and cold in the evening heat. He got up stiffly, feeling an utter loneliness and a terrible desire to weep. The only thing to lean on now the bollard was gone was the rear of that lethal white car. He leaned on it, feeling sick.

Presently he opened his eyes and moved slowly along the body of the car to where Wexford stood contemplating a girl's shaggy black head. This was no business of his, Archery's. He wanted no hand in it, only to ask Wexford where he could find an hotel for the night.

Something in the other man's expression made him hesitate. The big Chief Inspector's face was a study in irony. He watched Wexford tap on the glass. The window was slid back and the girl inside lifted to them a face drowned in tears.

'This is a bad business,' he heard Wexford say, 'a very bad business, Miss Crilling.'

'God moves in a mysterious way,' said Wexford as he and Archery walked over the bridge, 'His wonders to perform.' He hummed the old hymn tune, apparently liking the sound of his rather rusty baritone.

'That's true,' said Archery very seriously. He stopped, rested his hand on the granite parapet and looked down into the brown water. A swan sailed out from under the bridge, dipping its long neck into the drifting weed. 'And that is really the girl who found Mrs Primero's body?'

'That's Elizabeth Crilling, yes. One of the wild young things of Kingsmarkham. A boy friend — a very *close* friend, I may add — gave her the Mini for her twenty-first and she's been a menace in it ever since.'

Archery was silent. Tess Kershaw and Elizabeth Crilling were the same age. Their lives had begun together, almost side by side. Each must have walked with their mother along the grass verges of the Stowerton Road, played in the fields behind Victor's Piece. The Crillings had been comfortably off, middle-class people; the Painters miserably poor. In his mind's eye he saw again that tearwrecked face down which grease and mascara ran in rivulets, and he heard again the ugly words she had used to Wexford. Another face superimposed itself on Elizabeth Crilling's, a fair aquiline face with steady intelligent eyes under a page-boy's blonde fringe. Wexford interrupted his thoughts.

'She's been spoilt, of course, made too much of. Your Mrs Primero had her over with her every day, stuffing her with sweets and what-have-you, by all accounts. After the murder Mrs Crilling was always taking her to psychiatrists, wouldn't let her go to school till they had the kid-catcher down on her. God knows how many schools she *has* been to. She was what you might call the female lead in the juvenile court here.'

But it was Tess whose father had been a murderer, Tess who might have been expected to grow up like that. 'God knows how many schools she's been to . . .' Tess had been to one school and to one ancient, distinguished university. Yet the daughter of the innocent friend had become a delinquent; the killer's child a paragon. Certainly God moved in a mysterious way.

'Chief Inspector, I want very much to talk to Mrs Crilling.'

'If you care to attend the special court in the morning, sir, she'll in all likelihood be there. Knowing Mrs Crilling, I'd say you might again be called upon in your professional capacity and then, who knows?'

Archery frowned as they walked on. 'I'd rather it was all above-board. I don't want to do anything underhand.'

'Look, sir,' said Wexford in a burst of impatience, 'if you're coming in on this lark you'll have to be underhand. You've no real authority to ask questions of innocent people and if they complain I can't protect you.'

'I'll explain everything frankly to her. May I talk to her?'

Wexford cleared his throat. 'Are you familiar with *Henry the Fourth*, Part One, sir?'

Slightly puzzled, Archery nodded. Wexford stopped under the arch that led to the coaching yard of the Olive and Dove. 'The quotation I had in mind is Hotspur's reply to Mortimer when he says he can call spirits from the vasty deep.' Startled by Wexford's deep voice, a little cloud of pigeons flew out from the beams, fluttering rusty grey wings. 'I've found that reply very useful to me in my work when I've been a bit too optimistic.' He cleared his throat and quoted, ' "And so can I and so can any man. But will they come when you do call to them?" Good night, sir, I hope you find the Olive comfortable.'

57

CHAPTER SEVEN

Into how high a dignity . . . ye are called, that is to say to be
Messengers, Watchmen and Stewards . . .

The Ordering of Priests

Two people sat in the public gallery of Kingsmarkham court,
Archery and a woman with sharp, wasted features. Her long
grey hair, oddly fashionable through carelessness rather than
intent, and the cape she wore gave her a medieval look.
Presumably she was the mother of this girl who had just been
charged with manslaughter, the girl whom the clerk had named
as Elizabeth Anthea Crilling, of 24A Glebe Road, Kingsmarkham in the County of Sussex. She had a look of her mother and
they kept glancing at each other, Mrs Crilling's eyes flicking
over her daughter's string-thin body or coming to rest with
maudlin watery affection on the girl's face. It was a well-made
face, though gaunt but for the full mouth. Sometimes it seemed
to become all staring dark eyes as a word or a telling phrase
awakened emotion, sometimes blank and shuttered like that of
a retarded child with an inner life of goblins and things that
reach out in the dark. An invisible thread held mother and
daughter together but whether it was composed of love or
hatred Archery could not tell. Both were ill-dressed, dirty-look-
ing, a prey, he felt, to cheap emotion, but there was some
quality each had — passion? Imagination? Seething memory?
— that set them apart and dwarfed the other occupants of the
court.

   He had just enough knowledge of the law to know that this
court could do no more than commit the girl to the Assizes for
trial. The evidence that was being laboriously taken down on a
typewriter was all against her. Elizabeth Crilling, according to
the licensee of the Swan at Flagford, had been drinking in his
saloon bar since six-thirty. He had served her with seven double

whiskies and when he had refused to let her have another, she had abused him until he had threatened to call the police.

'No alternative but to commit you for trial at the Assizes at Lewes,' the chairman was saying. ' . . . Nothing to hope for from any promise of favour, and nothing to fear from any threat which may be . . .'

A shriek came from the public gallery. 'What are you going to do to her?' Mrs Crilling had sprung up, the tent-like cape she wore billowing out and making a breeze run through the court. 'You're not going to put her in prison?'

Hardly knowing why he did so, Archery moved swiftly along the form until he was at her side. At the same time Sergeant Martin took half a dozen rapid strides towards her, glaring at the clergyman.

'Now, madam, you'd far better come outside.'

She flung herself away from him, pulling the cape around her as if it were cold instead of suffocatingly hot.

'You're not going to put my baby in gaol!' She pushed at the sergeant who stood between her and her view of the bench. 'Get away from me, you dirty sadist!'

'Take that woman outside,' said the magistrate with icy calm. Mrs Crilling spun round to face Archery and seized his hands. 'You've got a kind face. Are you my friend?'

Archery was horribly embarrassed. 'You can ask for bail, I think,' he muttered.

The policewoman who stood by the dock came over to them. 'Come along now, Mrs Crilling . . .'

'Bail, I want bail! This gentleman is an old friend of mine and he says I can have bail. I want my rights for my baby!'

'We really can't have this sort of thing.' The magistrate cast an icy scornful look upon Archery who sat down, wrenching his hands from Mrs Crilling's. 'Do I understand you wish to ask for bail?' He turned his eyes on Elizabeth who nodded defiantly.

'A nice cup of tea, Mrs Crilling,' said the policewoman. 'Come along now.' She shepherded the demented woman out, her arm supporting her waist. The magistrate went into conference with the clerk and bail was granted to Elizabeth Crilling in her own recognisance of five hundred pounds and that of her mother for a similar sum.

'Rise, please!' said the warrant officer. It was over.

On the other side of the court Wexford shovelled his papers into his briefcase.

'A friend in need, that one,' he said to Burden, glancing in Archery's direction. 'You mark my words, he'll have a job getting out of old Mother Crilling's clutches. Remember when we had to cart her off to the mental unit at Stowerton that time? You were her friend then. Tried to kiss you, didn't she?'

'Don't remind me,' said Burden.

'Funny affair altogether last night, wasn't it? Him being on hand, I mean, to show that poor kid his way to heaven.'

'It was lucky.'

'I only remember that happening once before, except in the case of R.C.s, of course.' He turned as Archery slipped between the wooden forms and came up to them. 'Good morning, sir. I hope you slept well. I was just saying to the inspector, there was a fellow killed out Forby way soon after I came here. Must be all of twenty years. I've never forgotten it. He was just a kid too and got it in the neck from an army lorry. But he wasn't quiet, he was screaming. All about a girl and a kid it was.' He paused. 'Did you speak, sir? Sorry, I thought you did. He wanted a clergyman, too.'

'I hope and trust he got what he wanted.'

'Well, no he didn't as a matter of fact. He died — unshriven is the word, I think. The vicar's car broke down on the way. Funny, I've never forgotten it. Grace was his name, John Grace. Shall we go?'

The Crillings had departed. As they came out into the sunshine, the policewoman came up to Wexford.

'Mrs Crilling left a note with me, sir. She asked me to give it to a Mr Archery.'

'Take my advice,' said Wexford. 'Tear it up. She's as mad as a hatter.' But Archery had already opened the envelope.

Dear Sir, he read.

They tell me that you are a man of God. Blessed is he that sitteth not in the seat of the scornful. God has sent you to me and my baby. I will be at home this afternoon, waiting to thank you in person.

Your affectionate friend, Josephine Crilling

*

60

Archery's bedroom combined charmingly the best of old and new. The ceiling was beamed, the walls painted pink and decorated with a tooled design of chevrons, but there was also a fitted carpet, an abundance of lights on walls and bedhead and a telephone. He rinsed his hands at the pink washbasin (a private bathroom he felt to be an unwarranted extravagance), lifted the receiver and asked for a call to Thringford in Essex.

'Darling?'

'Henry! Thank heaven you've phoned. I've been trying over and over again to get you at that Olive Branch place or whatever it's called.'

'Why, what's the matter?'

'I've had a dreadful letter from Charles. Apparently poor darling Tess phoned her people late yesterday afternoon and now she's told Charles the engagement's definitely off. She says it wouldn't be fair on him or us.'

'And . . . ?'

'And Charles says if Tess won't marry him he's going to come down from Oxford and go out to Africa to fight for Zimbabwe.'

'How utterly ridiculous!'

'He says if you try and stop him he'll do something dreadful and get sent down.'

'Is that all?'

'Oh, no. There's lots and lots of it. Let me see. I've got the letter here. 'What's the use of Father always ballsing on' — sorry, darling, does that mean something awful? — 'on about faith and taking things on trust if he won't take Tess's word and her mother's? I've been into the whole fiasco of the case myself and it's full of holes. I think Father could get the Home Secretary to have the case re-opened if he would only make some sort of effort. For one thing there was an inheritance involved but it never came up at the trial. Three people inherited vast sums and at least one of them was buzzing around the place the day Mrs Primero died . . .'

'All right,' said Archery wearily. 'If you remember, Mary, I have a transcript of the trial myself and it cost me two hundred pounds. How are things apart from that?'

'Mr Sims is behaving rather oddly.' Mr Sims was Archery's

curate. 'Miss Bayliss says he keeps the communion bread in his pocket, and this morning she got a long blonde hair in her mouth.'

Archery smiled. This parish chit-chat was more in his wife's line than solving murders. It brought her to him visually, a handsome strong woman who minded the lines on her face that he never noticed. He was beginning to miss her mentally and physically.

'Now, listen, darling. Write back to Charles — be diplomatic. Tell him how well Tess is behaving and say I'm having some very interesting talks with the police. If there's the slightest chance of getting the case re-opened I'll write to the Home Secretary.'

'That's wonderful, Henry. Oh, there go your second lot of pips. I'll ring off. By the way, Rusty caught a mouse this morning and left it in the bath. He and Tawny are missing you.'

'Give them my love,' said Archery to please her.

He went downstairs into the dark cool dining room, ordered something called a *Navarin d'agneau*, and in a burst of recklessness, a half-bottle of Anjou. All the windows were open but on some of them the green shutters had been closed. A table in one of these embrasures reminded him with its white cloth, its tilted cane chairs and its vaseful of sweet peas of a Dufy that hung on the wall of his study at home. Filtered sunlight lay in primrose-pale bars across the cloth and the two places laid with silver.

But for himself and half a dozen elderly residents, the dining room was deserted, but presently the door from the bar opened and the head waiter ushered in a man and a woman. Archery wondered if the management would object to the apricot poodle the woman fondled in her arms. But the head waiter was smiling deferentially and Archery saw him pat the tiny woolly head.

The man was small and dark and would have been good-looking but for his glassy, red-rimmed eyes. Archery thought he might be wearing contact lenses. He sat down at the Dufy table, ripped open a packet of Peter Stuyvesant and poured the contents into a gold cigarette case. In spite of the man's obvious polish — his sleek hair, svelte suit, taut bone-smooth skin —

there was something savage in the way his white fingers tore the paper. A wedding ring and a big bold signet gleamed in the soft light as he tossed the mutilated packet on to the cloth. Archery was amused to see how much jewellery he wore, a sapphire tie pin and a watch as well as the rings.

By contrast the woman wore none. She was plainly dressed in a cream silk suit that matched her hair, and everything about her from the gauzy hat and hair to her crossed ankles was the colour of faint sunlight, so that she seemed to glow with a pale radiance. Outside the cinema and the pictures in Mary's magazines, she was the most beautiful woman he had seen for years. Compared to her Tess Painter was just a pretty girl. Archery was reminded of an ivory orchid or a tea rose which, when lifted from the florist's cube of cellophane, still retains its patina of dew.

He gave himself a little shake and applied himself determinedly to his *Navarin*. It had turned out to be two lamb chops in a brown sauce.

Between Kingsmarkham High Street and the Kingsbrook Road lies an estate of ugly terraced houses covered with that mixture of mortar and grit builders call pebble dashing. On a hot day when the roads are dusty and flickering with heat mirage these rows of dun-coloured houses look as if they have been fashioned out of sand. A giant's child might have built them, using his crude tools unimaginatively.

Archery found Glebe Road by the simple and traditional expedient of asking a policeman. He was getting into the habit of asking policemen and this one was low in the hierarchy, a young constable directing traffic at the crossroads.

Glebe Road might have been designed by the Romans, it was so straight, so long and so uncompromising. The sand houses had no woodwork about them. Their window frames were of metal and their porch canopies excrescences of pebbly plaster. After every fourth house an arch in the façade led into the back and through these arches sheds, coal bunkers and dustbins could be seen.

The street was numbered from the Kingsbrook Road end and Archery walked nearly half a mile before he found twenty-four. The hot pavements running with melted tar made his feet burn. He pushed open the gate and saw that the canopy covered not one front door but two. The house had been converted into two surely tiny flatlets. He tapped the chromium knocker on the door marked 24A and waited.

When nothing happened he tapped again. There was a grinding trundling sound and a boy on roller skates came out from under the arch. He took no notice at all of the clergyman. Could Mrs Crilling be asleep? It was hot enough for a siesta and Archery felt languid himself.

He stepped back and looked through the arch. Then he heard the door open and slam shut. So somebody was at home. He rounded the sandy wall and came face to face with Elizabeth Crilling.

At once he sensed that she had not answered, nor probably even heard, his knock. Evidently she was going out. The black dress had been changed for a short blue cotton shift that showed the outlines of her prominent hip bones. She wore backless white mules and carried a huge white and gilt handbag.

'What d'you want?' It was obvious she had no idea who he was. He thought she looked old, finished, as if somehow she had been used and wrecked. 'If you're selling something,' she said, 'you've come to the wrong shop.'

'I saw your mother in court this morning,' Archery said. 'She asked me to come and see her.'

He thought she had rather a charming smile, for her mouth was well-shaped and her teeth good. But the smile was too brief.

'That,' she said, 'was this morning.'

'Is she at home?' He looked helplessly at the doors. 'I — er — which one is it, which flat?'

'Are you kidding? It's bad enough sharing a house with her. Only a stone-deaf paralytic could stick living *underneath* her.'

'I'll go in, shall I?'

'Suit yourself. She's not likely to come out here.' The bag strap was hoisted on to the right shoulder, pulling the blue stuff tight across her breasts. Without knowing why, Archery remembered the exquisite woman in the dining room of the Olive and Dove, her petal skin and her easy grace.

Elizabeth Crilling's face was greasy. In the bright afternoon light the skin had the texture of lemon peel. 'Well, go on in,' she said sharply, unlocking the door. She pushed it open and turned away, her mules flapping and clacking down the path. 'She won't bite you,' she said over her shoulder. 'At least, I shouldn't think so. She bit me once, but there were — well, extenuating circumstances.'

Archery went into the hall. Three doors led off it but they were all closed. He coughed and said tentatively, 'Mrs Crilling?' The place was stuffy and silent. He hesitated for a moment, then opened the first of the doors. Inside was a bedroom divided into two by a hardboard partition. He had been wondering how the two women managed. Now he knew. The middle room must be where they lived. He tapped on the door and opened it.

Although the french windows were ajar the air was thick with smoke and the two ashtrays on a gateleg table were filled with stubs. Every surface was covered with papers and debris and the debris with dust. As he entered a blue budgerigar in a tiny cage broke into a stream of high brittle chatter. The cage swung furiously.

Mrs Crilling wore a pink nylon dressing gown that looked as if it had once been designed for a bride. The honeymoon, Archery thought, was long over, for the dressing gown was stained and torn and hideous. She was sitting in an armchair looking through the window at a fenced-in piece of land at the back. It could hardly be called a garden for nothing grew in it but nettles, three feet high, rose-pink fireweed, and brambles that covered everything with fly-infested tendrils.

'You hadn't forgotten I was coming, Mrs Crilling?'

The face that appeared round the wing of the chair was enough to intimidate anyone. The whites of the eyes showed all the way round the black pupils. Every muscle looked tense, taut and corrugated as if from some inner agony. Her white hair, fringed and styled like a teenager's, curtained the sharp cheekbones.

'Who are you?' She dragged herself up, clinging to the chair arm, and came slowly round to face him. The vee at the dressing gown front showed a ridged and withered valley like the bed of a long-dried stream.

'We met in court this morning. You wrote to me . . .'

He stopped. She had thrust her face within inches of his and seemed to be scrutinising it. Then she stepped back and gave a long chattering laugh which the budgerigar echoed.

'Mrs Crilling, are you all right? Is there anything I can do?'

She clutched her throat and the laugh died away in a rising wheeze. 'Tablets . . . asthma . . . ,' she gasped. He was puzzled and shocked, but he reached behind him for the bottle of tablets on the littered mantelpiece. 'Give me my tablets and then you can . . . you can get out!'

'I'm sorry if I've done anything to distress you.'

She made no attempt to take a tablet but held the bottle up against her quaking chest. The movement made the tablets rattle and the bird, fluttering its wings and beating against the bars, began a frenzied crescendo, half song and half pain.

'Where's my baby?' Did she mean Elizabeth? She must mean Elizabeth.

'She's gone out. I met her in the porch. Mrs Crilling, can I get you a glass of water? Can I make you a cup of tea?'

'Tea? What do I want with tea? That's what she said this morning, that police girl. Come and have a cup of tea, Mrs Crilling.' A terrible spasm shook her and she fell back against the chair, fighting for breath. 'You . . . my baby . . . I thought you were my friend . . . Aaah!'

Archery was really frightened now. He plunged from the room into the dirty kitchen and filled a cup with water. The window ledge was stacked with empty chemist's bottles and there was a filthy hypodermic beside an equally dirty eye dropper. When he came back she was still wheezing and jerking. Should he make her take the tablets, dare he? On the bottle label were the words: *Mrs J. Crilling. Take two when needed.* He rattled two into his hand and, supporting her with his other arm, forced them into her mouth. It was all he could do to suppress the shudder of distaste when she dribbled and choked over the water.

'Filthy . . . nasty,' she mumbled. He half-eased, half-rolled her into the chair and pulled together the gaping edges of the dressing gown. Moved with pity and with horror, he knelt down beside her.

'I will be your friend if you want me to be,' he said soothingly.

The words had the opposite effect. She made a tremendous effort to draw breath. Her lips split open and he could see her tongue rising and quivering against the roof of her mouth.

'Not my friend . . . enemy . . . police friend! Take my baby away . . . I saw you with them . . . I watched you come out with them.' He drew back from her, rising. Never would he have believed her capable of screaming after that spasm and when the scream came, as clear and ear-splitting as a child's, he felt his hands go up to his face. '. . . Not let them get her in there! Not in the prison! They'll find it out in there. She'll tell them. . . my baby . . . She'll have to tell them!' With a sudden galvanic jerk she reared up, her mouth open and her arms flailing. 'They'll find it all out. I'll kill her first, kill her . . . D'you hear?'

The french windows stood open. Archery staggered back into the sun against a stinging prickling wall of weeds. Mrs Crilling's incoherent gasps had swollen into a stream of obscenity. There was a gate in the wire netting fence. He unlatched it, wiping the sweat from his forehead, and stepped into the cool dark cave of the sand-walled arch.

'Good afternoon, sir. You don't look very well. Heat affecting you?'

Archery had been leaning over the bridge parapet, breathing deeply, when the detective inspector's face appeared beside him.

'Inspector Burden, isn't it?' He shook himself, blinking his eyes. There was comfort in this man's steady gaze and in the shoppers who flowed languidly across the bridge. 'I've just come from Mrs Crilling's and . . .'

'Say no more, sir. I quite understand.'

'I left her in the throes of an asthma attack. Perhaps I should have got a doctor or an ambulance. Frankly, I hardly knew what to do.'

There was a crumb of stony bread on the wall. Burden flicked it into the water and a swan dived for it.

'It's mostly in the mind with her, Mr Archery. I should have warned you what to expect. Threw one of her scenes on you, did she?' Archery nodded. 'Next time you see her I daresay she'll be as nice as pie. That's the way it takes her, up one minute, down the next. Manic-depressive is the term. I was just going into the Carousel for a cup of tea. Why don't you join me?'

They walked up the High Street together. Some of the shops sported faded striped sunblinds. The shadows were as black as night, the light cruelly bright under a Mediterranean blue sky. Inside the Carousel it was darkish and stuffy and it smelt of aerosol fly spray.

'Two teas, please,' said Burden.

'Tell me about the Crillings.'

'There's plenty to tell, Mr Archery. Mrs Crilling's husband died and left her without a penny, so she moved into town and got a job. The kid, Elizabeth, was always difficult and Mrs Crilling made her worse. She took her to psychiatrists — don't ask me where the money came from — and then when they made her send her to school it was one school after another. She was in St Catherine's, Sewingbury, for a bit but she got expelled. When she was about fourteen she came up before the juvenile court here as being in need of care and protection and she was taken away from her mother. But she went back eventually. They usually do.'

'Do you think all this came about because she found Mrs Primero's body?'

'Could be.' Burden looked up and smiled as the waitress brought the tea. 'Thanks very much, miss. Sugar, Mr Archery? No, I don't either.' He cleared his throat and went on, 'I reckon it would have made a difference if she'd had a decent home background, but Mrs Crilling was always unstable. In and out of jobs, by all accounts, until she ended up working in a shop. I think some relative used to give them financial assistance. Mrs Crilling used to take days off from work ostensibly on account of the asthma but really it was because she was crazy.'

'Is she certifiable?'

'You'd be surprised how difficult it is to get anyone certified, sir. The doctor did say that if ever he saw her in one of her tantrums he could get an urgency order, but they're cunning, you see. By the time the doctor gets there she's as normal as you or me. She's been into Stowerton once or twice as a voluntary patient. About four years ago she got herself a man friend. The whole place was buzzing with it. Elizabeth was training to be a physiotherapist at the time. Anyway, the upshot of it all was that the boy friend preferred young Liz.'

'*Mater pulchra, filia pulchrior,*' Archery murmured.

'Just as you say, sir. She gave up her training and went to live with him. Mrs Crilling went off her rocker again and spent six months in Stowerton. When she came out she wouldn't leave the happy couple alone, letters, phone calls, personal appearances, the lot. Liz couldn't stand it so eventually she went back to mother. The boy friend was in the car trade and he gave her that Mini.'

Archery sighed. 'I don't know if I ought to tell you this, but you've been very kind to me, you and Mr Wexford . . .' Burden felt the stirring of guilt. It wasn't what he would call kind. 'Mrs Crilling said that if Elizabeth — she calls her her baby — went to prison . . . it might mean prison, mightn't it?'

'It might well.'

'Then she'd tell you something, you or the prison authorities. I got the impression she'd feel compelled to give you some information Mrs Crilling wanted kept secret.'

'Thank you very much, sir. We shall have to wait and see what time brings forth.'

Archery finished his tea. Suddenly he felt like a traitor. Had he betrayed Mrs Crilling because he wanted to keep in with the police?

'I wondered,' he said, justifying himself, 'if it could have anything to do with Mrs Primero's murder. I don't see why Mrs Crilling couldn't have worn the raincoat and hidden it. You admit yourself she's unbalanced. She was there, she had just as much opportunity as Painter.'

Burden shook his head. 'What was the motive?'

'Mad people have motives which seem very thin to normal men.'

'But she dotes on her daughter in her funny way. She wouldn't have taken the kid with her.'

Archery said slowly, 'At the trial she said she went over the first time at twenty-five past six. But we've only her word for it.

Suppose instead she went at twenty to seven when *Painter* had already been and gone. Then she took the child back later because no-one would believe a killer would wittingly let a child discover a body she knew was there.'

'You've missed your vocation, sir,' said Burden, getting up. 'You should have come in on our lark. You'd have been a superintendent by now.'

'I'm letting my fancy run away with me,' Archery said. To avoid a repetition of the gentle teasing, he added quickly, changing the subject, 'Do you happen to know the visiting times at Stowerton Infirmary?'

'Alice Flower's next on your list, is she? I'd give the matron a ring first, if I were you. Visiting's seven till seven-thirty.'

CHAPTER EIGHT

The days of our age are threescore years and ten; and though men be so strong that they come to fourscore years, yet is their strength then but labour and sorrow.

Psalm 90. *The Burial of the Dead*

Alice Flower was eighty-seven, almost as old as her employer had been at the time of her death. A series of strokes had battered her old frame as tempests batter an ancient house, but the house was strong and sturdily built. No gimcrack refinements of decoration or delicacy had ever belonged to it. It had been made to endure wind and weather.

She lay in a narrow high bed in a ward called Honeysuckle. The ward was full of similar old women in similar beds. They had clean pink faces and white hair through which patches of rose-pink scalp showed. Every bed trolley held at least two vases of flowers, the sops to conscience, Archery supposed, of visiting relatives who only had to sit and chat instead of handling bed-pans and tending bed-sores.

'A visitor for you, Alice,' said the sister. 'It's no use trying to shake hands with her. She can't move her hands but her hearing's perfectly good and she'll talk the hind leg off a donkey.'

A most un-Christian hatred flared in Archery's eyes. If she saw it the sister took no notice.

'Like a good gossip, don't you, Alice? This is the Reverend Archery.' He winced at that, approached the bed.

'Good evening, sir.'

Her face was square with deeply ridged rough skin. One corner of her mouth had been drawn down by the paralysis of the motor nerves, causing her lower jaw to protrude and reveal large false teeth. The sister bustled about the bed, pulling the old servant's nightgown higher about her neck and arranging on the coverlet her two useless hands. It was terrible to Archery to have to look at those hands. Work had distorted them beyond hope of beauty, but disease and oedema had smoothed and whitened the skin so that they were like the hands of a misshapen baby. The emotion and the feel for the language of 1611 that was with him always welled in a fount of pity. Well done, thou good and faithful servant, he thought. Thou hast been faithful over a few things, I will make thee ruler over many things . . .

'Would it upset you to talk to me about Mrs Primero, Miss Flower?' he asked gently, easing himself into a bentwood chair.

'Of course it wouldn't,' said the sister, 'she loves it.'

Archery could bear no more. 'This is rather a private matter, if you don't mind.'

'Private! It's the whole ward's bedtime story, believe me.' She flounced away, a crackling navy and white robot.

Alice Flower's voice was cracked and harsh. The strokes had affected her throat muscles or her vocal cords. But her accent was pleasant and correct, learnt, Archery supposed, in the kitchens and nurseries of educated people.

'What was it you wanted to know, sir?'

'First tell me about the Primero family.'

'Oh, I can do that. I always took an interest.' She gave a small rattling cough and turned her head to hide the twisted side of her mouth. 'I went to Mrs Primero when the boy was born . . .'

'The boy?'

'Mr Edward, her only child he was.'

Ah, thought Archery, the father of rich Roger and his sisters.

'He was a lovely boy and we always got on a treat, him and me. I reckon it really aged me and his poor mother when he died, sir. But he'd got a family of his own by then, thanks be to God, and Mr Roger was the living spit of his father.'

'I suppose Mr Edward left him pretty well off, did he?'

'Oh, no, sir, that was the pity of it. You see, old Dr Primero left his money to madam, being as Mr Edward was doing so well at the time. But he lost everything on something in the city and when he was taken Mrs Edward and the three kiddies were quite badly off.' She coughed again, making Archery wince. He fancied he could see a terrible vain effort to raise those hands and cover the rattling lips. 'Madam offered to help — not that she had more than she needed — but Mrs Edward was that proud, she wouldn't take a penny from her mother-in-law. I never shall know how she managed. There was the three of them, you see. Mr Roger he was the eldest, and then there was the two little mites, ever so much younger than their brother, but close together if you take my meaning. No more than eighteen months between them.'

She rested her head back on the pillows and bit at her lip as if trying to pull it back into place. 'Angela was the oldest. Time flies so I reckon she'd be twenty-six now. Then there was Isabel, named after madam. They was just babies when their Daddy died and it was years before we saw them.

'It was a bitter blow to madam, I can tell you, not knowing what had become of Mr Roger. Then one day just out of the blue he turned up at Victor's Piece. Fancy, he was living in digs just over at Sewingbury, studying to be a solicitor with a very good firm. Somebody Mrs Edward knew had got him in. He hadn't no idea his granny was still alive, let alone in Kingsmarkham, but he was looking up somebody in the phone book, in the line of business, sir, and there it was: Mrs Rose Primero, Victor's Piece. Once he'd come over there was no stopping him. Not that we wanted to stop him, sir. Pretty nearly every Sunday he came and once or twice he fetched his little sisters all the way from London and brought them with him. Good as gold they were.

'Mr Roger and madam, they used to have some laughs together. All the old photographs they'd have out and the tales she used to tell him!' She stopped suddenly and Archery watched the old face swell and grow purple. 'It was a change for us to have a nice gentlemanlike young fellow about the place after that Painter.' Her voice changed to a shrill whistling shriek. 'That dirty murdering beast!'

Across the ward another old woman in a bed like Alice Flower's smiled a toothless smile as of one hearing a familiar tale retold. The ward's bedtime story, the sister had said.

Archery leant towards her. 'That was a dreadful day, Miss

Flower,' he said, 'the day Mrs Primero died.' The fierce eyes flickered, red and spongey blue. 'I expect you feel you'll never forget it . . .'

'Not to my dying day,' said Alice Flower. Perhaps she thought of the now useless body that had once been so fine an instrument and was already three-quarters dead.

'Will you tell me about it?'

As soon as she began he realised how often she must have told it before. It was likely that some of these old women were not absolutely bedridden, that sometimes in the evenings they got up and gathered round Alice Flower's bed. A tale, he thought, paraphrasing, to draw children from play and old women from the chimney corner.

'He was a devil,' she said, 'a terror. I was scared of him but I never let him know it. Take all and give nothing, that was his motto. Six pounds a year, that was all I got when I first went out into service. Him, he had his home and his wages, a lovely motor to drive. There's some folks want the moon. You'd think a big strong young fellow like that'd be only too glad to fetch the coal in for an old lady, but not Mr Bert Painter. Beast Painter was what I called him.

'That Saturday night when he never come and he never come madam had to sit all by herself in the icy cold. Let me go over and speak to him, madam, I said, but she wouldn't have it. The morning's time enough, Alice, she said. I've said to myself over and over again, if he'd come that night I'd have been in there with them. He wouldn't have been able to tell no lies then.'

'But he did come the next morning, Miss Flower . . .'

'She told him off good and proper. I could hear her giving him a dressing down.'

'What were you doing?'

'Me? When he come in first I was doing the vegetables for madam's lunch, then I popped on the oven and put in the meat tin. They asked me all that at the court in London, the Old Bailey it was.' She paused and there was suspicion in the look she gave him. 'You writing a book about it all, are you, sir?'

'Something like that,' said Archery.

'They wanted to know if I was sure I could hear all right.

74

My hearing's better than that judge's, I can tell you. Just as well it is. If I'd been hard of hearing we might have all gone up in smoke that morning.'

'How was that?'

'Beast Painter was in the drawing room with madam and I'd gone into the larder to get the vinegar for the mint sauce, when all of a sudden I heard a kind of plop and sizzle. That's that funny old oven, I said, and sure enough it was. I popped back quick and opened the oven door. One of the potatoes had kind of spat out, sir, and fallen on the gas. All in flames it was and sizzling and roaring like a steam engine. I turned it off quick and then I did a silly thing. Poured water on it. Ought to have known better at my age. Ooh, the racket and the smoke! You couldn't hear yourself think.'

There had been nothing about that in the trial transcript. Archery caught his breath in the excitement. 'You couldn't hear yourself think . . .' While you were choked with smoke and deafened by hissing you might not hear a man go upstairs, search a bedroom and come down again. Alice's evidence in this matter had been one of the most important features of the case. For if Painter had been offered and had taken the two hundred pounds in Mrs Primero's presence in the morning, what motive could he have had for killing her in the evening?

'Well, we had our lunch and Mr Roger came. My poor old leg was aching from where I'd bruised it the night before getting a few lumps in on account of Beast Painter being out on the tiles. Mr Roger was ever so nice about it, kept asking me if there was anything he could do, wash up or anything. But that isn't man's work and I always say it's better to keep going while you can.

'It must have been half past five when Mr Roger said he'd have to go. I was up to my neck what with the dishes and worrying if Beast would turn up like he'd promised. "I'll let myself out, Alice," Mr Roger said, and he come down to the kitchen to say good-bye to me. Madam was having a little snooze in the drawing room, God rest her. It was the last she had before her long sleep.' Aghast, Archery watched two tears well into her eyes and flow unchecked down the ridged sunken cheeks. 'I called out, "Cheeri-by, Mr Roger dear, see you next

Sunday", and then I heard him shut the front door. Madam was sleeping like a child, not knowing that ravening wolf was lying in wait for her.'

'Try not to upset yourself, Miss Flower.' Doubtful as to what he should do — the right thing is the kind thing, he thought — he pulled out his own clean white handkerchief and gently wiped the wet cheeks.

'Thank you, sir. I'll be all right now. You do feel a proper fool not being able to dry your own tears.' The ghastly cracked smile was almost more painful to witness than the weeping. 'Where was I? Oh, yes. Off I went to church and as soon as I was out of the way along comes Madam Crilling, poking her nose in . . .'

'I know what happened next, Miss Flower,' Archery said very kindly and quietly. 'Tell me about Mrs Crilling. Does she ever come to see you in here?'

Alice Flower gave a kind of snort that would have been comical in a fit person. 'Not she. She's kept out of my way ever since the trial, sir. I know too much about her for her liking. Madam's best friend, my foot! She'd got one interest in madam and one only. She wormed that child of hers into madam's good books on account of she thought madam might leave her something when she went.'

Archery moved closer, praying that the bell for the end of visiting would not ring yet.

'But Mrs Primero didn't make a will.'

'Oh, no, sir, that's what worried Mrs Clever Crilling. She'd come out into my kitchen when madam was sleeping. "Alice," she'd say, "we ought to get dear Mrs Primero to make her last will and testament. It's our duty, Alice, it says so in the Prayer Book." '

'Does it?'

Alice looked both shocked and smug. 'Yes, it does, sir. It says, "But men should often be put in remembrance to take order for the settling of their temporal estates whilst they are in health." Still I don't hold with everything that's in the Prayer Book, not when in comes to downright interference — saving your presence, sir. "It's in your interest too, Alice," she says. "You'll be turned out into the streets when she goes."

'But madam wouldn't have it, anyway. Everything was to go to her natural heirs, she said, them being Mr Roger and the little girls. It'd be theirs automatically, you see, without any nonsense about wills and lawyers.'

'Mr Roger didn't try to get her to make a will?'

'He's a lovely person is Mr Roger. When Beast Painter had done his murdering work and poor madam was dead Mr Roger got his bit of money — three thousand it was and a bit more. "I'll take care of you, Alice," he said, and so he did. He got me a nice room in Kingsmarkham and gave me two pounds a week on top of my pension. He was in business on his own then and he said he wouldn't give me a lump sum. An allowance, he called it, bless his heart, out of his profits.'

'Business? I thought he was a solicitor.'

'He always wanted to go into business on his own, sir. I don't know the ins and outs of it, but he came to madam one day — must have been two or three weeks before she died — and he said a pal of his would take him in with him if he could put up ten thousand pounds. "I know I haven't got a hope," he said, speaking ever so nice. "It's just a castle in the air, Granny Rose." "Well, it's no good looking at me," says madam. "Ten thousand is all I've got for me and Alice to live on and that's tucked away in Woolworth's shares. You'll get your share when I'm gone." I don't mind telling you, sir, I thought then, if Mr Roger liked to do his little sisters down he could try getting round madam to make that will and leave him the lot. But he never did, never mentioned it again, and he'd always made a point of bringing the two mites just whenever he could. Then Beast Painter killed madam and the money went like she said it would, to the three of them.

'Mr Roger's doing very well now, sir, very well indeed, and he comes to see me regular. I reckon he got the ten thousand from somewhere or maybe another pal came up with something else. It wasn't for me to ask, you see.'

A nice man, Archery thought, a man who had needed money perhaps desperately, but would do nothing underhand to get it; a man who provided for his dead grandmother's domestic while he was struggling to get a business going, who still visited her and who doubtless listened patiently over and over again to the tale Archery had just heard. A very nice man. If love, praise and devotion could reward such a man, he had his reward.

'If you should see Mr Roger, sir, if you want to see him about the story you're writing, would you give him my best respects?'

'I won't forget, Miss Flower.' He put his hand over her dead one and pressed it. 'Good-bye and thank you.' Well done, thou good and faithful servant.

It was gone eight when he got back to the Olive and Dove. The head waiter glared at him when he walked into the dining room at a quarter past. Archery stared about him at the empty room, the chairs arranged against the walls.

'Dance on tonight, sir. We did make a point of asking residents to take their dinner at seven sharp, but I expect we can find you something. In here, if you please.'

Archery followed him into the smaller of the two lounges that led off the dining room. The tables had been crammed in and people were hastily gobbling their meal. He ordered, and through the glass doors, watched the band take its place on the dais.

How was he to spend this long hot summer evening? The dancing would probably go on until half-past twelve or one and the hotel would be unbearable. A quiet stroll was the obvious thing. Or he could take the car and go and look at Victor's Piece. The waiter came back with the braised beef he had ordered, and Archery, resolutely economical, asked for a glass of water.

He was quite alone in his alcove, at least two yards from the next table, and he jumped when he felt something soft and fluffy brush against his leg. Drawing back, he put his hand down, lifted the cloth and met a pair of bright eyes set in a golden woolly skull.

'Hallo, dog,' he said.

'Oh I'm so sorry. Is he being a nuisance?'

He looked up and saw her standing beside him. They had evidently just come in, she, the man with the glassy eyes and another couple.

'Not a bit.' Archery's poise deserted him and he found himself almost stammering. 'I don't mind, really. I'm fond of animals.'

'You were here at lunch, weren't you? I expect he recognised you. Come out, Dog. He doesn't have a name. We just call him Dog because he is one and it's just as good a name as Jock or Gyp or something. When you said, "Hallo, dog," he thought you were a personal friend. He's very intelligent.'

'I'm sure he is.'

She gathered the poodle up in her arms and held him against the creamy lace of her dress. Now that she wore no hat he could see the perfect shape of her head and the high unshadowed brow. The head waiter minced over, no longer harassed.

'Back again, Louis, like the proverbial bad pennies,' said the glassy-eyed man heartily. 'My wife took a fancy to come to your hop, but we must have a spot of dinner first.' So they were married, these two. Why hadn't it occurred to him before, what business was it of his and, above all, why should it cause him this faint distress? 'Our friends here have a train to catch, so if you can go all out with the old speed we'll be eternally grateful.'

They all sat down. The poodle mooched between diners' legs, scavenging for crumbs. Archery was faintly amused to see how quickly their dinner was brought to them. They had all ordered different dishes, but there was little delay and at the same time little hustle. Archery lingered over his coffee and his bit of cheese. Surely he was no bother to anyone in his small corner. People were coming in to dance now, passing his table and leaving in their wake the faint scent of cigars and floral perfume. In the dining room, a ballroom, now, the garden doors had been opened and couples stood on the terrace listening to the music in the tranquillity of the summer night.

The poodle sat on the threshold, bored, watching the dancers.

'Come here, Dog,' said his owner. Her husband got up.

'I'll take you to the station, George,' he said. 'We've only got ten minutes, so get a wiggle on, will you?' He seemed to have a variety of expressions to imply the making of haste. 'You don't have to come, darling. Finish your coffee.'

The table was veiled in smoke. They had smoked

throughout the courses. He would be gone perhaps only half an hour but he bent over and kissed his wife. She smiled at him, lit another cigarette. When they had gone, she and Archery were alone. She moved into her husband's chair from where she could watch the dancers, many of whom she seemed to know, for she waved occasionally and nodded as if promising she would soon join them.

Archery suddenly felt lonely. He knew no one in this place except two rather hostile policemen. His stay might be for the whole fortnight. Why hadn't he asked Mary to join him? It would be a holiday for her, a change, and — heaven knew — she needed a change. In a minute, when he had finished his second cup, he would go upstairs and telephone her.

The girl's voice startled him. 'Do you mind if I have your ashtray? Ours are all full.'

'Of course not, take it.' He lifted the heavy glass plate and as he handed it to her the tips of her cool dry fingers touched his own. The hand was small, childlike, with short unpainted nails. 'I don't smoke,' he added rather foolishly.

'Are you staying here long?' Her voice was light and soft, yet mature.

'Just a few days.'

'I asked,' she said, 'because we come here so often and I hadn't seen you before today. Most of the people are regulars.' She put out the cigarette carefully, stubbing it until the last red spark was dead. 'They have these dances once a month and we always come. I love dancing.'

Afterwards Archery wondered what on earth had induced him, a country vicar nearly fifty years old, to say what he did. Perhaps it was the mingled scents, the descending twilight or just that he was alone and out of his environment, out of his identity almost.

'Would you like to dance?'

It was a waltz they were playing. He was sure he could waltz. They waltzed at church socials. You simply had to make your feet go one, two, three in a sort of triangle. And yet, for all that, he felt himself blush. What would she think of him at his age? She might suppose he was doing what Charles called 'picking her up'.

'I'd love to,' she said.

Apart from Mary and Mary's sister, she was the only woman he had danced with in twenty years. He was so shy and so overcome by the enormity of what he was doing, that for a moment he was deaf to the music and blind to the hundred or so other people who circled the floor. Then she was in his arms, a light creature of scent and lace whose body so incongruously touching his had the fluidity and the tenuousness of a summer mist. He felt that he was dreaming and because of this, this utter unreality, he forgot about his feet and what he must make them do, and simply moved with her as if he and she and the music were one.

'I'm not very good at this sort of thing,' he said when he found his voice. 'You'll have to overlook my mistakes.' He was so much taller than she that she had to lift her face up to him.

She smiled. 'Hard to make conversation when you're dancing, isn't it? I never know what to say but one must say something.'

'Like "Don't you think this is a good floor?" ' Strange, he remembered that one from undergraduate days.

'Or "Do you reverse?" It's absurd really. Here we are dancing together and I don't even know your name.' She gave a little deprecating laugh. 'It's almost immoral.'

'My name's Archery. Henry Archery.'

'How do you do, Henry Archery?' she said gravely. Then as they moved into a pool of sunset light, she looked steadily at him, the glowing colour falling on her face. 'You really don't recognise me, do you?' He shook his head, wondering if he had made some terrible *faux pas*. She gave a mock sigh. 'Such is fame! Imogen Ide. Doesn't it ring a bell?'

'I'm awfully sorry.'

'Frankly, you don't look as if you spend your leisure perusing the glossy magazines. Before I married I was what they call a top model. The most photographed face in Britain.'

He hardly knew what to say. The things that came to mind all had some reference to her extraordinary beauty and to speak them aloud would have been impertinent. Sensing his predicament, she burst out laughing, but it was a companionable laugh, warm and kind.

He smiled down at her. Then over her shoulder he caught sight of a familiar face. Chief Inspector Wexford had come on to the floor with a stout pleasant-looking woman and a young couple. His wife, his daughter and the architect's son. Archery supposed, feeling a sudden pang. He watched them sit down and just as he was about to avert his eyes, Wexford's met his. The smiles they exchanged were slightly antagonistic and Archery felt hot with awkwardness. Wexford's expression held a mocking quality as if to say that dancing was a frivolity quite out of keeping with Archery's quest. Abruptly he looked away and back to his partner.

'I'm afraid I only read *The Times*,' he said, feeling the snobbishness of the remark as soon as the words were out.

'I was in *The Times* once,' she said. 'Oh, not my picture. I was in the High Court bit. Somebody mentioned my name in a case and the judge said "Who is Imogen Ide?" '

'That really is fame.'

'I've kept the cutting to this day.'

The music that had been so liquid and lullaby-like suddenly jerked into a frightening tempo with a stormy undertone of drums.

'I haven't a hope of doing this one,' Archery said helplessly. He released her quickly, there in the middle of the floor.

'Never mind. Thank you very much anyway. I've enjoyed it.'

'So have I, very much indeed.'

They began to thread their way between couples who were shuddering and bounding about like savages. She was holding his hand and he could hardly withdraw it without rudeness.

'Here's my husband back,' she said. 'Won't you join us for the evening if you've nothing better to do?'

The man called Ide was coming up to them, smiling. His evenly olive face, dead black hair and almost feminine standard of grooming gave him the look of a waxwork. Archery had the absurd notion that if you came upon him at Madame Tussaud's the old joke of the naive spectator mistaking a model for a flesh and blood attendant would be reversed. In this case you would pass the real man by, thinking him a figure in wax.

'This is Mr Archery, darling. I've been telling him he ought to stay. It's such a beautiful night.'

'Good idea. Perhaps I can get you a drink, Mr Archery?'

'Thank you, no.' Archery found himself shaking hands, astonished because of his fantasy at the warmth of Ide's hand. 'I must go. I have to phone my wife.'

'I hope we shall see you again,' said Imogen Ide. 'I enjoyed our dance.' She took her husband's hand and they moved away into the centre of the floor, their bodies meeting, their steps following the intricate rhythm. Archery went upstairs to his bedroom. Earlier he had supposed that the music would annoy him but here in the violet-coloured dusk it was enchanting, disturbing, awakening in him forgotten, undefined longings. He stood at the window, looking at the sky with its long feathery scarves of cloud, rose pink as cyclamen petals but less substantial. The strains of the music had softened to match this tranquil sky and now they seemed to him like the opening bars of an overture to some pastoral opera.

Presently he sat down on the bed and put his hand to the telephone. It rested there immobile for some minutes. What was the point of ringing Mary when he had nothing to tell her, no plans even for what he would do in the morning? He felt a sudden distaste for Thringford and its small parochial doings. He had lived there so long, so narrowly, and outside all the time there had been a world of which he knew little.

From where he sat he could see nothing but sky, broken continents and islands on a sea of azure. 'Here will we sit and let the sound of music creep in our ears . . .' He took his hand from the telephone and lay back, thinking of nothing.

CHAPTER NINE

The words of his mouth were softer than butter, having war in his heart: his words were smoother than oil, and yet be they very swords.

Psalm 55, appointed for the Tenth Day.

'I suppose there isn't anything in it?'

'In what, Mike? Liz Crilling having some dark secret her mother doesn't want extorted from her under the third degree?'

Burden lowered the blinds against the brazen morning sky.

'Those Crillings always make me uneasy,' he said.

'They're no more kinky than half our customers,' Wexford said breezily. 'Liz'll turn up at the Assizes all right. If not for any other reason simply because Mrs Crilling doubts her ability to get a thousand quid out of her brother-in-law, or whoever it is supports them. And then if she's got something to tell us, she'll tell us.'

Burden's expression, though apologetic, was obstinate.

'I can't help feeling it's got some connection with Painter,' he said.

Wexford had been leafing through a thick orange-coloured trade directory. Now he dropped it on the desk with a deliberate bang.

'By God, I won't have any more of this! What is it, anyhow, some sort of conspiracy to prove I can't do my job?'

'I'm sorry, sir, you know I didn't mean that.'

'I don't know a damn' thing, Mike. I only know the Painter case was an open and shut affair, and nobody's got a hope in hell of showing he didn't do it.' He began to calm down slowly, and he spread his hands in two large implacable fans on the directory cover. 'Go and question Liz by all means. Or tell Archery to do it for you. He's a fast worker that one.'

'Is he? What makes you say so?'

'Never mind. I've got work to do if you haven't and . . .' said Wexford, splendidly co-ordinating his metaphors, 'I'm fed up to my back teeth with having Painter rammed down my throat morning, noon and night.'

Archery had slept deeply and dreamlessly. It occurred to him that he had done all his dreaming while he was awake and there was none left for sleep. The telephone roused him. It was his wife.

'Sorry it's so early, darling, but I've had another letter from Charles.'

There was a cup of cold tea by the bed. Archery wondered how long it had been there. He found his watch and saw that it was nine.

'That's all right. How are you?'

'Not so bad. You sound as if you're still in bed.'

Archery grunted something.

'Now, listen. Charles is coming down tomorrow and he says he's coming straight over to Kingsmarkham.'

'Coming *down*?'

'Oh, it's all right, Henry. He's going to cut the last three days of term. Surely it can't matter much.'

'As long as it isn't the thin end of the wedge. Is he coming to the Olive?'

'Well, naturally. He's got to stay somewhere. I know it's expensive, darling, but he's got himself a job for August and September — something in a brewery. It sounds awful but he's going to get sixteen pounds a week and he says he'll pay you back.'

'I hadn't realised I made such an avaricious impression on my son.'

'You know he doesn't mean that. You *are* touchy this morning . . .'

After she had rung off he still held the receiver for some moments in his hand. He wondered why he hadn't asked her to join him as well. He had meant to last night and then . . . Of course, he had been so drowsy while she was speaking that he hardly knew what he was saying. The operator's voice broke in.

'Have you finished or did you want to make a call?'

'No thank you. I've finished.'

The little sandy houses in Glebe Road seemed to have been bleached and dried up by the sun. This morning they looked even more like desert dwellings, each surrounded by its own scanty oasis.

Burden went first to number a hundred and two. An old acquaintance of his lived there, a man with a long record and a nasty sense of humour called by some 'Monkey' Matthews. Burden thought it more than likely that he was responsible for the home-made bomb, a bizarre affair of sugar and weed killer stuffed into a whisky bottle that a blonde woman of easy virtue had received that morning through her letter box. The bomb had done no more than wreck the hall of her flat, she and her current lover being still in bed, but Burden thought it might amount to attempted murder just the same.

He knocked and rang but he was sure the bell didn't work. Then he went round the back and found himself ankle-deep in garbage, pram wheels, old clothes, newspapers and empty bottles. He looked through the kitchen window. There was a packet of weed killer — sodium chlorate crystals — on the window sill and the top had been torn off. How confident could you get, or how stupid? He went back up the street to a call box and told Bryant and Gates to pick up the occupant of a hundred and two Glebe Road.

Twenty-four was on the same side. Now he was so near there would be no harm in having a chat with Liz Crilling. The front door was closed but the latch was down. He coughed and walked in.

In the back room a plastic transistor was playing pop music. Elizabeth Crilling sat at the table reading the Situations Vacant in last week's local paper and she was wearing nothing but a slip, its broken shoulder strap held together with a safety pin.

'I don't remember inviting you in.'

Burden looked at her distastefully. 'D'you mind putting something on?' She made no move but kept her eyes on the paper. He glanced around the dismal, untidy room, and from the various miscellaneous heaps of clothes, selected something that might have been a dressing gown, a pink floppy thing whose flounces recalled withered petals. 'Here,' he said, and he wondered if she were not quite well, for she shuddered as she put the dressing gown round her. It was far too big, obviously not her own.

'Where's your mother?'

'I don't know. Gone out somewhere. I'm not her keeper.' She grinned suddenly, showing her beautiful teeth. 'Am I my mother's keeper? That's good, don't you think? Which reminds me . . .' The smile died and she exclaimed sharply, 'What's that clergyman doing here?'

Burden never answered a question if he could help it.

'Looking for a new post, are you?'

She gave a sulky pout. 'I phoned my firm yesterday when I got back from that bloody court and they gave me the push. I've got you lot to thank for that.' Burden inclined his head politely. 'Well, I've got to have a job, haven't I? They want girls at the raincoat factory and they say you can pick up twenty quid a week with overtime.'

Burden remembered her education, the expensive schools the Crilling relatives had paid for. She stared at him boldly.

'I may as well go and see them,' she said. 'What's the harm? Life's hell anyway.' She gave a strident laugh, walked to the mantelpiece and leaned against it, looking down at him. The open dressing gown, the tatty underclothes were provocative in a raw, basic way, that seemed to go with the hot weather and the dishevelled room. 'To what do I owe the honour of this visit? Are you lonely, Inspector? I hear your wife's away.' She took a cigarette and put it between her lips. Her forefinger was rusty with nicotine, the nail yellow, the cuticle bitten. 'Where the hell are the matches?'

There was something in the quick wary look she gave over her shoulder that impelled him to follow her to the kitchen. Once there, she turned to face him, grabbed a box of matches and stood as if barring his way. He felt a thrill of alarm. She thrust the matches into his hand.

'Light it for me, will you?'

He struck the match steadily. She came very close to him and as the flame shrivelled the tobacco, closed her fingers over his hand. For a split second he felt what his rather prudish nature told him was vile, then that nature, his duty and a swift suspicion took over. She was breathing hard, but not, he was certain, because of his nearness to her. From long practice he side-stepped neatly, freeing the long bare leg from between his own, and found himself confronting what she perhaps had hoped to hide from him.

The sink was crammed with dirty crocks, potato peelings, tea leaves, wet paper, but the Crillings were long past middle-class concealment of squalor.

'You could do with a few days off, I should think,' he said loudly. 'Get this place in some sort of order.'

She had begun to laugh. 'You know, you're not so bad-looking on the other side of a smoke-screen.'

'Been ill, have you?' He was looking at the empty pill bottles, the one that was half full and the syringe. 'Nerves, I daresay.'

She stopped laughing. 'They're hers.'

Burden read labels, saying nothing.

'She has them for her asthma. They're all the same.' As he put out his hand to find the hypodermic she seized his wrist. 'You've no business to turn things over. That amounts to searching and for searching you need a warrant.'

'True,' said Burden placidly. He followed her back to the living room and jumped when she shouted at him:

'You never answered my question about the clergyman.'

'He's come here because he knows Painter's daughter,' said Burden guardedly.

She went white and he thought she looked like her mother.

'Painter that killed the old woman?'

Burden nodded.

'That's funny,' she said. 'I'd like to see her again.' He had a queer feeling she was changing the subject, and yet her remark was not inconsequential. She turned her eyes towards the garden. But it wasn't, he thought, the nettles, the brambles and the mean wire fence she could see. 'I used to go over to the coach house and play with her,' she said. 'Mother never knew. She said Tess wasn't my class. I couldn't understand that. I thought, how can she have a class if she doesn't go to school?' She reached up and gave the birdcage a vicious push. 'Mother

88

Respectability, always respectability.

'Did you ring me up about something special, Mr Archery, or was it just for a chat?'

'I wondered if you'd mind giving me your husband's business number?'

'If you two think you can get together,' she said more warmly, 'and have a go at patching things up, that would suit me down to the ground. I really can't contemplate the idea of my Tess being — well, thrown over.' Archery did not answer. 'The number's Uplands 62234,' she said.

Kershaw had an extension of his own and a bright cockney secretary.

'I want to write to Painter's commanding officer,' Archery said when the civilities had been exchanged.

Kershaw seemed to hesitate, then said in his usual eager vital voice, 'Don't know the bloke's name, but it was the Duke of Babraham's Light Infantry he was in. Third Battalion. The War Office'll tell you.'

'The defence didn't call him at the trial, but it might help me if he could give Painter a good character.'

'If. I wonder why the defence didn't call him, Mr Archery?'

The War Office was helpful. The Third Battalion had been commanded by a Colonel Cosmo Plashet. He was an old man now living in retirement in Westmorland. Archery made several attempts to write to Colonel Plashet. The final letter was not what he would have wished, but it would have to do. After lunch he went out to post it.

He strolled up towards the Post Office. Time hung heavy on his hands and he had no notion what to do next. Tomorrow Charles would come, full of ideas and extravagant plans, but comforting, an assistant. Or, knowing Charles, a director. He badly needed someone to direct him. Police work is for policemen, he thought, experts who are trained and have all the means for detection at their disposal.

Then he saw her. She was coming out of the florist's next door to the Post Office and her arms were full of white roses. They matched and mingled with the white pattern on her black dress so that you could not tell which were real and which a mere design on silk.

'Good afternoon, Mr Archery,' said Imogen Ide.

Until now he had hardly noticed the beauty of the day, the intense blue of the sky, the glory of perfect holiday weather. She smiled.

'Would you be very kind and open the car door for me?'

He jumped to do her bidding like a boy. The poodle, Dog, was sitting on the passenger seat and when Archery touched the door, he growled and showed his teeth.

'Don't be such a fool,' she said to the dog and dumped him on the back seat. 'I'm taking these up to Forby cemetery. My husband's ancestors have a sort of vault there. Very feudal. He's in town so I said I'd do it. It's an interesting old church. Have you seen much of the country round here yet?'

'Very little, I'm afraid.'

'Perhaps you don't care for clerestories and fonts and that sort of thing.'

'Quite the contrary, I assure you. I'll get the car and go over to Forby tonight if you think it's worth seeing.'

'Why not come now?'

He had meant her to ask him. He knew it and he was ashamed. Yet what was there to be ashamed about? In a way he was on holiday and holiday acquaintances were quickly made. He had met her husband and it was only by chance her husband was not with her now. In that case there was no harm in a man going on a little excursion with a woman. How many times had he picked up Miss Bayliss in Thringford village and driven her into Colchester to do her shopping? Imogen Ide was much farther removed from him in age than Miss Bayliss. She couldn't be more than thirty. He was old enough to be her father. Suddenly he wished he hadn't thought of that, for it put things in an unpleasant perspective.

'It's very good of you,' he said. 'I'd like to.'

She was a good driver. For once he didn't mind being driven, didn't wish he was at the wheel. It was a beautiful car, a silver Lancia Flavia, and it purred along the winding roads. All was still and they passed only two other cars. The meadows were rich green or pale yellow where they had been shorn of hay, and between them and a dark ridge of woodland ran a glittering brown stream.

'That's the Kingsbrook,' she said, 'the same one that passes under the High Street. Isn't it strange? Man can do almost anything, move mountains, create seas, irrigate deserts, but he can't prevent the flow of water. He can dam it, channel it, pass it through pipes, make bridges over it . . .' He watched her, remembering with wonder that she had been a photographic model. Her lips were parted and the breeze blew her hair. 'But still it springs from the earth and finds its way to the sea.'

He said nothing and hoped she could sense if not see his nod. They were coming into a village. A dozen or so cottages and a couple of big houses surrounded a sprawling green; there was a little inn and through a mass of dark green foliage. Archery could see the outlines of the church.

The entrance to the churchyard was by way of a kissing gate. He followed Imogen Ide and he carried the roses. The place was shady and cool but not well-tended and some of the older gravestones had tumbled over on their backs into the tangle of nettles and briars.

'This way,' she said, taking the left-hand path. 'You mustn't go widdershins around a church. It's supposed to be unlucky.'

Yews and ilexes bordered the path. Underfoot it was sandy, yet green with moss and the delicate tufts of arenaria. The church was very old and built of rough-hewn oaken logs. Its beauty lay in its antiquity.

'It's one of the oldest wooden churches in the country.'

'There's one like it in my county,' said Archery. 'At Greensted. I believe it's ninth century.'

'This one's Nine something. Would you like to see the leper squint?'

They knelt down side by side and, bending forward, he peered through the small triangular gap at the base of the log wall. Although it was not the first of its kind he had seen, it pained him to think of the outcast, the unclean, who came to this tiny grille and listening to the Mass, received on his tongue the bread that some believe is the body of God. It made him think of Tess, herself an outcast, condemned like the leper to an undeserved disease. Within he could see a little stone aisle, wooden pews and a pulpit carved with saints' faces. He shivered and he felt her shiver beside him.

93

They were very close together under the yew boughs. He had a strange feeling that they were quite alone in the world and that they had been brought here for the working out of some destiny. He lifted his eyes, and turning to her, met hers. He expected her to smile but instead her face was grave, yet full of wonder and a kind of fear. He felt in himself, without analysing it, the emotion he saw in her eyes. The scent of the roses was intoxicating, fresh and unbearably sweet.

Then he got to his feet quickly, a little quelled by the stiffness of his knees. For a moment he had felt like a boy; his body betrayed him as bodies always do.

She said rather brightly, 'Have a look inside while I put these flowers on the grave. I won't be long.'

He went softly up the aisle and stood before the altar. Anyone watching him might have taken him for an atheist, so cool and appraising was his glance. Back again to look at the unassuming little font, the inscriptions on the wall plaques. He put two half-crowns in the box and signed his name in the visitors' book. His hand was shaking so badly that the signature looked like that of an old man.

When he came out once more into the churchyard she was nowhere to be seen. The lettering on the older stones had been obliterated by time and weather. He walked into the new part, reading the last messages of relatives to their dead.

As he came to the end of the path where the hedge was and on the other side of the hedge a meadow, a name that seemed familiar caught his eye. Grace, John Grace. He reflected, searching his mind. It was not a common name and until quite recently he had associated it only with the great cricketer. Of course — a boy had lain dying in the road and that death and that boy's request had reminded Wexford of another similar tragedy. Wexford had told him about it in the court. 'Must be all of twenty years . . .'

Archery looked to the engraved words for confirmation.

Sacred to the Memory of
John Grace
Who departed This Life
February 16th, 1945

In the Twenty-First Year
of His Age

Go, Shepherd, to your rest;
Your tale is told.
The Lamb of God takes
Shepherds to his fold.

A pleasant, if not brilliant, conceit, Archery thought. It was apparently a quotation, but he didn't recognise it. He looked round as Imogen Ide approached. The leaf shadows played on her face and made a pattern on her hair so that it looked as if it was covered by a veil of lace.

'Are you reminding yourself of your mortality?' she asked him gravely.

'I suppose so. It's an interesting place.'

'I'm glad to have had the opportunity of showing it to you. I'm very patriotic — if that's the word — about my country though it hasn't been mine for long.'

He was certain she was going to offer herself as his guide on some future occasion and he said quickly: 'My son is coming tomorrow. We'll have to explore together.' She smiled politely. 'He's twenty-one,' he added rather fatuously.

Simultaneously their eyes turned to the inscription on the stone.

'I'm ready to go if you are,' she said.

She dropped him outside the Olive and Dove. They said good-bye briskly and he noticed she said nothing about hoping to see him again. He didn't feel like tea and he went straight upstairs. Without knowing why he took out the photograph he had of Painter's daughter. Looking at the picture, he wondered why he had thought her so lovely. She was just a pretty girl with the prettiness of youth. Yet while he looked he seemed to realise for the first time why Charles longed so passionately to possess her. It was a strange feeling and it had little to do with Tess, with Tess's appearance or with Charles. In a way it was a universal diffused empathy, but it was selfish too and it came from his heart rather than from his mind.

95

CHAPTER TEN

And if he hath not before disposed of his goods, let him be admonished to make his will . . . for the better discharging of his conscience and the quietness of his executors.

The Visitation of the Sick

'You don't seem to have got very far,' said Charles. He sat down in an armchair and surveyed the pleasant lounge. The maid who was operating a floor polisher thought him very handsome with his rather long fair hair and his scornful expression. She decided to give the lounge a more than usually thorough do. 'The great thing is to be businesslike about it. We haven't got all that long. I start at the brewery on Monday week.' Archery was rather nettled. His own parochial duties were being overlooked. 'I'm sure there's something fishy about that fellow Primero, Roger Primero. I rang him up before I got here last night and I've got a date to see him this morning at half eleven.'

Archery looked at his watch. It was almost ten.

'You'd better get a move on, then. Where does he live?'

'You see? Now if I'd been in your shoes that's the first thing I'd have found out. He lives at Forby Hall. I suppose he fancies himself as the lord of the manor.' He glanced at his father and said quickly, 'Be all right if I have the car?'

'I suppose so. What are you going to tell him, Charles? He might have you thrown out.'

'I don't think he will,' Charles said thoughtfully. 'I've found out a bit about him and it seems he's mad keen on publicity. Always trying to create an image.' He hesitated, then added boldly, 'I told him I was the top features man on the *Sunday Planet* and we were doing a series on tycoons. Rather good, don't you think?'

'It doesn't happen to be true,' said Archery.

Charles said rapidly, 'The end justifies the means. I thought

I could put across the line about his early life being dogged by misfortune, father dying, grandmother murdered, no prospects — that sort of thing. And look at him now. You never know what will come out. He's supposed to be very forthcoming to the Press.'

'We'd better go and get the car out.'

It was as hot as ever, but more sultry. A thin mist covered the sun. Charles wore an open necked white shirt and rather tapering trousers. Archery thought he looked like a Regency duellist.

'You won't want to start yet,' he said. 'Forby's only about four miles away. Would you like to look round the place?'

They walked up the High Street and over the Kingsbrook bridge. Archery was proud to have his son beside him. He knew they were very much alike but he didn't for a moment deceive himself they might be taken for brothers. The heavy muggy weather had brought on a twinge of lumbago and today he had utterly forgotten what it felt like to be twenty-one.

'You're reading English,' he said to Charles. 'Tell me where this comes from.' His memory hadn't begun to fail, at any rate. He was word perfect in the little verse.

> ' "Go, Shepherd, to your rest;
> Your tale is told.
> The lamb of God takes
> Shepherds to his fold." '

Charles shrugged. 'Sounds vaguely familiar, but I can't place it. Where did you see it?'

'On a gravestone in Forby churchyard.'

'You really are the end, Father. I thought you wanted to help me and Tess and all you've been doing is messing about in cemeteries.'

Archery controlled himself with difficulty. If Charles was going to take everything into his own hands there seemed no reason why he shouldn't just go back to Thringford. There was nothing to keep him in Kingsmarkham. He wondered why the prospect of returning to the vicarage seemed ineffably dull. Suddenly he stopped and nudged his son's arm.

'What's the matter?'

'That woman outside the butcher's, the one in the cape — it's that Mrs Crilling I told you about. I'd rather not come face to face with her.'

But it was too late. She had evidently seen them already, for with her cape flying, she came bearing down upon them like a galleon.

'Mr Archery! My dear friend!' She took both his hands in hers and swung them as if she were about to partner him in an eightsome reel. 'What a lovely surprise! I was only saying to my daughter this morning, I do hope I shall see that dear man again so that I can thank him for ministering to me in my wretched affliction.'

This was a new mood. She was like a dowager at a successful garden party. The cape was familiar but the dress she wore under it was an ordinary cotton frock, simple and dowdy, somewhat splashed with gravy stains on its front. She gave a broad, calm and gracious smile.

'This is my son, Charles,' Archery muttered. 'Charles, this is Mrs Crilling.'

To his surprise Charles took the outstretched, none-too-clean hand and half-bowed over it.

'How do you do?' Over her head he gave his father an angry glance. 'I've heard so much about you.'

'Nice things, I hope.' If it occurred to her that Archery had seen nothing nice about her to relate she gave no sign of it. She was quite sane, gay, even frivolous. 'Now, don't refuse to gratify my little whim. I want you both to come into the Carousel and take a wee cup of coffee with me. My treat, of course,' she added archly.

'Our time,' said Charles grandiloquently — absurdly, Archery thought, 'is quite at your disposal. Until eleven fifteen, that is. Don't let us discuss anything so absurd as treats in the company of a lady.'

Evidently it was the right line to take with her. 'Isn't he *sweet*?' she gurgled. They went into the cafe. 'Children are such a blessing, don't you think? The crown of the tree of life. You must be proud of him, even though he quite puts you in the shade.'

Charles pulled out a chair for her. They were the only customers and for a while no one came to take their order. Mrs Crilling leant confidingly towards Archery.

'My baby has got herself a situation and she starts tomorrow. An operative in a ladies' wear establishment. I understand the prospects are excellent. With her intelligence there's no knowing how far she can go. The trouble is she's never had a real chance.' She had been speaking in a low genteel voice. Suddenly she turned her back on him, banged the sugar basin on the table and screamed loudly in the direction of the kitchen:

'Service!'

Charles jumped. Archery shot him a glance of triumph.

'Always having her hopes raised and then it comes to nothing,' she went on just as if the scream had never happened. 'Her father was just the same — struck down with T.B. in the flower of his age and dead within six months.' Archery flinched as she jerked away from him once more. 'Where the flaming hell are those bloody girls?' she shouted.

A woman in a green uniform with Manageress embroidered on the bodice came out of the kitchen. The look she gave Mrs Crilling was bored and withering.

'I asked you not to come in here again, Mrs Crilling, if you can't behave yourself.' She smiled frostily at Archery. 'What can I get you, sir?'

'Three coffees, please.'

'I'll have mine black,' said Charles.

'What was I talking about?'

'Your daughter,' said Archery hopefully.

'Oh, yes, my baby. It's funny really she should have had such a bad break because when she was a little tot it looked as if everything in the garden was lovely. I had a dear old friend, you see, who simply doted on my baby. And she was rolling in money, kept servants and all that kind of thing . . .'

The coffee came. It was the espresso kind with foam on the top.

'You can bring me some white sugar,' said Mrs Crilling sulkily. 'I can't stomach that demerara muck.' The waitress flounced away, returned with another sugar bowl and banged it down on the table. Mrs Crilling gave a shrill little shriek as soon as she was out of earshot. 'Silly bitch!'

Then she returned to her theme. 'Very old my friend was and beyond being responsible for her actions. Senile, they call it. Over and over again she told me she wanted to do something for my baby. I passed it off, of course, having an absolute revulsion about stepping into dead men's shoes.' She stopped suddenly and dropped four heaped teaspoonfuls of sugar into her coffee.

'Naturally,' said Charles. 'The last thing anyone would call you is mercenary, Mrs Crilling.'

She smiled complacently and to Archery's intense amusement, leant across the table and patted Charles's cheek.

'You dear,' she said. 'You lovely, understanding dear.' After a deep breath she went on more practically, 'Still, you have to look after your own. I didn't press it, not till the doctor told me Mr Crilling had only got six months to live. No insurance, I thought in my despair, no pension. I pictured myself reduced to leaving my baby on the steps of an orphanage.'

For his part, Archery was unable to picture it. Elizabeth had been a sturdy youngster of five at the time.

'Do go on,' said Charles. 'It's most interesting.'

'You ought to make a will, I said to my friend. I'll pop down the road and get you a will form. A thousand or two would make all the difference to my baby. You know how she's gladdened your last years, and what have those grandchildren of yours ever done for you? Damn all, I thought.'

'But she didn't make a will?' Archery said.

'What do you know about it? You let me tell it in my own way. It was about a week before she died. I'd had the will form for weeks and weeks and all the time poor Mr Crilling was wasting away to a shadow. But would she fill it in? Not her, the old cow. I had to use all my most winning powers of persuasion. Every time I said a word that crazy old maid of hers would put her spoke in. Then that old maid — Flower, her name was — she got a bad cold and had to keep to her bed. "Have you thought any more about disposing of your temporal estates?" I said to my friend in a light-hearted, casual manner. "Maybe I should do something for Lizzie," she said and I knew my opportunity was at hand.

'Back across the road I flew. I didn't like to witness it myself, you know, on account of my baby being a beneficiary. Mrs White, my neighbour, came over and the lady who helped with her housework. They were only too delighted. You might say it brought a ray of sunshine into their humdrum lives.'

Archery wanted to say, 'But Mrs Primero died intestate.' He didn't dare. Any hint that he knew whom she was talking about and the whole narrative might be brought to a halt.

'Well, we got it all written out. I'm a great reader, Mr Archery, so I was able to put it in the right language. "Blood is thicker that water," said my old friend — she was wandering in her mind — but she only put the grandchildren down for five hundred apiece. There was eight thousand for my baby and I was to have charge of it till she was twenty-one, and a bit left over for the Flower woman. My friend was crying bitterly. I reckon she realised how wicked she'd been in not doing it before.

'And that was that. I saw Mrs White and the other lady safely off the premises — more fool I, though I didn't know it at the time. I said I'd keep the will safe and I did. She wasn't to mention it to anybody. And — would you believe it? — a week later she met with her death.'

Charles said innocently, 'That was a good start for your daughter, Mrs Crilling, whatever misfortunes came afterwards.'

He started as she got up abruptly. Her face had blanched to the whiteness it had worn in court and her eyes blazed.

'Any benefits she got,' she said in a choking voice, 'came from her dead father's people. Charity it was, cold charity. "Send me the school bills, Josie," her uncle'd say to me. "I'll pay them direct, and her auntie can go with her to get her uniform. If you think she needs treatment for her nerves her auntie can go with her to Harley Street, too." '

'But what about the will?'

'That bloody will!' Mrs Crilling shouted. 'It wasn't legal. I only found out after she was dead. I took it straight round to Quadrants, the solicitors that were in the High Street. Old Mr Quadrant was alive then. "What about these alterations?" he said. Well, I looked and, lo and behold, the old cow had scribbled in a lot of extra bits while I was at the front door with

Mrs White. Scribbled in bits and scratched out bits too. "These invalidate the whole thing," said Mr Quadrant. "You have to get the witnesses to sign them, or have a codicil. You could fight it," he said, looking me up and down in a nasty way, knowing I hadn't got a bean. "But I wouldn't say much for your chances." '

To Archery's horror she broke into a stream of obscenities, many of which he had never heard before. The manageress came out and took her by the arm.

'Out you go. We can't have this in here.'

'My God,' said Charles, after she had been hustled away. 'I see what you mean.'

'I must confess her language shook me a bit.'

Charles chuckled. 'Not fit for your ears at all.'

'It was most enlightening, though. Are you going to bother with Primero now?'

'It can't do any harm.'

Archery had to wait a long time in the corridor outside Wexford's office. Just as he was beginning to think he would have to give up and try again later, the main entrance doors opened and a little bright-eyed man in working clothes came in between two uniformed policemen. He was plainly some sort of criminal, but everyone seemed to know him and find him a source of ironic amusement.

'I can't stand these contemporary-type nicks,' he said impudently to the station sergeant. Wexford came out of his office, ignoring Archery, and crossed to the desk. 'Give me the old-fashioned kind every time. I've got a slummy mind, that's my trouble.'

'I'm not interested in your views on interior decoration, Monkey,' said Wexford.

The little man turned to him and grinned.

'You've got a nasty tongue, you have. Your sense of humour's sunk as you've gone up. Pity, really.'

'Shut up!'

Archery listened in admiration. He wished that he had the power and the authority to talk like that to Mrs Crilling, or that such authority could be vested in Charles, enabling him to question Primero without the inhibitions of subterfuge. Wexford, talking silkily about bombs and attempted murder, ushered the little man into his office and the door closed on them. Such things did go on, Archery thought. Perhaps his own new-forming theories were not so far-fetched after all.

'If I could just see Inspector Burden for a moment,' he said more confidently to the station sergeant.

'I'll see if he's free, sir.'

Eventually Burden came out to him himself.

'Good morning, sir. Doesn't get any cooler, does it?'

'I've got something rather important to tell you. Can you spare me five minutes?'

'Surely.'

But he made no move to take him into a more private place. The station sergeant occupied himself with perusing a large book. Sitting on a ridiculous spoon-shaped chair outside Wexford's office, Archery felt like a school boy who, having waited a long time to see the headmaster, is compelled to confide in and perhaps take his punishment from an underling. Rather chastened, he told Burden briefly about Mrs Crilling.

'Most interesting. You mean that when Mrs Primero was murdered the Crilling woman thought the will was valid?'

'It amounts to that. She didn't mention the murder.'

'We can't do anything. You realise that?'

'I want you to tell me if I have sufficient grounds to write to the Home Secretary.'

A constable appeared from somewhere, tapped on Wexford's door and was admitted.

'You haven't any circumstantial evidence,' Burden said. 'I'm sure the Chief Inspector wouldn't encourage it.'

A roar of sardonic laughter sounded through the thin dividing wall. Archery felt unreasonably piqued.

'I think I shall write just the same.'

'You must do as you please, sir.' Burden got up. 'Been seeing much of the country round here?'

Archery swallowed his anger. If Burden intended to terminate the interview with small talk, small talk he should have. Hadn't he promised his old friend Griswold and, for that matter, the Chief Inspector, not to make trouble?

'I went to Forby yesterday,' he said. 'I was in the church-

103

yard and I happened to notice the grave of that boy Mr Wexford was talking about in court the other day. His name was Grace. Do you remember?'

Burden's face was a polite blank but the station sergeant glanced up.

'I'm a Forby man myself, sir,' he said. 'We make a bit of a song and dance about John Grace at home. They'll tell you all about him in Forby for all it was twenty years ago.'

'All about him?'

'He fancied himself as a poet, poor kid, wrote plays too. Sort of religious mystic he was. In his day he used to try and sell his verses from door to door.'

'Like W. H. Davis,' said Archery.

'I daresay.'

'Was he a shepherd?'

'Not as far as I know. Baker's roundsman or something.'

Wexford's door swung open, the constable came out and said to Burden, 'Chief Inspector wants you, sir.'

Wexford's voice roared after him, 'You can come back in here, Gates, and take a statement from Guy Fawkes. And give him a cigarette. He won't blow up.'

'It seems I'm wanted, sir, so if you'll excuse me . . .'

Burden went with Archery to the entrance doors.

'You had your chat with Alice Flower just in time,' he said. 'If you had it, that is.'

'Yes, I talked to her. Why?'

'She died yesterday,' said Burden. 'It's all in the local rag.'

Archery found a newsagent. The *Kingsmarkham Chronicle* had come out that morning and fresh stacks of papers lay on the counter. He bought a copy and found the announcement at the bottom of the back page.

'Death of Miss A. Flower.'

He scanned it and took it back with him to the terrace of the hotel to read it properly.

'The death occurred today . . .' That meant yesterday, Archery thought, looking at the dateline. He read on. 'The death occurred today of Miss Alice Flower at Stowerton Infirmary. She was eighty-seven. Miss Flower, who had lived in the district for twenty-five years, will be best remembered for the part she played in the notorious Victor's Piece murder trial. She was for many years maid and trusted friend of Mrs Primero . . .'

There followed a brief account of the murder and the trial.

'The funeral will take place at Forby parish church on Monday. Mr Roger Primero has expressed a wish that the last rites may be celebrated quietly and that there will be no sightseers.'

Roger Primero, faithful to the end, Archery thought. He found himself hoping that Charles had done nothing to distress this kindly and dutiful man. So Alice Flower was dead at last, death had waited just long enough to let her tell him, Archery, all she knew. Again he seemed to feel the working of destiny. Well done, thou good and faithful servant. Enter thou into the joy of thy Lord!

He went in to lunch, feeling jaded and depressed. Where on earth was Charles? He had been gone more than two hours. By now Primero had probably seen through that absurd cover story and . . .

His imagination showing him his son being interrogated by Wexford at his nastiest, he was just picking at his fruit salad and warm ice-cream when Charles burst into the dining room, swinging the car keys.

'I was wondering where you'd got to.'

'I've had a most instructive morning. Anything happened here?'

'Nothing much. Alice Flower is dead.'

'You can't tell me anything about that. Primero was full of it. Apparently he was at her bedside for hours yesterday.' He threw himself into a chair next to his father's. 'God, it was hot in that car! As a matter of fact, her dying like that was a help if anything. Made it easier to get him on to the murder.'

'I didn't think you could be so callous,' said Archery distastefully.

'Oh, come off it, Father. She'd had her allotted span plus seventeen. She can't have wanted to live. Don't you want to hear what I got out of him?'

'Of course.'

'You don't want any coffee, do you? Let's go outside.'

There was no one on the terrace. A yellow climbing rose

had shed its petals all over the ground and the battered cane chairs. What residents there were had left possessions out here as if to reserve permanent perches, magazines, library books, a roll of blue knitting, a pair of glasses. Ruthlessly Charles cleared two chairs and blew away the rose petals. For the first time Archery noticed that he looked extremely happy.

'Well,' he said when they had sat down, 'the house first. It's quite a place, about ten times the size of Thringford Manor, and it's built of grey stone with a kind of pediment thing over the front door. Mrs Primero lived there when she was a girl and Roger bought it when it came up for sale this spring. There's a park with deer in it and a vast drive coming up from a pillared entrance. You can't see the house from the road, only the cedars in the park.

'They've got an Italian butler — not so classy as an English one, d'you think? But I suppose they're a dying race. Anyway, this butler character let me in and kept me hanging about for about ten minutes in a hall the size of the ground floor of our house. I was a bit nervous because I kept thinking, suppose he's rung up the *Sunday Planet* and they've said they've never heard of me? But he hadn't and it was all right. He was in the library. Superb collection of books he's got and some of them looked quite worn, so I suppose someone reads them, though I shouldn't think he does.

'It was all furnished in leather, black leather. You know that rather sexy modern stuff. He asked me to sit down and have a drink . . .'

'A bit early, wasn't it?'

'People like that, they slosh it down all day. If they were working class they'd be alcoholics, but you can get away with anything when you've got a butler and about fifty thousand a year. Then his wife came in. Rather a nice-looking woman — a bit past it, of course — but magnificent clothes. Not that I'd want Tess to dress like that . . .' His face fell and Archery's heart moved with pity. 'If I ever get a say in what Tess wears,' he added dolefully.

'Go on.'

'We had our drinks. Mrs Primero wasn't very talkative, but her husband was most expansive. I didn't have to ask him much, so you needn't get all steamed up about your conscience, and he got on to the murder, quite naturally. He kept saying he wished he hadn't left Victor's Piece so early that Sunday evening. He could easily have stayed.

' "I was only going to meet a couple of chaps I knew at a pub in Sewingbury," he said. "And, as it happened, it was a dead loss because they never turned up. Or, at least, they did turn up but I got the wrong pub. So I waited about for an hour or so and then I went back to my lodgings. I wonder," he said, "how many times I've cursed myself for not staying at Victor's Piece."

'What d'you think of that? I thought it was fishy.'

'He didn't have to tell you,' Archery said. 'In any case the police must have questioned him.'

'Maybe they did and maybe they didn't. He didn't say.' Charles lounged back in his chair, and swinging his feet up poked them through the trellis. 'Then we got on to money,' he said. 'Money, I may add, is the mainspring of his existence.'

Inexplicably, Archery felt himself marked out as Primero's defender. Alice Flower had painted him in such glowing colours. 'I had the impression he was rather a nice sort of man,' he said.

'He's all right,' Charles said indifferently. 'He's very modest about his success and about his money.' He grinned. 'The kind of character who cries all the way to the bank. Anyway, now we come to the crux of the whole thing.

'Just before Mrs Primero was killed some mate of his asked him if he'd like to go into business with him. Importing or exporting. I don't quite know what it was but it doesn't matter. The friend was to put up ten thousand and so was Primero. Well, Primero hadn't got it, hadn't got a smell of it. As far as he was concerned it was hopeless. Then Mrs Primero died.'

'We know all this,' Archery objected. 'Alice Flower told me as much . . .'

'All right, wait for it. Alice Flower didn't know this bit. "That was the making of me," he said very breezily. "Not that I wasn't devastated by my grandmother's death," he added as a sort of hasty afterthought. His wife was sitting there all the time with a blank look on her face. He kept looking at her uneasily.

' "I put up the money and we were away," he said, talking rather fast. "And since then I've never looked back."

'I was in a bit of a dilemma. Everything was going so smoothly and I didn't want to mess things up. I thought he was looking defiant and suddenly I realised why. *He didn't know how much I knew about Mrs Primero's money.* She died intestate, it was sixteen years ago, I was a newspaper reporter and for all he knew I was interested in him, not his grandmother.'

'A lot to read into a defiant look,' said Archery.

'Perhaps there was a bit of hindsight in that. But just wait a minute. Then I asked a question. It was a shot in the dark but it came off.

' "So you got your ten thousand just when you needed it?" I said casually. Primero didn't say anything, but his wife looked at me and said, "Just the exact sum after death duties. You should really be asking me. Roger's told me about it so often I know it better than he does."

'Well, I couldn't leave it there. I persisted. "I understand you've got two sisters, Mr Primero," I said. "I suppose they inherited similar amounts?" He began to look terribly suspicious. After all, it wasn't my business and it had nothing to do with the story I was supposed to be writing. "Are they successful in business too?" I asked, trying to justify myself. It was a stroke of genius. Sorry to be big-headed but it was. I could actually see him relax.

' "I really don't see much of them," he said. "Oh, Roger," said his wife, "you know me *never* see them." Primero gave her an icy look. "One's married," he said, "and the other has a job in London. They're much younger than I am." "It must be nice to inherit ten thousand pounds when you're still a child," I said. "I imagine it's always nice," he said, "but I've never had the pleasure of inheriting any more. Shall we leave the subject and get on with the story of my life?"

'I pretended to take notes. I was doodling really but he thought it was shorthand. When we'd finished he got up and shook hands and said he'd keep his eye open for the *Sunday Planet*. I felt a bit awkward at that and I didn't quite know what to say but his wife saved me by asking me to lunch. So I accepted and we had a splendid lunch, smoked salmon and enormous steaks, great sides of oxen they were, and raspberries in framboise liqueur.'

'You've got a nerve,' said Archery in grudging admiration. He pulled himself up. 'It was very wrong of you. Most unethical.'

'All in a good cause. You do see the point, don't you?'

Why do one's children always think one senile yet childish, dully practical yet irrational, capable of supporting them but unintelligent to the point of imbecility?

'Of course I do,' Archery said irritably. 'Alice Flower and Mrs Crilling both said Mrs Primero had only ten thousand to leave, but apparently Roger Primero didn't get only a third of that, he got the whole ten thousand.'

Charles jerked round to face him, scattering more rose petals from the trellis. 'Now, why? There definitely wasn't a will. I've checked on that. And there were just the three heirs, Roger, Angela and Isabel. Mrs Primero hadn't another relative in the world and according to the law it should have been divided between the three grandchildren. But Roger got the lot.'

'I can't understand it.'

'Neither can I — yet. Maybe I shall when I've seen the sisters. I couldn't ask Roger where they lived, but Primero isn't a common name and the single one may be in the London phone directory. I haven't quite made up my mind about the line I'll take with them, but I've got the glimmerings of an idea. I might say I've come from the Inland Revenue . . .'

'*Facilis descensus Averni.*'

'In matters of this kind,' Charles said crisply, 'you have to be bloody, bold and resolute. Can I have the car again tomorrow?'

'If you must.'

'I thought you might like to go out to Victor's Piece,' Charles said in a hopeful tone, 'and just have a look round. See if you can see if Primero could have hidden himself anywhere, sneaked upstairs or something instead of letting himself out of the front door that Sunday night.'

'Aren't you letting your imagination run away with you?'

'It's a family failing.' His eyes clouded suddenly and to Archery's dismay he put his head in his hands. Archery didn't know what to do. 'Tess hasn't spoken to me for two days,' the boy said. 'I can't lose her, I can't.' If he had been ten years younger his father would have taken him in his arms. But if he had been ten years younger the whole thing would never have happened.

'I don't give a damn,' Charles said, controlling himself, 'what her father was or what he did. I don't care if every one of her ancestors were hanged. But you do and she does and ... Oh, what's the use?' He got up. 'Sorry to make an exhibition of myself.' Still looking down, he scuffed his feet against the eddies of petals. 'You're doing all you can,' he said with a dreadful prim gravity, 'but you can't be expected to understand at your age.' Without looking at his father, he turned and went into the hotel.

CHAPTER ELEVEN

From fornication, and all other deadly sin; and from all the
deceits of the world, the flesh and the devil,
Good Lord, deliver us.

The Litany

Angela Primero lived in a flat at Oswestry Mansions, Baron's
Court. She was twenty-six years old and the elder of Mrs
Primero's granddaughters. That was all Charles Archery knew
about her — that and her telephone number which he had
easily found. He rang her up and asked if he could see her on
the following morning. Thinking better of his original plan, he
said he represented the *Sunday Planet,* and the death of Alice
Flower having brought once more into prominence Mrs Primero's murder, his newspaper were running a feature on the fate
of the other people concerned in the case. He was rather
pleased with that. It had the ring of verisimilitude.

Miss Primero had a grim voice for so young a woman. It
was gravelly, abrupt, almost masculine. She would be glad to
see him, but he did realise, didn't he, that her recollection of
her grandmother was slight? Just a few childhood memories
were what he wanted, Miss Primero, little touches to add colour
to his story.

She opened the door to him so quickly that he wondered if
she had been waiting behind it. Her appearance surprised him
for he had kept a picture of her brother in his mind and he had
therefore expected someone small and dark with regular features. He had seen a photograph of the grandmother too, and
though the old face was both wizened and blurred by age, there
were still to be seen vestiges of an aquiline beauty and a strong
resemblance to Roger.

The girl whose flat this was had a strong plain face with
bad skin and a big prognathous jaw. Her hair was a dull flat

brown. She wore a neat dark blue frock bought at a chain store and her figure, though over-large, was good.

'Mr Bowman?'

Charles was pleased with the name he had invented for himself. He gave her a pleasant smile.

'How do you do, Miss Primero?'

She showed him into a small very sparsely furnished sitting room. He could not help adding to the mystery by contrasting this with the library at Forby Hall. Here there were no books, no flowers, and the only ornaments were framed photographs, half a dozen perhaps, of a young blonde girl and a baby.

She followed his gaze towards the studio portrait of the same girl that hung above the fireplace. 'My sister,' she said. Her ugly face softened and she smiled. As she spoke there came from the next room a thin wail and the murmur of a voice. 'She's in my bedroom now, changing the baby's napkin. She always comes over on Saturday mornings.'

Charles wondered what Angela Primero did for a living. A typist perhaps, or a clerk? The whole set-up seemed too scanty and poor. The furniture was brightly coloured but it looked cheap and flimsy. In front of the hearth was a rug woven out of woollen rags. Needy nothing trimmed in joillity . . .

'Please sit down,' said Angela Primero.

The little orange chair creaked as it took his weight. A far cry, he thought, from the brother's voluptuous black leather. From the floor above he could hear music playing and someone pushing a vacuum cleaner.

'What do you want me to tell you?'

There was a packet of Weights on the mantelpiece. She took one and handed them to him. He shook his head.

'First, what you remember of your grandmother.'

'Not much. I told you.' Her speech was brusque and rough. 'We went there to tea a few times. It was a big dark house and I remember I was afraid to go to the bathroom alone. The maid used to have to take me.' She gave a staccato, humourless laugh and it was an effort to remember she was only twenty-six. 'I never even saw Painter if that's what you mean. There was a child across the road we used to play with sometimes and I believe Painter had a daughter. I asked about her once but my grandmother said she was common, we weren't to have anything to do with her.'

Charles clenched his hands. He felt a sudden desperate longing for Tess, both for himself, and also to set her beside this girl who had been taught to despise her.

The door opened and the girl in the photographs came in. Angela Primero jumped up at once and took the baby from her arms. Charles's knowledge of babies was vague. He thought this one might be about six months old. It looked small and uninteresting.

'This is Mr Bowman, darling. My sister, Isabel Fairest.'

Mrs Fairest was only a year younger than her sister, but she looked no more than eighteen. She was very small and thin with a pinkish-white face and enormous pale blue eyes. Charles thought she looked like a pretty rabbit. Her hair was a bright gingery gold.

Roger's hair and eyes were black, Angela's hair brown and her eyes hazel. None of them was in the least like either of the others. There was more to genetics than met the eye, Charles thought.

Mrs Fairest sat down. She didn't cross her legs but sat with her hands in her lap like a little girl. It was difficult to imagine her married, impossible to think of her as having given birth to a child.

Her sister scarcely took her eyes off her. When she did it was to coo at the baby. Mrs Fairest had a small soft voice, tinged with cockney.

'Don't let him tire you, darling. Put him down in his cot.'

'You know I love holding him, darling. Isn't he gorgeous? Have you got a smile for your auntie? You know your auntie, don't you, even if you haven't seen her for a whole week?'

Mrs Fairest got up and stood behind her sister's chair. They both gurgled over the baby, stroking its cheeks and curling its fingers round their own. It was obvious that they were devoted to each other, but whereas Angela's love was maternal to both sister and nephew, Isabel showed a clinging dependence on the older girl. Charles felt that they had forgotten he was there and he wondered how Mr Fairest fitted into the picture. He coughed.

'About your early life, Miss Primero . . . ?'

'Oh, yes. (Mustn't cry, sweetie. He's got wind, darling.) I really can't remember any more about my grandmother. My mother married again when I was sixteen. This is the sort of thing you want, is it?'

'Oh, yes.'

'Well, as I say, my mother married again and she and my stepfather wanted us to go out to Australia with them. (Up it comes! There, that's better.) But I didn't want to go. Isabel and I were still at school. My mother hung it out for a couple of years and then they went without us. Well, it was their life, wasn't it? I wanted to go to training college but I gave that up. Isabel and I had the house, didn't we, darling? And we both went out to work. (Is he going to have a little sleep, then?)'

It was an ordinary enough tale, fragmentary and very clipped. Charles felt that there was far more to it. The hardship and the privation had been left out. Money might have changed it all but she had never mentioned money. She had never mentioned her brother either.

'Isabel got married two years ago. Her husband's in the Post Office. I'm a secretary in a newspaper office.' She raised her eyebrows, unsmiling. 'I'll have to ask them if they've ever heard of you.'

'Yes, do,' said Charles with a suavity he didn't feel. He must get on to the subject of the money but he didn't know how to. Mrs Fairest brought a carry-cot in from the other room, they placed the baby in it, bending tenderly over him and cooing. Although it was nearly noon neither of them had mentioned a drink or even coffee. Charles belonged to a generation that has accustomed itself to almost hourly snacks, cups of this, glasses of that, bits and pieces from the refrigerator. So, surely, did they. He thought wistfully of Roger's hospitality.

Mrs Fairest glanced up and said softly, 'I do like coming here. It's so quiet.' Above them the vacuum cleaner continued to whirr. 'My husband and me, we've only got one room. It's nice and big but it's awfully noisy at weekends.'

Charles knew it was impertinent but he had to say it.

'I'm surprised your grandmother didn't leave you anything.'

Angela Primero shrugged. She tucked the blanket round the baby and stood up. 'That's life,' she said in a hard voice.

'Shall I tell him, darling?' Isabel Fairest touched her arm and looked timidly into her face, waiting for guidance.

'What's the point? It's of no interest to him.' She stared at Charles and then said intelligently, 'You can't put that sort of thing in newspapers. It's libel.'

Damn, damn, damn! Why hadn't he said he was from the Inland Revenue? Then they could have got on to money at once.

'But I think people ought to know,' said Mrs Fairest, showing more spirit than he had thought her capable of. 'I do, darling. I always have, ever since I understood about it. I think people ought to know how he's treated us.'

Charles put his notebook away ostentatiously.

'This is off the record, Mrs Fairest.'

'You see, darling? He won't say anything. I don't care if he does. People ought to know about Roger.'

The name was out. They were all breathing rather heavily. Charles was the first to get himself under control. He managed a calm smile.

'Well, I *will* tell you. If you put it in the paper and I have to go to prison for it, I don't care! Granny Rose left ten thousand pounds and we should all have had a share, but we didn't. Roger — that's our brother — he got it all. I don't quite know why but Angela knows the ins and outs of it. My mother had a friend who was a solicitor where Roger worked and he said we could try and fight it, but Mother wouldn't on account of it being awful to have a court case against your own son. We were just little kids, you see, and we didn't know anything about it. Mother said Roger would help us — it was his moral duty, even if it wasn't legally — but he never did. He kept putting it off and then Mother quarrelled with him. We've never seen him since I was ten and Angela was eleven. I wouldn't know him now if I saw him in the street.'

It was a puzzling story. They were all Mrs Primero's grandchildren, all equally entitled to inherit in the event of there being no will. And there had been no will.

'I don't want to see all this in your paper, you know,'

Angela Primero said suddenly. She would have made a good teacher, he thought, reflecting on waste, for she was tender with little children, but stern when she had to be.

'I won't publish any of it,' Charles said with perfect truth.

'You'd better not, that's all. The fact is, we couldn't fight it. We wouldn't have stood a chance. In law Roger was perfectly entitled to it all. Mind you, it would have been another story if my grandmother had died a month later.'

'I don't quite follow you,' said Charles, by now unbearably excited.

'Have you ever seen my brother?'

Charles nodded, then changed it to a shake of the head. She looked at him suspiciously. Then she made a dramatic gesture. She took her sister by the shoulders and pushed her forward for his inspection.

'He's little and dark,' she said. 'Look at Isabel, look at me. We don't look alike, do we? We don't look like sisters because we aren't sisters and Roger isn't our brother. Oh, Roger is my parents' child all right and Mrs Primero was his grandmother. My mother couldn't have any more children. They waited eleven years and when they knew it was no good they adopted me. A year later they took Isabel as well.'

'But . . . I . . .' Charles stammered. 'You were legally adopted, weren't you?'

Angela Primero had recovered her composure. She put her arm round her sister who had begun to cry.

'We were legally adopted all right. That didn't make any difference. Adopted children can't inherit when the dead person has died without making a will — or they couldn't in September 1950. They can now. They were making this Act at the time and it became law on October 1st, 1950. Just our luck, wasn't it?'

The photograph in the estate agent's window made Victor's Piece look deceptively attractive. Perhaps the agent had long given up hope of its being sold for anything but its site value, for Archery, enquiring tentatively, was greeted with almost fawning exuberance. He emerged with an order to view, a bunch of keys and permission to go over the house whenever he chose.

116

No bus was in sight. He walked back to the stop by the Olive and Dove and waited in the shade. Presently he pulled the order to view out of his pocket and scanned it. 'Splendid property of character,' he read, 'that only needs an imaginative owner to give it a new lease of life . . .' There was no mention of the old tragedy, no hint that violent death had once been its tenant.

Two Sewingbury buses came and one marked Kingsmarkham Station. He was still reading, contrasting the agent's euphemisms with the description in his transcript, when the silver car pulled into the kerb.

'Mr Archery!'

He turned. The sun blazed back from the arched wings and the glittering screen. Imogen Ide's hair made an even brighter silver-gold flash against the dazzling metal.

'I'm on my way to Stowerton. Would you like a lift?'

He was suddenly ridiculously happy. Everything went, his pity for Charles, his grief for Alice Flower, his sense of helplessness against the juggernaut machinery of the law. An absurd dangerous joy possessed him and without stopping to analyse it, he went up to the car. Its bodywork was as hot as fire, a shivering silver blaze against his hand.

'My son took my car,' he said. 'I'm not going to Stowerton, just to a place this side of it, a house called Victor's Piece.'

She raised her eyebrows very slightly at this and he supposed she knew the story just as everyone else did, for she was looking at him strangely. He got in beside her, his heart beating. The continual rhythmic thudding in his left side was so intense as to be physically painful and he wished it would stop before it made him wince or press his hand to his breast.

'You haven't got Dog with you today,' he said.

She moved back into the traffic. 'Too hot for him,' she said. 'Surely you're not thinking of buying Victor's Piece?'

His heart had quietened. 'Why, do you know it?'

'It used to belong to a relative of my husband's.'

Ide, he thought, Ide. He couldn't remember hearing what had become of the house after Mrs Primero's death. Perhaps it had been owned by some Ides before it became an old people's home.

'I have a key and an order to view, but I'm certainly not going to buy. It's just — well . . .'

'Curiosity?' She could not look at him while she was driving but he felt her thoughts directed on him more powerfully than any eyes. 'Are you an amateur of crime?' It would have been natural to have used his name, to end the question with it. But she didn't. It seemed to him that she had omitted it because 'Mr Archery' had suddenly become too formal, his Christian name still too intimate. 'You know, I think I'll come over it with you,' she said. 'I don't have to be in Stowerton until half-past twelve. Let me be your guide, may I?'

Imogen Ide will be my guide . . . It was a stupid jingle and it tinkled in his ears on a minor key like an old, half-forgotten madrigal. He said nothing but she must have taken his silence for assent, for instead of dropping him at the entry she slowed and turned into the lane where dark gables showed between the trees.

Even on this bright morning the house looked dark and forbidding. Its yellow-brown bricks were crossed with fretted half-timbering and two of its windows were broken. The resemblance between it and the agent's photograph was as slight as that of a holiday postcard to the actual resort. The photographer had cunningly avoided or else subsequently removed the weeds, the brambles, the damp stains, the swinging rotted casements and the general air of decay. The gates were broken down and she drove straight through the gap, up the drive and stopped directly before the front door.

This moment should have been important to him, his first sight of the house where Tess's father had committed — or had not committed — his crime. His senses should have been alert to absorb atmosphere, to note details of place and distance that the police in their jaded knowledge had overlooked. Instead he was conscious of himself not as an observer, a note-taker, but only as a man living in the present, dwelling in the moment and discarding the past. He felt more alive than he had done for years and because of this he became almost unaware of his surroundings. Things could not affect him, not recorded fact. His emotions were all. He saw and experienced the house only as a deserted place into which he and this woman would soon go and would be alone.

As soon as he had thought this in so many words he knew that he should not go in. He could easily say that he only wanted to look at the grounds. She was getting out of the car now, looking up at the windows and wrinkling her eyelids against the light.

'Shall we go in?' she said.

He put the key in the lock and she was standing close beside him. He had expected a musty smell from the hall but he was hardly aware of it. Shafts of light crossed the place from various dusty windows and motes danced in the beams. There was an old runner on the tiled floor and catching her heel in it, she stumbled. Instinctively he put out his hand to steady her and as he did so he felt her right breast brush his arm.

'Mind how you go,' he said, not looking at her. Her shoe had sent up a little cloud of dust and she gave a nervous laugh. Perhaps it was just a normal laugh. He was beyond that kind of analysis, for he could still feel the soft weight against his arm as if she had not stepped quickly away.

'Terribly stuffy in here,' she said. 'It makes me cough. That's the room where the murder was committed — in there.' She pushed open a door and he saw a deal board floor, marble fireplace, great bleached patches on the walls where pictures had hung. 'The stairs are behind here and on the other side is the kitchen where poor old Alice was cooking the Sunday dinner.'

'I don't want to go upstairs,' he said quickly. 'It's too hot and dusty. You'll get your dress dirty.' He drew a deep breath and, moving far from her, stood against the mantelpiece. Here, just on this spot, Mrs Primero had felt the first blow of the axe; there the scuttle had stood, here, there, everywhere, the old blood had flowed. 'The scene of the crime,' he said fatuously.

Her eyes narrowed and she crossed to the window. The silence was terrible and he wanted to fill it with chatter. There was so much to say, so many remarks even mere acquaintances could make to each other on such a spot. The noonday sun cast her shadow in perfect proportion, neither too tall nor grossly dwarfed. It was like a cut-out in black tissue and he wanted to fall to his knees and touch it, knowing it was all he would get.

It was she who spoke first. He hardly knew what he had expected her to say, but not this — certainly not this.

'You are very like your son — or he's like you.'

The tension slackened. He felt cheated and peeved.

'I didn't know you'd met,' he said.

To this she made no reply. In her eyes was a tiny gleam of fun. 'You didn't tell me he worked for a newspaper.'

Archery's stomach turned. She must have been there, at the Primeros'. Was he expected to sustain Charles's lie?

'He's so very like you,' she said. 'It didn't really click, though, until after he'd gone. Then, taking his appearance and his name together — I suppose Bowman's his pseudonym on the *Planet*, is it? — I guessed. Roger hasn't realised.'

'I don't quite understand,' Archery began. He would have to explain. 'Mrs Ide . . .'

She started to laugh, stopped when she saw the dismay in his face. 'I think we've both been leading each other up the garden,' she said gently. 'Ide was my maiden name, the name I used for modelling.'

He turned away, pressing the hot palm of his hand against the marble. She took a step towards him and he smelt her scent. 'Mrs Primero was the relative who owned this house, the relative who's buried at Forby?' There was no need to wait for her answer. He sensed her nod. 'I don't understand how I can have been such a fool,' he said. Worse than a fool. What would she think tomorrow when the *Planet* came out? He offered up a stupid ashamed prayer that Charles had found out nothing from the woman who was her sister-in-law. 'Will you forgive me?'

'There's nothing to forgive, is there?' She sounded truly puzzled, as well she might. He had been asking pardon for future outrages. 'I'm just as much to blame as you. I don't know why I didn't tell you I was Imogen Primero.' She paused. 'There was no deceit in it,' she said. 'Just one of those things. We were dancing — something else came up . . . I don't know.'

He raised his head, gave himself a little shake. Then he walked away from her into the hall. 'You have to go to Stowerton, I think you said. It was kind of you to bring me.'

She was behind him now, her hand on his arm. 'Don't look

like that. What are you supposed to have done? Nothing, nothing. It was just a — a social mistake.'

It was a little fragile hand but insistent. Not knowing why, perhaps because she too seemed in need of comfort, he covered it with his own. Instead of withdrawing it, she left her hand under his and as she sighed it trembled faintly. He turned to look at her, feeling shame that was as paralysing as a disease. Her face was a foot from his, then only inches, then no distance, no face but only a soft mouth.

The shame went in a wave of desire made the more terrible and the more exquisite because he had felt nothing like it for twenty years, perhaps not ever. Since coming down from Oxford he had never kissed any woman but Mary, scarcely been alone with any but the old, the sick or the dying. He did not know how to end the kiss, nor did he know whether this in itself was inexperience or the yearning to prolong something that was so much more, but not enough more, than touching a shadow.

She took herself out of his arms quite suddenly, but without pushing or struggling. There was nothing to struggle against. 'Oh, dear,' she said, but she didn't smile. Her face was very white.

There were words to explain that kind of thing away. 'I don't know what made me do that' or 'I was carried away, the impulse of the moment . . .' He was sick of even the suggestion of lying. Truth itself seemed even more compelling and urgent than his desire and he thought he would speak it even though tomorrow and in the days to come it too would appear to her as a lie.

'I love you. I think I must have loved you from the first moment I saw you. I think that's how it was.' He put his hands up to his forehead and his fingertips, though icy cold, seemed to burn just as snow can burn the skin. 'I'm married,' he said. 'You know that — I mean my wife is living — and I'm a clergyman. I've no right to love you and I promise I'll never be alone with you again.'

She was very surprised and her eyes widened, but which of his confessions had surprised her he had no idea. It even occurred to him that she might be amazed at hearing from him lucid speech, for up to now he had been almost incoherent. 'I mustn't suppose,' he said, for his last sentence seemed like vanity, 'that there's been any temptation for you.' She started to speak, but he went on in a hurry, 'Will you not say anything but just drive away?'

She nodded. In spite of his prohibition, he longed for her to approach him again, just touch him. It was an impossible hunger that made him breathless. She made a little helpless gesture as if she too were in the grip of an overpowering emotion. Then she turned, her face held awkwardly away from him, ran down the hall and let herself out of the front door.

After she had gone it occurred to him that she had asked no questions as to his reasons for coming to the house. She had said little and he everything that mattered. He thought that he must be going mad, for he could not understand that twenty years of discipline could fall away like a lesson imparted to a bored child.

The house was as it had been described in the transcript of the trial. He noticed its layout without emotion or empathy, the long passage that ran from the front door to the door at the back where Painter's coat had hung, the kitchen, the narrow, wall-confined stairs. A kind of cerebral paralysis descended on him and he moved towards that back door, withdrawing the bolts numbly.

The garden was very still, overgrown, basking under a brazen sky. The light and the heat made him dizzy. At first he could not see the coach house at all. Then he realised he had been looking at it ever since he stepped into the garden, but what he had taken for a great quivering bush was in fact solid bricks and mortar hidden under a blanket of virginia creeper. He walked towards it, not interested, not in the least curious. He walked because it was something to do and because this house of a million faintly trembling leaves was at least a kind of goal.

The doors were fastened with a padlock. Archery was relieved. It deprived him of the need for any action. He leant against the wall and the leaves were cold and damp against his face. Presently he went down the drive and through the gateless entrance. Of course, the silver car would not be there. It wasn't.

A bus came almost immediately. He had quite forgotten that he had omitted to lock the back door of Victor's Piece.

Archery returned the keys to the estate agent and lingered for a while looking at the photograph of the house he had just come from. It was like looking at the portrait of a girl you had known only as an old woman, and he wondered if it had perhaps been taken thirty years before when Mrs Primero had bought the house. Then he turned and walked slowly back to the hotel.

Half-past four was usually a dead time at the Olive and Dove. But this was a Saturday and a glorious Saturday at that. The dining room was full of trippers, the lounge decorously crowded with old residents and new arrivals, taking their tea from silver trays. Archery's heart began to beat as he saw his son in conversation with a man and a woman. Their backs were towards him and he saw only that the woman had long fair hair and that the man's head was dark.

He made his way between the armchairs, growing hot with trepidation and weaving among beringed fingers holding tea-pots, little asthmatic dogs, pots of cress and pyramids of sandwiches. When the woman turned he should have felt relief. Instead bitter disappointment ran through him like a long thin knife. He put out his hand and clasped the warm fingers of Tess Kershaw.

Now he saw how stupid his first wild assumption had been. Kershaw was shaking hands with him now and the man's lively face, seamed all over with the wrinkles of animation, bore no resemblance at all to Roger Primero's waxen pallor. His hair was not really dark but thin and sprinkled with grey.

'Charles called in on us on his way back from town,' Tess said. She was perhaps the worst dressed woman in the room in her white cotton blouse and a navy serge skirt. As if explaining this, she said quickly, 'When we heard his news we dropped everything and came back with him.' She got up, threaded her way to the window and looked out into the bright hot afternoon. When she came back she said, 'It feels so strange. I must have walked past here lots of times when I was little, but I can't remember it at all.'

Hand in hand with Painter perhaps. And while they

walked, the murderer and his child, had Painter watched the traffic go by and thought of the way he could become part of that traffic? Archery tried not to see in the fine pointed face opposite his own, the coarse crude features of the man Alice Flower had called Beast. But then they were here to prove it had not been that way at all.

'News?' he said to Charles and he heard the note of distaste creep into his voice.

Charles told him. 'And then we all went to Victor's Piece,' he said. 'We didn't think we'd be able to get in, but someone had left the back door unlocked. We went all over the house and we saw that Primero could easily have hidden himself.'

Archery turned away slightly. The name was now invested with many associations, mostly agonising.

'He said good-bye to Alice, opened and closed the front door without actually going out of it, then he slipped into the dining room — nobody used the dining room and it was dark. Alice went out and . . .' Charles hesitated, searching for a form of words to spare Tess. 'And, after the coal was brought in, he came out, put on the raincoat that was left hanging on the back door and — well, did the deed.'

'It's only a theory, Charlie,' said Kershaw, 'but it fits the facts.'

'I don't know . . .' Archery began.

'Look, Father, don't you want Tess's father cleared?'

Not, thought Archery, if it means incriminating *her* husband. Not that. I may already have done her an injury, but I can't do her that injury.

'This motive you mentioned,' he said dully.

Tess broke in excitedly, 'It's a marvellous motive, a *real* motive.' He knew exactly what she meant. Ten thousand pounds was real, solid, a true temptation, while two hundred pounds . . . Her eyes shone, then saddened. Was she thinking that to hang a man wrongfully was as bad as killing an old woman for a bag of notes? And would that too remain with her all her life? No matter which way things fell out, could she ever escape?

'Primero was working in a solicitor's office,' Charles was saying excitedly. 'He would have known the law, he had all the facilities for checking. Mrs Primero might not have known about it, not if she didn't read the papers. Who knows about all the various Acts of Parliament that are going to be passed anyway? Primero's boss probably had a query about it from a client, sent him to look it up, and there you are. Primero would have known that if his grandmother died intestate before October 1950 all the money would come to him. But if she died after the Act his sisters would get two-thirds of it. I've been looking it all up. This is known as the Great Adoption Act, the law that gave adopted children almost equal rights with natural ones. *Of course* Primero knew.'

'What are you going to do?'

'I've been on to the police but Wexford can't see me before two on Monday. He's away for the weekend. I'll bet the police never checked Primero's movements. Knowing them, I'd say it's likely that as soon as they got hold of Painter they didn't trouble with anyone else.' He looked at Tess and took her hand. 'You can say what you like about this being a free country,' he said hotly, 'but you know as well as I do that everyone has a subconscious feeling that "working class" and "criminal class" are more or less synonymous. Why bother with the respectable, well-connected solicitor's clerk when you've already got your hands on the chauffeur?'

Archery shrugged. From long experience he knew it was useless to argue with Charles when he was airing his quasi-communist ideals.

'Thank you for your enthusiastic reception,' Charles said sarcastically. 'What is there to look so miserable about?'

Archery could not tell him. A load of sorrow seemed to have descended on him and in order to answer his son, he sorted out from conflicting pain something he could express to them all.

'I was thinking of the children,' he said, 'the four little girls who have all suffered from this crime.' He smiled at Tess. 'Tess, of course,' he went on, 'those two sisters you saw — and Elizabeth Crilling.'

He did not add the name of the grown woman who would suffer more than any of them if Charles was right.

CHAPTER TWELVE

Is it not lawful for me to do what I will with mine own?

The Gospel for Septuagesima Sunday

The man who was shown into Wexford's office at nine on Monday morning was small and slender. The bones of his hands were particularly fine and with narrow delicate joints like a woman's. The dark grey suit he wore, very expensive looking and very sleek, made him look smaller than he actually was. He seemed to be surrounded, even so early in the morning and away from his own home, with a great many adjuncts of elegance. Wexford, who knew him well, was amused by the sapphire tie-pin, the two rings, the key chain with its heavy drop of chased — amber, was it? — the briefcase of some kind of reptile skin. How many years, he asked himself, was Roger Primero going to need to get used to wealth?

'Lovely morning,' said Wexford. 'I've just had a couple of days at Worthing and the sea was like a millpond. What can I do for you?'

'Catch a con man,' said Primero, 'a lousy little squirt posing as a journalist.' He unclipped his briefcase and flicked a Sunday newspaper across Wexford's desk. It slipped on the polished surface and fell to the floor. Raising his eyebrows, Wexford let it lie.

'Hell,' said Primero. 'There's nothing for you to see, anyway.' His glazed eyes had a sore look in the handsome expressionless face. The man's vanity had made him rebel against glasses at last, Wexford thought, blinking slightly behind his own heavy tortoise-shell frames. 'Look here, Chief Inspector, I don't mind telling you, I'm hopping mad. This is how it was. Mind if I smoke?'

'Not at all.'

A gold cigarette case spilled out from his pocket, followed

by a holder and a lighter in peculiar black and gold mosaic. Wexford watched this production of props, wondering when it was going to end. The man is furnished like a room, he thought.

'This is how it was,' he said. 'Character rang me up on Thursday, said he was on the *Planet* and wanted to do an article about me. My early life. You get the picture? I said he could come along on Friday and he did. I gave him a hell of a long interview, all the dope and the upshot of it was my wife asked him to lunch.' He screwed up his mouth and nose like a man smelling something offensive. 'Hell,' he said, 'I don't suppose he's ever seen a lunch like that in all his life . . .'

'But no article appeared and when you rang the *Planet* this morning they'd never heard of him.'

'How did you know?'

'It happens,' said Wexford dryly. 'I'm surprised at you, sir, a man of your experience. The time to ring the *Planet* was *Friday* morning.'

'It makes me feel such a frightful ass.'

Wexford said airily, 'No money passed, I daresay?'

'Hell, no!'

'Just the lunch, then, and you told him a lot of things you'd rather have left unsaid.'

'That's the thing.' His expression had been sulky, but suddenly he smiled and it was a likeable smile. Wexford had always rather liked him. 'Oh hell's bells, Chief Inspector . . .'

'Hell's bells, as you say. Still, you were wise to come to us, though I don't know that we can do anything unless he makes a move . . .'

'A move? What d'you mean, a move?'

'Well, let me give you an example. Nothing personal, you understand. Just supposing a wealthy man, a man who is somewhat in the public eye, says something a shade indiscreet to a reputable journalist. Ten to one he can't use it because he's laying his paper open to libel action.' Wexford paused and gave the other man a penetrating look. 'But if he says those same indiscreet things to an impostor, a confidence trickster . . .' Primero had grown very pale. 'What's to stop the impostor following a few leads and ferreting out something really damaging. Most people, Mr Primero, even decent law-abiding people,

127

have something in their pasts they'd rather not have known. You have to ask yourself, if he's not on the level, what's he up to? The answer is either he's after your money or else he's crazy.' He added more kindly, 'In my experience nine out of ten of them are just crazy. Still, if it'll help to set your mind at rest perhaps you could give us a description. I suppose he gave you his name?'

'It wouldn't be his real name.'

'Naturally not.'

Primero leant confidingly towards him. During the course of his long career Wexford had found it valuable to make himself *au fait* with perfumes and he noticed that Primero smelt of Lentheric's Onyx.

'He seemed nice enough,' Primero began. 'My wife was quite taken with him.' His eyes had begun to water and he put his fingers very cautiously up to them. Wexford was reminded of a weeping woman who dare not rub her eyes for fear of smudging mascara. 'I haven't told her about this, by the way. I passed it off. Wouldn't want to upset her. He was well-spoken, Oxford accent and all that. A tall fair fellow, said his name was Bowman, Charles Bowman.'

'A-ha!' said Wexford but not aloud.

'Chief Inspector?'

'Mr Primero?'

'I've just remembered something. He was — well, he was extraordinarily interested in my grandmother.'

Wexford almost laughed.

'From what you've told me I think I can assure you there won't be any serious repercussions.'

'You think he's a nut?'

'Harmless, anyway.'

'You've taken a load off my mind.' Primero got up, retrieved his briefcase and picked up the newspaper. He did it rather awkwardly as if he was unused to performing even so simple a service for himself. 'I'll be more careful in future.'

'An ounce of prevention, you know.'

'Well, I won't take up any more of your time.' He pulled a long, but possibly sincerely sad face. The watering eyes added to his look of melancholy. 'Off to a funeral, as a matter of fact. Poor old Alice.'

Wexford had noticed the black tie on which the sapphire glowed darkly. He showed Primero to the door. Throughout the interview he had kept a solemn face. Now he permitted himself the indulgence of gargantuan, though almost silent, laughter.

There was nothing to do until two o'clock except sight-seeing. Charles had been out early and bought a guide book. They sat in the lounge studying it.

'It says here,' said Tess, 'that Forby is the fifth prettiest village in England.'

'Poor Forby,' said Charles. 'Damned with faint praise.'

Kershaw began organising them.

'How about all piling into my car . . .' He stuck his finger on the map '. . . and going down the Kingsbrook road to Forby — keep clear of Forby Hall, eh, Charlie? — have a quick look at the church, and then on to Pomfret. Pomfret Grange is open every weekday in the summer — we might have a look over it — and back into Kingsmarkham along the main road.'

'Lovely,' said Tess.

Kershaw drove and Archery sat beside him. They followed the same route he had taken with Imogen Ide when she had come to put flowers on old Mrs Primero's grave. As they came within sight of the Kingsbrook he remembered what she had said about the implacability of water and how, notwithstanding the efforts of man, it continues to spring from the earth and seek the sea.

Kershaw parked the car by the green with the duckpond. The village looked peaceful and serene. Summer was not as yet so far advanced as to dull the fresh green of the beech trees or hang the wild clematis with its frosty greyish beard. Knots of cottages surrounded the green and on the church side was a row of Georgian houses with bow windows whose dark panes glistened, showing chintz and silver within. There were just three shops, a post office, a butcher's with a canopy and white colonnade, and a place selling souvenirs for tourists. The cottagers' Monday morning wash hung drying in the windless warm air.

They sat on the seat on the green and Tess fed the ducks from a packet of biscuits she had found on the shelf under the dashboard. Kershaw produced a camera and began taking photographs. Suddenly Archery knew he did not want to go any further with them. He almost shivered with distaste at the thought of trailing round the galleries of Pomfret Grange, gasping with false pleasure at the china and pretending to admire family portraits.

'Would you mind if I stayed here? I'd like to have another look at the church.'

Charles glared. 'We'll all go and look at the church.'

'I can't, darling,' said Tess. 'I can't go into a church in jeans.'

'Not in these trousers,' Kershaw quipped. He put away his camera. 'We'd better get moving if we're going to see the stately home.'

'I can easily go back on the bus,' said Archery.

'Well, for God's sake, don't be late, Father.'

If it was going to be any more than a sentimental journey, he too would need a guide. When the car had gone he made his way into the souvenir shop. A bell rang sweetly as he opened the door and a woman came out from a room at the back.

'We don't keep a guide to St Mary's, but you'll find them on sale inside the church door.'

Now he was here he ought to buy something. A postcard? A little brooch for Mary? That, he thought, would be the worst kind of infidelity, to commit adultery in your heart every time you saw your wife wearing a keepsake. He looked drearily at the horse brasses, the painted jugs, the trays of costume jewellery.

A small counter was devoted entirely to calendars, wooden plaques with words on them in pokerwork, framed verses. One of these, a little picture on a card, showing a haloed shepherd with a lamb, caught his eye because the words beneath the drawing were familiar.

'Go, Shepherd, to your rest . . .'

The woman was standing behind him.

'I see you're admiring the efforts of our local bard,' she said brightly. 'He was just a boy when he died and he's buried here.'

'I've seen his grave,' said Archery.

'Of course a lot of people who come here are under the impression he was a shepherd, you know. I always have to explain that at one time shepherd and poet meant the same thing.'

'Lycidas,' said Archery.

She ignored the interruption. 'Actually he was very well-educated. He'd been to High School and everyone said he should have gone to college. He was killed in a road accident. Would you like to see his photograph?'

She produced a stack of cheap framed photographs from a drawer beneath the counter. They were all identical and each bore the legend: John Grace, Bard of Forby. Those whom God loves, die young.

It was a fine ascetic face, sharp-featured and ultra-sensitive. It also, Archery considered, gave the impression that its owner suffered from pernicious anaemia. He had a curious feeling that he had seen it somewhere before.

'Was any of his work published?'

'One or two bits in magazines, that's all. I don't know the ins and outs of it because I've only been here ten years, but there was a publisher who had a weekend cottage here and he was very keen on making his poetry into a book when the poor boy died. Mrs Grace — his mother, you know — was all for it, but the thing was most of the stuff he'd written had disappeared. There were just these bits you see here. His mother said he'd written whole plays — they didn't rhyme, if you know what I mean, but they were kind of like Shakespeare. Anyway, they couldn't be found. Maybe he'd burnt them or given them away. It does seem a shame, though, doesn't it?'

Archery glanced out of the window towards the little wooden church. 'Some mute inglorious Milton here may rest . . .' he murmured.

'That's right,' said the woman. 'You never know, they may turn up, like the Dead Sea Scrolls.'

Archery paid five and sixpence for the picture of the shepherd and the lamb and strolled up towards the church. He opened the kissing gate and, walking in a clockwise direction, made for the door. What was it she had said? 'You must never go widdershins around a church. It's unlucky.' He needed luck for Charles and for himself. The irony was that however things fell out, one of them would lose.

131

There was no music coming from the church, but as the door opened he saw that some sort of service was in progress. For a moment he stood, looking at the people and listening to the words.

'If after the manner of men I have fought with beasts at Ephesus, what advantageth it me, if the dead rise not?'

It was a funeral. They were almost exactly halfway through the service for the burial of the dead.

'Let us eat and drink for tomorrow we die . . .'

The door gave a slight whine as he closed it. Now, as he turned, he could see the funeral cars, three of them, outside the other gate. He went to look again at Grace's grave, passed the newly dug trench where this latest coffin was to be laid, and finally sat down on a wooden seat in a shady corner. It was a quarter to twelve. Give it half an hour, he thought, and then he would have to go for his bus. Presently he dozed.

The sound of gentle footfalls awakened him. He opened his eyes and saw that they were carrying the coffin out of the church. It was supported by four bearers, but it was a small coffin, a child's perhaps or a short woman's. On it were a few bunches of flowers and a huge wreath of madonna lilies.

The bearers were followed by a dozen people, the procession being headed by a man and a woman walking side by side. Their backs were towards Archery and besides that the woman, dressed in a black coat, wore a large black hat whose brim curved about her face. But he would have known her anywhere. He would have known her if he were blind and deaf, by her presence and her essence. They could not see him, had no idea they were watched, these mourners who had come to bury Alice Flower.

The other followers were mostly old, friends of Alice's perhaps, and one woman looked as if she must be the matron of the Infirmary. They gathered at the graveside and the vicar began to speak the words that would finally commit the old servant to the ground. Primero bent down and, taking rather fastidiously a handful of black earth, cast it on to the coffin. His shoulders shook and a little hand in a black glove reached out and rested on his arm. Archery felt a savage stab of jealousy that took away his breath.

132

The vicar spoke the Collect and blessed´ them. Then Primero went a little way apart with him, they spoke together and shook hands. He took his wife's arm and they walked slowly towards the gate where the cars were. It was all over.

When they were out of sight Archery got up and approached the gradually filling grave. He could smell the lilies five yards off. A card was attached to them and on it someone had written simply: 'From Mr and Mrs Roger, with love.'

'Good day,' he said to the sexton.

'Good day, sir. Lovely day.'

It was gone a quarter past twelve. Archery hurried towards the kissing gate, wondering how often the buses ran. As he came out from under the arch of trees, he stopped suddenly. Charles was striding towards him up the sandy lane.

'Good thing you didn't come,' Charles called. 'The place was shut for redecorating. Can you beat it? We thought we might as well drift back and pick you up.'

'Where's the car?'

'Round the other side of the church.'

They would be gone by now. Just the same Archery wished he were safely back at the Olive and Dove eating cold beef and salad. As they rounded the yew hedge a black car passed them. He forced himself to look towards the gate. The Primeros were still there, talking to the matron. His throat grew suddenly dry.

'Let's cut across the green,' he said urgently.

'Mr Kershaw happens to be waiting on this side.'

They were now only a few yards from the Primeros. The matron shook hands and stepped into a hired limousine. Primero turned and his eyes met those of Charles.

He grew first white, then a curious vinegary purple. Charles went on walking towards him and then Primero too began to move. They were approaching each other menacingly, ridiculously, like two gunmen in a Western.

'Mr Bowman, of the *Sunday Planet*, I believe?'

Charles stopped and said coolly, 'You can believe what you like.'

She had been talking to the women in the car. Now she withdrew her head and the car began to move off. They were alone, the four of them, in the centre of the fifth prettiest village in England. She looked at Archery first with embarrassment, then with a warmth that conquered her awkwardness.

'Why, hallo, I . . .'

Primero snatched at her arm. 'Recognise him? I shall need you for a witness, Imogen.'

Charles glared. 'You what?'

'Charles!' said Archery sharply.

'Do you deny that you made your way into my home under false pretences?'

'Roger, Roger . . .' She was still smiling, but her smile had grown stiff. 'Don't you remember we met Mr Archery at the dance? This is his son. He's a journalist, but he uses a pseudonym, that's all. They're here on holiday.'

Charles said rigidly, 'I'm afraid that isn't quite true, Mrs Primero.' She blinked, her lashes fluttering like wings, and her gaze came to rest softly on Archery's face. 'My father and I came here with the express purpose of collecting certain information. That we have done. In order to do it we had to make our way into your confidence. Perhaps we have been unscrupulous, but we thought the end justified the means.'

'I'm afraid I don't understand.' Her eyes were still on Archery and he was unable to draw his own away. He knew that his face registered a tremendous plea for forgiveness, a disclaimer of Charles's statement and also registered the agony of love. There was, however, no reason why she should read there anything but guilt. 'I don't understand at all. What information?'

'I'll tell you . . .' Charles began, but Primero interrupted him.

'Since you're so frank, you won't have any objection to coming down to the police station right now and laying your "information" before Chief Inspector Wexford.'

'None at all,' Charles drawled, 'except that it happens to be my lunchtime and in any case I have an appointment with the Chief Inspector already. At two sharp. I intend to tell him, Mr Primero, just how opportunely for you your grandmother died, how — oh, perfectly legally, I admit — you managed to cheat your sisters out of their inheritance, and how you concealed yourself in Victor's Piece on a certain evening in December sixteen years ago.'

'You're out of your mind!' Primero shouted.

Archery found his voice. 'That's enough, Charles.' He heard her speak, a tiny disembodied sound.

'It isn't true!' And then, terribly afraid, 'It isn't true, is it?'

'I'm damned if I'll argue it out in the street with this crook!'

'Of course it's true.'

'It was all above board.' Primero suddenly broke. They were all hot, standing there in the noon sun, but only Primero's face showed actual sweat, water drops on the cheesy sallow skin. 'Hell, it was a matter of law,' he blustered. 'What's it got to do with you, anyway? Who *are* you?'

Without taking her gaze from Archery, she took her husband's arm. All the gaiety had left her face and she looked almost old, a faded blonde who was effaced by her black clothes. Because she had become ugly she suddenly seemed for the first time within Archery's reach, yet she had never been farther from it. 'Let's go home, Roger.' Her mouth trembled and cobweb lines had appeared at its corners. 'In the course of your enquiries, Mr Archery,' she said, 'I hope you managed to combine pleasure with business.'

Then they were gone. Charles gave a great gasp.

'I must say I rather enjoyed that. I suppose by pleasure she meant the lunch they gave me. You can rely on these tycoons' wives to tot up every egg in the caviare. Still it was hard on her. You needn't look so shattered, Father. It's awfully middle-class to have a phobia about scenes.'

CHAPTER THIRTEEN

I deal with the thing that is lawful and right . . . and all false
ways I utterly abhor.

Psalm 119, appointed for the 26th Day

'Public General Acts and Measures, 1950. Wexford took the
book — was it a White Paper? Archery was ashamed to confess
that he did not know — and read the title aloud. 'There's
something here you want me to look at?'

Charles found the page for him. 'Here.' Wexford began
to read. The silence was tense, almost agonised. Archery
looked surreptitiously at the others, Charles who was flushed
with eagerness, Kershaw trying to sit casually, but whose
bright darting eyes betrayed his anxiety, Tess who looked
confident, serene. Was it her mother in whom she trusted
so completely or was it Charles? A good deal of Charles's
poise had deserted him when on entering the office five
minutes before he had had to introduce Tess to the Chief
Inspector.

'Miss Kershaw,' he had said, 'my . . . the girl I'm going to
marry. I . . .'

'Ah, yes.' Wexford had been very urbane. 'Good afternoon,
Miss Kershaw, Mr Kershaw. Won't you sit down? Heat wave's
coming to an end at last, I'm afraid.'

And indeed a change had come over the bright blue
un-English sky. It had begun just after lunch with the appearance of a cloud that was truly no bigger than a man's hand, and
this cloud had been followed by more, driven by a sudden wind.
Now, as Wexford, frowning a little, read steadily, Archery
contemplated the window from which the yellow blind had
been fully raised, and through it the lumpy blotchy mass of
cumulus, hollowed and pock-marked with grey.

'Very interesting,' said Wexford, 'and new to me. I didn't

know the Primero sisters were adopted. Convenient for Primero.'

'Convenient?' said Charles. Archery sighed within himself. He could always tell when his son was going to be rude or what Charles himself called forthright. 'Is that all you've got to say?'

'No,' said Wexford. Few people have the confidence and the restraint to say 'yes' or 'no' without qualification. Wexford was big and heavy and ugly; his suit had seen better days, too many wet ones and too many hot dusty ones, but he radiated strength. 'Before we go any further on this tack, Mr Archery,' he said to Charles, 'I'd like to say that I've had a complaint about you from Mr Primero.'

'Oh, that.'

'Yes, that. I've been aware for some days that your father had made the acquaintance of the Primeros. Perhaps it wasn't a bad idea and I'm sure it wasn't an unpleasant one to do so through Mrs Primero.' Archery knew his face had become white. He felt sick. 'And let me say in all fairness,' Wexford went on, 'that I told him it was all right as far as I was concerned to make contact with the people concerned in the Primero case.' He glanced briefly at Tess, who didn't move. 'Make contact, I said, not make trouble. Your little escapade on Friday is what I call making trouble and that I won't have!'

Charles said sulkily, 'All right, I'm sorry.' Archery saw that he had to justify himself before Tess. 'You're not going to tell me that your people don't occasionally invent a cover story to get what they want.'

'My people,' Wexford snapped, 'happen to have the law on their side.' He added grandiloquently, 'They *are* the law.' The frown thawed. 'Now we've got the lecture over you'd better tell me just what you and your father have found out.'

Charles told him. Wexford listened patiently, but as the evidence against Primero mounted, instead of surprise, his face registered a strange blankness. The heavy features had become brutish, like those of an old bull.

'Of course, you'll say he had an alibi,' said Charles. 'I realise your people would have checked his alibi and after all these years it's going to be difficult to crack, but . . .'

'His alibi was not checked,' said Wexford.

'What did you say?'

'His alibi was not checked.'

'I don't understand.'

'Mr Archery . . .' Wexford got up and rested his massive hands on the desk, but he didn't move away from behind it. 'I am quite happy to discuss this whole matter with you, answer any questions you may like to ask.' He paused. 'But not in the presence of Miss Kershaw. If I may say so, I think you were unwise to bring her with you.'

Now it was Charles's turn to get to his feet.

'Miss Kershaw is going to be my wife,' he said hotly. 'Anything you say to me you can say to her. I won't have any secrets from her in this.'

Casually Wexford sat down again. He drew a bunch of papers from a desk drawer and began to study them. Then he lifted his eyes slowly and said: 'I'm sorry this has been a fruitless interview for you. With a little co-operation I think I could have saved you a lot of useless enquiry. But, if you'll forgive me, I'm a very busy man so I'll say good afternoon.'

'No,' said Tess suddenly. 'I'll go. I'll wait in the car.'

'Tess!'

'Of course I'm going, darling. Don't you see? He can't talk about my father in front of me. Oh, darling, be your age!'

He is being his age, thought Archery miserably. Wexford knew something — something that was going to be horrible. But why was he playing this pouncing cat and mouse game with them all, why had he played it with Archery all along? Confidence and strength — but did it cover a fierce inverted snobbism, a fear that the Archerys might shake his authority and trouble the still waters of his district? And yet the man held such sway and was, beyond a doubt, a good, just man. He would never lie or even shift truth to cover a lapse. 'His alibi was not checked . . .' If only they would stop fencing!

Then suddenly, Wexford stopped it.

'No need to leave the building, Miss Kershaw,' he said. 'If your — your father would care to take you upstairs — straight along the corridor and turn left when you come to the double doors — you'll find we've got quite a reasonable canteen, even for a lady. I suggest a cup of strong tea and an eccles cake.'

'Thanks.' Tess turned and just touched Kershaw's shoulder. He rose at once. Wexford closed the door after them.

Charles took a deep breath, and making a brave attempt to lounge casually in his chair, said, 'All right, then. What about this alibi that for some mysterious reason was never investigated?'

'The reason,' said Wexford, 'was not mysterious. Mrs Primero was killed between six-twenty-five and seven o'clock on the evening of Sunday, September 24th, 1950.' He paused to allow Charles's inevitable interruption of 'Yes', yes', uttered with fierce impatience. 'She was killed in Kingsmarkham and at six-thirty Roger Primero was seen in Sewingbury five miles away.'

'Oh, he was seen, was he?' Charles scoffed, crossing his legs. 'What do you think, Father? Doesn't it seem remotely possible to you that he could have fixed beforehand that he'd be "seen"? There's always some shifty mate who'll perjure himself and say he's seen you for twenty quid.'

'Some shifty mate, eh?' Wexford was now hardly bothering to conceal his amusement.

'Somebody saw him. All right. Who saw him?'

Wexford sighed and the smile was erased.

'I saw him,' he said.

It was a blow in the face. Archery's love for his son, dormant over the past days, rose within his breast in a hot tide. Charles said nothing, and Archery who had been doing this sort of thing rather a lot lately, tried hard not to hate Wexford. He had taken an unconscionable time coming to the point, but this, of course, was his revenge.

The big elbows rested on the desk, the fingers meeting and pressing together in an implacable pyramid of flesh. The law incarnate. If Wexford had seem Primero that night, there was no gainsaying it, for here was incorruptibility. It was almost as if God had seen him. Horrified, Archery pulled himself up in his chair and gave a dry painful cough.

'You?' said Charles at last.

'I,' said Wexford, 'with my little eye.'

'You might have told us before!'

'I would have,' said Wexford mildly and, oddly enough,

believably, 'if I'd had the remotest idea you suspected him. Chatting up Primero about his grandmother was one thing, pinning murder on him quite another.'

Polite now, stiff and very formal, Charles asked, 'Would you mind telling us the details?'

Wexford's courtesy matched his. 'Not at all. I intend to. Before I do, however, I'd better say that there was no question of hindsight. I knew Primero. I'd seen him in court with his chief on a good many occasions. He used to go along with him to learn the ropes.' Charles nodded, his face set. Archery thought he knew what was going on in his mind. Loss was something he knew about, too.

'I was in Sewingbury on a job,' Wexford continued, 'and I'd got a date to meet a man who sometimes gave us a bit of information. What you might call a shifty mate, but we never got twenty quidsworth out of him. The appointment was for six at a pub called the Black Swan. Well, I had a word with my — my friend, and I was due back in Kingsmarkham at seven. I walked out of the public bar at just on half past six and ran slap bang into Primero.

' "Good evening, Inspector," he said, and I thought he looked a bit lost. As well he might. I found out afterwards that he'd been going to meet some pals, but he'd got the wrong pub. They were waiting for him at the Black Bull. "Are you on duty?" he said. "Or can I buy you a short snort?" '

Archery nearly smiled. Wexford had given a very fair imitation of the absurd slang Primero still affected after sixteen years of affluence.

' "Thanks all the same," I said, "but I'm late as it is." "Good night to you, then," he said and he went up to the bar. I'd only been in Kingsmarkham ten minutes when I got called out to Victor's Piece.'

Charles got up slowly and extended a stiff, mechanical hand.

'Thank you very much, Chief Inspector. I think that's all anyone can say on the subject, don't you?' Wexford leaned across the desk and took his hand. A faint flash of compassion softened his features, weakened them, and was gone. 'I'm sorry I wasn't very polite just now,' Charles said.

'That's all right,' said Wexford. 'This is a police station, not a clerical garden party.' He hesitated and added, 'I'm sorry, too.' And Archery knew that the apology had nothing to do with Charles's ill manners.

Tess and Charles began to argue even before they had all got into the car. Certain that they had said it all or something very like it before, Archery listened to them indifferently. He had kept silent for half an hour and still there was nothing he could say.

'We have to be realistic about it,' Charles was saying. 'If I don't mind and Mother and Father don't mind, why can't we just get married and forget you ever had a father?'

'Who says they don't mind? That's not being realistic, anyway. I'm being realistic. One way or another I've had a lot of luck . . .' Tess flashed a quick watery smile at Kershaw. 'I've had more than anyone would have thought possible, but this is one bit I have to dip out on.'

'And what does that mean exactly?'

'Just that — well, it was ridiculous ever to imagine we could be married, you and I.'

'You and I? What about all the others who'll come along and fancy you? Are you going to go through the same melodrama with them or d'you think you'll weaken when the thirties rear their ugly heads?'

She winced at that. Archery thought Charles had almost forgotten they were not alone. He pushed her into the back seat of the car and banged the door.

'I'm curious, you see,' Charles went on, bitterly sarcastic. 'I'd just like to know if you've taken a vow of perpetual chastity. O God, it's like a feature in the *Sunday Planet* — Condemned to lonely spinsterhood for father's crime! Just for the record, since I'm supposed to be so far above you morally, I'd like to know the qualifications the lucky man has to have. Give me a specification, will you?'

Her mother had built up her faith, but the Archery family with their doubts had knocked it down; still it had lived until Wexford had killed it. Her eyes were fixed on Kershaw who had given her reality. Archery was not surprised when she said hysterically:

'I suppose he'd have to have a murderer for a father.' She gasped, for she was admitting it to herself for the first time. 'Like me!'

Charles tapped Archery's back. 'Just nip out and knock someone off,' he said outrageously.

'Oh, shut up,' said Kershaw. 'Give it a rest, Charlie, will you?'

Archery touched his arm. 'I think I'll get out, if you don't mind. I need some air.'

'Me too,' said Tess. 'I can't stand being boxed up in here any longer and I've got a ghastly head. I want some aspirins.'

'Can't park here.'

'We'll walk back to the hotel, Daddy. If I don't get out I'll pass out.'

Then they were all three on the pavement, Charles's face as black as thunder. Tess swayed a little and Archery caught her arm to steady her. Several passers-by gave them curious looks.

'You said you wanted aspirins,' said Charles.

It was only a few yards to the nearest chemist's, but Tess was shivering in her thin clothes. The air was heavy and cloying. Archery noticed that all the shopkeepers had furled their sunblinds.

Charles seemed about to begin again but she gave him a pleading look. 'Don't let's talk about it any more. We've said it all. I needn't see you again till October, not then if we're careful . . .'

He frowned silently, made a little gesture of repudiation. Archery held the shop door open for Tess to pass through.

There was no one inside but the assistant and Elizabeth Crilling.

She did not appear to be buying anything, just waiting and gossiping with the shop girl. It was the middle of a weekday afternoon and here she was shopping. What had become of the job in the 'ladies' wear establishment'? Archery wondered if she would recognise him and how he could avoid this happening, for he did not want to have to introduce her to Tess. It gave him a little thrill of awe when he realised what was happening in this small town shop, a meeting after sixteen years of the child who was Painter's daughter and the child who had discovered Painter's crime.

While he hovered near the door Tess went up to the counter. They were so close together that they were almost touching. Then Tess reached across in front of Liz Crilling to select one of the aspirin bottles, and in doing so brushed her sleeve.

'I beg your pardon.'

'That's O.K.'

Archery could see Tess had nothing smaller than a ten shilling note. His trepidation, his fears for the effect of illumination on Tess at this moment were so great, that he almost cried aloud, 'Never mind. Leave it! Only, please God, let us all get away and hide ourselves!'

'Haven't you anything smaller?'

'I'm sorry.'

'I'll just go and see if we've got any change.'

The two young women stood side by side in silence. Tess stared straight in front of her, but Liz Crilling was playing nervously with two little scent bottles displayed on a glass shelf, moving them about as if they were chessmen.

Then the pharmacist in his white coat came out from the back.

'Is there a Miss Crilling waiting for a prescription?'

Tess turned, her face flooded with colour.

'This is a repeat prescription, but I'm afraid it's no longer valid . . .'

'What d'you mean, no longer valid?'

'I mean that it can only be used six times. I can't let you have any more of these tablets without a fresh prescription. If your mother . . .'

'The old cow,' said Liz Crilling slowly.

The swift animation on Tess's face died as if she had been struck. Without opening her purse she tumbled the change loose into her handbag and hurried out of the shop.

The old cow. It was her fault, everything bad that had ever happened to you was her fault — beginning with the beautiful pink dress.

She was making it for you and she worked at the sewing machine all day that cold wet Sunday. When it was finished you put it on and Mummy brushed your hair and put a ribbon in it.

'I'll just pop over and show you off to Granny Rose,' Mummy said and she popped over, but when she came back she was cross because Granny Rose was asleep and hadn't heard when she'd tapped on the window.

'Give it half an hour,' Daddy said, 'and maybe she'll be awake then.' He was half asleep himself, lying in bed, white and thin on the pillows. So Mummy had stayed upstairs with him, giving him his medicine and reading to him because he was too weak to hold a book.

'You stay in the sitting room, Baby, and mind you don't get that frock dirty.'

You had done as you were told but it made you cry just the same. Of course you didn't care about not seeing Granny Rose, but you knew that while she was talking to Mummy you could have slipped out into the passage and down the garden to show it to Tessie, now, while it was brand-new.

Well, why not? Why not put on a coat and run across the road? Mummy wouldn't come down for half an hour. But you would have to hurry, for Tessie always went to bed at half-past six. Auntie Rene was strict about that. 'Respectable working class,' Mummy said, whatever that meant, and although she might let you into Tessie's bedroom she wouldn't let you wake her up.

But why, why, why had you gone?

Elizabeth Crilling came out of the shop and walked blindly towards the Glebe Road turning, bumping into shoppers as she went. Such a long long way to go, past the hateful little sand houses that were like desert tombs in this spectral storm light, such a long way . . . And there was only one thing left to do when you got to the end of the road.

144

CHAPTER FOURTEEN

It is lawful for Christian men ... to wear weapons and serve in the wars.

The Thirty-nine Articles

The letter with the Kendal postmark was awaiting Archery on the hall table when they got back to the Olive and Dove. He glanced at it uncomprehendingly, then remembered. Colonel Cosmo Plashet, Painter's commanding officer.

'What now?' he said to Charles when Tess had gone upstairs to lie down.

'I don't know. They're going back to Purley tonight.'

'Do we go back to Thringford tonight?'

'I don't know, Father. I tell you I don't know.' He paused, irritable, pink in the face, a lost child. 'I'll have to go and apologise to Primero,' he said, the child remembering its manners. 'It was a bloody awful way to behave to him.'

Archery said it instinctively, without thinking. 'I'll do that, if you like. I'll ring them.'

'Thanks. If he insists on seeing me I'll go. You've talked to her before, haven't you? I gathered from something Wexford said.'

'Yes, I've talked to her, but I didn't know who she was.'

'That,' said Charles, severe again, 'is you all over.'

Was he really going to ring her up and apologise? And why should he have the vanity to suppose that she would even come to the phone? 'In the course of your enquiries, Mr Archery, I hope you managed to combine pleasure with business.' She was bound to have told her husband what she had meant by that. How the middle-aged clergyman had suddenly gone sentimental on her. He could hear Primero's reply, his colloquialism, 'Didn't actually make the old pass, did he?' and her light dismissive laughter. His soul cringed. He went into the empty lounge and ripped open Colonel Plashet's letter.

145

It was handwritten on rough white vellum almost as thick as cartridge paper. By the occasional fading of the ink from deep black to pale grey Archery could tell that the writer had not used a fountain pen. An old man's hand, he thought, a military man's address, 'Srinagar', Church Street, Kendal . . .

Dear Mr Archery, he read,

I was interested to receive your letter and will do my best to provide you with what information I can on Private Herbert Arthur Painter. You may be aware that I was not called to give evidence as to character at Painter's trial, though I held myself in readiness to do so should it have been necessary. Fortunately I have retained in my possession certain notes I then made. I say fortunately, for you will appreciate that Private Painter's war service covered a period of from twenty-three to twenty years ago, and my memory is no longer what I should like it to be. Lest you should be under the impression, however, that I am the possessor of information sympathetic to Painter's relatives, I must reluctantly disabuse your mind. In deciding not to call me, Painter's defending counsel must have been aware that any statements I could truthfully have made would, instead of assisting their cause, have merely made the task of prosecution easier.

That was it, then. There would follow only another loathsome catalogue to Painter's propensities. Colonel Plashet's very idiosyncratic style of writing brought home to him, more forcibly than the cold print of the transcript had done, the kind of man Charles was prepared to accept as a father-in-law. Curiosity, not hope, made him read on.

Painter had been serving with His Majesty's Forces for one year when he entered my regiment. This was shortly prior to our embarkation for Burma as part of the Fourteenth Army. He was a most unsatisfactory soldier. We saw no action until we had been in Burma for three months, during which time Painter was twice put on a charge for being drunk and disorderly and sentenced to seven days' detention for gross insolence on an officer.

In action his manner and bearing improved considerably. He was a naturally pugnacious man, brave and aggressive. Soon after this, however, an incident occurred in the village in which we had our camp and a young Burmese woman was killed. A Court Martial was held before which

Painter was charged with her manslaughter. He was found not guilty. I think I had better say no more on this matter.

In February 1945, six months before the cessation of hostilities in the Far East, Painter succumbed to a certain tropical affliction which manifests itself in severe ulceration of the legs, accelerated, I am told, by his complete disregard of certain elementary hygienic precautions and his refusal to take a proper diet. He became seriously ill and responded badly to treatment. There was at this time a troopship lying off Calcutta, and as soon as Painter's condition allowed, he and certain other sick men were transported there by air. This troopship reached a United Kingdom port during the latter part of March, 1945.

I have no further information as to Painter's fate except that I believe he was shortly afterwards demobilised on health grounds.

If you have any other questions whatsoever to put to me regarding Painter's war service, you may be assured of my willingness to answer them to the best of my ability and discretion. You have my full permission to publish this letter. May I, however, ask your indulgence to an old man's whim, and request a copy of your book when it comes out?

> *Yours sincerely,*
>
> *Cosmo Plashet*

They all assumed he was writing a book. Archery smiled a little at the colonel's grandiose style, but there was nothing to smile at in the brief lines about the Burmese woman's death. The colonel's guarded, 'I think I had better say no more on this matter . . .' told him more than a page of explanations

Nothing new, nothing vital. Why, then, did he have this urgent sensation of having missed something of importance? But no, he couldn't see it . . . He looked again, not knowing what he was looking for. Then, as he stared at the spidery loops and whorls, he was engulfed by a hot wave of trepidation and longing. He was afraid to speak to her, yet he longed to hear her voice.

He looked up, surprised to find how dark it had become. The summer afternoon sky simulated dusk with its covering of slate-coloured cloud. Over the housetops away to the east it was leaden tinged with angry purple and as Archery began to fold the letter, a vivid flash of lightning shocked across the room, flashing the words on the paper into relief and bleaching his hands livid white. The thunder followed it as he reached the stairs, and echoes were still curling and growling round the old building when he entered his bedroom.

She could only refuse to speak to him. She wouldn't even have to do that herself, for she could send the Italian butler. There was no question of her berating or reproaching him personally — she could do it with far more crushing effect by proxy.

'Forby Hall. Mr Primero's residence.'

It *was* the butler. The Italian accent distorted every word except the name to which it gave true Latin emphasis.

'I should like to speak to Mrs Primero.'

'What name shall I say, sir?'

'Henry Archery.'

Perhaps she would not be with her husband when the message came. People situated as they were in an enormous house of many rooms tended to live individual lives, he in the library, she in the drawing room. She would send the butler back with a message. As a foreigner the butler would be without that intimate feel for the nuances of English and that would give her scope. She could tell him to say something subtle and apparently polite and he would not appreciate the cutting sting that underlay the words. He heard footsteps, echoing footsteps across the big hall Charles had described. The phone crackled, perhaps because of the storm.

'Hallo?'

Out of a bone-dry throat he tried to speak. Why hadn't he rehearsed something? Because he had been so sure she wouldn't come?

'Hallo, are you still there?'

'Mrs Primero . . .'

'I thought you might have got fed-up with waiting. Mario took so long about it.'

'Of course I waited.' Rain burst against his window, smacking and sobbing at the glass. 'I want to apologise to you for this morning. It was unforgivable.'

'Oh, no,' she said. 'I've forgiven you — for this morning. You didn't really take any part in it, did you? It was the other times that seem so — well, not forgivable, just incomprehensible.'

He could imagine her little helpless gesture, the white hands spreading out.

'One doesn't like to feel one's been used, you see. It's not that I'm hurt. I'm not likely to be hurt because I'm really very tough, much tougher than Roger. But I am a bit spoilt and I feel as if I've been kicked off my pedestal. Good for me, I expect.'

Archery said slowly, 'There's so much to explain, I thought I could explain on the phone, but now I find I can't.' And yet the violence of the storm made it easier for him. He could hardly hear his own words. 'I want to *see* you,' he said, forgetting his promise.

Apparently she had forgotten it too. 'You can't come here,' she said practically, 'because Roger's somewhere about and he might not look on your apology in the same light as I do. And I can't come to you because the Olive and Dove, being a respectable hostelry, doesn't allow visitors in residents' bedrooms.' He made an inarticulate murmur. 'That's the second cheap thing I've said to you today,' she said. 'Oh, my dear, you wouldn't want me to talk in the lounge among all the fuddy-duddies, would you? I know, what about Victor's Piece?'

'It's locked,' he said, adding stupidly, 'and it's raining.'

'I've got a key. Roger's always kept one. Shall we say eight? The Olive will be only too happy if you have an early dinner.'

He dropped the receiver almost guiltily as Charles put his head round the door. And yet the telephone call had not been clandestine but made at Charles's instigation.

'I think I've made it all right with the Primeros,' he said, and he reflected on words from an unremembered source. God gave men tongues that they might conceal their thoughts.

But Charles, with the quixotry of youth, had lost interest. 'Tess and her father are just off,' he said.

'I'll come down.'

They were standing in the hall, waiting. For what? Archery wondered. The storm to cease? A miracle? Or just to say goodbye?

'I wish we hadn't seen Elizabeth Crilling,' Tess said. 'And yet now I wish I'd talked to her.'

'Just as well you didn't,' said Archery. 'You're worlds apart.

The only thing you'd have in common is your age. You're both twenty-one.'

'Don't wish away my life,' Tess said oddly and he saw there were tears in her eyes. 'I'm not twenty-one till October.' She picked up the duffel bag that served her as a weekend case and held out her hand to Archery.

'We must love you and leave you,' said Kershaw. 'Doesn't seem anything more to be said, does there, Mr Archery? I know you hoped things would work out, but it wasn't to be.'

Charles was gazing at Tess. She kept her eyes averted.

'For God's sake say I can write to you.'

'What's the use?'

'It would give me pleasure,' he said tightly.

'I shan't be at home. I'm going to Torquay to stay with my aunt the day after tomorrow.'

'You won't be camping on the beach, will you? This aunt, doesn't she have an address?'

'I haven't got a piece of paper,' said Tess and Archery saw that she was near to tears. He felt in his pocket, pulled out first Colonel Plashet's letter — not that, not for Tess to see — then the illuminated card with the verse and the picture of the shepherd. Her eyes were misted and she scrawled the address quickly, handing it to Charles without a word.

'Come on, lovey,' said Kershaw. 'Home, and don't spare the horses.' He fished out his car keys. 'All fifteen of them,' he said, but no one smiled.

CHAPTER FIFTEEN

If he hath offended any other . . . ask them forgiveness; and
where he hath done injury or wrong to any man . . . make
amends to the uttermost of his power.

The Visitation of the Sick

It was raining so heavily that he had to dash from the car into
the dilapidated porch and even there the rain caught him,
blown by the gusty wind and tossed in icy droplets off the
evergreens. He leant against the door and staggered because it
gave with his weight and swung noisily open.

She must have arrived already. The Flavia was nowhere to
be seen and he felt a shiver of self-disgust and trepidation when
it occurred to him that she was being purposely discreet. She
was well known in the district, she was married and she was
having a secret meeting with a married man. So she had hidden
her conspicuous car. Yes, it was cheap, cheap and sordid, and
he, a priest of God, had engineered it.

Victor's Piece, dry and rotten in drought, smelt wet and
rotten now the rain had come. It smelt of fungus and dead
things. There were probably rats under these knotted flaking
floorboards. He closed the door and walked a little way down
the passage, wondering where she was and why she had not
come out to him when she heard the door. Then he stopped,
for he was facing the back door where Painter's raincoat had
hung, and there was a raincoat hanging there now.

Certainly nothing had hung there on his previous visit to
the house. He moved up to the raincoat, fascinated and rather
horrified.

Of course, it was obvious what had happened. Someone
had bought the place at last, the workmen had been in and one
of them had left his raincoat. Nothing to be alarmed about. His
nerves must be very bad.

'Mrs Primero,' he said, and then, because you do not call women with whom you have secret assignations by their surnames, 'Imogen! Imogen!'

There was no answer. And yet he was sure he was not alone in the house. What about knowing her if you were deaf and blind, jeered a voice within him, what about knowing her by her essence? He opened the dining room door, then the drawing room. A damp cold smell came to meet him. Water had leaked under the window sill and formed a spreading pool, dark in colour, hideously evocative. This and the rusty veining on the marble of the fireplace recalled to him splashed blood. Who would buy this place? Who could bear it? But someone had bought it for there was a workman's coat hanging behind the door . . .

Here she had sat, the old woman, and bade Alice go to church. Here she had sat, her eyes closing easily into sleep, when Mrs Crilling had come tapping at the window. Then he had come, whoever he was, with his axe and perhaps she had still been sleeping, on and on over the threats and the demands, over the blows of the axe, on and on into endless sleep. Endless sleep? *Mors janua vitae.* If only the gateway to life had not been through an unspeakable passage of pain. He found himself praying for what he knew was impossible, that God should change history.

Then Mrs Crilling tapped on the window.

Archery gave a start so violent and galvanic that he seemed to feel a hand squeeze his heart with slippery fingers. He gasped and forced himself to look.

'Sorry I'm late,' said Imogen Ide. 'What a ghastly night.'

She should have been on the inside, he thought, pulling himself together. But she had been outside, tapping, tapping, because she had seen him standing there like a lost soul. This way it altered the aspect of things, for she had not hidden the car. It stood on the gravel beside his own, wet, silver, glittering, like something alive and beautiful from the depths of the sea.

'How did you get in?' she said in the hall.

'The door was open.'

'Some workman.'

'I suppose so.'

She wore a tweed suit and her pale hair was wet. He had

152

been silly enough — bad enough, he thought — to imagine that when they met she would run to him and embrace him. Instead she stood looking at him gravely, almost coldly, two little frown lines between her brows.

'The morning room, I think,' she said. 'There's furniture in there and besides it doesn't have — associations.'

The furniture consisted of two kitchen stools and a cane-back chair. From the window, heavily encrusted with grime, he could see the conservatory to whose walls of cracked glass the tendrils of a dead vine still clung. He gave her the chair and sat down on one of the stools. He had a strange feeling — but a feeling not without a charm of its own — that they had come here to buy the house, he and she, had come early and were reduced to wait thus uncomfortably until the arrival of the agent who would show them round.

'This could be a study,' he would say. 'It must be lovely on a fine day.'

'Or we could eat in here. Nice and near the kitchen.'

'Will you able to bear getting up in the morning to cook my breakfast?' (My love, my love . . .)

'You were going to explain,' she said, and of course, there would never be a shared bed or a shared breakfast or any future at all. This was their future, this interview in a damp morning room, looking at a dead vine.

He began to tell her about Charles and Tess, about Mrs Kershaw's belief. Her face grew even harder and colder when he came to the bit about the inheritance and before he had finished, she said:

'You really meant to pin the murder on Roger?'

'What could I do? I was torn between Charles,' he said, 'and you.' She shook her head quickly, the blood running into her face. 'I beg you to believe I didn't try to know you because you were his wife.'

'I believe you.'

'The money . . . his sisters . . . you didn't know about that?'

'I knew nothing. Only that they existed and that he never saw them. Oh God!' She screwed up her face, pushed her hands over her cheeks, across her eyes and up to the temples. 'We've been talking about it all day. He can't see that he was morally obliged to help them. Only one thing matters to him, that Wexford won't take it seriously as a motive for murder.'

'Wexford saw him himself that night at the crucial time in Sewingbury.'

'He doesn't know or he's forgotten. He's going to go through hell until he can pluck up courage to ring Wexford. Some people might say that's his punishment.' She sighed. 'Are his sisters very badly off?'

'One of them is. She lives in a single room with her husband and her baby.'

'I've got Roger to agree to let them have what they should have had in the first place, three thousand, three hundred odd each. I think I'd better go to see them myself. He won't even notice it's gone. It's funny, you know, I knew he was unscrupulous. You can't make that amount of money without being, but I didn't know he'd stoop to that.'

'It hasn't made you . . . ?' He hesitated, wondering what he had destroyed.

'Never feel the same about him again? Oh, my dear, you are funny. Listen, I'll tell you something. Seven years ago it was the month of June. My face was on the cover of six separate magazines that month. The most photographed girl in Britain.'

He nodded, puzzled and out of his depth.

'If you reach a peak there's nothing left but to go downhill. In June of the next year I had my face on one magazine. So I married Roger.'

'You didn't love him?'

'I liked him, you know. He saved me in a way and all the time I'm saving him.' Archery knew what she meant, recalling her soft tranquillity in the Olive dining room, her hand touching a mourner's trembling arm. He expected always from her calm serenity and he was shocked when she raged suddenly: 'How was I to know there was a middle-aged clergyman waiting for me — a clergyman with a wife and a son and a guilt complex as big as a mountain?'

'Imogen!'

'No, you're not to touch me! It was stupid to come here and I should never have done it. O God, how I hate these sentimental scenes!'

He got up and walked as far from her as the little room allowed. It had stopped raining but the sky was sludge-coloured and the vine was as dead as a doornail.

'What will they do now,' she said, 'your son and this girl?'

'I don't think they know themselves.'

'And you, what will you do?'

' "Go to the wife of my bosom," ' he quoted, ' "the same as I ought to go." '

'Kipling!' She gave a hysterical laugh, and he was pained by the depths he was discovering too late. 'Kipling! That's all I need.'

'Good-bye,' he said.

'Good-bye, dear Henry Archery. I've never known what to call you. Do you know that?' She lifted his hand, kissed the palm.

'Perhaps it's not a name for dalliance,' he said ruefully.

'But it sounds well with Rev. in front of it.'

She went out, closing the door soundlessly behind her.

'Jenny kissed me,' he said to the vine. Jenny could just be short for Imogen. 'So what?'

Presently he came out into the hall and he wondered why the place seemed emptier and more lifeless than before. Perhaps it was his own fresh sense of loss. He turned towards the back door and then he saw. It was not an imagined but an actual diminishing. The raincoat had gone.

Had it ever been there or was his fancy, morbid and hypersensitive, creating hallucinations? It was a vision that might naturally come to someone involved as he was in Painter's story. But if the raincoat had never been there what would account for those penny-sized puddles on the floor, made surely by rain rivulets running from a sleeve?

He had no belief in the vulgar supernatural. But now as he stood looking at the hook where the raincoat had hung, he remembered how he had jumped at the tap on the window and had likened the marble veining to blood. It was not impossible that some evil hung over places such as this, fermenting the imagination and re-creating on the mind's retina images from a past tragedy.

The door was glazed in square panes. All were dirty yet all glinted faintly in the evening light — all but one. He peered, then smiled wryly at his absurd fancies. The glass had been completely removed from the frame nearest to the lock. An arm could have passed through it to turn the key and slide back the bolts.

It was unbolted now. He stepped out on to the flagged yard. Beyond, the garden lay enveloped in thin wet mist. The trees, the bushes, the lush blanket of weed sagged under their weight of water. Once he would have felt the responsible citizen's anxiety as to the whereabouts of whoever had broken that window, might even have considered going to the police. Now he was simply apathetic, indifferent.

Imogen filled his mind, but even on this subject, his thoughts were no longer passionate or ashamed. He would give her five more minutes to get away and then he would return to the Olive. Mechanically he stooped down and for something to do began carefully picking up the shards of broken glass, stacking them against the wall where no one, not even the burglar, might tread on them.

His nerves were bad, he knew that, but surely that was a footfall, the sound of indrawn breath.

She was coming back! But she must not — it was more than he could stand. The sight of her would be joy, but anything she said could only mean a fresh parting. He set his teeth, tightened the muscles of his hands and before he could stop himself his fingers had closed on a sliver of glass.

The blood came before the pain. He stood up, looking stupidly at his hand and saying, 'I've cut myself' aloud in that empty place, and he turned to meet the tap-tap of high heels.

Her scream burst in his face.

'Uncle Bert! Uncle Bert! Oh, my God!'

His hand was all bloody but he put it out, the hurt hand and the other, to catch Elizabeth Crilling as she fell.

'You ought to have it stitched,' she said. 'You'll get tetanus. You'll have an awful scar.'

He wrapped the handkerchief more tightly about the wound and sat grimly on the step, watching her. She had come round in seconds but her face was still white. A little gust of wind flicked through the tangled mass of green and showered them with water drops. Archery shivered.

'What are you doing here?' he asked.

She lay back in the chair he had fetched her from the morning room, her legs stretched out and limp. He noticed how thin they were, thin as the legs of an Oriental, the stockings wrinkled at the ankles.

'I've had a row with my mother,' she said.

He said nothing, waiting. For a moment she remained inert, then her body seemed to snap forwards, a trap with a steel spring. Instinctively, he shifted a little away from her, for she had brought her face towards his, her hands clutching each other between knees and breast. Her mouth moved before the words found sound.

'Oh Christ!' He kept still, controlling his inevitable reaction to the oath. 'I saw you with blood on you,' she said, 'and then you said it, what he said. "I've cut myself." ' A great shudder rocked her as if she had been grasped and shaken by an invisible force. Amazed, he watched her slacken again and heard her say in cold contrast, 'Give me a cigarette.' She tossed her bag to him. 'Light it!' The flame guttered in the damp air and the tugging wind. She cupped her thin hands with their big knuckles around it. 'Always snooping, aren't you?' she said, drawing back. 'I don't know what you thought you'd find, but this is it.'

Bewildered, he found himself staring at the garden, up at the overhanging gables, down at the wet broken paving.

'Me, I mean,' she said with savage impatience. 'You've been telling tales to the police about me and you don't even know what it's all about.' Again she snapped forward and shamelessly — he was horrified — pulled up her skirt and exposed her thigh above her stocking top. The white skin was covered all over with needle punctures. 'Asthma, that's what it's about. Asthma tablets. You dissolve them in water — and that's a hell of a job on its own — and then you fill up a hypodermic.'

Archery did not think himself easily shocked. But he was shocked now. He felt the blood run into his face. Embarrassment silenced him, then gave place to pity for her and a kind of diffused indignation with humanity.

'Does it have any effect?' he asked as coolly as he could.

'It gives you a lift, if you follow me. Much the same as you get from singing psalms, I expect,' she jeered. 'There was this man I lived with, he put me on to it. I was in the right place

157

for getting supplies, you see. Until you sent that bastard Burden down and he put the fear of God into my mother. She's got to get a new prescription every time she wants them now and she's got to collect them herself.'

'I see,' he said, and hope went. So that was what Mrs Crilling had meant. In prison there would be no tablets, no syringe, and because she had become addicted to them she would have to reveal her addiction or . . .

'I don't think the police can do anything to you,' he said, not knowing whether they could or not.

'What would you know about it? I've got twenty left in a bottle so I came here. I've made myself a bed upstairs and . . .'

He interrupted her. 'It's your raincoat?'

The question surprised her, but only for a moment, then scorn returned to make her look twice her age.

'Sure it is,' she said scathingly. 'Whose did you think it was, Painter's? I went out for a bit to get something from my car, left the door on the latch and when I came back you were here with that tarty piece.' He kept his eyes on her, controlling himself. For the only time in his life he felt an urge to strike another person's face. 'I didn't dare come back for a bit,' she said, returning to the only other mood she had, a self-pitying childishness. 'But I had to get my raincoat — the tablets were in the pocket.'

She inhaled deeply and flung the cigarette away from her into the wet bushes.

'What the hell were you doing, returning to the scene of the crime? Trying to get under his skin?'

'Whose skin?' he whispered urgently.

'Painter's of course. Bert Painter's. My Uncle Bert.' She was defiant again, but her hand shook and her eyes glazed. It was coming now. He was like a man awaiting bad news, knowing it was inevitable, knowing even exactly what it was going to be, but still hoping that there would be some detail, some facts to mitigate it. 'That night,' she said, 'he stood there just like you. Only he was holding a piece of wood and there was blood on it and all over him. "I've cut myself," he said. "Don't look, Lizzie, I've cut myself."'

CHAPTER SIXTEEN

When the unclean spirit is gone out of a man, he walketh through dry places seeking rest and finding none. He saith, I will return unto my house whence I came out.

The Gospel for the Fourth Sunday in Lent

She told it in the second person, 'You did this,' 'You did that.' Archery realised he was hearing what no parent and no psychiatrist had ever heard, and he marvelled. The peculiar use of the pronoun seemed to draw his own mind into the child's body so that he could see with her eyes and feel with her overweening terror.

She sat down in the damp dusk on the spot where it had all begun for her, utterly still now. Only her eyelids moved. Sometimes, at agonising moments in the narrative, she would close her eyes then open them again with a slow exhalation of breath. Archery had never been to a seance — would indeed disapprove of such a thing as being theologically untenable — but he had read of them. Elizabeth Crilling's steady outpouring of terrible events told in a flat monotone was reminiscent, he thought, of mediumistic revelation. She was coming to the end now and a weary relief crossed her face as of one shedding a load.

. . . You put your coat on, your best coat because it was your best frock, and you ran across the road, down the sideway and past the greenhouse. Nobody saw you because there was no one about. Or was there? Surely that was the back door closing softly.

You came very quietly around the side of the house and then you saw it was only Uncle Bert who had come out of the house into the garden.

'Uncle Bert, Uncle Bert! I've got my best frock on. Can I go and show it to Tessie?'

Suddenly you were very frightened, more frightened than you had ever been in all your life, because Uncle Bert was breathing in such a funny way, gasping and coughing like Daddy did when he had one of his attacks. Then he turned round and there was red stuff all over him, on his hand and all down the front of his coat.

'I've cut myself,' he said. 'Don't look, Lizzie. I've just cut myself.'

'I want Tessie! I want Tessie!'

'Don't you go up there!'

'You're not to touch me. I've got my new dress on. I'll tell my mummy.'

He just stood there with the red stuff on him and his face was like the face of a lion, big thick mouth, thick nose, curly tawny hair. Yes, it was like the lion in that picture book Mummy said you must not look at . . .

The red stuff had splashed on to his face and trickled to the corner of his mouth. He brought that dreadful face down close to yours and shouted right at you:

'You tell her, Lizzie Crilling, you stuck-up little snob, and d'you know what I'll do? Wherever I am — wherever, d'you hear me? — I'll find you and I'll give you what I gave the old girl.'

It was over. He could tell that by the way she came out of her trance, sat up and gave a kind of moan.

'But you went back,' Archery murmured. 'You went back with your mother?'

'My mother!' Weeping would not have surprised him. This violent bitter laughter did. On a high discordant peal, she stopped suddenly and rushed into her answer. 'I was only five, only a kid. I didn't know what he meant, not then. I was much more frightened of letting her know I'd been over there.' He noted that 'her' and knew intuitively she would not mention her mother by name again. 'You see, I didn't even know it was blood and I reckon I must have thought it was paint.

'Then we went back. I wasn't afraid of the house and I didn't know what he meant by the old girl. I think when he said about giving me what he'd given the old girl I thought he meant his wife, Mrs Painter. He knew I'd seen him hit her. I found the body. You knew that? God, it was terrible. I didn't understand, you see. D'you know what I thought at first? I thought she'd sort of burst.'

'Don't,' said Archery.

'If you can't take it now, what d'you think it was like for me? I was *five*. Five, my Christ! They put me to bed and I was ill for weeks. Of course, they'd arrested Painter, but I didn't know that. You don't tell children that sort of thing. I didn't know what had happened at all, only that Granny Rose had burst open and he had made it happen and if I said I'd seen him he'd do the same to me.'

'But afterwards. Didn't you tell anyone then?'

She had talked about finding the body and said it was terrible, but then there had been affectation in her voice. A child finding a murdered woman, he thought. Yes, all the world would recoil in shock from that. Yet for her that had not been the worst. Now as he asked her about afterwards he saw the trance begin once more to mist her face as the spectre of Painter — Painter on this very spot — rose before it.

'He'd find you,' she mumbled. 'He'd find you wherever you were, wherever he was. You wanted to tell *her,* but she wouldn't listen to you. 'Don't think about it, Baby, put it out of your mind.' But it wouldn't go *out* . . .' Her features worked and the blank eyes flickered.

'Miss Crilling, let me take you home.'

She was standing up now, moving mechanically towards the house wall, a robot whose programming has failed. When her hands touched the bricks she stopped and spoke again, talking to him but into the house itself.

'It wouldn't go out. It went in and in, till it was just a little black wheel spinning and playing the same thing over and over again.'

Had she realised she was speaking in metaphor? He had thought of a medium's utterances, but now he knew it had been more like a discordant record, playing the same horror each time it was pricked by the stylus of association. He touched her arm and was surprised when she followed him meekly and limply back to the chair. They sat in silence for some minutes. She was the first to speak and she was almost her normal self.

'You know Tessie, don't you? She's going to marry your son?' He shrugged. 'I think she was the only real friend I ever had,' she said quietly. 'It was her birthday the next week. She was going to be five, and I thought I'd give her one of my old dresses. Sneak it round when *she* was with the old girl. Generous little beast, wasn't I? I never saw her again.'

Archery said gently, 'You saw her this afternoon in the chemist's.'

Her new tranquillity was very finely balanced. Had he pushed it too far?

'In the white blouse?' she said in a dead even voice, so low that he had to lean forward and strain to catch it. He nodded.

'That girl who hadn't got any change?'

'Yes.'

'She was standing beside me and I never knew.' There was a long silence. The only sound was the faint rustling of wet bushes, water-loaded gleaming leaves on the coach-house walls. Then she tossed her head. 'I reckon I don't notice women much,' she said. 'I saw you all right and the boy that was with you. I remember I thought the talent's looking up in this dump.'

'The talent,' Archery said, 'is my son.'

'Her boy friend? I never would have told you!' She gave a low cry of exasperation. 'And, my God, I never would have told her — not if you hadn't caught me out like that.'

'It was chance, coincidence. Perhaps it's better that I do know.'

'You!' she said. 'That's all you think about, you and your precious son. What about me?' She stood up, looked at him and moved towards the door with the broken pane. It was true he thought, ashamed. He had been prepared to sacrifice all these other people to save Charles — the Crillings, Primero, even Imogen — but his quest had been doomed from the beginning because history could not be changed.

'What will they do to me?' Her face was turned away from him and she spoke softly. But there was such urgency and such fear in those six short words that their impact was as if she had shouted.

'Do to you?' He could do no more than get to his feet and stand helplessly behind her. 'Why should they do anything to you?' He remembered the dead man on the crossing and he remembered the needle punctures, but he said only, 'You've been more sinned against than sinning.'

'Oh, the Bible!' she cried. 'Don't quote the Bible to me.' He said nothing for he had not done so. 'I'm going upstairs now,' she said strangely. 'When you see Tess would you give her my love? I wish,' she said, 'I wish I could have given her something for her birthday.'

By the time he had found a doctor's house he felt all hand, nothing but hand, a throbbing thing that beat like a second heart. He recognised Dr Crocker at once and saw that he, too, was remembered.

'You must be enjoying your holiday,' Crocker said. He stitched the finger, filled a syringe with anti-tetanus serum. 'First that dead boy and now this. Sorry, but this may hurt. You've got thick skin.'

'Really?' Archery could not help smiling as he bared his upper arm. 'I want to ask you something.' Without stopping to explain he put the question that had been troubling him all the way from Victor's Piece. 'Is it possible?'

'Beginning of October?' Crocker looked closely and not unsympathetically at him. 'Look, how personal is this?'

Archery read his thoughts and managed a laugh. 'Not that personal,' he said. 'I am, as they say, enquiring for a friend.'

'Well, it's extremely unlikely.' Crocker grinned. 'There have been cases, very few and far between. They make minor medical history.'

Nodding, Archery got up to go.

'I shall want to see that finger again,' the doctor said. 'Or your local G.P. will. You'll need another couple of injections. See to it when you get home, will you?'

Home . . . yes, he would be home tomorrow. His stay in Kingsmarkham had not been a holiday, anything but that, yet he had that curious end-of-a-holiday feeling when the resort one has stayed in becomes more familiar than home.

He had walked along this High Street every day, more frequently even than he trod the main village street at Thringford. The order of the shops, chemist, grocer, draper, was as well known to him as to the housewives of Kingsmarkham. And the place was certainly pretty. Suddenly it seemed sad that he should hardly have noticed its prettiness — more than that really, for prettiness does not go with grace and dignity — but would associate it for ever with a lost love and a failed search.

Street lamps, some of them of ancient design and with wrought iron casings, showed him alleys winding between stone walls, coaching yards, flowers in a few cottage gardens. The weak yellow light bleached these flowers to a luminous pallor. Half an hour ago it had been just light enough to read print by; now the darkness had come down and lamps appeared in windows fronting the street. The sky had a rainy look and the stars showed only in the crevices between bulbous bloated cloud. There was no moon.

The Olive and Dove was brightly lit and the car park full. Glass doors separated the hall from the cocktail bar and he saw people sitting on high stools, gathered round the small black oak tables. Archery thought he would give everything he possessed to see Charles among them, throwing back his head in laughter, his hand resting on the shoulder of a pretty girl. Not a beautiful, intellectual, tainted girl — just someone pretty and dull and uncomplicated. But Charles was not there. He found him alone in the lounge writing letters. Only a few hours had elapsed since his parting from Tess, but already he was writing . . .

'What on earth have you done to your hand and where have you been?'

'Hacking away at the past.'

'Don't be cryptic, Father. It doesn't suit you.' His tone was bitter and sullen. Archery wondered why people say that suffering improves the character, why indeed he had sometimes thoughtlessly said it to his own parishioners. He listened to his son's voice, carping, querulous and selfish. 'I've been wanting to address this envelope for the past two hours, but I couldn't because I don't know where Tess's aunt lives.' Charles gave him a sour accusing look. 'You wrote it down. Don't say you've lost it.'

'Here.' Archery took the card from his pocket and dropped it on the table. 'I'm going to phone your mother, tell her we'll be home in the morning.'

'I'll come up with you. This place goes dead at night.'

Dead? And the bar crowded with people, some of whom were surely as exacting as Charles. If Tess had been with them it would not have been dead. Quite suddenly Archery made up his mind that Charles must be made happy, and if happiness meant Tess, he should have Tess. Therefore the theory he was formulating would have to be made to work.

He paused on the threshold of his bedroom, put his hand to the light switch but did not press it. There in the darkness with Charles behind him there flashed across his brain a picture of himself and Wexford that first day at the police station. He had been firm then. 'Bitterly, bitterly against this marriage,' he had told the Chief Inspector. How utterly he had come round! But then he had not known what it was to crave for a voice and a smile. To understand all was not merely to forgive all, it was utter identification of the spirit and the flesh.

Over his shoulder Charles said, 'Can't you find the switch?' His hand came up and met his father's on the dry cold wall. The room flooded with light. 'Are you all right? You look worn-out.'

Perhaps it was the unaccustomed gentleness in his voice that did it. Archery knew how easy it is to be kind when one is happy, how nearly impossible to feel solicitude in the midst of one's own misery. He was suddenly filled with love, an overflowing diffused love that for the first time in days had no specific object but included his son — and his wife. Hoping unreasonably that her voice would be soft and kind, he moved towards the telephone.

'Well, you are a stranger,' were the first words he heard and they were sharp with resentment. 'I was beginning to wonder what had happened to you. Thought you must have eloped.'

'I wouldn't do that, darling,' he said, sick at heart. And then, because he had to set his foot back on the path of constancy, he took a grotesque echo, 'Kingsmarkham isn't conspicuous for its talent. I've missed you.' It was untrue and what he was going to say next would also be a lie. 'It'll be good to be home with you again.' That lie would have to be changed into truth. He clenched his hand till the hurt finger burned with pain, but as he did so he thought that he and time could make it true . . .

'You do use some extraordinary expressions,' Charles said when he had rung off. 'Talent, indeed. Very vulgar.' He was still holding the card, staring at it with utter absorption. A week ago Archery would have marvelled that a woman's address and a woman's handwriting could provide such fascination.

'You asked me on Saturday if I'd ever seen this before. You asked me if I'd heard it. Well, now I've *seen* it, it's rung a bell. It's part of a long religious verse play. Part of it's in prose but there are songs in it — hymns really — and this is the last verse of one of them.'

'Where did you see it? In Oxford? In a library?'

But Charles was not listening to him. He said as if he had been meaning to say it for the past half-hour, 'Where did you go tonight? Had it any connection with me and — and Tess?'

Must he tell him? Was he obliged to root out those last vestiges of hope before he had anything real and proven to put in their place?

'Just to have a last look at Victor's Piece.' Charles nodded. He appeared to accept this quite naturally. 'Elizabeth Crilling was there, hiding.' He told him about the drugs, the wretched attempts to secure more tablets, but he did not tell him everything.

Charles's reaction was unexpected. 'Hiding from what?'

'The police, I suppose, or her mother.'

'You didn't just leave her there?' Charles asked indignantly. 'A crazy kid like that? God knows what she might do. You don't know how many of those tablets would poison her. She might take them deliberately to that end. Have you thought of that?'

She had accused him of not considering her but even that taunt had not prompted him. It had simply not crossed his mind that he was doing something irresponsible in leaving a young girl alone in an empty house.

'I think we ought to go to Victor's Piece and try to get her to come home,' Charles said. Observing the sudden animation on his son's face, Archery wondered how sincere he was and how much of this spurt of energy was due to a desire to do something, anything, because he knew that if he went to bed he would not sleep. Charles put the card away in his pocket. 'You won't like this,' he said, 'but I think we ought to take the mother with us.'

'She's quarrelled with her mother. She behaves as if she hates her.'

'That's nothing. Have you ever seen them together?'

Only a glance across a courtroom, a glance of indecipherable passion. He had never seen them together. He knew only that if Charles were alone somewhere and miserable, on the verge perhaps of taking his own life, he, Archery, would not want strangers to go to his succour.

'You can drive,' he said and he tossed the keys to his son. Mrs Crilling would be in bed. Then it occurred to him for the first time that she might be worrying about her daughter. He had never attributed to the Crillings ordinary emotions. They were different from other people, the mother deranged, the girl delinquent. Was that why, instead of being merciful, he had merely used them? As they turned into Glebe Road he felt a new warmth stir within him. It was not too late — especially now she had found some release — to bring Elizabeth back, to heal that old wound, to retrieve something out of chaos.

Outwardly he was cold. He was coatless and the night was chilly. You expect a winter's night to be cold, he thought. There was something depressing and wrong about a cold summer night. November with flowers, a November wind that ruffled the ripe leaves of summer. He must not find omens in nature.

'What d'you call it,' he said to Charles, 'when you ascribe emotions to nature? What's the expression?'

'The Pathetic Fallacy,' Charles said. Archery shivered.

'This is the house,' he said. They got out. Number twenty-four was in darkness upstairs and down.

'She's probably in bed.'

'Then she'll have to get up,' said Charles and rang the bell. He rang again and again. 'Pointless,' he said. 'Can we get round the back?'

Archery said, 'Through here,' and led Charles through the sandy arch. It was like a cavern, he thought, touching the walls. He expected them to be clammy but they were dry and prickly to the touch. They emerged into a dark pool among patches of light which came from french windows all along the backs of houses. A yellow square segmented by black bars lay on each shadowed garden but none came from Mrs Crilling's window.

'She must be out,' said Archery as they opened the little gate in the wire fence. 'We know so little about them. We don't know where she'd go to or who her friends are.'

Through the first window the kitchen and the hall showed dark and empty. To reach the french windows they had to push through a tangle of wet nettles which stung their hands.

'Pity we didn't bring a torch.'

'We haven't *got* a torch,' Archery objected. He peered in. 'I've got matches.' The first he struck showed him the room as he had seen it before, a muddle of flung-down clothes and stacked newspapers. The match died and he dropped it on wet concrete. By the light of a second he saw that on the table were the remains of a meal, cut bread still in its paper wrappings, a cup and saucer, a jam jar, a single plate coated with something yellow and congealed.

'We might as well go,' he said. 'She isn't here.'

'The door's not locked,' said Charles. He lifted the latch and opened it quietly. There came to them at once a peculiar and unidentifiable odour of fruit and of alcohol.

'You can't go in. There isn't the slightest justification for breaking in.'

'I haven't broken anything.' Charles's foot was over the threshold, but he stopped and said over his shoulder to his father, 'Don't you think there's something odd here? Don't you feel it?'

Archery shrugged. They were both in the room now. The smell was very strong but they could see nothing but the dim outlines of cluttered furniture.

'The light switch is on the left by the door,' he said. 'I'll find it.' He had forgotten that his son was a man, that his son's adult sense of responsibility had brought them there. In that dark, evilly scented place, they were just a parent and his child. He must not do as Mrs Crilling had done and let the child go first. 'Wait there,' he said. He felt his way along the side of the table, pushed a small armchair out of his path, squeezed behind the sofa and felt for the switch. 'Wait there!' he cried again, much more sharply and in a spasm of real fear. Previously in his passage across the room his feet had come into contact with debris on the floor, a shoe, he thought, a book dropped face-downwards. Now the obstruction was larger and more solid. His scalp crept. Clothes, yes, and within those clothes something heavy and inert. He dropped to his knees, thrusting forward hands to palpate and fumble. 'Dear God . . . !'

'What is it? What the hell *is* it? Can't you find the light?'

Archery could not speak. He had withdrawn his hands and they were wet and sticky. Charles had crossed the room. Light pouring into and banishing that darkness was a physical pain. Archery closed his eyes. Above him he heard Charles make an inarticulate sound.

He opened his eyes and the first thing he saw was that his hands were red. Charles said, 'Don't look!' and he knew that his own lips had been trying to frame those words. They were not policemen, not used to sights such as this, and each had tried to save the other from seeing.

Each had to look. Mrs Crilling lay spread on the floor between the sofa and the wall and she was quite dead. The chill of her body came up to Archery's hands through the pink flounces that covered it from neck to ankles. He had seen that neck and at once had looked away from the stocking that made a ligature around it.

'But she's got blood all over,' said Charles. 'It's as if — God! — as if someone had sprinkled her with it.'

CHAPTER SEVENTEEN

I held my tongue and spake nothing; I kept silence, yea, even from good words; but it was pain and grief to me.

Psalm 39. *The Burial of the Dead*

'It isn't blood,' said Wexford. 'Don't you know what it is? Couldn't you smell it?' He lifted the bottle someone had found under the sideboard and held it aloft. Archery sat on the sofa in Mrs Crilling's living room, worn, tired, utterly spent. Doors banged and footsteps sounded as Wexford's two men searched the other room. The people upstairs had come in at midnight, Saturday night happy, the man a little drunk. The woman had had hysterics during Wexford's questioning.

They had taken the body away and Charles moved his chair round so that he could not see the crimson splashes of cherry brandy.

'But why? Why did it happen?' he whispered.

'Your father knows why!' Wexford stared at Archery, his grey gimlet eyes deep and opaque. He squatted opposite them on a low chair with wooden arms. 'As for me, I don't know but I can guess. I can't help feeling I've seen something like this before, a long, long time ago. Sixteen years to be exact. A pink frilly dress that a little girl could never wear again because it was spoilt with blood.'

Outside the rain had begun again and water lashed against the windows making them rattle. It would be cold now inside Victor's Piece, cold and eerie like a deserted castle in a wood of wet trees. The Chief Inspector had an extra uncanny sense that almost amounted to telepathy. Archery willed his thoughts to alter course lest Wexford should divine them, but the question came before he could rid his mind of its pictures.

'Come on, Mr Archery, where is she?'

'Where is who?'

'The daughter.'

'What makes you think I know?'

'Listen to me,' said Wexford. 'The last person we've talked to who saw her was a chemist in Kingsmarkham. Oh, yes, we went to all the chemists first, naturally. This one remembers that when she was in the shop there were two men and a girl there too, a young man and an elder one, tall, fair, obviously father and son.'

'I didn't speak to her then,' Archery said truthfully. The smell sickened him. He wanted nothing but sleep and peace and to get out of this room where Wexford had kept them since they had telephoned him.

'Mrs Crilling's been dead six or seven hours. It's ten to three now and you left the Olive at a quarter to eight. The barman saw you come in at ten. Where did you go, Mr Archery?'

He sat silent. Years and years ago — Oh, centuries ago! — it had been like this in school. You own up, you betray someone, or everyone suffers. Funny, once before he had thought of Wexford as a kind of headmaster.

'You know where she is,' Wexford said. His voice was loud, threatening, ominous. 'D'you want to be an accessory? Is that what you want?'

Archery closed his eyes. Quite suddenly he knew why he was prevaricating. He wanted the very thing that Charles had warned him might happen and although it was contrary to his religion, wicked even, he wanted it with all his heart.

Charles said, 'Father . . .' and when he got no reply shrugged, turned his dull shocked eyes to Wexford. 'Oh, what the hell? She's at Victor's Piece.'

Archery realised that he had been holding his breath. He let it out in a deep sigh. 'In one of the bedrooms,' he said, 'looking at the coach house and dreaming of a heap of sand. She asked what they would do to her and I didn't understand. What will they do to her?'

Wexford got up. 'Well, sir . . .' Archery noted that 'sir' as one might notice the re-assuming of a velvet glove. 'You know as well as I do that it's no longer lawful to punish with death for certain . . .' His eyes flickered over the place where Mrs Crilling had lain. ' . . . certain heinous and grievous offences.'

171

'Will you let us go now?' Charles asked.

'Until tomorrow,' said Wexford.

The rain met them at the front door like a wave or a wall of spray. For the past half-hour it had been drumming on the roof of the car and seeping in through the half-open quarter light. There was water laying in a small pool at Archery's feet but he was too tired to notice or care.

Charles came with him into his bedroom.

'I shouldn't ask you now,' he said. 'It's almost morning and God knows what we'll have to go through tomorrow, but I have to know. I'd rather know. But what else did she tell you, that girl at Victor's Piece?'

Archery had heard of people pacing a room like caged beasts. He had never imagined himself so strung with tension that in spite of utter exhaustion he would have to find release by crossing and re-crossing a floor, picking up objects, replacing them, his hands shaking. Charles waited, too wretched even for impatience. His letter to Tess lay in its envelope on the dressing table and beside it the card from the gift shop. Archery picked it up and kneaded it in his hands, crumpling the deckle edging. Then he went up to his son, put his hands gently on his shoulders and looked into the eyes that were young replicas of his own.

'What she told me,' he said, 'needn't matter to you. It would be like — well, someone else's nightmare.' Charles did not move. 'If you will only tell me where you saw the verse that is printed on this card.'

The morning was grey and cool, such a morning as occurs perhaps three hundred times a year out of the three hundred and sixty-five, when there is neither rain nor sun, frost nor fog. It was a limbo of a morning. The policeman on the crossing had covered his shirt sleeves with his dark jacket, the striped shop blinds were rolled up and sluggish steps had grown brisk.

Inspector Burden escorted Archery along the drying pavements to the police station. Archery was ashamed to answer Burden's kindly question as to how he had slept. He had slept heavily and soundly. Perhaps he would also have slept dreamlessly had he known what the inspector now told him, that Elizabeth Crilling was alive.

'She came with us quite willingly,' Burden said and added rather indiscreetly, 'To tell you the truth, sir, I've never seen her so calm and sane and — well, at peace, really.'

'You want to go home, I suppose,' Wexford said when Burden had left them alone in the blue and yellow office. 'You'll have to come back for the inquest and the magistrates' court hearing. You found the body.'

Archery sighed. 'Elizabeth found a body sixteen years ago. If it hadn't been for her mother's self-seeking vanity, greed for something she had no claim to — that would never have happened. You might say that the greed reached out and destroyed long after its original purpose had been frustrated. Or you might say that Elizabeth bore her mother a grudge because Mrs Crilling would never let her talk about Painter and bring her terrors to the light of day.'

'You might,' said Wexford. 'It could be all those things. And it could be that when Liz left the chemist's she went back to Glebe Road, Mrs Crilling was afraid to ask for another prescription, so Liz, in the addict's frenzy, strangled her.'

'May I see her?'

'I'm afraid not. I'm beginning to guess just what she saw sixteen years ago and what she told you last night.'

'After I talked to her I went to see Dr Crocker. I want you to look at this.' Archery gave Wexford Colonel Plashet's letter, silently indicating the relevant passage with his bandaged finger. 'Poor Elizabeth,' he murmured. 'She wanted to give Tess a dress for her fifth birthday. Unless Tess has changed a lot it wouldn't have meant much to her.'

Wexford read, closed his eyes briefly and then gave a slight smile. 'I see,' he said slowly and restored the letter to its envelope.

'I am right, aren't I? I'm not juggling things, imagining things? You see, I can't trust my own judgement any more. I have to have an opinion from an expert in deduction. I've been to Forby, I've seen a photograph, I've got a letter and I've talked to a doctor. If you had the same clues would you have come to the same conclusions?'

'I'm sure you're very kind, Mr Archery.' Wexford gave a broad ironic grin. 'I get more complaints than compliments.

Now, as to clues and conclusions, I would, but I'd have been on to it a whole lot sooner.

'You see, it all depends on what you're looking for and the fact is, sir, you didn't know what you *were* looking for. All the time you were trying to disprove something in the face of — well, you said it — expert deduction. What you've found now achieves the same results as the other thing would have. For you and your son, that is. But it hasn't changed what for justice is the *status quo*. We would have made sure we knew precisely what we were looking for at the start, the basic thing. When you come down to that, it doesn't matter a damn to you who committed the crime. But you were looking through a pair of spectacles that were too big for you.'

'A glass darkly,' said Archery.

'I can't say I envy you the coming interview.'

'Strange,' said Archery thoughtfully as he got up to go, 'that although we both held such opposing opinions in the end we were both right.'

Wexford had said he must come back. He would make his visits short, though, short and blind, his eyes opening only in the court he could see out of this window, his words mere evidence. He had read stories of people transported to strange places, blindfolded and in shuttered cars, so that they should not see the country through which they passed. In his case he would be prevented from seeing visions and associations with those visions, by the presence of those he was legitimately allowed to love. Mary should come with him and Charles and Tess to be his shutters and his hood. Certainly he would never see this room again. He turned to give it a last glance, but if he hoped to have the last word he was disappointed.

'Both right,' said Wexford, giving Archery's hand a gentle clasp. 'I by reason and you by faith. Which, taken all in all,' he added, 'is only what one might expect.'

She opened the door to them carefully, grudgingly, as if she expected to see gypsies or a brush salesman from a disreputable firm.

'I hope you'll forgive us, Mrs Kershaw,' Archery said with

too loud heartiness, 'Charles wanted to see Tess and as we were coming this way . . .'

It is difficult to greet callers, even unwelcome callers, without some kind of a smile. Irene Kershaw did not smile, but she made muttering noises in which he caught the occasional word: 'very welcome, I'm sure,' 'unexpected . . .' and 'not really prepared . . .' They got into the hall, but it was an awkward manoeuvre and it almost involved pushing past her. She had grown rather red and she said to Charles, now quite coherently: 'Tess has popped down to the shops to get a few last-minute things for her holiday.' Archery could see that she was angry and that she did not know how to vent her anger on people who were at the same time adults and from a different background from her own. 'You've quarrelled, haven't you?' she said. 'What are you trying to do, break her heart?' Apparently she was capable of emotion, but once she had shown it, not capable of control. Tears welled into her eyes. 'Oh dear . . . I didn't mean to say that.'

Archery had explained everything to Charles in the car. He was to find Tess, get her alone and tell her. Now he said, 'You might go down the hill, Charles, and see if you can meet her coming up. She'll be glad of a hand with her basket.'

Charles hesitated, possibly because he was at a loss to answer Mrs Kershaw's accusation and could not bring himself to echo so exaggerated an expression as 'a broken heart'. Then he said, 'I'm going to marry Tess. That's what I've always wanted.'

The colour died out of her face and now that there was no occasion for them the tears trickled down her cheeks. Archery would, under no other circumstances, have been embarrassed. Now he realised that this mood of hers, tears, a lukewarm resentment that might be her nearest approach to passion, would make her receptive to what he had to say. A tired tigress apparently lurked under that dull suburban exterior, a mother beast capable of being roused only when its young was threatened.

Charles let himself out of the front door. Archery, left alone with her, wondered where the other children were and how soon Kershaw himself would return. Again he was finding himself, when in the sole company of this woman, at a loss for words. She made no effort to help him, but stood stiff and expressionless, dabbing at the tearmarks with the tips of her fingers.

'Perhaps we could sit down?' He made a vague gesture towards the glass door. 'I should like to have a talk, settle things, I . . .'

She was recovering fast, tunnelling back into the sanctuary of her respectability. 'You'd like some tea?'

The mood must not be allowed to peter out into small talk over the cups. 'No,' he said, 'no, really . . .'

She went before him into the living room. There were the books, the Reader's Digests, the dictionaries and the works on deep sea fishing. The portrait of Jill on the easel was finished and Kershaw had made the amateur's mistake of not knowing when to stop, so that the likeness had been lost in last-minute touches. In the garden which was spread before him with the unreality and the garish colours of a cushion cover in gros point, the Paul Crampel geraniums burned so brightly that they hurt his eyes.

Mrs Kershaw sat down genteelly and crimped her skirt over her knees. Today, now that it was cold again, she wore a cotton dress. She was that kind of woman, Archery thought, who would wear her winter clothes on and on cautiously until she was sure a heat wave was fully established. Then just as the hot weather was ending and the storm about to break, then at last the carefully laundered thin dress would be brought out.

The pearls had been restrung. She put her hand up to them and drew it away quickly, curbing temptation. Their eyes met and she gave a tiny nervous giggle, perhaps aware that he had noticed her tiny vice. He gave a small inner sigh, for all her emotion had gone and her face showed only the natural bewilderment of a hostess who does not know the purpose of a call and is too discreet to question the caller.

He must — he *must* — awaken something from behind that pale lined brow. All his carefully prepared openings died. In a moment she would begin on the weather or the desirability of white weddings. But she did not quite do that. He had forgotten the other stock remark that is so handy a conversation starter between strangers.

'And how did you enjoy your holiday?' said Irene Kershaw. Very well. That would do as well as anything.

'Forby is your native village, I believe,' he said. 'I went to see a grave while I was there.'

She touched the pearls with the flat of her hand. 'A grave?' For an instant her voice was as raw as when she had talked of a broken heart, then all passionless Purley again as she added, 'Oh, yes, Mrs Primero is buried there, isn't she?'

'It wasn't her grave I saw.' Softly he quoted, ' "Go, Shepherd, to your rest . . ." ' Tell me, why did you keep all the works he left behind him?'

That there would be reaction and that that reaction might be anger he had expected. He was prepared for a flouncing hauteur or even the damning, dulling response so dear to the heart of the Mrs Kershaws of this world: 'We needn't discuss that.' He had not thought she would be frightened and at the same time stricken with a kind of awe. She cowered a little in the armchair — if cowering is compatible with perfect stillness — and her eyes, wide and glistening now, had the utter immobility of the dead.

Her fear had the effect of frightening him. It was as communicable as a yawn. Suppose she were to have a fit of hysterics? He went on very gently:

'Why did you keep them hidden away in the dark? They might have been published, they might have been acted. He could have had posthumous fame.'

She made no answer at all, but now he knew what to do, the answer came to him like a gift of God. He only had to go on talking, gently, mesmerically. The words tumbled out, platitudes and clichés, praise of work he had never seen and had no reason to suppose he would admire, assurances and unfounded promises he might never be able to honour. All the time, like a hypnotist, he kept his eyes on her, nodding when she nodded, breaking into a wide fatuous smile when for the first time a tiny vague one trembled on her lips.

'May I see them?' he dared. 'Will you show me the works of John Grace?'

He held his breath while with torturing slowness she mounted a stool and reached for the top of the book case. They

were in a box, a large cardboard grocer's box that had apparently once contained a gross of tinned peaches. She handled it
with a peculiar reverence, her care all concentrated on it, so
that she let the magazines which had been stacked on it cascade
to the floor.

There must have been a dozen of them but only one cover
picture splashed at Archery like acid on the eyes. He blinked
away from the beautiful photographed face, the pale hair under
a hat of June roses. He had waited for Mrs Kershaw to speak
now and her words pulled him out of shock and misery.

'I suppose Tess told you,' she whispered. 'It was supposed
to be our secret.' She lifted the lid of the box so that he was
able to read the writing on the topmost sheet of manuscript.
The Fold. A Prayer in Dramatic Form by John Grace.' 'If you'd told
me before I would have shown them to you. Tess said I should
show them to anyone who would be interested and would —
would understand.'

Again their eyes met and Irene Kershaw's tremulous stare
was caught and steadied in his strong one. He knew his face was
mobile and expressive of his thoughts. She must have read them
for she said, thrusting the box towards him, 'Here, have them.
You can have them.' He drew away his hands and his body,
horrified and ashamed. At once he had realised what she was
doing, that she was trying to pay him off with her most precious
material possession. 'Only don't ask me.' She gave a little thin
cry. 'Don't ask me about him!'

Impulsively, because he could not bear those eyes, he
covered his own with his hands. 'I've no right to be your
inquisitor,' he murmured.

'Yes, yes . . . It's all right.' Her fingers touching his shoulder
were firm with a new strength. 'But don't ask me about him.
Mr Kershaw said you wanted to know about Painter — Bert
Painter, my husband. I'll tell you everything I can remember,
anything you want to know.'

Her inquisitor and her tormentor . . . Better a swift knife
thrust than this interminable twisting on the rack. He clenched
his hands till the only pain he could feel came from the wound
where the glass had gone in and he faced her across the
yellowing sheets of verse.

178

'I don't want to know about Painter any more,' he said. 'I'm not interested in him. I'm interested in Tess's father...' The moan she gave and the feel of those fingers scrabbling at his arm could not stop him now. 'And I've known since last night,' he whispered, 'that Painter *couldn't* have been her father.'

CHAPTER EIGHTEEN

... As ye will answer at the dreadful day of judgement when the secrets of all hearts shall be disclosed ...

The Solemnisation of Matrimony

She lay on the floor and wept. To Archery, standing by helpless, it was some measure of her total breakdown that she had come so far wide of her conventional limits as to lie there prone and shake with sobs. Archery had never in his life reached such a nadir of despair. He pitied with an anxiety that had something of panic in it this woman who cried as if the power to weep had long fallen into disuse, as if she were experimenting with some new and shattering exercise.

He did not know how long this abandonment to grief had lasted or would last. This room with all its apparatus for living what some call a 'full life' contained no clock and he had removed his watch to make room for the wrist anchorage of the bandage. Just as he was beginning to feel that she would never stop, she made a curious humping movement so that she rested like a flogged overburdened beast.

'Mrs Kershaw . . .' he said. 'Mrs Kershaw, forgive me.'

She got up slowly, her breast still heaving. The cotton dress was creased into a faded rag. She said something but he could not hear her at all and he realised what had happened. She had utterly exhausted her voice.

'Can I get you a glass of water, some brandy?'

Her head shook as if it were not part of her body but a separate thing quivering on a pivot. Her voice came in a hoarse croak. 'I don't drink.' Then he knew that nothing could fully pierce the layers of respectability. She fell into the chair from which his questions had prised her and let her arms hang limply over its sides. When he came back from the kitchen and gave her the glass of water she had recovered sufficiently to sip it and to rub with the old refinement at the corners of her lips. He was afraid to speak.

'Does she have to know?' The words had a hollow sound to them but the roughness had gone. 'My Tessie, does she have to know?'

He did not dare to tell her that Charles would have told her already. 'It's nothing these days,' he said, and shed with a word two thousand years' teaching of his faith. 'Nobody thinks anything of it any more.'

'Tell me what you know.'

He knelt at her feet, praying that all his guesses would approximate to the truth and that there would be few gaps for her to fill. If only he could deal well with this and save her the shame of confession. 'You and John Grace,' he said, 'lived close together in Forby. You were in love, but he was killed . . .'

On an impulse he took the manuscript in his hands and laid it gently on her lap. She took it as a religious takes a talisman or a relic and she said softly:

'He was so clever. I couldn't understand the things he wrote, but they were beautiful. His teacher wanted him to go to college but his mother wouldn't let him. You see, his father had a bakery business and he had to go into that.' Let her go on, he prayed, edging away to squat on the edge of his chair. 'He still wrote his poems and his plays,' she said, 'and in the evenings he used to study for some exam. He wasn't strong enough to go into the force, anaemia or something he had.' Her fingers tightened on the manuscript but her eyes were dry and drained. Archery had a quick vision of the pale pointed face in the souvenir shop picture, only now it was blending into and becoming one with Tess's.

He let his eyes linger on Irene Kershaw for a brief moment with painful compassion. They had reached a point in this telling where she must, unless he could save her, touch on that which would humiliate her most.

'You were going to be married,' he said.

Perhaps she was afraid to hear the words he might choose. 'We never did anything wrong but the once,' she cried. 'After-wards — well, he wasn't nasty like other boys, and he was just as ashamed as me.' Justifying herself, her head turned from him, she whispered, 'I've had two husbands and then there was John, but I've never been so much for that side of things.' Her head swung back and her face was aflame. 'We were engaged, we were going to be married . . .'

Archery knew he must rush on with his conjectures. 'After he was killed you knew you were going to have a child?' She nodded, silent now with the enormity of her embarrassment. 'You had nowhere to go, you were afraid so you married Painter. Let me see, John Grace was killed in February 1945 and Painter got home from Burma at the end of March. You must have known him before,' he said, guessing, improvising. 'Perhaps he was stationed at Forby before he went to the Far East?' A tiny nod rewarded him and he was prepared to go on, drawing someone else's story out of an inspired imagination, out of a letter from Kendal, a photographed face, the bruises on a woman's arm. He lifted his eyes from her and clasped his hands tightly to stop the sound that might have been no more than a sigh. Even a sigh would tell her. At the open french window, against the blaze of red petals, Kershaw was standing, silent, still and powerfully alert. How long had he been there? How much had he heard? Archery, transfixed, sought momentarily in his expression for suffering or anger and saw a sweetness that brought a sudden strength to his heart.

Perhaps he was betraying this woman, perhaps he was doing the unforgivable. It was too late for such recriminations.

'Let me try to finish,' he said, and he had no idea whether he kept his voice on the same level he had used before. 'You were married and you let him think he was Tess's father. But he suspected and that was why he never loved her as a father loves his child? Why didn't you tell Mr Kershaw?'

She leant forward and he could tell she had not heard the man behind her move almost soundlessly into the room. 'He never asked me about my life with Bert,' she said. 'But I was so ashamed of it, of being married to a man like that. Mr Kershaw's so good — you don't know him — he never asked me, but I had to tell him some of it, didn't I?' She was suddenly eloquent. 'Think what I had to tell him, think what I had to bring him — nothing! People used to point to me out in the street like I was a freak. He had to take that on his shoulders

— Mr Kershaw who'd never touched dirt in all his life. He said he'd take me away and give me a new life where no one'd know, he said I wasn't to blame, I was innocent. D'you think I was going to give up the one chance I'd ever had by telling him Tess was — was illegitimate?'

Archery gasped and staggered to his feet. By the power of his eyes and his will he had been trying to force the man behind her chair to retreat the way he had come. But Kershaw remained where he was, still, a man apparently without breath or heartbeats. His wife had been rapt, her own story dulling all outer stimuli, but now she seemed to sense the atmosphere in the room, the soundless passion of two other people whose sole desire was to help her. She twisted in her chair, sketched a strange little gesture of pleading and rose to confront her husband.

The scream Archery expected never came. She lurched a little, but whatever she was trying to gasp out was lost and muffled by Kershaw's strong embrace. He heard her say only, 'Oh, Tom, oh, Tom!' but his energy was so drained that his brain was filled with just one foolish thought. It was the first time he had ever heard Kershaw's christian name.

She did not come downstairs again for that time. Archery supposed that he would not see her again until they all met among flowers and bridesmaids and wedding cake. Tess sat pale-faced and almost shy, her hand clasped in that of Charles, the manuscript on her knees.

'I feel so strange,' she said. 'I feel I have a new identity. It's as if I had three fathers and the most remote of them was really my father . . .'

Charles said tactlessly, 'Well, wouldn't you choose to have had this one, a man who could write like this?' But Tess lifted her eyes momentarily to the man Archery would have to learn to call Tom and he knew she had made her choice.

Then she thrust the heavy stack of paper towards Archery. 'What can we do with them?'

'I could show them to a publisher I know. I once wrote part of a book myself . . .' He smiled. 'On Abyssinian cats. I do know someone who might be interested. Something I can do to make amends,' he said.

'You? You've got nothing to reproach yourself with.' Kershaw moved to stand between him and the lovers. Only marred one marriage to make another, Archery thought. 'Listen,' said Kershaw, his face scored with the lines of effort to make himself understood. 'You did nothing but what I should have done years ago, talked to her. I couldn't you see. I wanted to get off on the right foot. Now I can see you can be too tactful, too damned diplomatic. Oh, there were a thousand little things, how she'd never cared for Painter but he'd been pestering her to marry him. I never asked her what made her change her mind when he came home from Burma. God help me, I thought it wasn't my business! She didn't want me to tell Tess about Painter and I went through agony trying to put that across to a kid of twelve.' Here, unafraid of sentimentality, he caught his stepdaughter's free hand and held it briefly. 'I remember I even got mad at Rene because she seemed to be contradicting every blessed word I said.'

Tess quoted softly, ' "Never mind what Daddy says. Your father was no murderer." '

'And she was right but I turned a deaf ear. She'll talk to me now as she's never talked in all these years. She'll talk to you, Tess, if you'll go up to her now.'

Like a child she hesitated and her lips trembled into a nervous smile of indecision. But obedience — happy, reasonable obedience — was natural in that house. Archery had seen an instance of it before.

'I don't know what to say, how to begin,' she said, getting slowly to her feet. 'I'm so desperately afraid of hurting her.'

'Begin with your wedding, then,' Kershaw said robustly. Archery watched him stoop to the floor where the magazines had fallen. 'Show her this and let her dream of seeing you in something like it.'

Tess was in jeans and a white shirt, an Olivia or a Rosalind finding her lost birthright and with it a new womanhood. She took the magazine from Kershaw and glanced at the cover picture, the hat that was a pyramid of flowers crowning the most photographed face in Britain.

'That's not for me,' she said, but she took it with her and Archery watched them depart together, Charles's flesh and blood love and his own, a paper fantasy. Not for me, not for me . . .

'We must go soon,' he said to his son. 'It's time we shared all this with your mother.'

The Speaker of
Mandarin

For Don

Author's Note

For the transcribing of Chinese words and Chinese proper names into English I have used both the Wade-Giles and the Pinyin systems. While Pinyin is the officially endorsed system in the People's Republic, Wade-Giles, which was evolved in the nineteenth century, remains more familiar to Western readers. So I have used each where I felt it to be more appropriate and acceptable; e.g. the modern Pinyin for Lu Xing She, the Chinese International Travel Service, but Ching rather than Xing for the name of the last Imperial Dynasty, and I have used Mao Tse Tung in preference to the Pinyin Mao Zedong.

Acknowledgement

The poem quoted on p. 448, 'To Wang Lun' by Li Po, the poem quoted on pp. 484 and 493-94, 'Drinking Song' by Shen Hsun, and the two lines on p. 557 from the 'Song of a Chaste Wife' by Chang Chi, are all from the *Penguin Book of Chinese Verse'*, translated by Robert Kotewall and Norman L. Smith, translation © Norman L. Smith and Robert Kotewall, 1962, and are reprinted here by permission of Penguin Books Ltd.

Part One

1

The perfectly preserved body of the woman they call the
Marquise of Tai lay, sheathed in glass, some feet below them
on the lower level. Two thousand odd years ago when she
died she had been about fifty. A white shift covered her thin
seventy-five-pound body from neck to thighs. Her legs were a
fish-like pinkish-white much marked with striations, her right
arm, on account of a mended fracture, was rather shorter
than her left. Her face was white, puffy, the bridge of the
nose encaved, the mouth open and the tongue protruding,
the whole face bearing an expression of extreme agony as if
she had died from strangulation.

This, however, was not the case. According to the museum's
brochure and Mr Sung, the Marquise had suffered from tuber-
culosis and a diseased gall bladder. Just before she died of
some kind of heart attack she had consumed a hundred and
twenty water melon seeds.

'She have myocardial infarction, you know,' said Mr Sung,
quoting from memory out of the brochure, a habit of his.
'Very sick, you know, bad heart, bad insides. Let's go.'

They moved along to look down through a second aperture
at the Marquise's internal organs and *dura mater* preserved
in bottles of formaldehyde. Mr Sung looked inquiringly
into the face of his companion, hoping perhaps to see
there signs of nausea or dismay. But the other man's
expression was as inscrutable as his own. Mr Sung gave
a little sigh.

'Let's go.'

'I wish you wouldn't keep saying that,' said Wexford irritably. 'If I may suggest it, you should say, "Shall we go?" or "Are you ready?"'

Mr Sung said earnestly, 'You may suggest. Thank you. I am anxious to speak good. Shall we go? Are you leady?'

'Oh, yes, certainly.'

'Don't reply, please. I practise. Shall we go? Are you leady? Good, I have got it. Come, let's go. Are you leady to go to the site? Reply now, please.'

They got back into the taxi. Between the air-conditioned building and the air-conditioned car the temperature seemed that of a moderate oven, set for the slow cooking of a casserole. The driver took them across the city to the excavation where archaeologists had found the bodies of the Marquise, her husband and her son, clay figures of servants, provisions, artefacts to accompany them on their journey beyond the grave. The other bodies had been skeletons, their clothing fallen to dust. Only the Marquise, hideous, grotesque, staring from sightless empty eyes, had retained the waxen lineaments of life, wrapped in her painted gown, her twenty layers of silk robes.

Wexford and Mr Sung looked through the wooden grille at the great deep rectangular burial shaft and Mr Sung quoted almost verbatim a considerable chunk from *Fodor's Guide to the People's Republic of China*. He had a retentive memory and seemed to believe that Wexford, because he couldn't decipher ideographs, was unable to read his own language. It was even Wexford's *Fodor's* he was quoting from, artlessly borrowed the night before. Wexford didn't listen. He would have given a good deal to have been rid of baby-faced pink-cheeked slant-eyed Mr Sung. In any other country on earth a bribe equivalent to a month's wages – and here that would easily have been within Wexford's means – would have freed him for good of his guide-interpreter. Not in China, where even tipping was banned. Mr Sung was incorruptible. In spite of his youth, he was already a party member. A fanatical light came into his eyes and his flabby muscles tautened when he spoke of the great statesmen, Mao Tse Tung included, his own native place of Hunan Province had produced. Wexford sometimes wondered if the day would come, twenty years hence perhaps, when if he still lived he would open his *Times* and read that the new Chairman of the Chinese Communist Party was one Sung Lao Zhong, aged forty-seven, from Chang-sha. It was more than possible. Mr Sung came to the end of his memorized paragraph, sighed at the call of duty but refused to shirk it.

'Light,' he said. 'Shall we go? We visit now porcelain factory and before evening meal teacher training college.'

'No, we don't,' said Wexford. A mosquito bit him just above the ankle bone. The heat was enormous. Like the imagined casserole, he was slowly cooking, a gravy-like viscous sweat trickling stickily all over his body. It was the humidity as much as the ninety-eight degree temperature that did it. 'No, we don't. We go to the hotel and have a shower and a siesta.'

'There will be no other time for porcelain factory.'

'I can't help that.'

'It is most necessary to see college attended by Chairman Mao.'

'Not today,' said Wexford. The ice-cold atmosphere in the car stimulated a gush rather than a trickle of sweat. He mopped his face.

'Velly well. I hope you not leglet,' said Mr Sung, indignation, as any emotion did, causing acute confusion in the pronunciation of liquids. 'I aflaid you be solly.' His voice was vaguely threatening. Much more rebellion on the part of this obstinate visitor, Wexford thought, and Mr Sung might even insist that no such omissions were open to him. If Lu Xing She, the Chinese Tourist Board, whose vicar on earth, so to speak, Mr Sung was, required Wexford to see factories, kindergartens, colleges and oil refineries, these institutions he would see and no doubt about it.

Mr Sung turned away and looked out of the window. His face seldom expressed anything but a ruthless affability. The top of his head came approximately to Wexford's shoulder, though for a Southern Chinese he wasn't particularly short. He wore a cotton shirt, white as driven snow, a pair of olive-green baggy cotton trousers and sandals of chestnut-brown moulded plastic. His father, he had told Wexford, was a party cadre, his mother a doctor, his sister and own wife doctors.

They all lived together in a two-roomed apartment in one of the city's grey barrack-like blocks with Mr Sung's baby son, Tsu Ken.

Hooting at pedestrians, at cyclists who carried on their bikes anything from a couple of live fat piglets and a chicken to a suite of furniture, the car made its way through drab streets to the Xiangjiang Hotel. There were very few buildings in Chang-sha that pre-dated the Revolution of 1949, only the Kuomintang general's house with green curly roofs just by the hotel and a ruined European church of grey stucco whose provenance no one seemed to know anything of. Mr Sung got out of the car and came into the lobby with him. There he shook hands. Any more casual mode of behaviour wouldn't have satisfied his sense of duty. It was all Wexford could do to prevent his accompanying him to the eighth floor in the lift. He would be ready, please, by seven, said Mr Sung, for an open-air showing of a film about the history of the Revolution.

'Oh, no, thank you,' said Wexford. 'Too many mosquitos.'

'You take anti-malaria pill evly Fliday, I hope?'

'I still don't like being bitten.' Wexford's anklebone felt twice its normal size. 'Mysteriously enough – ' he caught sight in a rare mirror of his sweat-washed, sunburnt, never even adequately handsome face, ' – I am particularly attractive to *anopheles* but the passion isn't mutual.' Mr Sung looked at him with uncomprehending relentless amiability. 'And I won't sit in the open inviting them to vampirize me.'

'I see. Light. You come to cinema in hotel and see *Shanghai Girl* and Charlie Chaplin in *Great Dictator*. *Shanghai Girl* very good Chinese film about construction workers. I sit next so you don't miss storly.'

'Wouldn't you rather be at home with your wife and your baby?'

Mr Sung gave an enigmatic smile. He shook Wexford's hand once more. 'I do my job, light?'

Wexford lay on his iron-hard bed on a thin quilt. The undersheet, for some quaint reason, was a blue and white checked tablecloth. Cold air blew unevenly over him from the Japanese air conditioner, while outside the window the general's house and the brown pantiled roofs of Chang-sha lay baking in moist sizzling heat. He had made himself, with water from the thermos flask that was one of the amenities of his room, half a pint of green tea in a cherry-blossom painted cup with a lid. They made you eat dinner here at six (breakfast at seven, lunch, appallingly, at eleven-thirty) but there was still an hour and a half to go. He couldn't stomach the lemonade and strawberry pop and Cassia fizz you were expected to pour hourly into yourself to combat dehydration. He drank green tea all the time, making it himself and making it strong, or else he bought it from the street stalls for a single *fen*, something like a third of a penny, a glass.

Presently, after a second cup of tea, he dozed, but then it was time to shower and put on a fresh shirt for dinner. He would write to his wife later, there wasn't time now. Hong Kong, where she was staying, waiting for him, seemed infinitely far away. He went down to the dining room where he would eat at a table by himself with his own private fan, discreetly half-concealed from the only other foreign contingent, Italians sitting at the next broad round table by a bamboo screen. He sat down and asked the girl for a bottle of beer.

The Italians came in and said hallo to him. The girl turned their fan on, tucked their screen round them and began bringing Wexford's platters. Chicken and bamboo shoots im ginger sauce tonight, peanuts fried in oil, bright green nearly raw spinach, fried pumpkin and fried fish. Setting off with his nephew Howard and those other police officers who all ranked so much higher than he, he had brought a spoon and fork in his suitcase because he was afraid the Peking Hotel might not have Western cutlery. How green he had been, as green as the tea! The Peking Hotel was like an austere Ritz with arctic air conditioning and a huge shopping arcade and curtains that drew and undrew electrically. But somehow none of them had ever bothered with the silver that was offered them but had eaten from the first as the Chinese eat, and now he was as proficient with chopsticks as might have been any dignitary in the Forbidden City. He could even, he now discovered, pick up a slippery oil-coated peanut with chopsticks, so skilful had he become.

The girl brought him a bowl of rice and the big green bottle of Tsing-tao beer.

A feeling of tremendous well-being invaded him as he began to eat. He could still hardly believe after two weeks in China that he, Reg Wexford, a country policeman, was here in Tartary, in Cathay, had walked on the Great Wall, set foot on the Stone Boat in the Summer Palace, touched the scarlet columns in the Temple of Heaven, and was now touring southwards, seeing as many marvels and experiencing as many delights as Lu Xing She would permit.

When Chief Superintendent Howard Fortune of Scotland Yard, who was Wexford's dead sister's son, had first told a family gathering he was going to China in the summer of 1980, his uncle had felt something he wasn't usually a prey to – envy. Howard would spend a good deal of time, of course, over the conference table. The particular branch of the Chinese Government who were his hosts wanted advice on crime prevention and crime detection and they would no doubt want to indulge in that favourite communist pastime of showing off national institutions – in this case, probably, police stations, courts, prisons. But Howard and his team would still have leisure to see the Imperial Palaces, Coal Hill and the Marco Polo Bridge. All his life Wexford had wanted to see the Forbidden City and been pretty sure he never would. But he had said nothing of this and had jollied Howard along and told him, as everyone else did, to be sure to buy jade and silk and to bring back a fragment of the Great Wall as a souvenir.

A week after that Howard had rung up to say he had to go to Brighton and would call in on his uncle in Kingsmarkham on the way back. He walked in at about six on a Saturday night, a cadaverous giant of a man who, though perfectly healthy, had always contrived to look twenty years older than he actually was. His parents-in-law lived in Hong Kong. After the China trip he would be joining his wife in Hong Kong. What would his aunt Dora think of joining Denise out there for two or three weeks?

'Reg too?' Dora had said quickly. She was used to being

left for long hours, days, by him. But she would never go off and leave *him* of her own accord.

'Can't be done,' Howard said, shaking his head. 'He'll be occupied elsewhere.'

Wexford thought he meant Kingsmarkham. He cocked an eyebrow at his nephew, though, at this curious choice of words.

'I shall need him in Peking,' said Howard.

There was a silence. Wexford said, 'You have to be serious, don't you, Howard?'

'Of course I'm serious. I've got *carte blanche* to pick my own team and I'm picking you as about the best detection expert I know, bar none. And I'm giving you plenty of notice so that you can get your own visa. These group visas are such a bore if you want to go wandering off on your own round China, which I'm sure you will.'

And that was what he was doing now while Howard, the amateur antiquarian, prowled about the yellow-roofed pavilions of Peking at his ecstatic leisure, and the other team members, nursing incipient coronaries, hastened back over the skies of Asia to British worries and British crime. It was two weeks of his own annual holiday Wexford was taking now. He had flown down from Peking three days before and been met at Chang-sha airport by Mr Sung. He would never forget that flight, the stewardess bringing a strange meal of hard-boiled eggs and sponge cake and dried plums wrapped up like toffees, and the passengers – he had been the only Caucasian – the boys and girls in blue cotton, the high-ranking Korean army officers, military and correct in khaki-green uniforms, yet fanning themselves with fans of black silk trimmed with gold.

Wexford was disturbed in his reverie by a discreet cough. Mr Sung was standing over him, waiting no doubt to take him to the cinema. Wexford asked him to sit down and have a beer but Mr Sung wouldn't do that, he was a teetotaller. He did, however, sit down and began lecturing Wexford on higher education in China with particular reference to the Peking Institute of Foreign Languages which he referred to as his alma mater. Had Wexford visited the university while there? No? That was strange, he would certainly regret it, he would be sorry. Wexford drank two cups of green tea, ate four lichees and a piece of water melon.

'Mind you not swallow seeds like two-thousand-year-old lady,' said Mr Sung, who had a sense of humour of a kind.

The Great Dictator was dubbed in Chinese. Wexford stuck it for ten minutes. It seemed to him that all the children in Chang-sha must be in the cinema, all laughing so much that they nearly fell off their mothers' laps. He excused himself to Mr Sung, saying with perfect if strange truth that he was cold. The air conditioning was blasting away over his left shoulder and down his neck. He strolled out into the street where the air had a warm furry dusty feel to it like the inside of a muff. Opposite was a shop where they sold tea. Wexford thought he would buy more tea there in the morning, he had almost exhausted the packet the hotel supplied.

He walked. He had a good sense of direction which was as well since the ideographs in which the street signs were written rendered him illiterate. The city was dimly lit, a warren, exotic and fantastic without the least pretension to beauty. In a broad intersecting highway people were playing cards on the pavement by the light of streetlamps. Remembering what the hotel's name meant, he headed back for the river. Crowds thronged the streets, friendly people too polite to stare, though their children looked and pointed and giggled at this blue-eyed giant. Ten o'clock is the middle of the night when you have to be up again at six. Wexford made himself a cup of tea, went to bed and to sleep and plunged soon after into the kind of dream he never had, or hadn't had for years.

A nightmare. He was in China but it was the China of his own youth, before the Communists came to power, long before the Cultural Revolution destroyed the temples of Taoists and Buddha and Confucius, when the cities were still walled-in clusters of pagodas. And he was a young man, Chinese perhaps. At any rate he knew he was on the run – from the Nationalist soldiers, it could have been, or the Communists or the Japanese. He was walking barefoot and with a pack on his back along a path to the north of the city, outside the city walls.

The stone door in the hillside stood a little open. He went inside as into a place to shelter for the night, finding himself in a cavernous passage that seemed to lead into the heart of the hill. It was cold in the passage and close with a dank, ancient kind of smell, the smell of the Han Dynasty perhaps. On and on he walked, not exactly afraid, no more than apprehensive. The passage was dark, yet he had no difficulty in finding his way into the big rectangular chamber, its walls shored up with wood, its dimness relieved by the light from a single small oil lamp of green bronze.

The lamp burned by the side of a wooden table or bench that looked to him like a bed provided for his own night's rest. He went over to it, lifted off the painted silk cloth which covered it and looked down upon the Marquise of Tai. It was a sarcophagus that he had uncovered, set in a burial chamber. The dead woman's face was convulsed in a grimace of agony, the cheeks puffed, the eyes black and protruding, the lips curled back from shrunken gums and sparse yellowed teeth and swollen tongue. He recoiled and started back, for there came from the misty, gloomy depths of the coffin a sweetish smell of putrefaction. But as he took hold of the silk to cover once more that hideous dead thing, a shudder seemed to pass along the striated limbs and the Marquise rose up and laid her icy arms about his neck.

Wexford fought his way out of the dream and awoke with a cry. He sat up and put the light on and came round to the roar of the air conditioner and the beating of his own heart. What a fool! Was it going to the cinema or eating fried fish spiced with ginger or the heat that had brought him a dream straight out of *Curse of the Mummy's Tomb*? It certainly wasn't as if he had never seen a woman's corpse before, and most of those he had seen had been a good deal less well-preserved than that of the Marquise. He drank some water and put out the light.

It was on the following day that he first saw the woman with the bound feet.

2

She wasn't the first woman of her kind he had seen since coming to China. The first had been in Peking on one of the marble bridges that cross the moat towards the Gate of Heavenly Peace. She was a tiny little old woman, very shrunken as the Chinese become with age, dressed in a black jacket and trousers, clasping a stick in one hand and with the other holding the arm of her daughter or daughter-in-law, for she could do no more than hobble. Her feet were like nothing so much as hooves, dainty hooves perhaps when she was young, shuffling club feet now in pinkish stockings and black slippers the size for a five-year-old.

Wexford had felt fascination, then a rush of revulsion. Foot-binding had come in about AD 500, hadn't it, and gone out with the Kuomintang? At first only aristocrats had practised it but the fashion had caught on even among peasants, so that you could scarcely have found a girl in China with normal unrestricted feet. He wondered how old the woman was who crossed the marble bridge on her daughter's arm. Perhaps no more than sixty. They used to begin the tight bandaging of feet, turning the toes under and up into the sole, when a girl was little more than a baby and the bones were pliable. Such was the power of fashion that no man would have wanted a wife with normal feet, a wife who could walk with ease. In the nineteen thirties the custom had been banned by law and feet that were not beyond remedy unbound. Fascination conquered revulsion, pity and distaste, and Wexford stared. After all, everyone stared at *him*.

How would that woman feel now? What would she feel? Self-pity, resentment, envy of her freer descendants and, worse, her liberated near-coevals? Wexford didn't think so. Human nature wasn't like that. For all the pain she had suffered, the curtailment of movement, the daily agony of dressing and cleansing and rebandaging, no doubt she looked with scorn on those girls who ran across the bridge on large whole healthy feet, and with a sniff of snobbish contempt shuffled the more proudly on her own tiny pointed deformities.

She was the first of several such women he had seen, maybe ten in all. They had caused him to look with curiosity at the shapely flexed feet of the Marquise of Tai, even though he knew she had been born centuries before the custom came into vogue. His dream seemed to him ridiculous when he reviewed it in the morning. He didn't have nightmares, never had, and had no intention of starting on them now. It must have been the food.

Breakfast was by far the least palatable meal he got and he viewed the spread before him with resignation. Fried bread rolls, sliced soda bread, rancid butter, plum jam, chocolate cream cake and coconut biscuits. Tea was brought in an aluminium kettle and he drank two cups of it. Mr Sung was hovering before he had finished.

He had a fresh pink shirt on – he was one of the cleanest-looking people Wexford had ever seen – and his black hair was still damp from its morning wash. How could you achieve that sort of thing when you shared a bathroom not only with four or five members of your family but with the other tenants on the same floor besides? It was wholly admirable. Wexford now recalled uneasily how it was said that Westerners smelt bad to the Chinese, owing to their consumption of dairy products. If this was true his own smell must lately be much improved, he thought, pushing away the nearly liquid greenish butter.

'You will not mind come on bus with party?'

'Not at all. Why should I?'

As if Wexford had protested rather than concurred, Mr Sung said in a repressive scolding way, 'It is not economic drive bus fifty kilometre for one man. This is very wasteful.

Much better you come with party, very nice Europe and American people. Light?'

The very nice European and American people were trooping off to the bus as he came out of the hotel. They looked weary and somewhat dishevelled and as if the last thing they wanted was to be driven out into the scorching Chinese countryside to the scenes of Mao Tse Tung's birth and infancy. However, they had little choice about that. Their guide, with whom his own was chatting in rapid Mandarin over a post-breakfast menthol cigarette, looked as relentless, determined, cheerful and clean as Mr Sung. He was a little taller, a little thinner, his English a little worse, and was introduced to Wexford as Mr Yu. They shook hands. It turned out he was a fellow alumnus of Mr Sung's from the alma mater of foreign languages.

Of all green growing things the greenest is rice. Wexford looked out of the window at rice seedlings, rice half-grown, rice near to harvest. This was the very quintessence of greenness, perhaps Aristotle's perfect green which all other greens must emulate and strive for. Men and women in the age-old Chinese blue cotton and conical straw hats worked in the fields with lumbering grey water buffalos. To distract Mr Sung and Mr Yu from their enthusiastic disquisitions on Mao's political career, Wexford asked what the crops were and was told peanuts, aubergines, castor oil plants, cassava, taro and soya beans. Sheets of water – ponds, lakes, canals – studded the neat landscape like jewels on patterned silk.

After a while Mr Yu got up and went to the front of the bus and began translating items from a newspaper into bad English for the benefit of the tourists. Wexford was trying to decide what was meant by a pirates' strike in Hungary and measles in Afghanistan when one of the men from the party came and sat in the seat next to him. He was a small man with a lined red face and a shock of sandy hair.

'Mind if I join you?'

What could he say but that he didn't mind?

'My name's Lewis Fanning. It was either coming to sit with you or jumping screaming off the bloody bus. You can't be worse than that lot and there's a chance you're better.'

206

'Thanks very much.' Wexford introduced himself and asked for an explanation of Mr Yu's news disclosures.

'He means pilots and missiles. If I'd known he was coming on this jaunt I wouldn't have myself. I'd have stayed in my room and got pissed. As it is I don't reckon I'll make it sane to Canton.'

Wexford asked him why he had come if he hated it so much.

'Dear God in heaven, I'm not on my hols. I'm *working*. I'm the tour leader. I brought this lot here by train. D'you wonder I'm going bananas?'

'On the train from where?'

'Calais,' said Fanning. He seemed cheered by Wexford's incredulity. 'Thirty-six days I've been in trains, the Trans-Siberian Railway among others. Ten lunatics to shepherd across Asia. I nearly lost one of them at the Berlin Wall. They uncoupled the carriage and she got left in the other bit. She jumped out yelling and came running up along the track, it's a miracle she's still here. There's another one an alcoholic and one who can't leave the men alone. To my certain knowledge she's had four in various wagons-lits en route.'

Wexford couldn't help laughing. 'Where's your destination?'

'Hong Kong. We leave tomorrow night on the train via Kweilin. I'm sharing sleeping quarters with two guys who haven't been on speaking terms since Irkutsk.'

Wexford too would be on that train, sharing his four-berth compartment, so far as he knew, only with Mr Sung. But he hesitated over inviting Lewis Fanning to join them and in the end he didn't. Instead he listened to a long account of the alcoholic tourist's propensities, how she had drunk a bottle of whisky a day and had had to be carried by four men back on to the train at Ulan Bator. This lasted until they reached Shao-shan and were drinking tea before climbing the hill to the Mao farmstead. The countryside here had that fresh sparkling look you occasionally see in England on a rare fine day after a long spell of rain. In front of the house the lotus reared its round sunshade leaves and pink lily flowers out of a shallow pond. The rice was the soft tender green of imperial jade. But for all that the heat was intense.

Thirty-nine degrees, said Mr Yu, which Wexford, multiplying by nine, dividing by five and adding thirty-two, made out to be a formidable hundred and two Fahrenheit. In the shade it became suddenly and shockingly cool, but they weren't in the shade much and when they walked back down the hill, their heads stuffed with Maoism, they still had the museum of Maoiana to inspect, before lunch in the hotel.

Wexford was one of those Englishmen who aver they find a hot drink more cooling and refreshing than a cold one. Once they were in the dining room of the hotel he drank about a pint of hot strong tea. Mr Sung sat with Mr Yu at a table with two local guides. The train party, for some inscrutable, Chinese, culinary reason, were placed behind a screen and once more Wexford found himself alone.

He was rather annoyed at being so affected by the heat. He misquoted to himself, 'My mother bore me in a northern clime'. Was that the reason for his feeling felled and bludgeoned in this temperature? Behind him a fan moved the warm heavy air about. Two girls brought a banquet in to him, no less than seven platters. Hard-boiled eggs, battered and fried, lotus buds, pork and pineapple, duck with beansprouts, mushrooms and bamboo shoots, prawns with peas and raw sliced tomatoes. He asked for more tea. From the moment he picked up the carved wooden chopsticks and began to eat the sweat rolled off him, wetting the back of his chair through his shirt.

Across the room the guides were eating fried bread rolls and hundred-year-old eggs and what Wexford thought might be snake.

'As long as it moves they'll eat it,' Lewis Fanning had muttered to him on entering the room. 'They'll eat mice if they can catch them.'

A murmur of soft giggling voices came from the girls. It was like the twittering of birds at sundown. The men's voices rose and fell in the strange purity of ancient Mandarin. Wexford wondered how it had come about that Europeans called the Chinese yellow. The skins of those four were a clear translucent ivory, a red flush on their cheeks, their hands thin and brown. He turned away, compelling himself not to stare, and looking instead into the shadowy part of the room from which the waitresses emerged where he saw an old woman standing by the doorway.

She was looking at him intently. Her face was pale and pouchy, her eyes black as raisins. Chinese hair scarcely ever turns white, remains black indeed long into middle age, and hers, though her age seemed great, was only just touched with grey. She wore a grey jacket over black trousers and her bound feet were tiny and wedge-shaped in their grey stockings and black child's slippers. She stood erect enough but nevertheless supported herself on a cane.

The mother of the proprietor or the cook, Wexford supposed. Her stare was almost disconcerting. It was as if she wanted to speak to him, was girding herself up to find the courage to speak to him. But that was absurd. The overwhelming probability was that she spoke nothing but Chinese. Their eyes met once more. Wexford put down his chopsticks, wiped his mouth and got up. He would go to Mr Sung and ask him to interpret for them, so evident was it that she wished to communicate something.

But before he reached Mr Sung's table the woman was gone. He looked back to where she had stood and there was no longer anyone there. No doubt he had imagined her need. He wasn't in Kingsmarkham now, he reminded himself, where he was so often consulted, grumbled at, even pleaded with.

Lunch over, they went once again into the relentless sunshine to visit the school Mao had attended and the pond where he had swum. On the way back to the bus Wexford looked again for the old woman. He peered into the dim lobby of the hotel on the chance she might be there, but there was no sign of her. Very likely she had gazed so intently at him only from the same motive as the children's — because his height and size, his clothes, ruddy skin and scanty fair hair were as remarkable here as a unicorn galloping down the street.

'Now,' said Mr Sung, 'we go to Number One Normal School, Chairman Mao's house, Clear Water Pond.' He jumped on to the bus with buoyant step.

Wexford's last day in Chang-sha was spent at Orange Island and in the museum where artefacts from the tombs at Mawangdui were on show. There, reproduced in wax this time, lay the Marquise of Tai, still protected by glass but available for a closer scrutiny. Wexford drank a pint of green tea in the museum shop, bought some jade for Dora, a fan for his younger daughter made of buffalo bone that looked like ivory – Sheila the conservationist wouldn't have approved of ivory – and a painting of bamboo stems and grasshoppers with the painter's seal in red and his signature in black calligraphy.

There was an English air about the old houses on the island with their walled gardens, their flowers and vegetables, the river flowing by. Their walls were of wattle and daub like cottages in Sewingbury. But the air was scented with ginger and the canna lilies burned brick red in the hazy heat. Off the point where Mao had once swum, boys and girls were bathing in the river. Mr Sung took the opportunity to give Wexford a lecture on Chinese political structure to which he didn't listen. In order to get his visa he had had to put down on the application form his religion and politics. He had selected, not without humour, the most stolid options: Conservative, Church of England. Sometimes he wondered if these reactionary entries had been made known by a form of red grapevine to his guide. He sat down in the shade and gazed appreciatively at the arch with its green pointed roof, delicate and jewel-like against a silvery blue sky.

Through the arch, supported this time on a walking stick with a carved buffalo-bone handle, came the old woman with bound feet he had seen at the hotel in Shao-shan. Wexford gave an exclamation. Mr Sung stopped talking and said sharply, 'Something is wrong?'

'No. It just seems extraordinary. That woman over there, I saw her in Shao-san yesterday. Small world.'

'Small?' said Mr Sung. 'China is very big country. Why lady from Shao-shan not come Chang-sha? She come, go, just as she like, all Chinese people liberated, all Chinese people flee. Light? I see no lady. Where she go?'

The sun was in Wexford's eyes, making him blink. 'Over by the gate. A little woman in black with bound feet.'

Mr Sung shook his head vehemently. 'Very bad feudal custom, very few now have, all dead.' He added, with a ruthless disregard for truth, 'Cannot walk, all stay home.'

The woman had gone. Back through the arch? Down one of the paved walks between the canna lily beds? Wexford decided to take the initiative.

'If you're ready, shall we go?'

Astonishment spread over Mr Sung's bland face. Wexford surmised that no other tourist had ever dared anything but submit meekly to him.

'O.K., light. Now we go to Yunlu Palace.'

Leaving the island, they met the train party under the leadership of Mr Yu. Lewis Fanning was nowhere to be seen, and walking alongside Mr Yu, in earnest conversation with him, was the younger and better-looking of the two men who had quarrelled on the Trans-Siberian Railway. His enemy, a tall man with a Humpty-Dumpty-ish shape, brought up the rear of the party and gazed about him with a nervous unhappy air. The women's clothes had suffered irremediably from those thirty-six days in a train. They were either bleached and worn from too frequent washing or dirty and creased from not having been washed at all.

Already, and without difficulty, Wexford had decided which was the nymphomaniac and which the alcoholic: a highly-coloured woman and a drab one respectively. Apart from these four apparently single people, the party consisted of another lone, and much older, woman, and two elderly married couples, one set of whom were accompanied by their middle-aged daughter. On the whole, Wexford reflected, it would seem that the young and the beautiful couldn't afford five-week long tours across Asia.

That evening the screens were drawn closely around their table and he had no further sight of the party until he and they were boarding the bus for Zhuzhou where they would pick up the Shanghai to Kweilin train.

3

It would have been easier and quicker to fly. Fanning's party, of course, had to make every leg of their journey by train but Wexford would happily have gone on by air. It wasn't a matter of his will, though, but the will of Lu Xing She and Mr Sung.

He had a double seat to himself on the bus. Silently he observed his fellow passengers. A couple of days in the hotel at Chang-sha had gone a long way towards reviving them and they looked less as if they had been pulled through a hedge backwards.

Each of the enemies had also secured a double seat, one of them behind the driver, the other on the opposite side of the aisle to Wexford. Out of the corner of his eye Wexford read the label tied to the older man's handcase. A. H. Purbank, and an address somewhere in Essex. Purbank was perhaps forty-five, unhealthy-looking, thin, dressed in baggy jeans and an open-necked pale green shirt. His sprucer, dark-haired adversary was also in jeans, but a snugly fitting pair of denims which looked smart and suitable with a 'friendship' tee-shirt. He had swivelled round in his seat and was talking to the woman in the seat behind him. This was the daughter of one of the elderly couples and after a little while Wexford saw her get up and sit in the empty place beside him. Wexford, with another glance at Purbank, thought how uncomfortable it must have been travelling all those miles from Irkutsk away up there on Lake Baikal with a man with whom you weren't on speaking terms. What quarrel had sprung up between these inoffensive-seeming travellers? Both were English, both middle-class, prosperous presumably, adventurously inclined surely, having a fair bit in common, yet they had fallen out so bitterly as purposely not to have exchanged a word across all those vast stretches of eastern Asia. At table in the hotels they must have sat, if not together, near enough to each other, perhaps have been allotted adjoining rooms. Now they were to share a sleeping space some eight feet by five and lie breathing the same warm air in the rattling darkness for eight or nine hours. It was grotesque.

Was one of them or perhaps each of them among the four men with whom Fanning alleged that pretty, painted, ageing creature in the spotted blouse and white pants had engaged in sexual relations during the trip? Fanning, of course, exaggerated wildly. Certainly he couldn't have been indicating as among her partners the fair woman's father, asleep now with his white cotton hat drooped over his eyes, or the austere silver-haired man with the ugly wife. Of course, Wexford reflected, he hadn't exactly specified members of the party and presumably there had been plenty of other men in the Trans-Siberian train.

The bright sky had clouded over and a little warm rain had begun to fall. It was still raining lightly when they came on to the station platform. By each door of the train stood a girl attendant in grey uniform and with the red star of the People's Republic on her cap. Wexford was shown to the carriage that was to be his for the night. Though clean and with comfortable-looking berths it was insufferably hot, the thermometer on the wall telling him the temperature was two degrees short of a hundred. Once the train started, he opened the window and switched on the fan. A very slightly cooler air blew in through the fly screen.

As soon as they were off Mr Sung came in. Wexford, who had discovered a thermos flask and was busy with the Silver Leaf he had bought in Chang-sha, offered him a cup of tea but Mr Sung refused. Here, as elsewhere, he contrived to give the impression of always being busy and involved. The restaurant car would open at eight, he said, and drinks would be available: beer, red and white wine, Maotai, maybe Japanese whisky.

213

Wexford drank tea and read his *Fodor's*. It was dusk now, growing dark, and was no longer unpleasantly hot, though smuts came in through the fine mesh of the screen. Hunan Province, blanketed in darkness, fled past as the train reached a steady speed. After a while he went out into the corridor to establish the whereabouts of lavatory and bathroom.

Next to the bathroom, in the first compartment of the carriage, four Hong-Kong Chinese in Palm Beach shirts and white trousers sat playing cards. The door of the next one was opened as Wexford passed it and a voice said, 'Oh, excuse me. I wonder if we could possibly trouble you a moment?'

Wexford went in, not entirely reluctantly. He had been curious enough about these two women to want to make a closer personal estimate. The one he had privately styled the alcoholic was lying in one of the lower berths, her shoes tumbled on the floor and her swollen feet raised up on two pillows. She gave him a wan smile.

'It's so awful constantly trying to make oneself understood to these Chinese,' said the other, 'and that beastly Yu has disappeared again. He always disappears when you want him. I suppose he thinks playing hard to get makes him more desirable, do you think? Oh, by the way, I'm Lois Knox and this is Hilda Avory — I already know your name, I *spied* on your luggage — and now, please, please, do you think you could be awfully sweet and make our fan work?'

The attendant who had shown Wexford to his carriage had worked his fan for him, so he had no difficulty in finding the switch which was rather cunningly hidden under the back of the table.

Lois Knox clasped her hands together girlishly.

'And since you're so clever, could you be even more of an angel and find out how to suppress that bloody radio?'

The martial music which had greeted him on entering the compartment — interrupted now for what was presumably a political harangue — Wexford had supposed to be on at the desire of the occupants.

'Oh, no, we hate it, don't we, Hilda? There should be a knob under there but it's broken and it won't move. How shall we ever get a wink of sleep?' Her eyes were a brilliant sea-blue, large beautiful eyes which she fixed intensely on his face. The muscles of her face sagged rather and her jawline was no longer firm but she had something of a youthful look as the gyrating fan fluttered her black hair about. It was dyed hair, greyish-brown at the roots after five weeks away from a hairdresser.

'You're all by yourself, aren't you?' She didn't wait for confirmation. 'We're on that beastly train tour but never again, so help us God. How we should love an aircraft or even a humble bus for a change, shouldn't we, Hilda?'

Hilda Avory made no reply. She put out a hand for her teacup and drank from it with a shudder. She had a damp look, skin glistening, tendrils of hair clinging to her forehead, portions of her dress adhering to thin flesh, as if she had been out in the rain or had sweated profusely.

Wexford set about hunting for the controls of the radio. 'I could fix it for you if I had a pair of pliers.'

'Imagine trying to explain pliers to that inscrutable little Yu! Do have a cup of tea, won't you? Or some *laoshan*?'

'That's Chinese for mineral water,' said Hilda Avory, speaking for the first time. She had a gravelly voice, unexpectedly deep.

'I'm terribly afraid we haven't anything stronger but the fact is Hilda is drying out, aren't you, darling? And she doesn't feel it's very wise to have spirits about, such an awful temptation, you know.'

There seemed no answer to make to this. He accepted a cup of tea. The music burst forth once more in a kind of Chinese version of 'Washington Post'.

'What shall we do?' cried Lois Knox. She brought her hands together appealingly. The red nails were as long as a Manchu's. 'We shall be found stark raving mad in the morning.'

'How about cutting the wires?' said Wexford.

The deep voice from the other berth said, 'Not a good idea. I heard of someone who did that in China and they had to pay to have the whole train rewired. It cost them thousands of *yuan*.'

'I'll see what I can do,' said Wexford. He drank up his tea and went off down the corridor to find an attendant.

The only one he came upon, a very young boy, had nodded off to sleep, his head against the hard wall, in a little cubby-hole next to the bathroom. Wexford went on over the intersection into the next carriage, the sweat gathering on his body now and breaking out on his forehead and upper lip. Away from the fans the heat was as great as ever. There was nothing but dense blackness to be seen outside now and, dimly through the upper part of the windows, a few faint stars. In a compartment with Mr Yu and another young Chinese sat Mr Sung, the three of them poring over a map of the Li River spread out on the table.

'Restaurant will open eight o'clock,' said Mr Sung as soon as he saw him. All the guides seemed to think that visitors from the west needed to eat and drink all day long in order to maintain equilibrium, and that any requests they received from tourists must necessarily be for food or tea or beer. 'I come fetch you when restaurant open.'

'I want a pair of pliers,' said Wexford.

Mr Sung, Mr Yu and the other man looked at him in blank inquiry. Wexford recalled how, in Peking, he had asked an interpreter where he could buy a packet of aspirin and had been directed to an ice-cream shop.

'Players,' said Mr Sung at last.

'You want cigarettes?' said Mr Yu. 'You get plenty cigarettes when restaurant open.'

'I don't want cigarettes, I want pliers.' Wexford made pinching movements with his fingers, he mimed pulling a nail out of the wall. Mr Sung stared amiably at him. Mr Yu stared and then laughed. The other man handed him a large shabby book which turned out to be an English-Chinese dictionary. Wexford indicated 'pliers' and its ideograph with his fingertip. Everyone smiled and nodded, Mr Sung went off down the corridor and came back with a girl train attendant who handed Wexford a pair of eyebrow tweezers.

Wexford gave up. It was a quarter to eight and he began to look forward to a beer. In the intersection he met the little elderly woman who was travelling in what he had mentally dubbed – though it certainly was not – a *ménage à trois*. She was carrying a packet of teabags.

'Oh, good evening,' she said. 'This is quite an adventure,

isn't it?' Wexford wasn't sure if she spoke with seriousness or irony, still less so when she went on to say, her head a little on one side, 'We English must stick together, is what I always say.'

He knew at once then, he intuited, he hardly knew how, that she was getting at him. It was neither witty nor particularly clever, though she intended it to be both, and she was referring to his brief association with Lois Knox which she had perhaps observed from the corridor. Her expression was dry, her mouth quirked a little. She was as small and thin as a Chinese and the dark blue trouser suit she wore unsexed her. What was she to the man Fanning had told him was a retired barrister? Sister? Sister-in-law? Wife's confidante or best friend's widow? As she went on her way into the next compartment he observed that her left hand was ringless.

In the cubby-hole next to the bathroom the boy was still asleep with his head against the wall. Wexford saw what he hadn't noticed before, a cloth toolbag lying beside the boy's legs on the floor. He went in, opened the toolbag and helped himself to a pair of pliers.

Outside the windows a few feeble clusters of light showed. They were passing a village or small town. For a moment the outline of a mountain could be seen and then the darkness closed in once more as the train gathered speed. Wexford stood in the doorway of Lois Knox's compartment. The radio was still on, playing a selection from *Swan Lake*. Hilda Avory still lay in the lower berth and on the end of it, beside her feet, sat Purbank. He seemed to be addressing them on the very subject which had been the reason for Wexford's visit to China in the first place, crime prevention. Lois's face wore the expression of a woman who has been taught from childhood that men must at all costs be flattered. Hilda's eyes were closed and slightly screwed up.

'These Communists make a lot of high-flown claims about how they've got rid of crime. Now that's all very well but we know in practice it just isn't true. I mean, where did I have my watch pinched and my Diners Club card and all that currency? Not in Europe, oh, no. In the Union of Soviet Socialist Republics. And that, mark you, was in a train. Now why should it be any different here? Same lack of material possessions – worse, if anything – so you can bet your life they can't wait to get their hot little hands on rich capitalists' property – and that means yours. So don't leave it in the compartment, carry it with you, and when you . . .'

Wexford coughed. Lois saw him and jumped up, clasping her hands. In his absence she had put on more lipstick and eyeshadow and had changed into a low-necked dress of thin yellow material with a black pattern on it.

'Oh, what a fright you gave me! Tony has been scaring us out of our wits with tales of robbery and murder.'

Purbank gave a very *macho*, reassuring-the-little-woman haw-haw of a laugh. 'When did I mention murder now? I never said a word about murder. I merely counselled the inadvisability of leaving valuables around.'

'Quite right too,' said Wexford.

He groped under the table, got a grip on the broken knob with the pliers and wrenched it anticlockwise. The music stopped.

'Oh, you wonderful, wonderful man!' cried Lois. 'Listen to the blessed silence. Peace at last! Don't you adore the masterful way he *strode* into the compartment? You couldn't do that, Tony. All you could do was say we'd have to put up with it all night and get robbed as well.'

'Give the man a cup of tea,' muttered Hilda into her pillow.

'I'll give him anything he wants!' She extended the teacup to Wexford, holding it in both hands and bowing over it in what she perhaps thought was the manner of an emperor's concubine. 'Oh, if only you hadn't drunk up all the Scotch, Hilda!'

But at that moment Mr Yu appeared in the doorway, announced that the restaurant was open and please to follow him. Mindful perhaps of Purbank's warning, Lois gathered up purse, handbag, hand case and what looked like a jewel box. Wexford gulped down the by now lukewarm tea, realizing he was about to be trapped into a foursome with the two women and Purbank. This being China, though, the restaurant would hardly be open for long. Everywhere he had been so far what night life there was came to a halt at about ten. But was there much chance of sleep in this stuffy train?

He felt himself being overtaken by those sensations which result from an insufficiency of sleep, not so much tiredness as a lightness in the head and a feeling of unreality.

They walked down the corridor, Wexford at the rear with Lois immediately in front of him. The boy was still asleep, his head having slid down the wall and come to rest on the table. Wexford slipped in to replace the pliers in the toolbag. Lois hadn't noticed his absence and had gone on in the wake of the others. Wexford stood a moment by the window, trying to make out some indication of the terrain in the darkness that rushed past. He heard a footstep not far from him, the way they had come, turned round and saw approaching him, though still some yards away, the old woman with the bound feet.

This time she was without her stick. Had she followed him on to the train? He closed his eyes, opened them again and she was gone. Had she turned aside into one of the compartments? A hand, red-taloned, was laid on his arm, he smelt Lois Knox's perfume.

'Reg? Do come along, darling, we thought we'd lost you.'

He followed her down the corridor to the restaurant car.

Blue velvet curtains, lace curtains, and on the seats those dun-coloured cotton covers with pleated valances that cover the chairs all over China in waiting rooms and trains and airports and even aircraft. Lois patted the chair next to hers and he had no choice but to sit there. On the table were a plate of wrapped sweets, a plate of wedges of sponge cake, a wine bottle which contained, according to Purbank, spirit and a spirit bottle containing wine. Both liquids were the colour of a Riesling. Wexford asked the waiter for a bottle of beer. Purbank, lighting a cigar, began to talk about the frequent incidence of burglaries in metropolitan Essex.

The restaurant car was full. Chinese passengers sat eating noodles and vegetables out of earthenware bowls. The guides were drinking tea, whispering softly together in Pu Tong Hua. Behind Wexford the two married couples shared a table and the older of the men, in the high-pitched, jovially insensitive voice common to many surgeons, was instructing his companions in the ancient art of foot-binding. A gasp of revulsion came from the barrister's wife as he described toes atrophying.

The beer arrived. It was warm and sweetish. Wexford made a face and signalled to the waiter who was walking round with a tea kettle. Under the tablecloth Lois's knee touched his. 'Excuse me,' Wexford said and he got up and walked over to Mr Sung's table. 'Let me know when you're ready for bed. I don't want to keep you up.'

One of those complex misunderstandings now arose. Why did Wexford want him, Mr Sung, to go to bed? He was not ill. It was (in Mr Sung's words) only twenty-one hundred hours. The dictionary was again produced. Mr Yu smiled benignly, smoking a cigarette. At length it transpired that Mr Sung was not sharing Wexford's compartment for the night, had never intended to share his compartment, would instead be sharing with Mr Yu and the other man whom he introduced as Mr Wong. Because the train wasn't crowded Wexford had his accommodation to himself. He went over to Lewis Fanning and offered him one of the spare berths in his compartment.

But Fanning rejoined in a fashion very interesting to those who are students of character.

'Good God in heaven, I couldn't leave those two alone together! They'd be at each other's throats in two shakes of a turkey's tail. They'd tear each other to pieces. No, I'm frightfully grateful and all that but it'd be more than my life's worth.'

From which Wexford gathered that Fanning was by no means dreading the night ahead and looked forward to extracting from it the maximum of dramatic value for the delectation of those willing to listen to him. Mr Sung, Mr Yu and Mr Wong had begun to play cards. The surgeon was drawing diagrams of the metatarsals, before and after binding, on a table napkin. Wexford sat down again. His teacup had been refilled. Having apparently postponed her drying out, Hilda Avory was drinking steadily from a tumbler filled out of the wine bottle Purbank said held the Chinese spirit Maotai, while Purbank himself told anecdotes of thefts and break-ins he had known. Lois Knox's knee came back against Wexford's and he felt her bare toes nudge his ankle, her sandal having been kicked off under the table. The train ran on through impenetrable darkness, through a dark that showed no demarcation between land and sky and which was punctured by not a single light.

The little woman in the blue trouser suit came into the restaurant car and hesitated for a moment before making for the table where the two married couples sat. The barrister jumped up and pulled out a chair for her. And then Wexford understood it was she he had seen. It was she who had been coming down the corridor when he turned away from the window, she who, while his eyes were closed, had vanished into her own compartment. She too was a small slight creature, she too was dressed in a dark-coloured pair of trousers and a jacket, and though her feet had certainly never been subjected to binding, they were not much bigger than a child's and they too were encased in the black Chinese slippers on sale everywhere. He laughed inwardly at himself. He must be very weary and light-headed if he really believed that the Chinese woman he had seen in Shao-shan and then on Orange Island was following him by train to Kweilin. He drank his tea, accepted a glass of Maotai. Who knew? It might help him to sleep.

Hilda Avory got unsteadily to her feet. She said in a shaky tone, 'I think I could get a little sleep if I try now. Please don't be long, Lois. You'll wake me up if you come bursting in at midnight.'

'Darling, I never burst,' said Lois. She edged a little closer to Wexford. 'Be an angel and give her a hand, Tony, this awful awful train does jerk so.'

Purbank hesitated, torn between being a gentleman and ordering another bottle of laurel flower wine before the bar closed. Fanning, alerted, had half-risen from his seat. 'Allow me,' said Wexford, seizing his opportunity. Lois made a petulant little sound. He smiled at her, rather as one might at a difficult child who, after all, is not one's own and whom one may never meet again, and taking Hilda's arm, shepherded her away between the tables and out into the corridor.

She was sweating profusely, deodorized, French-perfumed sweat, that trickled down her arm and soaked through his own shirt sleeve. Outside the window a box of a building, studded all over with points of light, flashed out of the darkness and receded as the train passed. Wexford slid open the door of the compartment next to his own and helped her in. It was silent in there now. The fan had been switched off so that the air was heavy and thick and densely hot with a faint smell of soot. The thermometer read ninety-five degrees or thirty-five Celsius. He switched the fan on again. Hilda fell on to the left-hand berth and lay face-downwards. Wexford stood there for a few moments, looking at her, wondering if there was anything more he could do and deciding there wasn't, moistening his lips, passing his tongue over the dry roof of his mouth. The Maotai had set up a fresh thirst. He closed the door on Hilda and went into his own compartment.

The fan was off there too. Wexford switched it on and turned back the sheet on the lower left-hand berth. His thermos had been refilled and there were two teabags on the table. He had never cared for teabags. He put a big helping of Silver Leaf into the cup and poured on the near-boiling water. A pungent aromatic perfume came off the liquid, as unlike supermarket packet tea at home as could be. For a moment or two, drinking his tea, he peered into the shining, starless darkness that streamed past the window and then he pulled down the blind.

Lois Knox and Purbank were coming along the corridor together now. He could hear their voices but not what they said. Then Purbank spoke more loudly, 'Good night to you, ladies.' His footsteps pattered away.

Wexford waited for the corridor to empty. He made his way to the bathroom. The lavatory was vacant, the bathroom engaged, the barrister having stolen a march on him and got there first. In the lavatory it was hot and there was a nauseous smell of ammonia. The train rattled and sang. Wexford waited in the corridor, looking out of the window at nothing, saying goodnight to the doctor and his wife who passed him, waiting for the barrister to come out of the bathroom and leave it free. Purbank's enemy and the doctor's daughter, he reflected, hadn't been with the rest in the restaurant car. A holiday romance? The bathroom door opened, the barrister came out, said rather curtly, 'Good night to you,' and walked off, carrying his dark brown towel and tartan sponge bag.

Wexford washed his hands and face and cleaned his teeth, trying not to swallow any of the water. Of course he should have brought some of the water from the thermos flask with him.

All the compartment doors were shut. The light that burned in the corridor wasn't very powerful. Wexford wondered, not for the first time, if there were such a thing as a hundred-watt bulb in the whole of China. He slid open the door to his compartment.

In the right-hand berth, on her back, her striated pinkish-white legs splaying from under the white shift, her face white and puffy, the bridge of the nose encaved, the mouth open and the tongue protruding, lay the Marquise of Tai.

4

He didn't cry out or even gasp. He closed his eyes and held his fists tightly clenched. Without looking again at the dead thing, the mummified, two-thousand-year-old thing, he turned swiftly and went out into the corridor. He didn't know whether he shut the door behind him or not.

He walked down the corridor. The bathroom window was open and he went in, inhaling the cooler air. He put his head out of the window into the rushing darkness. None knew better than he that this was an unwise thing to do. Years ago, when he was young, he had been to an inquest on a man who put his head out of a train window and was decapitated as the train entered a tunnel. He breathed deeply, closed his eyes again. Any attempts at thinking were impossible. He would have to go back there and *do something*.

The bathroom door opened and someone said, 'Oh, sorry.' It was the old doctor.

'I'm just going,' said Wexford.

He wondered if his face was as white as it felt. The doctor didn't seem to notice anything. Humming to himself, he began to wash his hands. Wexford walked swiftly back down the corridor the way he had come, blindly as well as fast, for he almost collided with Lois Knox who was sliding open the door to her own compartment. She wore a short, white, crumpled negligee of broderie anglaise and her face had the stripped look women's faces have that are usually coated with make-up.

He apologized. She said nothing but drew the door across

224

with a slam. Drawing breath, tensing himself, he opened his own door and looked at the berth. It was empty.

Wexford sat down. He closed his eyes and opened them and looked at the berth and saw it was still empty. He would dearly have liked a stiff whisky or even a glass of Maotai, but he was pretty sure he wouldn't get either at this hour – it was after eleven – even if he knew how to summon an attendant, which he didn't. He scattered Silver Leaf into a clean cup and poured hot, no longer boiling, water on to it.

There was no doubt of what he had seen. The corpse had been lying there. And what he had seen had been precisely what he had seen when he had looked down through the cavity in the museum floor at the glass sarcophagus below. It had been the same even to the shortened right arm, the flexed feet, the yawning tongue-filled mouth. *He knew he had seen it.* And now, gingerly, then more firmly, touching the opposite berth, he saw that something had indeed lain there. There was a distinct indentation in the pillow and a creasing of the upper sheet. Something had lain there, been put there, and in his absence had been removed.

He found there was no way of locking his door, but it was possible by stuffing the side into which the door slid with the Peking *Blue News*, to prevent anyone's opening it from the outside. He drank his tea. The fan had gone off for the night and, in spite of the open window, a close heavy warmth filled the compartment. A nasty thought came to Wexford as he undressed. By means of the metal step which let down out of the wall, he climbed up and checked there was nothing in either of the upper berths. He had just recalled a particularly unpleasant story by F. Marion Crawford in which a traveller at sea finds a drowned corpse, or the ghost of a drowned corpse, in the upper berth of his cabin.

When he had had a second cup of tea he put out the light. After several hours of tossing and turning he got about an hour's sleep but no more. It was still only three when he awoke and he knew he wouldn't get any more sleep that night.

He sat up, switched the light on and asked himself a question. Was it possible that what he had seen lying in that berth was Lois Knox?

Wexford was a modest man with a humble idea of his own attractions insofar as he ever thought about them. To his own wife he seemed to be unfailingly attractive after thirty years of marriage, but this was something to be thankful for and dismissed rather than speculated about. His life hadn't been devoid of feminine admiration; he had taken none of it very seriously. He hadn't taken Lois Knox seriously at all, yet now he came to think of it . . . if what Fanning said was true, or even partly true, this holiday was for her a kind of sex tour. Wexford knew very well that a woman of this sort need not even find her selected partner attractive; it would be enough that he were a man and accessible, someone to boost her drooping ego, for an evening or an hour, someone to quell her panic, push old age and death an inch or two further away.

Foolishly, he had smiled at her on leaving the restaurant car. Had she taken this smile for an invitation? She had been in the corridor when he came back from the bathroom. She had been wearing a short white shift or at any rate a short white dressing gown, and she had seemed offended with him, in high dudgeon. Had it been she, then, lying in that berth, waiting for him? What must she have felt when he recoiled, closed his eyes in horror and stumbled out without a word?

Wexford was aware that a good many people would have found this funny. After all, the woman, no longer young, no longer attractive, but as forward and brazen as any young beauty, had only got what she deserved. At least, thank God, she didn't know he had mistaken her for a two-thousand-year-old, diseased, disembowelled corpse. But had he? Again, closing his eyes in the dim warm jogging compartment, he saw what he had seen. The Marquise of Tai. The face wasn't Lois's face – God preserve him! And that shortened right arm? Those thighs, scored with deep striations?

Perhaps he needed glasses for daily wear, not just for reading. Perhaps he was going mad. Presumably if you developed schizophrenia – which was quite possible, there was such a thing as spontaneous schizophrenia coming on in middle age – presumably then you had hallucinations and didn't know they were hallucinations and behaved, in short, just as he had. Don't be a fool, he told himself. Get some sleep. No wonder you see visions when you never get any sleep. Towards morning he dozed, until the sunrise came in and the fan came on again.

Things always seem different in the morning. We reiterate this truism always with wonder perhaps because it is such a remarkable truth. It is invariably so. The fearful, the anxious, the monstrous, the macabre, all are washed away in the cool practical morning light. The light which filled Wexford's compartment wasn't particularly cool but it performed the same cleansing function. He wasn't mad, he could see perfectly, and no doubt he shouldn't have drunk that big glass of Maotai on the previous evening.

Events quickly confirmed that it had been Lois Knox in the lower berth. In the restaurant car she and Hilda Avory were sharing their table with the barrister, his wife and the wife's friend, and all but Lois looked up to say good morning to him. Lois, who had been reading aloud from her guide to Kweilin, paused, stared out of the window, and once he had passed on, continued in a gushing voice.

Wexford took a seat opposite Fanning.

'How was your night? I see they haven't killed each other.'

'Mr Purbank and I slept soundly, thank you. Mr Vinald didn't honour us with his presence, thank God. As far as I can gather, and I can't say the subject fascinates me, he had the vacant berth in Dr Baumann's compartment.'

'Unconventional,' said Wexford.

'There's nothing like a few days on the Trans-Siberian Railway to make you forget all the dearest tenets of your upbringing. Not that there'd be anything like that with the Baumanns and Mr Vinald. Daddy and Gordon up top, Mummy and Margery down below.'

Wexford glanced at the plump fair-haired woman who now sat next to her father and opposite Gordon Vinald, eating the Chinese version of a Spanish omelette which always appeared under the sweeping generic title of 'eggs' and which was served up without fail each breakfast time wherever he had been. She was pleasant-looking with a serene face and she hadn't made the mistake which Lois had of cramming an hour-glass shape into trousers and tee-shirt. His glance now fell upon Lois herself. Her hair was carefully dressed, her face painted to a passable imitation of youth. She bore not the least resemblance to the Marquise of Tai and it would have been a cruel libel to suggest it. Her eyes met his and she looked away in calculated disdain.

'Mrs Knox given you the old heave-ho yet?' asked Fanning innocently.

'Good God, no,' said Wexford.

'I only wondered.'

Mr Sung, Mr Yu and Mr Wong were eating with chopsticks from bowls of noodles with rice and vegetables. Purbank came in and Wong immediately got up to speak to him. Whatever it was he said, it brought an expression of edginess to Purbank's face, for a moment he looked almost panicky. He walked away from the Chinese and sat at a table by himself.

Wexford felt relieved. He was noticing people's behaviour again, he was himself again, he had cleansed his thoughts of what hadn't, after all, been a corpse in the berth. He held out his cup as the waiter came by with the tea kettle.

Another grey barrack of a hotel, its design so uninspired that Wexford felt sure no true architect had had a hand in its building. But when he crossed his room and looked out of the window the view was enough to dispel any speculations about man-made things. The mountains that formed the skyline, and in front of the skyline a long ridge, were so fantastic in shape as to resemble almost anything but the karst formations the guidebook said they were. These mountains were shaped like cones, like cypress trees, like toadstools. They rose, tree-studded, vertically out of the plain, their sides straight and their peaks rounded curves. They were the mountains of Chinese paintings that Wexford had until now believed to be artists' stylizations. While you gazed at them you could forget the grey blocks, very like this hotel, that had sprung up too frequently all over the town, and see only those curvy cone mountains and the little red-brown roofs and the water everywhere in ponds and lakes and the Li River twining silver amongst it all.

It was unusual in China for one's guide to accompany one on a train journey. Generally, Mr Sung would have parted from him at Chang-sha station and would have been met by a fresh guide at Kweilin. It appeared, though, that Mr Sung was a native of Kweilin and hadn't been above fiddling this trip for reasons of his own. Mr Yu, in company with Mr Wong, had disappeared at Kweilin station and Fanning's party were now in the charge of a cadaverous man, exceptionally tall for a Chinese, called T'chung. This new guide had relentlessly organized his tourists into an excursion to caves.

They had only two days here. No doubt they had to make the most of it. Wexford eluded Mr Sung and took himself for a quiet walk about the town, under the cassia trees. You could get knocked down by the bicycles which thronged the streets here just as you could in Peking. Men with bowed shoulders and straining muscles pulled carts laden with concrete blocks while women, wearing the yoke pole with a loaded basket at each end of it, jogged by with their curious coolie trot. Among the cassia leaves flew green and black butterflies. Wexford paid a few *fen* to look at an exhibition of paintings and brush calligraphy and to walk in a bonsai garden. He went into one of the dark spice-scented grocery stores, stacked with sweet jars, and bought more green tea. In there he lingered, examining the wares, dried seaweed in bundles and barrels of rice, pickled fish, root ginger, casks of soya sauce, *tofu* in tanks of water. When he turned round to look at the cakes and pastries displayed under glass, he saw across the shop, leaning on her stick, peering as he had just been doing into a drum of rice, the old woman with the bound feet.

It was no more than a split second before he realized that this wasn't the same woman. She straightened and turned her head and he saw a face like a brown nut, scored with a hundred wrinkles, spectacles on her tiny snub nose. Her eyes passed indifferently over him, or at least there was no more in them than a spark of natural curiosity, and then she began speaking in a rapid sing-song to the assistant she had called over to her. The shops here were like they had been in England forty years ago, Wexford thought. This was the way they had been in his early youth. Assistants were polite to you, served you patiently, took trouble, made you into the customer who was always right. How times had changed! The old woman bought her rice, her two pastries, her bag of roasted soya beans, and set off at the clumping pony trot which is how you have to walk if you have no toes and your instep is bowed like a U.

At dinner he was glad they continued the discreet custom of giving him a fan and a carefully screened table to himself. On the other side of the screen he could hear Purbank and Lois Knox grumbling about the miles they had been expected to walk in those caves, and on top of that train journey too. The waitress brought him fried carp, pork and aubergines in ginger sauce, glass noodles with mushrooms, slices of duck, boiled eggs dipped in batter and fried. They made the tea very strong here and aromatic. When he had finished he went up on to the roof to the new bar the hotel seemed so proud of.

It was evident that its creators had never seen any sort of bar in the west. Perhaps they had read of bars or seen old films. The effect was of a mixture of a bunfight in an English village hall and a one-horse town saloon in a Western movie of the thirties. On the concrete of the roof with its concrete parapet, large bare trestle tables had been set out and folding wooden chairs. Light came from bare bulbs and the moon. At the counter you could buy fireworks and on a distant unlit part of the roof a group of Chinese were setting off firecrackers.

Whatever amenities the rooftop bar lacked was made up for by the view. The sky glowed with moonlight and above the river's thread the mountains floated like black stormclouds. As Wexford, a glass of cassia wine beside him on the parapet, leaned over to gaze at the town and the mountains, music burst forth from a record player set up on a card table. It was an LP of Christmas music they were playing. The syrupy voices of an angel choir began with 'Silent Night', went on to 'Santa Claus is Coming' and then Bing Crosby started his soft crooning of 'White Christmas'. It was hotter here than in Chang-sha, stickily humid, the treetops rich with foliage, a bright June moon illuminating it all. As the record went relentlessly on, the Americans at the next table to Wexford's began laughing. The neat smiling Chinese boy who supervised the player and had put the record on beamed at them with gratification. He had made the foreign tourists happy, he would make them even happier by starting it all over again.

As 'Silent Night', with all its evocations of bitter cold, of church bells, of the star of Bethlehem, crept for the second time over the still, hot air, Lois Knox came up the stairs from the floor below. She came from under the concrete canopy which sheltered the bar out on to the roof and she was accompanied by a large paunchy Australian with whom Wexford had gone down to dinner in the lift. Lois's make-up was fresh, she had at some time contrived to visit the hotel hairdresser, and she was wearing a newly pressed blue linen dress and high-heeled blue shoes. She was looking better than he had ever seen her and the Australian seemed smitten already. Wexford understood that he was forgiven, she could afford to forgive him now. She waved, calling out, 'We won't intrude on your reverie!' The Australian took her arm and led her away to a part of the roof where neither the moon nor the lights penetrated.

He sat down at a table alone. After last night it might be wise not to drink too much. Besides, the cassia wine was sweet to the point of cloyingness. Presently Gordon Vinald and Margery Baumann came up on to the roof together. He talked to them for a while and then he went off to green tea and bed.

Going out of the hotel in the morning was a little like walking into a cloud of steam. Already, at a quarter to eight, the temperature was soaring into the eighties. To Wexford it seemed absurd to board a bus for a three- or four-hundred-yard journey to the landing stage. He walked, attempting to shake off the light-headed unreal feeling that was still with him. The roar of his air conditioner had awakened him at two, and when he turned it off the oven temperature returned, closing in like a thick soft blanket. Moreover, the bed was the hardest he had ever attempted to sleep on, a wooden cot with a thin layer of cotton wadding over it. He had lain there, reading, shifting his aching limbs about. Having already got through most of what he had brought with him, *Vanity Fair* (a third reading), the poetry of Lu Yu (because he was coming to China) and last year's Booker winner, he had started on a weighty anthology called *Masterpieces of the Supernatural*. The first story in the collection was 'The Upper Berth' and he was glad he hadn't tried to read it in the train.

Gradually coming round, shaking off the miseries of the night, he walked along the avenue of cassia trees. The boat was in and the American party and the Australian businessmen were already going on board. As Wexford started to follow them the minibus drew up and Mr Sung came bounding out, cross and pompous.

'This is very bad. Must not go alone. Why not wait bus like I say? Cannot board ship without tickets.'

He thrust a piece of coloured cardboard at Wexford. Mr T'chung gathered up the train party by waving his arms like one making semaphore signals. Wexford took the ticket stub that was handed back to him. It had a map of the Li River on it and their route down to Yang-shuo marked, a number of ideographs in pink ink and the somewhat pretentious words printed: Ship's papers. But the boat itself was nice enough, a typical river boat, with a saloon and a big upper deck with deckchairs.

'Good scenery begin ten-thirty,' said Mr Sung.

'Isn't this good scenery?' Wexford asked as the gangway went up and they cast off. The Li River, broad and bronze-coloured, wound out of the town between green cone mountains.

'Ten-thirty,' said Mr Sung. 'Then you take photographs.'

Wexford was tired of explaining to him that he didn't have a camera. Impossible to make Mr Sung understand that to be without a camera was to be free. Gordon Vinald, the barrister's wife and her friend were already up on deck, grumbling, changing films, struggling with telescopic lenses. Wexford sat at a table in the saloon with Margery Baumann, drinking tea that was just being served. Sometimes it is possible for a middle-aged woman to look as fresh as a girl and that was how Margery Baumann, in blue and white checked cotton and with her fair hair newly washed, looked at eight-thirty in the morning on the Li River.

'I'm looking forward to this trip,' she said. 'It's going to be wonderful. And after that – well, we can't get home soon enough for me.'

'I don't imagine you're doing the homeward trip by train as well?'

'Oh, no, thank goodness.' She had a nice light laugh and laughed a good deal but not, Wexford thought, from any sort of nervousness. 'Train to Canton, train out of China to Hong Kong, then the flight home with dear old comfy Swissair.'

'You haven't enjoyed your holiday?'

'In some ways tremendously.' For a moment her eyes had a dreamy look as of delightful, perhaps romantic, things remembered. She became practical. 'But I've had enough, six weeks is too much really. And then I'm needed at home. I'm beginning to feel guilty.'

'What job do you have, Miss Baumann?'

'I'm a GP.' He didn't know why he was so surprised. The children of doctors are often doctors themselves. But she looked so much more the sort of woman who had devoted a gentle life to her old parents. 'I hadn't taken a holiday, not more than a long weekend, in three years. So I got a locum and took the lot owing to me in one – well, not fell, but super swoop!' She laughed.

'The practice is in London?' He really mustn't ask so many questions. It was the habit of an investigating officer. She didn't seem to mind.

'No, Guildford.'

'Really? I'm not far away in Kingsmarkham.'

'Then the Knightons are even nearer to you. They come from a place called Sewingbury.'

'The Knightons?'

'Those people,' she said, as the barrister and his wife walked past the windows. Lois Knox came into the saloon with her Australian. She introduced him as Bruce. Wexford, keeping a straight face, shook hands. Bruce began to talk loudly and vituperatively about Chinese double-think, the way everything was the people's – the people's money, the people's hotel, the people's school – while the people themselves had nothing. He buttonholed Mr T'chung who was peaceably drinking tea with Mr Sung.

'You say it was slave labour built the Ming Tombs, right? It's wrong to force men to build a grandiose tomb for some lousy emperor?'

'Of course,' said Mr T'chung.

'But it's O.K. to make men build a damn great tomb for Mao Tse Tung in Tienanmen Square, is it? What's the difference?'

Mr T'chung looked at him calmly. 'That is a question,' he said in his little clipped voice, 'no one can answer.'

Bruce threw up his hands and gave a bark of laughter.

'Don't let's talk dreary dreary politics,' said Lois.

Wexford went up on deck. The Knightons' friend and Hilda Avory were sitting in deckchairs, drinking tea and Maotai respectively. Hilda said in her gravelly voice with its dying fall, 'Some people who did the trip yesterday told me the boat broke down in mid-stream and they were three hours repairing it.'

'Then the odds are against its breaking down today.'

'It's not a matter of odds, it's a question of efficiency. My only comfort is this place isn't quite so bad as Russia.'

There were boys swimming in the river on one side and water buffalo on the other. High up on the cliffside, against the limestone, wheeled a pair of birds that might have been eagles. Wexford sat in silence, watching the life of the river go by, a village in which was a little curved bridge over an inlet, a temple with a blue roof that the Cultural Revolution had managed to miss, men fishing with cormorants . . .

He stayed up there in the sun for as long as he could stand the heat. Mrs Knighton came up on deck and indefatigably took pictures of everything she saw, water buffalo, cormorants, peasant farmers in the fields, boats with square orange sails, even a utilitarian building Wexford suspected might be a sewage works. By the time it was ten-thirty he had gone below, scorched off the deck. But it was true what Mr Sung had predicted. The scenery suddenly became spectacular, the mountains looping like fantastic clouds, the water clear as glass but with a fierce current running.

Lunch was served at the favourite Chinese time of eleven-thirty and it was the worst meal Wexford had so far eaten, the main course being mainly those organs and entrails which in the west are not eaten by human beings. It amused him to consider how Chinese food, which is usually thought of in Rupert Street or at Poon's as crisp and delicate, may have its slime and lights side too.

It was during lunch that, looking round, Wexford saw the man who had been introduced to him in the train as Mr Wong. He was very surprised. But perhaps it wasn't Mr Wong, perhaps he was confusing him with someone else. But he didn't think so. To say that all Chinese look alike to Europeans was as great a fallacy as that all Chinese had yellow skins. Ah, well, there must be some reason for his being there, not mysterious at all probably to Lu Xing She.

There was just room to wedge a chair into one of the shady companionways. He sat there sleepily while the boat chugged along from Kao Ping to Hua Shan through the deep water, past the drifting boats on which whole families lived, past the cormorant fishermen, between the domed mountains on which trees grew like moss on boulders. When he didn't want to sleep he couldn't keep awake . . .

A commotion awoke him to an immediate awareness that the boat was no longer moving. Normally, his was a quick rousing from sleep, but after so many white nights and in the slumbrous steamy heat he came to gradually and slowly. His first thought was that Hilda Avory had been right and the boat had broken down. But the engine room was just behind where he was sitting and, turning round, he saw it was deserted.

Then he saw the heads bobbing on the water. He got up and tried to go forward but after a few yards his passage was blocked by the press of people. The saloon was empty, twenty or thirty people were in the bows. Wexford turned back and made his way up on to the upper deck. Here too was a similar craning crowd but the river could be seen. He could see Mr Sung swimming, fully clothed, and what seemed like the entire crew of the boat in the water. And not only the crew – Margery Baumann, Gordon Vinald, Tony Purbank, all swimming or treading water, searching for something, someone . . .

Mrs Knighton, holding her camera in thick red hands, said to him, 'A man went overboard. He couldn't swim, they can't find him.'

'Who is it?'

She began to take pictures, and said with indifference, 'Not one of us. A Chinese.'

5

It was an hour before they gave up trying. Before that they had put one of the crew ashore and he had set off to walk, a distance of four or five miles, to the nearest place where there would be a telephone. Wexford watched the little figure in the blue shirt walking along between the river bank and the rice fields until it was swallowed up by the richer blue and the green.

Margery Baumann was the first of the would-be rescuers to reboard the boat. She was in a one-piece black swimsuit. Wexford thought she was exactly the sort of woman who would never take this sort of trip without wearing a bathing costume under her clothes. She said nothing, went down to the bathroom to get dried and dressed. Purbank came next, shivering in spite of the heat. The crew member who had stayed on board – young, though older than the others, who all looked to Wexford about eighteen – seemed to be the captain. He helped haul Purbank aboard, tried to say something to him in very halting English, failed, and shrugged, holding up his hands.

Gordon Vinald was still swimming among the reefs which reached in places almost to the surface of the water. But as, one by one, the Chinese gave up the search, he too swam reluctantly towards the boat in a slow crawl and allowed himself to be hauled in. Now the search had been abandoned, almost everyone had either gone up on deck or retreated into the saloon. The river was empty, a shining sheet of turquoise under a pale blue sky, the mountains behind making a horizon of misted blue loops. Such a beautiful, gently smiling river! A river artists had been painting for two thousand years and would paint, no doubt, for a thousand more. Under its silken rippling surface, trapped in the teeth of one of those reefs, hung a drowned corpse, small, thin, white as a root.

'What happened?' Wexford said to Purbank. 'I was asleep.'

Purbank, in blue underpants, the sun drying him, pushed his fingers through his wet hair. 'Nobody knows really. It's always like that, isn't it, when someone goes overboard? This chap was up here in the bows where we are now. He must have been alone and he was sitting on his haunches, I reckon, the way they all do, and somehow or other he toppled in. Couldn't swim, of course. Captain Ma got everyone who could swim to go in after him but he'd gone before I was even in the water.'

'Who was it?

'Who was what?'

'The man who was drowned. Who was he?'

'God knows. To tell you the truth I never asked. I mean, we wouldn't know anyway, would we? He was Chinese.'

'Not one of the crew?'

'I wouldn't know. Anyone would think you were a policeman, the questions you ask. I daresay we shall get enough of that from the Chinese cops when we get to what's it called, Yang Shuo.'

But Captain Ma, apparently, had no intention of continuing the journey to Yang Shuo. They were within a bend of the river of a village with a landing stage and it was to there, Mr Sung told Wexford, that they were now heading. The engines started up and the boat began to move. A bus would come and pick them up. It was best, there was nothing to worry about, the incident was unfortunate, that was all.

'Who was the drowned man?' Wexford asked. 'One of the crew?'

Mr Sung hesitated. He seemed to be considering and he looked far from happy. Wexford, from long practice in studying the reactions of men, thought that what he saw in Mr Sung's face was not so much sorrow at the death of a fellow human being as fear for his own skin. Eventually he said with reluctance, 'His name Wong T'ien Shui.'

'Mr Wong?'

Mr Sung nodded. He stood looking over the side at the reefs, one of which the boat's bottom had slightly scraped. 'Impossible navigate here at all January, February,' he said brightly.

Wexford shrugged. He went into the saloon and helped himself to one, then a second, cup of green tea. The pungent tea revived him with almost the stimulus of alcohol. The passengers were gathering up their belongings – bags, carriers, raincoats, umbrellas, maps – preparatory to landing.

'What the hell was that Wong doing on this trip anyway?' grumbled Fanning to Wexford. 'I thought he was supposed to be a student? I thought he was supposed to be at university in Chang-sha? Chinese can't just run about the country like that, going where they please. They're not *free*. I bet you fifty *yuan* there's going to be hell to pay. Heads will roll over this. Thank God I'm whizzing my little lot off to Canton tomorrow.'

They went ashore. On a little beach sat an old man with a sparse beard and two strands of moustache. Three small children played about him in the sand. The beach was also populated by a hundred or so chickens and ducks and two white goats. The old man looked at the people from the West with a kind of impassive polite curiosity. He put a few words to Captain Ma and nodded his head.

The village lay above them, at the top of a sloping lane. It was the hottest part of the day. Wexford had never before experienced the sun as an enemy, something to retreat from, to fear. The party wound its way up the street where mirages danced ahead of them in the light. The ground was thick with reddish-brown dust which rose in spirals at their tread. Dust coated everything, the hovels that lined the lane, the walls, the grass, even the legs and arms and faces of the children who came out of their houses, chewing on handfuls of glutinous rice, to stare at the visitors.

At the top of the hill half a dozen men and a girl were building an apartment block. The smell of the river and the dust gave place to a pleasanter one of sandalwood. There was a shop next door into which the entire party, with the exception of Wexford and Fanning, immediately disappeared, and at the end of the village a big house with a walled-in court which had perhaps once been the home of the local warlord. Fanning squatted, oriental fashion, on the broad veranda of the shop and lit a cigarette.

'I make call Yang Shuo,' said Mr Sung. 'Bus come very soon.'

'*I* make call,' Mr T'chung corrected him in a very admonitory voice. He began lecturing the other guide in a hectoring sing-song, wagging his finger. Wexford began to think that if it were to be a question of finding a new Chairman from this part of the world, T'chung Bei Ling might stand a better chance than Sung Lao Zhong.

It was too hot to explore the village, though Wexford walked down one or two narrow little lanes. Children followed him in a giggling huddle. As he returned once more to the square or market place where the shop was he saw an old woman standing in the deep shadow of an overhanging roof. He stood still and looked at her, from her black hair laced with grey, her white puffy face – the Marquise of Tai's face – down to her tiny wedge-shaped feet in child's slippers. He approached till he was no more than a yard from her.

'You want to speak to me?' he said, enunciating clearly.

She made no answer. He repeated what he had said. She seemed to shrink, from shyness or fear. From the other side of the square Mr T'chung began calling, 'Bus has come. Please come quick down hill to bus. Come along, bus has come.'

When Wexford turned from the voice and looked where the old woman had been she was gone. Into the house? It was impossible she should keep vanishing into the abodes of strangers. He went up to the dark doorway and looked inside. It was a dirty hovel in which a child sat eating rice on the floor and a small pig rooted in the far corner. No old woman and no other exit for her to have departed through. If for one moment he were prepared to entertain the idea of the supernatural . . .

Talking excitedly about their purchases, the drowned Wong for the time being forgotten, the train party and the Australians made their way down the hill to where the bus waited. It was parked by the beach and beside it was what was very evidently a police car. Police were on the boat, talking to Captain Ma. An officer came up to Mr T'chung and fired a string of questions at him.

'People's police will come to hotel this evening,' said Mr T'chung.

All this would normally have interested Wexford very much. The reason it didn't was that he had been aware, all the way down the hill, of the old woman with the bound feet following him at a distance. He turned round once or twice, like Shelley's traveller, he told himself, and saw not exactly a frightful fiend but this old creature, hobbling on her stick, who was becoming fiendish enough to him. Now about to enter the bus, the heat thick and gleaming, radiated off the still blue water in a dazzling glare, he made himself turn round and face behind him boldly. She was gone. There was nowhere for her to disappear to but she was gone.

For the rest of the passengers the bus ride back was as rewarding as the boat trip had been on account of the scenery through which the route passed. They drove along lush valleys, green with young rice. Wexford thought about the old woman whom he had now seen three, or possibly four, times. Was she real? Was she a real woman who, incredible as it might be, was for some reason following him across China? Or was she a hallucination such as he supposed schizophrenics might have?

He was sitting next to Tony Purbank who was as silent as he. Purbank was also a fair-skinned person who reacted badly to the sun and his face hadn't been protected as Wexford's had. Moreover, he had a big bald patch on top of his head. His forehead and his bald pate began to glow a fiery red as soon as he was in the air-conditioned shelter of the bus. He spoke not a word, he looked as if he were suffering from a mild degree of heatstroke. Mr Sung too made the return journey in total silence. From the back seats, where Lois Knox sat with Bruce and the Knightons, Wexford could hear a continuous hum of speculation as to how Mr Wong had come to fall overboard.

Wexford expected to see the old woman get off the bus after him but she didn't. It was an absurd relief. He went straight off upstairs and made himself a cup of Silver Leaf.

He lay on the bed, thinking about schizophrenia, wondering what he was going to do if she moved in with him, if she came into his room in the night and lay down in the other bed. Presumably, the truth was that she had never existed at all. He thought back. At Chang-sha he had heard the tap of her stick, her voice as she spoke to her companion. Besides, if his mind was going to produce figments to haunt him, why produce *her*? Out of what recesses of experience, unconscious processes, even trauma, was his mind conjuring an old Chinese woman?

The tea, as always, made him feel better. Could he convince himself it was a mirage he had seen in that river village, a trick of the heat and light?

'People's police say no need talk with you,' said Mr Sung, coming up to his table as dinner was being served. 'No need ask questions any tourists, ship's crew only.' He paused, said, carefully choosing his words, 'They have find dead body Wong T'ien Shui.'

'Poor chap,' said Wexford. 'He can't have been more than twenty or so.'

'Age I don't know,' said Mr Sung. 'Very young, yes. Body cut and – what you say? – brushed very bad by rocks.'

'Bruised?'

'Bruised, yes. Thank you. Many bad rocks there under river so body all cut and bad bruise.'

There was as usual a screen between Wexford and the table at which the train party sat. From beyond it he could only hear a general buzz of conversation. The girl came round with the tea kettle and he had two cups, strangely disturbed now by the death of Wong T'ien Shui. It was still only seven and the sun was just setting. He walked out of the hotel, crossed the road and took the little causeway to the island in the middle of the lake. Somehow – sentimentally, no doubt – he couldn't help imagining Wong as he must have been when a little boy, not so long ago, attending the kindergarten, being met by his mother with her hair in two braids, having a doughnut bought for him in a dark scented grocer's shop, flying a kite shaped like a butterfly or a dragon, going home to loving grandparents. It was a very young life to have been cut short like that.

It should have been pleasant out on the island but because of the weighty thickening humidity, it wasn't. The undulations of mountains looked blue now, veiled in mist, and the air hung full of sluggishly moving mosquitos. After being bitten for the second time he went back to the hotel. Malaria and dengue fever might now be avoidable, but you could still have a leg or an arm swell up like a balloon.

Up on the roof it was too high for the mosquitos. He knew he shouldn't drink, because of his blood pressure and an ever threatening weight problem, but he had to get some sleep somehow. He bought a smallish bottle of cassia wine. The Baumanns, the Knightons and Gordon Vinald called him over to the table they were sharing, only a second before he was similarly summoned to the other — necessarily a few yards away because of the Purbank-Vinald feud — shared by Lois Knox, Hilda Avory and Purbank. There was no sign of the Australians, Fanning or Mrs Knighton's friend. Lois looked sour and Hilda ill, and it was a relief to Wexford to follow the rule of first come, first served.

The people at the table he joined were indulging in the favourite tourist pastime of showing off to each other the souvenirs they had bought that day. As Gordon Vinald began talking, Mrs Baumann whispered to Wexford that he was an antique dealer.

'Jade is always cold to the touch,' he was saying. 'That's one of the best ways for the amateur to tell if it's jade or not. If it stays cold in a hot room or against the skin the chances are it's jade.'

He told them of various jade frauds. How the unscrupulous dealers of Hong Kong would arrange a display with five items of plastic to one of jade, five items of plastic to one of ivory. China was safe, though. The Chinese were either too high-principled to deceive or too innocent to understand the mechanics of deception. But if, of course, the jade they were selling had been imported into China they might themselves have been deceived . . . Wexford thought of the little pieces he had bought for Dora and Denise and his daughters. Were they cold to the touch? He couldn't remember. He put a tentative question about it to Vinald.

'You're in the room next to mine, aren't you?' Vinald

replied. 'No doubt we'll be keeping our usual nursery hours, so why don't you bring them in at the witching hour of nine-thirty and show me?'

Margery Baumann laughed. She took a tissue-wrapped parcel out of her handbag and out of it tumbled half a dozen little cups, medallions, a ring and a pendant in the shape of a turtle. She put the ring on to her finger. Vinald examined all the pieces and pronounced them to be jade, one indeed very close in colour to the imperial jade beloved by the emperors. Then suddenly, as if no one else was there, he lifted her hand in his and brought it up against his cheek. Ostensibly, he was testing the temperature of her ring on his own skin, yet the gesture had a very lover-like air to it. Wexford saw Mrs Baumann smile with pleasure and Margery blush.

Vinald released her hand. 'That's your true nephrite. You've done well, Margery. If you hadn't a worthier profession already I'd say you've a flair for my business.'

She said nothing, only laughed again. And yet the remark, delivered in such a tone and after such a gesture, could almost have been leading up to a proposal of marriage. Wexford thought he wouldn't be surprised if an announcement were made to the party on the following day.

He offered his wine round the table. The beer drinkers refused but Mrs Baumann and Mrs Knighton each took a glass. His bottle wasn't going to last long at that rate. He went off to the bar to get another as 'Silent Night' came crooning out of the record player.

Standing at the bar, in the company of an older woman, was the best-looking girl he had seen since he came to China.

The best-looking Caucasian, that is. Of Chinese beauties there had been plenty but it had seemed to him that women with the looks of his daughter Sheila or his niece Denise weren't interested in visiting the People's Republic.'

This girl, though, would have compelled glances in the most sophisticated milieu. She and the older woman were standing by the counter, talking to the three Australian businessmen about the topic which commanded the attention of the whole hotel, and probably the whole city of Kweilin, the drowning of Wong T'ien Shui. Wexford heard her say, 'There's always something with that boat. If I believed in things like that I'd say that boat had bad joss. Maybe the place they built it was on a dragon's eye or something.'

She laughed. The Australians laughed uproariously. Her accent, he thought, was that of New Zealand. The older woman — her mother? — spoke to her.

'Are you having that red wine again, Pandora, or the Japanese whisky stuff?'

Pandora pondered. She was tall and extravagantly slender, somewhere in her early twenties. Her hair was as black as Lois Knox's raven dye, but Pandora's was natural and it fell as straight to her shoulders as if it were wet. There was no make-up on the dazzling white skin but for a stroke of emerald green on her eyelids. Her eyes were hazel green and the lashes as thick and sooty as a black kitten's. She had on a bright green dress with a pink and black cummerbund and pink sandals. Deciding on the whisky, she turned away and walked out on to the roof. Bruce took a tray and piled bottles and glasses on to it.

Wexford bought his wine and went back. For a moment he thought he saw the old woman with the bound feet standing up against the parapet, but when he looked again he saw only a Chinese boy with a firecracker in his hand. Back at the table they were once more on the topic of Wong's death. Dr Baumann couldn't understand how anyone could have drowned where there were so many reefs to provide footholds. Margery wondered if he had struck his head on one of those reefs as he fell. Mrs Knighton, with an unpleasant little laugh, said be that as it might it had ruined what had promised to be an interesting day out. And then Wexford's attention was caught by the action of Lois Knox who, seeing her Australian come out on to the roof with a woman and two other men, seeing him home in on the table where Pandora had sat down, got up, muttered 'excuse me' to her companions and walked swiftly away towards the stairs. Purbank said something inaudible but Hilda Avory's reply carried on the night air.

'Of course it makes her unhappy. What does she expect if she goes on like that at her age?'

Knighton was staring ahead of him. He had contributed little to the conversation but now he had extracted himself from it entirely. Gazing across the roof like that, he looked as if he had had some transcending vision or had just seen a ghost. Abruptly he jerked his head aside and Wexford was astonished to see his enraptured expression. What had produced that?

His wife was showing family snapshots to Mrs Baumann. 'We've four children, three sons and a daughter, and four simply adorable grandchildren with another on the way.'

Mrs Baumann was beginning an appropriate comment when Knighton spoke. He seemed to be addressing no one in particular. He looked at the view, at the stars, and said:

'"I had gone aboard and was minded to depart,
When I heard from the shore your song with tap of foot.
The pool of peach blossom is a thousand feet deep
But not so deep as the love in your farewell to me." '

The Baumanns looked extremely embarrassed. A sheepish smile lingered on Vinald's face. Mrs Knighton looked at her friend and her friend looked at her and Mrs Knighton very slightly cast up her eyes.

'The work of Li Po,' said Knighton in his more usual cold and dry tone. 'The famous eighth-century Chinese poet.'

'I don't know about you, Irene,' said Mrs Knighton, 'but I feel like going up to my room.'

'Down,' said her friend.

'I mean down. Don't be late,' she said to her husband. 'You've had a long day.' She achieved, like someone doing facial exercises, a broad smile and said briskly, 'Good night, everyone.'

Knighton got to his feet with the air of someone following a weary old rule of politeness. But when the women had gone and the elder Baumanns had gathered up their things and started to follow them, instead of sitting down again, he walked away from the table to a distant part of the roof, leaned over the parapet and gazed at the moonlit landscape.

Wexford was left to play gooseberry to the lovers. He said

good night to Margery, went down to his room and made himself a cup of tea. The old woman with the bound feet had departed to wherever such materializations go when off-duty. Settled down with Poe's 'The Tell-tale Heart', he waited for Vinald's footfall in the corridor – unless, of course, he should forget his appointment and his footfall sound tonight in the corridor below, where Margery's room was.

But no more than half an hour had passed before he heard Vinald's light switch go on. Wexford collected his pieces of jade and knocked at the antique dealer's door.

6

Treasures set about the austere Chinese hotel bedroom had transformed it into something resembling a corner of a museum in the Forbidden City. There were dishes of *famille jaune*, pieces of blue and white ware, a magnificent tall pearl-coloured vase with a design on it of birds and ripe peaches on a peach tree, lacquer trays, boxes of chops in jade and carnelian and soapstone, three or four plain pale bowls of exquisite shape, a pair of carved jade vases with lids, and everywhere a scattering of tiny pieces of carved jade, of snuff bottles, seals and metal scent bottles.

'I confess to liking the gorgeous stuff best,' said Wexford. 'Does that prove me ignorant and undiscriminating?'

Vinald laughed. 'Not really. That vase is a lovely piece. I'm lucky to have found it. There are a pair just like it that were made for the Dowager Empress.'

'It's not so very old then?' Wexford knew that much.

'Under a hundred years.' Vinald handed his purchases back to him. 'Your jade's O.K. Frankly, I'd be surprised if it wasn't. Can I offer you a cup of tea?' When it was poured he began tidying the room. 'We're off again tomorrow, a ghastly round-about journey since there's no direct route from Kweilin to Canton. It seems that the mountains get in the way.' He was thrusting items from the desk into a hand case, a ball-point pen, a stick of red sealing wax, a note book, the hotel writing paper out of the blotter. Wexford was amused. How people loved acquiring something for nothing, even the wealthiest! Here was this evidently rich man pinching three sheets of

248

writing paper when there was little doubt he could have bought up all the notepaper stocks in Kweilin and given it back again without much noticing the loss.

Vinald took a drink of tea. 'I didn't exactly come to China to buy antiquities,' he said. 'I was in need of a holiday, I was literally dying on my feet for a holiday. But I had every intention of buying antiquities when I got here. I knew what a hoard China has, you see.'

Wexford raised his eyebrows enquiringly.

'Oh, yes. You can imagine the stuff that got pinched at the time of what they call Liberation, can't you? Not to mention the Cultural Revolution. They claim it has all passed through Government hands but the fact is they simply stole it from its rightful owners, and murdered them too if the truth were known.'

'The truth never really is known about China,' said Wexford. 'And that's not new, it's always been so.'

Vinald passed over the interruption with a slight impatient wave of his hand. 'I can tell you that if China chose to let loose what she's got on the world the bottom would fall slap bang out of the antiques market.'

'Which would hardly suit you, I suppose.'

'You're right there. I've helped myself to a few unconsidered trifles.' Vinald pulled tissue paper out of a drawer and started wrapping things up, packing them into boxes, some of which were padded with straw. 'Tell me,' he said, speaking rather abruptly, 'do you think it's wrong to buy something for fifty *yuan* – say fifteen pounds – when you know perfectly well its real worth would be five hundred pounds?'

'If by wrong you mean illegal, I shouldn't think that's illegal anywhere in the world. No doubt it's unethical, some would say it's taking advantage of innocence. Why? Have you done much of that sort of thing?'

'A bit,' said Vinald. 'They're so ignorant they don't know what they're offering you half the time. It might be unethical in some places, I don't think it is here. You can't think of yourself as taking an unfair advantage of the Chinese Government, can you? It's not as if it were some individual trying to make a living.'

'How about a nation trying to make a living?' Vinald

249

looked uncomprehending so Wexford turned aslant of the subject. 'I don't envy you carrying that lot home.'

'Most of it'll go in my suitcase.' Vinald packed the blue and white dishes, an ikon, a gleaming white bowl. 'I brought the minimum of clothes because I knew I'd want to fill up this end.'

'You don't anticipate trouble with the Customs?'

'I shan't fall foul of them. As long as you don't take anything out of China that's more than a hundred and twenty years old you're O.K.'

Wexford thanked him for his opinion and his tea and left him wrapping up and packing a blue, crimson and gold ikon. In his own room, standing in the corner by the air conditioner, was the old woman with the bound feet. He stared and she changed into the wooden coat stand over which he had hung his jacket.

Her shadow flitted across the window blind. He knew she wasn't real now and because of something that had happened to his eyes or his mind he was imagining her. In the book of supernatural stories he was reading was one by Somerset Maugham called 'The End of the Flight', which had nothing to do with aircraft but was about a man in the Far East who had done some sort of injury to an Achinese and thereafter, no matter where he fled to, was haunted by this Achinese or his spirit or ghost. He, Wexford, had of course never done any sort of injury to an old Chinese woman.

The room was empty again, not a trace of her. The air conditioning made it rather too cool. He went to bed, pulling the quilt up over his head. It was impossible to sleep, so in the middle of the night he got up again and made tea. There was no sign of the old woman but still he couldn't sleep, and to keep sleep still further at bay, at about four in the morning the drone of the air conditioner was augmented by a rushing roaring sound. It was raining.

When it began to get light he got out of bed and looked at the rain. He could see the rain crashing against the windows and that was about all he could see, the lake, the city roofs, the mountains were all blotted out by dense white fog.

It was absurd to attempt to go out unless one had to. The

train party had to. They were embarking on a journey to Canton that was only about two hundred miles as the crow flies but which would take two days in a train. Their luggage was piled in the hotel lobby. In twos and threes they came down in the lift to await Mr T'chung and the bus.

Wexford sat in a rattan chair, reading Maugham's story about the ghost of the Achinese. The Knightons came first with their friend, who was wearing her dark blue trouser suit but not looking much like the old woman with the bound feet. The bus had drawn up outside. Lois Knox came out of the lift with Hilda Avory behind her.

'I suppose we must say goodbye,' Lois said with a meaning look as if she and he had been on intimate terms.

Wexford shook hands with her, then with Hilda and Vinald. 'Have a good journey.'

'And you,' said Vinald. 'Flying off in a nice little Fokker Friendship aren't you? We should be so lucky.'

The Baumanns and Margery waved to him. Fanning got out of the lift with Mr T'chung. 'So help me God,' whispered Fanning to Wexford, 'but once I get home the furthest bloody abroad I'm going ever again will be the Isle of Wight.'

Under umbrellas held up by their guides they filed out to the bus, joined at the last moment by the two women from New Zealand. The beautiful Pandora was in tight yellow trousers and a yellow tee-shirt and Wexford saw Lois give her a glare of dislike.

The rain swallowed the bus as it went splashing off towards the railway station. Wexford drank some tea, tried to sleep, read a story by M.R. James about a man dogged by the ghost of a Swedish nobleman whom he had inadvertently released from a tomb. He didn't finish it. He had seen the old woman with the bound feet cross the lobby just after the bus had left and now he could see her most of the time hovering on the edge of his sight. When he stared hard she would disappear and then, as he looked away, he would be dimly aware of her waiting, so to speak, in the wings of his vision.

It was useless to worry about it. When he got home he would get Dr Crocker to send him to an oculist or specialist in allergies or maybe, if it had to be, a psychiatrist. Instead of worrying, or instead of worrying more than he could help, he began to wonder if he ought to go and call on the local police. After all, he had originally come to China because he was a policeman, he had come at the express invitation of the Ministry of Internal Affairs. Having actually been on the boat at the time of Wong's fatal accident, should he not go and inform them of this fact? Rather glumly he thought about it. With his lack of Chinese and their undoubted lack of English? With Mr Sung as his interpreter? And what help could he be? He had been asleep at the time.

No, he wouldn't go. Such an action would smack of 'putting himself forward', of showing off his greater sophistication and that of the nation he came from. Besides, he could do nothing, tell them nothing, beyond revealing himself as possibly the least effective witness on the boat.

It rained all day. But twenty-four hours later, when he was starting to think his flight would be cancelled because of the bad weather, the sky cleared, the sun came back and the looped mountains stood out so sharply against the translucent blue that it seemed one could pick out every tree on their slopes. Mr Sung escorted him to the airport in a taxi.

'I like to say,' said Mr Sung, 'the very great pleasure it has been to me to be your guide and I wish you good journey and pleasant stay in Guangzhou.'

This, Wexford knew, was what the Chinese called Canton, or perhaps it would be more correct to say that in trying to pronounce Guangzhou, Canton was the best those European merchants who had come there had been able to do.

'You will please convey best wishes to your friends and relations in UK and say they are welcome to China. All friends are welcome to China.'

The aircraft had no air conditioning. Once they were airborne steam poured across the non-pressurized interior and the passengers fanned themselves with fans painted with the Kweilin mountains which the stewardess provided. Wexford was the only European on board. He knew that the stewardess walking up and down the aisle with fans and sweets on a tray was a young girl in her early twenties but for a moment he had seen her as an old woman with bound feet.

Would he see her in Canton? In Hong Kong? Would he — like Maugham's man with the Achinese — would he see her in *England*?

At Canton he was met by his new guide, Lo Nan Chiao. Mr Lo shook hands and said he was welcome to Guangzhou and if he was agreeable, while his luggage went on to the hotel, they would proceed straight to Martyrs' Mausoleum.

The old woman with the bound feet was there waiting for him. He closed his eyes and opened them and she had changed back into the uniformed attendant. She emerged from the doors of the Sun Yat-sen Monument and came across the bridge from Sha Mian to meet him. By that time he would have been convinced of his own madness if Mr Lo hadn't gone up to speak to her, remarking afterwards to Wexford that she was an acquaintance of his mother's.

Wexford sweated. She wasn't *always* an acquaintance of Mr Lo's mother. It was even hotter here and the humidity was intense. When he tried to make tea he found the water in his thermos flask was only lukewarm and repeated requests to the hotel staff failed to produce boiling water. But at dinner he discovered a new brand of Lao Shan, the coldest and best mineral water he had so far tasted, and he bought a dozen bottles to the amazement of the waitress to whom such extravagance perhaps represented a week's wages. The food was good too and the coffee was drinkable.

He dozed in his bedroom and this time it might have been a dream and not a vision he had. He never knew. But he took the traditional action honoured in ghost stories. He threw something. Almost anywhere else in the world a holy book would have been provided in an hotel bedroom, the Bible or the Koran or the Gita, but here he had to make do with *Masterpieces of the Supernatural*. The old woman disappeared. Wexford felt worn out. He was sure he wouldn't sleep and he prepared for another white night, only to fall into a heavy dreamless slumber he didn't come out of until six when the phone rang.

'Good morning. Time to get up,' said a chirpy voice, habituated to the rhythms of Cantonese.

Wexford felt much better. The sun was shining on the green wooded mountains that he could see from his window.

Breakfast and then off to the porcelain factory with Mr Lo, to the factory at Fu-shan where all the great Chinese porcelain of the past was made and from where it had been exported to Europe, where the peach-blossom vase acquired by Gordon Vinald certainly had been shaped and painted and glazed.

It was while he was having dinner back once more at the Bai-yun Hotel that he realized he hadn't seen the old woman once she had scuttled out of sight at the factory behind a group of girls modelling figurines. She didn't appear in his room that evening nor next day in Tung Shan Park nor was she anywhere around to spoil the beauty of the orchid garden.

Mr Lo came with Wexford's exit visa and a packed lunch to eat on the train to Kowloon. They went to the station and the old woman wasn't there. She wasn't waiting for him in his carriage either. The train had dun-coloured cotton covers with pleated valances on the seats and net curtains and pale blue velvet curtains at the windows. There was closed-circuit television on which sometimes a girl announcer appeared and sometimes acrobats gyrated. Wexford couldn't yet believe the old woman had gone and he even tried to catch glimpses of her round the edges of his vision but he achieved nothing by this beyond a headache.

He was leaving China. Quietly, without pause or frontier fuss, the train crossed the border into the Hong Kong New Territories at Sum-chun. By now Wexford had a feeling of complete certainty he would never again see the old woman with the bound feet. Ghost or hallucination, for some reason she had come to him in Shao-shan and, equally inexplicably, left him in Canton. He felt tired, shaky, with relief. The cool airy train raced pleasantly along towards the Crown Colony, back to luxury, ordinariness, a 'too high' standard of living, soft beds, capitalism.

Dora was there to meet him on the platform at Kowloon Station. She had missed her husband and guessed he had missed her but they had been married, after all, for more than thirty years and so she was a little surprised by the ardour of his embrace.

Part Two

7

Thatto Hall Farm stands about a mile outside the small town of Sewingbury in pleasant hilly wooded country. The Hall itself was pulled down many years ago and the smaller house, which was bought by a London couple in 1965 and converted for use as a weekend residence, is now the only dwelling in Thatto Vale. Paunceley is the nearest village, a collection of cottages and a small council estate linked to Sewingbury by a B-class road and a system of footpaths that run close by the farmhouse.

It is a long low brick house, about a hundred and sixty years old, comprising six rooms, two bathrooms, a small washroom and a kitchen. The gardens have been well kept and the house has acquired a tended, even luxurious appearance. In October the Virginia Creeper which covers half the front of the house turns to a blaze of crimson and the two circular flowerbeds in the two front lawns are filled with dwarf Michaelmas daisies in shades of purple, rose and deep blue.

It was on a morning in October that Mrs Renie Thompson, the cleaner at Thatto Hall Farm, arrived at nine to find her employer lying dead on the dining-room floor.

Wexford got to work half an hour later and that was the first thing they told him. The name rang a bell and so did the address.

'*Who* is it that's dead?' he said to Detective Sergeant Martin.

'A Mrs Knighton, sir. A Mrs Adela Knighton. The woman who found her said she'd been shot.'

'And Inspector Burden's gone over there, has he, with the doctor and Murdoch? I think we'll go too.'

It was a fine sunny day, a little morning mist still lingering. The leaves had not yet begun to fall. Where the footpath met the road, just before the farmhouse, a man came over the stile, carrying a shotgun and with two dead rabbits slung over his shoulder. Thatto Hall Farm lay in a misty golden haze. On its well-trimmed dewy lawns lay a scattering of red and yellow fruit from crab apple trees. The front door was open and Wexford walked in.

Murdoch, the Scene-of-Crimes Officer, was in the dining room with Dr Crocker and the body. Naughton, the fingerprint man, was busy in the hall. At the kitchen table with Burden opposite her, drinking strong tea, sat Renie Thompson. She was much the same age as her dead employer had been, somewhere in the middle sixties, a big gaunt woman with dyed brown hair in a hairnet and wearing a skirt and jumper covered by a mauve flowered overall.

'Where is Mr Knighton?' Wexford asked.

'Don't ask me.' Mrs Thompson kept up a bold and truculent manner even while in shock. 'I always come in nine sharp Mondays, Wednesdays and Fridays and this is the first time I've known him not be here as well as her. I went upstairs and looked. I mean he might have been dead and laying up there too for all I knew. They had twin beds and his wasn't slept in. I've never known that before, not all the time I've worked here and that's donkey's years.'

Wexford went upstairs. The staircase was of polished oak, uncarpeted, and, though the bedrooms were carpeted, the spacious upper hall had a polished floor on which lay blue and silvery grey rugs. The principal bedroom, with its made bed and its unmade bed, was done in shades of rose, the other three in blue, green and gold respectively. Victorian furniture, chintz curtains pinch-pleated or on rings, Arthur Rackham drawings in narrow silver-coloured frames, on a console table a bunch of everlasting flowers in a Bing and Grondahl bowl, and in every bedroom a jar of pot-pourri. All very correct and tasteful. Wexford looked in all the cupboards, he even looked under the beds. He went downstairs and looked in the large, similarly conventionally furnished living room. Having looked in the bathrooms, he looked in the washroom where he noticed a pane of glass was missing from the window. Knighton, alive or dead, wasn't in the house.

Dr Crocker came out of the dining room and said, 'Old Tremlett's on his way. I managed to get him at home before he left for the infirmary.'

'Is it true she was shot?'

'Through the back of the head. He must have brought the barrel of the gun right up against the occipital itself. All her back hair was singed.'

'He shot her through the *back* of the head? Put the gun against the back of her head and shot her? The mind boggles a bit. What do you think, Sergeant, she heard a sound, came down to see what it was, he crept up behind her and shot her?'

'She might have heard glass breaking, sir. There's a piece of glass missing from the window in there.'

'Except that it was cut out. You can get together with Mrs Thompson and find out what sort of valuables they've got or had in this house.'

Wexford knelt down and looked at the body. It was cold and heavy to the touch and rigor was already established. What he had seen of Adela Knighton in China he hadn't cared for but he forgot that in a rush of pity. She was a sad sight and there was no dignity in her death. While alive and in health she had been a plain, stocky, rather aggressive, no-nonsense sort of woman. Now in death she lay as a flabby heap, her face having a look of half-melted wax, her grizzled sandy hair burned black at the nape of her neck and around the red, charred-edged hole the bullet had drilled there. She wore an expensive-looking nightgown of some thick, shiny, peach-coloured silky material with lace borders and lace insertions and over it a dressing gown of dark blue velour. On her feet were flat-heeled slippers of quilted black velvet. Her wedding ring, a chased platinum band worn down to the thinness of wire, was on her left hand.

'It doesn't look as if anything very alarming fetched her

down,' said Wexford. 'There's a phone extension by her bed and the wires haven't been cut.'

A black Daimler drew up on the gravel drive. Sir Hilary Tremlett, the pathologist, had arrived. Wexford went into the washroom off the hall. It contained a lavatory pan with low flush cistern, a vanity table with bowl insert, a small round mirror on the wall above the bowl. The window was the sash kind divided into four panes, each about fifteen inches square, and from one of these the glass had been cut. Wexford decided there was no way he himself could have squeezed through the aperture thus obtained but he was a large man with a big frame. Most women could have got through there and any average-sized man.

Directly below the window outside was a small narrow flowerbed in which pink sedum was blooming. Wexford knew there wouldn't be any footprints. He went out to look and there weren't, though someone had plainly kicked over the remains of what footprints there had been.

Mrs Thompson was telling Martin that the Knightons had never kept money in the house as far as she knew. Mrs Knighton, like a lot of well-off people, Renie Thompson implied, was always short of cash and as often as not would pay her with a cheque. No ornaments were missing, no attempt had been made to remove heavy equipment, television, record player or any kitchen machinery.

'Presumably she had some jewellery.'

'Must have done,' said Martin in a way that indicated he wouldn't have thought of it if his chief hadn't reminded him. 'How about jewellery, Mrs Thompson?'

'I only saw her in the mornings, didn't I? It's no good asking me what rings and whatnot she had.'

Wexford remembered, from China, a platinum watch and an engagement ring with, he thought, a square-cut stone. He mentioned those items to Mrs Thompson.

'If you say so. Don't ask me where she kept them.'

'Very well, we won't ask you,' said Wexford, irritated by her truculent huffy manner. 'We'll look. There are a limited number of places. She didn't keep them in the fridge or up a chimney.'

Sir Hilary had finished his preliminary examination and

they were about to take the body away. Murdoch was still meticulously at work on table surfaces, banisters, door jambs. The doctor, about to leave, said to Wexford, 'Did she live here alone?'

'There's a husband,' said Wexford.

'Where is he then?'

'I wish I knew.'

Martin came downstairs. 'There's no jewellery or jewel case in her room or any of the bedrooms, sir.'

'Right.' He said to Mrs Thompson, remembering a table on a hotel roof, a yellow envelope of snapshots, 'She had children. Where do they live?'

'The daughter in Sewingbury, that I do know. Don't ask me where you'll find the sons, all off abroad somewhere, I daresay. There might be numbers in that book.'

A leather-bound directory lay on a table by the telephone. Wexford himself held his daughters' phone numbers in his head. He was justly and secretly proud of his memory, knowing it to be exceptional.

'What's the daughter's married name?'

'Her *surname*? That I wouldn't know. I'd no reason ever to be told that, had I? Jennifer, they call her. Mr Knighton could tell you.'

'Yes, I've no doubt he knows his own daughter's name,' said Wexford. 'You can go home now, Mrs Thompson, if you like. I expect we'll want to see you again. We'll let you know.'

'Don't I get a lift home then?'

'I beg your pardon?'

'I should think the least you could do is one of you run me home. I reported finding her, didn't I? I've helped you with your enquiries. It's usual to arrange for transport under the circumstances.'

Wexford was amused. 'Not in this neck of the sticks it isn't. Maybe in Y Division or Los Angeles. You've been watching too many crime serials.'

Renie Thompson stuck her chin in the air and flounced out. Wexford laughed.

'She only lives in Paunceley,' said Burden. 'You don't think she could have done it?'

'Come on. She couldn't tell a Beretta from a bottle opener. Have you finished, Murdoch? Better get back then. Martin, I want Knighton's daughter found – she lives somewhere in Sewingbury – and the sons too if possible. I want a house-to-house between here and Sewingbury and the other side of Thatto Vale through Paunceley. Luckily, or maybe unluckily, there aren't that many houses.'

'What are we looking for, sir?'

'Any suspicious happenings during the night, any strange cars seen, strangers on foot yesterday or in the night. Oh, and we're looking for Knighton. Very keenly are we looking for Knighton.'

When they had gone Wexford began telling Burden about China. Not about the trip in general – with restraint he had done that weeks before – but everything he could recall of Adam and Adela Knighton. It wasn't much. By a curious irony he had paid more attention to the other members of the train party than he had to the Knightons and their friend. Perhaps it was because the others had been rather thrust upon him and when, belatedly, he had made the Knightons' acquaintance it was at a time when he was being most bedevilled, haunted, plagued by that fantasy or hallucination or whatever you liked to call it. To the women he had hardly spoken a word, to Knighton . . . What could he remember of him? A tall, thin, silver-haired man in his sixties who had looked for a moment as if he had seen a vision and who had recited, for no apparent reason, a strange little piece of Chinese poetry. To Burden, now that he told all this – leaving out only the bit about his own visions – and delved in that excellent memory of his, he was able to reproduce, accurately, he was sure, every sentence he had heard Adam and Adela Knighton utter.

'It may be useful,' said Burden not very encouragingly.

Wexford retorted rather obscurely, though Burden understood, 'Well, it wasn't a burglar, was it? She didn't get up and go down for a burglar. A burglar didn't come up behind her and stick a gun in the back of her head. It wasn't like that. And where the hell is Knighton?'

'Murdered his wife and run off with her friend. No, but seriously, it looks as if he might have. Not run off with the friend, I don't mean that. Not at their ages. But had a row with her in the night and shot her and then got the hell out. Why not? It's the most likely thing. He could be out of the country by now, probably is. People in his position always have wealthy and influential friends.'

'You don't need wealthy and influential friends,' snapped Wexford. 'You just need to buy a plane ticket. On American Express. It's all made so damned easy these days. O.K., I agree it's quite likely, though I'd have expected them to be upstairs having their row if she was in her nightdress, and I certainly wouldn't have expected an English gentleman like Knighton to shoot anyone, let alone his wife, through the *back* of the head.'

'That's going to bother you a lot, isn't it?'

'Of course.'

They were in the living room. Once three or four small rooms, now made into one, it was about thirty feet long with French windows at the back and casements giving on to the front lawns and the drive. A grandfather clock began chiming eleven with rich sonorous notes. Wexford heard another sound. He moved to one of the windows and looked out. A car was coming up the drive, a large dark blue Ford.

'That's one of the Kingsmarkham station taxis,' said Burden.

'Yes.'

The car drew up. A man got out of the back of it, paid the driver and picked up a black leather suitcase of overnight bag size which he had set down on the gravel for a moment, and walked towards the front door where he was lost to their view.

'Knighton,' said Wexford.

His key turned in the lock. The two policemen stood absolutely still, waiting. The front door opened and closed, footsteps sounded across the hall and Knighton's voice called, 'Adela!'

8

It was time to declare themselves. Wexford coughed but perhaps Knighton didn't hear, for when he saw the two men emerge from his living room he gave a violent start.

'What on earth . . . !'

'Good morning, Mr Knighton,' Wexford said. 'Yes, we've met before. In China. I see you recognize me as I do you. Chief Inspector Wexford of Kingsmarkham CID. This is Inspector Burden.'

'Mr Wexford, yes. I do remember you, though I had no idea . . . What are you doing in my house? Has there been some sort of robbery or what . . . ?'

'That we don't yet know. However, something very serious has taken place. You must be prepared for . . .'

'Where's my wife?'

Wexford told him. All the colour went out of Knighton's face. He walked into the living room and sat down in an armchair.

'Shot?' he said. 'Adela – shot?'

'I'm afraid it's true, sir.'

'Shot by some intruder? She's dead?'

'Yes, it appears she was shot by someone who forced an entry to this house during the night.'

Knighton passed a hand across his face. 'And you – you're a policeman in Kingsmarkham? You came in here and found my wife dead?'

'I among others. Your cleaner notified us.'

'Good God. Good God in heaven!'

Burden had sat down and now Wexford sat down too. Knighton's face was still paper-white, his eyes glassy with shock. Wexford could have sworn it had been a shock. He noticed something that hadn't really struck him while they were in China – his wretched preoccupation with the old woman with bound feet, no doubt, had distracted him – he noticed how extraordinarily good-looking Knighton was. He was still good-looking now, though he looked ill with shock. What must he have been like when young? He still had a boy's figure, a young man's lithe carriage, and his features were of the classical sort, grown somewhat marble-like with age. His golden locks time had to silver turned. Adela Knighton, on the other hand, had been very plain, ugly even. And hers was the kind of ugliness not created by time but bred in the bone.

All that, of course, might be quite irrelevant. Wexford asked the classic requisite question that always made him feel like a character in a detective story.

'Where were you last night, sir?'

'Where was I? Staying with a friend in London. Why do you ask?'

'Routine.'

'Good God.' A sort of horrified understanding twisted Knighton's mouth. 'I thought you said a burglar . . . '

'If you could just tell us where you were last night, sir, the name of your friend and so on, we should be able to get through this painful business a good deal faster.'

'Oh, very well.' Knighton hesitated a fraction. 'An old friend of mine, Henry Lacey,' he said, 'was giving a dinner party at a club to which both he and I belong. The Palimpsest in St James's. It was to celebrate his fifty years at the bar, what it would be the fashion to call a Golden Jubilee, I suppose. I was invited. On such occasions I stay in London as I have never cared to fetch my wife out with the car at one o'clock in the morning. And the station taxi service is not available at that hour, as you doubtless know.'

'You stayed at the club?'

'No, with a friend who has a flat in Hyde Park Gardens.' The phone rang. Knighton gave another violent start.

Wexford was rather surprised that he glanced at him for the go-ahead before answering it. He nodded.

Knighton gave the number in a steady low voice. Whoever was at the other end, unless exceptionally insensitive, would have recognized it as the voice of one recently bereaved. A cruel estimate, Wexford thought, but just. Knighton was shocked but he was not unhappy – perhaps unhappiness would come hereafter.

'Oh, Jennifer . . . ' It was the daughter. 'The police have told you? Have you talked to Rod? Yes, please do come . . .' He put the phone down, again touched his forehead with his hand. 'My son is coming and my daughter and son-in-law.'

'I understand you have four children?'

'A daughter and three sons. One is in America and one in Turkey.'

'While we're waiting for your son and Mr and Mrs . . . ?'

'Norris. My son-in-law is a solicitor with Symonds, O'Brien and Ames in Kingsmarkham.'

'While we're waiting for them, perhaps you'll give me the name of your friend in Hyde Park Gardens and the address of Mr Henry Lacey.'

Jennifer and Angus Norris got there first. She was a plain young woman, dumpy and freckled, who resembled her mother. She was also about seven months pregnant and Wexford remembered Adela Knighton speaking of another grandchild 'on the way'.

Her brother Roderick turned up soon afterwards in a yellow Triumph TR7, having driven very fast from London. He was handsome and tall like his father, though anxious-looking and a good deal older than his sister. A barrister also, Wexford gathered. The law was well represented in the Knighton family to whom this lawless thing had happened. The spry little son-in-law, no taller than his wife and with a shock of dark curly hair surrounding a bald spot, he had sometimes seen in the Magistrates' and Crown Courts.

Young Mrs Norris had a manner Wexford had met before in women of the upper middle class who have led indulged lives. She called her parents Mummy and Daddy and spoke of her family and its immediate circle as of an élite.

'It's so awful, I feel it just can't be happening to us. Daddy was at the criminal bar, you know, and I remember Mummy saying how that really brought home to one what a horrendous lot of murders there actually are. And Daddy used to say she needn't worry because only a fraction of those murders happened to people like us, they were nearly all confined to the lower classes. And now poor Mummy . . . I mean, it seems so unfair. You lead a decent life and try to keep up some sort of standard and then an appalling thing like this has to happen.'

No doubt she would have found the murder more comprehensible if Renie Thompson had been the victim. But for those remarks of hers Wexford might not have asked where she and her husband had been on the previous night.

'What sort of time had you in mind?' said Norris. 'What does "night" mean?' He spoke in the style he used when cross-examining nervous witnesses. 'What time did all this take place?'

'Let's just stick to "night" for the moment, Mr Norris.'

'I asked because it so happens I took my wife out for a while during the evening.'

Jennifer Norris made a sound which in the circumstances couldn't have been laughter but which came very near it, an unamused grim laugh. Her brother turned cold magisterial eyes on her.

'Yes, but really, Angus, *you* took *me* out! What he means, Rod, is that we walked down to the river and back and had a drink at the Millers', the usual extent of our wining and dining these days . . .'

Wexford coughed.

'Yes, well, Chief Inspector,' began Norris who had gone rather pink, 'we went to bed early, we . . .'

'Oh, Angus, let me tell him. My doctor gives me a mild sedative and the result is I sleep like a log. And lately we've been taking the phone off the hook, so if poor Mummy had tried to get through . . .' It was plain to Wexford that she couldn't for a moment imagine she or her husband might come under suspicion. This was murder in the course of robbery. This was a 'lower class' crime. 'We live in Springhill

Lane, actually,' she volunteered. 'In one of the *old* houses.' This was a facet of local snobbism Wexford had encountered once or twice before. People living in this prestigious district of Sewingbury had an edge on their neighbours if they possessed one of the original seventeenth-century houses. There were perhaps half a dozen of these, around and among which new building had taken place during the past twenty years.

'Mummy can't have heard that glass breaking. She had a phone by her bed and even if she couldn't get through to us she'd have tried to phone the police. I mean, how could she have hoped to deal with some rough type like that?'

'He forced an entry by breaking a window?' said Norris.

'Not exactly, Mr Norris. Rather let's say a pane of glass was cut out from a window. And what were your movements last night, Mr Knighton?'

Roderick Knighton had a breezy manner. He glanced frequently at his watch. Already he had made several phone calls, declaring during the intervals between them that he didn't know what use he could be here but if there was anything he could do his father, sister and the Chief Inspector had only to ask. He yawned, looked once more at his watch and replied to Wexford that he had hardly slept a wink on the previous night, he and his wife and the au pair having been up for most of it with the youngest child who was ill.

'Mumps, actually,' he said. 'Poor little scrap.'

Jennifer Norris had put her feet up. Her husband was standing by one of the windows, looking thoughtful. He seemed worried or puzzled, perhaps only concerned that a man in his position – as he would doubtless refer to himself – could suddenly find himself involved in so unsavoury a business. And Wexford's next remark made him turn slowly round to exchange with his wife a glance of dismay or possibly incredulity.

'I'd like to see what we can do by way of making an inventory of Mrs Knighton's missing jewellery.'

For Knighton this was a hopeless task. He now seemed stunned or bemused by what had happened and his face was drained of all colour and animation. He sat limply in an armchair, gazing at a fixed point and occasionally shaking himself out of his reverie with a shiver. Wexford's suggestion fetched from him a vague shake of the head. Roderick was on the phone again, whispering discreetly, sometimes cupping his hand round the mouthpiece.

'Is any jewellery actually missing?' said Norris in his courtroom drawl.

'One would suppose so. There's none in the house.' Wexford said dryly, 'I'm assuming Mrs Knighton possessed jewellery apart from her wedding ring.'

'Of course she did,' said Jennifer very sharply. Wexford wondered how much of that steel-trap snapping Norris had to put up with. 'There was a gold bracelet that had been my grandmother's,' she said, and added with a resounding lack of discretion, 'that she always said would be mine one day.' Norris closed his eyes and winced. 'And her pearls, of course. A few rings and brooches, a couple of watches. We aren't the sort of people who decorate ourselves like Christmas trees. Mummy thought it dreadfully vulgar to have your ears pierced.'

'I'd like you to do your best to make a list, Mrs Norris. No doubt your father gave her presents of jewellery over the years?'

Knighton said nothing. Wexford suddenly noticed the large, square-cut diamond on the daughter's small red left hand. 'I don't actually think he did much,' she said.

Dr Moss, who was Crocker's partner and Adam Knighton's GP, arrived at one and offered Knighton sleeping pills, tranquillizers and restrained sympathy. Roderick said he would be off but if there was anything he could do they had only to ring him. He left a string of phone numbers. Jennifer Norris remarked to her husband that they could phone her brother in Washington now, it would be eight in the morning in Washington. To her brother in Ankara she had sent a cable.

Wexford went back to the police station.

The house-to-house had produced nothing. Wexford hadn't thought it would. Thatto Hall Farm was too isolated. Pending Sir Hilary Tremlett's report, Crocker had volunteered that death had taken place approximately between two and four a.m. It would be at least tomorrow before they knew more:

the type of gun used, the precise cause of death, other injuries, if any, to the body.

'It wasn't a burglary, was it?' said Burden. 'It was a clumsy half-hearted attempt to make it look like a burglary.'

Wexford nodded. 'Possibly not even what Jennifer Norris calls a "rough type".'

'Knighton,' said Burden cautiously, 'is not what anyone would call a rough type.'

Wexford's eyebrows went up.

Burden sat down in the only other seat apart from Wexford's swivel one that might remotely be called an armchair. 'He's fixed himself up a wonderful alibi for an innocent man. Going up to London, dining in St James's, staying in Hyde Park Gardens. He hardly ever spends a night away from home but the very night he does his wife gets murdered. Would you have reckoned when you met him in China that he was — well, fond of his wife? I mean, was it a happy marriage?'

'Marriage is a funny old carry-on altogether, isn't it? Hard to say. I couldn't say.'

'Helpful. I really came to say do you feel like a spot of lunch? The Pearl of Africa? Oh, God, I can see it in your face, you want to go Chinese again. The day is coming when I shan't be able to face another crispy noodle.'

'I can't resist impressing people with my dazzling virtuosity with the chopsticks,' said Wexford as they walked down Queen Street towards the Many-Splendoured Dragon. 'D'you know, Mike, I wish I'd paid more attention to the Knightons in China. I've a feeling it would have been profitable. But all I can really remember is Knighton sitting at a table and suddenly looking as if he'd seen a ghost. Or maybe not a ghost.' He paused thoughtfully. 'Maybe the Holy Grail or the City of God or, if he were Dante, Beatrice.'

9

Lodged in the dead woman's skull, egress stopped by the frontal bone, was a bullet from a Walther PPK 9 mm automatic. She had been shot at the closest possible range, the barrel of the gun having been in contact with the back of her head.

Sir Hilary Tremlett's more precise assessment narrowed down the time of death to between 2.15 and 3.45 a.m. Adela Knighton had been a normal healthy woman of about sixty-five, somewhat overweight, who had borne several children and at several times in her life had undergone surgery. For mastoid, for varicose veins, appendicitis and, within the past four or five years, a hysterectomy. There was a mild degree of bruising on the upper left arm.

The fingerprints in Thatto Hall Farm proved to be those of the dead woman herself, Adam Knighton, Renie Thompson, Jennifer Norris and Angus Norris. On the evening of the day of her mother's death, Mrs Norris had provided Wexford with a list of all the jewellery she believed her mother had possessed. But by that time Wexford's officers, combing the grounds of Thatto Hall Farm, had found a green leather jewel case under the hedge by the front gates. Items from it also came to light, scattered haphazardly with no apparent attempt at concealment, in flowerbeds, under the same hedge, on the bank that bordered the road. Two watches, a gold bracelet, a string of pearls, two diamond and ruby rings in old-fashioned settings. Mrs Norris identified it all as having

271

belonged to her mother and told Wexford that nothing was missing.

He saw clearly what had happened. This was no burglar who had come into Thatto Hall Farm during the small hours. Whoever it was had taken the jewel case, having at the time the intention of making the intrusion look like robbery. Later, abandoning this idea as likely to deceive no one and not wishing to be encumbered with some not very valuable jewellery, he had thrown it away, item by item, as he fled from the house.

He had known the house, he had known about that window. He had known Mrs Knighton would be alone. He had cut out that pane of glass and rested the cut-out pieces neatly up against the wall, entered silently, gone upstairs and awakened the sleeping woman. She had been forced to get up and walk downstairs ahead of him at gunpoint. The gun had been pressed against the back of her skull and she had been gripped by the upper arm. There, in the dining room – because she had refused to show him something, tell him something, lead him somewhere, promise, betray, give? – he had pressed the trigger and she had fallen forward, dead on the floor.

That was what he thought had happened. It would do as a working hypothesis.

'Knighton,' said Wexford, 'says he left home at three on Tuesday afternoon, having phoned for a car to take him to Kingsmarkham station, and caught the three-twenty-seven train. He has a car, a Volvo estate, but he says his wife wanted to use it and if he had let her drive him to Kingsmarkham it would have delayed her.'

'Where was she going?' Burden asked. They were in the car, being driven to London.

'Shopping in Myringham. A regular Tuesday afternoon exercise, apparently. Knighton got to Victoria at four-fifteen and from there he went by tube to Lancaster Gate and walked the short distance to the flat of a friend of his called Adrian Dobson-Flint in Hyde Park Gardens, Dobson-Flint having arrived home a little earlier than usual to let him in.

'This dinner at the Palimpsest Club was at seven for

seven-thirty. He and Dobson-Flint left Hyde Park Gardens in a cab at ten to seven, remained at the club having their dinner and generally merry-making until eleven-thirty, at which time they left and walked home. There they had something to drink and went to bed at about half-past midnight. Dobson-Flint had to be in the Old Bailey by ten in the morning, so they were both up by eight. Dobson-Flint left soon after nine and Knighton about nine-twenty, catching the nine-forty train to Kingsmarkham from Victoria.'

'You suspect him,' said Burden.

'Not really. Only I don't know who else to suspect. Early days, I daresay. She left a will, by the way. Angus Norris told me all about it without waiting to be asked. His firm were her solicitors. Adela Knighton had quite a bit of money of her own, a few thousand inherited from an aunt, another few from an uncle, parents' property, as like as not some share in a family trust. Anyway, there was two hundred thousand and she left it equally between her four kids.

'Julian, the son in Washington, is married to an American woman whose father is some sort of millionaire. Roderick has a thriving law practice and his wife's got her own employment agency. Colum, the youngest – he's thirty – is an attaché at the British Embassy in Ankara and whether or not he was looking to his inheritance there's no doubt he was in Turkey at three on Wednesday morning.

'I jib a bit at the idea of a woman seven months pregnant killing her own mother. On the other hand, she wouldn't have had to get in the window. She, apart from Knighton himself and Mrs Thompson, was the only person to have a key to the house. She would certainly have known her father was going to be away for the night and her mother would be alone. But where's her motive? The fifty grand she would inherit? Norris is only an assistant solicitor but he's obviously no fool and likely to be a partner one day. They live in Springhill Lane which is hardly a milieu for people short of the ready. We can put them on one side for the moment. Julian and his wife were in Washington, Colum, as I said, in Ankara and Roderick is alibi'd – if he needs an alibi – by his wife, his au pair, his unfortunate GP and

273

no doubt would be by his mumps-stricken daughter if we asked her.'

The chambers of which Adrian Dobson-Flint was a member were those to which Adam Knighton had formerly belonged. It was the death, and such a death, of Knighton's wife which was presumably responsible for the expression of discreet woe on the face of the Clerk to Chambers, a man called Brownrigg, who showed Wexford and Burden into Dobson-Flint's room.

Adam Knighton's friend was some seven or eight years younger than he, a man who must have been improved by his barrister's wig, for he was almost totally hairless. Since his face was unlined, pink and youthful-looking, this gave him something of the appearance of a skinhead. His room too was untypical, neither dusty and dark nor a litter of books, but a coolly, creamily painted office with fawn carpet and mahogany furniture, a view of a little enclosed garden and a window that let in sunlight.

'In what way can I be of assistance to you gentlemen?'

The skinhead image was quickly dispelled by Dobson-Flint's gracious, modulated voice. It too held the requisite, muted note of sorrow. The baby face contorted into a twist of petulant distress.

'I must say this is really the most shocking and appalling thing I ever heard.'

Which, if it were true, would give a very curious slant to the man's courtroom activities over the past quarter of a century or so. Wexford asked him for an account of Tuesday evening. In discussing alibis, times, reasons why persons should be in such and such a place rather than in another, Dobson-Flint was very much at home. And in spite of having heard his voice raised in public almost every day for many years, he was still fond of the sound of it. He discoursed lucidly, mellifluously, on the dinner party, the date some weeks previously on which invitations to it had been received, the time of Knighton's arrival at his flat, the time of their departure for and arrival at the Palimpsest. There was a note of faint amusement, such as would have been present had he been playing with a witness like a fly fisherman tickling a salmon. Underlying it seemed to be the unspoken question:

274

Are you so obtuse that you can even remotely consider my old friend Adam Knighton under suspicion of murder?'

His distress at the death of his friend's wife, if he had ever felt it, now seemed forgotten. His pale blue eyes twinkled. He sat back in his chair with his legs crossed at the knees, one arm resting negligently on the arm of the chair, the other hand supporting his chin.

'It being a fine clear night,' he said, 'we resolved not to indulge ourselves with a cab but instead, in short, to walk it. We arrived on my doorstep at precisely two minutes to midnight. And now, Chief Inspector, you will ask me in time-honoured fashion how I can be so sure of the time, will you not? And my answer will be to you that as I raised my hand to insert my latchkey in the lock Mr Knighton informed me of the time, remarking that twenty-eight minutes from St James's to the Bayswater Road was not bad for two men no longer in their first or indeed second youth.'

With people of Dobson-Flint's kind Wexford generally allowed his own manner to become dull and dead-sounding, and it was in a leaden voice that he asked, 'You live alone, sir?'

'Oh, yes, and have done these twenty years since my wife and I reached an amicable agreement to part.'

Wexford made no comment on this marital revelation. Dobson-Flint said, 'Shall I proceed? Mr Knighton and I each took a glass of Chivas Regal whisky and retired to our beds at approximately twenty-past twelve. I say "approximately", because this time Mr Knighton did not happen to make any remark upon the time. At seven forty-five or thereabouts in the morning I rose up, took my bath, girded my loins and was about to enter Mr Knighton's room with a cup of China tea when he appeared, fully-dressed, and announcing his kind intention of taking breakfast with me. At nine-ten, as is my wont, I departed to win my bread, leaving Mr Knighton to go on his way rejoicing, though in point of fact it was rather to a weeping, a wailing and a gnashing of teeth.'

'Yes, sir. Did Mr Knighton often stay with you?'

'Often is an imprecise adverb,' said Dobson-Flint in his best Central Criminal Court manner. 'A man might say "I often go abroad", implying he leaves the country three or four times a year, but he may equally aver, "I often visit a cinema", meaning in this case that he attends a picture palace twice a week.' He smiled.

'And which would be true of Mr Knighton's overnight stays with you?'

'Neither!' said Dobson-Flint triumphantly. 'It would probably be true to say that, in the three years since his retirement and removal to the country, he has stayed with me on an average one and a half times per year.'

Wexford got up. 'I expect you'll be having a lunchtime break now, sir?'

'If you will excuse me, Chief Inspector.'

'I didn't quite mean that, Mr Dobson-Flint. I meant that since you'll no doubt be free for the next hour or so, we might use the time in having a look at this flat of yours. '

'Oh, come, is that necessary?'

In the same deadening voice Wexford said, 'It's essential. I have a car. You won't be much inconvenienced.'

Hyde Park Gardens, the mid-nineteenth-century terrace which faces the Bayswater Road and Hyde Park at the Lancaster Gate, is divided by Brook Street into two sections. The eastern part is older, larger and rather grander. Here the Sri Lankans have their embassy, and from a house once owned by the mysterious Duke of Portland (who went about always in a black veil) legend has it a secret passage runs underground to Baker Street. However, it was in the western terrace of Hyde Park Gardens that Adrian Dobson-Flint had his flat. Wexford had been into the block once before, years ago, and then had gone in through the front entrance, up the steps, through double doors, past the porters' office and up the wide curving staircase. He expected to do so again but Dobson-Flint directed the taxi into Stanhope Place which runs along the back of Hyde Park Gardens and led them up to the front door of a flat which though on the ground floor at the back would have to be designated 'basement' or 'lower ground floor' at the front. It took Wexford no more than a few seconds to realize that it was only from these flats which had access to Stanhope Place that occupants of Hyde Park Gardens could come and go without passing through the front entrance or chancing an encounter with porters.

On the doorstep Wexford said, 'What time did Mr Knighton get here on Tuesday afternoon?'

'I was back here by five,' said Dobson-Flint. 'Shall we say ten past? Yes, I should say about ten past.'

They went inside. There were two bedrooms, the spare one being the nearer to the front door. Dobson-Flint had dropped his keys into a shallow pewter dish which stood on a console table and which already contained another bunch of keys and car keys attached to a fob.

'Are you a heavy sleeper, Mr Dobson-Flint?' Burden asked.

'I succeed in sleeping through some of the worst traffic noise in London, so I should say yes, I am.'

There was nothing else of interest to see. Wexford said, 'I suppose Mr and Mrs Knighton were a happy couple?'

He didn't expect a frank answer but he wanted to see just what sort of answer he would get. Dobson-Flint replied with a kind of forced impatient enthusiasm.

'Oh, absolutely devoted. They simply adored each other. The Knightons were what is generally called a very united family. Until this fearful tragedy struck them Mr and Mrs Knighton lived for each other. I can't imagine either of them ever having had eyes for anyone else!'

He refused Wexford's offer of a lift back and departed in a taxi, leaving them in the street outside his front door.

Wexford said thoughtfully, 'He doth protest too much.'

'About the Knightons' mutual devotion, do you mean?' asked Burden.

'That was a strange remark. "I can't imagine either of them ever having had eyes for anyone else." It's not the sort of thing that would come to mind at all when considering the domestic happiness or otherwise of people in their sixties. Why did he mention it? It's a funny thing, Mike, but I keep having this feeling that what's happened in this case, and maybe is happening, ought to be to people thirty years younger than the Knightons. I've got a feeling this was a crime of passion, yet any less likely candidate for passion than Mrs Knighton I've yet to see.'

'And that bald-headed stuffed shirt feels it too?'

'Harsh words, Mike. But maybe, yes, I think he does.

277

Knighton could have gone back to Sussex during the night, shot his wife and returned here hours before Dobson-Flint started fiddling about with his Lapsang-Souchong.'

'How? There's no train between the twelve fifty-five and the six-forty.'

'It doesn't have to be by train. In fact, train would have been no use to him since he couldn't have got from Kingsmarkham to Sewingbury at the other end. But he could have done it by car.'

'We know he didn't. His car was in the garage at Thatto Hall Farm.'

'Listen, Mike. What was he doing between getting to Victoria at four-fifteen and arriving at Hyde Park Gardens at ten-past five? Fifty-five minutes to get from Victoria to Lancaster Gate? There's something he could have been doing. He could have been in a local car hire place, renting a car, and returning it next morning.

'All he had to do was book himself a car by phone and turn up to collect it at four forty-five, drive it here and leave it on a meter. It looks to me as if the whole of this area is metered, I noticed as we were coming along. Metering ends at six-thirty so he'd only have to put his money in for an hour and a half. After Dobson-Flint's gone to bed he leaves the flat, helping himself to a key out of that pewter plate thing, retrieves his hired car and drives to Sewingbury – an hour's drive at that time of night. He lets himself in by the front door, awakens Adela and shoots her, takes her jewel case. Then he cuts the pane out of the loo window. On his way back to the road where he has left the car parked on the verge he discards the jewellery and the case. An hour later he's back in Hyde Park Gardens and it's still only three-thirty. How about that?'

'He was taking a hell of a risk,' said Burden. 'Suppose Dobson-Flint had gone into his room?'

'Never! Can you imagine it? Not those sort of people, they never would. Their sons might, yes, but never those two. Dobson-Flint would have gone in there only if Knighton had cried out and even then he'd have hesitated.'

'By the way,' said Burden as they got back into the car, 'his son lives in London. Why couldn't he stay with him?'

'Roderick Knighton and his wife live in Mill Hill, quite a

way out. Too far out if you're depending on public transport and taxis. Or I think that's what Knighton would say. The truth may of course be that if he was planning a small hours murder trip the Bayswater Road is a good deal nearer to Sussex.'

Men were searching for the weapon in the grass verges, the hedges, the fields, the footpaths, even wading in the Kingsbrook itself where it flowed through Thatto Vale. Wexford asked himself if the gun had belonged to Knighton. A retired counsel who had been at the criminal bar might well know where to acquire an automatic. The little gun, it had been discovered from a hairline scratch on the bullet that had killed Adela Knighton, had a tiny pinhead-sized protuberance, a minute wart-like flaw, on the inside of its barrel.

It was a damp chilly day, rather colder than usual for the time of year and darker than usual for the time of day. The surrounding hills and woodland were blanketed in grey mist. The gun might be hidden anywhere in there, a tiny metal tube in innumerable tons of earth, leaf mould and water. Or it might be cleaned and polished, folded in a soft cloth, put away in a drawer. He went up the drive to Thatto Hall Farm.

Julian Knighton with his wife Barbara had arrived that morning from America. Julian was shortish, thick-set like his mother, moon-faced like his mother, perhaps forty years old. The Knightons had evidently belonged in that category of couples who, like the Queen, had had two families. The first pair, the two older sons, must surely have been about ten and eight years old before Jennifer was born, and then they had had another son two or three years later, the still absent Colum.

Adam Knighton looked ill, stricken with suffering. His face was drawn in under the cheekbones. Wexford remembered how astounded he had been, how disbelieving, when first told of his wife's death. Only a brilliant actor could have feigned that. He looked at the chief inspector with sunken haunted eyes. The pregnant Mrs Norris reclined in an armchair with her feet up. Barbara Knighton was drinking something from a glass that might have been iced tea or heavily diluted whisky. Her husband presented Wexford with a theory.

'It strikes me as being highly probable he expected to find a safe, Chief Inspector. My father did in fact have a safe in this house at one time but when break-ins became so frequent in Sewingbury he had it taken out. Its presence did seem to advertise that one had rather special things to protect.'

'It was while we were still using this house as a weekend retreat,' said his father. 'On a Sunday night before we left to go back to Hampstead I used to put our few valuables in the safe. Could he have been looking for that? Is that at all feasible? Do you think it conceivable my wife was shot by accident? That this man threatened her with the gun if she refused to reveal the whereabouts of the safe to him and when she did refuse the gun went off by accident? Is that at all a useful theory?'

The man had been a distinguished, even brilliant, counsel. It was hard to believe it in the face of this nonsense. Wexford remembered reading of him in the newspapers, 'Mr Adam Knighton, defending . . .' 'Mr Adam Knighton's masterly presentation of the prosecution's case . . .' Something soft and weak had come into the hard aquiline face. When they were in China it had been like the face of some noble bird of prey but now it was as if those features had been made of wax and a warm hand had passed, smudging, across them. There had been a pathetic loosening of the muscles around the mouth. The uncomfortable thought came to Wexford, became a conviction, that when he was alone, when he went to his bedroom and shut the door on all those sympathizing considerate children, he wept. His face was the face of a man who has soaked it with tears.

'Have you ever possessed a gun, sir?' The question was addressed to Julian Knighton who exclaimed, 'Good God, no! Certainly not!'

Wexford's eyes rested on Adam Knighton.

'When I first came here and fancied myself a week-end country gentleman I had a shotgun. I sold it five years ago.'

Jennifer Norris whispered something to her sister-in-law. They both looked truculently at Wexford.

'I should like to have another look over the house, if I may,' he said.

'I thought my brother made it plain the safe isn't here any more,' said Jennifer Norris in the tone of a nineteenth-century chatelaine addressing a bailiff.

'Quite plain, thank you.' Wexford looked at Adam Knighton.

'You must do as you please, Chief Inspector.'

Wexford closed the living-room door after him and went upstairs to the bedroom where Adela Knighton had slept alone that Tuesday night and from where she had been peremptorily and terrifyingly summoned. Since his last visit the bed had been made. There was nothing to be learned from a perusal of Mrs Knighton's clothes. Their pockets, as were her handbags, were empty. On the windowsill, between looped-up rose-printed curtains, stood a china candlestick, a pomander and book ends encompassing the reading matter of someone who stopped reading when she was in her teens: two or three Jeffery Farnols, *Precious Bane*, *The Story of an African Farm*, C.S. Lewis's *Mere Christianity*, Mrs Gaskell's *Cranford*. Wexford was looking for something he hadn't been consciously looking for when, two days before, he had searched the desk downstairs.

The dressing table had only one drawer. He opened it. Handkerchiefs, a box of tissues, a card of hairclips, two unused face flannels, a cardboard carton of cotton wool. Mahogany bedside cabinets supported pink porcelain lamps with pink tulle shades. Each cabinet had a drawer. In Mrs Knighton's were a bottle of aspirin, two more handkerchiefs, an old-fashioned silver-handled manicure set, nasal drops, a pair of glasses in a case; in Knighton's a pair of glasses in a case, two ballpoint pens, a scribbling pad, a tube of throat pastilles and a battery shaver in a leather case. Each cabinet had a cupboard under its drawer. Mrs Knighton's held a pair of black corded velvet bedroom slippers and a brown leather photograph album, Knighton's a stack of books, evidently his reading-in-bed for some weeks or months past, for the present and possibly the immediate future. They were, to Wexford, an unexpected collection.

Han Suyin's *A Mortal Flower* and a book of linguistics

called *About Chinese*. Understandable inclusions, those two. The man had recently been in China. *Anna Karenina*, *The Return of the Native*, Elizabeth Barrett's *Sonnets from the Portuguese* and *The Browning Love Letters*. Wexford looked at them, intrigued. 'Romantic' was the word that had come into his mind. With the exception of that linguistics book they were all voluptuously romantic. They seemed highly unlikely reading matter for that white-haired, dried-up, unhappy old lawyer downstairs. Yet they must be there because he had read them, was reading them now or had at any rate intended to read them.

He opened *Sonnets from the Portuguese* where the place ('If thou must love me, let it be for naught Except for love's sake only . . .') was kept by a marker. The marker was a scrap of paper torn from the scribbling pad and on it, in Knighton's stylized 'ronde' handwriting, were written a few lines of verse. Not Elizabeth Barrett, nor the piece Knighton had quoted leaning over the parapet in Kweilin, but a fragment that was also, unmistakably, Chinese poetry:

> Shoot not the wild geese from the south;
> Let them northward fly.
> When you do shoot, shoot the pair of them,
> So that the two may not be put asunder.

Very curious indeed. Of course it might be assumed that Knighton had written that down after his wife's death, after someone had in fact shot her and put the two of them asunder. Somehow Wexford didn't think so. Those words hadn't been written since Tuesday. The paper was creased from many usings, many insertions into that volume of sonnets. And when he went out on to the landing again and looked through the open doorway of the 'green' bedroom opposite, he saw the bedcover turned down and a brown plaid dressing gown lying over a chair. Temporarily, the widower had removed himself from the room he had shared with his wife.

They were still in the living room, all four of them. Jennifer Norris still reclined with her feet up. She and her father were drinking tea. Barbara Knighton was arranging the last roses of summer in a copper bowl, October blooms from a second or third flowering. They were a little pale and worn, those roses, with a papery look.

'Just one thing, Mr Knighton. What has become of the photographs you and Mrs Knighton took while you were on holiday?'

'Photographs?'

'They aren't in the album I found in Mrs Knighton's bedside table, though pictures from your previous holidays are.'

'Probably you didn't take any this time, did you, Father?'

Knighton hesitated. Wexford guessed he might clutch at the straw Julian offered him and to prevent this said firmly, 'I don't think there's much doubt that both you and Mrs Knighton took photographs, do you?'

Their eyes met. Wexford wondered if he was reading the other man's expression accurately. Or was he imagining the reaction that nothing could have been less fortunate than that he and this policeman had happened to encounter each other on that Chinese holiday? 'We did take a few snaps, yes,' he said languidly. 'If they came out, if they were ever developed, no doubt they're somewhere about the house.'

But they were not.

Wexford said no more about it. He pondered on Adam Knighton, his wistful predilection for romance, his listless, sometimes hag-ridden or haunted look, the possibility that he who loved poetry and the great love stories, had held a gun to his wife's scalp and sent a bullet into her brain.

The inquest was on Monday morning, the funeral the following day at All Saints, Sewingbury. By that time it had been established that no car hire company within a three-mile radius of Adrian Dobson-Flint's home had hired a car to a man answering Adam Knighton's description. By then the search for the gun in the vicinity of Thatto Vale had been called off.

Sewingbury has about four thousand inhabitants, a golf course, a convent and girls' school, a disused mill on the Kingsbrook and a huge market square, usually packed tight with parked cars. The church is half-way down the hill that leads to the river and the new 'weir'. Wexford's driver took the route along Springhill Lane, over the newly built bridge, along the river bank past where the footpath from Thatto Vale comes out and up River Street.

All the Knighton family were assembled, Adam, lean, gaunt, bareheaded, wearing a waisted black overcoat, Roderick in a dark suit with a black tie and Roderick's wife Caroline in a tight black suit and high-heeled black patent shoes. Julian and his wife were in light colours, grey and green respectively, but wore the most doleful expressions, perhaps to compensate. The fair young man with the beaky nose and the thin dark Greek-looking girl Wexford decided must be Colum and his wife. Only Jennifer was absent, though represented by her husband who arrived late and on foot.

Leaving the church when it was all over, after the family had filed out, Wexford, who had been sitting in the very back row, happened to look over his shoulder along the aisle. The small elderly woman he remembered from China as Adela Knighton's friend was walking towards him from where she had been sitting in one of the front pews. He had forgotten all about her until now.

He could tell she was astounded at seeing him. She looked at him as he must have looked when he saw his persecutor with the bound feet. And then her eyes turned sharply away.

Wexford went out and waited for her in the porch.

10

'My name is Irene Bell. I don't believe we were ever introduced in China.'

'Chief Inspector Wexford of Kingsmarkham CID. How do you do, Miss Bell?'

'So you're a policeman and living here. How very odd! That must have been quite a shock for poor Adam on top of everything else. He's very cut up, isn't he? Well, we all are. Adela and I were at school together, we'd known each other nearly all our lives. I suppose we'd been friends for something like half a century.'

'It's a long time,' said Wexford. 'Can you and I have a talk, Miss Bell?'

'Now, d'you mean? I suppose so. I wouldn't go back to the house anyway. I don't care for all this eating and drinking at funerals. People don't mean to be irreverent but somehow they forget what they're there for, someone starts laughing and before you know where you are it's turned into a party. I call that very bad taste.'

Wexford nodded in agreement. She seemed a woman of character. 'I'll see you get to Kingsmarkham station afterwards. You wouldn't think a cup of tea irreverent, would you?'

'I could do with a cup of good hot tea,' said Miss Bell.

She was short and sturdily built, though not fat, with a round sharp-featured face and dark hair that still hadn't much grey in it and was crisply permed. The blue trouser suit would have been unsuitable for today and in any case too light in weight, for the previous night had seen the first frost of the winter and a little white frost still lay in shady places. She had on a dark grey tweed suit, beige silk blouse and black court shoes that were nevertheless 'sensible' ones. Up until three years before, she told Wexford, she had been the manager of a travel agency at Swiss Cottage near where she lived. In fact it was this agency that had arranged the trans-Asia trip for her and the Knightons. It wasn't the first time the three of them had been away together. She had gone with them to Egypt as well as on various European holidays. It was company for Adela, she said, which Wexford thought an interesting remark.

Back in Kingsmarkham Wexford took her into the Willow Pattern, a café in the High Street, and ordered tea for two. Irene Bell refused food, perhaps once again on the grounds of the unsuitability of eating just after one has buried one's best friend. For this was what Mrs Knighton had evidently been, a devoted dear friend, as close as a sister, and when Miss Bell referred to her in this way a look of heavy bitter sadness came into her sharp face. She was, she said, godmother to Jennifer, 'Aunt Irene' to all the young Knightons, as nearly a member of the family as one could be who was not allied by blood. Wexford let her talk for a while about her long friendship with the dead woman, noting that though she referred to all Mrs Knighton's children by name and spoke of their children, Adam Knighton was never mentioned. He interrupted her by reverting to what she had said in the car.

'You said you were company for Mrs Knighton. Wasn't her husband company enough for her?'

She lifted her shoulders and gave a half-smile.

'Was it a happy marriage, Miss Bell?'

'Someone said the state of marriage is unhappy only insofar as life itself is unhappy.'

'Samuel Johnson said it. What do you say?'

'In general, Mr Wexford, I don't think much of it. It goes on too long. If it could be for five years, say, I think it would be an excellent institution. Who can stand the same person morning, noon and night for forty years? People think a single woman of my age hasn't married because she hasn't had the chance. That's not so of course.' Irene Bell chuckled. It was a grim chuckle that hadn't much to do with amusement or pleasure. 'I'm not much to look at and never have been but neither are most of the married women you see around you. If folks only got married because they were pretty or charming it'd be a world of singles. No, I never fancied marriage myself. I don't much like sharing. I don't like cooking or housework or babies or sex. Oh, yes, I've tried sex. I tried it three times forty years ago and those three times were enough for a lifetime in my opinion.

'But those are my views. That's marriage in general. In particular, which is what you're asking, I daresay the Knightons were as happy as most people. She was very fond of *him*, poor Adela. She made her choice and she stuck to it and she was a good wife, no one could have had a better wife.'

You don't like him, Wexford thought to himself. Or is it more complex than that? Is it that once you liked him too much?

'They never had much to say to each other. That's partly what I mean when I say I don't think much of marriage. How else do we communicate but in words when all's said and done? You hear a lot of nonsense about the language of the eyes, the language of love, silent communion, all that kind of thing. There wasn't anything of that sort with Adela and Adam, I can tell you. Adela wasn't that sort of woman anyway. Adam – well, it always seems a funny thing to me, a man who reads poetry.'

'Most of it was written by men.'

'That's different,' said Miss Bell. 'Don't confuse me. I mean it's not very robust, it's affected, if you ask me, a man reading – what d'you call 'em? – sonnets.'

Wexford said abruptly, 'Was he unfaithful to her? Did he have love affairs with other women?'

She was taken aback. She had been raising her teacup to her lips. The motion was arrested in mid-air then slowly she restored the cup to the saucer. 'Good God, no. What an extraordinary idea! He was sixty-three.'

'He wasn't always sixty-three. In any case he's a very handsome man, with what I'd call an attractive presence.' Wexford paused. How intimate they had become, how frank, in ten minutes over the teacups! It seemed at that moment as if there were nothing they couldn't have said to each other. It was a pity she hadn't more to say. 'There's many a man of sixty-three,' he said, 'would be horrified at a suggestion his emotional life was over.'

She gave a short, rather harsh, cackle. 'See the day looming yourself, can you? No, there was nothing like that with Adam, you can forget that. Who would he carry on with? Never saw a woman but the vicar's wife. If you're thinking he shot poor Adela to take up with someone else, you're cold like they say in "hunt the thimble", you're stone cold. Adam wouldn't point a gun at anyone, let alone fire it. He gave up shooting pigeons because he said it wasn't ethical. I once saw him get stung by a wasp trying to put it out of the window because he wouldn't kill it.' She laughed again, then set down her cup with a rattle. 'I knew it!' she said. 'This is turning into a party, a beanfeast, and I'm not having it. I call it very bad taste. It was good of you to give me tea but now you'll take me to the station, please.'

Wexford pleaded, 'Five more minutes, Miss Bell, and I promise I will. I want to ask you something about China. Do you remember when we were all sitting in that bar on the hotel roof in Kweilin?'

She was putting on her gloves. 'The temperature was ninety and they were playing "White Christmas". Of course I remember.'

'Mr Knighton had a shock. He went white. He saw something or someone and he was absolutely astounded by what he saw. Did you notice that?'

'I can't say I did.'

'A minute or two later Mrs Knighton said she thought she would go to bed and you and she got up to leave.'

'Maybe, but I don't remember.'

'And the next day he didn't mention it to you? Or to Mrs Knighton in your presence? I mean, he didn't say "Something I saw on the roof last night amazed me"?'

'No, he didn't. Why don't you ask *him*?'

'I will. You took a lot of photographs. So did Mrs Knighton. Did she show you the ones she took?'

'Weeks ago,' said Irene Bell. 'She came up to town. She

always had lunch with me when she did that. We had lunch and we looked at each other's snaps.'

'What did she do with hers?'

'Took them away, of course. She was going to put them in an album she'd got.'

Up in his office on the second floor of the police station he found Burden and Dr Crocker talking about guns. Burden even had a replica of a Walther PPK 9 mm, one which they had taken off a young tearaway who had threatened a visiting pop star with it and which, after the case was over, had unaccountably got into Wexford's desk drawer and remained there ever since.

'I feel more at home with a scalpel,' said the doctor. 'Had a nice funeral, Reg? It beats me why people who aren't religious have funerals. Boring, embarrassing, awkward affairs with no grace or beauty to them now the old prayer book's more or less gone.'

'You have to have a funeral, don't you?' said Burden.

'If you mean by law, certainly not. People have them because they think they've got to but they haven't. You can just get your undertaker to do a quiet little disposal when the crematorium's not busy. Nothing to it. Mind you, it'll cost you much the same. Five hundred quid give or take a little, that's what a funeral comes to these days.'

Wexford, who had been silent, sat down at his desk and, taking the replica gun, turned it slowly over and over in his hands, saying, 'He was sitting on that roof, drinking cassia wine, and suddenly he saw something that utterly astounded him. Not something unpleasant, mark you, rather the reverse. I could almost hazard a guess he saw something wonderful. But what did he see?'

'A pretty girl,' said the doctor.

'Oh, come on. You'd only look like that when you saw a pretty girl if you'd been shut up in solitary confinement for the past twenty years.'

'An old friend?' said Burden. 'Someone maybe he'd defended in court years ago and thought he'd never see again?'

'In that case why didn't he immediately get up and go and

speak to him? Why did he go and lean over the parapet and start muttering Chinese poetry?'

'You'd better ask him.'

'I will, but I'm sure he'll lie about it. One of the things we have to do is find out just who knew he was going to be away last Tuesday night. We haven't done much about that but it's on the cards a good many people did know. Everyone at that Golden Jubilee party at the Palimpsest Club for a start. Probably most of Mrs Knighton's acquaintances in Sewingbury. Friends or relations she may have written to or talked to on the phone.'

'You mean,' said the doctor, 'it's a bit fishy it happened that night. I mean here's a chap stays away from his home once a year and on the very night he's away his wife gets murdered.'

'At any rate it teaches us that it was planned. It may have been planned by one of those people who knew he'd be away or it may have been planned by Knighton himself in collusion with someone else or Knighton may have done it alone.'

'Everyone in Hyde Park Gardens,' said Burden, 'is being questioned as to the possibility of their having seen Knighton that night.' He hesitated, said in a rather embarrassed way, 'You may think this very far-fetched . . .'

Wexford countered, 'I'm the one that gets accused of that.'

'Maybe it's infectious. Maybe it's because I – well, I sort of read more than I used.' It was well-known that Burden's cultured wife was in the habit of recommending books to him, was one of those rare people who like being read to and had discovered in her husband an unexpected histrionic talent for reading aloud. Burden's face had become a little pink. 'Fiction, you know. I must admit to having read only novels lately.'

Wexford exploded into a quotation from Jane Austen.

'Only novels! Only some work in which the most thorough knowledge of human nature, the happiest delineation of its varieties, the liveliest effusions of wit and humour are conveyed to the world in the best chosen language!'

'O.K., let him tell us his idea,' said Crocker.

'It's just that – well, it sounds like something out of Conan

Doyle really. On the other hand, you do read in the papers sometimes . . . ' Seeing Wexford's eyes sharpening with rage, Burden went on hurriedly, 'You hear of old lags, or any villains really, getting sent down by a judge and swearing to get back at him later. Right? And I'm pretty sure I've come across actual cases – attempts anyway. It did strike me it might be something like that which had happened here.'

'Knighton wasn't a judge.'

'No, but someone accused of a crime in a case where he was prosecuting might feel much the same towards him as towards the judge. He might easily feel that Knighton's presentation of the evidence against him had more effect on the jury than the judge's summing up. Say that because of what Knighton said for the prosecution some guy either got convicted when he expected to be acquitted or got sent down for twice as long as he anticipated, mightn't he then resolve to get back at Knighton when he came out? And I reckon Knighton's prosecuted in dozens of possible cases. His name was always in the papers.'

'You mean this chap shot Mrs Knighton to get revenge on her husband?' Wexford was interested. He didn't dislike the idea. 'It's a possibility, especially if as you say Knighton got him put away for ten years instead of four or five. Wouldn't he shoot Knighton, though?'

'There's many a married man,' said Burden, 'whose life wouldn't be worth living without his wife.' He gave the doctor an uneasy look as if he expected to be laughed at. 'I know I felt that way when Jean died and if it doesn't sound too ridiculous I'd feel it now about Jenny.' The others didn't laugh but Burden himself did in a high embarrassed sort of way.

'Knighton had been married a very long time too,' said Crocker. 'If you believed the funny postcards and the cartoons and whatever you'd think that made people less fond. But it doesn't. The long habit of the years, the shared things, the curious kind of oneness – my God! You haven't had a chance yet, young Mike. You don't know the half of it.'

And nor did Irene Bell, thought Wexford. He quoted:

'Shoot not the wild geese from the south;

291

Let them northward fly.
When you shoot, shoot the pair of them,
So that the two may not be put asunder.'

'Where did you get that from?'

Wexford told them. 'I got the library here to trace it for me. It's a Chinese poem from a collection of T'ang verse, ninth century. The poet was called Shen Hsun and a curious note to it is that he and his wife were murdered by a slave.

'We keep coming back to China, don't we? I've got a feeling, I've had it almost since the murder really, that the key to all this was in China.'

'You can't very well go back there,' said the doctor.

'No, but I can at least see the people Adela Knighton travelled across Asia with. I met them too, remember. There were some strange things . . . ' He told them about the two men who hadn't spoken to each other from Irkutsk to Kweilin, about Wong who had drowned. 'She and he took photographs in China, they were always making with the camera. What's happened to those photographs? Why aren't they in her album or sculling about the house in packets? No, I'm more and more sure it's to China and what happened there that we have to look. I just wish I'd taken more notice. I wasn't to know, of course, but usually I like watching people, seeing how they behave. I was too damned preoccupied with that woman with the bound feet.'

Crocker looked at him. 'What woman?'

Diffidently Wexford told him. He had often felt he should have told him long before but he never had. When the symptoms disappear who cares about the cause of the disease? Crocker, who hadn't even smiled at Burden's marital confidings, now burst out laughing.

'What had you been reading?'

'O.K., I know, something called *Masterpieces of the Supernatural* and I never finished it.'

'I wouldn't have your imagination for all the tea in China.'

'Sure, but all hallucinations are from the imagination. That doesn't make them any less real to the hallucinator. D'you think it was just that book and lack of sleep?'

'And getting dehydrated and drinking that filthy Maotai you brought home a bottle of.'

'Start getting worried,' said Burden, 'when you see the lady tottering over the Kingsbrook Bridge.'

Wexford gave him a bland look. 'We mustn't risk not investigating the possibilities of this revenge motive, so you can make it your business to inquire into the present circumstances of every villain Knighton prosecuted in, say, the fifteen years prior to his retirement. And for good measure into those of every villain he failed successfully to defend. That should keep you busy for a bit.

'As for me, I shall "fire a mine in China here with sympathetic gunpowder".'

11

Donaldson went off to find somewhere to park the car and Wexford crossed Kensington Church Street to the shop above whose window in gilt Times Roman was the single name 'Vinald'. In the window itself, in solitary splendour, stood a vase. Not one of those Vinald had collected in China, but a vessel as tall as a small man and of dully gleaming black porcelain with a design on it of a blood-red gilt-clawed dragon.

Inside, deep soft black carpet like cat's fur. The place was discreetly lit by wall lights in gilt rococo brackets and by a single spot that fell upon a spinet or harpsichord or some such thing. A few other *objets d'antiquité* were set about the long room, wax fruit under a glass bell, a china clock around whose face a Chelsea china Eros and Psyche sported, a tall slender glass jug, and on a console table a book of Audubon prints open at a picture of green and yellow birds.

Wexford introduced himself to the woman in charge and asked for Gordon Vinald. She was afraid Mr Vinald was at a sale and not expected back until late afternoon. Was it very important? Wexford said yes but he would come back.

'Would it help to see Mrs Vinald? I know she's in. She phoned just a couple of minutes ago.'

Surely he hadn't been married when Wexford had last seen him? 'I didn't know there was a Mrs Vinald.'

She smiled in the way people do who find something sweet or touching about matrimony in its early stages. 'Mr and Mrs Vinald have only been married a month. Shall I give her a ring? Their house is just round the corner in Searle Villas.'

He realized what had happened. Hadn't he foreseen it? Vinald had married Margery Baumann.

'Mrs Vinald says if you'd like to go straight over, Mr Wexford, she'll be happy to see you.'

Searle Villas was indeed just round the corner. The garden of number sixteen must have backed on to the shop. It was a house in a Victorian terrace that no one would have looked at twice in Kingsmarkham but here was no doubt worth about half a million. He was admitted by a young black woman in jeans with a duster in her hand. She pushed a door open and said to him indifferently, 'She's in there.'

The room was a museum, seemingly furnished with over-flow from the shop. In the middle of the Chinese carpet sat a very large stout lushly-furred tabby cat which ceased washing itself to stare at him with glittering zircon eyes. Standing by the marble fireplace, one white arm extended along the mantel, was the beautiful black-haired Pandora.

She didn't recognize him. Probably she hadn't even noticed him on that previous occasion. While a man of Wexford's age will inevitably notice and remember such a woman, to her he may be invisible.

Her hair was longer, cut now with a fringe that curved symmetrically down into a page-boy, the Egyptian queen look. Her mouth was as red as cinnabar and her eyelids painted jade. Wexford felt that either he had seen her before – and he meant before the encounter on the hotel roof – or that she reminded him strikingly of some famous beauty. A film star from when he was young? Hedy Lamarr? Lupe Velez? She wore a clinging black silk jersey and a skirt of black and red printed velvet and her legs were the best he had ever seen, better even, he thought disloyally, than his daughter Sheila's.

'I think you've come to talk about the late Mrs Knighton. Am I right?'

He was surprised and his eyebrows went up.

'What else could it be?' Her twang brought her down to earth, made her less of a goddess. 'I travelled with her to

295

Hong Kong. Well, all the way to England, if you count being in the airplane. Don't you care to sit down?'

The cat leapt – gracefully for one of her girth – up on to the chair before he could sit in it.

'Oh, get out, Selima.' She picked it up and dumped it on to a chaise longue. 'She's called the Pensive Selima for some reason known to my husband, some poem.'

'Demurest of the tabby kind,' said Wexford.

'Maybe. I'm not poetical myself.' In a way she was, though. Any man would have wanted to write a poem to her or about her. But with a faint feeling of disappointment he saw what she meant. Despite her looks, the Hollywood profile, she was of the earth, earthy. 'So what can I do for you?'

'I don't know, Mrs Vinald, I'm a bit in the dark. You didn't travel on that train across Asia, did you?'

She shook her head. 'We met up with the train party in a place called Kweilin. I first met my husband in the hotel there. I was doing a kind of world tour. We'd come from Auckland to Jakarta, Jakarta to Singapore, Singapore to Peking. It was going to be Bombay after Hong Kong but – well, London suddenly seemed that much more attractive! But I have to tell you, I don't think I spoke one single word to that poor Mrs Knighton. I only know her name because Gordon said who she was after we saw in the papers about her getting murdered.'

Wexford thought it was time he explained that he too had been in China. She was astonished and then confused. Had he been there tailing Mrs Knighton, watching her or what? No, she couldn't follow it. He'd actually seen her, Pandora Vinald, before? It is always hard to understand that someone very beautiful, particularly someone with a sensitive face and a sweet expression, may be quite stupid. Pandora Vinald, he decided, was – to put it as kindly as possible – not very intelligent. Not a patch really – except in one vital way – on Margery Baumann.

'Have you seen any of the train party people since you came here?' he asked.

'No, we haven't. Gordon says holiday friendships are a dead loss, they never lead to anything.'

'Unlike holiday romances.'

It took her a moment to understand but when she did she broke into merry gratified laughter. The Pensive Selima sat up and began frantically washing her face in the way cats do, as if they have suddenly been warned by some inner voice of a disfiguring smut. Pandora Vinald said, 'We did have a photo sent us by a Mrs Knox. I mean Gordon did. We were in it, you see, and a lot of other people. You couldn't see us very well, it wasn't very good. Gordon said not to answer, it would only encourage her, but I didn't think that was very kind, I thought of how *she'd* feel, you see.' She smiled and said naively, 'So I wrote back and thanked her and said it was very nice, though it wasn't, and mentioned we were getting married.'

'Do you still have her address?'

The cat jumped off the chaise longue, stalked to the door and emitted a shrill impatient mew. Because the mew wasn't attended to she followed it up with a series of near-screams.

'Oh, Selima, you noisy beast. She's a terribly spoilt cat. Gordon's ex-wife let her do anything she wanted, scrape her claws down some practically priceless old pieces, just awful.' The door was opened and the cat went out with a slowness that was insolent. 'Address, did you say? I've got all their addresses, as a matter of fact. The tour company sent Gordon a list of the people going with their addresses before he went and it's right here in the top of the desk. Would that be of use to you?'

There they all were in alphabetical order:

Mrs H. Avory, 19 Oswestry Place, Rosia Bay, Gibraltar.
Dr and Mrs C. Baumann, Four Winds, Southwood Hill, Purley, Surrey.
Dr M. Baumann, 2 Crestleigh Drive, Guildford, Surrey.
Miss I.M. Bell, Flat 6, Meleager Court, Queen Charlotte Road, London NW3.
Mr L. Fanning (tour leader), 105a Kingsland House, New King's Road, London SW6.
Mr and Mrs A.D. Knighton, Thatto Hall Farm, Myringham Road, Sewingbury, Sussex.
Mrs L. Knox, 26 Redvers Lodge, Redvers Road, Rosia Bay, Gibraltar.

Mr A.H. Purbank, 10 Fairmead Farm Court, Disraeli Road, Buckhurst Hill, Essex.
Mr G.W.M. Vinald, 16 Searle Villas, London, W8.

He thanked Mrs Vinald and said goodbye to her. Outside, ornamenting the top of one of the columns that flanked the gate, sat Selima like a sphynx. Unwisely Wexford put out a hand to stroke her and got a scratch that made the blood run.

Only Lewis Fanning's wife was at home in the mansion flat down below the World's End, a stringy woman with grey roots showing in her henna'd hair. She was short with Wexford and indifferent. Her husband was away again, shepherding a party round the Aegean and wouldn't be back till the end of the month.

Purley, where the Baumanns lived, would be passed through on the homeward journey, it was on the route of the Brighton Road. Before that Wexford thought he might take a look at what had been the Knightons' home before their permanent removal to Sussex. He told Donaldson to take him up to Hampstead.

His knowledge of London was better than Burden's but it was still full of gaps. It was only seeing a sign to Swiss Cottage which reminded him that Irene Bell had said she lived there, though to him the postal address looked like Hampstead.

'See if you can find Queen Charlotte Road.'

But Donaldson who, long before he joined the force, had thought of being a London taxi driver and had gone so far as to ride round on a bicycle to acquire the 'knowledge', knew where it was without a map. Meleager Court was a block that seemed to be composed entirely of red brick balconies set among plane trees. Irene Bell looked more the way he remembered her today, in a grey trousered garment which, when he was young in the forties, had been called a 'siren suit'. She showed no great surprise at seeing him.

'I've just made a pot of our favourite poison, Chief Inspector. Come in. Mind the step. It takes a true-born Englishman to fancy tea at one pip emma, that's what I say. I've made a sandwich too or have you had lunch?'

'I was thinking of having it at my daughter's. She lives

up the hill in Keats Grove, only I've just remembered it's Thursday and she's got a matinee.'

'Sheila Wexford,' said Miss Bell. 'That's who you are, her father. I mean apart from what else you are. *Sluttish Time* still running, is it? Not my kind of play but I loved her in it, she's a joy to look at.'

Wexford felt that he really liked Irene Bell very much. He accepted tea and a ham sandwich. Perhaps she could tell him, he said, whereabouts in Hampstead the Knightons had lived. She told him, pouring a second cup for both of them.

'I should have been more forthcoming the other day,' she said. 'I was upset and it didn't seem right. But there's quite a bit more to say, though I don't know if it's the kind of thing you want to hear.'

'I want to hear everything.'

'Old stuff from years ago?' She frowned, thinking back. Then she said, 'I'd like you to find who killed Adela and I'd like him to get his just desserts. Not that that'll be much these days – five years inside doing an Open University degree, I daresay, and then let him out with a new suit and fifty quid out of the poor box.'

'Not quite that,' said Wexford who couldn't help smiling.

She said abruptly, 'They had to get married, you know.'

'I beg your pardon?'

'Adam and Adela. You know what the expression means, I suppose? They used it in your young days as well as mine. Don't any more of course. Girls have babies or abortions and as often as not from what I hear it's the boys who beg the girls to marry *them*. Adela fell in love with Adam the first moment she saw him. His sister had been at school with us too and she asked us to be her bridesmaids and that's how we came to meet Adam. We were all twenty-four and Adam was twenty-one. He was up at Oxford. Well, I've never been much for men as I think I said the other day but Adam was something else again as the young folks say. He wasn't handsome, he was beautiful. You hear people talk about "tall, dark and handsome" but to my mind there's nothing to beat a really good-looking *fair* man. Sound soppy, don't I, but he was like a god in a painting.

'I was very fond of Adela, very. Anyway I think she'd

have been the first to agree with me she was never much to look at. Mind you, she came from a very good family. The Aylhursts, you know. They're a cadet branch of the Staffordshire Aylhursts, nothing wrong there.' She hesitated. Wexford hadn't guessed her a snob and was surprised to find such frank snobbery in her. But there, she had been Mrs Knighton's closest friend . . . 'Gerald Aylhurst was her father. He was the Recorder of Salop. I can't tell you how Adam came to be interested in her. I don't know. Perhaps he was flattered because she was older or something. I've heard men of my generation say they used to suffer from terrible sex frustration when they were young – far cry from these days, eh? – so maybe it was that. Adela didn't say no, though you'll no doubt recall that nice girls usually did say no in 1939. Anyway she got pregnant and of course there were no two ways about it, Adam had to marry her. I don't think he ever questioned that he had to marry her but he told his sister and his sister told me that when they sort of first made it clear to him he decided he'd rather die. He said he was in love with someone else and he'd kill himself before he married Adela.'

'Who was the someone else?'

'Don't ask me. You needn't look like that. It wasn't *me*. Come on, Adam Knighton wouldn't have looked twice at me. I don't know who it was, some girl at Oxford, and it can't matter now, not after forty years.'

Wexford agreed that it couldn't matter now. Irene Bell went on, 'He didn't kill himself as we know. The Aylhursts fixed up a big white wedding at their village church. Very bad taste, with Adela four months gone and showing it. Adam went back to Oxford and took his finals, and got himself a First incidentally, and in September Julian was born.

'They must have got on well enough because the next year, in the November, Adela had Roderick. That was 1941 and Adam had to go off with his regiment to the Far East somewhere, Burma, I think it was. He was away four years. When he came home he went back to reading for the bar and he was called and everything and he made quite a success for himself, as we all know. I used to see quite a bit of them. I was sharing a flat with another girl in Maitland Park and they were living in one of those roads off Haverstock Hill near Belsize Park station. He had a funny way of treating her, sort of tolerant exasperated patience. I don't know if I make myself clear? These days they'd say he was always putting her down. I remember once – they'd just got their first TV set – he said he was going to watch *The Brothers Karamazov* and Adela said, "Is that from the London Palladium, darling?" Well, I happened to know it was a famous sort of Russian novel, though I'd never read it, but it was the kind of mistake anyone might make. It does sound like acrobats, doesn't it? Adam called the boys in and said, "Come and hear what your intellectual mama's just said," and then when that pansy phoned, that Dobson-Flint, he repeated it to him.

'Adela had the other two children. I think she did that to keep a hold on Adam. I don't know for sure but that's what I think.'

'You mean he was straying?'

'I don't know. It got so that he was never at home. Working, he used to say, and perhaps he was. He had to do a lot of entertaining too, he said, though Adela always entertained well at home for him. She was a good wife, like I said, she cared, she went to a lot of trouble. Anyway she had Jennifer and Colum but that didn't seem to have much effect on Adam. He slept at home, they'd moved to Fitzjohn's Avenue, and that's about all you can say. It'd be true that for – what? Five years? – anyway for years after Colum was born Adela had a husband insofar as there was a man sleeping in the other bed in her room.

'And then, suddenly, I remember it well, some time in the late fifties it must have been, he came back. He lived at home, he had his meals there, he started taking Adela out – the lot. It was as if he'd had a shock and come to his senses. It's my belief she threatened to leave him and take the children with her, take them away from him. He was fond of his kids all right. Anyway back he came and there he stayed. They were quite a model couple after that except that they never had anything to say to each other. All the old Adam had gone out of Adam, that's for sure. He was bored stiff but he was resigned. And poor old Adela, she went on beavering away at being a good loving wife, but she had to take me on holiday with her, there are limits to how much you can stand of a man who doesn't say two words to you for hours on end.

'Good God,' said Irene Bell, 'do you wonder I don't think much of marriage when that was the marriage I saw at close quarters?'

A fine house of many rooms, rose madder brick, Edwardian probably, with the gables and diamond panes the Edwardians loved. It stood about half-way up the big hill to Hampstead on the right-hand side. Its garden was a shrubbery of rhododendrons, an ilex, in the oval lawn a monkey puzzle. As Wexford looked from the car at the house where the Knightons had lived in such sad contiguity, a hooknosed man in a burnous came out of the front door. Only an Arab could have afforded to buy the house and live there now.

'Marriage,' murmured Wexford, as if to himself, 'is a desperate thing. The frogs in Aesop were extreme wise. They had a great mind to some water but would not leap into the well because they could not get out again.'

Donaldson said nothing to this. But he remarked some time afterwards to Loring that life was full of surprises, he had always thought the Chief Inspector got on O.K. with Mrs Wexford.

'Purley now, sir?' he said after a minute or two.

'Purley it is and then Guildford.'

But from that particular journey across Surrey they were to be saved. Just as Wexford had been taken aback *not* to see Margery Baumann open Vinald's front door to him, so he was surprised to see her open this one. She recognized him at once and was herself as astonished as anyone would be to find a man she had encountered by chance in China three months before standing on her parents' front doorstep.

He explained who he was and why he had come. Margery Baumann understood more readily than Pandora Vinald had done. Since she had no late surgery on Fridays, she said, she always spent those evenings with her father and mother. By that time they had passed through the panelled hall of the Baumanns' rather opulent thirties house and entered a living room where the Baumanns were having a thirties tea. Cucumber sandwiches, bread and butter, strawberry jam, Victoria sponge and custard creams. Dr Baumann wore grey flannels, white shirt, college tie, sports jacket, his wife a flowered afternoon dress and pearls. She was in the act of pouring from a silver teapot. It looked exactly like a stage set for a piece from the vintage days of drawing-room comedy, and but for the autumnal state of the garden and the grey of the sky, one would have expected at any moment the entry from the French windows of a young man in flannels holding a tennis racquet.

All this Wexford remarked while Margery went through the business of explaining to her parents his status and the reason for his visit. They seemed very little less puzzled when she had finished than when she began.

'Now you're here, do sit down and have a cup of tea,' said Mrs Baumann rather faintly.

'I expect he would like a piece of your splendid cake, Lilian.' Dr Baumann got up. 'I shall go and fetch him a plate. I can't say it's at all clear to me why he's here but he's not the man I take him for if he won't enjoy Mother's excellent cake.'

'Milk *and* sugar, Mr Wexford?'

'No sugar, thank you.'

'What exactly did you want us to tell you then?' Margery asked.

'For a start, everything you can remember about the Knightons. Oh, thank you, very kind of you.' Dr Baumann had returned with a tea plate and a small napkin with lace round it. Wexford, who was always more or less on a diet, was obliged to accept a large slice of yellow sponge cake with jam filling. 'You travelled in the train with them. I'd like to know whatever you can recall about them.'

'Aha,' said Dr Baumann, 'so that's what he wants. Well, my dear? Well, Margery? He'll be surprised to find what an observant couple of girls I've got, I daresay.' He barked at Wexford, 'How d'you find the cake?' It was the first time he had addressed him directly. Wexford had been beginning to think the doctor had acquired his habit of speaking in the third person from constant reference for the benefit of students to bedbound patients.

'Very nice. Do you think you could give me your impressions of the Knightons, Mrs Baumann?'

He had utterly floored her. 'I didn't have any impressions. They were just – well, quite nice, ordinary people. That's what we said, ˙ ʒasn't it, Cyril? At the time, I mean, when we were talking about the other people in the party, you know the way one does. I said to my husband that the Knightons seemed quite nice and that Miss Bell they were with, she seemed quite nice. Mr Knighton had been a lawyer, I remembered seeing his name in the papers. He was a very well-informed man, I thought.'

Margery said suddenly, 'She was anti-Semitic.'

A shadow passed across Mrs Baumann's face and was gone. Her husband smiled, a little too widely and tolerantly. It hadn't occurred to Wexford before that they were Jewish, but of course they were.

'That sort of thing is very nasty,' Margery said. 'It was embarrassing. *I* didn't like hearing somebody or other called a "Jewboy" and her call her husband an old Jew when he didn't want to spend money on something. But my mother lost all her family in the Holocaust – did Mrs Knighton consider how she must have felt?'

'That wasn't the first time your mother and I have had to put up with that kind of thing and it won't be the last.' Baumann took his wife's hand. 'He doesn't want to hear about that. He wants to hear about threats and blackmail and murder attempts. About revolvers fired at the dead of night and arsenic in the chop suey.'

'I hardly think . . .'

'Oh, good heavens, no. There was nothing of that. But I know what you chaps like, something to get your teeth into. He doesn't think I've ever read a detective story, Margery.'

Wexford suppressed a sigh. A light rain was falling now and the dusk was coming down. Margery switched on a couple of wall lights and a table lamp with a galleon painted on its parchment shade. 'We really didn't notice anything out of the ordinary about the Knightons, Mr Wexford.'

'Then let me ask you something else. Do you remember when we were all sitting at a table on the roof of the hotel at Kweilin? The three of you, I, Mr Vinald, the Knightons and

Miss Bell. Knighton saw something that astonished him, he looked as if he had had a tremendous, though not unpleasant, shock. I want to know what it was he saw.'

Dr Baumann laughed at that and shook his head from side to side several times as if at some amusing idiosyncrasy. The idiosyncrasy, though, he seemed to make clear, was Wexford's and not Knighton's. What a question to ask! What kind of answer could he expect?

'I can't say I noticed that,' said Mrs Baumann complacently.

Her daughter looked at Wexford. 'It was that very good-looking girl of course, the one that got so friendly with Gordon Vinald on our way home. Pandora Something. A girl from New Zealand. She walked out on to the roof and all the men were looking at her.' Her voice when she mentioned Vinald had an edge of awkwardness but not perhaps pain. 'I did happen to notice the expression on Mr Knighton's face. He was just startled at suddenly seeing such a very striking – well, beautiful girl.'

'I didn't even see her,' said Dr Baumann in a triumphant way.

'Well, maybe not, Dad, you wouldn't. But I should think every other man on that roof did. I know exactly what Mr Wexford means, I saw it just as he did. I expect Mr Knighton is very sensitive to beauty and there hadn't been much in that line, had there? What struck me about those tour parties was that we were all as old as the hills.'

'Margery!' said her mother. 'A young woman like you! I'm sure I didn't see much to write home about in that Miss Pandora Whatever-it-was.'

'Mrs Vinald now,' said Wexford.

Mrs Baumann looked cross, her daughter wryly amused. 'I'm sure he's welcome,' said Mrs Baumann. 'I never liked the man, he wasn't a nice man at all. And I'm sure he wasn't honest, I don't believe antique dealers ever are quite honest.'

'Oh, Mother! He was very kind to us. You know how pleased you are with that little vase and you never would have bought it if Gordon hadn't said it was worth far more than the man was asking. And it was too. My father had it valued, Mr Wexford, and the valuer put it at three hundred pounds. Not bad when Mother gave twenty for it.'

She picked up from a coffee table a small blue and white jar and handed it to Wexford. It was inconceivable to him that anyone would give three hundred pounds for such a thing, a whitish mottled thick piece of pottery with a blue bird and some squiggles on it. On its base was a small red seal.

'You can't take anything out of China that's more than a hundred and twenty years old,' Margery said. 'They put the red seal on an antique piece to show you it's within the limit and therefore all right.'

Wexford handed it back. 'Do you happen to know what it was Mr Vinald and Mr Purbank quarrelled about so that they didn't speak to each other after the train left Irkutsk?'

Now it was Margery's turn to laugh. 'I know they didn't but I haven't the faintest idea why. Gordon just said he was a "nasty piece of work" and left it at that.'

He went home to another good, almost elderly, marriage – his own. Dora was watching an old British film on television, *The Snow Moth* with Trevor Howard and Milborough Lang.

'I wonder if people will see old films of Sheila's in thirty years time.'

'Considering she's never made any,' said Wexford, 'they don't stand much chance. You don't want her going off to Hollywood, do you?'

'I'd like her to make just one or two really good films as well as acting on the stage. There's that old TV series of hers, of course, I don't count that. I'd like to think of her – well, her beauty recorded for posterity. In a lovely setting, in a sensitive film like this one. After all, what do you suppose Milborough Lang looks like now? She must be fifty-five.'

Wexford always did his best to jolly his wife out of these alas-for-my-lost-looks moods of hers. To him, of course, she looked much the same as she had done when he first married her. As the credit titles came up he switched off the set.

'I wish to God you'd been with me in Kweilin. You'd have observed people. You'd have talked to people, you always do, you'd have got to know them. You wouldn't have been distracted like I was by – hallucinations.'

She looked a little worried. 'Reg, I wish we knew what those hallucinations of yours actually were.'

'Lack of sleep; Maotai.'

'Oh, come on. I doubt if you had more than a couple of sips of the stuff.'

Wexford shrugged. 'You might have been able to tell me why a man who sees a pretty girl walk across a roof looks more like he's seen the Virgin Mary.'

The phone rang. It was Burden.

'I'm getting more help than I expected from that chap Brownrigg who's the Clerk to Chambers where Knighton used to be. He's a meticulous old boy and he's got records of all the cases they've handled back for twenty years. But what I'm phoning for is because a fellow by the name of Vinald's been on the blower for you three times since midday. I'll give you his number.'

Wexford dialled it. Vinald himself answered. 'Oh, Chief Inspector, how super of you to phone. I've been trying to get in touch ever since my wife said you'd been here.' The voice was hearty, ingratiating. It was also very nervous. 'I really did want to know precisely what you wanted of me.'

'Any little bits of help you or your wife could give me on the background of Mr and the late Mrs Knighton, Mr Vinald, that's all.'

There was a short silence. Vinald cleared his throat. 'There's more to it than that, though, isn't there? I don't think it can be just that, eh?'

Wexford thought quickly. He would play along, though in the dark. 'I expect,' he said, 'you remember that last evening in Kweilin as well as I do.'

'Oh, certainly. And I realize a fuller explanation is actually called for here. I suppose I should begin at the point we all met up in that roof bar place . . .'

'Mr Vinald,' said Wexford heavily, 'I don't want to hear this on the phone. I'll come along and see you tomorrow. I'll see you in your shop at noon sharp.'

'Well, of course. I'll make a point of being there. I can assure you there's a perfectly simple and reasonable explanation for the whole thing . . .'

'Good night, Mr Vinald,' Wexford said firmly. Far better to

confront the man in the morning and hear it face to face. He rather enjoyed the feeling of suspense, of revelation deferred. Tomorrow, perhaps, indeed probably, Vinald was going to tell him what had so affected Knighton on the roof.

But that, though not in detail, Wexford thought he already knew. Knighton had seen Pandora Vinald. Of course it wasn't the sight of a pretty girl which had brought that look to his face. The people who had suggested that to him simply hadn't thought what they were saying. It was *this particular pretty girl*, and Knighton hadn't looked like that because he was seeing her for the first time but because he was seeing her again, perhaps after the passage of years.

A girl who had once meant a great deal to him – whom he had loved? – had walked out on to that roof and by the merest chance he had been there, had looked up and with joy and wonder and fear had seen her.

Part Three

12

Inspector Burden was a conventional conservative man who believed passionately in law and order. The slightest offence against those principles irked him and he loathed crime. That curious understanding of the criminal mind and its workings which some policemen have to such a degree that there is not much to choose between them and their morality and the criminals and theirs, was foreign to Burden, was distasteful to him. That perhaps was why he was a less successful policeman than he might have been. For between them and him a great gulf was fixed which grew wider and deeper as he grew older.

He was insensitive and he lacked sympathy. Supporting a cliché he didn't know to be one, he would often say he reserved his compassion for the mugger's victim, the beleaguered householder or even the Inland Revenue. He was a believer in retribution and was one of that majority of policemen – to which Wexford did not belong – who favoured the reintroduction of capital punishment. And this not solely for the taking of the lives of policemen. That the French, who had been sensible enough to keep the guillotine for so long, were now proposing to get rid of it, was beyond his comprehension.

More even than young rioters and muggers he disliked recidivists. This was a word his wife had taught him, he had always called them old lags himself, but it came to the same thing. It was just his luck, as he remarked to Jenny on leaving the house, that he should have to spend

311

the day, maybe the next few days, hunting them out. And that without even the satisfaction of the housewife hunting cockroaches, in that there was nothing he could do to them when he found them.

He had taken an unprofessional dislike to Adam Knighton but he had to see him first. Renie Thompson opened the front door to him. She showed him into the living room where to his mild surprise he saw his chief already there, seated opposite Knighton and in the throes of an enquiry into the topic that was at present obsessing him. Knighton had grown gaunt in the past few days, his feet were in carpet slippers and a grey heavy knit cardigan was wrapped round his shoulders. He had become an old man, all that style and presence gone.

Wexford gave Burden a nod but the other man made a gesture of rising from his chair.

'Don't get up, Mr Knighton,' Wexford said. 'I'd like you to give a little more thought to what I've been asking, if you please.'

Knighton moved his shoulders. He was frowning. 'I told you, I remember very little about it. My memory has been affected by all this,' he said bitterly, as one recalling a tranquil time that can never return. 'It was all very beautiful, wasn't it? The most beautiful view I think I've ever seen. If I looked astonished up on that roof I suppose it was at the beauty of the sight.' A ghastly smile widened across his face and turned it into a death's-head.

With a shrug Wexford turned to Burden. He had tried his best. The man was lying, of course, or at least that last sentence of his was highly ambiguous. Burden suggested the possibility that the murder had been committed by someone out to 'get his own back' on the former prosecuting counsel. The smile shrivelled on Knighton's face, he looked almost faint. He took from Burden the lists Brownrigg had compiled.

It took him a few moments to collect himself. But he made the effort. He spoke in an almost normal conversational tone.

'I see Hayward's name is here. Gilbert or 'Gib' Hayward. He threatened me, actually threatened me in court. The jury had returned a verdict of guilty and he was awaiting sentence. When the judge asked him if he had anything to say he began shouting threats at me. It was really rather alarming, though of course there was nothing he could actually do.

'I've had anonymous letters too but they won't be much use to you, will they, since they were anonymous?' Knighton was burbling on in this half-crazed way, Burden thought, for the sake of saying something, anything, rather than reveal his true feelings, his deep fears. 'Oh, and there was this other chap here, one Peter Kevin Smith. I was *defending* him. For some reason he thought I hadn't done a good enough job. He went to prison for five years and the next day his mother came in to see me, made her way into chambers, if you please, burst in threatening he'd shoot me when he came out.'

'When you look at these names, sir, does any one or more of them give you a feeling that, yes, here's someone who might have done more than threaten?'

Knighton gave the lists back as if he didn't like holding them, as if he didn't care for the feel of them on his hands. 'None of them ever did. I can't imagine anyone carrying out such a threat against my – my wife. And do men have such long memories?'

'Some do,' Wexford said rather enigmatically, and he added, 'It depends on how much they want to remember.'

Now how to act on the information in the lists? Those people whom Knighton had successfully defended and those whom he had unsuccessfully prosecuted could be ignored. But this still left so many that Burden realized he was going to have to be ruthless, categorize them according to the circumstances of the case, perhaps decide to disregard all petty crime and go only for killers and perpetrators of manslaughter, robbery with violence and grievous bodily harm. Could he dare assume it wasn't a woman? For a start he thought he could. He just couldn't see a woman not personally antagonistic to Adela Knighton getting her out of bed and forcing her downstairs and shooting her in cold blood. A girlfriend of Knighton's who had had reason to hate or resent Adela, that would be a different thing. But Knighton had no girlfriend.

313

The murderer wasn't going to be in his dotage either. Knighton's own age was just about the oldest at which Burden could imagine anyone climbing up and squeezing through that window, and Knighton was a well-preserved thin sixty-three. The murderer was going to have to be thin, no more than middle-aged. He had started making his list and on it, prominently, were 'Gib' Hayward and Peter Kevin Smith, the former now fifty-two years old, the latter forty-six. They might be fat, though, they might even be dead.

Hayward had killed a man in a fight outside a West London pub and Peter Kevin Smith had hit an old woman im the stomach, rupturing her spleen, prior to breaking into the till in her tobacconist's shop. Narrowing down, rejecting women, people over sixty-five, forgers, con men, straight burglars, bank robbers — though he didn't know if he could afford to do this — he had ended up with a total of sixteen men. In fact there had been more clients in Brownrigg's records with reason to be grateful to Knighton than inimical towards him. Certainly he had been the kind of counsel newspapers and hardened villains adore, spectacular, unscrupulous, witty, savage and subtle.

He went up to London with Wexford where their ways diverged. Though he had set Martin on to 'Gib' Hayward in Brighton, he intended to see Peter Kevin Smith personally.

'He's still living with that loyal and supportive mother of his,' Burden said as they parted. Wexford kept the car and Burden got into the train for Mile End.

The Pensive Selima was sitting in the shop window this time. Not on the lofty vase's side but on the edge of the blue plush drapery that covered its plinth. She sat cosily folded up into roughly the shape of a fat tawny brown armchair. The woman in the big glasses wasn't there. If he hadn't been seeing him at the appointed time and in his natural habitat, Wexford might not have recognized Vinald. In China he had always worn jeans. He looked quite different in a suit of dark grey fine tweed, pure white shirt and grey tie with a silver zig-zag down it. He looked older, cleverer and much more suave.

'Chief Inspector, do sit down. It's good of you to come.'

Wexford thought this remark strange since it must have

been obvious to meaner intelligences that he had come out of duty rather than altruism. He chose a chair which, because he had once apprehended a man who had stolen half a dozen like it, he suspected of being by Hepplewhite. Vinald sat down opposite him on the yellow satin cushion of a love seat. He leant forward in an intimate fashion and, low-voiced, plunged into a – what? The answer to an unasked question? A lecture on iconoclasm? Or just a defence?

'Chief Inspector, China is an extremely long way away and pretty alien to us anyway, I'm sure you'll agree. And who knows how long the present regime will last? What's thirty years? Nothing in historical terms. The next lot to get into power would only do so by bloody revolution. And what's going to happen during any new insurrection? Much the same as happened during the Cultural Revolution. Anarchy. Armies of sixteen-year-old boys told by the highest authority to destroy anything old they could lay their hands on. Did you know that every village in China had its own temple, Taoist, Buddhist or Confucian, and many of them had all three? Where are they now? We know the answer to that. Destroyed. Razed to the ground and the very sites ploughed over as with ancient Carthage. When I hear sentimentalists groaning over our so-called thefts from China in, say, the Boxer Rebellion, I thank God for those – appropriations. Thank God we do have the Dowager Empress's throne in the British Museum. What do you suppose the Red Guards would have done with that?'

Wexford was not at all sure what Vinald was driving at but the man was evidently very very guilty over something. 'What indeed?' he said equably.

'Again only a romantic idealist would insist that the means are never justified by the end. The end here is to save priceless art treasures for the world. And these are not China's but indisputably the property of *all mankind*. They are our heritage, for in art all men are brothers. So therefore I maintain we should get our hands on what we can of it by fair means or foul – not that my means were foul, not at all.' Wexford's mystification, though veiled by experience, was now reaching him. 'And my scale is small enough,' he said more confidently. 'I would hardly have thought it worth anyone's while . . .'

'If we in the force decided that what you call things on a small scale weren't worth our while, Mr Vinald, I think we might very soon have anarchy in our own country.' He would get to the bottom of what Vinald was on about but not now. 'Since you're being so frank with me I'm sure you won't mind answering a couple of questions.' Vinald was looking very nervous indeed now. 'Like where you were on the night of October the first, for a start.'

It surprised him that Vinald didn't have to pause to think. Still, there were people with very good memories, people who in a flash could tell you exactly what they had been doing on any evening in the past fortnight. Wexford himself was one of them.

'I was at home with my wife. You know where I live, just round the corner in the Villas. My wife's mother brought a friend of hers round to meet us after dinner, a film cameraman or some such thing. They stayed till nearly midnight and after that my wife and I went to bed.'

Wexford asked him for his mother-in-law's address and was told she had a flat in Cadogan Avenue.

'I can't tell you where the guy she brought with her lives. His name's Phaidon, Denis Phaidon with a ph.'

As if to leave, Wexford got up and said with deceptive indifference, 'By the by, what *did* you and Mr Purbank quarrel about in the train on the way to Irkutsk?'

'*What?*

Patiently Wexford repeated his question.

'What can that possibly have to do with it?'

'To do with what, Mr Vinald?'

'My buying antiques,' Vinald muttered, 'or the fact that this Mrs Knighton was murdered.'

'It's just one of those small things we think it worth our while to bother about,' said Wexford.

Vinald shrugged. 'I don't remember anyway. It was a long time ago and no doubt I did my best to forget it and forgotten it I have. The man was simply a very nasty piece of work.'

Cats never make a sound when they move. Wexford was aware that the Pensive Selima had left the window only when he felt the faintest sussuration against his trouser leg. She stalked slowly into the back regions as if she owned the place and no one else was present.

The old woman herself came to the door, eyeing Burden with such contemptuous hatred that he knew it would be useless to place credence on any alibi she might produce for her son.

But as it had happened no alibi of hers was needed. For one thing, Peter Kevin Smith had grown far too fat in the ten years since he had come out of prison to have got through that window. For another, his right hand was in plaster and he was a right-handed man. He had broken it falling in the street – drunk, Burden supposed – and to prove the break had occurred before 1 October, exhibited an appointments card from an orthopaedic hospital with appointments listed back to 18 September.

Next on the list was Sidney Maurice Wills of Southwark. He was more interesting than Smith, being thin and wiry and in fit condition. Also he was still in his early thirties, having been out of prison not more than a year. Knighton had been prosecuting counsel in a curious case in which Wills had been found guilty of being an accessory to murder and of concealing a body. He had undertaken to dispose of the corpse of a woman stabbed to death by an acquaintance of his and had subsequently buried it among roadworks.

'What you want to do instead of wasting your time on me is find out who that bastard Knighton paid to do it for him.'

'Oh, he paid someone?'

'Only natural, isn't it? He wouldn't do it himself, no more than he'd fix up his electric wiring or service his own Rolls-Royce motor car himself. He'd call in a professional. Like Chipstead, for instance. Used to be with Lee's mob, could be dead for all I know, I never mix with them sort of people these days, but he's just an example. Christ, do I have to teach you your job?'

Wills had an alibi nearly as good as Smith's, or would have once it was verified. He had been on a week's holiday in Minehead with a girl he called his fiancée, returning to London on 3 October.

There were eight more Londoners to see. The other men on the list lived in the north of England and would be seen by their local police. Of the London eight, George Lake had been celebrating his Silver Wedding at a restaurant in his home suburb of Wandsworth until 1 a.m., Mojinder Singh, a Sikh from Southall, had been at home with his huge family of wife, parents-in-law, two brothers and six children, Norman Trimley and Brian Gage were far too fat, Henry Rossi was seventy-two and growing feeble, George Catchpole had been working a night shift, and Walter 'Silver' Perry . . .

'Silver do harm to Mr Knighton?' Mrs Perry screamed at him in the council flat on the top of the Bethnal Green tower. 'Silver worships the ground Mr Knighton treads on. Didn't he save his life?'

Burden nearly groaned aloud. He realized he had muddled the lists. That was what came of doing a task as distasteful to him as this was. Silver Perry had coshed and killed a night watchman and had done so some years before the abolition of capital punishment. Or it was generally believed by every newspaper reader in the country that this was what he had done, yet the skill of Adam Knighton had acquitted him. Burden vaguely remembered the man's story sold to the *News of the World* and, as he was recalling it, a scrapbook was thrust into his hands by Mrs Perry. There was the half page of cutting, the first instalment, yellowed by time. 'I firmly believe I owe Mr Knighton my sanity and indeed my very life . . .' These ghost writers! He was handing the scrapbook back when Perry himself walked in.

He was a tall man, getting on for sixty, with hair like that of an elderly woman who has just had a rinse, styling and 'set'. Silver's hair, however, was naturally metallic-looking and naturally wavy and had looked just the same, according to the *News of the World* photograph, when he was thirty-three. He gave Burden a parsonical look and said gravely, 'I would lay down my life for Mr Knighton.'

'Really? I don't know what use that would be to him.'

Silver went on as if Burden hadn't spoken. 'I was grieved to hear of his great loss, and him such a devoted husband by all accounts . . .'

Burden hadn't heard of Knighton as a devoted husband by any accounts. He left and when the lift didn't come walked down by the stairs, all the hundred and fifty feet.

There was one more man to see. Coney Newton, who also lived in the East End, had raped a girl and afterwards stabbed her, though not fatally. Nearly a year later, when the girl was at last recovered, Knighton had held her up to ridicule in the witness box, but the jury would have none of it and Newton had gone to prison for eight years. No one could say, except perhaps the paranoid Newton, that Knighton hadn't done his best for him.

'I don't bear a grudge, mind. I said to Silver, I don't bear a grudge and I don't hold you to blame . . .'

'Silver?' said Burden.

'Silver Perry. He's a mate of mine. It was on account of him, what he'd said in the papers like, that I was set on getting that Knighton to defend me. I said to them, I want a fella called Knighton and then I'll be O.K. I don't bear a grudge, mind, but I might have saved me breath. All that carry-on, that telling the jury the girl was asking for it, that wasn't to help me, that was just for show. Using a lot of long words and making her colour up and getting a laugh, that was for show. What he should have done, what I told him again and again, was just stick to it I wasn't *there*. That was the truth, I wasn't there. All I wanted was him to tell the true fact which was, I wasn't *there*.'

'I suppose that's what you'll say when I ask you where you were on the night of Tuesday, October the first?'

Coney Newton looked narrowly at Burden. He was a thin, gaunt, grey-headed man of perhaps fifty, with a rampart of prominent grey teeth. In every sense an ugly customer. 'I wasn't anywhere I shouldn't have been and that's for sure,' he said, and he went into an elaborate explanation of how on that evening he had been in a pub with someone called Rocky whose surname he didn't know, then at his sister's, then in a club round the back of Leicester Square with 'old Silver'.

'You were in a club with Silver Perry?'

'That's what I said.'

'Till when?'

'Maybe two,' said Newton and he gave Burden another narrow look.

It would have to be checked along with the alibis of Lake, Singh and Catchpole. The club, which Newton said was called the El Video, would very likely be closed at this hour, but Burden had time to kill before meeting Wexford. He got on a bus and went on to the upper deck, always his favourite way of jaunting around London.

Really he should have gone to see Newton first, then he could have checked that alibi with Perry. The last thing Perry would do, surely, was support the false story of someone intending harm to his hero. Still, the El Video first.

It was, as he had expected, closed. With the tightening up of the pornography law, the photographs in the narrow glass case beside the door had been softened to mere languishing close-ups of breast and buttock, succulent mouth and swelling flank. The door itself had a cardboard notice on it which said the club was strictly private and for members only and underneath that a poster advertising a rock concert. There were three bells and Burden rang the middle one.

After a while the door was opened by a young black woman in velvet knee breeches and a red tee-shirt. She looked at Burden, said there was nothing doing till six and then it was only by appointment, but then seemed to understand he meant the club. She giggled and said Moggy would be opening up at eight. Burden walked off up the Charing Cross Road, wondering how Wexford was getting on.

Purbank wouldn't tell him what the quarrel was about. He also said he had forgotten the reason for it, though being more restrained than Vinald, he didn't add that the other man was a nasty piece of work.

His flat, on the fringe of Epping Forest, was in an apartment block with huge picture windows which pictured panoramas of tree tops. Purbank turned out to be an accountant who operated from home, in a big room drably furnished in 'safe' shades of porridge, cardboard and mud. Like Vinald he was made highly nervous by Wexford's visit and, when asked if he had been in touch with any other members of the train party since their return, particularly if he had received photographs from any of them, he cried, 'No, no, no!' with the vehemence of someone pleading not to be assaulted.

But of the Knightons he seemed genuinely to know nothing. In the train it was the single people who had congregated, the married couples keeping a little apart, though the Knightons had always made a three with Irene Bell. On the hotel roof in Kweilin he disclaimed having noticed anything out of the way except what he called the 'silly' music and, remembering it, he gave a nervous bellowing laugh.

Wexford thought the chances of his having shot Adela Knighton were about as remote as they could be. But he was rather taken aback when Purbank was unable to account for his movements on the night of 1 October. He could only say that he had been at home alone, or so he supposed, he couldn't really recall, but he thought he had been at home alone and could recall no visitors or phone calls. He seemed a friendless man, not so much a recluse as one whose manner, both boring and blundering, had driven possible friends away.

His head full of China, remembering China and wondering where Adela Knighton's photographs of China had got to, Wexford walked across the lobby of the flats and came face to face with a Chinese man. In other circumstances, even in Kingsmarkham where there was at least a Chinese restaurant, he would scarcely have given him a second glance. But here, in spite of himself, he stared just as those Chinese in Chang-sha had stared at him.

The man spoke pleasantly in an English that was a little high-pitched. 'Good afternoon. Were you looking for someone?'

Wexford collected himself. 'No,' he said, 'thanks all the same.'

He was tall for a Chinese, about forty, professional-looking, in a dark suit and plum silk tie and carrying a dark red leather briefcase. His English was accented but absolutely fluent and idiomatic. 'Nasty day,' he said. 'It's getting very chilly out,' and with a smile walked away to the lift.

Wexford had a look at the names above the doorbells outside. Number 7: Y.S. and M. Hsia. That would be it. And Purbank lived at number 8. Of course there was no reason why Purbank shouldn't have a Chinese next-door neighbour. There must be many thousands of immigrants from Hong Kong, Taiwan and Singapore in this country. They mostly lived in cities and city suburbs, just as well in a flat in Buckhurst Hill as elsewhere. And yet it *was* odd. It made him look on Purbank, whom he had almost dismissed as of nugatory interest, with new eyes.

He picked up Burden at the appointed place by London Bridge. By now it was raining hard and the inspector was standing under his umbrella.

'We'll have a look at Knighton's bank account,' said Wexford. 'See if any large sums have gone out since he got back from China.'

Burden said rather gloomily, 'Can you see that guy hiring an assassin?'

'The wine he drinks is made of grapes. Other men in his station and class of life have done murder. Whatever he may have said on the subject to his wife and children, murder is by no means confined to the working class. And, you know, Mike, it ill becomes him to have said so, it was a fault of character in him that he could say that and it makes me feel his guilt more likely. I don't agree with you, I feel it's more likely he'd have hired someone than done it with his own hand.'

'Well,' said Burden with unexpected shrewdness, 'that might account for why he's so ashamed, why he seems to *hate himself so much.*'

13

If he was more interested in the Vinald family than in other members of the train party this was because he was coming to believe that it was the sight of Pandora Vinald, then unmarried, which had occasioned that look of ecstatic shock on Knighton's face. Somewhere, somehow, Knighton had seen her before, and if that look was anything to go by, had done more than see her. The next step would be to call on Jennifer Norris in her 'old' house in Springhill Lane.

Today she looked more like her mother than ever. Her hair had received a recent perm and her face was as shiny as a new coin. He had expected to be admitted by a cleaner or the present-day equivalent of a maid and into opulent luxury. It was rather a surprise to find her alone and the room into which she took him sparsely furnished. She didn't ask him to sit down.

'Where did my parents go on previous holidays? Do you mean since Daddy retired?'

'Go back five years, would you, Mrs Norris?' How old was Pandora? Younger than Jennifer certainly. Perhaps no more than twenty-four.

She didn't immediately answer him. It was impossible for her to miss an opportunity of dilating on her family's prosperity and social advantages. 'Mummy had what she called her holiday fund, you know. It was her way of getting the best out of her own money. She wanted real travel, you see, not just the usual winter sports in January and some Mediterranean beach in the summer everyone has.' This last sentence nearly took Wexford's breath away. He said nothing. 'So Angus invested this fund for her and she drew on it whenever they wanted to go anywhere – well, really super, you know. Like China. Mummy adored travel.'

Wexford nodded. 'Where did they go the first time after this – er, fund was started?'

'Egypt, I think, or it might have been Thailand and Java. I think they went to Mexico some time but I can't be absolutely sure. And once they just went to Jugoslavia and Corfu.' The Balkans were dismissed and put on a level with Bognor Regis. 'But that was at least six years ago.'

Keeping his patience, Wexford asked if they had ever been to New Zealand.

'People don't go to New Zealand for holidays, do they?' She was a girl of limited horizons. 'We have some sort of remote cousin in Sydney or it may be Melbourne, some place down there, and they did go to him for a while, maybe a month.'

'They spent a month in Australia? When was that?'

'Oh, years and years ago, six or seven years.'

It was stretching things a bit. Wexford found it hard to imagine the fifty-six-year-old Knighton popping across from Sydney to Auckland and there falling in love with a girl of seventeen. And what was being suggested, after all? That the girl had still loved him after seven years, had been reunited with him in China and then shot the rival wife?

'Mummy wanted to go to India and Nepal next,' said Jennifer Norris. 'She wanted to go in February, poor Mummy.' For the first time he saw signs of real emotion in her face.

He noticed something on the walls of a kind of study as they passed back through the hall to the front door which set him inquiring of Sergeant Johnson of the uniformed branch as soon as he was back in the station. But Johnson knew all about it.

'He's got a gun licence all right, sir, had one for years. Had one long before he was married when he was living in a flat in the High Street here. We do inspect, check he keeps the lethal stuff under lock and key. What you saw on his wall is mostly old fowling pieces, flintlock stuff and so on. He does have modern weaponry. I've a list of what he's got kept up to date.'

'But no Walther PPK?'

Johnson shook his head. 'He was the first one I checked on when your directive went round at the start of the case.'

Of course.

Wexford walked into his office and found two parcels awaiting him with the rest of the post. One had come by post, the other, in a large brown envelope and unsealed, by hand. He looked into that one first. The envelope contained a secondhand copy of the collected short stories of that Victorian writer of the macabre, Sheridan Le Fanu, and a bit of paper torn from a prescription pad with *Len* scrawled across it. Wexford wondered what Dr Crocker could be up to but he had never read any Le Fanu and thought this would do very well for relaxation during the Saturday afternoon and Sunday which he intended to take off.

In the other package, the one that had come by post, there was no clue to the identity of its sender. Wexford removed from their brown paper wrapping eight cardboard folders, the kind that film processors use. The name 'Knighton' was written across the top of each of them. Undoubtedly, these were the snapshots the Knightons had taken during their holiday, sent to him from an unknown source. His name on the wrapping and the address of Kingsmarkham Police Station had been printed. The postmark was a London one, Chingford, E.4.

Carefully, he went through the photographs. But it didn't take much perspicacity to tell that some, three or four, were missing. The appropriate negatives had also gone, the strip of celluloid cut through. It wasn't then just a failure to 'come out' that accounted for their disappearance. But which ones weren't there?

The first six envelopes were all of Eastern Europe and Russia, including one of a Russian railway station which the authorities would certainly have pounced on had they known of its existence. It was from the photographs in the other two folders, the Chinese ones, that the shots were missing. He recognised Chang-sha, the Marquise of Tai's tomb at Mawangdui, the Mao birthplace at Shao-shan. There were several shots of loop-shaped mountains in Kweilin, all apparently taken from the hotel roof. Then nothing till the Five Goats statue in Canton. What had become of the Li River excursion then, the most spectacular trip to be taken between Peking and Hong Kong? Had the Knightons left their camera behind? Wexford knew they hadn't. He could remember Adela Knighton taking shots on deck – of the cormorant fishers, the villages, the boats with their square orange sails. Someone, the sender of this parcel, had for a reason as yet unfathomable to Wexford, abstracted those pictures and doubtless destroyed them along with their negatives.

Knighton put up no opposition to the suggestion that his financial circumstances be examined. Without expression he handed Wexford his latest bank statements, of which he received one every month. When Wexford asked why he had statements so often he explained that this was because, a year ago, owing to a standing order for a direct debit he had forgotten about, he had been briefly overdrawn. Since then his bank had kept him up to date with frequent statements. Prior to his retirement he had had a private account but since then he and his wife had used only their joint account. It was for this account that the statements had been issued. Knighton telephoned his bank and asked the manager to tell Wexford the facts about the private account, that it had been closed for three years.

There was nothing in the statements for the past year to indicate that any large sum which couldn't be accounted for had been withdrawn. A substantial monthly sum was paid in which Wexford took to be from some pension or annuity of Knighton's, and there were injections of larger sums, presumably from interest on Knighton's or his wife's investments. Four thousand pounds had been paid into the account in April, very obviously from Mrs Knighton's holiday fund, and a similar amount withdrawn two weeks later to pay in advance for the train tour. It was evident that Knighton had parted with nothing in fee to an assassin.

Of course there was no way of knowing whether this particular account was the only one he had. But in his previous exploration of the house and its desk and drawers, Wexford had found no cheque book or paying-in book for any account apart from this one and the closed private account of which Knighton had kept his final cheque book.

'Mr Knighton, I'd like you to come down to the police station with me so that we can have a talk. I think it would be profitable for you to have a talk with me and my colleague, Inspector Burden.'

'I see no reason why you can't talk to me here.'

'Perhaps not but I do. It will be more straightforward for all of us at the police station.'

'You mean more intimidating for me? I am quite sufficiently intimidated, I assure you.' Knighton made a weary movement of his head. 'I don't know if it's fear or shock or what it is, but I seem to be suffering from some kind of amnesia, what a mad doctor would call a fugue.' Knighton used the quaint and old-fashioned expression for an alienist without awkwardness. 'I seem to live in a stupefied daze,' he said.

Wexford noted he hadn't included grief among the emotions which distressed him.

'If I am going to be interrogated, I think I should have legal advice.' It seemed a strange thing for such as he had been to say. 'My legal adviser should be present,' he said.

'That's entirely your privilege, sir,' said Wexford more blandly than he felt.

It was a curious interview. And this was because of Knighton's frankness in certain areas and obtuse caginess in others. However, no legal adviser was present. Perhaps he thought that with a lifetime of experience behind him he could advise himself.

They used one of the less cell-like interview rooms. It had a rug on the floor. The chairs had straight backs but padded seats. Knighton sat on one side of the table and Wexford and Burden faced him. He looked ill, his eyes were fast becoming dark holes in his face, some sort of remorse was piling years on him as cancer does. He looked as if he had reached the end of his tether or some eleventh hour. Yet he could make a pedantic lawyer's joke.

It was chilly in the room. The central heating was not due

to be started until 1 November. Wexford had a small electric heater brought in and apologized to Knighton for the cold and general mild discomfort.

'*De minimis non curat lex*,' said Knighton with his death's-head grin.

The law may take no account of trifles but lawyers do. In accordance with Wexford's expressed wish, Knighton went into long detailed theories of how a potential killer might have known he was to be away on the night of 1 October. Once again he named the people to whom he had spoken of his projected trip to London, his wife, his daughter, son-in-law, village cronies, his son Roderick, and his daughter Jennifer. His host naturally had known of it and Dobson-Flint. Whom those people had told he couldn't begin to guess. Suddenly he said, 'You've asked my children and Miss Bell and Adrian Dobson-Flint and a good many others too, I suspect, if my marriage was a happy one. You haven't asked me.'

'In the circumstances,' said Burden, 'we took it for granted you'd say it had been.'

'In a murder inquiry, Inspector, you shouldn't take anything for granted. It was not a happy marriage. It never was. For years it was common knowledge I didn't get on with my wife. My wife felt towards me as many women feel towards their husbands. I was her possession and her protector and she had a right to my continued presence in her life. I don't suppose she ever thought whether she cared for me or not. I disliked her. As the years went by I disliked her more and more.'

Temporarily this silenced Burden. It took more than that to nonplus Wexford.

'Perhaps you feel like making a new statement, Mr Knighton?'

'I'm not going to confess to anything if that's what you mean. I disliked my wife but I bitterly regret her death. I would give everything I have — ' he hesitated and Wexford thought he was going to say 'to bring her back' but he ended ' — to turn time back to before the first of October.'

Wexford said, 'You were an unwilling husband. Were you a faithful one?'

'For twenty-five years I was. Before that — there was someone I wished to marry but it was impossible and we parted.
I had my children to think of.'

'And your career, I daresay,' said Wexford.

Knighton winced. He made a vague gesture in front of
his face. 'And my career, yes. I was thinking of a judgeship.
As it happened, it never came. Let me say that I knew it
wouldn't come if I deserted my wife and children for a young
actress.'

They talked to him for a further hour. Gates came in with
coffee and a plate of ham and cheese sandwiches. Knighton
took the coffee but refused to eat anything. Wexford asked
him about his knowledge of guns. Knighton said he knew
nothing about the Walther PPK beyond that in fiction it was
the gun used in the later James Bond books and that in fact
it was used by the Stockholm police force. As the afternoon
wore on to five o'clock they let him go home.

Two things of significance happened on Monday morning.
One was the collapse of Gordon Vinald's alibi. Mrs Ingram
and Denis Phaidon had been sounded out and both agreed
that they had been to visit the Vinalds for coffee and drinks
but it had been on Wednesday, 2 October, not Tuesday, 1
October. And Phaidon, in all innocence, made matters rather
worse for Vinald by saying that they had originally intended
to go there on the Tuesday but had been put off until the
next night because, according to Pandora, her husband had
been called away on business to Birmingham.

Wexford was reading the report on this and thinking about
it, when Detective Constable Archbold who, with Bennett
and Loring, was still pursuing a house-to-house enquiry in
Sewingbury, came in to tell him it seemed they had at last
found a witness. Thomas Bingley, an old man, retired, a
one-time agricultural labourer. He had been in the wood
through which the footpath from Sewingbury to Thatto Vale
ran . . .

'An old man?' Wexford interrupted. 'In a wood at half-past
two in the morning? What the hell for?'

'Well, sir, for poaching. Pheasants, it would seem. That's
why it's taken us so long to find him, he's been lying low. It

was his niece put us on to him, thought we ought to know uncle was often out on that path at night at this time of year. Apparently he sets running snares and goes to fetch his booty in the small hours.'

'And he was there on October the first, was he? I call that adding insult to injury, poaching a man's birds on the very first day shooting officially begins.'

'Cheeky,' Archbold agreed. 'The point is, sir, he says he saw a man on that path. It was a clear night and the moon was shining and he says he saw a tall thin man with grey or white hair walking rapidly along the path towards Sewingbury.'

'With a smoking automatic in his hand, I daresay,' said Wexford.

By chance, thanks to the anonymous parcel, Wexford had photographs of several possible suspects in his possession. In the single living room of Bingley's unsavoury cottage down by Sewingbury Mill he showed the old man a picture of Knighton. Bingley looked at it and scratched his head and said that could have been the man he saw, though he thought he wasn't so tall. Purbank, pictured on the Kweilin hotel parapet in conversation with Irene Bell, he looked at and seemed to consider as a possibility. Then he hesitated and pointed with his little finger, a dirty finger with a broken nail, at someone in the background of the photograph, a man whose hair was covered by a straw sun hat. It was Vinald.

'This feller I saw looked a lot like him.'

'You can't put any credence on anything a bloke like that says,' said Burden when they were outside by the river bank.

'It's a muddled effort to please us in case we do him for poaching. He's one of those who thinks we won't love him if he says he doesn't know.' Wexford surveyed the recently completed concrete embankments, already known locally as 'the weir', through which the Kingsbrook had now been made to pass. There had been considerable controversy over whether it should be done at all. The river which, three weeks before, had flowed between reedy (and often litter-strewn) banks, was trammelled into a symmetrical gorge with a paved sitting area, holes in the paving for trees and a new brickwork arch to the bridge that carried Springhill Lane.

'It doesn't look all that bad now it's finished,' Wexford said. There came into his mind a vision of the Li River and its landscape of looped mountains, the porcelain blue sky, the rippling water – and Wong drowned. 'Purbank has grey hair,' he said.

'Oh, come *on*. Any port in a storm, that is.'

'Not a bit of it. Purbank has no alibi for that night. And he may have a motive.' They strolled over to the car that was waiting for them at the point where the footpath to Thatto Vale joined the road. 'Three or four photographs and their negatives are missing from this set of Knighton's. Suppose it was to Purbank that Adela Knighton sent her pictures? The postmark on the package returned to me was Chingford, and Chingford, according to my map of Greater London, is pretty well next door to Buckhurst Hill where Purbank lives. Suppose one or more of those snaps showed Purbank in a compromising situation, a situation which he would do a great deal to avoid having made public.'

'Like what?'

'That I don't know. I haven't seen them. But Purbank might conceivably have thought Adela Knighton sent them to him, not out of kindness or interest, but to inform him what she knew. *And perhaps she did.*'

'So what do we do about that?'

'Nothing, at the moment. First we're going to find out why Vinald lied and said he was at home having cosy little drinks parties when in fact he was in Birmingham. Or Herstmonceux or Mevagissey. There's no knowing with a liar of his calibre. The really interesting thing about that alibi of his, though, was that it alibi'd Pandora as well. And now it doesn't, nothing and no one does.'

In Birmingham, it appeared, Vinald had done no more than meet the agent of a South American collector of porcelain. He had taken with him certain of the pieces he had brought out of China and two vases more recently acquired. In saying that this had taken place on the evening of 2 October instead of the true date, 1 October, he had made a simple mistake.

Vinald brought all this out very glibly but he couldn't conceal a terrible underlying nervousness. He was afraid of something and his fear was mounting. Wexford and Burden saw him at home, not in the shop, and Pandora came into the room while they were talking. Was it for her that he was afraid?

She was in a dress of white knitted wool today, bronze belt and shoes, her black glossy hair in the current fashion of smooth top and the sides a Renaissance frizz. She looked calm, not at all nervous. Wexford was suddenly sure he had been quite wrong in connecting her with Knighton. It was most probable they had never even spoken to each other.

'So you and your wife were alone here on the Tuesday night?'

They both said yes to that rather quickly and in unison. Their haste made them break off and smile awkwardly at each other. Pandora shrugged, opening her eyes wide.

'I'm going to have to insist on your telling me the cause of your quarrel with Mr Purbank.'

Vinald waited a moment. He smiled stoically, making the best of things.

'If you must know, he persistently made remarks insinuating I was turning the trip into what he called a buying spree.'

'And if you were, how did that affect him?'

'He suggested that every time we went sight-seeing and had a choice of what to visit I opted for the places where there would be artefacts for sale rather than for museums or panoramic views or whatever.'

'That may have been irritating to you but it was hardly offensive, was it?'

'It was the way he said it. It was more in the implication than what was actually said.'

'Mr Purbank says he has forgotten the cause of your quarrel.'

There was no mistaking the satisfaction this afforded Vinald. He smiled gaily. He put his arm through his wife's. 'He's a very nasty piece of work. Frankly, when he said he'd tell our guide it was my object to turn other people's holidays into a commercial venture to feather my own nest, I'd had enough. I slapped him down and we – exchanged no further words.'

Wexford knew he was lying, or rather that he was telling a heavily diluted version of whatever the truth was. As they left going down the steps, Wexford paused to stroke the head of the Pensive Selima who was sitting among some dead lobelias in an urn. She suffered his attentions, shook herself distastefully, jumped out of the urn and skittered down into the area.

'Not all that tempts your wandering eyes,' said Wexford, 'and heedless hearts is lawful prize . . .'

'What's that?'

'The poem the cat gets her name from. Come on, we're going to the V and A.'

Once Burden wouldn't have been quite sure. His wife had altered all that. 'The Victoria and Albert Museum,' he said to that London expert, Donaldson, and to Wexford, 'What are we going there for?'

'China's gayest art,' said Wexford.

That night, tired but not particularly late home, he finished Le Fanu's novella of vampires, 'Carmilla', and went on to the next story in the collection, 'Green Tea'.

14

He didn't tell Burden. He didn't tell anyone but his wife. Sitting up in bed reading Le Fanu beside Dora reading Charlotte Brontë, he came wonderingly to the end of the story and started to laugh.

'You mean,' said Dora as he explained, 'that this man was writing a book and he got overtired and he kept himself going by drinking green tea? Tremendous quantities of it as a sort of stimulant?'

'You might say he chain-drank cups of green tea. And he was very much frightened by a monkey-like creature he began seeing in the corner of his room. Then he saw it in the street and it got on an omnibus with him. Well, I saw an old woman with bound feet.'

'I suppose it was Len Crocker sent you the book.'

'Of course it was. He realized I'd made myself hallucinate in the same way as the Reverend Mr Jennings did in Le Fanu's story. I chain-drank green tea too, you know. I must have been drinking a couple of gallons a day.'

He laughed, remembering. But thinking about it before he fell asleep, he wasn't entirely satisfied with the explanation. He was relieved, it took a niggling little load off his mind, it was obvious it had been the green tea that produced the visions – but was that really all there had been to it? Surely there had to be more, though he might never find out what.

It made him feel a little strange about drinking his breakfast cup of tea, though this was Twining's Assam and in no way green. After breakfast he looked among his books, found *Masterpieces of the Supernatural*, and saw as he suspected that the last story in the collection was 'Green Tea'. If only he had read on to the end he would have known the answer when his anxiety was at its height.

Now what to do about what the poacher saw? About Purbank and the photographs? Burden was busy with reports from Middlesbrough, Manchester and Newcastle, all of them clearing the remaining men whom Knighton had prosecuted, respectively, on charges of murder, arson and grievous bodily harm. Back in the cottage down by Sewingbury weir, Wexford struggled to get something more satisfactory out of Bingley. But the old man again picked Vinald out from the photograph, qualifying his selection by saying the man he had seen looked more like Vinald than anyone else there. All he was positive about was that he had seen a man walking along the footpath at three in the morning or thereabouts and that man had been walking *back* from Thatto Vale.

Wexford and Burden had lunch together im the Many-Splendoured Dragon. Spring rolls, beef and onions, beansprouts, water chestnuts, Chinese mushrooms. Burden had a pot of jasmine tea but with a restrained shudder Wexford stuck to Perrier. He had been back in his office five minutes when the switchboard told him there was a girl downstairs wanting to see him. A Miss Elf.

'A Miss what?'

'Elf, Mr Wexford. Like, you know, gnomes and fairies.'

He nearly said, 'Is she pale green?' but green for the moment was a dirty word with him. 'Get someone to bring her up.'

Loring brought her in and left at a nod from Wexford. She was a small fair girl, perhaps five feet tall, and she looked very young. Fourteen or fifteen was his first impression. Her face was babyish, innocent, with large soft blue eyes. She wore jeans, a red sweat shirt and a red and white track suit top, blue and white canvas and rubber running shoes and, carrying no handbag, came in with her hands in her pockets.

'Miss Elf?' Wexford said.

335

'That's right.' Her voice didn't quite match the appearance. 'What can I do for you?'

'It's more what I can do for you. O.K. if I sit down? I've got some info for you. A friend of mine – well, more a client – he said the police here were looking for this old guy hanging about H.P.G. in the night time on October the first. So I never let on to my client but I reckoned I'd better present myself to you seeing as I did. Did see him, I mean.'

It was all very unclear. Miss Elf had aged in his estimation about two years but he was still mystified. 'You live in Hyde Park Gardens or Stanhope place? Your parents live there?'

She broke into laughter. 'No, no. I'd better begin at the beginning, hadn't I? Tell you who I am and what I am and what I was doing there at that hour, right?'

'What are you?' Wexford said slowly.

'I'm a whore,' said Miss Elf.

Wexford had begun to guess it. He disliked people trying to shock him, he wondered when they would ever learn he couldn't be shocked and hadn't been shockable these thirty years.

'I suppose you mean you're a prostitute, a call girl?'

'Right.'

'You look very young for that.'

'Well, that's the point, isn't it? I mean, me looking young. That's what you might say got me into it, me looking so young always. I'd got a rare commodity to sell and it was a sellers' market. I'm twenty-four actually. But wanting to screw twelve-year-olds didn't go out with the Victorians, you know, and I looked twelve when I started. I'd pass for fifteen now, wouldn't you say?'

Wexford nodded. He couldn't resist asking, 'Is your name really Elf?'

Her laughter was loud and harsh, with a coarse note. 'Really and truly. I was born Elf, the only daughter of Mr and Mrs Elf. Piece of luck, wasn't it? But I don't insist on it, you can call me Sharon.'

Of this offer he resolved not to avail himself. He was thinking that most of her clients were probably men of his age and he knew enough of prostitutes to be aware that she would look on him with the same eyes as she looked on them, believe him subject to the same desires and the same perverse needs that made them want little girls. He felt a bit angry and a bit sick over it all and then he told himself that at any rate what went on now was ten thousand times better than in the days when it was really little girls they had.

'So to the night of October the first,' he said coldly.

Sharon Elf fixed her large blue eyes on him. 'This client of mine in Stanhope Place, he's one of my regulars, reminds me a bit of you actually.' She didn't see Wexford wince, or if she did, didn't care. 'He gave me a buzz around eight that night and said would I come and see him at midnight. Half twelve would be better if I could make it on account of he'd got people for dinner and by twelve-thirty they were sure all to have gone.'

'Where exactly does this client of yours live?'

'One of those houses facing the back of H.P.G.'

'Hyde Park Gardens, yes, I see.'

'As it happened, I could make it very well. I'd got another client at eleven, that was up in St John's Wood, so I left there around twelve-twenty, twelve twenty-five and I got a cab and it got me round to Stanhope Place just before twenty to one. I know you're going to ask me how I can be so sure of the time. The fact was I didn't want to embarrass my client — you know, if his guests hadn't gone on the dot like he said. So I kept looking at my watch and it was just before twenty to one we got there.

'I took a look at my client's house and I saw the light on in the hall and the bedroom but not the lounge, so I knew that was O.K. Anyway, I was paying off the driver when this old fella came out of the back of H.P.G., one of the lower ground floor flats — well, basements really. He came across the road and took my taxi.'

'Did you hear where he asked the driver to go to?'

'Sorry. There I can't help you. I wasn't interested, you see, didn't know any reason why I should be. Not then.'

'How exactly do you know now?' Wexford asked.

She said simply, 'My client in Stanhope Place gave me a buzz last night and I went round around ten. He told me the fuzz had been asking questions. It was the first time I'd seen him for three weeks, you see, or I reckon he'd have told me before.'

Wexford could almost have blessed Purbank or whoever it was had sent him those photographs. They were coming in very handy. There was one of the whole train party together on the Kweilin hotel roof. Only Adela Knighton, who had taken the shot, was missing. Unhesitatingly Sharon Elf picked out Knighton.

'That's him.'

'You're quite sure that's the man you saw in Stanhope Place at twenty minutes to one on the night of October the first?'

'Positive,' she said cheerfully. 'I had a good look. You see, I rather fancied him.'

Wexford's brain reeled. Did it work both ways then? If tired old men were looking for girls too young to criticize or have standards, were the girls looking for surrogate grand-fathers? He was glad, though, to see the back of Miss Elf and feeling a fool, asking himself who was he to sit in judgement, nevertheless opened his window for a little while after she had gone. Perhaps it was only to blow away the smell of rubber soles and Palmolive soap.

He turned his thoughts to what she had told him. There was Bingley's evidence and now this. He pressed his buzzer and said, if Inspector Burden was about, would they ask him to come up? Burden came in carrying a report on the last man on his list, a certain Dudley Preston whom Knighton had defended on charges of manslaughter and drunk driving but had failed to save from three years in prison.

'Do you know your window's wide open? It's like an icebox in here.'

'You can shut it if you like.' Wexford told him about Sharon Elf and what she had seen.

Burden's mouth went down at the corners. But that, Wexford thought, was more on account of Miss Elf's profession than the destruction of Knighton's alibi.

'You believe her? A woman like that?'

'Sometimes you talk like a mid-Victorian beadle. I don't see why a call girl shouldn't be as truthful as anyone else. Look at it how you will, it's an honest trade, it parts with what it's paid for. Enough of this rubbish anyway. She picked him out from a group photograph, so of course I have to believe her.'

Burden shrugged. 'If it's true, and I suppose it is, things look bad for Knighton. The presumption would be that immediately he and Dobson-Flint had retired to their rooms, he prepared to go out again. No doubt he hung about while Dobson-Flint used the bathroom, then he slipped out, taking with him one of the bunches of keys from the hall table. It was too late for a train, so he must have had the taxi take him to wherever he had a rented car waiting. Who knows? He might have rented a car somewhere near Victoria Station and left it parked and waiting for him. He'd have hired that when he got to London and put enough in the meter to last him till six-fifteen. With meter charges stopping at six-thirty he wouldn't have had to worry. I suppose that means checking on the car hire places round Victoria now.

'If he took the taxi at twenty to one he would have been in Victoria by ten to. I may be ignorant of London but even I know there wouldn't be much traffic at that time of night. By one at the latest he would have been in that car and starting his drive. It wouldn't take him more than an hour so we'll say he got there at two.'

'A quarter of an hour to cut out the pane of glass, maybe a few minutes to steel himself – yes, it just about works out.'

'He didn't have to get through the window, he had a key.'

'He still had to cut out the glass.'

'Of course he did,' said Burden. 'I'm a fool. Of course he did. And he wouldn't have done it *after* he'd killed her. There's one thing, though – can you imagine him hoicking her out of bed and bringing her downstairs and shooting her through the back of the head?'

'There are a lot of things I can't imagine human beings doing but still they do them, Mike.'

'Well, I can't swallow it. Not a woman you'd been married to for over forty years. Not your own *wife*. And Knighton's not one of these yobs I've been hob-nobbing with, is he? Wouldn't we, I mean wouldn't anyone, call him a *civilized* sort of man?'

'Look, there are a lot of things I don't like too. I don't like any of it much but this is evidence we've got, Mike. Sharon Elf saw him at twelve-forty slipping out of Dobson-Flint's flat. Bingley saw a man walking back to Sewingbury around three and it wasn't Vinald he saw. Adela Knighton died between two-fifteen and three-thirty. The timing works out very neatly. What was he doing, taking a taxi at twenty to one in the morning when his friend thought him in bed asleep if he wasn't going clandestinely back to Sussex? We have to see him, we have to get him down here again. We have to know where that gun is now.'

'I don't see any motive.'

'Motive sometimes has a way of showing itself rather late in the day. Anyway, someone said that every married man has a motive for murder.'

But as Wexford reached for the phone, it rang. The switchboard again, announcing a second visitor.

'There's a Mr Shah here, sir, asking to see you.' The voice went lower. 'A Chinese.'

'He doesn't sound Chinese.'

Sha? *Shah?* Did they mean Indian or maybe Tibetan? For a moment Wexford was mystified. Then a little tug of excitement caught at his throat. The name might be pronounced more or less Shah but in fact it was Hsia.

His visitor was Purbank's next-door neighbour in Fairmead Farm Court, Buckhurst Hill.

'I'd like you to stay,' he said to Burden.

The tall man in the dark suit that Wexford had encountered in the lobby of the flats came into the office. He was wearing a dark suit of a slightly different shade today and he still carried his briefcase. His black hair was so smooth and sleek it seemed to have been painted on his scalp. His eyes were mild, intelligent, his expression one of gentle impassivity. He held out to Wexford a narrow pale brown hand on which he wore a signet ring in obsidian and gold.

'My colleague, Inspector Burden,' said Wexford. 'Mr Hsia.'

Hsia sketched a slight bow. 'It's Chief Inspector Wexford, I believe? I hope I haven't come at an inconvenient time?'

'Not at all. Won't you sit down? I think we might all

have some tea, don't you?' Wexford put his finger on the buzzer.

Sitting down, Hsia kept his arms tensely along the arms of the chair, then, as if by some oriental relaxation technique, lifted them and laid his hands calmly in his lap.

'Chief Inspector, I have come here to tell you something my friend and neighbour Mr Purbank cannot bring himself to tell you. It may seem I am betraying a trust, you see, but while this secrecy goes on I fear very much he will become ill. He is very much frightened, you see, so for his relief I must speak the whole truth to you.' Hsia's face relaxed and he gave a sort of rueful chuckle. 'You may feel, you see, that I am the one who should need to keep the secret, for I am the criminal. May I begin now?'

Wexford nodded. The tea came in. It rather surprised Wexford to see Hsia take milk and two lumps of sugar.

'My name is Hsia Yu-seng,' he began. 'You know where it is I live. I work for the Kowloon and Fuchow Bank in London Wall.' He paused and Wexford thought that 'work for' was probably a modest understatement. 'Most people,' Hsia went on, 'suppose that I am originally from Hong Kong or Taiwan, you see, but this isn't so. I was born in Shao-shan in the People's Republic – in fact, you know, in the very birthplace of the late Chairman, Mao Tse Tung. I was born in that place ten years before what they call liberation.'

'How did you come to leave China?' Wexford asked.

Hsia raised his teacup to his lips and drank a little. 'May I?' he said, reaching the ringed hand out for a Garibaldi biscuit. 'I committed a crime,' he said. 'I was twenty-one. If I had been caught – and I should have been caught, there is no hiding such things in China, you see – I would have been executed.'

Wexford moistened his lips. Inescapably, he associated capital punishment with murder. 'What crime?'

'I raped someone,' said mild sleek Mr Hsia, and he turned up the corners of his mouth in an apologetic smile.

15

Burden made a choking sound over his tea. He wiped his mouth with a crisp white initialled handkerchief. 'Excuse me.'

'*You raped someone?*' Wexford said.

'I and three others. You don't know how it was, the life there, the deprivation, the oppression, the *re*pression. This girl, she asked us, you see, she teased us, it was an invitation with the eyes, the walk. And then, when it is happening first with my friend, then with me, she is frightened and later she tells her father who is Party cadre.' With the stress of telling, Hsia's English worsened, approaching pidgin. He recovered himself and loosened his clenched hands. 'For this in China there is execution. There was then and there is now. My uncle, my mother's brother, he was a truck driver, driving every week to Canton. He took me in the truck, hid me, and from Canton I got into the New Territories. I am cutting a long story short, you see, but that was how it was. I walked to the border, crossed into the New Territories and came to Hong Kong. English I could speak a little, I had studied it at the University of Chang-sha, so after a while I came to England with my wife that I had married in Hong Kong, you see, and whose father is director of the Kowloon and Fuchow Bank. And from then on all goes very well for me.' He smiled again and this time slightly inclined his head.

Wexford looked at him, the bland parchment-coloured face, the still features that have led to 'inscrutable' being the adjective invariably associated with the Chinese. Undreamt-of adventures, terrors, privations, struggles, lay hidden between the lines of that long story cut short. A less likely rapist than Hsia Yu-seng, Wexford had never seen.

'This is all very interesting,' he said, 'but what has it to do with Mr Purbank?'

'I am coming to it,' Hsia said, nodding. 'I have said all goes well for me and this is true, you see, except in one respect. That is my mother. My father died, you see, in the fighting of 1949 and my mother is widow, living with my brother and his family. But I was her favourite and always I have been very sad that I cannot get news to her. Always I have been afraid for her sake, you see, to send a letter and it is out of question for me ever to set foot in People's Republic. Often I have been thinking of ways to get news but find nothing better than what my father-in-law already has done − send her message only that I am alive. Then one day my neighbour Mr Purbank says to my wife that he is going in a train to China.'

'I begin to see,' said Wexford. 'Mr Purbank's itinerary would take him to Shao-shan and you asked him to deliver a message to your mother.'

'I asked him if he would take a *letter* to my mother. I had heard through my father-in-law that my brother's wife is cook in Wu Jiang Hotel, you see, so I thought to myself, there can be no trouble for Mr Purbank, who will surely eat there when he visits Mao's birthplace, to ask for the cook in order to praise his meal. He was to ask her name and if she answers, 'Mrs Hsia,' to slip her my letter.

'But all this goes wrong, you see, for Mr Purbank lost my letter when some things were stolen from his bags in Russia. And this made him very nervous and anxious to do the right thing, but he didn't know how to do it, you see. So he asked the interpreter to say to the cook, 'Your brother's friend is here,' which he does and my sister-in-law, very excited, you see, sends home for my mother who is an old woman now, more than seventy years old.'

With bound feet, Wexford thought. And when he had seen her that first time, then, when he had seen her as he was lunching in the Wu Jiang Hotel, it was no green tea hallucination. It had been a real woman that time that he had seen standing by the screen and waiting for news of her son. 'Go on,' he said.

'Well, then it was that Mr Purbank became really frightened, for whatever he said he must say through this interpreter, this official guide and interpreter from Lu Xing She. He knew I had been criminal, you see, and feared that if this was known he and the party might be expelled from China, so to my mother and sister-in-law, through the interpreter, he says that he has made a mistake, there has been a misunderstanding.

'But with this my mother was not content. She guessed, I think, that Mr Purbank has much to say but was frightened to say it, so next day when my cousin, the son of my uncle who saved my life, when he drives to Chang-sha she goes with him to look for Mr Purbank . . .'

The second sighting, Wexford thought, on Orange Island.

' . . . and there she finds him but they cannot communicate, you see, except by signs and by then both are afraid, Mr Purbank and my poor mother. Then, as luck would have it, while Mr Purbank is walking in the street in Chang-sha a student called Wong comes to him and asks to practise his English.' Hsia had gone entirely into the present tense now and Wexford remembered reading somewhere that Mandarin has no tenses. 'Perhaps this happens often in present-day China?' Hsia asked.

'Yes, it does.'

'So Mr Purbank has bright idea, you see, of asking this Wong to be interpreter for him. My mother still sits, waiting, in lobby of Wu Jiang Hotel. Mr Purbank tells Wong all about me, how I live in England, work in Kowloon and Fuchow Bank, have wife, have two boys at boarding school, everything about me, and Wong tells my mother who is made very happy and goes off full of happiness when my cousin calls back for her. But this is not, you see, the end of the story for Mr Purbank.

'This Wong is himself perhaps a criminal element or perhaps it's true he wants only to escape from People's Republic. Again to cut the story short, he follows Mr Purbank on the train to Kweilin, pleading with him to get him out of China. Also, Mr Purbank says, he asks always for money, you see, as if to threaten Mr Purbank that he has done a wrong thing that will get him in trouble unless he gives money.'

'You mean this Wong was blackmailing Mr Purbank? Unless Mr Purbank agreed to help get him out of China and gave him money, he would make the whole story of your contact with your mother known?'

'Something of that kind, yes. Mr Purbank was very frightened by now, always to be followed everywhere by this Wong, and although it was dreadful thing to happen he wasn't so very distressed when there was accident on the Li River boat and Wong was drowned.' The still features widened into a reflective smile. 'Mr Purbank then thought his troubles at an end till when he got home, a good while after, this Mrs Knighton whom someone has shot sends him photographs of the Li River trip. In them he is talking with Wong and Mr Purbank is very afraid once more . . .'

'Did you see these photographs, Mr Hsia?'

'No, I didn't but I was told of them. Mrs Knighton's husband, you see, is in some way connected with the law and Mr Purbank thinks, suppose this whole story comes out and causes international incident, you see. So he burns the pictures and the negatives and sends the rest back to you and then he becomes nervous again in case you think he shot this Mrs Knighton . . .'

Wexford very nearly laughed. There was something he knew and Hsia very evidently didn't which stopped him laughing.

'It was wise of you to come to me,' he said.

'I thought it best. And now I shall tell you where Mr Purbank was on the night of October first till after midnight – with me and my wife in our flat.' Getting up to leave, extending his hand, Hsia added, 'I fear he thinks it safer to be suspected of Mrs Knighton's murder than have it known he associates with such politically dangerous people as ourselves.'

From the window Wexford watched him cross the police station forecourt and get into this year's registration dark blue BMW. Strange to reflect that this sleek capitalist was the son of that old woman with the hoof-like mincing feet, that forerunner and instigator of hallucinations.

'Can you believe that?' Burden said. 'Can you believe Purbank was actually afraid of high-level repercussions because photographs existed of himself in conversation with a dissident Chinese?'

'Hsia believes it.'

'Sure he does. He grew to manhood in a country with perhaps the most repressive political system on earth.'

'I'll tell you what I think for what it's worth,' said Wexford. 'I'll never be able to prove it, I've nothing to go on but my own feelings, but it's my belief Purbank pushed Wong overboard. He was harassed by Wong's persecution and when they were on the boat and he came up behind Wong squatting down in the bows, he gave him a shove and pushed him overboard. Not intending to kill, I daresay, intending to frighten, to show Wong in his muddled way that he wasn't going to be used and battened on in the way Wong hoped.

'Back home I expect he soon forgot about it. We all know the old postulation: if by raising your hand you could acquire a million pounds and kill a Chinaman, would you do it? It's generally believed that few would hesitate long. Maybe it seemed a little like that to Purbank. After Wong was drowned I asked Adela Knighton what had happened and she said indifferently that someone had been drowned – "not one of us" she said "a Chinese". Purbank had raised his hand and acquired peace if not money and it was all twelve thousand miles off and there are a lot of Chinese anyway . . . until the picture came with his hand reaching towards Wong's back.'

Burden nodded. It was likely enough. Suspects were being cleared, others implicated. Rape had reminded him of Coney Newton and what he had to tell Wexford of the El Video Club. Loring had been there the night before, making inquiries.

'It's managed by a man called Jimmy Moglander – 'Moggy' to his associates. Newton was in there all right. He and three or four other men he was with were there until they closed on the Wednesday morning. The lives these villains lead! Moglander and the barman both remember Newton being there. So that seems to clear each and every old lag that might have had a grudge against Knighton.'

'So how about Knighton?'

'He'll keep till the morning, I should think.'

'You're right.' Wexford thrust back his chair and got up. 'I'm going home, Mike. If I hang about here someone'll be bound to drop in and tell me how he saw an old woman with bound feet climbing in through Knighton's loo window. We'll leave Knighton till tomorrow.'

But for Adam Knighton tomorrow never came. It was like *déjà vu*, Wexford thought in the morning, or the rerun of a tape. It was like going to see a film and sitting through the whole programme to see the beginning again. Only you usually did that because you liked the film. He hadn't liked this one the first time round, and as for the second . . .

The same credit titles, the same opening. It started with Renie Thompson phoning the police station at nine, with Burden and the fingerprint man and the scene-of-crimes man and Dr Crocker all going up to Thatto Hall Farm. The sun was shining and there was dew on the grass, and if the Michaelmas daisies were a little more mature and frost had shrivelled the leaves of the dahlias, if the sun was a little higher because the clocks had gone back an hour, only a purist would have noticed. All things up until this point seemed the same. They found a divergence only when they were inside the house, for this time it was Knighton who lay dead and by his own hand.

'Two times in a month,' said Mrs Thompson. 'It makes you think twice about going into a person's house. I thought he must be having a lay-in but the bedroom door wasn't shut, it was like on the jar, so I just gave a tap and put my head round . . .'

Since Wexford's last visit, Knighton had moved back into the room he had shared with his wife and there, on the evening before, he had undressed, put on blue cotton pyjamas and a brown wool dressing gown, lain on his bed and surrendered himself to death. On the bedside table beside him was an almost empty brandy bottle, an empty wine, not brandy, glass, and a cylindrical plastic container that had once held fifty capsules of tuinal.

'His doctor prescribed that for insomnia, presumably.'

'Not me, thank God,' said Crocker. 'I'd have given him mogadon. The only way you can kill yourself with mogadon is stuff down so many you choke to death.'

He closed Knighton's pale blue staring eyes. On the dressing table were two sealed envelopes, both addressed in Knighton's bold and beautiful hand. One of them was to the coroner.

'Who's Mrs M. Ingram?' said Crocker.

'God knows.' Wexford read the address, Thain Court, Cadogan Avenue, London, SW1, and then he knew. 'It would seem she's the mother-in-law of an antique dealer I happen to know. I see he's provided a stamp but I think I'll deliver this by hand.' Outside, below the window, the gravel crunched. Wexford looked out. 'Angus and Jennifer,' he said and he stuffed the letters into his pocket.

Knighton's yellowish-white waxen face looked as long dead as the Marquise of Tai's. It looked as if it were made of porcelain but a porcelain they had forgotten to colour before the glaze went on.

'Poor devil,' Wexford said. 'There was no loophole left for him.'

'He did kill her then?'

'I didn't mean that. I've a feeling his predicament was a moral one, that it was his conscience he couldn't escape.' They left the room and closed the door. 'I never thanked you for the book.'

'I'm not sure if it would really happen.'

'Well, yes and no,' said Wexford cryptically.

Jennifer and her husband were in the hall. Her expression was as surly as ever. As he came down the stairs Wexford heard the tail end of what she was saying to Mrs Thompson, something about having no help in the house and a shock like this being enough to send her into premature labour. But Angus Norris looked as shocked and distressed as if Knighton had been his own father.

'This is a bad business, Mr Norris,' Wexford said. It was a phrase he used when he found himself in these or similar circumstances. Non-committal, it nevertheless expressed everything needful.

Norris took it *au pied de la lettre*. He spoke with a kind of tragic enthusiasm. 'A dreadful business, dreadful.' His face was rather pale and lined in a way some adolescents' faces are, though this ages them not at all. He looked round for his wife, to comfort her perhaps or be comforted, but Jennifer had gone into the living room and was lying in a chair with her feet up.

He said carefully, in a more controlled tone, 'Was there — a suicide note or anything of that sort?'

'Something of that sort,' said Wexford and he followed the doctor out through the front door.

Roderick Knighton's yellow TR7 had just joined the Norrises' worn-out Citroën on the gravel drive. The barrister got out of it and rushed into the house, closing the front door behind him with almost a slam.

The letters burned Wexford's pocket. He would have been justified in opening the envelope addressed to Mrs Ingram and reading the contents. A suicide has forfeited his right to privacy and this suicide was also a prime suspect in a murder case. Who *was* Mrs Ingram, apart from being Pandora Vinald's mother? What had she been to Adam Knighton that he had written her a letter from his deathbed?

He wouldn't open it without phoning her first. He picked up the phone to ask the switchboard to find her number for him, then put it down again. On the hotel roof in Kweilin there had been another woman with Pandora, a much older woman, white-haired. In all the thought he had given to the events of that evening at the rooftop bar, in all his recollections of the people involved, that woman had never figured. The beauty of Pandora had eclipsed her.

For him perhaps, for almost everyone who saw them together, but not for Knighton. Knighton, sitting at that table with his wife, had seen her as Dante saw Beatrice and in a moment his life and his hopes had been transformed. But unlike Dante he wasn't seeing her for the first time. Wexford was sure of that. There was a romantic side to his nature that had a weakness for the phenomena of passion, yet he couldn't admit of the possibility of a man of Knighton's age falling in love at first sight with a woman of Mrs Ingram's.

He must have known her before, perhaps years ago. When they had interrogated him he had said that his career would have been damaged if he had 'deserted my wife and children for a young actress'. Mrs Ingram would have been young then, when the Knightons lived in Hampstead during the week and Sussex at the weekends, when Jennifer and Colum were babies, when Knighton by his eloquence was saving at least one murderer from execution.

The interesting thing was that the first time he saw her in London Pandora had reminded him of some famous beauty of thirty years back. He had thought of Hedy Lamarr or Lupe Velez. Thou art thy mother's glass and she in thee calls back the lovely April of her prime . . . Mrs Ingram had friends in the film world. She had brought a film cameraman to meet her daughter and son-in-law.

'What do you suppose Milborough Lang looks like now?' Dora had said, watching *The Snow Moth*. 'She must be fifty-five.'

The letter to the coroner, Dr Neville Parkinson, Wexford delivered in person. Then he went off to meet Burden for lunch at the Many-Splendoured Dragon.

'It's unlike you not to be hungry,' said Burden.

Wexford was picking rather listlessly at his food. 'It's Setzuan here too,' he said. 'Nicer than the Hunan we mostly got served with.'

Burden looked impressed. 'Have you ever heard of a play called *The Good Woman of Setzuan* by a chap called Brecht? The drama society here is doing it at the end of the month. You ought to go.'

'I suppose your wife's playing the lead?' Wexford could tell from Burden's sheepish look that he had guessed right. He dipped in his chopsticks to catch a curl of okra while Burden, resigned to a spoon, watched him warily. Wexford dismissed the versatile Jenny Burden with a wry smile. 'Fishing for trouts in a peculiar river,' he said. 'Knighton was too old for that kind of thing. He was too old to have a mistress and too old to murder his wife.'

'What did Parkinson's letter say?'

'It was very short. I can probably quote it from memory.

"This is to inform you that on the morning of 2 October I killed my wife, Adela Knighton, by shooting her with a Walther PPK automatic pistol. As a consequence of that act I shall, by the time you read this, have taken my own life." And he signed it. That was all.'

Burden poured himself a glass of mineral water. 'I wonder where he got the gun and, come to that, what he did with it afterwards.'

'I wonder about a lot of things. Frankly, Mike, I think it's all these doubts I have that are making me – well, I won't say upset. Uneasy.'

'You don't mean you think it's a false confession?'

Wexford didn't answer him directly. 'He was devoured by guilt, wasn't he? You could tell that.' He pushed away his plate. For a moment he hesitated, then he asked the waiter to bring a pot of green tea. 'And certainly he wanted her dead. He left Dobson-Flint's and came back here that night. He must have killed her. Why say so if he hadn't? It's not your run-of-the-mill false confession. The man killed himself. The whole point of a false confession is to attract attention and the kind of hysteric who does that doesn't defeat his own object by committing suicide immediately afterwards.'

'Certainly not,' said Burden firmly.

'Let's go. I have to phone Mrs Ingram and then I have to see her.'

16

Fashion had come full circle and the clothes she wore were
not unlike those she had been dressed in for her films, a little
grey flannel suit with a straight skirt, a pearl-coloured silk
blouse with a high pleated neckline, stockings with seams,
high-heeled shoes. Her figure seemed unchanged. But that
kind of black silk hair is perhaps of all shades the most
vulnerable to time. It was whiter than her skin now and
that skin itself webbed with lines.

She hadn't sounded surprised by his phone call. Why
should she have been? For weeks now she must have been
waiting for the police to come to her. *Why* he had come, that
was something else again. She greeted him with a gentle, ever
so slightly ironical, friendliness.

They went into a living room. The flat was in a small
block of apartments for rent on short leases, smart, even
luxurious, in one of the most highly desirable residential areas on earth. It lacked any particle of character.
It was a suite of motel rooms, biscuit-coloured Wilton
on the floors, chocolate-coloured linen at the windows
and upholstering the furniture, here and there murals that
were blends of Samuel Palmer and Rowland Hilder or
montages of beaten tin cans and bits of bamboo. She
had added pieces of her own, a pair of water colours,
a red, blue and gold ikon, a vase or two that very likely
came from Vinald, and flowers in abundance. She had
filled vases and bowls with what October afforded in the
way of dahlias and chrysanthemums and what October

couldn't afford but she evidently could, roses and gladioli and carnations.

She sat down on the sofa, her knees together, her body held a little to one side, her head up, a very Milborough Lang attitude. Suddenly Wexford's heart felt heavy. He was desperately sorry for her.

'I believe you knew Adam Knighton well?' he began.

She was immediately apprehensive. '"Knew"?' she said. 'What does "knew" mean? I know him, yes.'

This was how the man felt who drew Priam's curtain in the dead of night. And like Priam, she had begun to guess. 'Mrs Ingram, I used the word advisedly. I have bad news for you. I think it will be bad news.' She was very still, her eyes on him. 'You must prepare yourself for a shock. Mr Knighton is dead.'

Her lips parted. She brought her hands together.

'He was found dead this morning,' Wexford said.

'Do you mean – he killed himself?'

'I am afraid so.'

'How?' she asked softly.

'Brandy and an overdose of sleeping pills. He left a note for the coroner and a note for you. I have brought yours with me.'

On the third finger of the thin veined hand she put out to him was a diamond cluster as big as a grape. She wore a diamond watch and diamond earrings. From the neck up she had grown some ten years older since he had told her of Knighton's death.

'It was kind of you to come personally to tell me.' She started to get up. She was politely dismissing him.

'I'm sure you would like to read your letter in private,' he said, 'but after that I'm afraid I shall have to see it.'

She held it against her breast, her hands crossed over it in the traditional gesture of a girl keeping a love letter from father or husband. She was still an actress.

'I shall have to see it, Mrs Ingram. It may be of great relevance to Mrs Knighton's murder. I must see the letter and then you and I must have a talk.'

'If I don't show it to you, could you get an order or a warrant or something like that to force me to?'

He nodded. 'Something like that. But I'm sure you'll let me see it without that, won't you?'

'Yes.' She pushed her thumbnail under the flap of the envelope and began to open it. 'Excuse me if I go away to read it.'

He was taking a small risk but he hadn't the heart to refuse her. While she was absent, the door between the communicating rooms left ajar as if she guessed what he slightly feared, he thought of what Irene Bell had told him about Knighton's attitude towards his family in the past. 'For five years after Colum was born Adela had a husband insofar as there was a man sleeping in the other bed in her room.' Colum Knighton would be about thirty. It fitted. 'And then suddenly Adam came back. He lived at home, he had his meals there, he started taking Adela out – the lot.' What else had she said? 'It was as if he'd had a shock and come to his senses.' What in fact had happened was that after a five-year-long love affair Milborough Lang had left him and married someone else.

She came back and gave him the letter in a quick, almost disdainful gesture. A lamp was on but he took it to the window and read it by the dying daylight.

My darling, I shall be dead when you come to read this. I had dreamed of our being so happy together, I had longed for it and it really did seem within our grasp for a little while. I believed I could live with anything so long as you and I had each other at last, but I was wrong. The love I have for you is the strongest emotion I have ever felt for anyone, stronger than my feeling for my children. I have loved you for thirty years and kept the image of you always in my mind.

But remorse is stronger than love. When I killed Adela I did not know myself. Though I had spent a lifetime in association with evil, I did not know how insidious evil is, how it destroys the joy of everything, even the joy of love. I had never considered that this act which was designed to bring me happiness would instead show me a hell of shame and self-hatred, a hell that is with me night and day, every moment of every day.

That is not something I can live with or expect you to

share with me. Therefore I have resolved to put an end to it. Twenty-five years ago my children and my responsibilities and my own fear held me back. This time I think I shall have the courage. Not so much courage, perhaps, as the lack of it, lack of fortitude for a continuance of the life I am living now.

Do you remember how we read the Chinese poems together? Here are two lines from Chang Chi.

So I now return your shining pearls with a tear on each.
Regretting that we did not meet while I was still unwed.
Good night, my darling, and God bless you, Adam.

She hadn't cried when she read the letter but the sight of him reading it brought the tears. They fell silently, she hardly seemed aware of them.

'Please sit down, Mrs Ingram. Do you feel able to talk about this or would you rather wait a while?'

'It may as well be now.' She spoke the ungracious words graciously. She sat down. 'I should like my letter back, please.'

'Later. You shall have it before I go. Now I should like you to tell me the whole story.'

She made a movement of recoil, she shook her head. 'He didn't kill her, whatever he says. He *couldn't* have killed her.'

'I'm afraid you're going to have to accept that he could and did. Now you're going to tell me about yourself and him. It will be good for you as well as for me. Have you anyone else you can tell it to? Anyone at all who will care enough to listen?'

'No,' she whispered.

He had been thirty-two, she twenty-five. They had met at a dinner party given by that very Henry Lacey who had entertained Knighton on the eve of his wife's death. Adela had been there too. The young Milborough Lang had become famous overnight when her first film was shown, a curious and almost mystical story of a deaf girl called *The Snow Moth*, and she had followed this with a stage success as Petra in Ibsen's *An Enemy of the People.* Wexford remembered seeing *The Snow Moth* when it first came out. As was probably true of Garbo, it was the star's beauty and grace of movement and look of other-worldliness which had brought her fame rather than her acting ability. Milborough Lang had been wonderfully beautiful.

'We were a handsome couple,' she said, seeming to read his thoughts. 'Isak Dinesen says that life is but a process for turning frisky young puppies into mangy old dogs. Only we never were a couple really. Adam had Adela and he had four children. Colum had been born just three months before we met. He told me Adela had had his two younger children to ensure he stayed with her, and it worked, it did ensure that.

'We saw as much of each other as we could. Technically, he still lived with Adela, he slept under her roof. It was very cruel, it was a hateful way to behave to her, I know that. I think I felt more guilty than he did.' She paused and put her fingers to her cheeks to wipe away the drying tears. 'We paid for it, of course. We were punished. The times we had together were always a rush, always a race against the clock. He had to get back to work, to court, to Adela, and I had my career too. I got this Hollywood offer and I went to Hollywood and made that terrible *Mind Over Matter*, but I couldn't stay there without Adam.

'I was the one who made the break. We couldn't have gone on like that. It had been five years but Colum was still only five, and it would have meant another fifteen years maybe of rush and subterfuge and passion and mad muddle. Besides, it had never had the chance to become a real workaday relationship, it was a romance.

'I met Ryan Ingram. He wanted to marry me and take me away to New Zealand. I think he saw himself, poor dear Ryan, as a sort of new world Prince Rainier, transporting his beloved from the rat race of the screen into a life of wealth and peace. I seem to be predisposed to these romantic men, don't I? Anyway, I did marry him and I did go away with him and Adam and I didn't write to each other or see each other for twenty-five years – until I walked out on to the roof in that place in China.'

*

Ryan Ingram had died of a coronary three years before. Their daughter Pandora had made a mistaken marriage when nineteen. It was partly to distract her mind from this and from the subsequent divorce that she and her mother had come on the trip that had been intended to take them round the world but had ended, in each case because of a love affair, in London.

'Adam recognized me at once. It must be true that love is blind because I think I've altered more than most people do in twenty-five years. I recognized him, of course. It was an extraordinary sensation, seeing him sitting there, still with Adela.'

She got up and drew the curtains on the dark late afternoon. When the lamp underneath it went on the rich colours of the ikon, the gold in its border and the Virgin's crown, glowed in the light. Wexford suddenly recalled reading an illustrated article in a Sunday supplement about ikons that looked like that and which came from the neighbourhood of Lake Baikal . . . Milborough Ingram smiled, a little sadly, a little ruefully, and went on, 'Adela went to bed. He came over to our table and said – to be prudent, you know. Oh, that eternal prudence! – "Miss Lang, we met years ago at Henry Lacey's house in London. I don't suppose you remember." "I remember," I said. Pandora was talking to some Australians, I don't think she noticed Adam. The young don't notice, they aren't interested in us. Why should they be? He said – his voice was shaking – "May I buy you a drink?" I excused myself to the others and we went inside the hotel. I never had that drink – I think I'd like one now, though. Will you?'

Wexford nodded. She fetched ice and poured whisky on to it in big glasses.

'We found a sort of banqueting room, a great empty gloomy place, and we went in there and talked. You were in that hotel too, Adam said. Isn't that strange? I wonder where you were then.'

'Being shown his porcelain collection by your son-in-law.'

The delicate dark eyebrows went up. 'He's scared stiff of you because he thinks you're after him for selling something or other to an American. Are you?'

Wexford smiled. 'I think the Chinese would be after him if they knew. China's a long way away.'

'Yes.' Her voice grew grave again. 'China's a long way away. Adam once told me about the Chinese mandarin, how most people wouldn't think twice about killing a Chinese mandarin if they could get a million pounds by doing so. China is so far away, so remote, even today. If one just had to make a sign, he said . . .' She sat down again, looking at him. 'In China, that night, everything seemed simple. Adam could leave Adela. Time had sorted things out for us and we could be together.'

'You still wanted to? After a quarter of a century? After your marriage?'

She delayed answering, drank some of her drink. 'I will be honest,' she said at last. 'I didn't feel the same as I had. How could any ordinary realistic person feel the same? Adam wasn't an ordinary realistic person. I'm not flattering myself when I say he felt just the same, perhaps even more so.

'I wanted to make him happy. I would have liked to remarry and to be married to him. Oh, yes, I would have liked it.'

'So he went home and you and your daughter went to England all on the same plane. Did you speak to Adela Knighton?'

'No. She had seen me once, thirty years ago at a dinner party and naturally she had forgotten me. Adam and I didn't speak to each other again until we saw each other in London. Pandora and Gordon were instantly attracted to each other. That was why it was easy to get straight to London, Pandora wanted it, she would have gone without me if I'd objected. In London I took a lease of this flat and Adam came to see me here. He and Adela used to have days out in London, they'd come up together on the train and he'd go and look up various old cronies while she went shopping and called on some friend of hers in Primrose Hill. I replaced the old cronies.

'It was very much like it had been twenty-five years ago. Patterns repeat themselves, don't they? There was I with my flat and there was Adam living with his wife. We were ruled by the clock as we had been. Almost from the first I knew he

wasn't going to leave Adela. I tackled him about it and he –
he wept, he actually cried, poor Adam, it was dreadful. He
couldn't leave her, he said, not after forty years. He couldn't
face her and his children with a thing like that. That quarter
of a century might never have been. I'd married and had a
child and lived on the other side of the world and he'd become
a QC and retired and was a grandfather – but everything was
just the same, it was uncanny. And yet he did love me, he
loved me more than I loved him, poor Adam.

'And then I tried to break it off just as I had before. I said
it was hopeless going on in this way, simply history repeating
itself. I said I was too old for that kind of thing and when
the lease of this place was up I'd go home to my house in
Auckland.'

'You mean you held that over him as a threat?'

She lifted her shoulders and there came to her lips the
ghost of a Milborough Lang smile. 'He knew I'd go unless
things could be made more permanent, yes.'

The smile angered him. 'You might say then, Mrs Ingram,
that you share some of the responsibility for Adela Knighton's
murder and hence for Adam Knighton's own death.'

She jumped up, her serenity gone, and cried out to him,
'That's not true! Adam didn't kill her. Haven't I told you he
couldn't have killed her?'

'He's admitted it. Before his confession we were pretty certain – all the evidence, circumstantial and otherwise, pointed
to his having killed her. He had motive and opportunity and
he was there.'

'He was not there,' she said more calmly. 'He was here
with me.'

17

'It sounds ridiculous,' she said, 'a man of over sixty sneaking out of his friend's house and dashing across London in a taxi to be with the woman he loves – a woman of fifty-five. To spend the night with her and go back at dawn. A superannuated Romeo and Juliet. It really does happen, it did happen.'

He believed her. It was so evidently true. 'What time did he come?'

She replied at once. Had it been the only whole night they had spent together? 'A few minutes after one.'

Knighton wasn't the first man to confess to a murder he hadn't committed, Wexford thought. And yet . . .

'No doubt you saw him several times after that?'

'We talked a lot on the phone. I saw him – oh, three times? Four?'

'He never said anything to you to suggest he had killed his wife?'

'How could he have when I knew he was here with me at the time? I could tell he was unhappy, he seemed tormented. But his wife had been murdered and however he felt about her and me, she *was* his wife.' Milborough Ingram put her hand to her forehand and leaned her face forward on it. Her voice had taken on a faltering note. 'He never said any more about our marrying, about our being together. He was different, changed. I thought he was ill. I said he ought to have a holiday and I'd go with him. He just stared at me, he held my hand and stared at me.' She reached for her whisky. 'Oh, God, I mustn't have any more to drink. I'll get drunk and that won't help. Ever since I was eighteen I've had it dinned into me I mustn't drink because it'd spoil my figure and my face, and it dies hard, all that. What does it matter now?'

He got up to go. She was composing herself but hysteria trembled beneath the surface of her composure.

'Would you like me to get your daughter to come to you?'

'I'm better alone. Really.'

He turned his eyes away from that ravaged, once-beautiful face. They lighted on the ikon. He remembered where he had seen it before – in Vinald's bedroom in the Kweilin Hotel.

'I gave my son-in-law two hundred pounds for that.'

Wexford heard a rasp in her voice. 'I'm sure it's worth it,' he said politely.

'Oh, no doubt. Only Pandora told me afterwards he gave two pairs of jeans for it and one of those wasn't even his own.'

She had spoken in the bitterness of her heart. It was an anger with the injustice of the world she was venting on Gordon Vinald. Already she looked ashamed of her indiscretion.

'What does it matter now?' she said again.

Wexford made no reply. He said goodbye to her and went down to where Donaldson and the car waited.

Tabard Road, Kingsmarkham, the bungalow that was almost as familiar to Wexford as his own home over the other side of the town. Dora Wexford had dealt with the problem of being a policeman's wife by acceptance, by patience, but Jenny Burden solved it more positively, filling her evenings with learning – and teaching – at classes, with drama groups and string trios. She was out this evening, at a rehearsal, Burden said. He fetched two cans of beer from the fridge.

'Knighton wasn't mad,' Wexford said. 'It wasn't a matter of having some sort of delusion he'd done it. He knew he hadn't held the gun and squeezed the trigger and shot her. He meant he was morally responsible, he instructed someone else to do it.'

'Not someone he paid. We know he parted with no large sums.'

Wexford said thoughtfully, 'I don't think it was anything as direct as that. I think it was more a matter of nodding, of raising one's hand and killing the mandarin.'

'I don't follow you.' Burden had put on his obtuse look, the one he wore less and less since his second marriage. Once it had inspired Wexford to say he was reminded of Goering who said that whenever he heard the word culture he reached for his gun. Sometimes it came back to make the Inspector's normally intuitive face mulish. 'I haven't a clue what all that means,' he said.

'I can't enlighten you. I'm not being purposely obscure, I don't know any more yet. Let me tell you about Vinald and Purbank instead. I can tell you what they quarrelled about. Vinald pinched a pair of Purbank's jeans to pay for an ikon.'

'He did *what*?'

'I imagine he discovered this ikon in the possession of some peasant in the far east of Russia. Russians are crazy to get their hands on denim jeans, or so I've heard. Probably Vinald hadn't got very long there, wherever it was, or the ikon vendor wouldn't hang about, so Vinald went back to the train and fetched a pair of his own jeans. Because he hadn't any more of his own clean or didn't want to part with them or something he took Purbank's. No doubt he explained to Purbank afterwards and maybe offered to pay for them but Purbank was outraged and refused to have any more to do with him.'

Burden laughed. 'But why not tell us?'

'Vinald wouldn't because it makes him look such a crook. Purbank wouldn't because it makes him look a fool. What could be more undignified than someone nicking a pair of your trousers? It's a kind of vicarious debagging.'

'I suppose it is,' Burden said. 'Put that cat down if you don't want it.'

Jenny's Abyssinian, as lithe and sinuous as the Pensive Selima was stout, had sprung up delicately on to Wexford's lap. He drew his hand down the smooth slippery back.

'Is Vinald a crook, d'you think?'

'D'you remember when we went to the V and A I paid particular attention to the Sung ware? Celadon, they call it. White or pale grey or pale green, an attempt to imitate jade, around a thousand years old. While we were in Kweilin Vinald showed me the Celadon ware he'd bought, trusting, and rightly, to my ignorance. He said it was a hundred years old, Ching stuff, and of course I believed him. He had a whitish bowl, a dull plain thing, and I remember thinking to myself that Dora wouldn't have given it house room. You wouldn't reckon on anyone paying ten thousand pounds for a thing like that, would you?'

'Ten grand? For a white pot a hundred years old?'

'Well, not a hundred years old, Mike. That's rather the point. Say eight hundred? I saw the stick of red sealing wax in Vinald's hotel room and it meant nothing to me. I didn't know then that any antique you bring out of China has to have the government's red seal on it. Vinald was getting hold of priceless pieces from people who didn't know any better, paying virtually nothing for them, and then putting the red seal on himself. Especially that bowl – which he took up to Birmingham on October the first and sold to the agent of a South American purchaser for ten thousand pounds.'

'Can we do anything to him?'

'Like what? Extradite him to China? Do you know what he'd answer if we said to him what I've just said to you? That he gave a fair price for the bowl, believing it to be Ching. Of course it had the seal on it. What can we mean? It was only when he got it home and examined it carefully that he discovered he'd paid five quid for a piece of Sung.'

As Wexford stroked it the cat began emitting a harsh rumbling purr. Still shaking his head over man's chicanery, Burden fetched more beer. Wexford changed the subject. 'When you went hunting up those old lags – what you might call recidivisiting – you had two lists, didn't you? The men Knighton had helped send down and those that had got off or got off lightly because of his defence?'

'That's right.'

'What was the point of the alternative list?'

'You mean the ones he got off?'

'I mean, what was the point of l.sting people who have had no motive for revenge on him?'

'There wasn't a point really. Brownrigg and I simply made a note of every case Knighton had been involved in that we thought important enough. I put those friendly to Knighton in the right-hand column and those – well, possibly revengeful on the left. I got them muddled too, I . . .'

But Wexford didn't want to hear about that. 'You've still got the lists?'

'Of course I have.'

In the morning Wexford looked at them.

'This Coney Newton seems to be on both lists. What did he get sent down for?'

'Rape and attempted murder,' said Burden. 'He's on both lists because – well, I thought he might have reason to be grateful to Knighton for getting him off with only seven years or vindictive towards Knighton for not getting him off altogether. And funnily enough, he didn't seem vindictive, he just seemed to think Knighton hadn't made a very efficient job of his defence. Anyway, he's got a good alibi for that night and he alibi's Silver Perry.'

'That's fine for him then, isn't it, having his word backed up by a really exemplary citizen like that?'

'They were in a club together,' Burden said slightly offendedly. 'I went to the club. There's no question . . .'

'All right. Who's Henry Thomas Chipstead?'

'Once upon a time he was an East End of London gangster. Around twenty years ago he was up on a charge of grievous bodily harm and Knighton got him off. Wills –' Burden indicated with his finger the name in the left-hand column. 'Wills suggested to me that Knighton might have called in "a professional like Chipstead". Those were his words, not mine. He said Chipstead had been with Lee's mob, might be dead now for all he knew. He's not dead, though, he's alive and living in Leytonstone. But he's over seventy now and in any case we know Knighton didn't pay anyone.'

'And what was this Wills's contribution to the disintegration of society?'

Burden grinned wryly. 'Aiding and abetting. He didn't

actually kill this woman but he was an accessory. He concealed the body by night in roadworks on a motorway, only one of the workmen discovered it before they laid the road surface . . . What's the matter?'

'I know where he put that gun,' Wexford said slowly.

'Where who put it?'

'Ah, that's something else. I mean I know where whoever our perpetrator is put the weapon. You just told me. What you said about this Wills and roadworks told me.'

'It did?'

'The weir, Mike, the weir at Sewingbury Mill.'

It was a long shot. Burden's opinion was that 'they' would never be got to demolish all that concrete and brickwork, embankment and paving, for the sake of finding a gun, it wasn't as if it was a body. And the chances, he said pessimistically, were that the gun wasn't there anyway.

'Once I've got a warrant,' said Wexford, 'they'd get on with the demolition if it was a pin they were looking for and Sewingbury Agricultural College they were demolishing.'

Colonel Charles Griswold, the Chief Constable of Mid-Sussex, was as uneasy about it as Burden. And perhaps Wexford would never have been allowed to swear out that warrant but for the clerk of works who had supervised the construction of the 'weir' for the county authority telling the chief constable that, when the workmen knocked off for the day at five on 1 October, only the paved area remained to be completed. At that time, on that afternoon, he said, the areas waiting to be paved had lain open and uncovered except for a foundation of 'hard core' spread on the soil.

'Suppose we say he left his car in the market square in Sewingbury,' Wexford said. 'He made his way by the foot-path to Thatto Vale and got to Thatto Hall Farm at about two. There he either entered by the washroom window or let himself in with a key, having made it appear as if he entered by the window. He woke Mrs Knighton, brought her downstairs at gun-point, shot her, feebly faked a burglary and returned by the path where he was seen by Bingley at around three. At the Sewingbury end of the footpath he spotted the nearly completed paving work on the weir and it would have been the work of only a few moments to bury the gun in the soil under the hard core.'

It was a cold day with a bitter wind blowing. The Kingsbrook, swollen by recent rains, rushed and tumbled under the Springhill bridge and through the new channel constructed for it. The same contractors that had built the 'weir' came to knock part of it down again. As soon as they had the paving stones up Sergeant Martin and Archbold were to go along and grub about under the hard core for the gun. Wexford looked in for a few moments at the inquest on Adam Knighton. Angus Norris was there but otherwise the family was not represented.

Wexford knew there could be no possible outcome but that the inquest be adjourned. Dr Parkinson was reading aloud Knighton's confession and now and then quoting Wexford's own words that Knighton could not himself have been physically responsible for his wife's death. Wexford crept out of the court. At the far side of the quadrangle that divided the courts from the police station Donaldson was awaiting him at the wheel of his car, Burden already seated in the back. The wind struck him with a sharp gust and blew out his scarf like a flag.

'The river bank is no place to be this morning,' said Burden, rubbing his hands.

'You sound like Mole.'

'Who?'

'It doesn't matter. We're going up to the Smoke anyway. Or near enough. The Haze, we should maybe call it. Is Leytonstone the sort of place we can get lunch in, Donaldson?'

But the London expert, to his own evident chagrin, didn't know, he had never been there.

'Chipstead, I suppose,' Burden said.

'Henry Thomas Chipstead, fifty-two Dogshall Road, Leytonstone. He's seventy-three and doesn't seem to have been up to anything in the hit man line since Knighton got him off the hook when he was fifty. But he'll do for a start.'

'I wish you'd explain to me what you meant about that killing the mandarin.'

They were on the motorway now, heading for London.

366

The wind was so strong that gusts of it shifted and swayed the heavy car. Occasionally spatters of rain in large drops dashed against the windscreen.

'I think that years and years ago,' Wexford said, 'Knighton had reason to be in contact with some villain who was a professional assassin or hit man. Defended him, presumably. After the case he went to Knighton and said to him something on the lines of, if there's ever anything I can do for you, Mr Knighton sir, you've only to say the word, you know what I mean, nudge, nudge, anything you want done on the quiet, and Knighton, no doubt, got all upstage with moral indignation, but later on he got to thinking about it. Much later on and when it would really have suited him to have someone put out of the way.

'No money would have to pass, you see. That would be the beauty of it. He wasn't going to have to be specific with this old lag, wasn't going to have to give him three or four grand in used oncers or anything like that. Beforehand he might even be able to think he wasn't really the instigator. Suppose it was no more than a matter of making a phone call and saying something like, My wife's going to be alone on the night of October the first? Suppose it was even more subtle and slight than that?

'But afterwards the remorse and the guilt, to a man like Knighton, would be as great as if he had paid an assassin or pulled the trigger himself.'

'Well, he'd be just as guilty,' said Burden.

'Of course he would, but a good many men wouldn't *feel* just as guilty. That's the analogy with the mandarin. One of China's teeming thousand millions is just as much a human life as one's wife or child, but it doesn't feel like that because it's so remote, so far out of sight. And if one only has to raise one's hand . . . I think maybe Knighton only had to raise his hand, or do something as slight as that, to rid himself of his wife and have Milborough Ingram.'

They came into London through the Blackwall Tunnel. From its northern end it wasn't far to Leytonstone. Dead leaves from the fringe ends of Epping Forest whirled in the wind. Dogshall Road was a long straight street that passed with a hump over one suburban railway line and in a dip under another. The gutters were choked with leaves, the trees in the pavement, three times as tall as the little squat terraces of houses, were shedding leaves into the wind. There was a red brick church and a pre-fab church hall with an asbestos roof but nothing else to relieve the long monotony of Victorian terraces, the long double row of parked cars. Donaldson pulled into a gap a little way down from number seventeen.

'Moralizing would be out of place,' said Wexford, 'but this is a fine illustration of how crime *doesn't* pay, don't you think? Chipstead made his living for years, for most of his life, out of violent crime. I'm not saying it was in vain, it wasn't, it caused a lot of suffering, it damaged society, provoked fear, made work for the police, cost the taxpayer money. But it didn't profit Chipstead himself much, did it?'

The three men looked at what Chipstead had got out of it, a hundred-year-old brown brick box with six feet of concrete, on which stood a dustbin and a dead geranium in a tub, separating it from the street. There were only three windows at the front of the house and at all of them the curtains were drawn. Wexford got out of the car and Burden followed him.

The house had a dead empty look as if its occupants had closed it up and gone away, and Wexford, banging hard on the knocker, for there was no bell, had very little hope of an answer. But after a moment or two a woman's voice was heard saying something and then footsteps sounded on the stairs.

The door was opened to them by Renie Thompson.

18

'Henry was my brother,' she said.

They stood in the hall. There was a light on upstairs and women whispering.

'Was?' said Wexford.

'He's dead, isn't he? You mean you didn't know? Today's the funeral. To tell you the truth, when you knocked I thought it was the undertakers come.' She wore a grey coat and a black felt hat. She looked at them truculently, at their dubious suspicious faces. 'You'd like to make something out of it, wouldn't you? I know. There's nothing to make.'

'Give us the raw materials, Mrs Thompson, and we'll decide that.'

A woman had begun coming down the stairs, evidently a sister. She stood there, staring, listening, holding the banister.

'I'd worked for Mrs Knighton since nineteen sixty. Him and her, they was the best employers you'd find anywhere. Henry had to come up in court for something he never done and I said, you want Mr Knighton to speak up for you and he got Mr Knighton, Mr Knighton was on his side on account of knowing *me*, and he got Henry off, of course he did, considering Henry never done it.'

The woman on the stairs clicked her tongue.

'Henry thought the world of Mr Knighton.'

'So did you too, Renie,' said the woman on the stairs.

'You a Sewingbury family, are you?' Burden asked. They

both nodded, eyeing him warily. 'Had your brother been ill prior to his death?'

The third sister now came down, buttoning herself into a black astrakhan coat.

'In the hospital six months,' said Renie Thompson. 'He had it in his chest, you see, the lung, and then it went to his spine.'

The door knocker rattled. The woman in astrakhan went to the door and the wind blew a dead leaf in to cling to her coat. Two men in black stood outside, their hats in their hands.

'All right,' said Wexford, 'we won't trouble you any more at the moment.'

Among the other parked cars two black Daimlers now waited, one empty, one bearing the body of the former gangster in a coffin laden with flowers. Wexford and Burden went back to their car. Donaldson said a message had come through on the radio that the gun had been found under the paving stones at the 'weir'.

Wexford nodded. He was watching Chipstead's house. Until now it hadn't occurred to him that there had been others inside as well as the three sisters. These people, no doubt, had been sitting in silence behind the bay window with the drawn curtains, waiting to follow Chipstead's body to the grave or the fire. They came trooping down the path, an elderly man and woman arm-in-arm, a boy of eighteen in a borrowed black jacket and tie, a little man with red hair, a fat man with practically no hair, a tall man with silver hair.

'Silver Perry,' Burden said.

'Were they old pals or something?'

'Evidently. It wouldn't surprise me.'

The Daimler took the sisters and the old couple. The rest of the mourners got into an old dark blue Ford Popular.

'Where do you suppose they're going, Donaldson?' said Wexford.

'City of London Crematorium, Manor Park, sir,' Donaldson said promptly. 'Twenty minutes there, twenty minutes for a hymn and our-dear-brother-to-the-fire, twenty minutes back.'

'We may as well go and have lunch then.'

*

370

The wind had dropped and it became very dark, dark enough to have the light on in the front room at 52 Dogshall Road. The light shimmered through unlined green curtains. The boy was the first to leave, dressed in leathers now and carrying a crash helmet. He got on the Yamaha parked next to the Ford Popular and roared off in the direction of the bridge. A little while later the front door opened again and Silver Perry came out. Conventionally dressed in a dark suit and dark waisted overcoat, he had something of a look in the fading light of Adam Knighton, but of Knighton debased, vulgarized, roughened. He was a little less tall and lacked the presence of the man for whom he had said he would do anything, would lay down his life.

'He used those words?' Wexford said.

'Well, in a newspaper,' said Burden. 'I was going to tell you, I nearly did tell you only you interrupted me with your idea about the gun, they remember Coney Newton being in the El Video till three or whatever and Newton says he was there with Perry but no one in the club said a word to me about seeing Perry.'

On the doorstep Perry kissed Renie Thompson and then walked quickly away. Wexford thought he would get into the Ford but evidently it wasn't his, he had come on foot. And on foot he was departing through the thin grey drizzle that had now begun to fall steadily. The street lights had come on, lozenges of fruit drop orange among the stripped branches of the trees. Perry turned up the collar of his coat and trudged along, hands in pockets. He was heading, probably, for the tube station, a quarter of a mile up the hill past the hump in the road.

The car crawled after him, Donaldson driving very slowly. A van behind started hooting but Donaldson took no notice.

'He thinks he's going to cross here,' said Wexford. 'Pull round the corner.'

Donaldson turned sharply to the left just as Perry approached the edge of the pavement to cross the street. The side of the car presented itself in front of him like a wall. Silver Perry took a step back as the car door was thrown open and Wexford got out.

'Care for a lift, Silver?'

Wexford had his warrant card out but he need not have troubled. Perry belonged in that category of men who could pick out a policeman on a nude beach or at a fancy dress ball. It was child's play to him to detect three of them in a London suburb, in a car, in the rain. For all that, he looked for a split second as if he might try making a run for it. In that second his face showed the spark of hope, the flare of panic, the commonsense realization that quenched them. He shrugged and got into the car. Rain was running off the glossy white cap of hair.

'D'you know where Cyril Street, Bethnal Green is, Donaldson?' said Burden.

'I can find it, sir.'

'Off Globe Road,' said Perry.

'Or do we take him straight back with us? Your gun's been found, Perry. Shooters usually do turn up in the long run.'

'Shooter? What shooter?' said Perry.

'Cyril Street first, I think,' Wexford said, 'and then maybe we can think again. Enjoy yourself at the funeral, did you, Silver? By God, but you niff of Cyprus sherry.'

'I suppose you think you're funny. I didn't go to enjoy myself. Henry Chipstead was a lifelong friend.'

'And we all know how good you are to your friends. Laying down your life and so forth. Or laying down other people's lives.' Wexford looked into the man's pale blue eyes, watery eyes, narrower and shiftier than Knighton's. 'You've no alibi for the night of October the first. And you were seen near Thatto Hall Farm. You were seen walking along the footpath to Sewingbury from Thatto Vale at three in the morning.'

Silver Perry said nothing. The car wound its way along a one-way street system, through back doubles, from the eastern suburbs into the East End of London. It was raining hard now and the wipers were on at high speed.

'You left your car in the market square at Sewingbury,' said Burden. 'You must know the area well.'

Perry admitted nothing. In a low voice he said, 'Renie and me — like a hundred years ago I used to know Renie pretty well.'

'When you came back you saw the building works and

you buried the gun, knowing it would be concreted in next day.'

Perry tapped Donaldson's back. 'Second one on the left now, son.'

'I reckon Knighton must have given you something for your trouble,' said Burden. 'Reimbursed you for the shooter at any rate.'

Perry sighed. 'The wife's out, round at her sister's. I wouldn't want her brought in on this.'

The tall stalk of a tower, punctured all over now with squares of light, and its fellow stalks, vertical dormitories. There were several hundred cars now on the shiny black wet tarmac that was clean of shed leaves since there were no trees here to shed them. Wexford sent Donaldson off for a cup of tea in a Globe Road café. The lift took them up what felt like ten miles to Perry's eyrie and the kind of view that would once have made men gasp but now is a commonplace to air travellers and frequenters of revolving restaurants.

No one was at home. The place was dark. Perry put on a light or two and took them into the room that had nothing in common with the accepted notion of a penthouse except altitude. He said, 'I'll tell you about it. It's too late to worry about Mr Knighton now. There's nothing can harm him where he's gone.'

The cheap sentimentality of these people! Wexford thought. It was typical. Perry had once shot a man in cold blood, had since then done appalling violence, to say nothing of accepting Knighton's commission to kill his wife, yet he talked like some guiltless and gullible old woman.

'You, however,' said Wexford, 'aren't yet in that happy hereafter and there's plenty of harm can come to you.'

'You mean you're going to caution me?'

Wexford shook his head. 'Not yet. Tell us about when you first knew Mr Knighton.'

'It's twenty-five years. More. But for him they'd have hung me.' Silver looked at Burden. 'You know how it was. I wrote my story for the paper and I cut the piece out and sent it to Mr Knighton. He never answered, naturally he didn't, a man in his position. I waited for him in Lincoln's Inn one evening and we got talking.'

'Just like that?' Wexford tried to imagine it, this shifty tyke and Knighton meeting, getting 'talking'. Knighton would surely have frozen him with a stare and if he persisted, threatened him with the police.

'Not "just like that",' Silver said. 'I never pestered him, I never annoyed him. I just said I wanted to thank him properly, I said it quiet like. I told him there was nothing in the world I wouldn't do for him.'

And then Wexford did see. Knighton's integrity was already shaky, he was already becoming corrupted. For five years he had been Milborough Lang's lover but by then he knew they couldn't continue on that impermanent, uneasy basis. She would go and he would be left with Adela. Unless . . .

'By all this "anything in the world" claptrap you meant you'd get rid of his wife for him, didn't you?'

Silver winced at the plain speaking. 'He knew what I meant. I knew and he knew, there wasn't no need to put it into words. Help him get what he wanted, that's what I meant and he knew what I meant.'

'How did you know what he wanted?' asked Burden.

'I said I waited for him. It was a few times I did that and I followed him before I got him alone and we got talking. A couple of times I saw him meet this girl. Actress, she was, world-famous.'

'Still, Knighton didn't take you up on your generous offer?'

'He had a lot of scruples, had Mr Knighton,' said Silver with a kind of sage reverence. 'Well, you have to in his position. I said to him I'd never forget what he'd done for me and any time he wanted you know what, any time, he'd only to let me know. I wouldn't bother him, I said. I knew a man in his position don't want to be seen with the likes of me, I understood that. I was living in rooms in Cambridge Heath then. When the council put us in here I dropped him a line with my address and my phone. He never answered, naturally he didn't.' Silver looked up, straight into Wexford's eyes. 'It used to bother me, I used to think about it a lot, the fact that I'd never done a thing to repay him, I had it on my conscience.'

'Your *what*?'

'I know the meaning of gratitude, the same as other folks.'

'No, not the same as other folks, Silver,' said Wexford. 'The way you know it is pathological.' He shook his head reflectively. 'What was he supposed to do, give you a ring and say he'd changed his mind?'

'I told you we never put it into words. It was subtle like, we understood each other. He had to give me a ring, yes. I arranged it, I knew he wouldn't want to ask me outright.' Silver shifted in his seat. He had kept his black overcoat on but now he pulled himself out of it and threw the coat across the arm of a chair. Behind him the glittering view twinkled like a million fallen stars. 'I said to him, if ever you want you-know-what, you give me a tinkle. He never said a word. I looked him in the eye. You don't even have to say it, I said. You dial my number, I said, and when I answer you say one word. Any word you like, I said, so long as I know it.' There were beads of sweat on Silver's forehead now, up near the wig-like white hairline. 'He never answered me direct. He just looked at me and started telling some story about a Chinese mandarin, I don't recall the ins and outs of it now. That's it, I said, mandarin. You give me a call and when I answer you say "Mandarin" and I'll know. That was all of twenty-five years ago, nearer twenty-six. "Mandarin", I said, "any time, you say that one word and I'll know – and I'll do it".'

What had passed through Knighton's mind at the time? Had he conceived it as possible even in those days? Or had he merely been humouring Silver Perry, jollying him along, preparatory to getting rid of him for good? Wexford supposed they had been in a pub or even on a park bench somewhere. Just the one meeting, he was sure of that. Perry eager, grateful, gratified that this august man would conde-scend to converse with him, Knighton inexpressibly shocked, horrified, yet tempted. Raise the hand, say the word, do nothing more and she will die and you may have your heart's desire. What evil wicked nonsense! Better take one's own life in one's misery than countenance this, than even stay here listening to this. But 'Mandarin', one word . . .

'But one day, not long ago, he did ring you and he did say the word,' said Burden.

'Early in September it was. I picked up the phone and no one spoke for a bit, though you could hear breathing, and I was just thinking this was some joker when this voice says it. Stuttered a bit and spoke very low. The funny thing was, I'd *forgotten*. I mean I'd never seen Mr Knighton all that time, I'd never heard his voice. I'd had a bit of news via Renie over the years, but not for a long time, I never even knew he was retired, I never knew they lived in Sussex permanent like.

'The voice said this word. I could hear it started "man" and I thought what it said was "managing", but the receiver was put back before I could say anything. But I must have like recognized it in my subconscious or whatever on account of it kept haunting me all day. And suddenly it came to me. After all those years I could repay Mr Knighton at last, I could fulfil my promise.'

Wexford got up and turned his back. 'You make me sick.' He stood at the window, looking down on lurex-embroidered London, up at a homing aircraft laden with lights, breathing steadily to command his anger. 'Get on with it,' he said, 'and we can dispense with the noble sentiments.'

'You went ahead on that single word, a word you didn't even hear properly?' Burden put in.

'I *knew*,' said Silver. 'I hung about his chambers but he never come out and then I saw his name gone from the list at the door. I went up to Hampstead but I only had to take one look to see the place was full of bleeding Arabs. A couple of times I rung Thatto Hall Farm and he answered the first time and she answered the second but that didn't help me any.'

'Help you?'

'I had to know her movements, didn't I? I had to get her alone. Then one day I saw him. Coming out of Victoria Station it was, round about four in the afternoon, Wednesday, October the first. He was carrying this overnight bag, I knew he'd gone away for the night.'

'What were you doing at Victoria?'

'I have to work, don't I? I've got my living to earn. I was driving the mini-cab, I'd just dropped a fare. He was looking for a taxi, Mr Knighton was, and I thought to myself, why

376

don't I offer him a lift to wherever he's going? But I knew I was the last person he'd want to be seen with. Besides, I'd had a better idea. Seeing that overnight bag gave it to me. He'd come up to town for the night and she'd be alone. I reckoned on her being alone. I'd been to see poor old Henry in the hospital, you see, a couple of weeks before, and Renie was there and she said the daughter was married and expecting a kid and all. So I reckoned on the old woman being alone. I reckoned if I was going to do it I'd better get on with it, I'd better get it over with that night.'

Wexford thought he heard the front door click. There were sounds of movement in the hall and the woman who had screamed at Burden came in. Like her husband, she knew policemen by instinct and she gave Wexford a look others reserve for a thief or a vagrant. Wexford and Burden went out into the hall.

'Do we take him back with us and charge him?'

Wexford shrugged. 'Nothing to charge him with. I doubt if we could even make conspiracy stick.'

When they went back into the room the woman had disappeared and Silver Perry was drinking something that looked like whisky. It appeared to have been rationed out to him, as if for medicinal purposes.

'I was working till midnight. I got on to a pal of mine, never mind who, it don't matter now, I got on to him to say I'd been with him at the El Video if there was questions asked. Anyway, my last fare kept me a good half-hour over the odds and it was gone two, more like two-fifteen, two-twenty, before I got to Sewingbury. I left my vehicle in the market square and I walked. I came back by the footpath but I went by the road, not being too sure of my bearings if the moon was to go in.

'It was well after three when I got to Thatto Hall Farm. I got out my glass cutter and cut out that pane in the toilet window. Must have taken me ten minutes, maybe fifteen. The house wasn't that dark inside because of the moon shining in. I took my shoes off and went upstairs.

'All the bedroom doors was open and I went in the big front one, thinking to find her there. There was twin beds and one of them had the bedclothes turned back. I went back there later and took her jewel box and chucked some of her bits and pieces away to make it look like an outside job. He was an amateur, you see, he didn't know what's what. But first I looked in the other rooms and when I couldn't find her I went downstairs again. I was beginning to wonder what was up, I can tell you.'

Silver drank his drink and put the glass down heavily.

'I found her on the floor. She was dead, she'd been shot dead. I knew what it was right away, Mr Knighton had got there before me and done it himself.'

19

Wexford held the gun in his hands. Everything that could be deduced from an examination of it was in the report on the desk in front of him. It was a Walther PPK 9 mm automatic and approximately half-way along the barrel, on the underside, was a minute wart-like fault in the metal which would mark each bullet that passed through it with a fine hairline scratch. Burden, looking over his shoulder, said, 'What was Perry going to use? His bare hands?'

'I daresay. They're weapons you don't have to dispose of. A strange business, wasn't it? Perry was sure Knighton had killed her, not knowing she didn't die till some eleven hours after Knighton's departure for London. He thought Knighton had got tired of waiting for him to keep his promise and had killed her himself.' Wexford put the gun down on the desk. 'I've no time for a villain like that, Mike, but I believe him when he says he was ashamed of himself for having failed Knighton. Because he had shilly-shallied since the beginning of September, Knighton had been driven to do it himself. And because he thought Knighton hadn't done a sufficient job of faking a break-in and burglary, hadn't done any sort of job of that at all, he himself took the jewel box out of the house and having no great opinion of our acumen, scattered its contents about the front garden.'

According to Perry, in spite of his ploy with Mrs Knighton's pieces of jewellery, in spite of the evidence of break-in, he had expected Knighton to be arrested and charged with his wife's murder almost at once. He had cursed himself for

379

the delay which he saw as having led Knighton to commit the crime. When nothing had happened to Knighton he had simply put this down to police ineptitude. If he had ever doubted Knighton's guilt, that doubt had been dispelled by his suicide.

'And certainly Knighton believed Perry had killed her,' Wexford went on. 'From the moment he came home on October the second and I told him his wife had been shot he believed Perry had done it and done it on his instructions. That accounts for the feeling we always had of his being surprised yet not surprised, guilty yet innocent. That day he phoned Perry at the beginning of September – I wonder what impelled him to do that, what particular thing happened? We shall never know now. Had Adela found out about Milborough Ingram and threatened or ridiculed? Had Mrs Ingram begun to talk of going home? Or had Adela begun talking of another long holiday – we know she wanted to go to India and Nepal in February – which would take him away from Milborough again? Whatever it was, a temptation that was a quarter of a century old came back and this time he succumbed. But I can't think he really believed in it, Mike. It must have seemed like fantasy. With anyone but Silver Perry, who isn't, I think, quite sane, it would have been fantasy.

'You can imagine him leaving Milborough Ingram's flat late one afternoon, going off to meet Adela and travel home with her. Maybe it was on a street corner or in a station that he saw the empty call box and remembered the past, remembered "Mandarin".

'Of course it was all nonsense, it could never happen now. "Mandarin" was all he had to say and the murder would be done and his happiness secured. In fantasy, in dreams, not really. But he went into the phone box and he dialled and he said it. At any rate he said something like it and then he went off and met Adela and no doubt told himself what a fool he was.'

Burden came round the desk and sat down. He was frowning.

'He must have wondered if anything would happen.'

'Perhaps. Nothing did, though, did it? Three or four

weeks went by and nothing had happened. He must have thought Silver Perry had forgotten "Mandarin" or got old or reformed or had never really meant it in the first place. But as soon as Adela was killed he knew. But happiness wasn't secured. There was no freedom, no future, no joyful looking-forward. Not happiness, but remorse. For he believed Perry had done it on *his* word, though that word was a muttered whisper given after a gap of twenty-five years.'

'He killed himself in vain,' said Burden. 'He killed himself for an illusion. He might have been happy, he might have re-married. He'd done nothing and Perry had done nothing.'

'The intention was there, Mike,' Wexford said thoughtfully. 'And it was more than just a wish for his wife to die, wasn't it? However slight, it was an express instruction and he had delivered it to a dirty little crook and murderer he shouldn't have lowered himself to speak to. Even if we'd found someone for this job while he was alive he'd still have had that on his mind, wouldn't he? On his conscience, disgusting him with himself and, I suspect, pretty well poisoning the feelings he had for the great love of his life. Men like Knighton had better not commit crimes even vicariously, they had better not be involved im crimes they *imagine* they have committed vicariously.'

Burden looked at his watch. 'He should be in by now. It's just gone ten.' When Wexford didn't respond he said more sharply, 'The one that really committed it, I mean. You said you didn't want him fetched from home.'

'Not in the circumstances, no.' Wexford sighed. 'Not that it's going to make much difference, maybe a couple of hours. I'm not planning on talking to him much, we don't need a confession. It's all as clear as glass. I should have seen it from the start, only China intruded, China and what went on there confused me. Not that China didn't have a good deal to do with his motive, it did.'

'He bought the gun,' said Burden, 'quite openly from a very respectable gunsmith's, Warrington Weapons of London Wall. It was easy. And it makes our task easier.'

'The books he was keeping, or not keeping, are going to be pretty damning evidence too. We'll be spending the rest of the day looking into his financial juggling, Mike. Come on, then, let's go and take him.'

They had finished. There was nothing more to do until the special court in the morning. It had been dark for hours, the damp foggy dark of November. Wexford picked up his coat and slung it over him. 'I feel like a drink.'

'Come back to my place,' Burden said.

Wexford felt deeply tired, as tired as he had been after those white nights in China. His head floated, it seemed full of a crowding of figures and prevarications and lies. Yet there was nothing to think of or talk about except what they had done that day and he went on talking about it.

'But surely it was Perry that Bingley saw in the wood?' Burden had asked.

'How can it have been? Confused as Bingley was, he was sure the man he saw was walking back from Thatto Vale, not going towards it. Besides that, Perry went by the road and only came back by the footpath. Now if Perry didn't get to Thatto Hall Farm till three, took ten to fifteen minutes cutting out that glass and another ten going over the house and finding the body, it would have been more like ten to four before he passed the spot where Bingley was. Or had been, for by that time Bingley had certainly gone off home.'

They got into Wexford's car. Jenny had taken Burden's. Wexford drove slowly because he was tired.

'It was a grey-haired man he saw,' Burden insisted.

'But was it? He came to see us in the first place because his niece told him he ought to. He had seen a man walking that footpath back to Sewingbury at three in the morning of October the second. But he was nervous about coming to us because he'd been poaching. So to please us he makes his story as near to what he thinks we want as he can. Knighton is tall and has grey or silver hair. He either knows Knighton by sight or has seen his picture in the paper. Therefore he describes the man he saw as tall and with grey hair. But when I show him photographs that's a different matter. He is reminded then of what the man in the wood *really* looked

382

like. Of the figures in the pictures he's shown he doesn't pick out Knighton who resembles Silver Perry more than any of them. He picks out Gordon Vinald who doesn't resemble him at all but is youngish, dark, rather short and slightly built.'

Burden's porch light was on. The bungalow itself was in darkness. Wexford got out of the car and walked up the path towards the light and something soft and slinky came out of the shadows and rubbed itself against his trouser leg. He jumped because he was weary and it had been a long day. Burden unlocked the front door and Wexford followed him into the house, holding the cat in his arms.

'Bingley couldn't pick out the man who killed Adela Knighton from the photographs because he wasn't in them. So he picked out the man most nearly like him. He chose the only man in the group who was also young, dark, short and slight.'

The centre light in the living room came on but the bulb in the table lamp flashed, fizzled and went dark. The bright glare from the middle of the ceiling made Wexford wince and blink. Burden switched it off.

'I'll get another bulb. I'll just have to think where it is Jenny keeps them. And then what? Scotch?'

'I shouldn't,' said Wexford in much the same way Milborough Ingram had, though he was thinking more of his health than his face and figure. 'But I will.'

He sat in the dark, a little light coming in from the hall. The back door slammed as Burden went out to the garage. The cat began doing that uncanny things cats do, staring at nothing, following nothing round the room with its eyes. It slid off Wexford's lap and sat with its tail faintly moving, gazing towards the doorway and the light.

An old Chinese woman with bound feet, in dark trousers and a quilted jacket, walking with small mincing steps, came out of the light – out of nowhere, it seemed – and stood on the threshold. His heart simply stopped. It felt as if it had stopped and the restarting, the thuds of its beat, were almost painful.

'Why are you sitting in the dark?' Jenny Burden said. 'Where's Mike?'

He managed to speak in his normal voice. 'Gone to find a light bulb.'

She retreated into the kitchen, the high wooden-soled sandals she wore restricting her walk, and came back at once with a bulb. The table lamp came on and showed him Burden's wife, made up to look Chinese but not to look old, a black wig covering her fair hair. The cat rubbed itself against her, winding in and out between her ankles.

'The Good Woman of Setzuan, I presume?'

'It was our dress rehearsal. It was dark so I thought I might as well come home just as I was.' She kissed Burden who came in with their drinks. 'If you'll excuse me, I'll go and take all this lot off.'

'My God,' said Burden. 'I wonder you didn't think you were hallucinating again.'

Wexford said nothing. He took his whisky with a steady hand.

'So it *was* Angus Norris that Bingley saw?' Burden said.

'Of course. Having let himself' into Thatto Hall Farm with his wife's key, got his mother-in-law out of bed, brought her downstairs and shot her, he made his way home again along that footpath, thus enabling Bingley to see him at three o'clock.

'I suppose he told her,' said Burden, 'that his wife had been taken ill or gone into early labour or some such thing and they hadn't been able to get through on the phone. He shot her through the back of the head because, like the gentleman he is, he let a lady precede him into a room. And that wife of his is having a baby any minute . . .'

'I hope it may be a consolation to her,' Wexford said sombrely. 'Mother, father and now this. Norris was shattered by Knighton's suicide. Did you see his face? He hadn't expected that. I daresay he thought he was doing Knighton a favour, killing Adela. Mind you, I don't think he planned it, or not very far in advance. He didn't go up to London and Warrington Weapons and buy the gun with that in mind. He bought the gun because he collects firearms. Then – maybe not till the very day of October the first – his wife told him her father would be going to London for the night.

'Jennifer slept soundly because she was sedated. She would have been unaware of it if he was absent for an hour. I think he was desperate. He had married someone who expected to be kept in the style of her mother, of her older brothers and their wives, but he couldn't make the grade. He had only what he earned as an assistant solicitor with Symonds, O'Brien and Ames. I'm guessing here but I hardly think it can be otherwise, that he bought that house on a mortgage far above what he could afford. The cost of living went on rising and mortgage interest rates edged up too. It's apparent the house isn't even adequately furnished. We've seen enough of his financial affairs today to know that he was substantially in debt. And now there was a baby on the way which probably meant Jennifer would demand some sort of living-in help.

'He was frantic with money worries. He took his gun and walked to Thatto Hall Farm and killed Jennifer's mother, believing it would be thought she had come down and admitted some stranger who had knocked at the door. Norris, you see, is tarred with the same brush as his wife's family – he thinks he belongs to an élite that is above suspicion of criminality.'

Burden said, 'His firm were Mrs Knighton's solicitors, they drew up her will for her, so he knew what was in it – fifty thousand pounds for his wife.'

'That was a contributory motive only. That was a bonus. His motive was Mrs Knighton's holiday fund.'

'We didn't find a single record of that, not a word referring to it.'

'I daresay Norris felt it was safer that way. I daresay he even had a bold dream that if ever it came to the crunch he could deny that his mother-in-law had entrusted him with a large sum to invest. But to do that would have meant cutting himself and his wife off from her family entirely and certainly losing that future inheritance. Anyway, he didn't have the nerve. He only had nerve enough to kill her.'

'I suppose he had drawn on the fund for his own use and was hoping against hope that by some means or other he could make up the deficit before Adela demanded a really large sum.'

Wexford nodded. 'After all, last April he had had to provide her with four thousand pounds to go to China, a substantial amount for one holiday.'

'But that was more than six months ago. Why kill her now?'

'Because she asked for more. She wanted to go to India and Nepal in February. What would that have cost for the two of them? At least as much as the China trip. Very likely he didn't even have that much remaining in the fund. With Jennifer's inheritance he could pay his debts. He could make good what he had helped himself to out of the fund and present the money intact as soon as Knighton or a brother-in-law started asking questions.'

'Strange, isn't it, that a man would rather do murder and thereby shut himself up for fifteen years, not to mention losing his wife and child – for I'm sure he will – he'd rather do that than stand up and confess to having lost a sum of money?'

Wexford shrugged. 'We're all cowards one way or another.' He looked up and smiled as Jenny came back dressed as herself.

Wolf to the Slaughter

I think the Vessel, that with fugitive
Articulation answer'd, once did live,
And merry-make; and the cold Lip I kiss'd
How many Kisses might it take—and give!

For Don

'Tis all Chequer-board of Nights and Days
Where Destiny with Men for pieces plays:
Hither and thither moves, and mates, and slays,
And one by one back in the Closet lays.

The Rubaiyát of Omar Khayyám

CHAPTER ONE

They might have been going to kill someone.

The police would possibly have thought so if they had stopped the car that was going too fast along the darkening road. The man and the girl would have had to get out and explain why they were carrying an offensive weapon. Explanation would have had to come from the man, for the girl could not have answered them. In the gathering dusk, watching the thin rain trickle down the glass, she thought that the raincoats they wore looked like a disguise, gangster garments, and the knife unsheathed for use.

'Why do you carry it?' she asked, speaking for the first time since they had left Kingsmarkham and its street lamps drowned in drizzle. 'You could get into trouble having a knife like that.' Her voice was nervous, although the nerves were not for the knife.

He pressed the switch that worked the windscreen wipers. 'Suppose the old girl turned funny?' he said. 'Suppose she changed her mind? I might have to put the fear of God into her.' And he drew his fingernail along the flat of the blade.

'I don't like it much,' the girl said, and again she did not only mean the knife.

'Maybe you'd rather have stayed at home, with him liable to come in at any minute? It's a miracle to me you ever got around to using his car.'

Instead of answering him, she said carefully, 'I mustn't see this woman, this Ruby. I'll sit in the car out of the way while you go to the door.'

'That's right, and she'll nip out the back. I got the whole thing arranged on Saturday.'

Stowerton was seen first as an orange blur, a cluster of lights swimming through the mist. They came into the town centre where the shops were closed but the launderette still open. Wives who worked by day sat in front of the machines, watching their washing spin round inside the portholes, their faces greenish, tired in the harsh white light. On the corner at the crossroads, Cawthorne's garage was in darkness, but the Victorian house behind it brightly illuminated and from its open front door came the sound of dance music. Listening to this music, the girl gave a soft giggle. She whispered to her companion, but because she had only said something about the Cawthornes having a party, nothing about their own destination and their purpose, he merely nodded indifferently and said:

'How's the time?'

She caught sight of the church clock as they turned into a side street. 'Nearly eight.'

'Perfect,' he said. He made a face in the direction of the lights and the music and raised two fingers in a derisive gesture. 'That to old Cawthorne,' he said. 'I reckon he'd like to be in my shoes now.'

The streets were grey and rain-washed and they all looked the same. Stunted trees grew from the pavements at four-yard intervals and their struggling roots had made cracks in the tarmac. The squat houses, unbroken rows and rows of them, were all garageless and there was a car stuck half-way on the pavement outside nearly every one.

'Here we are, Charteris Road. It's number eighty-two, the one on the corner. Good, there's a light in the front room. I thought she might have done the dirty on us, got cold feet or something and gone out.' He put the knife into his pocket and the girl watched the blade flick back to bury itself in the shaft. 'I shouldn't have liked that,' he said.

The girl said quietly, but with an undercurrent of excitement in her voice, 'Nor should I now.'

The rain had brought night early and it was dark in the car, too dark to see faces. Their hands met as together they fumbled to make the little gold cigarette lighter work. In its flame she saw his dark features glow and she caught her breath.

'You're lovely,' he said. 'God, you're beautiful.' He touched her throat, moving his fingers into the hollow between the horizontal bones. They sat for a moment looking at each other, the flame making soft candlelight shadows on their faces. Then he snapped the lighter closed and pushed open the car door. She twisted the gold cube in her hands, straining her eyes to read its inscription: For Ann who lights my life.

A street lamp on the corner made a bright pool from the kerb to the gate. He crossed it and it threw his shadow black and sharp on this evening of blurred outlines. The house he had come to was poor and mean, its front garden too small to have a lawn. There was just an earth plot, an area ringed with stones, like a grave.

On the step he stood a little to the left of the front door so that the woman who would come to answer his knock should not see more than she need, should not, for instance, see the tail of the green car, wet and glistening in the lamplight. He waited impatiently, tapping his feet. Raindrops hung from the window sills like chains of glass beads.

When he heard sounds of movement from within, he stood stiffly and cleared his throat. The footsteps were followed by sudden illumination of the single diamond pane in the door. Then, as the latch clicked, that pane became a frame for a wrinkled painted face, businesslike but apprehensive, crowned with ginger hair. He thrust his hands into his pockets, feeling a smooth polished hilt in the right-hand one, and willing things to go right for him.

When things went wrong, hideously wrong, he had a terrible sense of fate, of inevitability. It would have happened sometime, sooner or later, this way or the other. They got into their coats somehow and he tried to staunch the blood with his scarf.

'A doctor,' she kept moaning, 'a doctor or the hospital.' He didn't want that, not if it could be avoided. The knife was back in his pocket and all he wanted was air and to feel the rain on his face and to get to the car.

The terror of death was on both their faces and he could not bear to meet her eyes, staring and red as if the blood were reflected in the pupils. Down the path, they held on to each other, staggering past the little bit of earth like a grave, drunk with panic. He got the car door open and she fell across the seat.

'Get up,' he said. 'Get a grip on yourself. We've got to get out of here,' but his voice sounded as far off as death had once seemed. The car jerked and shuddered up the road. Her hands were shaking and her breath rattled.

'You'll be all right. It was nothing — that tiny blade!'

'Why did you do it? Why? Why?'

'That old girl, that Ruby . . . Too late now.'

Too late. A blueprint for last words. Music came out from Cawthorne's house as the car went past the garage, not a dirge but music for dancing. The front door stood open and a great band of yellow light fell across the puddles. The car went on past the shops. Beyond the cottages the street lamps came to an end. It had stopped raining but the countryside was shrouded in vapour. The road was a tunnel between trees from which the water dripped silently, a huge wet mouth that sucked the car along its slippery tongue.

Across the band of light and skirting the puddles, party guests came and went. Music met them, hot dry music in sharp contrast to the night. Presently a young man came out with a glass in his hand. He was gay and full of *joie de vivre* but he had already exhausted the possibilities of this party. The drunk he spoke to in a parked car ignored him. He finished his drink and put the glass down on top of a diesel pump. There was no one to talk to except a sharp-faced old girl, going home, he guessed, because the pubs were shutting. He hailed her, declaiming loudly:

'Ah, make the most of what we yet may spend,
Before we too into the dust descend!'

She grinned at him. 'That's right, dear,' she said. 'You enjoy yourself.'

He was hardly in a fit state to drive. Not at the moment. Besides, to remove his own car would necessitate the removal of six others whose owners were all inside enjoying themselves. So he began to walk, buoyantly and in the faint hope of meeting someone rather special.

It had come on to rain again. He liked the cool feeling of the drops on his hot face. The road to Kingsmarkham yawned at him. He walked along it happily, not at all tired. Far away in the distance, in the throat as it were of this deep wet mouth, he could see the lights of a stationary car.

'What lamp,' he said aloud, 'had destiny to guide
Her little children stumbling in the dark?'

CHAPTER TWO

A high east wind blowing for a day and night had dried the streets. The rain would come again soon but now the sky was a hard bitter blue. Through the centre of the town the Kingsbrook rattled over round stones, its water whipped into little pointed waves.

The wind was high enough to be heard as well as felt. It swept between the alleys that divided ancient shops from new blocks and with a sound like an owl's cry made leafless branches crack against the slate and brick. People waiting for the Stowerton bus going north and the Pomfret bus going south turned up collars to shelter their faces. Every passing car had its windows closed and when cyclists reached the summit of the bridge over that rushing stream, the wind caught them and stopped them for a moment before they battled against it and wobbled down past the Olive and Dove.

Only the daffodils in the florist's window showed that it was April and not December. They looked as sleek and smug behind their protective glass as did the shopkeepers and office workers who were lucky enough to be indoors on this inclement morning. Such a one, at least for the moment, was Inspector Michael Burden, watching the High Street from his well-insulated observatory.

Kingsmarkham police station, a building of startling modernity, commands a view of the town although it is separated from its nearest neighbour by a strip of green meadow. A horse was tethered there this morning and it looked as cold and miserable as Burden had felt on his arrival ten minutes before. He was still thawing out by one of the central heating vents which blew a stream of warm air against his legs. Unlike his superior, Chief Inspector Wexford, he was not given to quotation, but he would have agreed on this bitter Thursday morning, that April is the cruellest month, breeding, if not lilacs, grape hyacinths out of the dead land. They clustered beneath him in stone urns on the station forecourt, their flowers smothered by a tangle of battered foliage. Whoever had planted them had intended them to blossom as blue as the lamp over the canopy, but the long winter had defeated them. Burden felt that he might have been looking upon tundra rather than the fruits of an English spring.

He swallowed the last of the hot sugarless tea Sergeant Camb had brought him. The tea was sugarless because Burden preferred it that way, not from motives of self-denial. His figure remained lean naturally, no matter what he ate, and his greyhound's face thin and ascetic. Conservative in dress, he was wearing a new suit this morning, and he flattered himself that he looked like a broker on holiday. Certainly no one seeing him in this office with its wall-to-wall carpet, its geometrically patterned curtains and its single piece of glass sculpture would have taken him for a detective in his natural habitat.

He restored the tea cup to its saucer of black Prinknash pottery and his gaze to a figure on the opposite pavement. His own sartorial correctness was uppermost in his mind today and he shook his head distastefully at the loiterer with his long hair and his unconventional clothes. The window was beginning to mist up with condensation. Burden cleared a small patch fastidiously and brought his eyes closer to the glass. He sometimes wondered what men's clothes were coming to these days — Detective Constable Drayton was just one example of contemporary sloppiness — but this! An outlandish jacket of spiky fur more suited to an eskimo, a long purple and yellow scarf that Burden could not excuse by connecting it with any university, pale blue jeans and suede boots. Now he was crossing the road — a typical jay walker — and entering the station forecourt. When he bent down and snapped off a grape hyacinth head to put in his buttonhole, Burden almost opened the window to shout at him, but remembered about letting warm air out and stopped in time. The scarf was the last he saw of him, its purple fringe flying out as its wearer disappeared under the canopy.

Might as well be in Carnaby Street, Burden thought, recalling a recent shopping trip to London with his wife. She had been more interested in the cranky-looking people than the shops. When he got home he would tell her there was no need to go fifty miles in a stuffy train when there were funnier sights on her own doorstep. Even this little corner of Sussex would soon be infested with them, he supposed as he settled down at his desk to read Drayton's report on the theft of some Waterford glass.

Not bad, not bad at all. Considering his youth and his inexperience, Drayton was shaping up well. But there were gaps, vital facts omitted. If you wanted anything done in this world, he thought aggrievedly, you mostly had to do it yourself. He took his raincoat from the hook — his overcoat was at the cleaner's. Why not, in April? — and went downstairs.

After days of being almost obscured by muddy footmarks, the foyer's black and white checkerboard floor was highly polished this morning. Burden could see his own well-brushed shoes reflected in its surface. The long ellipse of the counter and the uncomfortable red plastic chairs had that chill clear-cut look wind and dry air give even to an interior.

Also contemplating his reflection in the mirror-like tiles, his bony hands hanging by his sides, sat the man Burden had seen in the street. At the sound of footsteps crossing the floor, he glanced up vaguely to where Sergeant Camb was on the phone. Apparently he needed attention. He had not come, as Burden had formerly supposed, to collect garbage or mend fuses or even sell shady information to Detective Sergeant Martin. It seemed that he was an authentic innocent member of the public in some sort of minor trouble. Burden wondered if he had lost a dog or found a wallet. His face was pale and thin, the forehead bumpy, the eyes far from tranquil. When Camb put the receiver down, he approached the counter with a curious sluggish irritability.

'Yes, sir?' said the sergeant, 'What can I do for you?'

'My name is Margolis, Rupert Margolis,' It was a surprising voice. Burden had expected the local brand of country cockney, something to go with the clothes, anything but this cultured effeteness. Margolis paused after giving his name, as if anticipating some startling effect. He held his head on one side, waiting perhaps for delighted gasps or extended hands. Camb merely gave a ponderous nod. The visitor coughed slightly and passed his tongue over dry lips.

'I wondered,' he said, 'if you could tell me how one goes about finding a charwoman.'

Neither dogs nor wallets, fuses nor undercover information. The man simply wanted his house cleaned. An anti-climax or a salutary lesson in not jumping to obvious conclusions. Burden smiled to himself. What did he think this was? The Labour Exchange? A Citizen's Advice Bureau?

Seldom disconcerted, Camb gave Margolis a genial smile. The enquirer might have found it encouraging, but Burden knew the smile covered a philosophical resignation to the maxim that it takes all sorts to make a world.

'Well, sir, the offices of the Ministry of Labour are only five minutes from here. Go down York Street, past Joy Jewels and you'll find it next to the Red Star garage. You could try there. What about advertising in the local rag or a card in Grover's window?'

Margolis frowned. His eyes were a very light greenish-blue, the colour of a bird's egg and like a bird's egg, speckled with brown dots. 'I'm very bad at these practical things,' he said vaguely, and the eyes wandered over the foyer's gaudy decor. 'You see, normally my sister would see to it, but she went away on Tuesday, or I suppose she did.' He sighed, leaning his whole weight against the counter. 'And that's another worry. I seem to be quite bogged down with care at the moment.'

'The Ministry of Labour, sir,' Camb said firmly. He recoiled, grabbing at fluttering papers, as Detective Constable Drayton came in. 'I'll have to see to those doors. Sheer waste running the heating.' Margolis made no move to go. He watched the sergeant twist the chrome handles, crouch down to examine the ball catch.

'I wonder what Ann would do,' he said helplessly. 'It's so unlike her to go off like this and leave me in a mess.'

His patience rapidly going, Burden said, 'If there aren't any messages for me, Sergeant, I'm off to Sewingbury. You can come with me, Drayton.'

'No messages,' said Camb, 'but I did hear Monkey Matthews was out.'

'I thought he must be,' said Burden.

The car heater was a powerful one and Burden found himself weakly wishing Sewingbury was fifty miles away instead of five. Their breath was already beginning to mist the windows when Drayton turned up the Kingsbrook Road.

'Who's Monkey Matthews, sir?' he asked, accelerating as they passed the derestriction sign.

'You haven't been with us all that long, have you? Monkey's a villain, thief, small-time con man. He went inside last year for trying to blow someone up. In a very small way, mind, and with a home-made bomb. He's fifty-odd, ugly, and he has various human weaknesses, including womanising.'

Unsmiling, Drayton said, 'He doesn't sound very human.'

'He looks like a monkey,' Burden said shortly, 'if that's what you mean.' There was no reason to allow a simple request for official information to grow into a conversation. It was Wexford's fault, he thought, for taking a liking to Drayton and showing it. Once you started cracking jokes with subordinates and being matey, they took advantage. He turned his back on Drayton to stare at the landscape of chilly fields, saying coldly, 'He smokes like a chimney and he's got a churchyard cough. Hangs around the Piebald Pony in Stowerton. Keep on the look-out for him and don't think you won't encounter him because you're bound to.' Better let him hear it and hear it without sentimentality from him than Wexford's highly coloured version. The Chief Inspector enjoyed the peculiar *camaraderie* he had with characters like Monkey and it was all right for him in his position. Let Drayton see the funny side and goodness knew where he would end up. He stole a glance at the young man's dark hard profile. Those cagey contained ones were all the same, he thought, a mass of nerves and complexes underneath.

'First stop Knobby Clark's, sir?'

Burden nodded. How much longer was Drayton going to let his hair grow? For weeks and weeks until he looked like a drummer in one of those pop groups? Of course Wexford was right when he said they didn't want all and sundry picking out an obvious cop from his raincoat and his shoes, but that duffel coat was the end. Line Drayton up with a bunch of villains and you wouldn't be able to tell the sheep from the goats.

The car drew up outside a small shabby jeweller's shop. 'Not on the yellow band, Drayton,' Burton said sharply before the hand brake was on. They went inside. A stout man, very short of stature, with a purple naevus blotching his forehead and the greater part of his bald pate, stood behind a glass-topped table, fingering a bracelet and a ring.

'Nasty cold morning,' Burden said.

'Bitter, Mr Burden.' Knobby Clark, jeweller and occasional receiver of stolen goods, shifted a step or two. He was too short to see over the shoulder of the woman whose trinkets he was pricing. His whole massive head came into view and it resembled some huge root vegetable, a swede perhaps or a kohl rabi, this impression being enhanced by the uneven stain of the birthmark.

'Don't hurry yourself,' Burden said. 'I've got all day.'

He transferred his attention to a display of carriage clocks. The woman Knobby was haggling with was, he could have sworn, utterly respectable. She wore a thick tweed coat that reached below her knees although she was a youngish woman, and the handbag from which she had produced the jewellery, wrapped in a thin plain handkerchief, looked as if it had once been expensive. Her hands shook a little and Burden saw that she wore a wedding ring on each. The shaking might have been due to the intense cold of Knobby's unheated shop, but only nerves could have been responsible for the tremor in her voice, nerves and the natural reluctance of such a woman to be there at all.

For the second time that day he was surprised by a tone and an accent. 'I was always given to understand the bracelet was valuable,' she said and she sounded ashamed. 'All my husband's gifts to me were very good.'

'Depends what you mean by valuable,' Knobby said, and Burden knew that the ingratiating note, the servility that covered granite imperviousness to pleading, was for his benefit. 'I'll tell you what I'll do. I'll give you ten for the lot.'

In the icy atmosphere her quickly exhaled breath hung like smoke. 'Oh, no, I couldn't possibly.' She flexed her hands, giving them firmness, but still they fumbled with the handkerchief and the bracelet made a small clink against the glass.

'Suit yourself,' said Knobby Clark. He watched indifferently as the handbag closed. 'Now, then, Mr Burden, what can I do for you?'

400

For a moment Burden said nothing. He felt the woman's humiliation, the disappointment that looked more like hurt love than wounded pride. She edged past him with a gentle, 'Excuse me', easing on her gloves and keeping that curious custody of the eyes that is said to be a nun's discipline. Going on for forty, he thought, not pretty any more, fallen on evil days. He held the door open for her.

'Thank you so much,' she said, not effusively but with a faint surprise as if once, long ago, she had been acustomed to such attentions and thought them lost for ever.

'So you haven't seen any of this stuff?' Burden said gruffly, thrusting the list of stolen glass under Knobby's bulbous nose.

'I already told your young lad, Mr Burden.'

Drayton stiffened a little, his mouth muscles hard.

'I think I'll take a look.' Knobby opened his mouth to complain, showing tooth fillings as richly gold as the metal of the clocks. 'Don't start screaming for a warrant. It's too cold.'

The search yielded nothing. Burden's hands were red and stiff when they came out of the inner room. 'Talk about Aladdin's cave in the Arctic,' he grumbled. 'O.K., that'll do for the time being.' Knobby was an occasional informer as well as a fence. Burden put his hand to his breast pocket where his wallet slightly disturbed the outline of the new suit. 'Got anything to tell us?'

Knobby put his vegetable-like head to one side. 'Monkey Matthews is out,' he said hopefully.

'Tell me something I don't know,' Burden snapped.

The swing doors had been fixed when they got back. Now it was difficult to open them at all. Sergeant Camb sat at his typewriter with his back to the counter, one finger poised in the warm air, his expression bemused. When he saw Burden he said as wrathfully as his bovine nature permitted:

'I've only just this minute got shot of him.'

'Shot of who?'

'That comedian who came in when you went out.'

Burden laughed. 'You shouldn't be so sympathetic.'

'I reckon he thought I'd send Constable Peach down to his cottage to clean up for him if he went on long enough. He lives in Quince Cottage down in Pump Lane, lives there with his sister only she's upped and left him to his own devices. Went to a party on Tuesday night and never came back.'

'And he came in here because he wanted a *charwoman*?' Burden was faintly intrigued, but still they didn't want to add to their Missing Persons list if they could avoid it.

'I don't know what to do, he says. Ann's never gone off before without leaving me a note. Ann this and Ann that. Talk about Am I my brother's keeper?'

The sergeant was a loquacious man. Burden could hardly help wondering how much Camb's own garrulity had contributed to Rupert Margolis's long diatribe. 'Chief Inspector in?' he asked.

'Just coming now, sir.'

Wexford had his overcoat on, that hideous grey overcoat which would never be at the cleaner's during cold spells because it was never cleaned. Its colour and its ridged, hide-like texture added to the elephantine impression the Chief Inspector made as he strode heavily down the stairs, his hands thrust into his pockets which held the shape of those fists even when empty.

'Carousel for a spot of lunch, sir?' said Burden.

'May as well.' Wexford shoved the swing door and shoved again when it stuck. With a half-grin, Camb returned smugly to his typewriter.

'Anything come up?' Burden asked as the wind hit them among the potted hyacinths.

'Nothing special,' Wexford said, ramming his hat more firmly on his head. 'Monkey Matthews is out.'

'Really?' said Burden and he put out his hand to feel the first spots of icy rain.

CHAPTER THREE

That Chief Inspector Wexford should be sitting at his rosewood desk reading the *Daily Telegraph* weekend supplement on a Friday morning was an indication that things in Kingsmarkham were more than usually slack. A cup of tea was before him, the central heating breathed deliciously and the new blue and grey folkweave curtains were half-drawn to hide the lashing rain. Wexford glanced through a feature on the beaches of Antigua, pulling down an angle lamp to shed light on the page. His little eyes, the colour of cut flints, held a mocking gleam when they lighted on a more than usually lush advertisement for clothes or personal furnishings. His own suit was grey, double-breasted, sagging under the arms and distorted at the pockets. He turned the pages, slightly bored. He was uninterested in after-shave, hair-cream, diets. Corpulent and heavy, he had always been stout and always would be. His was an ugly face, the face of a Silenus with a snub nose and wide mouth. The classics have it that Silenus was the constant companion for Bacchus, but the nearest Wexford ever got to Bacchus was an occasional pint with Inspector Burden at the Olive and Dove.

Two pages from the end he came upon an article which caught his eye. He was not an uncultured man and the contemporary fashion of investment by buying pictures had begun to interest him. He was looking at coloured photographs, two of paintings and one of a painter, when Burden came in.

'Things must be quiet,' Burden said, eyeing the *Weekend Telegraph* and Wexford's pile of scattered correspondence. He came up behind the Chief Inspector and glanced over his shoulder. 'Small world,' he said. Something in his tone made Wexford look up and raise one eyebrow. 'That bloke was in here yesterday.' And Burden stabbed his finger at the photographed face.

'Who? Rupert Margolis?'

'Painter, is he? I thought he was a Mod.'

Wexford grinned. 'It says here that he's a twenty-nine-year-old genius whose picture, "The Dawn of Nothing", has just been bought by the Tate Gallery.' He ran his eye down the page. ' "Margolis, whose 'Painting of Dirt' is contemporaneous with the Theatre of Cruelty, uses coal dust and tea leaves in his work as well as paint. He is fascinated by the marvellous multifarious textures of matter in the wrong place, etcetera, etcetera." Come, come, Mike, don't look like that. Let us keep an open mind. What was he doing in here?'

'Looking for some home help.'

'Oh, we're a domestic service agency now, are we? Burden's Buttling Bureau.'

Laughing, Burden read aloud the paragraph beneath the Chief Inspector's thick forefinger. ' "Some of Margolis's most brilliant work is the fruit of a two-year sojourn in Ibiza, but for the past year he and his sister Anita have made their home in Sussex. Margolis works in a sixteenth-century studio, the converted living room of Quince Cottage, Kingsmarkham, and it is here under the blood-red quince tree that he has given birth after six months' painful gestation to his masterpiece, or 'Nothing' as he whimsically calls it." '

'Very obstetric,' said Wexford. 'Well, this won't do, Mike. We can't afford to give birth to nothing.'

But Burden had settled down with the magazine on his knees. 'Interesting stuff, this,' he said. ' "Anita, a former model and Chelsea playgirl, is often to be seen in Kingsmarkham High Street, shopping from her white Alpine sports car...." I've never seen her and once seen never forgotten, I should think. Listen. "Twenty-three years old, dark and exquisite with arresting green eyes, she is the Ann of Margolis's portrait for which he was offered two thousand pounds by a South American collector. Her devotion to Margolis's interests is the inspiration of some of his best work and it is this which, some say, led to the breaking off six months ago of her engagement to writer and poet Richard Fairfax." '

Wexford fingered his own sample of the glass sculpture which with the desk and the curtains had just been allocated to the station. 'Why don't you buy the *Telegraph* yourself if you're so keen,' he grumbled.

'I'm only reading it because it's local,' Burden said. 'Funny what goes on around you and you don't know it.'

Wexford quoted sententiously, 'Full many a gem of purest ray serene the dark unfathomed caves of ocean bear.'

'I don't know about dark unfathomed caves.' Burden was sensitive to criticisim of his hometown. He closed the magazine. 'She's a gem all right. Dark and exquisite, arresting green eyes. She goes to parties and doesn't come home. . . .'

The glance Wexford gave him was sharp and hard and the query cracked out like a shot. 'What?'

Surprised, Burden looked up. 'I said she goes to parties and doesn't come home.'

'I know you did.' There was a hard anxious edge to Wexford's impatience. The teasing quality present in his voice while they had been reading was quite gone and from facetious mockery he had become suddenly alert. 'I know what you said. I want to know what made you say it. How d'you know?'

'As I said, genius came hunting for a charwoman. Later he got talking to Camb and said his sister had been to a party on Tuesday night and he hadn't seen her since.'

Wexford got up slowly. The heavy lined face was puzzled and there was something else there as well. Doubt? Fear? 'Tuesday night?' he said, frowning. 'Sure it was Tuesday night?'

Burden did not care for mysteries between colleagues. 'Look, sir, he didn't even report her missing. Why the panic?'

'Panic be damned!' It was almost a shout. 'Mike, if her name is Ann and she went missing Tuesday night, this is serious. No picture of *her,* is there?' Wexford flicked expertly through the magazine, having snatched it roughly from Burden. 'No picture,' he said disgustedly. 'What's the betting the brother hasn't got one either?'

Burden said patiently, 'Since when have we got all steamed up because a single girl, a good-looking, probably rich girl, takes it into her head to run off with a boy friend?'

'Since now,' Wexford snapped. 'Since this morning, since this.' The correspondence, Wexford's morning post, looked like a pile of litter, but he found the envelope unerringly and held it out to Burden. 'I don't like this at all, Mike.' He shook out a sheet of thick folded paper. The glass sculpture, indigo blue and translucent, shed upon it a gleaming amorphous reflection like a bubble of ink. 'Things are slack no longer,' he said.

It was an anonymous letter that lay where the magazine had been and the words on it were handwritten in red ball-point.

'You know what a hell of a lot of these we get,' Wexford said. 'I was going to chuck it in the basket.'

A back-sloping hand, large writing, obviously disguised. The paper was not dirty nor the words obscene. The distaste Burden felt was solely on account of its author's cowardice and his desire to titillate without committing himself.

He read it to himself.

A girl called Ann was killed in this area between eight and eleven Tuesday night. The man who done it is small and dark and young and he has a black car. Name of Geoff Smith.

Discarding it with a grimace, he turned to the envelope. 'Posted in Stowerton,' he said. 'Twelve-fifty yesterday. Not very discreet of him, writing it. In our experience, the usual line is to cut words out of newspapers.'

'Assuming the infallibility of handwriting experts?' Wexford scoffed. 'Have you ever heard one of those johnnies give a firm opinion one way or the other, Mike? I haven't. If your recipient hasn't got a sample of your normal handwriting you might just as well save your newspaper and your scissors. Slope backwards if you normally slope forwards, write large if you usually write small, and you're perfectly incognito, safe as houses. No, I'll send this down to the lab but I'll be very much surprised if they can tell me anything I haven't deduced for myself. There's only one thing I haven't deduced for myself. There's only one thing here that'll lead me to my correspondent.'

'The paper,' Burden said thoughtfully. He fingered its thick creamy surface and its silky watermark.

'Exactly. It's handmade, unless I'm much mistaken, but the writer isn't the kind of man to order handmade paper. He's an uneducated chap; look at that "done it".'

'He could work in a stationers,' Burden said slowly.

'More likely work for someone who ordered this paper specially from a stationers.'

'A servant, d'you mean? That narrows the field a lot. How many people around here employ menservants?'

'Plenty employ gardeners, Mike. The stationers should be our starting point and we'll only need to tackle the high-class ones. That leaves out Kingsmarkham. I can't see Braddon's supplying handmade paper and certainly not Grover's.'

'You're taking this whole thing very seriously, sir.'

'I am. I want Martin, Drayton, Bryant and Gates up here because this is one anonymous letter I can't afford to treat as a practical joke. You, Mike, had better see what you can get out of the twenty-nine-year-old genius.'

He sat beside Burden behind the desk when they were all assembled. 'Now, I'm not taking you off your regular work,' he began. 'Not yet. Get hold of the electoral register and make a list of all the Geoffrey Smiths in the district. Particularly in Stowerton. I want them all looked up during the course of the day and I want to know if any of them are small and dark and if any of them has a black car. That's all. No frightening of wives, please, and no insisting on looking into garages. Just a casual survey. Keep your eyes open. Take a look at this paper, Sergeant Martin, and if you find any like it in a stationers I want it brought back here for comparison . . .'

After they had gone, Burden said bitterly, 'Smith! I ask you, Smith!'

'Some people really are called Smith, Mike,' Wexford said. He folded up the colour supplement with Margolis's photograph uppermost and tucked it carefully in a drawer of the rosewood desk.

'If I could only find the matches,' Rupert Margolis said, 'I'd make you a cup of coffee.' He fumbled helplessly among dirty crockery, topless bottles of milk, crumpled frozen food cartons on the kitchen table. 'There were some here on Tuesday night. I came in about eleven and all the lights had fused. That's not unusual. There was an enormous pile of newspapers on here and I picked them up and chucked them outside the back door. Our dustbins are always full. However, I did find the matches then, about fifteen boxes where the papers had been.' He sighed heavily. 'God knows where they are now. I haven't been cooking much.'

'Here,' said Burden and handed him one of the match books the Olive and Dove gave away with drinks. Margolis poured a percolator full of black liquid sprouting mould down the sink. Grounds clung to the sink side and to an aubergine floating in dirty dishwater. 'Now, let me get this straight.' It had taken him half an hour to get the salient facts out of Margolis and even now he was not sure if he had them sorted out. 'Your sister, whose name is Anita or Ann, was going to a party given by Mr and Mrs Cawthorne of Cawthorne's service station in Stowerton on Tuesday night. When you got home at eleven, having been out since three, she was gone and her car also, her white Alpine sports car which is usually parked outside in the lane. Right?'

'Right,' said Margolis worriedly. The kitchen had no ceiling, only a roof of corrugated metal supported by ancient beams. He sat on the edge of the table staring at the cobwebs which hung from them and moving his head gently in time to the movement of those swinging grey ropes, agitated by the rising steam from the coffee pot.

Burden went on firmly. 'You left the back door unlocked for her and went to bed but you were awakened soon afterwards by Mr Cawthorne telephoning to ask where your sister was.'

'Yes. I was very annoyed. Cawthorne's a terrible old bore and I never talk to him unless I have to.'

'Weren't you at all concerned?'

'No. Why should I be? I thought she'd changed her mind and gone off somewhere else.' The painter got down from his perch and ran the cold water tap over two filthy tea cups.

'At about one o'clock,' Burden said, 'you were awakened again by lights passing across your bedroom ceiling. These you assumed to be the lights of your sister's car, since no one else lives in Pump Lane, but you did not get up . . .'

'I went straight off to sleep again. I was tired, you see.'

'Yes, I think you said you'd been in London.'

The coffee was surprisingly good. Burden tried to ignore the incrustations on the cup rim and enjoy it. Someone had been dipping wet spoons in the sugar and at times it had apparently been in contact with a marmalade-covered knife.

'I went out at three,' Margolis said, his face vague and dreamy. 'Ann was here then. She told me she'd be out when I got back and not to forget my key.'

'And had you forgotten it, Mr Margolis?'

'Of course I hadn't,' the painter said, suddenly sharp. 'I'm not crazy.' He drank his coffee at a gulp, and a little colour came into his pale face. 'I left my car at Kingsmarkham station and went to see this man about a show I'm having.'

'A show?' Burden said, bewildered. The word conjured up in his mind visions of dancing girls and dinner-jacketed comedians.

'An exhibition, then,' Margolis said impatiently. 'Of my work. Really, you are a bunch of philistines. I thought so yesterday when nobody seemed to know who I was.' He favoured Burden with a look of dark suspicion as if he doubted his efficiency. 'As I was saying, I went to see this man. He's the manager of the Morissot Gallery in Knightsbridge and when we'd had our talk he rather unexpectedly gave me dinner. But I was absolutely exhausted with all this travelling about. This gallery man's a fearful bore and it got very tedious just sitting there listening to him talking. That's why, when I saw Ann's car lights, I didn't bother to get up.'

'But yesterday morning,' Burden said, 'you found her car in the lane.'

'All wet and revolting with the *New Statesman* plastered across its windscreen.' Margolis sighed. 'There were papers all over the garden. I don't suppose you could send someone to clear them up, could you? Or get the council to?'

'No,' said Burden firmly. 'Didn't you go out at all on Wednesday?'

'I was working,' said Margolis. 'And I sleep a lot.' He added vaguely, 'At odd times, you know. I thought Ann had come and gone. We go our own ways.' His voice rose suddenly to a shrill pitch. Burden began to wonder if he might be slightly mad. 'But I'm lost without her. She never leaves me like this without a word!' He got up abruptly, knocking a milk bottle on to the floor. The neck broke off and a stream of sour whey flowed across coconut matting. 'O God, let's go into the studio if you don't want any more coffee. I don't have a photograph of her, but I could show you my portrait if you think it would help.'

There were probably twenty pictures in the studio, one of them so large that it filled an entire wall. Burden had only once in his life seen a larger and that was Rembrandt's *Night Watch* viewed reluctantly on a day trip to Amsterdam. To its surface, giving a three-dimensional look to the wild cavorting figures, other substances apart from paint adhered, cotton wool, slivers of metal and strips of tortured newspaper. Burden decided that he preferred the *Night Watch*. If the portrait was in the same style as this picture it would not be helpful for the purposes of identification. The girl would have one eye, a green mouth and a saucepan scourer sticking out of her ear.

He sat down in a rocking chair, having first removed from its seat a tarnished silver toast rack, a squashed tube of paint and a wooden wind instrument of vaguely Mediterranean origin. Newspapers, clothes, dirty cups and saucers, beer bottles, covered every surface and in places were massed on the floor. By the telephone dead narcissi stood in a glass vase half-full of green water, and one of them, its stem broken, had laid its wrinkled cup and bell against a large wedge of cheese.

Presently Margolis came back with the portrait. Burden was agreeably surprised. It was conventionally painted rather in the style of John, although he did not know this, and it showed the head and shoulders of a girl. Her eyes were like her brother's, blue with a hint of jade, and her hair, as black as his, swept across her cheeks in two heavy crescents. The face was hawk-like, if a hawk's face can also be soft and beautiful, the mouth fine yet full and the nose just verging on the aquiline. Margolis had caught, or had given her, a fierce intelligence. If she were not already dead in her youth, Burden thought, she would one day be a formidable old woman.

He had an uneasy feeling that one ought always to praise a work when shown it by its creator and he said awkwardly:

'Very nice. Jolly good.'

Instead of showing gratitude or gratification, Margolis said simply, 'Yes, it's marvellous. One of the best things I've ever done.' He put the painting on an empty easel and regarded it happily, his good humour restored.

'Now, Mr Margolis,' Burden said severely, 'in a case like this it's normal practice for us to ask the relatives just where they think the missing person might be.' The painter nodded without turning round. 'Please concentrate, sir. Where do you personally think your sister is?'

He realised that his tone had become more and more stern, more schoolmasterish, as the interview progressed, and suddenly he wondered if he was being presumptuous. Since his arrival at Quince Cottage he had kept the newspaper feature in mind, but only as a guide, as information on the brother and sister that could only have been elicited from Margolis after hours of probing. Now he remembered why that feature had been written and what Margolis was. He was in the presence of genius, or if that was journalist's extravagance, of great talent. Margolis was not like other men. In his fingers and his brain was something that set him apart, something that might not be fully recognised and appreciated until long after the painter was dead. Burden experienced a sense of awe, a strange reverence he could not reconcile with the seamy disorder that surrounded him or with the pale-faced creature that looked like a beatnik and might be a latter-day Rembrandt. Who was he, a country policeman, to judge, to mock and put himself among the philistines? His voice softened as he repeated his question.

'Where do you think she is, Mr Margolis?'

'With one of her men friends. She's got dozens.' He turned round and his opalescent eyes seemed to go out of focus and into some dreamy distance. Did Rembrandt ever come into contact with whatever police they had in those days? Genius was more common then, Burden thought. There was more of it about and people knew how to deal with it. 'Or I *would* think so,' Margolis said, 'but for the note.'

Burden started. Had he also received an anonymous letter? 'What note? A note about your sister?'

'That's the point, there isn't one, and there should be. You see, she's often popped off like this before and she wouldn't disturb me if I was working or sleeping.' Margolis passed his fingers through the long spiky hair. 'And I don't seem to do much apart from working and sleeping,' he said. 'She always leaves a note in a very prominent position, by my bed or propped up somewhere.' Memories seemed to come to him of such former examples of his sister's solicitude. 'Quite a long detailed note usually, where she'd gone and who with and what to do about cleaning the place and — and, well, little things for me to do, you know.' He gave a small doubtful smile which clouded into sourness as the telephone rang. 'That'll be dreary old Russell Cawthorne,' he said. 'He keeps bothering me wanting to know where she is.'

He reached for the receiver and rested his elbow against the chunk of mouldering cheese.

'No, she isn't here. I don't know where she is.' Watching him, Burden wondered exactly what were the 'little things' his sister would recommend him to do. Even so small a thing as answering the telephone seemed to throw him into a state of surly misanthropy. 'I've got the police here, if you must know. Of course I'll tell you if she turns up. Yes, yes, yes. What d'you mean, you'll be seeing me? I shouldn't think you will for a moment. We never do see each other.'

'Oh, yes, you will, Mr Margolis,' Burden said quietly. 'You and I are going to see Mr Cawthorne now.'

CHAPTER FOUR

Thoughtfully Wexford compared the two sheets of paper, one piece with red ballpoint writing on it, the other new and clean. The texture, colour and watermark were identical.

'It was from Braddon's, after all, sir,' said Sergeant Martin. He was a painstaking officer whose features were permanently set in an earnest frown. 'Grover's only sell pads and what they call drawing blocks. Braddon's get this paper specially from a place in London.'

'D'you mean it's ordered?'

'Yes, sir. Fortunately they only supply it to one customer, a Mrs Adeline Harper who lives in Waterford Avenue, Stowerton.'

Wexford nodded. 'Good class residential,' he said. 'Big old-fashioned houses.'

'Mrs Harper's away, sir. Taking a long Easter holiday, according to the neighbours. She doesn't keep a manservant. In fact the only servant she does have is a char who goes in Mondays, Wednesdays and Fridays.'

'Could she be my correspondent?'

'They're big houses, sir, and a long way apart. Waterford Avenue's not like a council estate or a block of flats where everyone knows everyone else. They keep themselves to themselves. This char's been seen to go in and out, but no one knows her name.'

'And if she has a way of snapping up unconsidered trifles like expensive writing paper, her employer and the neighbours don't know about it?'

'All the neighbours know,' said Martin, a little discomfited by the paucity of his information, 'is that she's middle-aged, showily dressed and got ginger hair.'

'Mondays, Wednesdays and Fridays . . . I take it she goes in while her employer's away?'

'And today's Friday, sir. But, you see, she only goes in mornings and she was gone before I got there. "I've just seen her go by", the neighbour said. I nipped up the road smartish but she was out of sight.'

Wexford turned his attention once more to the sheets of paper and to the lab report on that paper. No fingerprints had been found on the anonymous letter, no perfume clung to it; the pen with which it had been written was a cheap ballpoint such as could be bought in every stationers in the country. He had an inventive imagination but he could not visualise the concatenation of happenings that must have been the prerequisite to this letter. A ginger-haired charwoman, whose own conduct was apparently not above reproach, had seen something or heard something that had led her to write to the police. Such communication would necessarily be alien to a woman of her type, a woman found to be an occasional thief. And yet she, or someone closely associated with her, had written it. Fear or spite might have prompted her action.

'I wonder if it could be blackmail,' Wexford said.

'I don't quite follow you, sir.'

'Because we always think of blackmail being successful or, at any rate, successful for a time. Suppose it isn't successful at all. Suppose our ginger-haired woman tries to put the squeeze on Geoff Smith, but he won't play. Then, if she's vindictive, she carries out her threat.'

'Blackmailers always are vindictive, sir,' Martin said, sagely unctuous. 'A nasty spiteful thing, if ever there was one. Worse than murder, sir.'

An excessive show of respect always grated on Wexford, especially as in this case when it was associated with the imparting of platitudes he had heard a thousand times before. 'Here endeth the first lesson,' he said sharply. 'Answer that, will you?'

Martin leapt to the phone before the end of the second double peal. 'Inspector Burden for you, sir.'

Wexford took the receiver without getting up. The stretched coil lead passed dangerously near his glass sculpture. 'Move that thing,' he said. The sergeant lifted it and stuck in on the narrow window sill. 'Well?' Wexford said into the mouthpiece.

Burden's voice sounded dazed. 'I'm off to have a word with

Cawthorne. Can we spare someone to come down here and fetch Miss Margolis's car? Drayton, if he's not tied up. Oh, and the cottage'll have to be gone over.' Wexford heard his tone drop to a whisper. 'It's a proper shambles, sir. No wonder he wanted a char.'

'We want one, too,' Wexford said crisply, 'a snappy dresser with ginger hair.' He explained. The phone made crackling sounds. 'What's going on?'

'The cheese has fallen into a flower pot.'

'My God,' said Wexford. 'I see what you mean.'

Mark Drayton came down the police station steps and crossed the road. To reach Pump Lane he had to walk the whole length of the High Street and when he came to Grover's the newsagent he stopped for a moment to glance at its window. It seemed incredible to him that Martin had for a moment considered this place as the possible purveyor of handmade paper. It had the shady, almost sordid, aspect of a shop in the slum streets of some great city. A high brick wall towered above it and between it and the florist's next door a brown cobbled alley plunged deep into a dubious hinterland of dustbins and sheds and a pair of garages.

In the shop window the displayed wares looked as if they had been arranged there some years before and since left utterly untended. Easter was not long past and the Easter cards were topical. But it seemed to him that their topicality must be an accident in the same way as a stopped clock must be right twice a day, for there were Christmas cards there as well, some fallen on their sides and filmed with dust.

Dying houseplants stood among the cards. Perhaps they were for sale or perhaps misguidedly intended for decoration. The earth around their roots had shrunk through dehydration, leaving an empty space between soil and pot. A box containing a game of snakes and ladders had come open, so that the coloured board hung from a shelf. The counters lay on the floor among rusty nails, spilt confetti and shed leaves. Drayton thought he had seldom seen anything which could be regarded as an advertisement so repellent and so discouraging to those shoppers who passed this way.

He was going to walk on with a shrug of disgust when, through the dirty glass panel that separated this window from the interior of the shop, he caught sight of a girl behind the counter. He could only see her dimly, the shape of her, and her pale bright hair. But, as he hesitated, his interest faintly aroused, she approached the panel and opening it, reached for a pack of cards which lay to the left of the snakes and ladders box. That she made no attempt to retrieve the counters or blow the dust from the box lid, annoyed him. He was meticulous in his own work, tidy, attentive to the tools of his life and his trade.

Because he felt distaste and a desire to make plain the disapproval of at least one potential customer, he raised his eyes coldly and met hers. At once he knew who she was. A face which had haunted him for four days and which was faintly familiar but not specifically identifiable was confronting him. He stared at her and felt the hot blood rush into his cheeks. She could not know that he had seen her before, or if she did know it, could not be aware of the thoughts, many of them dreamlike, searching, sensuous, which had accompanied his constant evoking of her image on to his mind's eye. She could not know it, but he felt that she must do so, that such vivid violent imaginings could not be contained within the brain that conceived them and must by some telepathic process be communicated to their object.

She gave no sign. Her grey eyes, large and listless, met his only for a moment. Then she took the pack of playing cards, kneeling among the dust and the confetti to reach them, and retreated to serve a waiting customer. Her legs were long and rather too thin. The dust had left circular grey patches on her knees. He watched the panel swing slowly shut behind her, its fingermarked, bluish translucency obscuring all but the blur of her silver-gold hair.

Drayton crossed the alley, avoiding puddles on whose scummy surface spilt oil made a rainbow iridescence. He glanced at the garage doors, wondering why no one painted them when paint was cheap and the making of things clean and fresh so satisfying. From the stall outside the florist's he could smell daffodils. They and the girl he had just seen shared the same quality of untouched exquisite freshness and like the girl they flowered in squalor. The roughly made dirty wooden box was to them what the sordid newsagents was to her, an ugly unfitting background for breathless beauty.

Was everything he saw going to remind him of her? Had he felt like this before Monday night? As he came to the parapet of the bridge and looked down the river path he asked himself the question again. Certainly he had noticed her shopping in the town. She was the sort of girl any man would notice. For months now she had held for him a vague attraction. Then, on Monday night, he had passed this spot and seen her on that path kissing another man. It had given him a strange feeling to watch her, disarmed, vulnerable, abandoned to a passion anyone walking by in the dusk might witness. It showed that she was flesh and blood, subject to sensuality and therefore attainable, accessible to him.

Their figures had been reflected in the dark water, the man's which he had disregarded, and hers, slim, long, quivering. From that moment her image had haunted him, lying just above the surface of his conscious mind to trouble him when he was alone.

His own reflection, sharper and more real in the afternoon light than theirs had been at twilight, stared back at him coldly from the stream. The dark Italianate face with its guarded eyes and its curved mouth showed nothing of his thoughts. His hair was rather long, much too long for a policeman, and he wore a dark grey duffel coat over slacks and sweater. Burden objected to the coat and the hair, but he could find no fault with Drayton's economy of speech, nor with his reserve, although it was a different brand from his own.

The mirrored head and shoulders crumpled and retreated into the parapet of the bridge. Drayton felt in his pockets to make sure he had remembered his gloves. It was a formality only; he seldom forgot anything. He looked back once, but he could only see shoppers, prams, bicycles, a tall brick wall and an alley with wet litter on its cobbles. Then he made his way to the outskirts of the town and Pump Lane.

This by-way into Kingsmarkham's countryside was new to him, but like the other lanes it was just a tunnel between green banks topped with high trees, a roadway scarcely wide enough for two cars to pass. A cow peered at him over the hedge, its feet in primroses. Drayton was not interested in natural history nor given to pastoral reflection. His eye was drawn to the white sports car, parked half on the verge, half on the road, the only man-made thing in sight. The cottage itself was not immediately visible. Then he discerned, among tangled greening hawthorn and white sloe blossom, a small rickety gate. The branches were spiny and wet. He lifted them, drenching his shoulders. Apple trees, their trunks lichened to a sour pulpy green, clustered in front of the house whose shabby whiteness was relieved by the flame-coloured flowers of a tall shrub growing against it, the quince — though Drayton did not know it — from which the cottage took its name.

He slipped on his gloves and got into the Alpine. Possessing little of his own, he nevertheless had a respect for material things. This car would be a delight to own, a pleasure to drive. It irked him that its owner appeared to have used it as a kind of travelling dustbin, throwing cigarette packets and match ends on to the floor. Drayton knew better than to touch more than was needful, but he had to remove the torn newspaper from the windscreen before he could see to drive. Hawthorn boughs scraping the roof hurt him almost as much as if they had scoured his own skin.

The temptation to take the longer way round by Forby had to be resisted. Traffic was not heavy at this time of day and his only excuse would be that he wanted to enjoy himself. Drayton had trained himself stoically to resist temptation. One, he knew, he would soon succumb to, but not such a triviality as this.

There was a yellow and brown spotted fur coat slung across the passenger seat. It had a strong heady scent, the smell of a beautiful woman, evoking in Drayton's mind past and future love. The car moved smoothly forward. He had reached the centre of the High Street before he noticed the needle on the gauge climbing swiftly and alarmingly. It was almost at danger level. There were no service stations in this part of the main road, but he remembered seeing a garage in York Street, just past Joy Jewels and the labour exchange.

When he reached it he got out and lifted the hood. Steam billowed at him and he stepped back.

'Radiator's leaking,' he said to the pump attendant.

'I'll get you some water. She'll be all right if you take her slow. Far to go?'

'Not far,' said Drayton.

The water began to leak out as soon as they poured it in. Drayton was almost within sight of the police station. He passed Joy Jewels with its windows full of rhinestones on crimson velvet and he passed Grover's but he did not look. Poetry was not among his considerable and heterogeneous reading matter, but he would have agreed that man's love is of man's life a thing apart. He would go there later when his work was done.

Cawthorne's garage was an altogether grander affair than the modest place to which Drayton had taken Anita Margolis's car. It commanded Stowerton crossroads. From the roof of the showroom to the pinnacle of the little glass cubicle where Cawthorne sat at the receipt of custom, hung a yellow and scarlet banner: *Treble stamps with four gallons*. These colours matched the paint on the eight pumps and the neon tubing on the arch to the service entrance. Burden could remember when, not so long ago, a copse of silver birches had stood here and he remembered the efforts of the rural preservation society to prevent Cawthorne's coming. The last of the birches huddled by the showroom wall like bewildered aborigines crowded out by a conqueror from the new world.

By contrast the house behind was old. A triumph of the gothic revival, it sported pinnacles, turrets, gables and aggressive drainpipes. Formerly known as Birch House, the home of two spinster sisters, it had been furnished by Cawthorne and his wife with every conceivable Victorian monstrosity. The mantelpieces were fringed and set about with green glass fluted vases, stuffed birds and wax fruit under domes. Cawthorne, after a dubious look at Rupert Margolis, took them into a sitting room and went away to fetch his wife.

'It's the latest fad,' Margolis said morosely. 'All this Victorian junk.' Above the fireplace hung an oleograph of a woman in grecian dress holding a lily. He gave it an angry glance. 'Cawthorne must be sixty and his wife's a hag. They're mad about young people. I expect the young people think they had this stuff for wedding presents.' And he laughed vindictively.

Burden thought he had seldom met anyone so uncharitable, but when Mrs Cawthorne came in he began to see what Margolis meant. She was extravagantly thin and her dress had a very short skirt and very short sleeves. Her hair was tinted primrose and styled like the head of a feather duster.

'Why, hallo, Roo. You are a stranger.' Burden was suddenly sure that she had met Margolis perhaps only once before, and here she was giving him pet names like a character out of *Winnie the Pooh*. A lion hunter. She bounced into a quilted and buttoned armchair, showing a lot of scrawny leg. Margolis took absolutely no notice of her. 'What's all this about Ann, then?'

'We hope you'll be able to help us, Mrs Cawthorne,' Burden said heavily, but it was to her husband that he turned his eyes. He was an elderly, white-moustached man, with a decided military bearing. If the growing fashion among the young of wearing soldier's uniforms spread to older generations, Cawthorne ought to catch on. He would look fine in a hussar's tunic. 'You had a party on Tuesday evening, Mr Cawthorne. Miss Margolis was invited. I understand she didn't turn up.'

'Right,' Cawthorne said briskly. 'She dropped in in the afternoon, said she'd be sure to be here. Never turned up. I've been damned worried, I can tell you. Glad to see you folk have been called in.'

'Yes, and Dickie Fairfax came all the way down from London just to see her.' Mrs Cawthorne moved closer to Margolis's side. 'They used to be friends. Very close friends, I may add.' She fluttered her beaded eyelashes.

'Fairfax, the writer?' Burden had never heard of him until that morning, but he did not wish to be branded a philistine for the second time that day.

Mrs Cawthorne nodded. 'Poor Dickie was rather peeved when she didn't turn up and drifted away around eleven.'

'Left one of my best brandy glasses on a diesel pump,' said Cawthorne gruffly. 'Damned inconsiderate blighter.'

'But he was here all the evening?' Between eight and eleven, Burden thought. That was the crucial time if the anonymous letter was to be trusted.

'He was here all right. Came on the dot of eight and got started in on the hard stuff right away.'

'You are so mean,' Mrs Cawthorne said unpleasantly. 'Mean and jealous. Just because Ann preferred him.' She gave a tinny laugh. 'She and Russell have a sort of thing.' Burden glanced at Margolis but the painter had gone off into a brooding abstraction. Mrs Cawthorne thrust a bony finger into her husband's ribs. 'Or that's what he kids himself.' The blood rushed into Cawthorne's already pink face. His hair was like white wool or the coat of a West Highland terrier.

Suddenly Margolis roused himself. He addressed Burden, rather as if there was no one else in the room.

'Ann gave Dickie the out months ago. There's someone else now. I'm trying to remember his name.'

'Not Geoff Smith, by any chance.' Burden watched the three faces, saw nothing but blankness. He had memorised the message in that letter. *He is small and young and dark and he has a black car. Name of Geoff Smith.* Of course, it wouldn't be his real name. Smith never was.

'All right. That's all for now. Thanks for your help.'

'I don't call that help.' Mrs Cawthorne giggled. She tried to take Margolis's hand but failed. 'You'll be lost without her, Roo,' she said. 'Now, if there's anything Russell and I can do. . . .'

Burden expected Margolis to maintain his silence, or possibly say something rude. He gave Mrs Cawthorne a blind hopeless stare. 'Nobody else has ever been able to do anything,' he said. Then he walked out of the room, his shoulders straight. For a brief moment he had attained Burden's notion of the heights of genius. He followed, Cawthorne behind him. The garage owner's breath smelt of whisky. His was a soldier's face, brave, hearty, a little stupid. The military air about him extended, Burden thought, even to his name. All those years ago his mother had called him Russell because it sounded so well with Cawthorne, auguring great things. General Sir Russell Cawthorne, K.C.B., D.S.O. . . . Burden knew something of his history. The man had never won a battle or even led a troop. He kept a garage.

'I'm looking for a Geoff Smith who might be a friend of Miss Margolis's.'

Cawthorne gave a braying laugh. 'I daresay he might, only

I've never heard of him. She's got a lot of boy friends. Lovely girl, lovely little driver and a good head for business. I sold her that car of hers. That's how we met. Haggled, you know, drove a hard bargain. I admire that. Only natural she'd have a lot of boy friends.'

'Would you include yourself among them?'

It was grotesque. The man was all of sixty. And yet boy friend could be applied these days to a lover of any age. It was in two senses a euphemism.

For a moment it seemed that Cawthorne was not going to reply and when he did it was not to answer the question.

'Are you married?'

'Yes, I am.'

'Horrible business, isn't it?' He paused and gazed lugubriously at a pump attendant giving green stamps with change. 'Growing old together . . . Horrible!' He braced his shoulders as if standing to attention. 'Mind you, it's your duty to stay young as long as you can. Live it up, keep going, go around with young people. That's half the battle.' The only one he was ever likely to fight.

'Did you "go around" with Miss Margolis, Mr Cawthorne?'

The garage proprietor brought his face and his whisky breath closer to Burden. 'Once,' he said. 'Just the once. I took her out to dinner in Pomfret, to the Cheriton Forest Hotel. Stupid, really. The waiter knew me. He'd seen me there with my wife. I was ordering, you see, and he said, "Will your daughter have smoked salmon too, sir?" '

Why do it, then? Why make such a crass fool of yourself? Burden had no temptations, few dreams. He got into the car beside Margolis, wondering why the defenceless put themselves into the firing line.

There were pictures on the stairs and pictures on the landing. The light was fading and Sergeant Martin stumbled over a pile of washing on the floor outside Anita Margolis's bedroom door.

'No letters and no diaries, sir,' he said to Burden. 'I never saw so many clothes in all my life. It's like a — a draper's shop in there.'

'A boutique, you mean,' said Drayton.

'Been in many, have you?' Burden snapped. Drayton looked the type who would buy black nylon underwear for his women and not turn a hair. Through the half-open door, propped ajar with a gilt sandal, he caught sight of garments spread on the bed and hung, crammed closely, in two wardrobes. 'If your sister went away of her own accord,' he said to Margolis, 'she'd have taken clothes with her. Is anything missing?'

'I really wouldn't know. It's absolutely useless asking me things like that. Ann's always buying clothes. She's got masses of them.'

'There's just one thing,' Drayton said. 'We can't find a raincoat.'

Martin nodded agreement. 'That's right. Furs and suede things and all sorts, but no woman's raincoat. It was raining cats and dogs on Tuesday night.'

'Sometimes she takes clothes,' said Margolis, 'and sometimes she doesn't. She's quite likely to have gone just as she was and then buy anything she needed.'

Leaving them to finish their search, Burden followed the painter downstairs. 'She had money then?' The woman in the portrait, the woman who possessed this vast and apparently expensive wardrobe, would hardly be content with something off the peg from Marks and Spencer. Or was the lover expected to cough up? In this set-up anything was possible. 'How much money did she have on her?'

'One of her cheques came on Monday. She has this money of her own, you see. My father left all the money to her. He didn't like me and I couldn't stand him, so he left it all to Ann. They pay it out every three months.'

Burden sighed. Anyone else would have spoken of a private income, of payments made quarterly.

'Do you know how much this cheque was for?'

'Of course I do,' Margolis said crossly. 'I'm not a half-wit. It's always the same, five hundred pounds.'

'And she had this cheque with her?' Here, at last, was something for him to get his teeth into. The beginning of a motive loomed.

'She cashed it as soon as it came,' Margolis said, 'and she put the money in her handbag.'

'All five hundred!' Burden gasped. 'You mean she set off for a party with five hundred pounds in her handbag?'

'Bound to have done. She always carried it about with her,' Margolis said casually, as if it were the most natural thing in the world. 'You see, she might be out and see something she wanted to buy and then she'd have the money on her, wouldn't she? She doesn't like paying for things with cheques because then she gets overdrawn, and Ann's rather middle-class in some ways. She gets worried if she's overdrawn.'

Five hundred pounds, even if it was in fivers, would make a big wad in a woman's handbag. Would she be careless about where she opened the handbag and to whom she revealed the contents? The woman was thoroughly immoral too. Decent women had clean tidy homes. They were either married or had jobs or both. They kept their money in the bank. Burden thought he could see just what had happened to Anita Margolis. She had gone into a shop or a garage on her way to the party, opened her bag and its contents had been seen by that villain Smith. A good-looking plausible villain, probably. Young, dark and with a black car. They had gone off together and he had killed her for the money. The letter writer had got wind of it, maybe tried blackmail, blackmail which hadn't worked?

But a casual pick-up would be next to impossible to find. A regular boy friend, especially if he was down on his luck, might fill the bill.

'Have you remembered the name of Fairfax's successor?' he asked.

'Alan Something. He's got no money and he's very provincial. I don't know what she sees in him, but Ann's rather inclined to go slumming, if you know what I mean. Fitz something. Fitzwilliam? It isn't exactly Fitzwilliam but it's something like that. I've only spoken to him once and that was enough.'

Burden said tartly, 'You don't seem to like anyone very much, sir.'

'I like Ann,' Margolis said sadly. 'I tell you who might know. Mrs Penistan, our late char. I should go and ask her, and if she's just pining to come back and clean this place, don't discourage her, will you?'

A chill grey drizzle was falling as they emerged from the cottage door. Margolis accompanied Burden to the garden gate. 'You haven't found a charwoman, then?'

From behind him the painter's voice held a note of childlike pride. 'I put an advertisement in Grover's window,' he said. 'I wrote it on a little card. Only half-a-crown a week. I really can't imagine why people spend all that money on the agony column of *The Times* when this way is so cheap and easy.'

'Quite,' said Burden, stifling an incipient desire to roar and stamp. 'This Mrs Penistan, she hasn't got ginger hair, has she?'

Margolis stood against the hedge, picking the new shoots off a hawthorn bush. These he put into his mouth and began to chew them with evident relish. 'She always wore a hat,' he said. 'I don't know what colour her hair is, but I can tell you where she lives.' He paused for congratulation perhaps on this unlooked-for feat of memory. Burden's expression seemed to gratify him, for he went on, 'I know that because I drove her home once when it was raining. It's in Glebe Road, on the left, past the fifth tree and just before you get to the pillar box. Red curtains downstairs and . . .'

Burden cut him short with a snort of exasperation. If this was genius he had had enough of it. 'I'll find it.' He could have recourse to the electoral register himself. Penistan was surely as rare a name as Smith was common.

CHAPTER FIVE

Mark Drayton rented a room down by Kingsmarkham station. His landlady was a motherly woman who liked to make her lodgers feel at home. She hung pictures on the walls, provided flowered counterpanes and scattered little ornaments about like seeds. As soon as he moved in Drayton put all the vases and ashtrays into the bottom of the cupboard. There was nothing to be done about the counterpane. He wanted the room to look like a cell. Someone — it was a girl — had told him he had a cold nature and he had since cultivated his personality in this direction. He liked to think he was austere and without emotion.

He was very ambitious. When he had first come to Kingsmarkham he had set out to make Wexford like him and he had succeeded. He carried out all Wexford's instructions meticulously, absorbing the Chief Inspector's homilies, lectures, digressions and pleasantries with courteously inclined head. The district was now as familiar to him as his own hometown and he used his library tickets for works on psychology and forensic medicine. Sometimes he read a novel, but nothing lighter than Mann or Durrell. One day he hoped to be a commissioner. He would marry the right wife, someone like Mrs Wexford, good-looking, quiet and gracious. Wexford had a daughter, a pretty girl and clever, they said. But that was a long way off. He had no intention of marrying until he had attained distinguished rank.

His attitude to women was a source of pride to him. Being intensely narcissistic, he had little admiration left over, and his idealism was reserved for his own career. His affairs had been practical and chilly. In his vocabulary love was a banned verb, the most obscene of the four letter words. He had never used it between 'I' and 'you'. If he ever felt anything stronger than a physical need he called it desire with complications.

That, he thought, was what he felt for the Grover girl. That was why he was going into the shop now to buy his evening paper. Maybe she would not be there. Or maybe when he saw her close-to, not through glass or in someone else's arms, it would all fade away. On the whole he hoped that would happen.

The shop squatted under a towering wall of brown brick. It seemed to lurk there as if it had something to hide. A street lamp in a black iron cage stuck out beside its door but the lamp was still unlit. As Drayton opened this door a little bell made a cold tinkle. The interior was dim and it smelt unpleasant. Behind the paperback stand and a rusty refrigerator hung with lop-sided ice-cream posters, he could see the shelves of a lending library. The books were the kind you buy at jumble sales, nineteenth century three-volume novels, explorer's reminiscences, school stories.

A thin dried-up woman was behind the counter, standing under a naked light bulb. Presumably this was her mother. She was serving a customer with tobacco.

'How's the governor?' said the customer.

'Ever so bad with his back,' said Mrs Grover cheerfully. 'Hasn't left his bed since Friday. Did you say Vestas?' Drayton noted with distaste the girlie magazines, the stand of paper patterns (two swinging mini-skirts to cut out and sew in an evening), the ninepenny thrillers, *Ghosty Worlds, Cosmic Creatures*. On a shelf among mock-Wedgwood ashtrays stood a pottery spaniel with artificial flowers growing from a basket on his back. The flowers were furred with dust like a grey fungoid growth. 'That's five and three, then. Thanks very much. It's what they call a slipped disc. He just bent over fiddling with the car and — crack!'

'Nasty,' said the customer. 'You thinking of letting your room again? I heard your young man had gone.'

'And good riddance. I couldn't take another one on, dear, not with Mr Grover laid up. Linda and me have got enough on our hands as it is.' So that was her name, Linda. Drayton turned away from *Ghosty Worlds*. Mrs Grover looked at him indifferently. 'Yes?'

'*Standard*, please.'

There was only one left and that was in the rack outside the shop by the advertisement case. Drayton followed her out and paid for his newspaper on the doorstep. He would never go back in there, inefficient, ill-mannered lot! Perhaps he never would have done and his life would have pursued its ordered, uninterrupted course towards its goal. He lingered only for a moment. The lamp had come on and his eyes was caught by a familiar name on one of the cards. Margolis, Quince Cottage, and beneath a plea for a charwoman. The door opened and Linda Grover came out. Even so quickly can one catch the plague . . .

She was as tall as he and her short grey dress made her look taller. The damp wind blew the stuff against her body, showing the shape of her little breasts and the long slender thighs. She had a small head set on a thin neck and her pale hair was drawn back so tightly that it pulled the skin and stretched wide the smooth dove-coloured eyebrows. He had never seen a girl so completely clothed look so naked.

She opened the card case, removed one and replaced it with another. 'Raining again,' she said. 'I don't know where it all comes from.' An ugly voice, half-Sussex, half-Cockney.

'The sky,' said Drayton. That was the only answer to such a stupid remark. He could not imagine why she had bothered to speak to him at all, unless she had seen him that night and was covering embarrassment.

'Very funny.' Her fingers were long and the hand had a wide octave span. He observed the bitten nails. 'You'll get soaked standing there,' she said.

Drayton put up his hood. 'How's the boy friend?' he asked conversationally. Her reaction pleased him. He had flicked her on the raw.

'Is there one?' Her ugly accent grated on him and he told himself it was this and not her proximity which made him clench his hands as he stood looking at the cards offering prams for sale and council flats to be exchanged.

'A good-looking girl like you?' he said, turning sharply to face her. It was not Mann or Durrell, just standard verbal practice, the first preliminary love play. 'Get away.'

Her smile began very slowly and developed with a kind of secrecy. He noticed that she smiled without showing her teeth, without parting her lips, and it devastated him. They stood

428

looking at each other in the rainy dusk. Drizzle spattered the tiers of newspapers. Drayton shifted his gaze rudely and deliberately back to the glass case.

'You're very interested in those cards, I must say,' she said sharply. 'What's so fascinating about a load of second-hand stuff?'

'I shouldn't mind it being second-hand,' he said, and when she blushed he knew she had seen him witness that kiss.

A charwoman with ginger hair. It might be. Everything pointed that way. Mrs Penistan seemed to fill the requirements. She had cleaned for Anita Margolis, why should she not also clean for Mrs Harper of Waterford Avenue? A woman who lived in unsalubrious Glebe Road might steal paper from one employer to write anonymous letters about another. In Glebe Road they were no strangers to crime, even to murder. A woman had been killed down there only last year. Monkey Matthews had once lived there and it was behind one of these squat stuccoed façades that he had mixed up sugar and sodium chlorate to make his bomb.

Burden tapped smartly on the door of the small terraced house. A light came on, a chain was slipped, and before the door opened he saw a little sharp face peering at him through the glass panel.

'Mrs Penistan?'

Her mouth snapped open like a spring trap and there came forth a voluble stream of words. 'Oh, here you are at last, dear. I'd nearly given you up. The Hoover's all ready for you.' She produced it, an enormous, old-fashioned vacuum cleaner. 'I reckon it's a bit of grit caught up in the motor. My boys don't care what muck they bring in on their shoes. Won't be a long job, will it?'

'Mrs Penistan, I haven't come to service your cleaner. I'm not a . . .'

She peered at him. 'Not a Jehovah Witness, I hope?'

'A police officer.' They sorted it out, Mrs Penistan laughing shrilly. Even in her own house, she still wore a hat. The hair which showed under its brim was not ginger but grey. You could neither describe her as middle-aged, nor showily dressed. In addition to the pudding basin hat, she wore a cross-over sleeveless overall, patterned in mauve and black, over a green cardigan. Burden thought she was approaching seventy.

'You won't mind coming in the kitchenette, will you, dear? I'm getting me boys' tea.' On the cooker chips were frying. She lifted out the wire basket, replenished it with a fresh mound of wet cut potatoes. 'How about a nice cuppa?'

Burden accepted the offer and when the tea came it was hot and strong. He sat down on a grubby chair at the grubby table. The frowsty appearance of the place surprised him. Somehow he expected a charwoman's house to be clean, just as a bank manager's account should always be in the black.

'Smith?' she said. 'No, it doesn't ring a bell.'

'Fitzwilliam?'

'No, dear. There was a Mr Kirkpatrick. Would it be him?'

'It might be.' Knowing Margolis, it very well might be.

'Lives in Pomfret somewhere. Funny you should ask about him because it was on account of him I left.'

'How was that, Mrs Penistan?'

'I don't know why I shouldn't tell you. Missing, you said? Well, it don't surprise me. It wouldn't surprise me if he'd done her in like he said he would.'

'He did, did he?'

'Threatened her in my hearing. D'you want to hear about it?'

'I do indeed, but first I'd like to hear about her, what you thought of her, that kind of thing.'

'She was a nice enough girl, mind, no side to her. First day I came I called her Miss and she just screamed out laughing. 'Oh, Mrs P., darling,' she said, 'you call me Ann. Everyone calls me Ann.' One of the free and easy ones she is, takes things as they come. Mind you, they've got money, got wads of it, but they're not always free with it, that kind. The clothes she gives me, you wouldn't believe. I had to let most of them go to my granddaughter, being a bit past wearing them trouser suits and skirts up to me navel.

'She'd got her head screwed on the right way, mind. Very sharp way she'd got with the tradesmen. She always bought the best and she liked to know what she was getting for her money.

You'd have to get up early in the morning to put anything over on her. Different to him.'

'Mr Margolis?'

'I know it's easy to say, but I reckon he's mental. All of a year I was there and he never had a soul come to see him. Paint, paint, paint, all the blessed day long, but when he'd done you couldn't see what it was meant to be. "I wonder you don't get fed up with it," I says to him once. "Oh, I'm very fecund, Mrs Penistan," he says, whatever that may mean. Sounded dirty to me. No, his mind's affected all right.' She piled the chips on to two plates and began cracking eggs which she sniffed suspiciously before dropping them into the pan.

Burden had just begun to ask her about Kirkpatrick's threats when the back door opened and two large bull-necked men in working clothes came in. Were these the boys who didn't care what they brought in on their feet? Both looked years older than Burden himself. With a nod to their mother, they tramped across the kitchen, taking no notice at all of her visitor. Perhaps they also concluded that he had come to service the vacuum cleaner.

'Hang on a minute, dear,' said Mrs Penistan. A plate in each hand, she disappeared into the living room. Burden finished the last of his tea. Presently one of the boys came back for the tea pot, followed by his mother, now all smiles.

'You can't get a word out of them till they've got a meal inside them,' she said proudly. Her son ignored her, marched off, banging doors behind him. 'Now, dear, you wanted to know about Mr Kirkpatrick. Let's see, where are we now? Friday. It would have been last Wednesday week. Mr Margolis had gone down to Devon for a painting holiday. I come in a couple of days before and I says to her, "Where's your brother, then?" "Dartmoor," she says, and *that* I could believe, though Broadmoor was more his mark.' She let out a shrill laugh and sat down opposite Burden, her elbows on the table. 'Well, two days later on the Wednesday there comes a knock at the door in the afternoon. "I'll go," she says and when she opens the door there's this Kirkpatrick. "Good afternoon," she says, sort of cool but in ever such a funny way I can't describe. "Good afternoon," he says and they just stand there looking at each other. Anyway, as I say, there's no side to her and she introduces me very nice. "Penistan?" he says. "That's a real local name. We've got some Penistans living opposite us in Pomfret," and that's how I know where he come from. Well, I was getting on with cleaning the silver so I went back into the kitchenette.

'No more than five minutes later I hear them go upstairs. Must be going to look at his paintings, I thought in my ignorance. There was paintings all over the place, dear, even in the bathroom. About half an hour after that they come down again and I'm beginning to wonder what's in the air. Then I heard them start this arguing.

' "For God's sake don't drool all over me, Alan," she says sharpish. "Love," she says, raising her voice. "I don't know what that is. If I love anyone it's Rupert." Rupert being her mental brother. Well, this Alan, he flies right off the handle and he starts shouting. All sorts of horrible expressions he used as I couldn't repeat. But she didn't turn a hair. "I'm not ending anything, darling," she says. "You can go on having what you've just had upstairs." I can tell you, dear, all the blood rushed to my head. This is the last time you set foot in here, Rose Penistan, I says to myself. My boys are very particular. They wouldn't want me going where there was immorality. I was going to march right in on her and that Kirkpatrick and tell her there and then when I heard him say, "You're asking to get yourself killed, Ann. I might do it myself one of these fine days."

'Anyway, the upshot was that he just went off in a huff. I could hear her calling out after him, "Don't be so silly, Alan, and don't forget we've got a date Tuesday night." '

'Tuesday?' Burden interjected sharply. 'Would that have been last Tuesday?'

'Must have been. People are funny, aren't they, dear? As business-like as they come, she is, and good too in a sort of way. Collected for Oxfam and the sick animals, read the newspaper from cover to cover and very hot about what she called injustice. Just the same, she was carrying on proper with this Kirkpatrick. It's a funny old world.'

'So you left?'

'That very day. After he'd gone she come out into the

kitchenette just as if nothing had happened. All cool and serene she was, smiling and talking about the horrible weather her poor Rupert was having down on the Moor. I don't know what it is, dear, but I reckon that's what they mean when they talk about charm. I couldn't have it out with her. "I'll finish out the week," was all I said, "and then I'll have to give up. This place is getting too much for me." And I never spoke a truer word.'

'Do you work anywhere else, Mrs Penistan? Stowerton, for instance?'

'Oh, no, dear. It wouldn't be worth my while going all that way. Not that my boys wouldn't fetch me in the van. Always thinking of their Mum, they are.' She accompanied him into the hall where they encountered one of her sons, returning to the kitchen with his empty plate. This he deposited silently on the table. Although he still took no notice at all of his mother, beyond pushing her aside as he passed through the doorway, the meal he had 'got inside him' had effected a slight improvement in his temper, for he remarked gloomily to Burden:

'Nasty night.'

Mrs Penistan smiled at him fondly. She lugged the vacuum cleaner out of the way and opened the front door on to squally rain. Strange how it always came on to pour in the evenings, Burden thought. As he walked along Glebe Road with his head lowered and his collar turned up, he reflected on the awkwardness of questioning Kirkpatrick when they had no body and no more proof of death than an anonymous letter.

CHAPTER SIX

Two men called Geoffrey Smith lived in Kingsmarkham, one in Stowerton and two more in Sewingbury. The only dark-haired one was six feet two; the only one under thirty-five had a blond beard; none possessed a black car. The enquiry had been fruitless, as unsatisfactory as the search of Margolis's house. His sister's note had not come to light, but then neither had anything else which might suggest foul play.

'Except the five hundred quid,' said Burden.

'A very nice sum to go on holiday with,' Wexford said firmly. And then, with less certitude, 'Have we worried Margolis in vain, Mike?'

'Hard to say whether he's worried or not. I don't understand the fellow, sir. One minute I think he's pulling my leg and the next — well, he's just like a child. I daresay that's what they mean by genius.'

'Some say there's a knife edge between it and madness, others that it's an infinite capacity for taking pains.'

If there was anything Burden did understand it was taking pains. 'It looks as if he pours that paint and muck on like you or I might slop sauce on fish and chips,' he said. 'All those paintings are beyond me. I'd say they were just another way of conning the public. How much do they charge to go into the Tate Gallery?'

Wexford roared with laughter. 'Nothing, as far as I know. It's free.' He tightened the thin shiny rag he called a tie. 'You remind me of that remark of Goering's,' he said. 'Whenever I hear the word culture I reach for my gun.'

Burden was offended. He went out into the corridor, looking for someone on whom to vent his temper. Bryant and Gates, who had been chatting up the sergeant, tried to look busy as soon as they saw him. Not so Mark Drayton. He was standing a little apart from the others, staring down at his feet and apparently deep in thought, his hands in the pockets of his duffel coat. The sight of his black hair sticking out over the hood lining inflamed Burden still further. He marched up to Drayton, but before he could speak, the young man said casually:

'Can I have a word with you, sir?'

'The only person you need a word with is a barber,' Burden snapped. 'Four words to be precise. Short back and sides.' Drayton's face was impassive, secretive, intelligent. 'Oh, very well, what is it?'

'An advert in Grover's window. I thought we might be interested.' From his pocket he took a neat flat notebook and opening it, read aloud: 'Quiet secluded room to let for evenings. Suit student or anyone wanting to get away from it all. Privacy guaranteed. Apply, 82, Charteris Road, Stowerton.'

Burden's nostrils contracted in distaste. Drayton was not responsible for the advertisement, he told himself, he had only found it. Indeed it was to his credit that he *had* found it. Why then feel that this kind of thing, so squalid, so redolent of nasty things done in nasty corners, was right up his street?

'Grover's again, eh?' said Wexford when they told him. 'So this is their latest racket, is it? Last year it was — er, curious books. This place gets more like the Charing Cross Road every day.' He gave a low chuckle which Burden would not have been surprised to hear Drayton echo. The fellow was a sycophant if ever there was one. But Drayton's olive-skinned face was wary. Burden would have said he looked ashamed except that he could not think of any reason why he should be.

'Remember the time when all the school kids were getting hold of flick knives and we knew for sure it was Grover but we couldn't pin it on him? And those magazines he sells. How would you like your daughter to read them?'

Wexford shrugged. 'They're not for daughters, Mike, they're for sons, and you don't *read* them. Before we get around to convening the purity committee, we'd better do something about this ad.' He fixed his eyes speculatively on Drayton. 'You're a likely lad, Mark.' It irked Burden to hear the Chief Inspector address Drayton, as he very occasionally did, by his christian name. 'You look the part.'

'The part, sir?'

'We'll cast you as a student wanting to get away from it all, shall we, Inspector Burden?' Still viewing Drayton, he added, 'I can't see any of the rest of us capering nimbly in a lady's chamber.'

The first time they went to the door there was no answer. It was a corner house, its front on Charteris Road, its side with a short dilapidated fence, bordering Sparta Grove. While Burden waited in the car, Drayton followed this fence to its termination in a lane that ran between the backs of the gardens. Here the stone wall was too high to see over, but Drayton found a gate in it, locked but affording through its cracks a view of the garden of number eighty-two. On a clothes line, attached at one end to the wall and at the other to a hook above a rear window of the house, hung a wet carpet from which water dripped on to a brick path.

The house was seventy or eighty years old but redeemed from the slumminess of its neighbours by a certain shipshape neatness. The yard was swept — a clean broom stood with its head against the house wall — and the back step had been whitened. All the windows were closed and hung with crisp net curtains. As Drayton contemplated these windows, a curtain in one, probably the back bedroom, was slightly raised and a small wizened face looked out. Drayton put his foot on a projecting hunk of stone and hoisted himself up until his head and shoulders were above the grass-grown top of the wall. The brown simian face was still there. Its eyes met his and there appeared in them a look of terror, surely out of proportion to the offence or to the retribution for that offence the occupants of the house might be supposed to have committed. The face disappeared quickly and Drayton returned to the car.

'There's someone in,' he said to Burden.

'I daresay there is. Apart from the fact that we can't force an entry over a thing like this, making a rumpus would rather defeat the object of the exercise, wouldn't it?'

Theirs was just one of twenty or thirty cars lining Sparta Grove. At this end of the street there were neither garages nor space for them.

'Someone's coming now,' Drayton said suddenly.

Burden looked up. A woman pushing a shopping basket on

wheels was opening the gate of the corner house. Her head was tied up in a coloured scarf and she wore a coat with a huge showy fur collar. As the door closed behind her, he said:

'I know her. Her name's Branch, Mrs Ruby Branch. She used to live in Sewingbury.'

'Is she one of our customers?'

This use, on Drayton's lips, of one of Wexford's favourite terms, displeased Burden. It seemed not so much an accidental echo as a calculated and ingratiating mimicry of the Chief Inspector's racy style. 'We've had her for shoplifting,' he said stiffly, 'larceny as a servant and various other things. This is a new departure. You'd better go in and do your stuff.'

She subjected him to a careful and at first alarmed scrutiny through the glass panel of the door before opening it. The alarm faded and the door gave a few inches. Drayton put his foot on the mat.

'I understand you have a room to let.' He spoke pleasantly and she was disarmed. She smiled, showing excellent false teeth with lipstick on them. The scarf and the coat had not yet been removed and between the feather boa-like sides of her collar he could see a frilly blouse covering a fine bosom. The face was middle-aged — early fifties, Drayton thought — and bravely painted particularly about the eyelids. 'I happened to see your advert in Grover's window, Mrs Er . . . ?'

'No names, no pack drill, dear,' she said. 'Just call me Ruby.'

'O.K., Ruby.'

The door was closed behind him and he found himself in a tiny narrow hall, its floor covered in cheap bright red nylon carpet. On the threshold of the front room he stopped, staring, and his face must have shown his astonishment, for she said quickly:

'Don't take any notice of the bare boards, duckie. I like everything to be spick and span, you see, and I'm just giving the carpet a bit of an airing.'

'Spring-cleaning, eh?' Drayton said. All the furniture had been moved against the walls. There was a three-piece suite, covered in moquette, whose pattern showed what seemed like, but surely could not be, blue fishes swimming through a tangle of red and pink climbing roses. On a huge television set stood a naked lady in pink porcelain whose eternally raised right arm held aloft a lamp in a plastic shade. The wallpaper was embossed in gilt and the single picture was of the late King George the Fifth and Queen Mary in full court regalia. 'I can see you keep it nice,' he said heartily.

'You wouldn't get things nicer in any of your hotels. When did you think of coming? Any night would be convenient to me.' She gave him a long look, partly coy, partly assessing. 'You'll be bringing a young lady with you?'

'If you haven't any objection. I thought perhaps this evening. Say eight till eleven. Would you . . . ?'

'I'll get my things on by eight sharp,' she said. 'If you'll just tap on the door you needn't bring the young lady in till after I've gone. Some do feel a bit shy-like. Say a fiver?'

Burden had agreed to give him ten minutes. Things could hardly have gone more smoothly. He glanced up at the window and saw the inspector approaching the front door. That she had seen him too and knew who he was he guessed from the little gasp of fear that came from her.

'What's going on, then?' she said, her voice dying to a whimper.

Drayton turned and addressed her severely. 'I am a police officer and I have reason to believe you are engaged in keeping a disorderly house . . .'

Ruby Branch sat down on the red and blue sofa, put her head in her hands and began to cry.

Drayton had expected they would simply take her down to Kingsmarkham and charge her. It was all cut and dried and there had been neither denial nor defiance. She had put the advertisement in Grover's window to make a little extra money. What with freezes and squeezes, it was a job to make ends meet . . . Burden listened to it all. His eyes were on the scarf Ruby Branch had unwound from her head and was using to wipe her eyes, or perhaps on the ginger curls the removal of that scarf had revealed.

'You were a blonde last time I saw you, Ruby,' he said.

'Since when do I have to ask your permission when I want to have my hair tinted?'

'Still working for Mrs Harper in Waterford Avenue, are you?'

She nodded tearfully, then glared at him. 'What business is it of yours who I work for? If it wasn't for you I'd still have my job at the supermarket.'

'You should have thought of that,' Burden said, 'before your little *contretemps* with six dozen packets of soap powder. You always were houseproud and it's been your undoing. Quite a vice with you, isn't it? I see you've been at it again.'

He stared at the bare boards and thence from Ruby's varicose veined legs in their thin black nylons to her suddenly terrified face. To Drayton he said conversationally:

'There's not many working women would find the time to wash a big carpet. Go over it with a damp cloth, maybe. That's what my wife does. Let's go outside and see what sort of a job she's made of it, shall we? It's not a bad morning and I could do with a spot of fresh air.'

Ruby Branch came with them. She tottered in her high-heeled shoes and it seemed to Drayton that she was dumb with terror. The kitchen was neat and fresh and the step so clean that Burden's not very dirty shoe made a black print on it. Of the man seen at the window — husband? lodger? — there was no sign.

Drayton wondered that the clothes line was strong enough to bear the weight of the carpet, for it was soaking wet and looked as if it had been totally immersed in a bath. The high wind hardly caused it to sway. Burden advanced on it curiously.

'Don't you touch it,' Ruby said shrilly. 'You'll have the lot down.'

Burden took no notice of her. He gave the carpet a twitch and suddenly, as she had predicted, the line snapped. Its load subsided with a squelch, half on to the path and half on to the lawn, giving off from its heavy soaking folds a strong animal smell of sodden wool.

'Look what you've done! What d'you want to come out here poking about for? Now I'll have to do it all again.'

'No, you won't,' Burden said grimly. 'The only people who are going to touch that are scientific experts.'

'Just giving it an airing?' Drayton exclaimed.

'Oh, my God!' Ruby's face had become a yellowish white against which the quivering red lips stood out like a double gash. 'I never meant any harm, I was scared. I thought maybe you'd pin it on me, maybe you'd get me for a — a . . .'

'An accessory? That's a good idea. Maybe we shall.'

'Oh, my God!'

Back in the disarranged sitting room, she sat for a moment in petrified silence, twisting her hands and biting what remained of the lipstick from her mouth. Then she said wildly:

'It's not what you're thinking. It wasn't blood. I was bottling raspberries and I . . .'

'In April? Do me a favour,' said Burden. 'You can take your time.' He looked at his watch. 'We've got a very slack morning, haven't we, Drayton? We can sit here till lunchtime for all I care. We can sit here till tomorrow.'

Again she said nothing and in the renewal of silence shuffling footsteps were heard outside in the passage. The door opened cautiously and Drayton saw a little man with thin grey hair. The face was the face he had seen at the window. With its prognathous jaw, its many furrows in dark brown skin, and its bulbous nose and mouth, it was not prepossessing. The terrified expression had undergone a change. The eyes were fixed on Drayton just as they had been previously, but the agony of fear had been replaced by a kind of gloating horror comparable to that of a man shown a five-legged sheep or a bearded lady.

Burden got up and, because the newcomer seemed inclined to make a bolt for it, closed his hand over the door knob.

'Well, if it isn't Mr Matthews,' he said. 'Can't say I think much of your coming-out togs. I thought they made them to measure these days.'

The man called Matthews said in a feeble grating voice, 'Hallo, Mr Burden,' and then automatically, as if he always did say it, just as other men say, 'How are things?' or 'Nice day', 'I haven't done nothing.'

'When I was at school,' said Burden, 'they taught me that a double negative makes an affirmative. So we know where we are, don't we? Sit down, join the gathering. There aren't any more of you, are there?'

Monkey Matthews skirted the room carefully, finally sitting

down as far as possible from Drayton. For a moment nobody said anything. Matthews looked from Burden to Ruby and then, as if unwillingly compelled, back again at Drayton.

'Is that Geoff Smith?' he asked at last.

'You see,' said Ruby Branch, 'he never saw them. Well, come to that, *I* never saw the girl.'

Wexford shook his head in exasperation. His whole body had shaken with fury when Burden first told him, but now his anger had begun to abate, leaving a sour disgust. Four days had passed since Tuesday, four days of doubt and disbelief. Half a dozen men had been wasting their time, working in the dark and perhaps asking the wrong questions of the wrong people. And all because a silly woman had been afraid to go to the police lest the police stop a racket that promised to be lucrative. Now she sat in his office snivelling into a handkerchief, a scrap of cotton and lace streaked with make-up that the tears had washed away.

'This Geoff Smith,' Wexford said, 'when was the first time you saw him?'

Ruby rolled the handkerchief into a ball and gave a deep choking sigh. 'Last Saturday, Saturday the 3rd. The day after I put the advert in. It was in the morning, about twelve. There was a knock at the door and there was this young chap wanting the room for Tuesday night. He was dark and ever so nice-looking and he spoke nice. How was I to know he was a killer?' She shifted in Wexford's yellow chair and crossed her legs. ' "My name's Geoff Smith," he said. Proud of it, he was. I didn't ask him for his name. Well, he said eight till eleven and I said that'd cost him five pounds. He didn't argue so I saw him off the premises and he got into this black car.

'On Tuesday he came back like he said, at eight sharp. But I never saw any car this time and I never saw his girl. He give me five pounds and said he'd be gone by eleven and when I came back he *had* gone. Now, I'd left the room like a new pin, as good as a hotel it was . . .'

'I doubt if the court will look on that as a mitigating circumstance,' Wexford put in coldly.

At this hint of the revenge society intended to take on her, Ruby gave another loud sniff. 'Well,' she gulped, 'they'd messed it up a bit, moved the furniture, and of course I started putting the room to rights . . .'

'D'you mind sparing me all these asides? I'm a detective, not a domestic science examiner.'

'I have to tell you, don't I? I have to tell you what I did.'

'Tell me what you found.'

'Blood,' Ruby said. 'I moved back the sofa, and there it was, a great big stain. I know I ought to have come to you, Mr Wexford, but I panicked. I was dead scared. All those convictions you've pinned on me. They'll get me for an accomplice or whatever it is, I thought. Then, there was him, Geoff Smith. It's all very well you saying you'd have looked after me. You and me, we know what that amounts to. You wouldn't have put a bodyguard on my place night and day. I was scared stiff.' She added in a querulous whimper, 'Still am, come to that.'

'Where does Matthews come into all this?'

'I was all on my own. I kept going to the window to see if I could see a little dark fellow watching the house. He's killed one girl, I thought. The odds are he won't think twice about finishing me off. George and me, we'd always been good friends.' For a moment Wexford wondered who she meant. Then he recalled Monkey's long disused christian name. 'I'd heard he'd come out and I found him in the Piebald Pony.' She put her elbows on Wexford's desk and fixed him with a long supplicating stare. 'A woman needs a man about at a time like this. I reckon I thought he'd protect me.'

'She wanted someone to protect her,' said Monkey Matthews. 'Can I have another fag? I hadn't got nowhere to go, being as my wife won't have me in the house. Mind you, Mr Burden, I don't know as I'd have gone back with Rube if I'd known what was waiting for me.' He banged his thin concave chest. 'I'm no bodyguard. Got a light?' Unashamed, no longer afraid since he had been assured that any possible resemblance between Drayton and Geoff Smith was coincidental, he sat jauntily in his chair, talking with animation.

Burden struck a match to light the fourth cigarette he had had since his arrival and pushed an ashtray pointedly towards him.

'It was blood on the carpet all right,' Monkey said. The

cigarette adhered to his lower lip and the smoke made him screw up his eyes. 'I didn't believe her at first. You know what women are.'

'How much blood?' Burden asked tightly as if the very effort of questioning this man hurt him.

'Good deal. Nasty it was. Like as if someone had been playing silly beggars with a knife.' He shuddered, but he cackled at the same time. The cigarette fell. When he had retrieved it, but not before it had marked the carpet, he said, 'Rube was scared stiff of this Smith coming back, wanted to come to you. "That's no bloody good," I said, "not after all this time," but not one to flout the law when it's a matter of real downright crime I thought I'd better give you a hint there was a body knocking about. So I wrote to you. Rube had got some paper about. She always has things nice.'

He gave Burden an ingratiating smile, hideously distorting his face. 'I knew you'd only need a hint to get your hands on him. Anyone who finds fault with our local police, I always say, Mr Wexford and Mr Burden, they're real educated tip-top men. They'd be up in London at the Yard if there was any justice in this world.'

'If there's any justice in this world,' Burden said furiously, 'it'll put you away for the biggest stretch you've ever done for this.'

Monkey contemplated Burden's green glass statuette as if he hoped to identify it with some known form of human or animal life. 'Now don't be like that,' he said. 'I haven't done nothing. You could say I'd put myself out to help you. I never even set eyes on this Geoff Smith, but if he'd come back snooping around, I'd have been up the creek just the same as Rube.' He gave a deep theatrical sigh. 'It was a real sacrifice I made, helping you with your enquiries, and where's it got me?'

The question was rhetorical but Burden answered it sharply. 'A nice comfortable house to kip down in, for one thing. Maybe you're putting the squeeze on this Smith and you only made your "real sacrifice" when he wouldn't play.'

'It's a dirty lie,' said Monkey passionately. 'I tell you I never saw him. I thought that young bloke of yours was him. God knows, I reckoned I could spot a copper a mile off, but then

443

they tog themselves up so funny these days. Rube and me we'd been scared stiff and then there he was, poking his long nose over the wall. I tell you, I thought my number was up. Put the squeeze on him! That's a proper laugh. How could I put the squeeze on him when I never set foot in Rube's place before Wednesday?' More ape-like than ever, he scowled at Burden, his eyes growing bulbous. 'I'll have another fag,' he said in an injured tone.

'When did you write the letter?'

'Thursday morning while Rube was out working.'

'So you were all by yourself?'

'Yes, on my tod. I wasn't putting Mr Geoff Smith through the third degree if that's what you're getting at. I leave that kind of thing to you.' Indignation brought on a coughing fit and he covered his mouth with deeply stained yellowish-brown fingers.

'I reckon you must have D.T.s of the lungs,' Burden said disgustedly. 'What d'you do when you're — er, behind bars? Start screaming like an addict in a rehabilitation centre?'

'It's my nerves,' Monkey said. 'I've been a mass of nerves ever since I saw that blood.'

'How did you know what to put in the letter?'

'If you're going to trap me,' Monkey said with distant scorn, 'you'll have to be more bloody subtle than that. Rube told me, of course. Be your age. Young, dark and got a black car, she says. Name of Geoff Smith. Come in at eight and was due out at eleven.'

His dog-end was stubbed out on the base of the glass sculpture. Lacking for a brief moment its customary cigarette, Monkey's face reminded the inspector of a short-sighted man without his glasses. There was about it something naked yet unnatural.

'O.K.,' he said. 'You know all this about him, because Ruby told you, but you never saw him and you never saw the girl.' At the last word Monkey's indignant eyes wavered. Burden was not sure whether this was from apprehension or because he was in need of further stimulation. He snatched the cigarette box and put it in the drawer. 'How did you know her name was Ann?' he said.

CHAPTER SEVEN

'How did you know her name was Ann?' Wexford asked.

The look Ruby Branch gave him was one of simple incomprehension. She appeared not merely unwilling to answer his question: She was utterly at sea. With Geoff Smith and his description she had been on firm ground. Now he had plunged her into uncharted and, for some reason possibly known to her, dangerous waters. She turned away her eyes and contemplated one of her veined legs as if she expected to see a ladder running up the stocking.

'You never even saw that letter, did you, Ruby?' He waited. Silence was the worst thing, the thing all policemen fear. Speech, no matter how clever and how subtly phrased, is necessarily a betrayal. 'Geoff Smith never told you that girl's name. How did you know? How does Matthews know?'

'I don't know what you're getting at,' Ruby cried. She clutched her handbag and shrank away from him, her mouth trembling. 'All those sarcastic things you say, they go in one ear and out the other. I've told you all I know and I've got a splitting headache.'

Wexford left her and went to find Burden. 'I don't even begin to understand this,' he said. 'Why does Geoff Smith tell her his name? She didn't want to know. 'No names, no pack drill' is what she said to Drayton.'

'Of course it's an assumed name.'

'Yes, I expect it is. He's an exhibitionist who uses an alias for fun, even when no one's interested.'

'Not only does he give his name unasked, he gives his girl friend's too.'

'No, Mike,' Wexford said crossly, 'my credulity won't stretch that far. "My name's Geoff Smith and I'll be bringing Ann with me." Can you visualise it? I can't. Besides, I've been over and over it with Ruby. I'd stake a year's salary on it. He never told her the girl's name and the first time she heard it was from me in there just now.'

'But Monkey knew it,' said Burden.

'And Monkey wasn't even there. I don't think Ruby's lying. She's scared to death and late in the day though it is, she's throwing herself on our mercy. Mike, would Ann Margolis go to a place like that? You know what the paper said. 'Ex-model and Chelsea playgirl!' Why wouldn't she just take her boy friend home with her?'

'She likes slumming,' said Burden. 'Margolis told me that. Smith, so-called, booked the room on Saturday. Anita knew Margolis would be out on Tuesday evening but she probably thought he'd come home fairly early. He didn't know and she didn't know the gallery manager would ask him out to dinner.'

'Yes, it ties up. Have they started going over Ruby's place?'

'Taking it apart now, sir. The carpet's gone down to the lab. Martin's found a neighbour who saw something. Old girl called Collins. She's waiting for us now.'

She was nearly as large as Wexford himself, a stout old woman with a square jaw. Before he began to question her, she launched forth on a long account of her suffering consequent on being Ruby Branch's next-door neighbour. Hardly an evening passed without her having to bang on the common wall between the houses. Ruby worked all day and did her cleaning after six. The television was always full on and often the vacuum cleaner at the same time. Monkey she knew. He had lived there from Ruby's arrival two years before until six months before he went to prison. It was disgusting, a crying scandal. As soon as she saw him come home with Ruby on Wednesday morning she knew trouble would start. Then there was a married niece and her husband from Pomfret way — if they *were* married — who came a couple of times a week, and who got drinking and laughing until the small hours.

'That's who I thought it was I saw leaving on Tuesday,' she said. 'Staggering down the path and holding on to each other. As much as they could do to walk it was.'

'Two of them?' Wexford said, his voice rising. 'You saw two of them?'

Mrs Collins nodded emphatically. 'Yes, there was two. I didn't look long, I can tell you. I was too disgusted.'

'Did you see them come?'

'I was in my kitchen till gone nine. I come into the front and I thought, thank the Lord she's gone out. There was dead silence until half past. I know I'm right about the time on account of looking at the clock. There was something on telly I wanted at twenty-five to. I'd just got up to switch it on when there comes this great mighty crash from next-door. Here we go, I thought, more hi-jinks, and I banged on the wall.'

'Go on,' Wexford said.

'For two pins, I said to myself, I'll go in and have it out with her. But you know how it is, you don't like to make trouble with the neighbours. Besides, there was three of them and I'm not so young as I used to be. Anyway, I got so far as putting my coat on and I was standing just inside the front door, sort of hesitating, when I saw these two come down the path.'

'How well did you see them?'

'Not that well,' Mrs Collins admitted. 'It was through the little glass bit in the door, you see. They was both in macs and the girl had a scarf on her head. His hair was dark, that I do know. I never saw their faces, but they were drunk as lords. I thought the girl was going to fall flat on her face. And she did fall when he got the car door open, fell right across the front seat.' She nodded indignantly, her expression smug and self-righteous. 'I gave them five minutes to get out of the way and then I went next-door, but there was no answer and I saw her come in myself at eleven. What's been going on? I thought. It wasn't the married niece from Pomfret. She never had no car. Couldn't keep money in her pocket long enough to get one.'

'This was a black car you saw them get into, Mrs Collins?'

'Black? Well, it was under one of them street lamps, and you know what they are, make you go all colours.' She paused, searching in her mind. 'I'd have said it was green,' she said.

Linda Grover flushed when Drayton told her to take the advertisement out of the window. The blood poured into her madonna's face and he knew it was because his explanation had been too crude.

'Didn't you realise what it meant?' he said harshly. 'I

should have thought one look at that old tart would have told you she wasn't a legitimate landlady.'

They were alone in the shop. She stood behind the counter, her eyes on his face and her fingers picking at the dog-eared corner of a magazine. 'I didn't know you were a policeman,' she said in a voice which had grown throaty.

'You know now.'

On his way here from Ruby Branch's house he had stopped at the library, not for the sake of the crime section this time, but to look at the big coloured books of paintings by old masters. There, amid the Mantegnas, the Botticellis and the Fra Angelicos, he had found her face under cracked haloes and he had stared at it in a kind of wonder before rage had taken over and he had slammed the book shut so that the librarian looked up with a frown.

'Is that all you came for?' Her first fright was gone and her voice took on an aggressiveness as he nodded. 'All that song and dance about an old advert card?' With a shrug, she walked past him and out of the shop, her body held straight as if she had an invisible weight on her head. He watched her come back, fascinated by the clean, pure curves of jaw and arm and thigh and by the small graceful movements her hands made as she tore Ruby's card into shreds.

'Be more careful next time,' he said. 'We'll be keeping an eye on you.' He saw that he had made her angry, for the colour faded utterly from her face. It was as if she had blushed white. There was a thin silver chain round her neck. As a schoolboy, Drayton had read the Song of Songs, hoping for something salacious. A line came back to him. He had not known what it meant, but now he knew what it meant for him. Thou hast ravished my heart with the chain of thy neck. . . .

'An eye on us?'

'This shop's got a bad enough reputation as it is.' He didn't give a damn about the shop's reputation, but he wanted to stay there, hang it out as long as he could. 'If I were your father with a nice little business like this I wouldn't touch that filth.'

She followed his glance at the magazines. 'Some like them,' she said. Her eyes had returned to his face. He had the notion that she was digesting the fact that he was a policeman and

searching for some brand mark he ought to carry about on him.
'If you've finished with the sermon, I've got Dad's tea to get and
I'm going to the pictures straight after. Last house is seven
thirty.'

'Mustn't keep what's-his-name waiting,' Drayton sneered.

He could see he had nettled her. 'His name's Ray if you
must know and he lodged with us,' she said. 'He's gone, left.
Oh, come off it. You needn't look like that. I know you saw me
with him. So what? It's not a crime, is it? Don't you ever stop
being a cop?'

'Who said anything about a crime? I get enough crime in
the daytime without the evenings.' He went to the door and
looked back at her. The grey eyes were large and luminous and
they had a trick of appearing always full of unshed tears.
'Maybe I wished I'd been in his shoes,' he said.

She took a step towards him. 'You're kidding.'

'Men usually kid you about that, do they?'

Her fingers went up to the little insincere smile that was just
beginning and she tucked one of the bitten nails between her
lips.

'What exactly are you trying to say?'

Now she looked frightened. He wondered if he had been
wrong about her and if she were really as inexperienced and
innocent as a tempera madonna. There was no gentleness in
him and he did not know how to be soft and kind.

'If I'm kidding,' he said, 'I won't be outside the cinema at
seven thirty.' Then he slammed the door and the bell tinkled
through the old sagging house.

'Believe it or not,' Wexford said, 'Monkey doesn't want to go
home. He's had a nice comfortable bed at Ruby's and God
knows how many free meals, but he'd rather spend his weekend
in what he calls "this contemporary-type nick". He's scared stiff
of coming face to face with Ruby. Just as well, since I haven't
the faintest idea what to charge him with.'

'Makes a change,' Burden grinned, 'our customers appreci-
ating the amenities. Maybe we could get ourselves in the A.A.
Guide, three-star hotel, specially adapted for those with previous convictions. Anything from the lab yet?'

'No, and I'll take my oath there won't be. We've only got Ruby's and Monkey's word that it was blood at all. You saw it, you saw what she'd done to that carpet. Char-ing may be a lowly trade, but Ruby's at the top of it. If I were Mrs Harper I wouldn't grudge a few sheets of handmade paper to get my house cleaned like that. She must have nearly killed herself washing that carpet. The lab say she used every cleanser in the book short of caustic soda. Oh, sure, they can sort out the Chemiglo from the Spotaway. The trouble is they can't sort out the blood, can't even say what group it is.'

'But they're still working on it?'

'Be working on it for days. They've got buckets full of muck from the pipes and drains. I'll be very surprised if they find anything. It's my bet our couple never went anywhere but that room in which they doubtless left a couple of hundred finger-prints . . .'

'All carefully removed by the Queen of the Chars,' Burden finished for him. 'The girl may be still alive, sir.'

'Because they left together and because the man's getting her out of there at all seems to show regret at what he'd done? I've had all the hospitals and all the G.P.s checked, Mike. They haven't had sight nor sound of anyone with stab wounds. And it must have been a stabbing, a blow on the head and that much loss of blood and the victim would never have been able to stand up, let alone stagger to a car. Moreover, if she's alive, where is she? It may only be assault we're up against or unlawful wounding, but whatever it is, we have to clear it up.'

Monkey Matthews gave them a crafty look when they returned to him.

'I've run out of fags.'

'I daresay Detective Constable Bryant will get you some if you ask him nicely. What d'you want. Weights?'

'You're joking,' said Monkey, stuffing a grubby paw into his jacket pocket. 'Forty Benson and Hedges Special Filter,' he said importantly and he brought out a pound note from a rustling mass that might indicate the presence of others like it. 'Better make it sixty.'

'Should last you till breakfast,' said Wexford. 'Rolling in it, aren't you? I can't help wondering if that's Geoff Smith's fee for silence you're sending up in smoke.' Stroking his chin, his head on one side, he looked speculatively into the other's simian face. 'How did you know her name was Ann?' he asked almost lightly and with a deceptive smoothness.

'Oh, you're round the twist,' Monkey said crossly. 'You don't listen to what you're told.'

When they came out of the cinema a light rain was falling, very little more than a clammy mist. Lamps glowed through the translucence, orange, gold and pearl-coloured. The cinema traffic coming from the car park swam out of the mist like subaqueous creatures surfacing with a gurgle and a splash. Drayton took the girl's arm to shepherd her across the road and left it there when they reached the pavement. This, the first contact he had ever had with her body, sent a tremor through him and made his mouth dry. He could feel the warmth from her skin just beneath the armpit.

'Enjoy the picture?' he asked her.

'It was all right. I don't like sub-titles much, I couldn't understand half of it. All that stuff about the woman letting the policeman be her lover if he wouldn't tell about her stealing the watch.'

'I daresay it happens. You don't know what goes on in these foreign places.' He was not displeased that the film had been sexy and that she wanted to talk about the sexiest part of the plot. With girls, that kind of talk was often an indication of intent, a way of getting on to the subject. Thank God, it wasn't the beginning of the week when they'd been showing that thing about a Russian battleship. 'You thinking of nicking any watches?' he said. She blushed vividly in the lamplight. 'Remember what the character in the film said, or what the sub-title said he said. "You know my price, Dolores."'

She smiled her close-lips smile, then said, 'You are awful.'

'Not me, I didn't write the script.'

She was wearing high heels and she was almost as tall as he. The perfume she had put on was much too old for her and it had nothing to do with the scent of flowers. Drayton wondered if her words had meant anything and if the perfume had been specially put on for his benefit. It was hard to tell how calculating girls were. Was she giving him an invitation or was the scent and the pale silvery stuff on her eyelids worn as a uniform might be, the battledress of the great female regiment who read the magazines she sold?

'It's early,' he said, 'only a quarter to eleven. Want to go for a walk down by the river?' It was under the trees there that he had seen her on Monday. Those trees arched dripping into the brown water, but under them the gravel path was well-drained and here and there was a wooden seat sheltered by branches.

'I can't. I mustn't be late home.'

'Some other night, then.'

'It's cold,' she said. 'It's always raining. You can't go to the pictures every night.'

'Where did you go with him?'

She bent down to straighten her stocking. The puddles she had stepped in had made dark grey splashes on the backs of her legs. The way she stretched her fingers and drew them up the calves was more provocative than all the perfume in the world.

'He hired a car.'

'I'll hire one,' Drayton said. They had come to the shop door. The alley between Grover's and the florist's next door was a walled lane that ended in a couple of garages. Its cobbles were brown and wet like stones on a cave floor that the tide has washed. She looked up at the high wall of her own home and at the blank unlit windows.

'You don't have to go in for a bit,' he said. 'Come under here, out of the rain.' There was no more shelter there than in the open street but it was darker. At their feet a little gutter stream flowed. He took her hand. 'I'll hire a car tomorrow.'

'All right.'

'What's the matter?' He spoke harshly, irritably, for he wanted to contemplate her face in repose, not working with anxiety, her eyes darting from one end of the alley to the other and up at the rain-washed wall. He would have liked eagerness, at least complaisance. She seemed afraid that they were watched and he thought of the thin beady-eyed mother and the mysterious father lying sick behind the brick bastion. 'Not scared of your parents, are you?'

452

'No, it's you. The way you look at me.'

He was nearly offended. The way he looked at her was something calculated and studied, a long, cold and intense stare that a good many girls had found exciting. A stronger desire than he had ever felt was increasing that intensity and making a contrived mannerism real. The poverty of her response almost killed it and he would have turned away from her to walk off alone into the wet night but for the two little hands which touched his coat and then crept up to his shoulders.

'It's you that frighten me,' she said. 'But that's what you want, isn't it?'

'You know what I want,' he said and brought his mouth down on hers, holding her body away from the cold, clammy wall. At first she was limp and unresisting. Then her arms went around him with a fierce abandon and as her lips parted under his, he felt a great thrill of triumph.

Above them a light appeared as a bright orange rectangle on the dark bricks. Before he opened his eyes Drayton felt it like pain on his eyelids.

She pulled away from him slowly with a long 'Aah!' of pleasure, a sigh of pleasure only begun to be cut short. 'They're waiting up for me.' Her breath was light and fast. 'I must go in.'

'Tomorrow,' he said, 'tomorrow.'

She could not find her key at first and it excited him to see her fumbling and hear her swearing softly under her breath. He had caused this sudden gaucheness, this disorientation, and it filled his masculine ego with the joy of conquest.

'Tomorrow, then.' The smile came, shy and tantalising. Then the door closed on her and the bell made its cold harsh music.

When he was alone in the alley and the light from above had gone out, he stood where they had kissed and passed his forefinger across his lips. The rain was still falling and the street lamp glowed with a greenish sulphurous light. He came out into this light and looked at his finger with the long smear of pale lipstick. It was not pink but the colour of suntanned flesh and he fancied that with it she had left on his mouth something of herself, a grain of skin or a trace of sweat. On the front of his

453

coat was a long fair hair. To have these vestiges of her was in itself a kind of possession. Alone in the wet street, he passed his tongue lightly across his finger and he shivered.

A cat came out of the alley and slunk into a doorway, its fur dewed with fine drops. There was no visible sky, just vapour, and beyond the vapour blackness. Drayton put up his hood and walked home to his lodgings.

CHAPTER EIGHT

To the south of Kingsmarkham and overshadowing the eastern
and southern sides of Pomfret lie twenty or thirty square miles
of pine woods. This is Cheriton Forest. It is a man-made
plantation, consisting mostly of firs and larches, and it has a
stark un-English beauty, giving to the green plains beneath it
the appearance of an Alpine meadow.

A new estate of small white houses has sprung up on the
Pomfret side of the forest. With their coloured front doors and
their decorations of cedar board they are not unlike chalets. To
one of these, a yellow-painted house with a new car port,
Detective Sergeant Martin took himself on Sunday morning,
looking for a man called Kirkpatrick.

The door was opened promptly by a girl of about seven, a
child with large eyes and a cowed look. Martin waited on the
doorstep while she went to find her mother. The house was built
on an open plan and he could see a little boy, as pale and wary
as his sister, playing apathetically on the floor with alphabet
bricks. The woman who came at last had a pugnacious face.
She had the roseate breathless look of those who suffer from
high blood pressure. Her blonde hair was dressed in tight shiny
curls and she wore red-rimmed glasses. Martin introduced
himself and asked for her husband.

'Is it about the car?' Mrs Kirkpatrick said savagely.

'In a way.'

The children crept up to their mother and stood staring.

'Well, you can see he isn't here, can't you? If he's crashed
the car I can't say I'm sorry. I'd say good riddance. I hope it's
a total write-off. When he brought it home here last Monday, I
said, "Don't think you'll get me to go joy-riding in that thing.
I'd rather walk. If I wanted to make an exhibition of myself in
a pink and white car with purple stripes I'd go on the dodgems
at Brighton," I said.'

Martin blinked at her. He had no idea what she meant.

'The other thing he had,' she said, 'that was bad enough.

Great old-fashioned black Morris like a hearse. God knows, we must be the laughing stock of all the neighbours.' She suddenly became aware of the staring listening children. 'How many times have I told you not to come poking your noses into my private business?' she said viciously. The boy wandered back to his bricks, but it took a savage push to move the little girl. 'Now, then,' she said to Martin. 'What's he done? What d'you want him for?'

'Just to talk to him.'

Mrs Kirkpatrick seemed more interested in listening to the sound of her own voice and airing grievances than eliciting reasons from Martin. 'If he's been speeding again,' she said, 'he'll lose his licence. Then he'll lose his job.' Far from being concerned, her voice held a note of triumph. 'A firm like *Lipdew* aren't going to keep on a salesman who can't drive a car, are they? Any more than they're going to give their people great showy cars for them to smash to smithereens just when it takes their fancy. I told him so before he went to Scotland. I told him on Tuesday morning. That's why he never came in for his dinner Tuesday night. But he can't be told. Pig-headed and stubborn he is and now it's got him into trouble.'

Martin backed away from her. A barrage of gunfire would be preferable to this. As he went down the path he heard one of the children crying in the house behind him.

Monkey Matthews was lying on his bed, smoking, when Wexford went into the cell. He raised himself on one elbow and said, 'They told me it was your day off.'

'So it is, but I thought you might be lonely.' Wexford shook his head reprovingly and looked round the small room, sniffing the air. 'How the rich live!' he said. 'Want me to send out for more of your dope? You can afford it, Monkey.'

'I don't want nothing,' Monkey said, turning his face to the wall, 'except to be left alone. This place is more like a goods yard than a nick. I never got a wink of sleep last night.'

'That's your conscience, Monkey, the still, small voice that keeps urging you to tell me something, like, for instance, how you knew the girl's name was Ann.'

Monkey groaned. 'Can't you give it a rest? My nerves are in a shocking state.'

456

'I'm delighted to hear it,' Wexford said unkindly. 'Must be the result of my psychological warfare.' He went out into the corridor and upstairs to Burden's office. The inspector had just come in and was taking off his raincoat.

'It's your day off.'

'My wife was threatening to cart me off to church. This seemed the lesser evil. How are we doing?'

'Martin's been talking to Mrs Kirkpatrick.'

'Ah, the wife of Anita Margolis's current boy friend.'

Burden sat down by the window. This morning the sun was shining, not after the fashion of fitful April sunshine but with the strength and warmth of early summer. He raised the blind and opened the window, letting in with the soft light the clear crescendo of bells from Kingsmarkham church steeple.

'I think we may be on to something there, sir,' he said. 'Kirkpatrick's away, travelling for his firm in Scotland. He went off on Tuesday and the wife hasn't seen him since. Moreover, he used to have a black car, had it up until last Monday, when his firm gave him a new one, white thing apparently, plastered all over with advertising gimmicks,' he chuckled. 'The wife's a harridan. Thought he'd smashed the car when she saw Martin, but she didn't turn a hair.' His face hardening slightly, he went on, 'I'm not one to condone adultery, as you know, but it looks as if there may have been some justification for it here.'

'Is he small and dark?' Wexford asked with a pained look at the open window. He moved closer to the central heating vent.

'Don't know. Martin didn't care to go into too many details with the wife. It's not as if we've much to go on.' Wexford nodded a grudging approval. 'Ah, well,' Burden said, getting up. 'Margolis may be able to help us there. For an artist he's a rotten observer, but he has *seen* the man.' He reached for his coat. 'Lovely sound those bells.'

'Eh?'

'I said the bells were lovely.'

'What?' said Wexford. 'Can't hear a word you say for the sound of those bloody bells.' He grinned hugely at the ancient joke. 'You might have a look-in on Monkey on your way out. Just in case he's getting tired of holding out on us.'

After careful examination by the police and a session at a

garage to have its radiator repaired, Anita Margolis's Alpine had been restored to its parking place on the grass verge outside Quince Cottage. Burden was not surprised to find it there, but his eyebrows went up as he saw ahead of him the rears of not one white car but two. He parked his own behind them and came out into the sunshine. As he walked up to it he saw that the new arrival was white only in that this was its background colour. Along its sides a band perhaps a foot wide had been painted in bright pink, adorned with sprays of purple flowers. This particular shade of purple had been used for the lettering above it: *Lipdew, Paintbox for a Prettier You.*

Burden grinned to himself. Only a brazen extrovert would enjoy being seen about in this car. He glanced through a side window at the pink seats. They were littered with leaflets and on the dashboard shelf were samples of the stuff the driver peddled, bottles and jars presumably, done up in mauve packages and tied with gold cord.

There could hardly be two cars in Sussex like this. Kirkpatrick must be somewhere about. Burden unlatched the gate and entered the cottage garden. The wind had scattered the petals of quince blossom and underfoot the ground was slippery scarlet. When nobody answered his knock, he went round the side of the house and saw that the doors of the garage where Margolis kept his own car were open and the car gone.

Fat buds on the apple branches brushed his face and all around him he could hear the soft twittering of birds. The atmosphere and appearance of rustic peace were somewhat marred by the ragged sheets of paper, vestiges of Margolis's inexpert tidying up, which still clung to bushes and in places fluttered in the treetops. Burden stopped by the back door. A man in a stone-coloured belted raincoat was standing on a wooden box and peering in at the kitchen window.

Unseen, Burden watched him in silence for a moment. Then he coughed. The man jumped, turned to face him, and came slowly down from his perch.

'There's nobody in,' he said diffidently, and then, 'I was just checking.' The man was undeniably good-looking, pale, dapper and with curling dark brown hair. The chin was small, the nose straight and the eyes liquid and lashed like a girl's.

'I'd like a word with you, Mr Kirkpatrick.'

'How d'you know my name? I don't know you.' Now that they were standing level with each other, Burden noted that he was perhaps five feet eight inches tall.

'I recognised your car,' he said. The effect of this was electric. Two dark red spots appeared on Kirkpatrick's sallow cheekbones.

'What the hell does that mean?' he said angrily.

Burden looked at him mildly. 'You said no one was in. Who were you looking for?'

'That's it, is it?' Kirkpatrick took a deep breath, clenching his fists. 'I know who you are.' He nodded absurdly and with grim satisfaction. 'You're a snooper, what they call an enquiry agent. I suppose my wife put you on to me.'

'I've never seen your wife,' said Burden, 'but I'm certainly an enquiry agent. More commonly called a police officer.'

'I overheard you asking the sergeant where you could hire a car,' Wexford said.

'In my lunch hour, sir,' Drayton replied quickly.

Wexford shook his head impatiently. 'All right, man, all right. Don't make me out an ogre. You can hire an articulated lorry for all I care and you won't do it in your lunch hour, you'll do it now. There are only three firms in the district doing car hire, Missal's and Cawthorne's in Stowerton and the Red Star where you took Miss Margolis's in York Street here. What we want to know is if anyone hired a green car from them last Tuesday.'

After Drayton had gone, he sat down to think it all out and try to solve the enigma of the cars. The man called Geoff Smith had used a black car on Saturday, a green one on Tuesday, if Mrs Collins could be believed. He thought she could. Last night he and Bryant had tested a black car under the pearly lamplight in Sparta Grove and it had remained black. He had looked at it through clear glass and through stained glass. No amount of contriving or exercise of the imagination could make it green. Did that mean that Geoff Smith possessed two cars, or that on Sunday or Monday he had sold the black one and bought a green? Or could it be that because this new car was conspicuous, he had hired the green one for his dubious and clandestine adventure?

Drayton, too, asked himself these questions as the tumultuous ringing of the church bells ceased and he turned the corner into York Street. In the strengthening sunshine the rhinestone ropes glittered at him from the window of Joy Jewels. He thought of the silver chain Linda wore around her neck and simultaneously of that smooth warm skin, silky to his touch.

He had to shake himself and tighten his mouth before going into Red Star Garage. They showed him two ageing red Hillmans and he turned away to catch the bus for Stowerton. There he found Russell Cawthorne in his office. On the one bit of solid wall behind his head was a calendar of a girl wearing three powder puffs and a pair of high-heeled shoes. Drayton looked at it with contempt and a certain unease. It reminded him of the magazines in Grover's shop. Cawthorne sat up stiffly when Drayton told him who he was and gave a brisk nod, the C in C receiving a promising subaltern.

' 'Morning. Sit down. More trouble brewing?'

Affected old bore, Drayton thought. 'I want to ask you about hiring cars. You do hire cars, don't you?'

'My dear boy, I thought you were here in your official capacity, but if you just . . .'

'I am. This is an official question. What colour are they, these hire cars of yours?'

Cawthorne opened a fanlight. The fresh air made him cough. 'What colour are they? They're all the same. Three black Morris Minors.'

'Were any of them hired on Saturday, the 3rd?'

'Now when would that have been, laddie?'

'Last week. There's a calendar behind you.' Cawthorne's face darkened to an even maroon. 'It'll be in the book,' he muttered.

The book looked well-kept. Cawthorne opened it and turned back a few pages, frowning slightly. 'I remember that morning,' he said. 'I lost my best mechanic. Impertinent young devil, treating the place like he owned it. I gave him the push, lost my temper . . .' Drayton fidgeted impatiently. 'About the cars,' Cawthorne said moodily. 'No, they were all in.'

'What about sales? You wouldn't have sold anyone a green car about that time?'

One of the veined, not very steady hands, went up to twitch at his moustache. 'My business hasn't been exactly booming.' He hesitated, eyeing Drayton warily. 'I'll tell you frankly,' he said, 'I haven't made a sale since Mr Grover took delivery of his Mini in February.'

Drayton felt his face grow hot. The name was enough to do it. 'I want to hire a car myself,' he said. 'For tonight.'

Blustering, confident as only the weak can be, Alan Kirkpatrick stood defiantly in Wexford's office. He had refused to sit down and a constantly reiterated, 'Rubbish' and 'I don't believe it' had greeted Wexford's hints as to Anita Margolis's probable death.

'In that case,' Wexford said, 'you won't mind telling us about your movements last Tuesday, the night you had a date with her.'

'A date?' Kirkpatrick gave a short sneering laugh. 'I like the way you put it. I got to know that woman solely because I'm keen on art. The only way to get into that place and look at Margolis's pictures was through her.'

Burden got up from his corner where he had been sitting quietly and said, 'Interested in his work, are you? So am I. I've been trying to remember the name of that thing he's got in the Tate. Perhaps you can refresh my memory.'

That it was so obviously a trap did not derogate from its significance as a question and a question which, if Kirkpatrick were to sustain his role as a seeker after artistic enlightenment, must be answered. His soft mobile mouth twitched.

'I don't know what he calls them,' he muttered.

'Funny,' said Burden. 'Any admirer of Margolis would surely know "Nothing".' For a moment Wexford himself stared. Then he recalled the *Weekend Telegraph* lying close to his hand in the desk drawer. As he listened to the inspector who had suddenly launched into an esoteric review of modern art, he was lost in admiration. Instead of reaching for his gun, Burden had evidently reached for a work of reference. Kirkpatrick, also perhaps overcome, sat down abruptly, his face puzzled and aggressive.

'I don't have to answer your questions,' he said.

'Quite right,' Wexford said kindly. 'As you rightly say, we can't even prove Miss Margolis is dead.' And he nodded sagely as if Kirkpatrick's wisdom had recalled him from sensational dreams to reality. 'No, we'll just make a note that you were probably the last person to see her alive.'

'Look,' said Kirkpatrick, on the edge of his chair but making no move to get up, 'my wife's a very jealous woman . . .'

'Seems to be infectious in your family. I'd have said it was jealousy made you threaten Miss Margolis a couple of weeks ago.' Wexford quoted Mrs Penistan. ' "I might kill you myself one of these fine days". Was last Tuesday one of those fine days? Funny way to talk to a woman you were only interested in because of her brother's painting, wasn't it?'

'That date, as you call it, she never kept it. I didn't go out with her.'

Ruby would know him again. Wexford cursed the paucity of their evidence. He did not think it would be an easy matter to persuade this man to take part in an identification parade. Kirkpatrick's confidence had been slightly shaken by Burden's questions, but as he sat down again some of his bravado seemed to return. With a look that was part impatience, part resignation, he took out a pocket-comb and began to arrange his curly hair.

'We're not interested in your wife's possible divorce proceedings,' Wexford said. 'If you're frank with us there's no reason why it should go further, certainly not to your wife's ears.'

'There's nothing to be frank about,' Kirkpatrick said in a less belligerent tone. 'I was going up North on Tuesday for my firm. It's true I'd arranged to meet Miss Margolis before I went. She was going to show me some of Margolis's — er, early work. He wouldn't have had it if he'd been there but he was going out.' Wexford raised his eyes and met Burden's calm, polite gaze. How green and gullible did this cosmetic salesman think they were? This story which seemed to fill its teller with pride was so near what Wexford called the 'old etching gag' that he could hardly suppress a chuckle of derision. Early work, indeed! 'I was going home first for a meal but I was late and it was seven when I got to Kingsmarkham. Grover's were closing and I remember that girl made a bit of a scene because I wanted my evening paper. There wasn't time to go home then, so I went straight round to Pump Lane. Ann — Miss Margolis, that is — had forgotten all about me coming. She said she was going to a party. And that's all.'

During the latter part of this explanation Kirkpatrick's face had grown red and he fidgeted uneasily.

'It can't have been more than half-past seven, if that,' Wexford said. He was wondering why Burden had gone to the window and was staring down, his expression amused. 'Surely there was time for your artistic researches, especially as you'd missed your evening meal?'

The flush deepened. 'I asked her if I could come in for a bit and then I said I'd take her out for a meal before the party. She had her ocelot coat on ready to go out, but she wouldn't let me in. I suppose she'd just changed her mind.'

Burden turned from the window and when he spoke Wexford knew what he had been scrutinising. 'How long have you had this car?'

'Since last Monday. I sold my own and got this one from my firm.'

'So Miss Margolis had never seen it before?'

'I don't know what you're getting at.'

'I think you do, Mr Kirkpatrick. I think Miss Margolis wouldn't go out with you because she didn't care to be seen about in such a conspicuous car.' The shot had gone home. Again Wexford marvelled at Burden's perspicacity. Kirkpatrick, who blushed easily at mild slights, had now grown white with anger and perhaps with mortification.

'She was a woman of taste,' Burden said. 'I shouldn't be surprised to hear she burst out laughing when she saw all your pink and mauve decorations.'

Apparently this was the salesman's soft spot. Whether he was a connoisseur of modern painting or just a philanderer, there was no room in either image for this ridiculous vehicle. It was the scar of the branding iron, the yellow armband, the shameful card of identity.

'What's so funny about it?' he said aggressively. 'Who the

hell did she think she was, laughing at me?' Indignation began
to rob him of caution. 'It doesn't alter my personality, make me
into a different man, just because I have to have a car with a
slogan on it. I was good enough for her before, my money was
good enough to spend on her . . .' He had said too much, and
his rage gave place to a sudden recollection of where he was
and to whom he was speaking. 'I mean, I'd given her a few
samples in the past, I . . .'

'For services rendered, no doubt?'

'What the hell does that mean?'

'You said she showed you her brother's paintings without his
knowledge. A kindly act, Mr Kirkpatrick. Worth a pot of nail
varnish or some soap, I should have thought.' Wexford smiled at
him. 'What did you do, borrow a more innocuous car?'

'I tell you, we didn't go anywhere. If we had, we could have
gone in hers.'

'Oh, no,' Wexford said softly. 'You couldn't have used hers.
The radiator was leaking. I suggest you got hold of a green car
and used this to drive Miss Margolis into Stowerton.'

Still smarting from the derision his car had aroused,
Kirkpatrick muttered, 'I suppose someone saw me in Stowerton,
did they? Cawthorne, was it? Come on, you may as well tell me
who it was.'

'Why Cawthorne?'

Kirkpatrick flushed patchily. 'He lives in Stowerton,' he
said, stammering a little over the dentals and the sibilant. 'He
was giving that party.'

'You were on your way to Scotland,' Wexford said thoughtfully. 'You must have made a detour to go through Stowerton.'
He got up ponderously and went over to the wall map. 'Look,
here's the London Road and you'd have to go that way, or east
into Kent, if you wanted to by-pass London. Either way,
Stowerton was miles off your route.'

'What the hell does it matter?' Kirkpatrick burst out. 'I had
the whole evening to kill. There was nothing else to do. I didn't
want to land up in Scotland in the small hours. I should have
thought the main thing was Ann wasn't with me. My God, she
wasn't even in Stowerton, she didn't go to that party!'

'I know,' Wexford said, returning to his chair. 'Her brother

464

knows and Mr Cawthorne knows, but how do you know? You never got back into Sussex till this morning. Now listen, an identification parade would clear the whole thing up. Do you object?'

Suddenly Kirkpatrick looked tired. It could have been mere physical exhaustion or that the strain of lying — and lying ineffectually — was telling badly on him. His good looks were particularly vulnerable to anxiety. They depended on a swagger in the tilt of his head, a laugh on his full mouth. Now there was sweat on his upper lip and the brown eyes, which were his most compelling feature, looked like those of a dog when someone had trodden on its tail.

'I'd like to know what it's in aid of,' he said sullenly. 'I'd like to know who saw me where and what I'm supposed to have been doing.'

'I'll tell you, Mr Kirkpatrick,' said Wexford, drawing up his chair.

'When am I going to get my carpet back?' said Ruby Branch.

'We're not cleaners, you know. We don't do an express service.'

She must be lamenting the days, Burden thought, when women wore veils as a matter of course, as often as not just to go out in the public street. He could remember one his grandmother had had on a toque, a thick, seemingly opaque curtain which when lowered was a perfect disguise for its wearer.

'Pity we're not in Morocco,' he said, 'you could put on your yashmak.'

Ruby gave him a sulky glance. She pulled down the brim of her hat until it almost covered her eyes and muffled her chin with a chiffon scarf.

'I shall be a marked woman,' she said. 'I hope you lot realise that. Suppose I pick him out and he escapes? The jails can't hold them these days. You've only got to look at the papers.'

'You'll have to take your chance on that,' said Burden.

When they were in the car she said diffidently, 'Mr Burden? You never told me whether you're going to do anything about that other thing, that keeping a what-d'you-call-it house?'

'That depends. We shall have to see.'

'I'm putting myself out to help you.'

They drove in silence until they reached the outskirts of Kingsmarkham. Then Burden said, 'Be honest with me, Ruby. What's Matthews ever done for you except take your money and pretty well break up your marriage?'

The painted mouth trembled. There were callouses and the long grey indentations housework makes on the fingers that held the scarf to her lips. 'We've been so much to each other, Mr Burden.'

'That was a long time ago,' he said gently. 'You've got yourself to think of now.' It was cruel what he had to say. Perhaps justice always is and he was used, if not to administering it, at least to leading people to its seat. Now, to find out what he wanted, he would lead Ruby away from it and cruelty would have to be his means. 'You're nearly ten years off your pension. How many of those women you work for would employ you if they knew what you'd been up to? They will know, Ruby. They read the papers.'

'I don't want to get George into trouble.' It took him, as it had Wexford, a moment's reflection before he remembered that George was Monkey's christian name. 'I was crazy about him once. You see, I never had kids, never had what you'd call a real husband. Mr Branch was old enough to be my father.' She paused and with a tiny lace handkerchief dabbed at the tear-stained space between scarf and hat brim. 'George had been in prison. When I found him he seemed — well, so kind of happy to be with me.' In spite of himself, Burden was moved. He could just recall old Branch, doddery and crotchety in advance of his years. 'Four quid George had off me,' she said unevenly, 'and all the drink I'd got in the place and God knows how many good dinners, but he wouldn't lie down beside me. It's not nice, Mr Burden, when you've got memories and you can't help . . .'

'He's not worth your loyalty. Come on now. Cheer up. Mr Wexford'll think I've been giving you the third degree. You never heard that Geoff Smith call the girl Ann, did you? It was all made up to save Monkey.'

'I reckon it was.'

'That's a good girl. Now then, did you search the room at all when you'd found the stain?'

'I was too scared for that. Look, Mr Burden, I've been thinking and thinking about it. George was alone in there for hours and hours on the Tuesday doing that letter while I was out at work. I think he must have found something they'd left behind them.'

'I've been thinking, too, Ruby, and I think great minds think alike.'

When they got to the police station a dozen men were lined up in the yard. None was more than five feet nine and all had hair of shades between mid-brown and coal-black. Kirkpatrick stood fourth from the end on the left. Ruby came hesitantly across the concrete, cautious, absurd in her high heels and with her swathed face. Wexford, who had not heard her story, could hardly keep himself from smiling, but Burden watched her rather sadly. Her eyes flickered across the first three men on the left and came to rest for a brief moment on Kirkpatrick. She came closer and walked slowly down the line, occasionally turning to look over her shoulder. Then she turned back. Kirkpatrick looked afraid, his expression bewildered. Ruby stopped in front of him. A spark of recognition seemed to pass between them and it was as marked on his part as on hers. She moved on, lingering longest of all in front of the last man on the right.

'Well?' said Wexford just inside the door.

'For a minute I thought it was the one on the end.' Wexford sighed softly. 'The one on the end' was Police Constable Peach. 'But then I knew I'd got it wrong. It must be the one with the red tie.'

Kirkpatrick.

'Must be? Why must it be?'

Ruby said simply, 'I know his face, I don't know none of the others. His face is kind of familiar.'

'Yes, yes, I daresay. My face ought to be familiar to you by this time, but I didn't hire your knocking shop last Tuesday.' Under the veil Ruby looked resentful. 'What I want to know is, is he Geoff Smith?'

'I don't know. I wouldn't know him if I saw him now. Ever since then I've been dead scared every time I've seen a dark man in the street. All I know is I saw that fellow with the red tie somewhere last week. Maybe it was Tuesday. I don't know. He knew me too. You saw that?' She made a little whimpering, snivelling sound. Suddenly she was a little girl with an old face. 'I want to go home,' she said, darting a vicious glance at Burden. He smiled back at her philosophically. She was not the first person to make a confession to him and then regret it.

Kirkpatrick came back into Wexford's office, but he did not sit down. Ruby's failure to identify him had restored his confidence and for a moment Wexford thought that he was going to add further touches to the image he had tried to create of himself as a patron or connoisseur of the arts. He picked up the blue glass sculpture and fingered it knowingly while giving Wexford a sullen glance.

'I hope you're satisfied,' he said. 'I think I've been very patient. You could see that woman didn't know me.'

You knew *her*, Wexford thought. You were in Stowerton and although you were not at the party nor in her brother's confidence, you knew Anita Margolis never went there.

Kirkpatrick was relaxed now, breathing easily. 'I'm very tired and, as I say, I've been particularly patient and forthcoming. Not many men who'd just driven four hundred miles would be as accommodating as I've been.' The foot-high chunk of glass was carefully replaced on the desk and he nodded as if he had just subjected it to expert evaluation. You poseur, thought Wexford. 'What I want now is a good sleep and to be left in peace. So if there's any more you want you'd better speak now.'

'Or else hereafter for ever hold our peace? We don't work that way, Mr Kirkpatrick.'

But Kirkpatrick hardly seemed to have heard. 'In peace, as I say. I don't want my family bothered or frightened. That woman not identifying me should settle the matter for good and all. I . . .'

You talk too much, Wexford thought.

'The Vine had struck a Fibre; which about
If clings my being — let the Sufi flout;
Of my base metal may be filed a Key,
That shall unlock the Door he howls without.'

CHAPTER NINE

After the rain the town looked cleansed. The evening sun made the pavements gleam like sheet gold and a thin vapour rose from them. It was mild, warm even, and the air heavy with damp. Excitement made a hard knot in Drayton's chest as he drove up the High Street in Cawthorne's hire car and parked it in the alley. He wanted to fill his lungs with fresh air, not this cloying stuff that made him breathless.

Seeing her was a shock. He had had fantasies about her in the intervening time and he had expected reality to disappoint. She was just a girl he fancied and would possess if he could. It had happened to him a dozen times before. Why then, although the shop was full of customers and pretty girls among them, were they all faceless, all so many zombies? The sensuality which had flooded into him last night outside the shop and had since been transmuted into a clinical tickling calculation, came back like a blow and held him, staring at her, while the doorbell rang in his ears.

Her eyes met his and she gave him the faint secret smile that was just a lifting of the corners of her mouth. He turned away and killed time playing with the paperback stand. The shop had an unpleasant smell, food stench that came perhaps from whatever they ate in those back regions, the sickliness of unwrapped sweets, dirt that filled up the corners where no one tried to reach. On the shelf above his head the china spaniel still carried his pot of dusty flowers. Nobody would ever buy him just as nobody would buy the ashtray and the jug which flanked him. What connoisseur of Wedgwood — what conoisseur of anything, come to that — would even enter this shop?

More and more customers kept coming in. The constant tinkling of the bell set Drayton's nerves on edge. He spun the stand and the coloured covers flickered in a bright senseless kaleidoscope, a gun, a skull under a stetson, a girl who lay in blood and roses. His watch told him that he had been in the shop only two minutes.

Only one customer left now. Then a woman came in to buy a dress pattern. He heard Linda say softly, even scornfully, 'Sorry, we're closed.' The woman began to argue. She had to have it that night, a matter of urgency. Drayton felt Linda's shrug, caught a firm phrase of denial. Was it thus, with this cool dogged patience, that she habitually refused demands? The woman went out, muttering. The blind rattled down the window and he watched her turn the sign.

She came away from the door and walked towards him quite slowly. Because her face had lost its smile and her arms hung stiffly at her sides, he thought that she was about to speak to him, perhaps apologise or state conditions. Instead, without a word or a movement of her hands, she lifted her mouth to his, opening her lips with a kind of sensuous gasp. He matched his mood to hers and for a moment they were joined only by the kiss. Then he took her in his arms and closed his eyes against the parody that mocked him from the book jackets, the orgy of writhing lovers, coupling above, below, beside each other, a massed fertility rite in modern undress.

He released her and murmured, 'Let's go.' She gave a soft giggle which drew from him a low, reluctant laugh. They were laughing, he knew, at their own weakness, their defencelessness under the grip of emotion.

'Yes, let's go.' She was breathing hard. The short staccato giggle she had given had nothing to do with amusement. 'Mark,' she said, faintly interrogative, and then, 'Mark' again, as if the repetition of his name settled something for her. To him it seemed like a promise.

'We'll go to Pomfret,' he said. 'I've got the car.'

'To Cheriton Forest?'

He nodded, feeling a stab of disappointment. 'You've been there before?'

The implication in the question was not lost on her. 'With Mum and Dad on picnics.' She looked at him gravely. 'Not like this,' she said. It might mean so much or so little. It might mean she had never been there with a boy friend, with any man, to make love or just to walk hand in hand. Words were a disguise for thought and for intention.

She got into the car beside him and went through a small

ritual of arranging her skirt, removing her gloves, placing her handbag under the dashboard. What strange compulsion women had with their genteelisms, their attention to their personal furnishings! And how seldom they abandoned themselves. The face which she had put on was not the one he had seen as they came out from their embrace, but a prideful smug mask arranged, as it were, in the framing of the car window so that the world might observe her serenity out in a car with a man.

'Where would you like to eat?' he asked. 'I thought of the Cheriton Hotel, just where the Forest begins?'

She shook her head. 'I'm not hungry. We could have a drink.'

A girl like this, had she ever been in such a place before? Could she resist being seen there? With all his heart he despised her for her origins, her poverty of conversation, the pitiful smallness of her world. And yet her physical presence excited him almost beyond bearing. How was he to endure an hour with her in an hotel lounge, what would they talk about, how could he keep from touching her? He had nothing to say to her. There were rules in this game, prescribed amorous badinage, corresponding to courtship in the ornithological world, a kind of dancing and fluffing out of feathers. Earlier in the evening, before he had come into the shop, Drayton had to some extent rehearsed these preambles, but now it seemed to him that they had passed beyond them. The kiss had brought them to the threshold. He longed for a little gaiety from her, a spark of joy that might change his excitement from lust into something more civilised.

'I don't know,' he said dully. 'The evening I get the car is the first one it hasn't rained for weeks.'

'We couldn't have come here without it.' Ahead of them the lights of Pomfret glimmered in the dusk through the greening trees. 'It's getting dark,' she said.

Driven to despair for something to talk about, he broke a rule. 'We've been questioning a fellow called Kirkpatrick today,' he said. It was unorthodox, perhaps even wrong, to talk police business. 'He's a customer of yours. D'you know him?'

'They don't give their names,' she said.

'He lives around here.' Exactly here, he thought. This must be it. The black escarpment of the forest rose before them and in front of it, lying like boxes dropped in a green meadow, were a dozen white and blue dwellings, styled 'village houses'.

'Oh, look!' she said. 'That car.' There it was on one of the drives, its pink and lilac turned sickly in the light of a porch carriage lamp. 'That's the man you mean, isn't it? Fancy driving around in a thing like that. I nearly killed myself laughing.' Her animation over something so puerile chilled him. He felt his mouth go stiff. 'What's he done?' she asked.

'You mustn't ask me that.'

'You're very careful,' she said and he sensed that her eyes were on him. 'Your bosses, they must think a lot of you.'

'I hope so.' He thought she was smiling at him, but he dared not turn. It came to him suddenly that her silence and her dullness perhaps sprang from the same source as his own and the thought rocked him. The road was dark here where the pinewoods began, too dark for him to take his eyes from it for an instant. In the distance, between black billows of conifers, he could see the lights of the hotel. She put her hand on his knee.

'Mark,' she said, 'Mark, I don't want that drink.'

It was nearly nine when the call from the station came through to Burden's house.

'Ruby Branch is back again, sir.' The voice was Martin's. 'She's got Knobby Clark with her and she wants to see you. I can't get a word out of them.'

He sounded apologetic and as if he expected a reprimand. But all Burden said was, 'I'll be straight down.'

At his throat, he could feel that odd little stricture, that nervous pull, which meant something was going to happen at last. His tiredness went.

Ruby was in the police station foyer, her attitude abject, almost martyred, and on her face an expression of stoicism. Beside her, on a spoon-shaped red chair inadequate to contain his bulky rotund body, sat the fence from Sewingbury. Looking at him, Burden recalled their last encounter. Knobby looked nervous now and he had the air of a suppliant, but on that previous occasion it was he who had been in a position to exercise scornful contempt, to bargain and reject. In his mind's eye, Burden saw again the shy ladylike woman who had come to sell the jewels that were her husband's gifts. His heart hardened and he was seized with a sudden anger.

'Well?' he said. 'What d'you want?'

With a heavy mournful sigh, Ruby surveyed the colourful appointments of the hall where they sat and it was these she seemed to address. 'A nice way to talk when I've taken the trouble to come all this way. It's a real sacrifice I've made.'

Knobby Clark said nothing. His hands were in his pockets and he appeared to be concentrating on retaining his balance on a seat constructed for narrower buttocks than his own. The little eyes in cushions of fat were still and wary.

'What's he doing here?' Burden asked.

An apparently self-appointed spokeswoman for both of them, Ruby said, 'I guessed George'd go to him, them being old buddies. I had a bus ride to Sewingbury after I'd been here.' She paused. 'After I'd been helping you,' she said with heavy meaning. 'But if you don't want to know, that's O.K. by me.' Clutching her handbag, she got up. Her fur collar undulated at the quivering of the big bosom beneath it.

'You'd better come into my office.'

Still silent, Knobby Clark hoisted himself carefully from his chair. Burden could look down easily on to the top of his head. All that remained of his hair was a feathery tuft, again evocative of the stubbly crown on a great misshapen swede.

Intent on wasting no more time, he said, 'Well, let's see it, then. What is it?' He was rewarded by nothing more than a slight tremor in Knobby's mountainous shoulders.

'D'you mind shutting the door?' said Ruby. Here the lights were brighter and her face looked ravaged. 'Show it to him, Mr Clark.'

The little jeweller hesitated. 'Now, look, Mr Burden,' he said, speaking for the first time. 'You and me, we've had no trouble for a long time, have we? Must be seven or eight years.'

'Six,' said Burden crisply. 'Just six next month since you had your little spot of bother over receiving those watches.'

Knobby said resentfully, 'That was when I come out.'

'I don't see the point of it, anyway.' Ruby sat down,

gathering confidence. 'I don't see the point of trying to make him look small. I come here of my own free will . . .'

'Shut up,' Burden snapped at her. 'D'you think I don't know what's been going on? You're narked with your boyfriend, you want to do him down. So you took yourself over to this little rat's shop in Sewingbury and asked him just what Monkey Matthews flogged to him last Thursday. Make him look small! That's a laugh. If he was much smaller we'd trip over him.' He swallowed hard. 'It wasn't public spirit, it was spite. Naturally Clark came with you when you told him we'd got Monkey here. Now you can fill in the rest but spare me the sob stuff.'

'Knobby wants to make sure there won't be no trouble for him,' Ruby said, now reduced to a tearful whimpering. 'He wasn't to know. How was I to know? I left George alone for a couple of hours on Thursday while I was working, making money to keep him in luxury . . .' Perhaps she recalled Burden's caution as to sentimentality, for she went on more calmly, 'He must have found it down the side of one of my chairs.'

'Found what?'

A fat hand returned to a shapeless pocket, emerged and dropped something hard and shiny on to Burden's desk. 'There's a lovely piece of workmanship for you, Mr Burden. Eighteen carat gold and the hand of a master.'

It was a cigarette lighter of gleaming red-gold, the length and breadth of a matchbox but thinner, its sides delicately chased with a design of grapes and vineleaves. Burden turned it over and pursed his lips. On its base was an inscription: 'For Ann who lights my life'.

A big split opened in Knobby's face, the rift in the mangold that has grown too pulpy for its skin. He was smiling. 'Thursday morning it was, Mr Burden.' The bloated hands spread and quivered. "Take a butcher's at this," Monkey says to me. "Where d'you get it?" I says, knowing his reputation. "All that glisters is not gold," I said . . .'

'But if it wasn't gold,' said Burden nastily, 'it could glisten on till kingdom come for all you cared.'

Knobby looked at him narrowly. ' "My old auntie left it me," he says, "my auntie Ann." "Lively old geezer she must have been," I said. "She leave you her cigar case and her hip

476

flask as well?" But that was only my fun, Mr Burden. I never thought it was hot. It wasn't on the list.' His face split again, virtuously this time. 'I gave him twenty for it.'

'Don't be childish. I'm not senile and you're no philanthropist.' Again Burden remembered the woman with the jewels. 'You gave him ten,' he said contemptuously.

Knobby Clark did not deny it. 'It's my loss, Mr Burden. Ten or twenty, it doesn't grow on trees. You won't make anything of it? No trouble, eh?'

'Oh, get out,' Burden said tiredly. Knobby went. He looked smaller than ever, yet he seemed to be walking on his toes. When he had gone Ruby put her ginger head in her hands.

'It's done then,' she said. 'My God, I never thought I'd shop George.'

'Hear the cock crowing in the distance, can you?'

'You're a hard man. You get more like your boss every day.'

Burden was not displeased at this. 'You can go, too,' he said. 'We won't say any more about the other thing. You've wasted enough public time and public money as it is. I should stick to char-ing in future.' He grinned, his good temper almost restored. 'You've got a genius for cleaning up other people's mess.'

'Would you let me see George?'

'No, I wouldn't. Don't push your luck.'

'I didn't think you would.' She sighed. 'I wanted to say I was sorry.' Her face was ugly and painted and old. 'I love him,' she said and her voice sounded very tired. 'I've loved him for twenty years. I don't reckon you can understand that. You and the others, it's a dirty joke to you, isn't it?'

'Good night, Ruby,' he said. 'I've got things to do.' Wexford would have managed things better. He would have said something ironic and tough — and tender. It was as she had said. He, Burden, could not understand, never would, did not want to. To him that kind of love was a closed book, pornography for Grover's library. Presently he went down to see Monkey Matthews.

'You ought to get yourself a lighter, Monkey,' he said through the smoke, viewing the litter of match ends.

'Can't seem to get on with them, Mr Burden.'

'Not even a nice gold one? Or would you rather have the lolly?' He let it lie in the palm of his hand, then raised it to catch the light from the bare bulb. 'Stealing by finding,' he said. 'What a come-down!'

'I don't suppose it's any use asking you how you found out?'

'Not a bit.'

'Ruby wouldn't do that to me.'

Burden hesitated for a second. She had said he was getting like Wexford and he had taken it as a compliment. Perhaps it was not only the Chief Inspector's toughness he could emulate. He opened his eyes wide in wrathful indignation. 'Ruby? I'm surprised at you.'

'No, I don't reckon she would. Forget I said it. Different to that lousy old git, Knobby Clark. He'd sell his own grandmother for cats' meat.' With slow resignation, Monkey lit another cigarette. 'How long'll I get?' he asked.

The car lights were off. He had parked in a clearing surrounded by dense trees, tall black firs and pines, grown for ship's masts and flagpoles. Their trunks looked grey but even these straight shapes were indiscernible a few yards in from the edge of the wood. Beyond them there was neither night nor day, only a dark labyrinth.

He held her in his arms and he could feel her heart beating. It was the only sound. He thought it would be dark when he opened his eyes — their kiss had been long and blind — and the pallid dusk was a shock.

'Let's walk,' he said, taking her hands. They were all right now. It had come right. He did not know why, but instead of triumph there descended upon him a subtle and hitherto unexperienced fear. It was not in any sense a fear of physical inadequacy, nor of psychological failure, but an apprehension rather of some terrible involvement. Until now his sexual adventures had been transient, sometimes gay, never the spur to introspection. But he felt that they had not in any way been a practice or a rehearsal. Indeed the feelings they had evoked and those by which they had been promoted were quite unlike the sensations he now had both in kind and in degree. He was totally engulfed by something new and terrifying. It might almost have been the first time for him.

'It's like a foreign country,' she said.

It was. An uncharted place, alien, with an untranslatable language. That she should feel what he felt, identically, telepathically, made him gasp. Then he looked at her and, following her gaze upwards to the crowns of the trees, knew with a sudden sense of let-down that she meant the forest itself, and not a state of mind.

'Have you ever been in one?'

'No,' she said, 'but it's like that. And it's like last night. Alone with you between high walls. Did you think of that when you brought me here?' They had begun to climb an avenue which, cutting into the hillside so evenly and precisely, resembled an incision in thick black flesh or a sewn wound. 'Did you think of that?'

'Perhaps.'

'That was clever of you.' She was breathing shallowly, although the ascent was steep. To the left of them and a little way ahead, a tiny footpath threaded between the trees.

'But there aren't any windows here, are there?' More than anything in the world, more at that moment even than absolute possession of her, he wanted to see that covert smile, that uplifting of the lips without parting them. She had not smiled at all since they had entered the forest and that look of hers was the essence, the very nucleus of her appeal to him. Without it he could kiss her, even achieve that culmination for which this visit had been contrived, but he would lose the savour and the scent and half his pleasure — or perhaps be saved. Already he was the slave of a fetish.

Echoing him, she said softly, 'No windows . . . No one to watch you or stop you.' She added breathlessly, turning to face him so that their bodies and their eyes were close, 'I'm tired of being watched, Mark.'

A little orange square in a wall, a bell that always jangled, a querulous voice calling.

'You're with me,' he said, 'and nobody watches me.' Usually he was subtle, but her nearness deprived him of restraint and brought out the swagger of the male animal. Before he could stop himself the appeal came out. 'Smile for me,' he said in a hard whisper. Her fingers closed on his shoulders, not firmly or passionately but with a light, almost calculatingly seductive pressure. The look in her eyes was quite blank and the invitation in them came entirely from the tremor of half-closed heavy lids. 'Oh, smile . . .'

Then suddenly he was rewarded. A terrible urgency possessed him, but for all that he took her slowly in his arms, watching the smile that was the focal point of all his desire, and then bringing his own mouth down to meet it.

'Not here,' she whispered. 'In the dark. Take me into the dark.' Her response was strong yet fluid. The words, spoken against his lips, seemed to flow into his body like wine and fill him with heat.

The thread of a path beckoned him and he held her against himself, half carrying her into the deep shadows of the forest edge. Above them the pine needles whispered and the sound was like the distant voices of doves. He took off his coat and spread it on the sandy floor. Then he heard her whispering to him words he could not catch but which he knew were no longer hesitant or passive. Her hands reached for him to pull him down beside her.

The darkness was almost absolute and it was this anonymous secret blackness which she seemed to have needed just as he had needed her smile. Her coquetry, her shy silence, had given place to a feverish hunger. That it was neither false nor simulated he knew when she took his face in the long hands that had become strong and fierce. He kissed her throat and her breasts and she gave a long sigh of pleasure. The darkness was a warm river to drown in. They call it the little death, he thought, and then the power to think at all melted away.

CHAPTER TEN

There was scarcely any delay between his knocking and the opening of the cottage door. A bright shaft of sunshine fell upon a black and mauve spotted overall and a sharp red face.

'Turned up again like a bad penny,' said Mrs Penistan. Burden blinked. He hardly knew whether her remark referred to his arrival or her own unexpected appearance. She clarified with one of her shrill laughs. 'I saw Mr M's advert and I took pity on him, said I'd come back till *she* turns up.' Leaning towards him, her broom held aloft like a spear, she whispered confidingly, 'If she turns up.' She stood aside for him to enter. 'Mind the bucket,' she said. 'We're all at sixes and sevens in here. Good thing my boys can't see what I have to contend with. If they set eyes on this place they'd have their mum out before you could say knife.' Remembering the ox-like Penistan men, not surely conspicuous for filial piety, Burden could only give a neutral smile. Their mother thrust her face into his and with a laugh, this time so cheerful as to amount to glee, said, 'Wouldn't surprise me if there was bugs in them walls.' A shrill peal of giggles pursued him into the studio.

Her efforts seemed to have made as yet small improvement in the general dirty disarray. Perhaps she had only just arrived. Nothing had been tidied or dusted and to the normal unpleasant smell had been added a sour stench, possibly coming from the dregs which still remained in the dozen or so empty cups on the tables and the floor. Here, as nowhere else, Ruby's vigour and acumen were needed.

Margolis was painting. In addition to the tubes of oil colour arranged about him were various small pots of unidentifiable matter. One seemed to contain sand, another iron filings. He looked up when Burden entered.

'I've decided not to think about it,' he said with as near an approach to firmness as could be imagined. 'I'm simply getting on with my work. Ann'll be back.' He added as if this clinched the matter, 'Mrs Penistan agrees with me.'

It was hardly the impression Burden had received on the doorstep. Without comment — let the man be cheerful while he could — he held out the lighter. 'Ever seen it before?'

'It's a cigarette lighter,' Margolis said sagely. So might some authoritative archaeologist identify an obscure find in an ancient barrow.

'The point is, is it your sister's?'

'I don't know. I've never seen it before. People are always giving her things.' He turned it over. 'Look, it's got her name on it.'

'It's got Ann on it,' Burden corrected him.

A poised broom preceded Mrs Penistan's entry into the studio. She seemed to find amusement not so much in her employer's remarks as in his very existence, for, standing behind him as he contemplated the lighter, she favoured Burden with a slow deliberate wink.

'Here, let's have a look,' she said. One glance satisfied her. 'No,' she said, 'no.' This time her laughter seemed aimed at his own gullibility or possibly at his supposing Margolis to be capable of identifying anything. Burden envied her ignorance. Not for her the dilemma of wondering how to contend with genius. Here was a man, inept in practical matters, vague in his speech; therefore he was a lunatic, affording mirth and a kind of rough pity. 'She never had nothing like that,' she said firmly. 'Her and me, we used to have our coffee break mid-morning. Always had a cigarette with it, she did. You need one of them lighters, I said, seeing the way she got through umpteen boxes of matches. Get some young fellow to give you one. It was way back around Christmas, you see, and her birthday was in Jan.'

'So she may have had it for her birthday?'

'If she did, she never showed it to me. Never had a gas lighter, neither. My boy could get you one cost price, him being in the trade, I said, but she . . .'

Burden cut her short, his ears painfully anticipating the strident laugh the end of this story, however humourless, would certainly provoke. 'I'll see myself out,' he said.

'Mind the bucket!' Mrs Penistan called after him cheerfully. He went out among the daffodils. Everything was gold this morning, the sunshine, the pale bright flowers of spring and the little object in his pocket.

Kirkpatrick's car was on his driveway. Burden edged past it, his coat brushing the lettering and the mauve flowers.

'He says he's ill,' Mrs Kirkpatrick said in a loud harsh voice.

Burden showed her his card. It might have been an advertising brochure for all the notice she took of it.

'He says he's got a cold.' Into this last word she put an infinite scorn as if a cold were of all afflictions the least credible and the most bizarre. She let Burden in and, leaving him alone with the two wide-eyed silent children, said, 'You might as well sit down. I'll tell him you're here.'

Two or three minutes later Kirkpatrick came down. He was wearing a silk dressing gown under which he appeared to be fully clothed. Burden recalled similarly attired figures, but gayer and more debonair, who featured in those bedroom comedies of the thirties, still ruthlessly acted by local dramatic societies, to whose performances he was sometimes dragged by his wife. The setting of chintz-covered chairs and mock wood panelling enhanced this impression, but Kirkpatrick had a hangdog look. Had this been a real stage, the audience would have supposed him to have forgotten his opening lines. His face was unshaven. He managed a smile for his children and just touched the little girl's long fair hair.

'I'm going to make the beds,' said Mrs Kirkpatrick. It was not, Burden thought, a statement normally capable of being interpreted as a threat, but she succeeded in putting into it an almost sinister menace. Her husband gave her an encouraging nod, smiling as might one who wishes to foster his wife's interest in some unusual intellectual pursuit.

'I'm sorry to hear you're feeling unwell.'

'I expect it's psychological,' Kirkpatrick said. 'Yesterday afternoon upset me a good deal.'

A psychological cold, Burden thought. That's a new one. 'Pity,' he said aloud, 'because I'm afraid you may have to go through the mill again. Don't you think it would be better if we were to stop this farce about your being interested in Miss

Margolis for the sake of her brother's paintings?' Kirkpatrick's gaze travelled to the ceiling. From above violent noises could be heard as if his wife were not so much making the beds as breaking the furniture. 'We know very well you were her lover,' Burden said roughly. 'You threatened to kill her. On your own admission you were in Stowerton on Tuesday night.'

'Not so loud,' Kirkpatrick said, an agonised note in his voice. 'All right. It's all true. I've been thinking — that's why I feel so bloody — I've been thinking I'll have to tell you. It's not *her,*' he said, and he looked at the boy and girl. 'It's my kiddies. I don't want to lose my kiddies.' In a low voice he added, 'They always give custody to the mother, never mind what sort of mother she is.'

Burden gave an impatient shrug. 'Ever seen this before?'

The colour which flooded Kirkpatrick's face was the outward sign of an emotion Burden could not define. Guilt? Horror? He waited.

'It's Ann's.'

'Sure of that?'

'I saw her with it.' Dropping pretence, he said, 'She flaunted it in my face.'

Although it was warm in the office, Kirkpatrick kept his raincoat on. He had come of his own free will, Burden told Wexford, to talk in comparative comfort away from his wife.

'Did you give this lighter to Miss Margolis?' Wexford asked.

'Me? How could I afford a thing like that?'

'Tell me how you know it's hers.'

Kirkpatrick folded his hands and bowed his head.

'It was about a month ago,' he said, his voice scarcely above a whisper. 'I called for her but she was out. Margolis didn't seem to want to know me and I sat out in the car waiting for her to come back. Not this car,' he said with a small painful frown, 'the other one I had, the black one.'

He sighed and went on, his voice still low, 'She came back in hers about half an hour later — she'd been getting it serviced. I got out and went up to her. That lighter you've got there, it was on the shelf in her Alpine and I picked it up. I knew she hadn't had it before and when I saw the inscription,

"For Ann who lights my life", well, I knew her and I knew what sort of terms she'd be on with the giver.' A tiny thread of hysteria crept into his tone. 'I saw red. I could have killed her then. Christ, I didn't mean that!' He passed his hand across his mouth as if by this action he could wipe away the injudicious words. 'I didn't mean that. You know I didn't, don't you?'

Wexford said very smoothly, 'I know very little about you, Mr Kirkpatrick. You seem to have a split personality. One day you tell me Miss Margolis was merely the key into her brother's art gallery, the next that you were passionately jealous of her. Which personality is — er, the dominant one?'

'I loved her,' he said stonily. 'I was jealous.'

'Of course you were,' Wexford said scornfully, 'and you don't know a Bonnard from a bull's foot.'

'Go on about the lighter,' said Burden.

Instead of continuing, the man said wretchedly, 'My wife mustn't know. God, I was mad, crazy, ever to go near that girl.' Perhaps he noticed that Wexford made him no promises of discretion, noticed and understood the implication, for he said wildly, 'I didn't kill her, I don't know anything about it.'

'For a man in love you're not showing much grief, Mr Kirkpatrick. Let's go back to the lighter, shall we?'

Kirkpatrick shivered in the warm room. 'I was jealous as hell,' he said. 'She took the lighter from me and looked at it in a peculiar way.'

'What d'you mean, a peculiar way?'

'As if there was something to laugh at,' he said savagely, 'as if it was all one hell of a big joke.' He passed his hand across his forehead. 'I can see her now in that spotted fur coat, beautiful, free . . . I've never been free like that. She was holding that little bit of gold in her hand. She read out those words on the bottom, read them aloud, and went on laughing. "Who gave it to you?" I said. "He's got a pretty turn of phrase, my generous friend, hasn't he?" she said. "You'd never think of anything like that, Alan. All you ever do is add two and two and make it come to about sixteen." I don't know what she meant.' His fingers had left white marks where they had pressed the skin. 'You talk about showing grief,' he said. 'I loved her all right, or I thought I did. If you love someone you ought to be sorry when

485

they're dead, oughtn't you? But, my God, if I couldn't have her, just me all to myself, I'd rather she was dead!'

'What were you doing in Stowerton on Tuesday night?' Wexford snapped.

'I don't have to tell you that.' He said it limply, not defiantly. Then he unbuttoned his coat as if he had suddenly grown hot.

'I wouldn't do that,' said Burden, 'not if you're going. As you said yesterday we can't keep you here.'

Kirkpatrick stood up. He looked weary to the point of distress. 'I can go?' He fumbled with his coat belt, his fingers jerking. 'There's nothing more I can tell you anyway.'

'Perhaps it'll come to you,' Wexford said. 'I'll tell you what, we'll drop by later in the day.'

'When the children are in bed,' Burden added. 'Maybe your wife knows what you were doing in Stowerton.'

'If you do that,' Kirkpatrick said fiercely, 'you'll lose me my children.' Breathing heavily, he turned his face to the wall.

'He can cool off in there with Drayton for company,' Wexford said over a cup of coffee in the Carousel Café. It was opposite the police station and he preferred it to their canteen. His entry always had the effect of clearing the place of less desirable elements and now they were alone with the espresso machine, the rubber plants and the juke box playing Mantovani.

'Funny Ruby recognising him like that,' said Burden, 'yet not being sure she recognised him as Geoff Smith.'

'I don't know, Mike. According to your moral code and maybe mine too, his behaviour wasn't exactly ethical, but it wasn't suspicious. She wouldn't have taken much notice of him.'

'Enough to know he was short, young and dark. Kirkpatrick's not that short, must be five feet eight or nine. It's the alias that puzzles me. Smith's obvious, but why Geoff? Why not John, for heaven's sake, or William?'

'Maybe Geoffrey is Kirkpatrick's middle name. We'll have to ask him.' Wexford drew his chair in from the gangway. A slim fair girl in skirt and sweater had come into the cafe and was making for a table beyond the room divider. 'Little Miss Grover,' he whispered. 'Let off the lead for once. If her father was up and about she wouldn't have the chance to pop out even for five minutes.'

'I've heard he's a bit of a tyrant,' Burden said, watching the girl. Her expression was dreamy, far away. 'Wonder what he was up to, slipping a disc? It's not as if he did manual work.'

'Save your detecting for what you get paid for,' said Wexford with a grin.

Linda Grover had ordered a raspberry milk shake. Burden watched her suck it up through a straw and look round with faint embarrassment as the straw made gurgling sounds in the dregs. A little drift of pink foam clung to her upper lip. Her hair, soft and satiny as a child's, was yet another golden eye-catcher on this golden day. 'Regular customer of theirs, Kirkpatrick,' he said. 'Buys his evening paper there. I wonder if he bought a knife too?'

'Let's go back and see,' said Wexford. The sun and the warmth made their walk across the street too short. 'Makes all the difference to the place, doesn't it?' he said as they passed up the steps and the cold stone walls of the police station enclosed them.

Drayton sat at one end of the office, Kirkpatrick at the other. They looked like strangers, indifferent, faintly antagonistic, waiting for a train. Kirkpatrick looked up, his mouth twitching.

'I thought you were never coming,' he said desperately to Wexford. 'If I tell you what I was doing in Stowerton you'll think I'm mad.'

Better a madman than a murderer, Wexford thought. He drew up a chair. 'Try me.'

'She wouldn't come out with me,' Kirkpatrick mumbled, 'on account of that damned car. I didn't believe she was going to that party, so,' he said defiantly, 'I went to Stowerton to check up on her. I got there at eight and I waited for hours and hours. She didn't come. God, I just sat there and waited and when she didn't come I knew she'd lied to me. I knew she'd found someone richer, younger, harder — Oh, what the hell!' He gave a painful cough. 'That's all I did,' he said, 'waited.' He lifted his eyes to Burden. 'When you found me yesterday morning at the cottage, I was going to tell her, ask her who she thought she was to cheat on me!'

Black against the sunlight, Drayton stood staring his contempt. What was he thinking? Wexford wondered. That he with his dark glow of virility, a glow that today was almost insolent, could never be brought so low?

'It got dark,' Kirkpatrick said. 'I parked my car by the side of Cawthorne's under a tree. They were making a hell of a racket in there, shouting and playing music. She never came. The only person to come out was a drunk spouting Omar Khayyam. I was there for three hours, oh, more than that . . .'

Wexford moved closer to the desk, folded his hands and rested his wrists on the rosewood. 'Mr Kirkpatrick,' he said gravely, 'this story of yours may be true, but you must realise that to me it sounds a bit thin. Can you produce anyone who might help to verify it?'

Kirkpatrick said bitterly, 'That's my affair, isn't it? You've done your job. I've never heard of the police hunting up witnesses to disprove their own case.'

'Then you have a lot to learn. We're not here to make "cases" but to see right is done.' Wexford paused. Three hours, he thought. That covered the time of arrival at Ruby's house, the time when the neighbour heard the crash, the time when two people staggered from the house. 'You must have seen the party guests arriving. Didn't they see you?'

'I put the car right down the side turning till it got dark, down by the side of the launderette.' His face grew sullen. 'That girl saw me,' he said.

'What girl?'

'The girl from Grover's shop.'

'You saw her at seven when you bought your evening paper,' Wexford said, trying to keep his patience. 'What you were doing at seven isn't relevant.'

A sulky flush settled on Kirkpatrick's face. 'I saw her again,' he said. 'In Stowerton.'

'You didn't mention it before.' This time impatience had got the upper hand and every word was edged with testiness.

'I'm sick of being made to look a fool,' Kirkpatrick said resentfully. 'I'm sick of it. If I get out of this I'm going to chuck in my job. Maybe someone's got to flog soap and powder and

488

lipstick, but not me. I'd rather be out of work.' He clenched his hands. 'If I get out of this,' he said.

'The girl,' said Wexford. 'Where did you see the girl?'

'I was down the side road by the back of the launderette, just a little way down. She was coming along in a car and she stopped at the traffic lights. I was standing by my car, then. Don't ask me what time it was. I wouldn't know.' He drew his breath in sharply. 'She looked at me and giggled. But she won't remember. I was just a joke to her, a customer who'd kept her late. She saw me standing by that thing and it was good for a laugh. *Lipdew!* I reckon she thinks about me and has a good laugh every time she washes her . . .'

Drayton's face had gone white and he stepped forward, his fingers closing into fists. Wexford interposed swiftly to cut off the last word, the word that might have been innocent or obscene.

'In that case,' he said, 'she will remember, won't she?'

CHAPTER ELEVEN

Sunshine is a great healer, especially when it is the first mild sunshine of spring. Paradoxically it cooled Drayton's anger. Crossing the street, he was once more in command of himself and he could think calmly and even derisively of Kirkpatrick. The man was an oaf, a poor thing with a pansy's job, emasculate, pointed at and pilloried by women. He had a pink and mauve car and he peddled cosmetics. Some day a perfume plutocrat would make him dress up in a harlequin suit with a powder puff on his head, make him knock on doors and give soap away to any housewife who could produce a coupon and sing out a slogan. He was a puppet and a slave.

The shop was empty. This must be a time of lull, lunchtime. The bell rang loudly because he was slow to close the door. Sunlight made the shop look frowstier than ever. Motes of dust hung and danced in its beams. He stood, listening to the pandemonium his ringing had called forth from upstairs, running feet, something that sounded like the dropping of a saucepan lid, a harsh bass voice calling, 'Get down the shop, Lin, for God's sake.'

She came in, running, a tea towel in her hand. When she saw him the anxiety went out of her face and she looked petulant. 'You're early,' she said, 'hours early.' Then she smiled and there was something in her eyes he was not sure that he liked, a look of conquest and of complacency. He supposed that she thought him impatient to be with her. Their date was for the evening and he had come at half past one. That was what they always wanted, to make you weak, malleable in their long frail hands. Then they kicked you aside. Look at Kirkpatrick. 'I can't come out,' she said. 'I've got the shop to see to.'

'You can come where I'm taking you,' Drayton said harshly. He forgot his rage at Kirkpatrick's words, the passion of last night, the tenderness that had begun. What was she, after all? A shop assistant — and what a shop! — a shop girl, afraid of her father, a skivvy with a tea cloth. 'Police station,' he said.

Her eyes went very wide. 'You what? Are you trying to be funny or something?'

He had heard the stories about Grover, the things he sold over the counter — and under it. 'It's nothing to do with your father,' he said.

'What do they want me for? Is it about the advert?'

'In a way,' he said. 'Look, it's nothing, just routine.'

'Mark,' she said, 'Mark, you tried to frighten me.' The sun flowed down her body in a river of gold. It's only a physical thing, he thought, just an itch and a rather worse one than usual. Repeat last night often enough and it would go. She came up to him, smiling, a little nervous. 'I know you don't mean it, but you mustn't frighten me.' The smile teased him. He stood quite still, the sun between them like a sword. He wanted her so badly that it took all his strength and all his self-control to turn and say, 'Let's go. Tell your parents you won't be long.' She was gone two minutes, leaving behind her a breath of something fresh and sweet to nullify the smell of old worn-out things. He moved about the shop, trying to find things to look at that were not cheap or meretricious or squalid. When she came back he saw that she had neither changed her clothes nor put on make-up. This both pleased and riled him. It seemed to imply an arrogance, a careless disregard of other people's opinion, which matched his own. He did not want them to have things in common. Enough that they should desire each other and find mutual satisfaction at a level he understood.

'How's your father?' he said and when he said it he realised it was a foolish catch-phrase. She laughed at him.

'Did you mean that or were you fooling?'

'I mean it.' Damn her for reading thoughts!

'He's all right,' she said. 'No, he's not. He says he's in agony. You can't tell, can you, with what he's got? It's not as if there was anything to show.'

'Seems to me he's a slave driver,' he said.

'They're all slave drivers. Better your own dad than some man.' At the door she basked in the sun, stretching her body like a long golden animal. 'When they talk to me,' she said, 'you'll be there, won't you?'

'Sure I'll be there.' He closed the door behind them. 'Don't do that,' he said, 'or I'll want to do what I did last night.' You could want it like mad, he thought, and still laugh. You could with this girl. My God, he thought, my God!

There was, Wexford thought, something between those two. No doubt Drayton had been chatting her up on the way. Only that would account for the look she had given him before sitting down, a look that seemed to be asking for permission. Well, he had always supposed Drayton susceptible and the girl was pretty enough. He had seen her about since she was a child but it seemed to him that he had never before noticed the exquisite shape of her head, the peculiar virginal grace with which she moved.

'Now, Miss Grover,' he said, 'I just want you to answer a few routine questions.' She smiled faintly at him. They ought not to be allowed to look like that, he thought wryly, so demure, so perfect and so untouched. 'I believe you know a Mr Kirkpatrick? He's a customer of yours.'

'Is he?' Drayton was standing behind her chair and she looked up at him, perhaps for reassurance. Wexford felt mildly irritated. Who the hell did Drayton think he was? Her solicitor?

'If you don't recognise the name, perhaps you know his car, You probably saw it outside just now.'

'A funny pink car with flowers on it?' Wexford nodded. 'Oh, I know *him*.'

'Very well. Now I want you to cast your mind back to last Tuesday night. Did you go to Stowerton that evening?'

'Yes,' she said quickly, 'I always do on Tuesdays. I take our washing to the launderette in my dad's car.' She paused, weariness coming into her young fresh face. 'My dad's ill and Mum goes to a whist drive most nights.'

Why play on my sympathies? Wexford thought. The hint of tyranny seemed to be affecting Drayton. His dark face looked displeased and his mouth had tightened. 'All right, Drayton,' he said, not unpleasantly, 'I shan't need you any longer.'

When they were alone, she said before he had time to ask her, 'Did Mr What's-his-name see me? I saw him.'

'Are you sure?'

'Oh, yes. I know him. I'd served him with an evening paper earlier.'

'It wasn't just the car you identified, Miss Grover, not just an empty car?'

She put up one hand to smooth the soft shiny knob of hair. 'I didn't know the car. He used to have a different one.' She gave a nervous giggle. 'When I saw him in it and knew it was his it made me laugh. He thinks such a lot of himself, you see, and then that car . . .'

Wexford watched her. She was far from being at ease. On her answer to his next question, the significant question, so much depended. Kirkpatrick's fate hung upon it. If he had lied . . .

'What time was it?' he asked.

'Late,' she said firmly. Her lips were like two almond petals, her teeth perfect. It seemed a pity she showed them so seldom. 'I'd been to the launderette. I was going home. It must have been just after a quarter past nine.' He sighed within himself. Whoever had been at Ruby's had certainly been there at nine fifteen. I'd stopped at the traffic lights,' she said virtuously. God, he thought, she's like a child, she doesn't differentiate between me and a traffic cop. Did she expect him to congratulate her? 'He'd parked that car down by the side of the garage . . .'

'Cawthorne's?'

She nodded eagerly. 'I saw him in it. I know it was him.'

'Sure of the time?'

He had noticed she wore no watch on the slender wrist.

'I'd just come from the launderette. I'd seen the clock.'

There was nothing more he could do. Perhaps it was all true. They had no body, no real evidence against Kirkpatrick after this. A fatherly impulse made him smile at her and say, 'All right, Miss Grover, you can run along now. Mr Kirkpatrick ought to be grateful to you.'

For a moment he thought the shot had gone home, then he wasn't sure. The look in her big grey eyes was hard to interpret. He thought it might be a relieved happiness, no doubt because he was terminating the interview. Her departure seemed to deprive the office of some of its brightness, although the sun still shone. Her scent remained, a perfume that was too old for her innocence.

'That girl was got at,' Burden said wrathfully.

'You could be right there.'

'We should never have let Kirkpatrick out of here yesterday afternoon.'

Wexford sighed. 'What had we got to hold him on, Mike? Oh, I agree he probably thought up that alibi between yesterday afternoon and this morning. I daresay he went straight round to Grover's when he left here. That girl wasn't at ease.'

'Show me a Grover who wouldn't do anything for money,' Burden said. 'Like father, like daughter.'

'Poor kid. Not much of a life for her, is it? Cooped up all day in that dirty little hole and carting the washing about in the evenings because her mother's playing whist.'

Burden eyed him uneasily. The expression on his chief's face was tolerant, almost tender, and it puzzled him. If he had not known Wexford to be almost as uxorious a husband as himself, he might have believed . . . But, no, there were limits.

'If he was outside Cawthorne's, sir,' he said, 'and if he was there at half-past nine, he's clear and we're wasting our time with him. But if the girl's lying and he did it, he could have disposed of Anita's body practically anywhere between here and the Scottish border. She could be lying in a ditch anywhere you can name in half a dozen counties.'

'And where the body is the weapon is, too.'

'Or he could have gone home to a place he knew and dumped her in the thickest part of those pine woods in Cheriton Forest.'

'But until we know more, Mike, searching for that body is impracticable, sheer waste of time.'

'I wouldn't mind having a go at Kirkpatrick over it,' Burden said with sudden ferocity. 'Having a go at him in his wife's presence.'

'No. We'll give him a rest for a while. The king-size question is, did he bribe that girl?' Wexford grinned sagely. 'I'm hoping she may feel inclined to confide in Drayton.'

'*Drayton?*'

'Attractive to the opposite sex, don't you think? That sulky brooding look gets them every time.' Wexford's little glinting eyes were suddenly unkind. 'Unless you fancy yourself in the role? Sorry, I forgot. Your wife wouldn't like it. Martin and I aren't exactly cut out to strut before a wanton ambling nymph . . .'

'I'd better have a word with him then.'

'Not necessary. Unless I'm much mistaken, this is something we can safely leave to Nature.'

CHAPTER TWELVE

The lighter had been lying on the desk in the sun and when Wexford picked it up it felt warm to his hand. The tendrils and leaves of its vine design glowed softly. 'Griswold's been getting at me,' he said. At the mention of the Chief Constable's name Burden looked sour. 'According to him, this is not to be allowed to develop into a murder enquiry. Evidence inconclusive and so on. We can have a couple more days to scout around and that's our lot.'

Burden said bitterly, 'The whole place turned upside-down just to get Monkey Matthews another few months inside?'

'The stain on the carpet was from the fruit of Ruby's imagination, Anita Margolis is on holiday, the couple who staggered down the path were drunk and Kirkpatrick is simply afraid of his wife.' Wexford paused, tossing the lighter up and down reflectively. 'I quote the powers that be,' he said.

'Martin's watching Kirkpatrick's house,' said Burden. 'He hasn't been to work today. Drayton's still presumably hanging around with that girl. Do I call them off, sir?'

'What else is there for them to do? Things are slack enough otherwise. As for the other questions I'd like answered, Griswold isn't interested and I can't see our finding the answer to them in two days, anyway.'

Silently Burden put out his hand for the lighter and contemplated it, his narrow lips pursed. Then he said, 'I'm wondering if they're the same questions that are uppermost in my mind. Who gave her the lighter and was it sold around here? Who was the drunk outside Cawthorne's, the man who spoke to Kirkpatrick?'

Wexford opened his desk drawer and took out his *Weekend Telegraph*. 'Remember this bit?' he asked. 'About her breaking off her engagement to Richard Fairfax? I'll bet it was him. Mrs Cawthorne said he left the party around eleven and Cawthorne said he dumped a brandy glass on one of his diesel pumps.'

'Sounds like a poet,' Burden said gloomily.

496

'Now, then, remember what I said about Goering.' Wexford grinned at the inspector's discomfiture. 'According to Kirkpatrick he was spouting Omar Khayyám. I used to be hot on old Khayyám myself. I wonder what he said?

' "I often wonder what the vintners buy.
One half so precious as the goods they sell?"'

'Or maybe he scattered and slayed with his enchanted sword.'

Burden took this last seriously. 'He can't have done that. He got to Cawthorne's at eight and he didn't leave till eleven.'

'I know. I was fooling. Anyway, Griswold says no hunting up of fresh suspects without a positive lead. That's my directive and I have to abide by it.'

'Still, I don't suppose there'd be any objection if I went to enquire at a few jewellers, would there? We'd have a positive lead if anyone remembered selling it to Kirkpatrick or even Margolis himself, come to that.' Burden pocketed the lighter. Wexford's face had a dreamy look, preoccupied but not discouraging, so he said briskly, 'Early closing today. I'd better get cracking before all the shops shut.'

Left alone, the Chief Inspector sat searching his mind for a peculiarly significant couplet. When he found it, he chuckled.

'What lamp has destiny to guide
Her little children stumbling in the dark?'

There ought to be an answer. It came to him at last but it was not inspiring. 'A blind understanding, Heaven replied,' he said aloud to the glass sculpture. Something like that was what they needed, he thought.

Kirkpatrick was leaning against the bonnet of his car which he had parked on the forecourt of the Olive and Dove, watching the entrance to Grover's shop. Ever since breakfast time Detective Sergeant Martin had been keeping his house and his gaudy car under observation. Mrs Kirkpatrick had gone shopping with the children and just as Martin, from his vantage point under the perimeter trees of Cheriton Forest, was beginning to abandon hope, the salesman had emerged and driven off towards Kingsmarkham. Following him had been easy. The car was a quarry even an intervening bus and hostile traffic lights, changing to red at the wrong moment, could not protect for long.

It was a warm morning, the air soft and faintly scented with the promise of summer. A delicate haze hung over Kingsmarkham which the sun tinted a positive gold. Someone came out from the florist's to put a box of stiff purple tulips on the display bench.

Kirkpatrick had begun to polish the lenses of a pair of sun glasses on the lapel of his sports jacket. Then he strolled to the pavement edge. Martin crossed the road before him, mingling with the shoppers. Instead of making directly for the newsagent's, Kirkpatrick hesitated outside the flower shop, looking at wet velvety violets, hyacinths in pots, at daffodils, cheap now because they were abundant. His eyes went to the alley wall no sun ever reached, but he turned away quickly and hurried into the York Street turning. Martin took perhaps fifteen seconds to make up his mind. He was only a step from Grover's. The bell rang as he opened the door.

'Yes?' Linda Grover came in from the door at the back.

Blinking his eyes to accustom himself to the dimness, Martin said vaguely, 'Just looking.' He knew her by hearsay but he was sure she didn't know him. 'I want a birthday card,' he said. She shrugged indifferently and picked up a magazine. Martin wandered into the depths of the shop. Each time the bell tinkled he glanced up from the card stand. A man came in to buy cigars, a woman with a pekingese which snuffled among the boxes on the floor. Its owner passed the card stand to browse among the dog-eared books in Grover's lending library. Martin blessed her arrival. One person dawdling in the shadows was suspicious, two unremarkable. He hoped she would take a long time choosing her book. The dog stuck its face up his trouser leg and touched bare flesh with a wet nose.

They were the only customers when, five minutes later, Alan Kirkpatrick entered the shop with a red and gold wrapped parcel under his arm.

Red and gold were the trade colours of Joy Jewels. Scarlet

carpet covered the floor, gilt *papier mâché* torsos stood about on red plinths, each figure as many-armed as some oriental goddess. Pointed, attenuated fingers were hung with glittering ropes of rhinestone. Schitz and quartz and other gems that were perhaps no more than skilfully cut glass made prisms which caught and refracted the flickering sunlight. On the counter lay a roll of wrapping paper, bright red patterned with gold leaves. The assistant was putting away his scissors when Burden came in and held up the lighter between them.

'We don't sell lighters. Anyway, I doubt if anyone round here would stock a thing like that.'

Burden nodded. He had received the same answer at four other jewellers' already.

'It's a work of art,' the assistant said, and he smiled as people will when shown something beautiful and rare. 'Eight or nine years ago it might have come from this very place.'

Eight or nine years ago Anita Margolis had been little more than a child. 'How come?' Burden asked without much interest.

'Before we took over from Scatcherd's. They were said to be the best jeweller's between London and Brighton. Old Mr Scatcherd still lives overhead. If you wanted to talk to him . . .'

'Too long ago, I'm afraid,' Burden cut in. 'It'd be a waste of my time and his.' Much too long. It was April and at Christmas Anita Margolis had been lighting her cigarettes with matches.

He walked up York Street under the plane trees. The misty sun shone on their dappled grey and yellow bark and their tiny new leaves made an answering shadow pattern on the pavement. The first thing he noticed when he came into the High Street was Kirkpatrick's car outside the Olive and Dove. If Martin had lost him . . . But, no. There was the sergeant's own Ford nudging the end of the yellow band. Burden paused on the Kingsbrook Bridge, idling his time away watching the swans, a cob and a pen wedded to each other and to their river. The brown water rippled on gently over round mottled stones. Burden waited.

The girl's face became sullen when she saw Kirkpatrick. She looked him up and down and closed her magazine, keeping her place childishly with one finger poked between the pages.

'Yes?'

'I was passing,' Kirkpatrick said awkwardly. 'I thought I'd come in and thank you.'

Martin selected a birthday card. He assumed a whimsical, faintly sentimental expression so that the woman with the pekingese might suppose he was admiring the verse it contained.

'This is for you, a token of my gratitude.' Kirkpatrick slid his parcel between the newspapers and the chocolate bar tray.

'I don't want your presents,' the girl said stonily. 'I didn't do anything. I really saw you.' Her big grey eyes were frightened. Kirkpatrick leaned towards her, his brown curls almost touching her own fair head.

'Oh, yes,' he said insinuatingly, 'you saw me, but the point is . . .'

She interrupted him sharply, 'It's all over, it's done with. They won't come bothering me any more.'

'Won't you even look inside the box?'

She turned away, her head hanging like a spring flower on a delicate stalk. Kirkpatrick took off the red and gold wrapping, the tissue paper and from a box padded with pink cotton wool, produced a string of glittering beads. They were little sharp metallic stones in rainbow colours. Rhinestones, Martin thought.

'Give it to your wife,' the girl said. She felt at the neck of her sweater until something silvery trickled over her thin fingers. 'I don't want it. I've got real jewellery.'

Kirkpatrick's mouth tightened. He stuffed the necklace into one pocket, the mass of crumpled paper into the other. When he had gone, banging the shop door behind him, Martin went up to the girl, the birthday card in his hand.

She read the legend. "My darling Granny"?' she said derisively and he supposed she was looking at his greying hair. 'Are you sure it's this one you want?' He nodded and paid his ninepence. Her eyes followed him and when he looked back she was smiling a little closed-lip smile. On the bridge he encountered Burden.

'What's this then?' said the inspector, eyeing the card with the same mockery. Drayton, he thought reluctantly, would have been more subtle. He stared down at the river bed and the stone arch reflected in brown and amber, while Martin told him what he had heard.

'Offered her a necklace,' Martin said. 'Showy sort of thing wrapped up in red and gold paper.'

'I wonder,' Burden said thoughtfully. 'I wonder if he always shops at Joy Jewels, if he bought a lighter there years and years ago when it was Scatcherd's . . .'

'Had it engraved recently for this girl?'

'Could be.' Burden watched Kirkpatrick seated at the wheel of his car. Presently he got out and entered the saloon bar of the Olive and Dove. 'There goes your man,' he said to Martin, 'drowning his sorrows. You never know, when he's screwed up his courage he may come offering his trinkets to the Chief Inspector. He certainly won't give them to his wife.'

The mist had begun to lift and there was real warmth in the sunshine. Burden took off his raincoat and laid it over his arm. He would have one last go at finding where that lighter came from, make one last enquiry, and if it was fruitless, give up and meet Wexford for lunch at the Carousel. But was there any point, was it too long a shot? He could do with a cup of tea first and the Carousel would already be serving lunches. The thought came to him that there was a little place, not a hundred yards from the bridge, a small café where they served good strong tea and pastries at all hours. He cut up the path between the cottages and came out in the Kingsbrook Road. Just past the bend it was, in the ground floor of one of the Georgian houses.

Strange how heavily the mist seemed to lie in this part of the town, on high ground too and coloured a deep ochreish yellow. He passed the big houses and stopped on the brow of the low hill.

Through the clouds of what he now realised to be not mist but plaster dust, a contractor's board faced him: *Doherty for Demolition. What Goes Up Must Come Down!* Beyond, where the block which had housed his cafe had stood, was a cliff-face of battered wall, roof, floors, façade torn from it. Among the rubble of what had once been elegant stonework stood a wooden hut on the threshold of which three workmen sat eating sandwiches.

Burden shrugged and turned away. The old town was going, gradually and cruelly. Beauty and grace were inconvenient. They pulled down the old buildings, put up splendid new ones like the police station. New buildings needed new drains and new wiring and digging up the roads killed the old trees. New shops replaced the old, rhinestones and gilt goddesses the best jeweller's between London and Brighton . . . That reminded him. It was useless to waste time regretting the past. If he was to get no tea he certainly wasn't going to delay his lunch. One more enquiry first, though.

Mr Scatcherd reminded Burden of a very old and very amiable parrot. The big curving nose came down over a genial mouth and the bird-like impression was sustained by a bright yellow waistcoat and baggy, shaggy trousers suggestive of plumage. The rooms over the shop might have been a perch or an eyrie, they were so airy and lofty, and their windows looked into the tops of whispering greening trees.

He was shown into a living room apparently unchanged since it had been furnished in the eighties. But instead of the drab browns and reds associated with the nineteenth century, here in the plush and velvet was peacock green, glowing puce and blue. A chandelier that hung from the ceiling winked in the blaze of sun like a handful of diamonds dropped and suspended in space. Fat cushions with gold tassels had cheeks of shiny green shot-silk. There were pieces here, Burden thought as he sat down in a brocade wing chair, that Cawthorne would give his sodden blue eyes to possess.

'I usually have a glass of madeira and a biscuit about this time,' said Mr Scatcherd. 'Perhaps you'll do me the honour of joining me?'

'It's very kind of you,' Burden said. The former variety of refreshment he had never sampled and he was still regretting the depredations which had deprived him of his tea as well as the town of its glory. 'I'd like to.'

A sweet smile told him he had been right to accept. 'Just the shade of a garnet,' the old jeweller said when he brought the wine on a japanned tray. 'Not a ruby.' A severity, the didactic crispness of the connoisseur, had entered his rather fluting voice. 'A ruby is quite different. What have you brought me to look at?'

'This.'

The hand that took it was grey and clawed, the nails long but scrupulously clean.

'Could it have come from around here? Or do you only get things like this in London?'

Mr Scatcherd was not listening to him. He had taken the lighter to the window and he was nodding his head precisely while screwing his old eye up against a pocket glass.

' "*Les grappes de ma vigne*",' he said at last. Burden sat up eagerly. 'That's the name of the design, you know. The grapes of my vine. Baudelaire, of course. Perhaps you are not familiar with the poem. Highly appropriate for a lover's gift.' He smiled with gentle pleasure, turning the lighter over. 'And it was a lover's gift,' he said as he read the inscription. 'A pretty greeting for a lady.'

Burden had no idea what he meant. 'You know it?' he said. 'You've seen it before?'

'Several years ago.' The chandelier flashed pink, violet and green prism spots on the walls. 'Seven, eight years.' Mr Scatcherd put away his glass and beamed with satisfaction. The rainbow lights flickered on his bald head. 'I know the design,' he said, 'and I well remember the inscription.'

'But that engraving was done recently!'

'Oh, no. Before I retired, before Joy Jewels took over.' A smile of mocking disparagement curved his mouth and made his eyes twinkle as he spoke the name. 'My dear inspector,' he said. 'I ought to know. I sold the thing.'

CHAPTER THIRTEEN

'Who did he sell it to? Kirkpatrick?'

Burden hung up his raincoat on the office rack and decided to do without it for the rest of the day. He glanced at the lab reports Wexford was studying and said:

'I don't understand it. Old Scatcherd hasn't sold anything for more than seven years and at that time Anita wasn't here, probably didn't even know such a place as Kingsmarkham existed. Kirkpatrick wasn't here either. Those houses where he lives have only been up a year. Besides, Scatcherd's got a wonderful memory for a man of his age and he's never had a customer called Kirkpatrick.'

'Look, Mike,' Wexford said, giving his reports a glance of disgust, 'are we going to be able to find out who did buy this damned lighter?'

'Scatcherd's looking it up in his books. He says it'll take him a couple of hours. But, you know, sir, I'm beginning to think Anita just found it, picked it up in the street and kept it because the inscription was appropriate.'

'Found it!' Wexford roared. 'You mean someone lost it and Anita found it and then she lost it again at Ruby's? Don't be so daft. It's not a key or an old umbrella. It's a valuable article and I reckon it's the key to this whole thing. If it was lost, why wasn't the loss reported to us? No, you get back to old Scatcherd, assist him with your young eyes.' Burden looked pleased at this as Wexford had known he would. 'You never know what you may discover,' he said. 'Cawthorne may have bought it for her or Margolis himself or at any rate someone who owns a green car. In all this we have to remember that however oddly Kirkpatrick may be behaving he doesn't have and never had a green car.'

When Burden had gone he returned to his perusal of the lab reports. He read them carefully, suppressing a disgusted rage. Never in all his experience had he come across anything so negative. The evidence the carpet afforded would have been satisfactory only to the manufacturers of Ruby's favourite detergents. Fingerprints on her car corresponded to those in Anita Margolis's bedroom. They were hers and hers alone. The ocelot coat gave even less information. An analyst had suggested that the scent with which it was redolent might be Guerlain's *Chant d'Aromes*. Wexford, who was good on perfumes, could have told them that himself. In one pocket was a crumpled sheet of trading stamps. She had probably bought her petrol at Cawthorne's. Wexford sighed. Who had brought that car back at one in the morning and where had it been all the evening? Why had her killer, Kirkpatrick or another, called himself Geoff Smith when it would have been so much more natural and indeed expected for him to remain anonymous?

A pile of thick books, some of them ancient and all bound in dark green morocco, was stacked at Mr Scatcherd's feet. Burden stepped over them and sat down in the brocade chair.

'I've been completely through the last three,' Mr Scatcherd said, showing no sign of a diminution of patience. 'That takes us right back to nineteen fifty-eight.' He had perched a pair of gold-rimmed glasses on his parrot's nose and he glanced over the top of them, smiling pleasantly.

Burden shrugged. It was all getting beyond him. Nine years ago Anita Margolis had been fourteen. Did men give valuable gold cigarette lighters — any cigarette lighters, come to that — to girls of fourteen? Not in his world. Whatever world this was in which he found himself, it was a topsy-turvy one of nightmare inconsistency. The lighter had been sold in Kingsmarkham and in Kingsmarkham its recipient had lived and gone out to meet her death. Simple on the face of it, but for ages and times and a host of confusing facts . . .

'I thought it was new,' he said.

'Oh, no. I knew the artist who made it. He's dead now but in his day he was a fine goldsmith. His name was Benjamin Marks but when I called him Ben it was another master I thought of. Perhaps you can guess whom I mean.' Burden looked at him blankly. 'Cellini, inspector,' Mr Scatcherd said almost reverently. 'The great Benvenuto. My Ben was a naturalist too in his way. It was always to Nature that he went for his inspiration. I remember a standard rose, designed for a lady's powder case. You could see the stamens in the heart of each tiny flower. He made this and inscribed it. It was done to a gentleman's order . . .'

'But whose order, Mr Scatcherd? Until I know that I'm no further.'

'We shall find it. It helps my memory to talk about it.' Mr Scatcherd turned the thick watered pages, running a long fingernail down the margins. 'We're coming up to the end of nineteen fifty-eight now. Do you know, each time I come to the end of a book I feel I'm getting warm. I have a faint recollection of Christmas and I seem to remember selling a fine ring at the same time.' The last page. Burden could see a date in December printed at the top of it. He had a wild sensation that if the record of the sale could not be found in this book or the next, Mr Scatcherd would keep on searching, for hours perhaps or days, until he came back to the first entry made by his father in eighteen eighty-six.

The jeweller looked up with a smile but he had worn this continually and Burden could see no particularly encouraging sign of gratification on his wrinkled face. 'Ah, yes, here we are,' he murmured. 'The ring I mentioned. A diamond and sapphire hoop to Mr Rogers of Pomfret Hall. For his wife, no doubt, or that poor daughter of his. There was insanity there, if I remember.' Nodding sagely, he continued his scanning. 'Not the same day, I'm sure. Perhaps the next day . . . Now, inspector, we're getting somewhere.'

Hope surging back, Burden got up to take the book from him but Mr Scatcherd held fast to it. 'Here we are,' he said again, but this time with a note of quiet triumph. 'Gold cigarette lighter to order: *"Les grappes de ma vigne"*, Benjamin Marks; inscribed: "For Ann who lights my life". Not much help to you, I'm afraid. Such a common name. Still, there's an address.'

Burden was unbearably intrigued. 'What name?' he asked excitedly.

'Smith. It was sold on December 15th, 1958 to a Mr Geoffrey Smith.'

No doubt about it, Drayton was taking his duties seriously,

Wexford thought as he came into the Carousel Café for his lunch. Behind the room divider a hooded coat could be seen lying over the back of a chair, one of its sleeves caught on the fleshy leaves of a rubber plant. Drayton's back was towards the door but there was something concentrated and intense in the set of his shoulders. He seemed to be in animated, not to say amorous, conversation with his companion, for their faces were close. It afforded Wexford considerable amusement to see Drayton raise his hand to cup the girl's white chin and to watch her delicate tentative smile. They had not observed him. Indeed, he thought, it would not be stretching a point to say they had eyes only for each other. A bit hard on the girl, he reflected, and he was wondering how much longer this simulated attention would be necessary when Burden found him.

'What are you eating?'

'Shepherd's pie,' said Wexford. 'Must be ten minutes since I ordered.' He grinned. 'I daresay they've had to go out and shoot a shepherd.'

'I've found him,' Burden explained and while he did so the Chief Inspector's expression changed from interest to scowling incredulity.

Burden said apologetically, 'You said yourself, sir, some people really are called Smith.'

'That was a funny,' Wexford growled. 'Where does he live?'

'Sewingbury.' The shepherd's pie came and Burden ordered a portion for himself. 'I don't understand why he isn't on the electoral register. He can't very well be under age.'

'Not unless we're dealing with a little boy buying cigarette lighters for a little girl.' Wexford raised a forkful of his pie to his mouth and made a face. 'I'd like to get our lab to work on this mashed potato,' he said. 'If I'm not mistaken it's been in a packet since it was dug out of the ground.' He pushed the bowl of green pepper salad the Carousel served with everything to the extreme edge of the table. 'Smith could be a foreigner who's changed his name but never got naturalised.'

Burden pondered. He felt he would think better on a full stomach. The mashed potato might be suspect but it was brown and crisp and the savoury smell whetted his appetite. 'We've assumed all the time Smith was a pseudonym,' he said, brightening as the hot steaming plate was set before him. 'Now it suddenly looks as if everything is going to be plain sailing. How about this, sir? Smith's known Anita for years and the friendship was renewed when she and Margolis came to live here. He booked the room on Saturday, going to Ruby's in his black car which he sold the following day or the Monday, exchanging it for a new green one. But when he gave his name to Ruby he had no idea he'd have anything to hide. An attack on Anita was the last thing he planned.' When Wexford nodded, he continued more confidently. 'She broke her date with Kirkpatrick, not on account of his car, but just because she was fed-up with him and because she'd made a new one with Smith. She met Smith somewhere, parked her own car and went to Stowerton with him in his. They quarrelled in Ruby's room, very likely over Kirkpatrick, and he attacked her with a knife or a razor. He managed to get her out of the house and into the car, but she died and he dumped her body or hid it at this place of his in Sewingbury. Later, when there weren't many people about, he collected her car and returned it to Pump Lane.'

'Who knows?' Wexford pushed aside his empty plate. 'It fits. Kirkpatrick comes into it only as a rival and all his worries are genuinely caused by fear of his wife's revenge.'

It was at this point that Burden, reaching for the pepper, saw Drayton. 'Then we can nip that little intrigue in the bud,' he said.

'Before he gets carried away, eh?' Wexford stood up. 'Yes, we'll accept Kirkpatrick's story for the time being. I don't fancy Griswold will consider Smith a new suspect, do you?' How preoccupied Drayton looked, almost entranced. 'I don't know that I want my young men amorously involved with a Grover, except in the line of business.' He crossed to the cash desk to pay the bill and dropped on one knee to tie his shoelace. Beneath the tablecloth he saw a long bare leg pressed against Drayton's knee. Playing footsie, he said to himself. He took his change and, approaching the two in the corner, gave a slight cough. Drayton lifted his face and instead of cold efficiency Wexford saw a dreamy rapture. 'Feel like a trip to Sewingbury, Drayton?'

The boy was on his feet before the words were out and once more the mask was assumed.

'I'm just coming, sir.'

'Finish your coffee.' By God, that girl was a beauty! The kind that bloomed for half a dozen years and then shrivelled like a straw before they were thirty, the golden kind that came to dust.

Geoffrey Smith's flat was one of four in a converted mansion on the far side of Sewingbury, a gracious Georgian house built perhaps at the same time as St Catherine's convent on to which it backed. A stately staircase took them up to a gallery. The wall facing them had once contained several doors but these had been boarded up and now only two remained, the entrances to flats one and two. Number two was on the left. Wexford rang the bell.

The grandeur of the place scarcely fitted in with Burden's theory of a knife or a razor. On the other hand, a customer of Mr Scatcherd's might well live here. All the same, Burden was not prepared for the lofty space which opened before them when the door swung inwards, and for a moment he looked not at the woman who stood on the threshold, but at the vast apartment behind her which led into another as large and ended finally in a pair of immense windows. It was more like a picture gallery — but for its bare walls — than a flat. Light fell from the windows in two huge twin rectangles and she stood in the darker split between them.

As soon as he met her eyes Burden knew that he had seen her before. She was the woman who had tried to sell her jewels to Knobby Clark.

'Mrs Smith?' Wexford said.

Burden had scarcely expected her to welcome them, but her reaction astonished him. There was shock and horror in her eyes. It was as if, he thought, analysing, she had been tortured for years and then, just as the respite had come, someone had threatened her with a renewal of torment.

'What do you mean?' she said, and she enunciated each word separately and slowly.

'I asked you if you are Mrs Smith, Mrs Geoffrey Smith?'

Her tired, once pretty face grew hard. 'Please go,' she said tightly. Wexford gave her one of his tough implacable looks and showed her his card. It had seldom evoked so gratifying a response. The hard look went with a gasp of relief. She smiled wryly, then laughed. 'You'd better come in.' Suddenly she was cordial, the ladylike creature Burden had seen in Knobby Clark's shop. 'I can't think what you want,' she said. He was sure she had not recognised him. 'But I'm evidently not in danger from you. I mean — well, before I knew who you were, I thought you were rather a lot of strange men for a lone woman to let into her home.'

A thin excuse for such a display of disgusted horror. In spite of the sun it was cold inside the flat. In winter it would be unbearable. They could see no sign of a radiator as they tramped through the first huge room and came into the place where the long windows were. Ivory-coloured double doors, the paint chipped on their mouldings, closed behind them. The furniture was much too small and much too new, but not new enough to be smart. No attempt had been made to achieve harmony between furniture and a noble decor. The elegant gleaming windows towered and shone between skimped bits of flowered cotton like society women fallen on evil days.

'I'd like to see Mr Smith. When do you expect him back?'

'I'd like to see him too.' Now her brown-skinned curly face was alight with a curious half-amused rue. The glasses bobbed on her short nose. Since she had discovered who they were all her fear had gone and she looked like a woman infinitely capable of laughter, a great deal of which might be directed against herself. 'Geoffrey divorced me five years ago,' she said.

'Do you know where he is now, Mrs Smith?'

'Not Mrs Smith, Mrs Anstey. Noreen Anstey. I married again.' She gave Wexford a wise elderly look, a look of wide and perhaps unpleasant experience. 'I think you might tell me why you want him.'

'Routine enquiries, Mrs Anstey.' She was the last woman in the world to be fobbed off with that one, he thought. Her eyes clouded with reproach.

'It must be something very mild,' she said, the gentle mocking smile sending sharp wrinkles up around her eyes. 'Geoff is one of the most honest people I ever met. Don't you think he looks honest?'

Wexford was greedy for the photograph and when it was handed to him, a large studio portrait, he almost grabbed it. A swarthy, pleasant face, black hair, a pipe in the mouth. The Chief Inspector was too old a hand at the game to give opinions as to honesty on this evidence. He was still studying it when Burden said:

'Have you ever seen this before?' He put the lighter into her hands. They shook a little as she took it and she gave a gasp of delight, bringing it close to her face. 'My lighter!' He stared at her. 'And I thought it had gone for ever!' She tried to make it ignite, shrugged, her face still radiant. 'Where did you find it? This is wonderful! Won't you have a cup of tea? Do let me make you some tea.'

She sat on the edge of her chair and she reminded Wexford of a child on Christmas morning. Smith's photograph was in her lap, the lighter in her hand. He had guessed her age at thirty-eight or thirty-nine but suddenly she looked much younger. There was a wedding ring on each hand. One was chased and patterned rather like the lighter she held, the other more like a Woolworth curtain ring.

'Now, let's get this clear,' Wexford said. 'This lighter is yours? You said your name was Noreen.'

'So it is.' He was sure he could believe her. Every word she spoke had the clear ring of honesty. 'Noreen Ann Anstey. I always used to be known as Ann. First I was Ann Greystock and that was fine; then Ann Smith which is dull but not so bad. But Ann Anstey? It's terrible, it's like a stammer. So I use my first name.'

'Your first husband gave you the lighter?' Burden put in.

'For Christmas. Let me see — nineteen fifty-eight it must have been.' She hesitated and her smile was rueful. 'We were getting on fine in those days. I lit his life.'

'How did you come to lose it?'

'How does one lose anything? It was last November. I had a handbag with a faulty clasp. I always carried it about with me even though I can't afford to smoke these days.' Wexford just glanced at the bare shabby furniture and then was sorry he had done so. Very little escaped her and now she was hurt.

With a brief frown, she went on, 'One day the lighter was there and the next it wasn't. I'd lost a necklace, a silver thing, the week before. Same old way. Some of us never learn.' She fingered the lighter lovingly and met Burden's censorious eye. 'Oh, I know it's valuable,' she said hastily. 'Everything Geoff gave me was pretty valuable. He isn't rich but he's the soul of generosity. I was his wife and nothing was too good for me. I've sold most of my other stuff . . .' Pausing, she glanced at him again and he knew she was remembering their encounter. 'I've had to,' she said. 'I'm a teacher at St Catherine's, but I don't manage very well. I don't know why I kept this.' She lifted her shoulders in the manner of one who regrets but regards regret as a waste of time. 'Perhaps because it was so very personal.' Her sudden smile was a flash of philosophy. 'Ah, well, it's nice to have been loved and remember it when it's gone.'

You didn't lose it, Wexford thought. Don't strain my credulity too far. You may have lost it and Anita Margolis may have lost it, but you didn't both lose it and within six months of each other.

'Mrs Anstey,' he said, 'as his divorced wife, you must know where Mr Smith is now.'

'He never paid me — what-d'you-call-it? — alimony. It was enough for me that he gave us the flat to live in.' She caught her lower lip in small white teeth. 'Ah, I see why you want him. Some tax thing because he's an accountant. Well, if anyone's been fiddling his returns it's nothing to do with Geoff.'

'Where can we find him?'

'Back where you come from, Kingsmarkham.' Wexford listened incredulously, recalling the visits they had paid to every Geoff Smith in the district. 'Twenty-two, Kingsbrook Road, Old Kingsbrook Road, that is. He lived in Kingsmarkham before we married and after the divorce he went back there.'

'Have you ever heard him speak of a Miss Anita Margolis?'

The mention of another woman's name did not please her. He could see that by the way the eager smile faded and her hands came tightly together. But she had an answer, an antidote, he thought, for every hint of poison. 'Is she the girl who's been fiddling her tax?'

'Mrs Anstey, has your ex-husband a key to this flat?'

She wrinkled the already lined brown forehead. Her eyes were teak-coloured but glowing with life. It wouldn't matter what she wore, Wexford reflected, you'd never notice. Her personality, her vitality — for Ann who lights up my life — made of her clothes something she put on to keep her warm. For the first time he observed them, a pullover and an old pleated skirt.

'A key?' she said. 'I shouldn't be surprised. If he has, he doesn't use it. Sometimes . . .' She looked up at him under lowered lashes, but not coyly, not artfully, rather as if she doubted his ability to understand. 'Sometimes I wish he would,' she said. 'One doesn't care to mess up someone else's life. It doesn't matter about me. Contrary to the general opinion, there's a whole heap of consolation in knowing one's only getting what one thoroughly deserves. Geoff deserved the best and he got a kick in the teeth. I'd like to know things had got better for him, that's all.' She had been lost and now she seemed to recollect the company she was in. 'You must think I'm crazy talking like this. Sorry. When you're alone a lot you get garrulous with visitors. Sure you won't have that tea?'

'Quite sure, thank you.'

'When you see him,' she said, 'you might give him my — er, best wishes. Still, maybe you don't carry messages and maybe he's forgotten the past.' Her face was full of tiny crinkles, a map of experience, and not all those lines, Wexford thought, were capable of being shrugged away.

'For Ann who messed my life,' said Burden when they were in the car. 'What did he do, sir, come back and nick the lighter because he'd found another girl who might appreciate it?'

'Let's not sentimentalise him, shall we? He made a nasty mess himself — out of the girl he did give it to. I suppose he remembered that he'd once given a present to his wife that was highly appropriate as a gift to another Ann. Not all that generous and high-minded, is he, if he sneaked back to his ex-wife's flat and stole it?'

'At any rate, we don't have to worry about him giving it to Anita Margolis nine years ago. He needn't have given it to her till a few months ago. Probably didn't even meet her till then.'

'Fair enough,' said Wexford. 'I go along with that, don't you, Drayton?'

Burden looked offended that Drayton had been considered worthy of consultation. 'I daresay he killed her with one of those flick knives from Grover's shop,' he said sourly. Drayton's back grew if anything slightly more rigid. Faintly amused, Wexford cleared his throat.

'Take the Stowerton Road,' he said to Drayton. 'We'll show this photo to Ruby Branch.'

She contemplated it and Wexford knew that it was hopeless. Too much time had passed, too many faces had been brought to her notice. The identity parade which should have settled things had merely unsettled her. She gave Wexford the photograph, shaking her ginger curls, and said:

'How many more of you are going to come calling?'

'What's that supposed to mean?'

Ruby shifted on the blue and red sofa and stared bitterly at the uncarpeted floor.

'Fellow called Martin,' she said, 'he's only been gone ten minutes. He's one of your lot, isn't he?' Wexford nodded, mystified. 'First there comes this great big car, pink and mauve with letters on it and this fellow gets out . . .'

'What fellow?' Not Martin, he thought. What the hell was going on?

'No, no, that chap with the red tie in your parade. As soon as I saw his car I remembered where I'd seen him before. Twice I saw him on that Tuesday night. Outside Cawthorne's he was when I went by at ten past eight and I saw him again at eleven, sitting in his car, staring at everyone, like he was going off his head. But I told your bloke Martin all that just now.'

It was all Wexford could do to quell the laugh that rose in his throat. Ruby's painted face was pink with indignation. Trying to sound severe, Wexford said:

'You wouldn't be saying all this because Mr Kirkpatrick asked you to, would you? You wouldn't be led into temptation by a nifty rope of rhinestones?'

'Me?' Ruby drew herself up virtuously. 'I never even spoke to him. He was just getting out of that daft car of his when your man drives up. Back he nips like one o'clock and off down the street. That Martin,' she said, very aggrieved, 'he was nasty to me. Some would call it threatening.'

'And others,' said Wexford, 'would call it saving weaker vessels from their baser instincts.'

At Stowerton crossroads Cawthorne was nowhere to be seen, but his wife, bony knees displayed and ear-rings big as Christmas tree baubles dangling beneath yellow curls, had perched herself on a diesel pump to flirt with an attendant. In the launderette the portholes still whirled.

'You can consider yourself absolved from laundry duty tonight, Drayton,' Wexford said, chuckling.

'I beg your pardon, sir?'

'Miss Grover always comes over here to do her washing on Tuesdays, doesn't she?'

'Oh, yes, sir. I see what you mean.' There was no need for him to flush quite so deeply, Wexford thought. The dark red colour had spread to the back of his neck.

'Kirkpatrick's safe all right,' he said. 'His bribes fell on stony ground.' The metaphor sounded wrong and he added quickly, 'Those two women saw him outside Cawthorne's right enough. He's just a fool who can't leave well alone. It's the inside of a divorce court he's afraid of, not a jail.'

'Straight to the Old Kingsbrook Road, sir?' Drayton asked stiffly.

'Number twenty-two's this end.' As they passed the Methodist church, Wexford leaned forward, a dull leaden weight diving to the pit of his stomach. He had feared this when Mrs Anstey gave him the address, feared it and dismissed his fear as jumping to conclusions.

'Look at that, Mike.'

'As if a bomb had dropped,' Burden said tiredly.

'I know. I feel like that too. Rather nice Georgian houses and the whole block's nearly demolished.' He got out of the car, Burden following him. In the mild afternoon light the last remaining wall stared at them. It was the inside that was displayed, green wallpaper above, then pink, stone-coloured on the ground. A dozen feet from the top an iron fireplace still clung to the plaster, and where the plaster had been stripped, to bare bricks. A great cable wrapped it and the cable was attached to a tractor, lurching through dust. Through the ochreish clouds they could see a painted board, *Doherty for Demolition,* and underneath the slogan, *What Goes Up Must Come Down!*

Burden's eye caught the number on the remaining doorpost, twenty-two. He looked disconsolately from the wall to the cable, the cable to the tractor. Then with a jerk of his head he beckoned the tractor driver.

'Police,' Burden said sharply into a red pugnacious face.

'O.K., O.K. Only I've got my work to do, same as anyone else. What were you wanting?'

Burden looked past him to the number on the doorpost.

'There was an accountant here, chap called Smith. D'you know where he went to?'

'Where you'll never find him.' The smirk was unpleasant. 'Underground.'

'Come again?'

'He's dead,' said the tractor driver, rubbing his dusty hands.

CHAPTER FOURTEEN

'He can't be dead,' Burden said aghast.

'Can't he? I'm only telling you what the old girl in the tea-place told me.' Cocking his head towards where the little café had been, the workman fished in his pocket for a large filthy handkerchief and blew his nose. 'Before her place come down it was. Poor Mr Smith, she says, he'd have hated to see the old house go. All he'd got left what with his wife doing him dirt and him all on his own.'

'What did he die of? A broken heart?'

'Something to do with his heart. The old girl could tell you more than I can.'

'You don't know when he died?' Wexford put in.

'A year, eighteen months. The place stood empty ever since and a proper mess it was in.' Burden knew the truth of this. Where the rubble now was he had often sat having his tea and, leaving, had passed boarded-up windows. 'There's the undertakers up on the corner. They'd know. Always go to the nearest, I reckon.'

The man went back to his tractor and, puffing heavily as if determined to move the wall by his own unaided effort, edged the vehicle forward over mounds of brick-filled loam. Burden went over to the undertakers. The cable pulled taut. Wexford stood watching it and listening to the groans of crumbling mortar until the inspector came back.

'He's dead all right,' Burden said, picking his way through the debris. 'Died last February twelvemonth. They remember the funeral. No one there but that old woman and a girl who used to do Smith's typing. Our surefire suspect is in a grave in Stowerton cemetery.'

'What did he die of?'

'Coronary,' said Burden. 'He was forty-two.' A low crunching tremor like the first cracking that precedes an earthquake made him look behind him. In the wall of Smith's house a fissure had appeared, running between green wallpaper and pink. From the centre of this rift brown plaster dust began to vomit down the patchy brick. 'As I see it, sir,' he said, 'the Geoff Smith business is coincidence. We have to forget him and begin again.'

'Coincidence! No, Mike, I won't have that. Its arm isn't that long. A man came to Ruby's house and said he was Geoff Smith and after he'd gone a lighter was found in that house that a man called Geoff Smith had bought eight years before. We *know* those things if we don't know anything else and you can't get away from them. It was in Stowerton and a man called Geoff Smith had lived in the next town, knew the place like you and I know it. The man is dead, was dead when the lighter went missing from Mrs Anstey's flat, dead before Anita came to live here and stone cold dead as a doornail last Tuesday. But to deny he had any connection with the case on the grounds of coincidence is crazy. That way madness lies.'

'Then Mrs Anstey's lying. She sold Anita the lighter — she admits she's sold a lot of stuff — and happened to tell her all about her first husband at the same time. That wouldn't be coincidence, that'd be normal behaviour for her. Anita told her boy friend the name and it stuck in his subconscious.'

'Why should she lie?' Wexford scoffed. 'What would be the point? I ask you, Mike, did she impress you as a liar?'

Burden shook his head doubtfully and began to follow the Chief Inspector back to Drayton and the waiting car. 'I don't believe her when she says she lost the lighter, at any rate,' he said.

'No, but she thinks she did,' Wexford said quickly. 'The truth is, somebody nicked it. Who? An old mate of Smith's? You know what we're going to have to do, don't you? Every friend of Smith's, every friend of Mrs Anstey's and all Anita's associates are going to have to be hunted up just to see if there's the tiniest tie-up between them.'

A shout from behind made them quicken their pace. 'Stand clear!' The tractor gave a final heave, and with a rumble that grew into a roar, the cable sliced through the wall like a grocer's wire cutter through a piece of cheese. Then everything vanished behind a huge yellow cloud. Where the house had been there was now nothing but a pillar of mud-coloured vapour through which could be seen clean blue sky.

'The last of Geoffrey Smith,' said Wexford. 'Come on. I want my tea.'

There was no future in it, Drayton thought. His ambitions had no place in them for such a girl as Linda Grover. Not even a single rung of his ladder could be spared to bear her weight. Now, looking back over the days, he saw that he had been culpable in associating himself at all with a girl whose father was eyed antagonistically by his superior officers, blameworthy for taking her out, appallingly foolhardy to have made himself her lover. The word with its erotic, insinuating associations made him shiver and the shiver was not for his future and his career.

It seemed that she was bribable, corruptible. He knew only that she, like her surroundings, was corrupting. And Wexford knew it too. Wexford had told him, although not knowing just what his prohibition entailed, to leave her alone. This was his chance, to obey, to yield, and in this yielding to put up a resistance to her spell sanctioned by authority.

He took his hooded coat and went down the police station steps. The evening was too warm to put it on. Cawthorne would have to go without his car hire fee tonight. Drayton made his way to the library where he got out a book on abnormal psychology.

It was seven when he came out and the library was closing. Grover's would be closed too and he would be safe if he went back to his lodgings by way of the High Street. The Stowerton to Forby bus came in as he approached the stop and he felt a strange urge to get on it and be carried far away into the anonymous depths of the countryside. Instead of the intellectual concentration abnormal psychology would demand, he wanted to lose himself and his identity; he wanted oblivion in the warm quiet air. But even as he thought this, he knew with a sudden conviction almost amounting to horror that he could not escape like this, that the wide green world was not big enough to contain him and her unless they were together. He grew cold and he began to hurry, like a man quickening his steps to stimulate circulation on a cold day.

Then he saw her. She was getting off the Stowerton bus and a young, good-looking man was helping her down with a wheel-basket full of bundled washing. Drayton saw her smile as she thanked him and it seemed to him that her smile was more coquettish and more seductive than any she had ever given him. Jealousy caught at him like a punch at the throat.

Avoidance was impossible. He had lost the will and the desire to avoid. Wexford's words — that apt crack about laundry duties — he recalled as he might remember a sermon so boring, so spurious that it sent you to sleep. But he was awake now, uncaringly reckless.

'Carry your bag, lady? Or should I say, push it?'

She smiled, a shadow of the look she had given the man on the bus. It was enough. The fetters were back. He seemed to feel their cold enclosing touch.

'My boss said I'd be a laundryman tonight,' he said, and he knew he was gabbling foolishly, wooing her anew as he did each time they met. 'He was right. Who's looking after the shop?'

'Your boss thinks a lot of you,' she said and he detected the proprietory note, the tone of satisfaction. 'I could tell that in the café today.' Her face clouded. 'Dad's up,' she said. 'His back's awful, but he says he can't trust us to mind the business.'

Drayton felt a curious desire to see the father. He sighed within himself. It was not thus that he had envisaged so crucial and significant a meeting, not in these circumstances nor in this place. Ten years hence, he thought, and a nice educated girl; a tall scholarly father with a degree, pearls round the mother's neck; a half-timbered country house with gardens and perhaps a paddock. She unlocked the shop door and the old grey smell came out to meet him.

Grover was behind the counter, shovelling up sweets some-one had spilt. His hands looked dirty and there were rust marks round the rim of the jar he held. Drayton had expected him to be older. The man looked no more than forty, if that. There was no grey in the lustreless dark hair and signs of age showed only in his face muscles, screwed up in pain. When he saw his daughter he put down the jar and clapped his hand to the small of his back.

'Your mum's just off to her whist drive,' he said and Drayton thought his voice horrible. 'She wants them things ironed tonight.' He spoke to his daughter as if she were alone with him and he gave her a surly glance.

'You ought to be in bed,' Linda said.

'And let the business go to pot? Fine mess you've got these books in.' Though he was dark and she fair, the resemblance between father and daughter was so strong that Drayton had to turn away deliberately to stop himself from staring. If the man smiled he thought he would cry aloud in anguish. But there was little chance of Grover's smiling. 'This is the end of me taking things easy,' he said. 'I can see that. Back to the grindstone tomorrow.' He came out from behind the counter as if he were going to pounce on her and, indeed, his crooked movements to some extent suggested those of a crippled and cornered animal. 'Then I'll get the car out,' he muttered. 'Don't suppose you've cleaned it since I was laid up.'

'The doctor'll have something to say about that,' she said and Drayton heard weariness in her voice. 'Why don't you go back to bed? I'm here. I'll manage.'

She took his arm as if he were in fact the ancient broken creature Drayton had imagined. Alone in the shop he felt desolate. This was no place for him and as always when here he felt a compulsion to wash his hands. Perhaps she would forget he was there, engulfed as she always was by her domestic duties, and he would be left among the suspect magazines — the hidden knives? — until night came to deepen this darkness. For he knew that he was a prisoner and that he could not leave without her.

It seemed an age before she returned and when she came he felt his face must betray God knew what enslavement, an end-of-his-tether abandonment to longing.

'I had to hang up the washing,' she said. 'Not that it'll dry tonight. I should have taken it in the afternoon like I did last week.' As she came close to him, he put up his hands to her face, touching it as a blind man might. 'No car tonight?' she asked him. He shook his head. 'We'll take Dad's,' she said.

'No,' he said. 'We'll go for a walk.'

He knew that she could drive; she had told Wexford. What puny power remained to him would be utterly lost if he allowed her to drive him about the countryside in her father's car.

'Tomorrow, then,' she said and she looked long into his eyes. 'Promise you will tomorrow, Mark, before Dad gets mobile — and commandeers it.'

He thought that at that moment he would have promised her his own life if she had asked for it. 'Look after me,' she said, a sudden agony in her voice. Upstairs he could hear the crippled man moving. 'Oh, Mark, Mark . . .'

The river beckoned them with its quiet sheltered path.

Drayton took her in his arms on the spot where he had seen that other man kiss her, but he had forgotten this and everything else which had passed before they met. Even the desire for immediate physical gratification was less strong. He had reached a stage when his paramount wish was to be alone with her in silence, holding her to him, and in silence enclosing her mouth with his.

'I think I was justified in calling you out,' Burden said. He stood up to let Wexford take his seat beside him on the window settle. As usual at this time, the saloon bar of the Olive and Dove was crowded.

'Wouldn't keep till the morning, I suppose,' Wexford grumbled. 'Don't sit down. You can get me a beer before you start expounding.'

Burden came back with two beers in tankards. 'Bit crowded and noisy in here, sir, I'm afraid.'

'Not half so crowded and noisy as my place. My daughter Sheila's having a jam session.'

'No,' said Burden with a smile, 'they don't call it that any more.'

Wexford said belligerently from behind his beer, 'What do they call it, then?'

'Search me.'

They moved into a quieter corner. Wexford lifted the hem of a curtain and looked out at the street. It was dark and there were few people about. Half a dozen youths loitered at the entrance to the cinema car park, pushing each other about and laughing.

'Look at all those bloody green cars,' the Chief Inspector said disgustedly. 'For all we know, he's out there, driving around or in the pictures.'

'I think I know who he is,' Burden said quietly.

'Well, I didn't suppose you'd dragged me down here for the sake of the booze. Let's have it.'

Burden looked speculatively at the heavy wrinkled face. Its expression was not encouraging. For a moment he hesitated, fidgeting with his tankard. His idea had come to him, or rather had crystallised, after three hours of arguing it out with himself. When he had formulated it and catalogued the details he had become so excited that he had to tell someone. The obvious someone now sat opposite him, already derisive and certainly prepared to scoff. The Chief Constable had evidently made up his mind that the whole investigation was so much hot air. Just as the cold light of morning is said to dispel fancies of the night before, so the atmosphere of the Olive and Dove, the sudden bursts of raucous laughter and Wexford's doubting look robbed his ingenious solution of everything cogent and left only the ingenuity. Perhaps it would be better if he drank up his drink and went without another word. Wexford was tapping his foot impatiently. Clearing his throat, Burden said lamely:

'I think it's Mrs Anstey's husband.'

'*Smith?* My God, Mike, we've been through that. He's dead.'

'Smith is, but Anstey isn't. At any rate, we've no reason to suppose so.' Burden lowered his voice as someone passed their table. 'I think it could be Anstey. Shall I tell you why?'

Wexford's spiky eyebrows went up. 'It had better be good,' he said. 'We don't know anything about the fellow. She hardly mentioned him.'

'And didn't you think that was funny?'

'Perhaps it was,' Wexford said thoughtfully. 'Perhaps it was.' He seemed to be about to go on. Burden did not wish to have the wind taken out of his own sails and he said hastily:

'Who does she give the impression of being more fond of, the man who divorced her five years ago or the man she's married to now? She regrets that divorce, sir, and she doesn't mind making it clear to three strangers who didn't even want to know. 'It's nice to have been loved and remember it when it's gone,' she said. Are those the words of a happily married woman? Then what was all that about being alone a lot? She's a teacher. A married woman with a job isn't alone a lot. She'd be hardly alone at all.'

'You think she and Anstey are separated?'

'I do,' said Burden with decision. Wexford showed no inclination to laugh and he began to gather confidence.

'We don't believe she lost the lighter, but she believes it. If she didn't lose it but just left it lying about or in her handbag, who's the most likely person to have it in his possession? The errant husband. Very probably Smith divorced her on Anstey's account. That means adultery, and a man who'll commit it once will commit it again.'

'Thus speaks the stern moralist,' said Wexford, smiling. 'I don't know that I'd go along with that. Your point is, of course, that Anstey took up with Anita and gave her the lighter. Mike, it's all right as far as it goes, but you haven't got any real reason for thinking Anstey's left her. Don't forget the Easter holidays are on and a married woman teacher would be alone a lot in the holidays.'

'Then why does she say she's only got her salary to live on?' Burden asked triumphantly. 'It's quite true what she says about selling jewellery. I saw her in Knobby Clark's shop.'

'I'll buy you a drink,' said Wexford, and now he looked pleased.

'Scotch,' said Burden when he came back. 'Very nice. Cheers.'

'To detection.' Wexford raised his glass. 'Where's Anstey now?'

Burden shrugged. 'Around here somewhere. Just getting on with whatever job he does.'

'Since you're so clever, you'll no doubt be able to tell me why a man called Anstey gives the name of his wife's former husband when he goes out on the tiles with another girl? Not just Smith, mind, *Geoff Smith*.'

'I can't tell you that,' Burden said, less happily.

'Or why he killed the girl. What was his motive?'

'When we suspected Kirkpatrick, we assumed the motive was jealousy. We lost sight of the five hundred pounds Anita was carrying in her handbag.'

'In that case, Mike, why didn't he wait until they were back in the car, drive to some lonely place and kill her there? You don't murder a woman in someone else's house by a method which leaves incriminating traces behind, when you could do it, for example, in Cheriton Forest. Which brings me back to another point. Ruby and Monkey both thought he'd go back. It was because they wanted him caught before he could go back that Monkey wrote to me. Why didn't he?'

'Scared, I suppose. We don't know where he is. For all we know he may have gone home, at least for a time.'

Burden shook his head regretfully. 'I don't know,' he said, and he added, repeating himself, 'I can't tell you that.'

'Perhaps Mrs Anstey can. Drink up. They're closing.'

Out in the street Wexford sniffed the soft April air. The sky which had been clear was now becoming overcast and clouds crossed the moon. They came to the bridge. A swan sailed out from the tunnel, into lamplight and then into their twin shadows. Wexford surveyed the almost empty High Street, the pearly white and yellow lamps and the dark holes made by the unlit alleys.

In the high wall that reared ahead of them an open window twenty feet up disclosed a girl leaning out, her arm dangling as over the rail of a stage balcony. On a bracket below was a lamp in an iron cage, and half in its light, half in velvet shadow, stood a man gazing upwards.

'Ah, moon of my delight,' Wexford quoted softly, 'who know'st no wane . . .'

With a sourness he did not bother to hide, Burden said, 'Drayton was told to leave her alone,' and he scowled at the yellow, cloud-scarred moon.

Indeed the Idols I have loved so long
Have done my Credit in Men's Eye much wrong:
Have drowned my Honour in a shallow cup,
And sold my reputation for a Song.

CHAPTER FIFTEEN

In the morning the rain came back. From the look of the sky it seemed to be one of those mornings when it rains from streaming dawn to dripping, fog-filled dusk. Wexford, dialling Sewingbury, held the receiver gripped under his chin and reached out to lower the venetian blind. He was listening to the ringing tone when Drayton came in.

'That Mrs Anstey to see you, sir. I passed her as I came in.'

Wexford put the phone down. 'For once the mountain has come to Mahomet.'

'Shall I bring her up?'

'Just a minute, Drayton.' It was a command, rather sharp and with a hint of admonition. The young man stopped and turned obediently. 'Enjoy yourself last night?'

If possible, Drayton's face became more than ever a cipher, secret, cautious, but not innocent. 'Yes, thank you, sir.' The rain drummed against the window. It had grown quite dark in the office as if night was coming at nine thirty in the morning.

'I don't suppose you've got to know many young people around here yet?' The question demanded an avuncular heartiness but Wexford made it sound menacing.

'Not many, sir.'

'Pity. God knows, my young daughter seems to know enough. Always having a' — no, not a jam session. Burden had corrected him on that. '— a get-together at our place. Quite a decent bunch if you don't mind noise. I daresay you don't.'

Drayton stood, silence incarnate.

'You must join in one of these nights.' He gave the young man a grey cold stare. 'Just you on your own,' he said.

'Yes, sir. I'd like that.'

'Good, I'll get Sheila to give you a tinkle.' Severity had gone and urbanity replaced it. 'Now for Mrs Anstey,' said the Chief Inspector.

The rain gave him a sensation of almost claustrophobic confinement as if he were enclosed by walls of water. He could hear it streaming from the sills and pouring over the naked stone bodies on the frescoes. Pity it never seemed to wash them properly but just left grey trails on shoulders and haunches. He switched on the lights as Burden came in with Mrs Anstey in his wake, each as wet as creatures from the depths of the sea. Mrs Anstey's umbrella hung from her arm and dripped water in a trickle at her heels.

'I had to come,' she said. 'I had an impulse. After you'd gone I got to thinking what on earth you could have meant about some girl you mentioned.' Her laughter sounded itself like water, fresh bubbling, yet a little hesitant. 'I got the first bus.' She shed her grey mackintosh and stripped a hideous plastic hood from her brown hair. There were raindrops on her nose and she wrinkled it as might a little dog. 'Geoff and a girl. I didn't like that. Dog in a manger, aren't I? The fact is, I just have to see him. I've waited long enough. I'm going there now, but I thought I ought to see you first.' Without explanation, she laughed again and this time her laugh held a nervous break. 'Has he got a girl?' she asked and that explained it.

The first bringer of unwelcome news, thought Wexford, has but a losing office. How did it go on? Something about his voice sounding ever after as a sullen warning bell. That didn't matter. Only the present pain mattered. For the first time since he and Burden had discussed Smith's death, his particular duty was brought home to him. He was going to have to tell her. That she was only an ex-wife would, he was sure, make no difference.

'Has he?' she said again and now she was pleading.

'I wasn't able to see him, Mrs Anstey.'

No lying, no prevaricating. None of that would be possible with this woman. Burden had turned his back.

'What is it? There's something bad. . . .' She got up, the plastic thing from her head stretched taut in her fingers. 'He's ill, he's . . .'

'He's dead.' No matter how prepared you were, it was still a shock. You could never be sufficiently prepared. Until the words were said, hope was invincible. 'I'm sorry,' he said quickly. 'I'm very, very sorry. It was a coronary, bit over a year ago. I'm sure it was quick.'

'He can't be dead!' The words were an echo of Burden's.

He could not have been dead for Burden because that made nonsense of a theory; he could not be dead for her because she had a theory too, a theory of re-shaping her life?

'Not dead!' Wexford heard the thin thread of hysteria, the burning electric shock wire.

'Please sit down. I'll get you something to drink.'

With a kind of horror, he watched her feel blindly behind her for the chair she had sat in, find it, kick it away and lurch at the wall. Her fists clenched, she struck her head against the plaster, then the fists themselves came up, pounding and beating on the hard surface.

Wexford took a step towards her. 'Better get one of the W.P.C.s,' he said to Burden. Then she began to scream with a throaty frenzy.

The policewoman took the tea cup from her and replaced the sodden handkerchief with a clean one of her own.

'Bit better now?'

Noreen Anstey nodded. Her face was pink and swollen and her hair, though wet from rain, gave the illusion of being, like her cheeks, soaked with tears. She was all tears, all grief.

Suddenly she said quite coherently, 'I can never ask him to forgive me now.' For a moment she had breath enough only for this. Sobs succeeded it. They were like blood pumping from a vein. 'I won't cry any more.' The sobs were involuntary. Eventually they would subside. 'I'll go to my grave,' she said, 'knowing he never knew I was sorry.' Wexford nodded to the policewoman and she went out with the tea cup and the wet handkerchief.

'He forgave you,' he said. 'Didn't he give you the flat?'

She hardly seemed to hear him. 'He died and I didn't even know.' Wexford thought of the two women at Smith's funeral, the old neighbour and the girl who did his typing. 'You don't even know what I did to him, do you? We'd been married eight years, the perfect couple, the happy couple. That's what everyone said and it was true.' The sobs made a rattle in her throat. 'He used to buy me presents. Unbirthday presents, he called them. You couldn't have that many birthdays. You'd get old too fast.' She covered her eyes, shaking her head from side to side. 'We lived in a house with his office in it. There was a garage next door. I could see it from my window. I'd given up work, teaching was my work. No need when I had Geoff to look after me.' The sentences jerked out, short, ragged, staccato. Wexford moved his chair close and sat looking down into his lap. 'Ray Anstey worked at the garage. I used to watch him. You know the way they lie on their backs with their heads thrown back? My God!' She shivered. 'You don't want to hear all this. I'd better go.' Her things were still wet, the raincoat, the umbrella that had dripped and made a puddle on the floor like a blister. She dabbed feebly at the sides of the chair, feeling for her handbag.

'We'll take you home, Mrs Anstey,' Wexford said gently. 'But not quite yet. Would you like to have a rest? Two questions only and then you can rest.'

'He's dead. Beyond your reach. Why did you want him?'

'I think,' Wexford said slowly, 'that it's your second husband we want.'

'Ray?'

'Where is he, Mrs Anstey?'

'I don't know,' she said tiredly. 'I haven't seen him for months. He left me at the end of last year.'

'You said he worked in a garage. Is he a mechanic?'

'I suppose he is. What else could he do?' Her gloves were on the floor at her feet. She picked them up and looked at them as at two wet dead things, dredged up from the bottom of a pond. 'You wanted him all along?' Her face went a sickly white and she struggled up out of the chair. 'It was my *husband* you wanted, not Geoff?' Wexford nodded. 'What's he done?' she asked hoarsely.

'A girl is missing, probably dead . . .'

'The knife,' she said. Her eyes went out of focus. Wexford took a step towards her and caught her in his arms.

'Where did your sister get her car serviced?' Burden said. Margolis looked up from his late breakfast of coffee, orange juice and unappetising hard-boiled eggs, his expression helplessly apathetic.

'Some garage,' he said, and then, 'It would be Cawthorne's, wouldn't it?'

'Come, Mr Margolis, you must know. Don't you have your own car seen to?'

'Ann looked after that side of things. When it wanted doing, she'd see to it.' The painter turned the eggshells upside down in their cups like a child playing April Fool tricks. 'There was something, though . . .' His long fingers splayed through his hair so that it stood up in a spiky halo. 'Some trouble. I have a remote recollection of her saying she was going to someone else.' He put the tray on the sofa arm and got up to shake crumbs from his lap. 'I wish I could remember,' he said.

'She took it to that Ray, Mr M.,' said Mrs Penistan sharply. 'You know she did. Why don't you pull yourself together?' She shrugged at Burden, turning her little eyes heavenwards. 'He's gone to pieces since his sister went. Can't do nothing with him.' She settled herself beside Margolis and gave him a long exasperated stare. Burden was reminded of a mother or a nanny taking a recalcitrant child to a tea party, especially when she bent over him and, with a sharp clucking of her tongue, pulled his dressing gown over to hide his pyjama legs.

'Ray who?'

'Don't ask me, dear. You know what she was like with her christian names. All I know is she come in here a couple of months back and says. "I've had about as much as I can stand of Russell's prices. I've a good mind to get Ray to do the cars for me." "Who's Ray?" I says, but she just laughed. "Never you mind, Mrs P. Let's say he's a nice boy who thinks the world of me. If I tell you who he is he might lose his job." '

'Did he come here to service the cars?'

'Oh, no, dear. Well, he wouldn't have the facilities, would he?' Mrs Penistan surveyed the studio and the window as if to imply that nothing of practical use to a sane human being could be found in cottage or garden. 'She always took them to him. He lived local, you see. Somewhere local. I'd see her go off but I'd always gone when she got back. *He'd* have been here.' She shoved her elbow into Margolis's thin ribs. 'But he don't listen to what folks tell him.'

Burden left them together, sitting side by side, Mrs Penistan coaxing Margolis to finish his coffee. The heavy rain had made the path slippery and there were wet petals everywhere underfoot. The garage doors were open and for the first time Burden saw Margolis's own car and saw that it was green.

He was beginning to discern a pattern, a way that it could all have been done. Now he thought he could understand why a black car and a green car had been used and where Anita's white car had been until the small hours. A new excitement made him walk jauntily to the cottage gate. He opened it and the hawthorn bush showered him with water as effectively as if someone had put a tilted bucket in its branches.

This is how it must feel to be a psychiatrist, Wexford thought. Noreen Anstey lay on the couch in the rest room, staring at the ceiling, and he sat beside her, letting her talk.

'He always had a knife,' she said. 'I saw it that first day, the first time he came up from the garage. Geoff was working downstairs. I used to take coffee down to him and then I started talking to Ray as well. One day he came up instead.' For a while she was silent, moving her head from side to side. 'God, he was beautiful. Not handsome, beautiful, perfect. Like people ought to be, like I never was. Not very tall, black haired, red mouth like a flower . . .' He didn't want to interrupt, but he had to. He wasn't a real psychiatrist.

'How old is he?'

'Ten years younger than me,' she said and he knew it hurt her to say it. 'He came up that day. We were quite alone and he had this knife, a little flick knife. He took it out of his pocket and put it on the table. I'd never seen one before and I didn't know what it was. We didn't talk much. What was there for us to talk about? We didn't have anything in common. He sat there smiling, making little sort of sly innuendoes.' She almost laughed but it was a gasp Wexford heard. 'I was sick with wanting him.' Her face turned to the wall, she went on, 'I'd had that lighter a few months and I remember lighting a cigarette for Ray. He said, "No, light it in your mouth". He looked at the lighter and he said, "He give you this? Does he give you toys because he can't give you anything else?" That wasn't true, but it must have been the way it looked, the way I looked. "I've got a toy too", he said, and he picked up the knife and held it against my throat. The blade came out. I kept still or it would

532

have cut me. My God, I was a teacher of French in a girl's school. I'd never been anywhere or done anything. You'd have thought I'd have screamed. D'you know, I'd have let him kill me, then? Afterwards, after he'd gone, there was blood on my neck from a little scratch and I knew he'd been looking at it all the time he was making love to me.'

'Smith divorced you?' Wexford said to fill up the great silence.

'He found out. That wasn't difficult. I've never been much good at hiding my feelings. Geoff would have forgiven me and started afresh. He couldn't believe I'd want to marry a man ten years younger than myself, a garage hand . . . I was mad to have him. I knew he was a sadist and a moron. He'd cut me, really cut me since then.' She pulled open her dress. On the left breast, where the flesh swelled under the collarbone, was a small white cicatrice. For all his years of experience, Wexford felt sickness catch at the back of his throat like a fingernail plucking.

'You were always unhappy?'

'I was never *happy* with him.' She said it almost reproachfully. 'I don't think there was a moment when I could say I was *happy*. He loathed Geoff. D'you know what he used to do? He'd give Geoff's name, pretend he was Geoff.' Wexford nodded, guessing this was to come. 'When the phone rang he'd pick it up and say — well, sort of absent-mindedly, "Geoff Smith speaking". Then he'd correct himself and say he'd made a mistake. Once he took some clothes to the cleaners, filthy overalls, and when I went to collect them they couldn't find the ticket. It was made out to Smith, you see. Anything a bit nasty or disreputable he was involved in and he'd always give Geoff's name. A girl came round once — she couldn't have been more than seventeen — and asked if this was where Geoff Smith lived. He'd dropped her and she wanted him back, even though he'd used the knife on her too. She showed me a scar on her neck. I told him he'd go too far one day. He'd kill one of them or she'd go to the police.'

'He's gone too far,' Wexford said.

'He had to see their blood, you see.' She spoke very calmly, without horror. Not for the first time Wexford pondered on the dulling effect of custom, how habit dulled the edge of shock. All pity choked with custom of fell deeds . . . 'I used to think,' she said, 'that one day there'd be a girl who wasn't mesmerised by him but just plain frightened and that maybe she'd turn the knife on him. He wasn't big and strong, you see, not powerful physically. His power was the other sort. I used to take the knives away but he always got new ones. Then he left me.'

'This must have been about the time you lost your lighter.'

Noreen Anstey raised herself on one elbow, then turned and swung her legs on to the floor. 'I've been thinking about that,' she said. 'Ray must have taken it. He took things from Geoff and me when we were still married. I couldn't prove it, but I thought he had, jewellery, things like that.' She sighed, covered her face and then brought her hands down again. 'I suppose Geoff guessed too. There were so many things,' she said, 'we both knew and never put into words. Oh, I'm sorry!' she cried, clenching her fists and pressing them into her lap. 'I'm so bitterly sorry. I want to find where he's buried and lie on his grave and cry into the earth that I'm sorry!'

So many women who were sorry, Wexford thought, Noreen Anstey because she had thrown away love for love's ugly shadow, Ruby Branch because she had betrayed an old crook, and Anita Margolis? The dead have no regrets. She could not be sorry that she had played her dangerous game once too often, played it with a man and a knife.

CHAPTER SIXTEEN

'Have you got a friend who could stay with you?' Wexford asked. 'Mother, sister, a neighbour?'

Noreen Anstey seemed to have shrunk. Deprived of her vitality, she was just a little plain woman wilting into middle-age. 'My mother's dead,' she said. 'Ray lost me most of my friends.'

'A policewoman will go back with you. She'll try and find someone to keep you company.'

'And when you find him?' she asked with wistful bitterness.

'We'll keep in touch, Mrs Anstey. Why do you suppose he ever came to Kingsmarkham?'

She shrugged her shoulders, pulling the creased raincoat tightly around her. Every movement now was a kind of shiver, a hunching and shrinking of her body in a gradual process of contraction. 'If I say to haunt him,' she said, 'you'll think I'm mad. But that would be like Ray. He'd go to — to Geoff and say he'd wrecked two lives, but he'd left me now and all the agony was for nothing. He's a sadist. Then he'd have started it all over again, that business of giving Geoff's name, telling girls he was Geoff and giving them his address.'

'Mrs Anstey, you thought we were friends of your husband, didn't you? When we called and asked if you were Mrs Smith. You thought Anstey had put us on to you.'

She nodded limply.

'He must have known Mr Smith was dead. Would he give his name, knowing he was dead?'

'He might have done. Not to a girl. There wouldn't be any point in that. But if he was going to do something disreputable or underhand, he might then. It would be a joke to him, dishonouring Geoff's memory. And it would be a habit too.'

'I wonder why he stayed.'

'I suppose he liked it here or got a good job that suited him. His idea of heaven would be an easy-going employer who'd pay him well and turn a blind eye if Ray took his customers away from him and serviced their cars on the cheap. That was always one of the ways he got to know his girls.'

Wexford did not want to hurt her more than he need, but he did not think she would sustain any further injury from a recital of Anstey's misdemeanours.

'By going round to their homes while their husbands were at work, I imagine?' he said. 'Sitting in their cars with them, the personal touch?'

'He wasn't doing too well in Sewingbury,' she said. 'People got to know too much about him. Some of these garage proprietors give their mechanics a car or let them borrow one. Ray's boss got hard about that when he smashed up a hire car. No, you can be sure he found a job and a good one.' She turned away from him and covered her eyes. 'If Geoff had been alive,' she whispered. 'Oh, if only he'd been alive! Ray wouldn't have been able to hurt him or me any more. When Geoff had seen him, seen him once and heard he'd left me, he'd have come back to me. I often used to think, he'll find out, he'll know sooner or later. We used to be able to read each other's minds. Married people can. He's lonely too, I thought. He's been lonely longer than I have.' She began to cry softly, the calm gentle tears of a grief beyond consolation. 'It's a fallacy that, about reading thoughts. He was dead.' She spoke evenly, as if she were just talking and not crying as well. 'And I sat and waited for him, quite happy really and peaceful. I didn't long for him or feel passionate or anything. I had peace and I thought, one day, this week, next week, sometime — well, it was never, wasn't it?' Her fingers dabbed the tears. 'May I have my lighter?' she said.

He let her hold it but shook his head at the request. 'In a little while.'

'The name of the design,' she said, 'came from a poem of Baudelaire. Geoff knew I loved that verse. "... *et tes seins*",' she quoted, '"*Les grappes de ma vigne.*" ' Wexford's French wasn't up to much but he could just understand. She had shown him the scar Anstey, the thief and the sadist, had made with his knife. He turned away his eyes.

It looked as if Russell Cawthorne had a young girl in the office

536

with him. Her back was to the door and she wore a red mac, the glistening hot red of a fire engine with the paint still wet. Burden drove through the rain and up under the trading stamps banner. He and Wexford dived for the office. The girl opened the door for them and illusion snapped, for it was Mrs Cawthorne's face that appeared between the scarlet collar and the frothy yellow hair.

'Better go into the house,' said Cawthorne. He heaved himself up, grunting. 'Come on, troops, run for it!'

In the living-room the Pre-Raphaelite lady contemplated her lily with pitying scorn. She had seen plenty in that room, she seemed to be saying, most of it unedifying. Mrs Cawthorne took off the red coat and stood revealed in lemon wool. Her Christmas tree ear-rings hung to her shoulders. Red and shining, they reminded Wexford of toffee apples.

'Ray Anstey was with me for six months,' Cawthorne said. 'He was a good lad, knew his job.' They sat down among the piecrust tables, the wax fruit, the candelabra. My God, thought Wexford, is it all coming back? Is this the way my Sheila will do up her house when the time comes? 'When he came he said he wanted something temporary. He'd only come here to hunt up a friend, but then he said the friend had died and he'd like to stay on.' Geoff Smith, Wexford reflected, Smith, the injured, the bait, the perpetually fascinating.

'Much of a one for the women?' he asked.

'I wouldn't say that.' Cawthorne gave Burden a sidelong glance. Perhaps he was remembering enquiries into his own proclivities in that direction. He shook himself and added in the tone of a colonel discussing with an officer of equal or even superior rank the naughtiness of a subaltern, 'Good-looking young devil, though.'

Mrs Cawthorne wriggled. Wexford looked at her. He had seen a similar expression in his seventeen-year-old Sheila's eyes when she was discussing with triumph a boy's unsuccessful advance. Here was the same half-smile, the same mock-anger. But surely he wasn't expected to believe . . . ? He was.

'You wouldn't say that?' she enquired archly of her husband. 'Then all I can say is, you don't listen to a word I say.' Cawthorne's sick glare made this seem more than probable.

'Why, the way he looked at me sometimes!' She turned to Wexford. 'I'm used to it, of course. I could see what young Ray was after. Not that he actually said anything. It was more than his job was worth to go chasing the boss's wife.'

Her husband turned his eyes towards the ceiling where he fixed them on a plaster cherub. 'Oh God,' he said softly.

'When did he leave?' Wexford put in quickly.

His wife's insinuation had temporarily thrown Cawthorne off balance. He went to the sideboard and poured himself a whisky before replying. 'Let's see now,' he said when half the drink had gone down. 'It'd be last Saturday week.' The day he booked Ruby's room, Wexford thought. 'I remember thinking what a bloody nerve he'd got.'

'In what way? Because he left you?'

'Not only that. It was the way he did it. Now I'm in the habit of letting any of my staff borrow a car when they're in need and provided they give me fair warning. It's hard on a young kid, wants to take his girl out.' He smiled philanthropically, the friend of youth, and drained his glass. 'Anstey was one of the kind that take advantage. Night after night he'd have one of the cars and it was all the same to him whether I knew or whether I didn't. Well, on that Saturday morning we were a bit short-handed and I noticed Anstey wasn't about. Next thing he came sweeping in in one of the Minors, all smiles and not a word of excuse. Said he'd been to see a friend on business.'

'A Minor?'

'Black Minor Thousand, one of the three I keep for hiring out. You've seen them out the front.' Cawthorne raised a thick eyebrow like a strip of polar bear fur. 'Drink?' Wexford shook his head for both of them. 'Don't mind if I do, do you?' His glass refilled, he went on, ' "Business?" I said. "Your business is my business, my lad," I said, "and just you remember it." "Oh," he said in a very nasty way, "I wonder how much business you'd have left if I didn't have scruples." Well, that was a bit much. I told him he could have his cards and get out.'

The ear-rings swung as Mrs Cawthorne gave a small theatrical sigh. 'Poor lamb,' she said. Wexford did not for a moment suppose she referred to her husband. 'I wish I'd been kinder to him.' There was no doubt what she meant by that. It was grotesque. God help him, he thought. Surely he wasn't going to have another regretful woman on his hands? What value they all put on themselves, all sorry, all wanting to reverse the hands of the clock.

'Scruples,' he said. 'What did he mean by that?'

Again Cawthorne favoured them with that curious narrowing of the eyes.

'Been taking away your business, had he?' Burden put in quickly, remembering Mrs Penistan.

'He was a good mechanic,' Cawthorne said. 'Too good.' This last perhaps reminded him of the whisky, for he poured himself some more, first half-filling the glass, then, with a quick reckless tilt to the bottle, topping it to the brim. He sighed, possibly with pleasure, possibly with resignation at another temptation unresisted. 'What I mean to say is, he was too much of a one for the personal touch.' Mrs Cawthorne's laugh cut off the last word with the shrill screeching whine of a circular saw. 'Ingratiated himself with the customers,' he said, ignoring her. 'Madam this and madam that, and then he'd open the doors for them and compliment them on their driving. Damn it all, it's not necessary for a thousand mile service.'

'Harmless, I should have thought.'

'Call it harmless, do you, when a little squirt like that takes away your business? The next thing I knew — heard by a roundabout route . . .' He scowled, the general in Intelligence. 'I have my spies,' he said absurdly. 'I could see it all. "Why not let me do it privately for you, madam. I'd only charge ten bob." ' He took a long pull at his drink. 'And there's not a damn thing I could do about it, what with my overheads. I'm out of pocket if I charge less than twelve and six. A good half-dozen of my customers he got away from me like that, and good customers too. I taxed him with it but he swore they'd taken to going to Missal's. But there was Mrs Curran, to give you an example, and Mr and Miss Margolis . . .'

'Ah!' said Wexford softly.

Cawthorne went pink and avoided his wife's eye.

'You might think she was flighty,' he said, 'but you didn't know her. It wasn't easy come, easy go with her. Oh, it came easily enough, but young Anita watched the spending of every penny. For all we'd been close friends for a year, she didn't think twice about going to Anstey on the sly. Still came to me for petrol, mind.' He belched and changed it to a cough. 'As if there was anything to be made on juice!'

'Were they friendly?'

'Anita and young Ray? Show me the man under fifty she wasn't friendly with. He'd have to have a hump or a hare lip.' But Cawthorne was over fifty, well over, and his age was his own deformity.

'He left you on the Saturday,' Burden said slowly. 'Where would he go?' It was a rhetorical question. He did not expect Cawthorne to answer it. 'D'you know where he was living?'

'Kingsmarkham somewhere. One of my boys might know.' His sodden face fell and he seemed to have forgotten his former attack on Anita Margolis's character. 'You think he killed her, don't you? Killed little Ann . . .'

'Let's find that address, Mr Cawthorne.'

The ear-rings bounced. 'Is he on the run?' Mrs Cawthorne asked excitedly. Her eyes glittered. 'Poor hunted creature!'

'Oh, shut up,' said Cawthorne and went out into the rain.

CHAPTER SEVENTEEN

They stood in the porch while Cawthorne questioned the men. The rain was passing now and the clouds splitting. Over Kingsmarkham they could see that patches of sky were showing between the great banks of cumulus, a fresh bright sky that was almost green.

'One hundred and eighty-six, High Street, Kingsmarkham,' Cawthorne said, trotting up to them and making a little final spurt for cover. 'That's his headquarters, or was.'

'One eight six,' said Burden quickly. 'Let's see now. The news block's one five eight to one seven four, then the chemist and the florist . . .' He ticked the numbers off on his fingers. 'But that must be . . .'

'Well, it's Grover's the newsagents.' Cawthorne looked as if it was only what he had expected. 'They let one of their attic rooms, you know. A couple of my chaps have lodged there before and when Anstey lost his first billet down the road here, someone suggested Grover's might fill the bill. Mind you, he was only there a month.'

'On our own doorstep!' Wexford said with an angry snort when they were in the car. 'You can see that place from our windows. A fat lot of use our observatory's been to us.'

'It's common knowledge they take lodgers, sir,' Burden said apologetically, but he did not know for whom he was making excuses and he added in his own defence, 'I daresay we've all seen a young dark fellow going in and out. We'd no cause to connect him with this case. How many thousands of little dark chaps are there in Kingsmarkham alone?'

Wexford said grimly, 'He didn't have to go far to see Ruby's ad., did he? He was in the right place to replace his knife, too. What happens now to your theory about the cars? Anstey didn't even own one, let alone swop black for green.'

'Anita got five hundred pounds the day before they went to Ruby's. Mrs Penistan says she was generous. Maybe she bought him a car.'

They pulled up on the police station forecourt. Burden turned his head to see a man come out of Grover's with an evening paper. As they went up the steps under the broad white canopy, water dripped from it on to their coat collars.

'Maybe she bought him a car,' Burden said again. 'You could buy a very decent second-hand car for five hundred.'

'We're told she was generous,' Wexford said on the stairs. 'We're also told she was hard-headed and careful with her money. She wasn't an old woman with a kept man. Young girls don't buy cars for their boy friends.'

It was warm and silent in Wexford's office. The chairs were back against the walls and the papers on the rosewood desk neatly arranged. Nothing remained to show that earlier it had been the scene of a tragic drama. Burden took off his raincoat and spread it in front of the warm air grille.

'Kirkpatrick saw her at twenty past seven,' he said. 'She was at Ruby's by eight. That gave her forty minutes to change her coat, get down to Grover's, leave her Alpine there for him to mend at some future time and drive to Stowerton. It could easily be done.'

'When Kirkpatrick saw her she was wearing that ocelot thing. You'd naturally expect her to change into a raincoat in the cottage, but the ocelot was *on the passenger seat of her car*. It's a small point, but it may be important. Then we come to this question of time. Your theory only works if Anita and Anstey already had a green car available. Maybe they did. We shall see. But if, at that juncture in the proceedings, they had to borrow or hire a car, it couldn't be done.'

'It could be done if they used Margolis's car,' said Burden.

Drayton and Martin interrupted them and moved in on the conference. The four of them sat round the desk while Wexford put the newcomers in the picture. He watched Drayton's face grow hard and his eyes stony when Grover's shop was mentioned.

'Right,' he said, looking at his watch. 'We'll give them a chance to close up and then we'll all go over. Grover's more or less bedridden at the moment, isn't he?' He gave Drayton a sharp look.

'Up and about again now, sir.'

'Good,' Wexford nodded. 'Now,' he said to Burden. 'What's all this about Margolis's car? Margolis was in London.'

'He'd left his car at Kingsmarkham station and it *is* a green car. Wouldn't Anita be just the kind of girl to go a couple of hundred yards down York Street to the station approach and borrow her brother's car? They could have got it back by the time he wanted it.'

'Don't forget they thought he'd want it at nine, not eleven. No one knew he'd be dining with this gallery manager.'

'So what?' Burden shrugged. 'If ever there was an easy-going slapdash pair it's Margolis and his sister. If his car wasn't there he'd probably think he hadn't left it there or that it had been stolen. And he'd never do anything about that until he saw her. Anstey dumped her body, returned Margolis's car to the station car park and when everyone was in bed and asleep, filled up the Alpine radiator, taking a can of water with him to be on the safe side, and drove it back to Quince Cottage.'

He expected to see on Wexford's face a look of pleasure and approval comparable to that he had shown the previous night at the Olive and Dove. Everything was beginning to fit beautifully, and he, Burden, had dovetailed it. Why then had Wexford's mouth settled into those dubious grudging creases? He waited for comment, for some sort of agreement that all this was at least possible, but the Chief Inspector said softly:

'I have other ideas, I'm afraid.'

The shop was closed. In the alley water lay in puddles that mirrored the greenish lamplight. Two bins had been moved out in front of the garage doors for the dust collection in the morning. A cat sniffed them, leaving wet paw marks on some-one's discarded newspaper.

Drayton had not wanted to come with them. He knew who Ray Anstey was now, the man he had seen her kissing by the bridge, the man who lodged with them and who had borrowed his employer's cars to take her out. Perhaps they had used that very car in which Drayton himself had driven her to Cheriton Forest. He had deceived her with Ann Margolis and she him with a young policeman. It was a roundabout, a changing spinning thing that sometimes came to a long pause. He felt that he had reached a halt and that they must alight from it together, perhaps for life.

But he had not wanted to come. Undesired things would be revealed to him and she who would be questioned might speak of a love he wanted to forget. He stood at the rear while Burden banged on the glass and as he waited it came to him suddenly that it would not have mattered whether Wexford had brought him or not. Where else had he to go in the evenings? He would have come here anyway, as he always came.

It was Grover himself who came to let them in. Drayton expected him to be antagonistic, but the man was ingratiating and the oiliness of his greeting was more repulsive than hostility. His black hair was flattened down and combed to cover a small bald spot and it smelt of violet oil. One hand clamped to the small of his back, he ushered them into the shop and put on a light.

'Ray was here a month,' he said in answer to Wexford's question. 'Cawthorne gave him the push on the Saturday and he left here on the Tuesday. Or so Lin and the wife said. I never saw him, being as I was laid up.'

'I believe he had one of your attic rooms.'

Grover nodded. He was not an old man but he dressed like one. Drayton tried to keep his eyes still and his face expressionless as he noted the unbuttoned cardigan, the collarless shirt and the trousers that had never been brushed or pressed. 'His room's been done,' the newsagent said quickly. 'Lin cleaned it up. He never left nothing behind so it's no use you looking.'

'We'll look,' Burden said lightly. 'In a minute.' His cold eyes skimmed the magazines and then he strolled down to the dark corner where the library was. Grover followed him, hobbling.

'I've got nothing to tell you, Mr Burden,' he said. 'He didn't leave no forwarding address and he'd paid up his next month's rent in advance. There was three weeks to run.'

Burden took a book from the shelf and opened it in the middle, but his face did not change. 'Tell me about Tuesday evening,' he said.

'Tell you what? There's nothing to tell. Lin was in and out all afternoon. We wanted some bread and it's early closing here on Tuesdays — not for us, we don't close. She popped into Stowerton. The wife went to her whist drive around half seven and Lin was off somewhere — the launderette, that was it.' He paused, looking virtuous. Drayton felt angry and bewildered. The anger was for the way Grover used her as a maid of all work. He could not account for the bewilderment unless it was because he could not understand her father's lack of appreciation. 'I never saw Ray all day,' Grover said. 'I was in bed, you see. You'd have thought he'd have looked in on me to say good-bye and thank me for all I'd done for him.'

'Like what?' Burden snapped. 'Providing him with a lethal weapon, that sort of thing?'

'I never gave him that knife. He had it when he first come.'

'Go on.'

'Go on with what, Mr Burden?' Grover felt his back, gingerly probing the muscles. 'I told you I never saw Ray after the Monday. The doctor came before the wife went out and said I was to stop in bed . . .'

'Anyone else call? During the evening, I mean?'

'Only that girl,' Grover said.

Burden blew dust off the book he was holding and replaced it on the shelf. He came close to Grover and stood over him. 'What girl? What happened?'

'I was in bed, you see, and there was this banging on the shop door.' The newsagent gave Wexford a sly yet sullen glance. 'I thought it was you lot,' he said. 'It's all very well the doctor saying not to get out of bed on any account, but what are you supposed to do when someone comes banging fit to break the door in?' He winced, perhaps at the memory of an earlier and more acute pain. 'One of his customers it was. I'd seen her about before. Tall, good-looking piece, but older than my girl. You want to know what she looked like?'

'Of course. We haven't come here for social chit-chat, Grover.'

Standing by the paperback stand, Drayton felt almost sick. Burden's reprimand, far from disconcerting Grover, had provoked a sycophantic grin. His lips closed, he stretched them wide, half-closing one eye. This mockery of a smile seemed the ghost of Linda's own. In fact it was the begetter, and Drayton felt nausea rise in his throat.

'Bit of all right she was,' Grover said, again sketching his wink. 'Kind of white skin and black hair with two curly bits coming over her cheeks.' He seemed to reflect and he wetted his lips. 'Got up in black trousers and a spotted fur coat. "What d'you mean banging like that?" I said. "Can't you see we've closed?" "Where's Ray?" she says. "If he's in his room I'll go up and root him out." "You'll do no such thing," I said. "Anyway, he's not there." She looked proper put out at that so I asked her what she wanted him for. I don't know whether she didn't like me asking or whether she was thinking up some excuse. "I'm going to a party," she says, "and I'm bloody late as it is and now my car radiator's sprung a leak." Mind you, I couldn't see no car. Go up to his room, would you? I thought, and him going steady with my Linda.'

Drayton gave a small painful cough. It sounded like a groan in the silence which had fallen. Wexford looked at him and his eyes were cold.

Grover went on after a pause, ' "In that case you'd best take it to a garage," I said, and then I come out on to the pavement in my dressing gown. There was this white sports job stuck in my sideway with a pool of water underneath it. "I daren't drive it," she said. "I'm scared it'll blow up on me." '

'Did she go away?' Burden asked, discreetly jubilant.

'I reckon she did, but I didn't wait to see. I locked up again and went back to bed.'

'And you heard nothing more?'

'Nothing till the wife came in. I do remember thinking I hoped she'd got that white car of hers out on account of Lin not being able to get mine into the garage if it was there. But I dropped off to sleep and the next thing I knew was the wife getting into bed and saying Lin had come in half an hour before. D'you want to see his room now?'

Frowning slightly, Burden came out of his dark corner and stood under the light that hung above the counter. He glanced down the passage towards the side door that led to the alley. For a moment Drayton thought he had seen someone coming. Linda herself perhaps, and he braced himself to face the shock of her entrance, but Burden turned back to the newsagent and said:

'Where did he do this car servicing of his?'

'In my spare garage,' Grover said. 'I've got the two, you

see. My own car's in one and the other used to be let, but I lost my tenant and when young Ray said he wanted it I let him have it.' He nodded smugly. Perhaps this was the favour, or one of the favours, for which he had claimed Anstey's gratitude. 'I only charged him five bob a week extra. Mind you, he had plenty of customers. Been doing the same thing at his old digs, if you ask me.'

'I'd like to see both garages,' Burden said. 'Keys?'

'The wife's got them.' Grover went into the passage and took an old overcoat down from a wall hook. 'Or maybe Lin has. I don't know, I haven't had the car out for the best part of a fortnight, my back's been so bad.' He got into the coat with difficulty, screwing up his face.

'Keys, Drayton,' Wexford said laconically.

Half-way up the stairs, Drayton met Mrs Grover coming down. She looked at him incuriously and would have passed him, he thought, without a word.

'Can you let me have your garage keys, Mrs Grover?' he asked. Linda must have told her who and what he was.

'In the kitchen,' she said. 'Lin left them on the table.' She peered at him short-sightedly. Her eyes were as grey as her daughter's, but passionless, and if they had ever held tears they had long been swept away. 'I'm right in thinking you're her young fellow, aren't I?' Who he was, Drayton thought, but not what he was. 'She said you and her'd want the car tonight.' She shrugged. 'Don't let her dad know, that's all.'

'I'll go up, then.'

Mrs Grover nodded indifferently. Drayton watched her go down the stairs and leave by the side door. The kitchen door was open and he went in. Out of her parents' presence, his sickness went, but his heart was beating painfully. The keys lay on the table, one for each garage and one ignition key, and they were attached to a ring with a leather fob. Beside them was a pile of unfolded, unironed linen, and at the sight of it he felt a return of that bewilderment he had experienced in the shop. The keys were in his pocket and he had reached the head of the stairs when a door facing him opened and Linda came out.

For the first time he saw her hair hanging loose, curtaining her shoulders in a pale bright veil. She smiled at him softly and shyly but all the coquetry was gone.

'You're early,' she said as she had said that day when he had come to take her to Wexford. 'I'm not ready.' It came to him suddenly that she, like her mother, had no idea why he was there or that others of his calling were down below in the shop. Perhaps she need not know and the knowledge of what probably lay in one of those garages be kept from her a little longer. 'Wait for me,' she said. 'Wait in the shop. I won't be long.'

'I'll come back later,' he said. He thought he could go back to them without touching her, but he could neither move nor take his eyes from the spell of the tiny wavering smile and the golden cloak of hair.

'Mark,' she said and her voice was breathless. She came towards him trembling. 'Mark, you'll help me out of — out of all this, won't you? The linen on the table, the shop, the chores. He nodded, committing himself to what? To a yet unconsidered rescue? To marriage? 'You do love me, then?'

For once the question was not a signal for evasion and ultimate departure. That she should love him and want his love was to confer upon him an honour and to offer him a privilege. He took her in his arms and held her to him, touching her hair with his lips. 'I love you,' he said. He had used the forbidden verb and his only sensation was a breathless humble longing to give and give to the utmost of his capacity.

'I'd do anything for you,' he said. Then he let her go and he ran down the stairs.

Faded green paint was peeling from the garage doors. From their roof gutters water streamed out of a cracked drainpipe and made a scummy pool around the dustbins. Drayton let himself into the alley by the side door. His hands were shaking because of what had passed upstairs and because here, a few yards from where Grover and the policemen stood, he had first kissed her. He raised his hood against the drizzle and handed the keys to Wexford.

'You took your time about it.'

'We had to look for them,' Drayton muttered. Whether it was that 'we' or the badly told lie that gave rise to that chilly glance Drayton did not know. He went over to the dustbins and began shoving them out of the way.

'Before we open the doors,' Wexford said, 'there's one little point I'd like cleared up.' Although it was not cold, Grover had begun to rub his hands and stamp his feet. He gave the Chief Inspector a sour disgruntled look. 'Inspector Burden was about to ask you what time Miss Margolis, the girl with the white car, called on you. He was about to ask, but something else came up.'

'Let me refresh your memory,' Burden said quickly. 'Between seven thirty and eight, wasn't it? More like half past seven.'

The hunched shivering figure galvanised into sudden life.

'Half seven?' Grover said incredulously. 'You're joking. I told you the wife and Lin came in just after. Half seven, my foot. It was all of ten.'

'She was dead at ten!' Burden said desperately and he turned to appeal to Wexford who, bland and urbane, stood apparently lost in thought. 'She was dead! You're wrong, you mistook the time.'

'Let us open the doors,' said Wexford.

Drayton unlocked the first garage and it was empty. On the concrete floor was a black patch where oil had once been.

'This the one Anstey used?'

Grover nodded, viewing the deserted place suspiciously. 'There's only my car in the other one.'

'We'll look, just the same.'

The door stuck and Drayton had to put his shoulder to it. When the catch gave, Burden switched on his torch and the beam fell on an olive-green Mini.

It was Wexford who opened the unlocked boot and revealed two suitcases and a canvas bag of tools. Muttering, Grover prodded the bag until Burden removed his hand roughly. Through the rear window something could be seen lying on the passenger seat, a stiff bundle, one arm in a raincoat sleeve outflung, black hair from which the gloss had gone.

Wexford eased his bulky body between the side of the car and the garage wall. He pressed his thumb to the handle and opened the door as widely as he could in that confined space. His mouth set, for he could feel a fresh onset of nausea, Drayton followed him to stare over the Chief Inspector's shoulder.

The body which was sprawled before them had a blackened stain of dried blood across the breast of the raincoat and there was blood on the hilt and the blade of the knife someone had placed in its lap. Once this corpse had been young and beautiful — the waxen features had a comeliness and a symmetry about them even in death — but it had never been a woman.

'Anstey,' said Wexford succinctly.

A dark trickle had flowed from one corner of the dead man's mouth. Drayton put his handkerchief up to his face and stumbled out of the garage.

She had come from the side door and her hair was still loose, moving now in the faint wind. Her arms were bare and on them and on her face gooseflesh had arisen, white and rough, like a disease. Incredible that that mouth had once smiled and kissed.

When he saw her Drayton stopped. In the wind and the rain a death's head was confronting him, a skull staring through stretched skin, and it was much more horrifying than what he had just seen in the car. She parted the lips that had smiled for him and been his fetish and gave a scream of terror.

'You were going to save me! You loved me, you'd do anything for me . . . You were going to save me!' He put out his arms, not to enclose her but to ward her off. 'I went with you because you said you'd save me!' she screamed, and flinging herself upon him, tore at his cheeks with the bitten nails that could not wound. Something cold struck his chin. It was the silver chain that Anstey had stolen from his wife.

When Burden pulled her away and held her while she kicked and sobbed, Drayton stood with his eyes closed. He could sort out nothing from her cries and the harsh tumult of words, only that she had never loved him. It was a revelation more unspeakable than the other and it cut into his ears like a knife slitting membrane. He turned from the watching eyes, the man's stern, the girl's unbearable, stumbled from the alley into the backyard and was sick against the wall.

CHAPTER EIGHTEEN

She was waiting in Wexford's office. Two minutes before, down in the foyer, he had been warned of her presence, so he was able to repress natural astonishment and approach her with the aplomb of a Stanley.

'Miss Margolis, I presume?'

She must have been home. After arriving from wherever she had been, she must have called at the cottage to collect the ocelot coat. It was slung across her shoulders over a puce and peacock trouser suit. He noted her tan and the bronze glaze a hotter sun than that of Sussex had given to her dark hair.

'Rupert said you thought I was dead,' she said. 'But he does tend to be unsure of things. I thought I ought to come and clarify.' She sat on the edge of his desk, pushing papers out of her way. He felt like a guest in his own office and he would not have been surprised if she had asked him in just this imperiously gracious tone to sit down.

'I think I know most of it,' he said firmly. 'Suppose I tell you and you correct the more crashing howlers.' She smiled at him with catlike enjoyment. 'You've been in Spain or Italy. Perhaps Ibiza?'

'Positano. I flew back this morning.' She crossed her legs. The trousers had bell bottoms with pink fringes. 'Dickie Fairfax got through a hundred and fifty quid of my money in a week. You might not think it to look at me but I'm very bourgeois at heart. Love's all very well but it's abstract if you know what I mean. Money's concrete and when it's gone it's gone.' She added thoughtfully, 'So I abandoned him and came home. I'm afraid he may have to throw himself on the mercy of the consul.' Black eyebrows met over the bridge of that pretty hawk's nose. 'Perhaps Dickie's name doesn't mean anything to you?'

'Wild conjecture,' said Wexford, 'leads me to suppose that he is the young man who went to the Cawthornes' party and when he found you weren't there, sallied forth to find you, chanting passages from Omar Khayyám.'

'How clever of you!' If she looked at them like this, Wexford thought, and flattered them like that, it was no wonder they came to her purring and let her devour them. 'You see,' she said, 'I had every intention of going to the party but that bloody stupid car of mine broke down. I hadn't a clue there was anything wrong with it until after half past nine when I left for the party. It was boiling like a kettle all the way down the road. Then I thought of Ray. I knew he'd fix it for me . . . Oh, but you were going to do the talking!'

Wexford returned her smile, but not enthusiastically. He was growing tired of young women, their ways, their wiles, their diverse characteristics. 'I can only guess,' he said. 'Anstey was out. Then I think you tried to drive to the party but the car died on you . . .'

'You've left something out. I saw Ray first. I was trying to get the car out of the alley when the Grover girl came along in hers. Ray was in the passenger seat, looking terrible. She said he was drunk but, my God, he looked as if he was dying! She wouldn't let me go near him, so I just backed the car out and left them.'

'He *was* dying,' Wexford said, 'or dead already.' Her eyebrows went up to meet the bronzy fringe but she said nothing. 'You might have come to us, Miss Margolis. You're supposed to have a reputation for being public-spirited.'

'But I did tell you,' she said softly, 'or I told Rupert. When I left Grover's I got about a hundred yards up the road and the car conked out. Well, I got some water from a cottage and filled up the radiator. I sort of crawled about half way to Stowerton and I was sitting in the damn thing cursing my luck when Dickie came along, singing at the top of his voice about being merry with the fruitful grape. We'd had a sort of affair about six months ago, you see, and we sat in the car talking. I had all that money in my bag. Talk about sugar for the horse. He's always on the breadline and when he knew I was flush he said, what about you and me going off to Italy? Well, it is a bloody climate here, isn't it?'

Wexford sighed. She was her brother's sister all right.

'He was terribly sloshed,' she went on artlessly. Wexford thanked God Burden was otherwise engaged. 'We sat about for hours. In the end when he'd sobered up he went back to Cawthorne's for his car and I drove mine home. It must have been about one. Rupert was in bed and he hates being disturbed, so I wrote him a note, telling him where I was going and then I remembered about Ray. Go round to Grover's, I wrote, and see if Ray's all right because I don't like it . . .'

'Where did you leave it?'

'Leave what?'

'The note.'

'Oh, the note. I wrote it on a big sheet of cartridge paper and stuck it in front of a pile of newspapers on the kitchen counter. I suppose it got lost.'

'He threw it away,' said Wexford. 'The lights fused and he threw it away in the dark with the newspapers. He had an idea we might have sent someone to clear it all up for him.' He added thoughtfully, 'We thought it infra dig. Perhaps we should be more humble.'

'Well, it might have saved a lot of trouble,' said Anita Margolis. Suddenly she laughed, rocking back and forth so that the glass sculpture shook precariously. 'That's so like Roo. He thinks the world owes him a regiment of slaves.' She seemed to remember that the question under discussion was no laughing matter and she grew quickly serious. 'I met Dickie in the High Street,' she said, 'and we drove straight to London Airport.'

'Why did you change your coat?'

'Change my coat? Did I?'

'The one you're wearing now was found on the passenger seat of your car.'

'I remember now. It was raining like mad, so I put on the one raincoat I've got, a red vinyl thing. You see, Dickie's car makes such a racket I didn't want him disturbing the peace and waking Rupert, so I arranged to meet him in the High Street.'

She looked at him impishly. 'Have you ever sat for three hours in a car in a soaking wet fur coat?'

'I can't say I have.'

'The proverbial drowned rat,' she said.

'I suppose you fetched your passport at the same time.' She nodded and he asked in some exasperation, 'Don't you ever send postcards, Miss Margolis?'

'Oh, do call me Ann. Everyone does. As to postcards, I might if I was enjoying myself, but what with Dickie getting through simply millions of horrid little *lire*, I never got around to it. Poor Roo! I'm thinking of carrying him off to Ibiza tomorrow. He's so very disturbed and, anyway, I can't wear all my lovely new clothes here, can I?'

She slithered languidly from the desk and, too late to stop it, Wexford saw the hem of her spotted coat catch at fragile glass. The blue sculpture did a nose-dive, rising slightly in the air, and it was her lunge to save it that sent it crashing against the leg of his desk.

'God, I'm terribly sorry,' said Anita Margolis.

She retrieved a dozen of the larger fragments in a half-hearted, well-meaning way. 'What a shame!'

'I never liked it,' Wexford said. 'One thing before you go. Did you ever own that lighter?'

'What lighter?'

'A gold thing for Ann who lights someone's life.'

She bent her head thoughtfully and the big crescents of hair swept her cheeks. 'A lighter I once showed to Alan Kirkpatrick?' Wexford nodded. 'It was never mine,' she said. 'It was Ray's.'

'He serviced the car and left the lighter in it by accident?'

'Mm-hm. I returned it to him the next day. Admittedly, I more or less let Alan think it was mine.' She wriggled her toes in gilt-strapped sandals, grinding glass into Wexford's carpet. 'He was always so jealous, a natural bait for a tease. Have you seen his car? He wanted to take me out in it. Just what do you think I am? I said, an exhibit in the Lord Mayor's show? I do tease people, I'm afraid.'

'You have teased us all,' said Wexford severely.

The letter of resignation had been pushed aside with the other papers on his desk. It was still unopened, a thick white envelope with the Chief Inspector's name on it in a clear upright hand. Drayton had used good paper and he had used ink, not a ballpoint. He liked, Wexford knew, the good things of life, the best and beautiful things. You could get too fond of beauty, seduced and intoxicated.

Wexford thought he understood, but understanding would not stop him accepting that resignation. He only thanked God that it had all come to light in time. Another day and he'd have asked Drayton if he'd care to make one of a group of young people Sheila was organising to the theatre in Chichester. Another day . . .

Anita Margolis had left perfume behind her. *Chant d'Arômes* that Wexford's nose detected better than an analyst's tests. It was a breath of frivolity, expensive, untender, like herself. He opened the window to let it out before the coming interview.

Drayton came in five minutes before the appointed time and Wexford was on the floor, gathering up broken glass. The young man had not caught him at a disadvantage. Wexford, in getting down to this menial task, had considered any occupation preferable to pacing up and down because a raw detective constable had made a fool of himself.

'You're resigning, I see,' he said. 'I think you're doing the wisest thing.'

Drayton's face was almost unchanged, perhaps a little paler than usual. Four red marks showed on each cheek, but the girl's nails had been too short to break the skin. His expression held neither defiance nor humility. Wexford had expected embarrassment. A violent outburst of emotion, long contained, would not have surprised him. Perhaps that would come. For the moment he sensed a self-control so regulated that it seemed like ease.

'Look, Drayton,' he said heavily, 'no one supposes you actually made that girl any promises. I know you better than that. But the whole thing — well, it smells and that's a fact.'

The narrow contained smile might have been the rejoinder to a wary joke. 'The stink of corruption,' Drayton said and his tone was cooler than the smile. Between them the lingering French scent hung like the perfume of a judge's posy, shielding him from contamination.

'I'm afraid we all have to be beyond reproach.' What else was there to say? Wexford thought of the pompous sermon he had prepared and it sickened him. 'My God, Mark!' he burst out, moving around the desk to stand in front of and tower above Drayton. 'Why couldn't you take the hint and drop her when I told you? You knew her, she talked to you. Couldn't you put two and two together? That alibi she gave to Kirkpatrick and we thought he'd got at her — she was alibi-ing herself! It was eight when she saw him, not nine thirty.'

Drayton nodded slowly, his lips compressed.

Splinters of glass crunched under Wexford's shoes. 'She was on her way to Ruby's house when she saw him and Anstey was with her, only Kirkpatrick didn't notice. Grover told us she went out on Tuesday afternoon, to go shopping, he said. That was when she took the washing, in the afternoon, not in the evening.'

'I began to guess that,' Drayton murmured.

'And you said not a word?'

'It was just a feeling of unease, of something not being right.'

Wexford set his teeth. He had almost gasped with annoyance. Some of it was for his own folly in that, while disapproving, he had entered with a certain romantic and conspiratorial delight into Drayton's love affair.

'You were nosing around that place for God knows how long and all the time that fellow's body was lying in the garage. You knew her, you knew her damn' well . . .' His voice rose and he knew he was trying to spark off in Drayton an answering show of passion. 'Didn't natural curiosity make you want to know who her ex-boy friend was? They'd had a lodger for four weeks, a small dark lodger who disappeared on the night of the murder. Couldn't you have told us?'

'I didn't know,' Drayton said. 'I didn't want to know.'

'You have to want to know, Mark,' Wexford said tiredly. 'It's the first rule of the game.' He had forgotten what it was like to be in love, but he remembered a lighted window, a girl leaning out and a man standing in the shadows beneath. It distressed him to know that passion could exist and grief beside it, that they could twist a man's bones and not show on his face. He had no son, but from time to time it is given to every man to be another's father. 'I should go away from here,' he said, 'right away. No need for you to appear in court. You'll forget it all, you know. Believe me, you will.'

'What did she do?' Drayton said very quietly.

'Anstey held the knife to her throat. He relied on a girl's fear and his own attraction to make her acquiescent. She wasn't, you see. She got it away from him and stabbed him in a lung.'

'Was he dead when they got home?'

'I don't know. I don't think she does. Perhaps we never shall know. She left him and ran upstairs to her father, but the next day she couldn't go back. I can understand that. The time would come when her father would want the car and Anstey would be found. Before that happened she hoped for a miracle. I think you were to be that miracle. You were to help her get him away, but we got there first.'

'She had the car keys out ready for me.' He looked down and now his voice was almost a whisper.

'We came half an hour too soon, Drayton.'

The boy's head jerked up. 'I would never have done it.'

'Not when it came to the final crunch, eh? No, you would never have done it.' Wexford cleared his throat. 'What will you do now?'

'I'll get by,' Drayton said. He went to the door and a sliver of glass snapped under his shoe. 'You broke your ornament,' he said politely. 'I'm sorry.'

In the hall he put on his duffel coat and raised the hood. Thus dressed, with a lock of black hair falling across his forehead, he looked like a mediaeval squire who has lost his knight and abandoned his crusade. When he had said good night to Sergeant Camb who knew nothing but that young Drayton was somehow in hot water, he came out into the wet windy street and began to walk towards his lodgings. By a small detour he could have avoided passing Grover's shop, but he did not take it. The place was in total darkness as if they had all moved away and in the alley the cobbles were wet stones on the floor of a cave.

Two months, three months, a year perhaps, and the worst would be over. Men have died from time to time and worms have eaten them, but not of love . . . The world was full of jobs and full of girls. He would find one of each and they would do him very well The daffodils in the florist's window had an untouched exquisite freshness. He would always think of her whenever he saw something beautiful in an ugly setting.

But you got over everything eventually. He wished only that he did not feel so sick and at the same time so very young. The last time he had felt like this was fourteen years ago when his mother had died and that also was the last time he had wept.

PUT
ON BY
CUNNING

For Simon

So shall you hear . . .
Of deaths put on by cunning and forc'd cause;
And, in this upshot, purposes mistook
Fall'n on th'inventors' heads — all this can I
Truly deliver.

Hamlet

Part One

CHAPTER ONE

Against the angels and apostles in the windows the snow fluttered like plucked down. A big soft flake struck one of the Pre-Raphaelite haloes and clung there, cotton wool on gold tinsel. It was something for an apathetic congregation to watch from the not much warmer interior as the rector of St Peter's, Kingsmarkham, came to the end of the second lesson. St Matthew, chapter fifteen, for 27 January.

'For out of the heart proceed evil thoughts, murders, adulteries, fornications, thefts, false witness, blasphemies. These are the things which defile a man. . . .'

Two of his listeners turned their eyes from the pattern the snow was making on a red and blue and yellow and purple 'Annunciation' and waited expectantly. The rector closed the heavy Bible with its dangling marker and opened an altogether more mundane-looking, small black book of the exercise variety. He cleared his throat.

'I publish the banns of marriage between Sheila Katherine Wexford, spinster, of this parish, and Andrew Paul Thorverton, bachelor, of the parish of St John, Hampstead. This is the first time of asking. And between Manuel Camargue, widower, of this parish, and Dinah Baxter Sternhold, widow, of the parish of St Mary, Forby. This is the third time of asking. If any of you know cause or just impediment why these persons should not be joined together in holy matrimony, ye are to declare it.'

He closed the book. Manuel Camargue resigned himself, for the third week in succession, to the sermon. As the congregation settled itself, he looked about him. The same crowd of old faithfuls came each week. He saw only one newcomer, a beautiful fair-haired girl whom he instantly recognized without being able to put a name to her. He worried about this a good deal for the next half-hour, trying to place her, annoyed with himself because his memory had become so hopeless and glasses no longer did much for his eyes.

The name came to him just as everyone was getting up to

leave. Sheila Wexford. Sheila Wexford, the actress. That was who it was. He and Dinah had seen her last autumn in that Somerset Maugham revival, though what the name of the play had been escaped him. She had been at school with Dinah, they still knew each other slightly. Her banns had been called before his but her name hadn't registered because of that insertion of Katherine. It was odd that two people as famous as they should have had their banns called simultaneously in this country parish church.

He looked at her again. She was dressed in a coat of sleek pale fur over a black wool dress. Her eye caught his and he saw that she also recognized him. She gave him a quick faint smile, a smile that was conspiratorial, rueful, gay, ever so slightly embarrassed, all those things expressed as only an actress of her calibre could express them. Camargue countered with a smile of his own, the best he could do.

It was still snowing. Sheila Wexford put an umbrella up and made an elegant dash towards the lychgate. Should he offer her a lift to wherever she lived? Camargue decided that his legs were inadequate to running after her, especially through six-inch deep snow. When he reached the gate he saw her getting into a car driven by a man at least old enough to be her father. He felt a pang for her. Was this the bridegroom? And then the absurdity of such a thought, coming from him, struck him forcefully and with a sense which he often had of the folly of human beings and their blindness to their own selves.

Ted was waiting in the Mercedes. Reading the *News of the World*, hands in woollen gloves. He had the engine running to work the heater and the wipers and the demisters. When he saw Camargue he jumped out and opened the rear door.

'There you are, Sir Manuel. I put a rug in seeing it's got so perishing.'

'What a kind chap you are,' said Camargue. 'It was jolly cold in church. Let's hope it'll warm up for the wedding.'

Ted said he hoped so but the long range weather forecast was as gloomy as per usual. If he hadn't held his employer in such honour and respect he would have said he'd have his love to keep him warm. Camargue knew this and smiled to himself. He pulled the rug over his knees. Dinah, he thought, my Dinah.

Towards her he felt a desire as passionate, as youthful, as intense, as any he had known as a boy. But he would never touch her, he knew better than that, and his mouth curled with distaste at the idea of it, of him and her together. It would be enough for him that she should be his dear companion — for a little while.

They had entered the gates and were mounting the long curving drive that led up to the house. Ted drove in the two channels, now filling once more with snow, which he had dug out that morning. From the smooth, pure and radiant whiteness, flung like a soft and spotless cloth over the hillocks and little valleys of Camargue's garden, rose denuded silver birches, poplars and willows, and the spikes of conifers, dark green and slate-blue and golden-yellow, as snugly clothed as gnomes.

The jam factory came into view quite suddenly. Camargue called it the jam factory, or sometimes the shoebox, because it was unlike any of the houses around. Not mock or real Tudor, not fake or genuine Georgian, but a long box with lots of glass, and at one end, dividing the original building from the newer wing, a tower with a peaked roof like an oast house. Perched on the weathervane, a facsimile of a treble clef in wrought iron, was a seagull, driven inland in its quest for food. It looked as white as the snow itself against the cinder-dark sky.

Ted's wife, Muriel, opened the front door. You entered the house at the lower level, where it was built into the hillside. There was a wide hall here which led through an arch into the dining room.

'It's so cold, sir,' said Muriel, 'that I'm cooking you a proper lunch since you said you wouldn't be going to Mrs Sternhold's.'

'Jolly thoughtful of you,' said Camargue, who no longer much cared what he ate. Muriel took his coat away to dry it. She and Ted lived in a house in the grounds, a period piece and as much unlike the jam factory as could be. Camargue liked her to have her afternoons off and all of her Sundays, but he couldn't be always checking her generous impulses. When he was half-way up the stairs the dog Nancy came down to meet him, wide smiling mouth and eager pink tongue and young strong paws capable of sending him flying. She was his fifth alsatian, a rich roan colour, just two years old.

The drawing room, two of its walls entirely glass, shone with the curious light that is uniquely reflected off snow. The phone began to ring as he stepped off the top stair.

'Were they well and truly called?'

'Yes, darling, the third time of asking. And at St Peter's?'

'Yes. My word, it was cold, Dinah. Is it snowing in Forby?'

'Well, it is but not all that heavily. Won't you change your mind and come? The main roads are all right and you know Ted won't mind. I do wish you'd come.'

'No. You'll have your parents. They've met me. Let them get over the shock a bit before Saturday.' Camargue laughed at her exclamation of protest. 'No, my dear, I won't come today. Muriel's cooking lunch for me. Just think, after Saturday you'll have to have all your meals with me, no excuses allowed.'

'Manuel, shall I come over this evening?'

He laughed. 'No, please.' It was strange how his accent became more marked when he talked to her. Must be emotion, he supposed. 'The villages will be cut off from Kingsmarkham by tonight, mark my words.'

He went into the music room, the dog following him. Up inside the cone-shaped roof of the tower it was dark like twilight. He looked at the flute which lay in its open case on the table, and then reflectively, no longer with pain, at his clawed hands. The flute had been exposed like that to show to Dinah's mother and Muriel would have been too much in awe of it to put it away. Camargue closed the lid of the case and sat down at the piano. He had never been much of a pianist, a second-class concert average, so it brought him no frustration or sadness to strum away occasionally with those (as he called them) silly old hands of his. He played *Für Elise* while Nancy, who adored piano music, thumped her tail on the marble floor.

Muriel called him to lunch. He went downstairs for it. She liked to lay the big mahogany table with lace and silver and glass just for him, and to wait on him. Far more than he had ever been or could ever be, she was aware of what was due to Sir Manuel Camargue. Ted came in as he was having coffee and said he would take Nancy out now, a good long hike in the snow, he said, she loved snow. And he'd break the ice at the edge of the lake. Hearing the chain on her lead rattle, Nancy nearly fell downstairs in her haste to be out.

Camargue sometimes tried to stop himself sleeping the afternoons away. He was rarely successful. He had a suite of rooms in the wing beyond the tower; bedroom, bathroom, small sitting room where Nancy's basket was, and he would sit determinedly in his armchair, reading or playing records — he was mad about James Galway at the moment. Galway, he thought, was heaps better than he had ever been — but he would always nod off. Often he slept till five or six. He put on the Flute Concerto, Köchel 313, and as the sweet, bright, liquid notes poured out, looked at himself in the long glass. He was still, at any rate, tall. He was thin. Thin like a ramshackle scarecrow, he thought, like an old junk-shop skeleton, with hands that looked as if every joint had been broken and put together again awry. *Tout casse, tout lasse, tout passe.* Now that he was so old he often thought in one or other of the two languages of his infancy. He sat down in the armchair and listened to the music Mozart wrote for a cantankerous Dutchman, and by the time the second movement had begun he was asleep.

Nancy woke him, laying her head in his lap. She had been back from her walk a long time, it was nearly five. Ted wouldn't come back to take her out again. Camargue would let her out himself and perhaps walk with her as far as the lake. It had stopped snowing, and the last of the daylight, a curious shade of yellow, gilded the whiteness and threw long blue shadows. Camargue took James Galway off the turntable and put him back in the sleeve. He walked along the passage and through the music room, pausing to straighten a crooked picture, a photograph of the building which housed the Camargue School of Music at Wellridge, and passed on into the drawing room. As he approached the tea tray Muriel had left for him, the phone rang. Dinah again.

'I phoned before, darling. Were you asleep?'

'What else?'

'I'll come over in the morning, shall I, and bring the rest of the presents? Mother and Dad have brought us silver pastry forks from my uncle, my godfather.'

'I must say, people are jolly generous, the second time

round for both of us. I'll have the drive specially cleared for you. Ted shall be up to do it by the crack of dawn.'

'Poor Ted.' He was sensitive to the slight change in her tone and he braced himself. 'Manuel, you haven't heard any more from — Natalie?'

'From that woman,' said Camargue evenly, 'no.'

'I shall have another go at you in the morning, you know, to make you see reason. You're quite wrong about her, I'm sure you are. And to take a step like changing your will without . . .'

His accent was strong as he interrupted her. 'I saw her, Dinah, not you, and I know. Let's not speak of it again, eh?'

She said simply, 'Whatever you wish. I only want what's best for you.'

'I know that,' he said. He talked to her a little longer and then he went downstairs to make his tea. The tranquillity of the day had been marred by Dinah's raising the subject of Natalie. It forced him to think of that business again when he had begun to shut it out.

He carried the teapot upstairs and lifted the folded napkin from the plate of cucumber sandwiches. That woman, whoever she was, had made the tea and brought the pot up, and it was after that that she had looked at Cazzini's golden gift on the wall and he had known. As is true of all honest and guileless people, Camarge resented attempts to practise deceit on him far more than do those who are themselves deceitful. It had been a hateful affront, and all the worse because it had taken advantage of an old man's weakness and a father's affection. Dinah's plea did not at all alter his feelings. It only made him think he should have told the police or his solicitors, after all. But no. He had told the woman that he had seen through her and he had told her what he meant to do, and now he must do his best to forget it. Dinah was what future he had, Dinah would be his daughter and more than daughter.

He sat by the window with the curtains undrawn, watching the snow turn blue, then glow dully white again as the darkness closed in. The moon was coming up, a full, cold, midwinter's moon, a glowing greenish-white orb. At seven he took the tea things down and fed Nancy a large can of dog meat.

By the light of the moon he could see the lake quite clearly

568

from the drawing-room window. To call it a lake was to flatter it, it was just a big pond really. It lay on the other side of the drive, down a shallow slope and ringed with willow trees and hawthorn bushes. Camargue could see that Ted, as good as his word, had been down to the pond that afternoon and broken the ice for air to get in to the fish. There were carp in the pond, some of them very large and very old. Ted's footprints led down to the water's edge and back up again to the drive. He had cast the ice on to the bank in great grey blocks. The moon showed it all up as well as any arc lamp. Nancy's pawprints were everywhere, and in places in the drifts there were signs of where she had plunged and rolled. He stroked her smooth brown head, drawing her against him, gently pushing her to settle down and sleep at his feet. The moon sailed in a black and shining sky from which all the heavy cloud had gone. He opened his book, the biography of an obscure Romanian composer who had once written an étude especially for him, and read for an hour or so.

When it got to half-past eight he could feel himself nodding off again, so he got up and stretched and stood in the window. To his surprise he saw it was snowing once more, snow falling out of the wrack which was drifting slowly over the clear sky and towards where the moon was. The conifers were powdered again, all but one. Then he saw the tree move. He had often thought that by night and in the half-light and through his failing eyes those trees looked like men. Now he had actually mistaken a man for a tree. Or a woman for a tree. He couldn't tell whether it had been Ted or Muriel that he had seen, a trousered figure in a heavy coat moving up now where the path must be towards the birch copse. It must have been one of them. Camargue decided to postpone letting Nancy out for ten minutes. If Ted saw him he would take over and fuss and probably insist on giving the dog a proper walk which she didn't need after all the exercise she had had. If Muriel saw him she would very likely want to come in and make him cocoa.

The figure in the garden had disappeared. Now the moon was no longer so bright. He couldn't remember that he had ever before seen such snow in all the years he had lived in Sussex. In his youth, in the Pyrenees, the snows had come like this with an even more bitter cold. It was remembering those days that had made him plant in this garden all the little fir trees and yews and junipers. . . .

He could have sworn he saw another tree move. How grotesque was old age when the faculties one took for granted like trusted friends began to play on one malicious practical jokes. He called out:

'Nancy! Time to go out.'

She was there at the head of the stairs long before he was. If he had gone first she would have knocked him over. He walked down behind her, propelling her with his toe when she looked anxiously back and up at him. At the foot of the stairs he switched on the outside light to illuminate the wide court into which the drive led. The snowflakes danced like sparks in the yellow light but when he opened the door the sharp cold of the night rushed in to meet him. Nancy bounded out into the whirling snow. Camargue took his sheepskin coat and gloves and a walking-stick from the cloaks cupboard and followed her out.

She was nowhere to be seen, though her paws had ploughed a path down the slope towards the lake. He fastened his coat and pulled the woollen scarf up around his throat. Nancy, though well aware this outing was no regular walk but merely for the purpose of stimulating and answering a call of nature, nevertheless would sometimes go off. If the weather conditions were right, damp and muggy, for instance, or like this, she had been known to go off for half an hour. It would be a nuisance were she to do that tonight when he felt so tired that even on his feet, even with this icy air stinging his face, he could feel drowsiness closing in on him.

'Nancy! Nancy, where are you?'

He could easily go back into the house and phone Ted and ask him to come over and await the dog's return. Ted wouldn't mind. On the other hand, wasn't that yielding to the very helplessness he was always striving against? What business had he to be getting married, to be setting up house again, even recommencing a social life, if he couldn't do such a little thing for himself as letting a dog out before he went to bed? What he would do was return to the house and sit in the chair in the hall and wait for Nancy to come back. If he fell asleep her scraping at the front door would awaken him.

Even as he decided this he did the very opposite. He followed the track she had made down the slope to the lake, calling her, irritably now, as he went.

The marks Ted had made when he broke the ice at the water's edge were already obliterated by snow, while Nancy's fresh tracks were fast becoming covered. Only the stacked ice showed where Ted had been. The area he had cleared was again iced over with a thin grey crust. The lake was a sombre sheet of ice with a faint sheen on it that the clouded moon made, and the willows, which by daylight looked like so many crouched spiders or daddy-long-legs, were laden with snow that clung to them and changed their shape. Camargue called the dog again. Only last week she had done this to him and then had suddenly appeared out of nowhere and come skittering across the ice towards him.

He began breaking the new ice with his stick. Then he heard the dog behind him, a faint crunching on the snow. But when he turned round, ready to seize her collar in the hook of the walking-stick, there was no dog there, there was nothing there but the gnome conifers and the light shining down on the white sheet of the circular courtyard. He would break up the rest of the thin ice, clear an area a yard long and a foot wide as Ted had done, and then he would go back into the house and wait for Nancy indoors.

Again the foot crunched behind him, the tree walked. He stood up and turned and, raising his stick as if to defend himself, looked into the face of the tree that moved.

CHAPTER TWO

The music met Chief Inspector Wexford as he let himself into his house. A flute playing with an orchestra. This was one of Sheila's dramatic gestures, he supposed, contrived to time with his homecoming. It was beautiful music, slow, measured, secular, yet with a religious sound.

His wife was knitting, on her face the amused, dry, very slightly exasperated expression it often wore while Sheila was around. And Sheila would be very much around for the next three weeks, having unaccountably decided to be married from home, in her own parish church, and to establish the proper period of residence beforehand in her father's house. She sat on the floor, between the log fire and the record player, her cheek resting on one round white arm that trailed with grace upon a sofa cushion, her pale gold water-straight hair half covering her face. When she lifted her head and shook her hair back he saw that she had been crying.

'Oh, Pop, darling, isn't it sad? They've had this tremendous obituary programme for him on the box. Even Mother shed a tear. And then we thought we'd mourn him with his own music.'

Wexford doubted very much if Dora, a placid and eminently sensible woman, had expressed these extravagant sentiments. He picked up the record sleeve. Mozart, Concerto for Flute and Harp, K 229; the English Chamber Orchestra, conductor, Raymond Leppard; flute, Manuel Camargue; harp, Marisa Roblès.

'We actually heard him once,' said Dora. 'Do you remember? At the Wigmore Hall it was, all of thirty years ago.'

'Yes.'

But he could scarcely remember. The pictured face on the sleeve, too sensitive, too mobile to be handsome, the eyes alight with a kind of joyous humour, evoked no image from the past. The movement came to an end and now the music became bright, liquid, a singable tune, and Camargue, who was dead, alive again in his flute. Sheila wiped her eyes and got up to kiss her father. It was all of eight years since he and she had lived under the same roof. She had become a swan since then, a famous lady, a tele-face. But she still kissed him when he came and went, putting her arms around his neck like a nervous child. Wryly, he liked it.

He sat down, listening to the last movement while Dora finished her row in the Fair Isle and went to get his supper. Andrew's regular evening phone call prevented Sheila from getting full dramatic value out of her memorial to Camargue, and by the time she came back into the room the record was over and her father was eating his steak-and-kidney pie.

'You didn't actually know him, did you, Sheila?'

She thought he was reproaching her for her tears. 'I'm sorry, Pop, I cry so easily. It's a matter of having to learn how, you know, and then not being able to unlearn.'

He grinned at her. 'Thus on the fatal bank of Nile weeps the deceitful crocodile? I didn't mean that, anyway. Let me put it more directly. Did you know him personally?'

She shook her head. 'I think he recognized me in church. He must have known I come from round here.' It was nothing that she should be recognized. She was recognized wherever she went. For five years the serial in which she played the most beautiful of the air hostesses had been on television twice a week at a peak-viewing time. Everybody watched *Runway*, even though a good many said shamefacedly that they 'only saw the tail-end before the news' or 'the kids have it on'. Stewardess Curtis was famous for her smile. Sheila smiled it now, her head tilted reflectively. 'I know his wife-that-was-to-be personally,' she said. 'Or I used to. We were at school together.'

'A young girl?'

'Thank you kindly, father dear. Let's say young to be marrying Sir Manuel. Mid-twenties. She brought him to see me in *The Letter* last autumn but I didn't talk to them, he was too tired to come round afterwards.'

It was Dora who brought them back from gossip to grandeur. 'In his day he was said to be the world's greatest flautist. I remember when he founded that school at Wellridge and Princess Margaret came down to open it.'

'D'you know what its pupils call it? Windyridge.' Sheila mimed the blowing of a woodwind, fingers dancing. Then, suddenly, the tears had started once more to her eyes. 'Oh, to die like that!'

Who's Who is not a volume to be found in many private houses. Wexford had a copy because Sheila was in it. He took it down from the shelf, turned to the C's and read aloud:

'Camargue, Sir Manuel, Knight. Companion of Honour, Order of the British Empire, Chevalier of the Legion of Honour. British fluteplayer. Born Pamplona, Spain, 3 June, 1902, son of Aristide Camargue and Ana Parral. Educated privately with father, then at Barcelona Conservatoire. Studied under Louis Fleury.

'Professor of Flute, Madrid Conservatoire, 1924 to 1932. Fought on Republican side Spanish Civil War, escaped to England 1938. Married 1942 Kathleen Lister. One daughter. Naturalized British subject 1946. Concert flautist, has toured Europe, America, Australia, New Zealand and South Africa. Founded 1964 at Wellridge, Sussex, the Kathleen Camargue School of Music in memory of his wife, and in 1968 the Kathleen Camargue Youth Orchestra. Recreations apart from music: walking, reading, dogs. Address: Sterries, Ploughman's Lane, Kingsmarkham, Sussex.'

'They say it's a dream of a house,' said Sheila. 'I wonder if she'll sell, that one daughter? Because if she does Andrew and I might really consider . . . Wouldn't you like me living just up the road, Pop?'

'He may have left it to your friend,' said Wexford.

'So he may. Well, I do hope so. Poor Dinah, losing her first husband that she *adored* and then her second that never was. She deserves some compensation. I shall write her a letter of sympathy. No, I won't. I'll go and see her. I'll phone her first thing in the morning and I'll . . .'

'I'd leave it a day or two if I were you,' said her father. 'First thing in the morning is going to be the inquest.'

'*Inquest?*' Sheila uttered the word in the loaded, aghast tone of Lady Bracknell. 'Inquest? But surely he died a perfectly natural death?'

Dora, conjuring intricately with three different shades of

wool, looked up from her pattern. 'Of course he didn't. Drowning, or whatever happened to him, freezing to death, you can't call that natural.'

'I mean, he didn't do it on purpose and no one did it to him.'

It was impossible for Wexford to keep from laughing at these ingenuous definitions of suicide and homicide. 'In most cases of sudden death,' he said, 'and in all cases of violent death there must be an inquest. It goes without saying the verdict is going to be that it was an accident.'

Misadventure.

This verdict, which can sound so grotesque when applied to the death of a baby in a cot or a patient under anaesthetic, appropriately described Camargue's fate. An old man, ankle-deep in snow, had lost his foothold in the dark, slipping over, sliding into water to be trapped under a lid of ice. If he had not drowned he would within minutes have been dead from hypothermia. The snow had continued to fall, obliterating his footprints. And the frost, ten degrees of it, had silently sealed up the space into which the body had slipped. Only a glove — it was of thick black leather and it had fallen from his left hand — remained to point to where he lay, one curled finger rising up out of the drifts. Misadventure.

Wexford attended the inquest for no better reason than to keep warm, the police station central heating having unaccountably broken down the night before. The venue of the inquest (Kingsmarkham Magistrates' Court, Court Two, Upstairs) enjoyed a reputation for being kept in winter at a temperature of eighty degrees. To this it lived up. Having left his rubber boots just inside the door downstairs, he sat at the back of the court, basking in warmth, surreptitiously peeling off various disreputable layers, a khaki green plastic mac of muddy translucency, an aged black-and-grey herringbone-tweed overcoat, a stole-sized scarf of matted fawnish wool.

Apart from the *Kingsmarkham Courier* girl in one of the press seats, there were only two women present, and these two sat so far apart as to give the impression of choosing each to ostracize the other. One would be the daughter, he supposed, one the bride. Both were dressed darkly, shabbily and without distinction. But the woman in the front row had the eyes and profile of a Callas, her glossy black hair piled in the fashion of a Floating World geisha, while the other, seated a yard or two from him, was a little mouse, headscarfed, huddled, hands folded. Neither, as far as he could see, bore the remotest resemblance to the face on the record sleeve with its awareness and its spirituality. But when, as the verdict came, the geisha woman turned her head and her eyes, dark and brilliant, for a moment met his, he saw that she was far older than Sheila, perhaps ten years older. This, then, must be the daughter. And as the conviction came to him, the coroner turned his gaze upon her and said he would like to express his sympathy with Sir Manuel's daughter in her loss and a grief which was no less a personal one because it was shared by the tens of thousands who had loved, admired and been inspired by his music. He did not think he would be exceeding his duty were he to quote Samuel Johnson and say that it matters not how a man dies but how he has lived.

Presumably no one had told him of the dead man's intended re-marriage. The little mouse got up and crept away. Now it was all over, the beauty with the black eyes got up too — to be enclosed immediately in a circle of men. This of course was chance, Wexford told himself, they were the escort who had brought her, her father's doctor, his servant, a friend or two. Yet he felt inescapably that this woman would always wherever she was be in a circle of men, watched, admired, desired. He got back into his coverings and ventured out into the bitter cold of Kingsmarkham High Street.

Here the old snow lay heaped at the pavement edges in long, low mountain ranges and the new snow, gritty and sparkling, dusted it with fresh whiteness. A yellowish-leaden sky looked full of snow. It was only a step from the court to the police station, but a long enough step in this weather to get chilled to the bone.

On the forecourt, between a panda car and the chief constable's Rover, the heating engineer's van was still parked. Wexford went tentatively through the swing doors. Inside it was as cold as ever and Sergeant Camb, sitting behind his counter, warmed mittened hands on a mug of steaming tea. Burden, Wexford reflected, if he had any sense, would have taken himself off somewhere warm for lunch. Very likely to the Carousel Cafe, or what used to be the Carousel before it was taken over by Mr Haq and became the Pearl of Africa.

This was a title or sobriquet given (according to Mr Haq) to Uganda, his native land. Mr Haq claimed to serve authentic Ugandan cuisine, what he called 'real' Ugandan food, but since no one knew what this was, whether he meant food consumed by the tribes before colonization or food introduced by Asian immigrants or food eaten today by westernized Ugandans, or what these would be anyway, it was difficult to query any dish. Fried potatoes and rice accompanied almost everything, but for all Wexford knew this might be a feature of Ugandan cooking. He rather liked the place, it fascinated him, especially the plastic jungle vegetation.

Today this hung and trembled in the steamy heat and seemed to sweat droplets on its leathery leaves. The windows had become opaque, entirely misted over with condensation. It was like a tropical oasis in the Arctic. Inspector Burden sat at a table eating Nubian chicken with rice Ruwenzori, anxiously keeping in view his new sheepskin jacket, a Christmas present from his wife, which Mr Haq had hung up on the palm tree hatstand. He remarked darkly as Wexford walked in that anyone might make off with it, you never could tell these days.

'Round here they might cook it,' said Wexford. He also ordered the chicken with the request that for once potatoes might not come with it. 'I've just come from the inquest on Camargue.'

'What on earth did you go to that for?'

'I hadn't anything much else on. I reckoned it would be warm too and it was.'

'All right for some,' Burden grumbled. 'I could have found a job for you.' Since their friendship had deepened, some of his old deference to his chief, though none of his respect, had departed. 'Thieving and break-ins, we've never had so much of it. That kid old Atkinson let out on bail, he's done three more jobs in the meantime. And he's not seventeen yet, a real little villain.' Sarcasm made his tone withering. 'Or that's what I call him. The psychiatrist says he's a pathological kleptomaniac with personality-scarring caused by traumata broadly classifiable as paranoid.' He snorted, was silent, then said on an altered note, 'Look, do you think you were wise to do that?'

'Do what?'

'Go to that inquest. People will think . . . I mean, it's possible they might think . . .'

'People will think!' Wexford scoffed. 'You sound like a dowager lecturing a debutante. What will they think?'

'I only meant they might think there was something fishy about the death. Some hanky-panky. I mean, they see you there and know who you are and they say to themselves, he wouldn't have been there if it had all been as straightforward as the coroner . . .'

He was saved from an outburst of Wexford's temper by an intervention from outside. Mr Haq had glided up to beam upon them. He was small, smiling, very black yet very Caucasian, with a mouthful of startlingly white, madly uneven, large teeth.

'Everything to your liking, I hope, my dear?' Mr Haq called all his customers 'my dear', irrespective of sex, perhaps supposing it to be a genderless term of extreme respect such as 'excellency'. 'I see you are having the rice Ruwenzori.' He bowed a little. 'A flavourful and scrumptious recipe from the peoples who live in the Mountains of the Moon.' Talking like a television commercial for junk food was habitual with him.

'Very nice, thank you,' said Wexford.

'You are welcome, my dear.' Mr Haq smiled so broadly that it seemed some of his teeth must spill out. He moved off among the tables, ducking his head under the polythene fronds which trailed from polyethylene pots in polystyrene plant-holders.

'Are you going to have any pudding?'

'Shouldn't think so,' said Wexford, and he read from the menu with gusto, 'Cake Kampala or ice cream eau-de-Nil — does he mean the colour or what it's made of? Anyway, there's enough ice about without eating it.' He hesitated. 'Mike, I don't see that it matters what people think in this instance. Camargue met his death by misadventure, there's no doubt about that.

Surely, though interest in the man will endure for years, the manner of his death can only be a nine days' wonder. As a matter of fact, the coroner said something like that.'

Burden ordered coffee from the small, shiny, damson-eyed boy, heir to Mr Haq, who waited at their table. 'I suppose I was thinking of Hicks.'

'The manservant or whoever he was?'

'He found that glove and then he found the body. It wasn't really strange but it might look strange the way he found the dog outside his back door and took her back to Sterries and put her inside without checking to see where Camargue was.'

'Hicks's reputation won't suffer from my presence in court,' said Wexford. 'I doubt if there was a soul there, bar the coroner, who recognized me.' He chuckled. 'Or if they did it'd only be as Stewardess Curtis's dad.'

They went back to the police station. The afternoon wore away into an icy twilight, an evening of hard frost. The heating came on with a pop just as it was time to go home. Entering his living room, Wexford was greeted by a large, bronze-coloured alsatian, baring her teeth and swinging her tail. On the sofa, next to his daughter, sat the girl who had crept away from the inquest, Camargue's pale bride.

CHAPTER THREE

He had noticed the Volkswagen parked in the ruts of ice outside but had thought little of it. Sheila got up and introduced the visitor.

'Dinah, this is my father. Pop, I'd like you to meet Dinah Sternhold. She was engaged to Sir Manuel, you know.'

It was immediately apparent to Wexford that she had not noticed him at the inquest. She held out her small hand and looked at him without a flicker of recognition. The dog had backed against her legs and now sat down heavily at her feet, glaring at Wexford in a sullen way.

'Do forgive me for bringing Nancy.' She had a soft low unaffected voice. 'But I daren't leave her alone, she howls all the time. My neighbours complained when I had to leave her this morning.'

'She was Sir Manuel's dog,' Sheila explained.

A master-leaver and a fugitive, Wexford reflected, eyeing the alsatian who had abandoned Camargue to his fate. Or gone to fetch help? That, of course, was a possible explanation of the curious behaviour of the dog in the night.

Dinah Sternhold said, 'It's Manuel she howls for, you see. I can only hope she won't take too long to — to forget him. I hope she'll get over it.'

Was she speaking of the dog or of herself? His answer could have applied to either. 'She will. She's young.'

'He often said he wanted me to have her if — if anything happened to him. I think he was afraid of her going to someone who might not be kind to her.'

Presumably she meant the daughter. Wexford sought about in his mind for some suitable words of condolence, but finding none that sounded neither mawkish nor pompous, he kept quiet. Sheila, anyway, could always be relied on to make conversation. While she was telling some rather inapposite alsatian anecdote, he studied Dinah Sternhold. Her little round sallow face was pinched with a kind of bewildered woe. One might almost believe she had loved the old man and not merely been in it for the money. But that was a little too much to swallow, distinguished and reputedly kind and charming as he had been. The facts were that he had been seventy-eight and she was certainly fifty years less than that.

Gold-digger, however, she was not. She appeared to have extorted little in the way of pre-marital largesse out of Camargue. Her brown tweed coat had seen better days, she wore no jewellery but an engagement ring, in which the ruby was small and the diamonds pinheads.

He wondered how long she intended to sit there, her hand grasping the dog's collar, her head bowed as if she were struggling to conquer tears or at least conceal them. But suddenly she jumped up.

'I must go.' Her voice became intense, ragged, charged with a sincerity that was almost fierce. 'It was so *kind* of you to come to me, Sheila. You don't know how grateful I am.'

'No need,' Sheila said lightly. 'I wanted to come. It was kind of *you* to drive me home. I had a hire car, Pop, because I was scared to drive in the snow but Dinah wasn't a bit scared to bring me back in the snow and the dark.'

They saw Dinah Sternhold out to her car. Ice was already forming on the windscreen. She pushed the dog on to the back seat and got to work competently on the windows with a de-icing spray. Wexford was rather surprised that he felt no compunction about letting her drive away, but her confidence seemed absolute, you could trust her somehow to look after herself and perhaps others too. Was it this quality about her that Camargue had needed and had loved? He closed the gate, rubbed his hands. Sheila, shivering, ran back into the house.

'Where's your mother?'

'Round at Syl's. She ought to be back any minute. Isn't Dinah nice? I felt so sorry for her, I went straight over to Forby as soon as the inquest was over. We talked and talked. I think maybe I did her a bit of good.'

'Hmm,' said Wexford.

The phone started to ring. Andrew, punctual to the minute. 'Oh, darling,' Wexford heard Sheila say, 'do you remember my

telling you about someone I know who was going to marry . . .'
He began picking alsatian hairs off the upholstery.

Father and daughter is not the perfect relationship. According to Freud, that distinction belongs to mother and son. But Wexford, looking back, could have said that he had been happy with his daughters and they with him, he had never actually quarrelled with either of them, there had never been any sort of breach. And if Sheila was his favourite he hoped this was so close a secret that no one but himself, not even Dora, could know it.

Any father of daughters, even today, must look ahead when they are children and anticipate an outlay of money on their wedding celebrations. Wexford realized this and had begun saving for it out of his detective inspector's salary, but Sylvia had married so young as almost to catch him napping. For Sheila he had been determined to be well prepared, then gradually, with wonder and a kind of dismay, he had watched her rise out of that income bracket and society in which she had grown up, graduate into a sparkling, lavish jet set whose members had wedding receptions in country mansions or else the Dorchester.

For a long time it had looked as if she would not marry at all. Then Andrew Thorverton appeared, a young businessman, immensely wealthy, it seemed to Wexford, with a house in Hampstead, a cottage in the country somewhere that his future father-in-law suspected was a sizeable house, a boat and an amazing car of so esoteric a manufacture that Wexford had never before heard of it. Sheila, made old-fashioned and sentimental by love, announced she would be married from home and, almost in the same breath, that she and Andrew would be paying for the entertainment of two hundred people to luncheon in the banquet room of the Olive and Dove. Yes, she insisted, it must be so and Pop must lump it or else she'd go and get married in a register office and have lunch at the Pearl of Africa.

He was slightly humiliated. Somehow he felt she ought to cut garment according to cloth, and his cloth would cover a buffet table for fifty. That was absurd, of course. Andrew wouldn't even notice the few thousand it would cost, and the bride's father would give her away, make a speech and hang on to his savings. He heard her telling Andrew she would be coming up to spend the weekend with him, and then Dora walked in.

'She won't be supporting her friend at the cremation then?'

Sheila had put the phone down. She was sometimes a little flushed and breathless when she had been talking to Andrew. But it was not now of him that she spoke. 'Dinah's not going to it. How could she bear it? Two days after what would have been their wedding day?'

'At least it's not the day itself,' said Wexford.

'Frankly, I'm surprised Sir Manuel's daughter didn't fix it on the day itself. She's capable of it. There's going to be a memorial service at St Peter's on Tuesday and everyone will be there. Solti is coming and probably Menuhin. Dinah says there are sure to be crowds, he was so much loved.'

Wexford said, 'Does she know if he left her much?'

Sheila delivered her reply slowly and with an actress's perfect timing.

'He has not left her anything. He has not left her a single penny.' She sank to the floor, close up by the fire, and stretched out her long legs. 'Her engagement ring and that dog, that's all she's got.'

'How did that come about? Did you ask her?'

'Oh, Pop darling, of course I did. Wasn't I with her for hours and hours? I got the whole thing out of her.'

'You're as insatiably inquisitive as your father!' cried Dora, revolted. 'I thought you went to comfort the poor girl. I agree it's not like losing a young fiancé, but just the same . . .'

'Curiosity,' quoted Wexford, 'is one of the permanent and certain characteristics of a vigorous intellect.' He chuckled. 'The daughter gets it all, does she?'

'Sir Manuel saw his daughter a week before he died and that was the first time he'd seen her for nineteen years. There'd been a family quarrel. She was at the Royal Academy of Music but she left and went off with an American student. The first Camargue and his wife knew of it was a letter from San Francisco. Mrs Camargue — he wasn't a Sir then — got ill and died but the daughter didn't come back. She didn't come back at all till last November. Doesn't it seem frightfully unfair that she gets everything?'

'Camargue should have made a new will.'

'He was going to as soon as they were married. Marriage invalidates a will. Did you know that, Pop?'

He nodded.

'I can understand divorce would but I can't see why marriage.' She turned her legs, toasting them.

'You'll get scorch marks,' said Dora. 'That won't look very nice on the beach in Bermuda.'

Sheila took no notice. 'And what's more, he was going to cut the daughter out altogether. Apparently, that one sight of her was enough.'

Dora, won uneasily on to the side of the gossips, said, 'I wish you wouldn't keep calling her the daughter. Doesn't she have a name?'

'Natalie Arno. Mrs Arno, she's a widow. The American student died some time during those nineteen years. Dinah was awfully reticent about her, but she did say Camargue intended to make a new will, and since he said this just after he'd seen Natalie I put two and two together. And there's another thing, Natalie only got in touch with her father after his engagement to Dinah was announced. The engagement was in the *Telegraph* on 10 December, and on the 12th he got a letter from Natalie telling him she was back and could she come and see him? She wanted a reconciliation. It was obvious she was scared stiff of the marriage and wanted to stop it.'

'And your reticent friend told you all this?'

'She got it out of her, Dora. I can understand. She's a chip off the old block, as you so indignantly pointed out.' He turned once more to Sheila. 'Did she try to stop it?'

'Dinah wouldn't say. I think she hates discussing Natalie. She talked much more about Camargue. She really loved him. In a funny sort of daughterly, worshipping, protective sort of way, but she did love him. She likes to talk about how wonderful he was and how they met and all that. She's a teacher at the Kathleen Camargue School and he came over last Founder's Day and they met and they just loved each other, she said, from that moment.'

The somewhat cynical expressions on the two middle-aged faces made her give an embarrassed laugh. She seemed to take her mother's warning to heart at last, for she got up and moved away from the fire to sit on the sofa where she scrutinized her smooth, pale golden legs. 'At any rate, Pop darling, it's an ill wind, as you might say, because now the house is bound to be sold. I'd love to get a look at it, wouldn't you? Why wasn't I at school with Natalie?'

'You were born too late,' said her father. 'And there must be simpler ways of getting into Sterries.'

There were.

'You?' said Burden first thing the next morning. 'What do *you* want to go up there for? It's only a common-or-garden burglary, one of our everyday occurrences, I'm sorry to say. Martin can handle it.'

Wexford hadn't taken his overcoat off. 'I want to see the place. Don't you feel any curiosity to see the home of our former most distinguished citizen?'

Burden seemed more concerned with dignity and protocol. 'It's beneath you *and* me, I should think.' He sniffed. 'And when you hear the details you'll feel the same. The facts are that a Mrs Arno — she's the late Sir Manuel's daughter — phoned up about half an hour ago to say the house had been broken into during the night. There's a pane of glass been cut out of a window downstairs and a bit of a mess made and some silver taken. Cutlery, nothing special, and some money from Mrs Arno's handbag. She thinks she saw the car the burglar used and she's got the registration number.'

'I like these open-and-shut cases,' said Wexford. 'I find them restful.'

The fingerprint man (Detective Constable Morgan) had already left for Sterries. Wexford's car only just managed to get up Ploughman's Lane, which was glacier-like in spite of gritting. He had been a determined burglar, Burden remarked, to get his car up and down there in the night.

The top of the hill presented an alpine scene, with dark-green and gold and grey conifers rising sturdily from the snow blanket. The house itself, shaped like a number of cuboid boxes pushed irregularly together and with a tower in the midst of them, looked not so much white as dun-coloured beside the dazzling field of snow. A sharp wind had set the treble-clef weathervane spinning like a top against a sky that was now a clear cerulean blue.

Morgan's van was parked on the forecourt outside the front door which was on the side of the house furthest from the lane. Some attempt had been made to keep this area free of snow. Wexford, getting out of the car, saw a solidly built man in jeans and anorak at work sweeping the path which seemed to lead to a much smaller house that stood in a dip in the grounds. He looked in the other direction, noting in a shallow tree-fringed basin the ornamental water newspapers had euphemistically called a lake. There Camargue had met his death. It was once more iced over and the ice laden with a fleecy coat of snow.

The front door had been opened by a woman of about forty in trousers and bulky sweater whom Wexford took to be Muriel Hicks. He and Burden stepped into the warmth and on to thick soft carpet. The vestibule with its cloaks cupboard was rather small but it opened, through an arch, into a hall which had been used to some extent as a picture gallery. The paintings almost made him whistle. If these were originals . . .

The dining-room was open, revealing pale wood panelling and dark red wood furnishing, and in the far corner Morgan could be seen at his task. A flight of stairs, with risers of mosaic tile and treads that seemed to be of oak, led upwards. However deferential and attentive Mrs Hicks may have been towards Sir Manuel — and according to Sheila he had been adored by his servants — she had no courtesy to spare for policemen. That 'she' was upstairs somewhere was the only introduction they got. Wexford went upstairs while Burden joined Morgan in the dining room.

The house had been built on various different levels of land so that the drawing room where he found himself was really another ground floor. It was a large, airy and gracious room, two sides of which were made entirely of glass. At the farther end of it steps led down into what must surely be the tower. Here the floor was covered by a pale yellow Chinese carpet on which stood two groups of silk-covered settees and chairs, one suite lemon, one very pale jade. There was some fine *famille jaune* porcelain of that marvellous yellow that is both tender and piercing, and suspended from the ceiling a chandelier of startlingly modern design that resembled a torrent of water poured from a tilted vase.

But there was no sign of human occupation. Wexford stepped down under the arch where staghorn ferns grew in troughs at ground level and a *Cissus antarctica* climbed the columns, and entered a music room. It was larger than had appeared from outside and it was dodecagonal. The floor was of very smooth, polished, pale grey slate on which lay three Kashmiri rugs. A Broadwood grand piano stood between him and the other arched entrance. On each of eight of the twelve sides of the room was a picture or bust in an alcove, Mozart and Beethoven among the latter, among the former Cocteau's cartoon of Picasso and Stravinsky, Rothenstein's drawing of Parry, and a photograph of the Georgian manor house in which the music school was housed at Wellridge. But on one of the remaining sides Camargue had placed on a glass shelf a cast of Chopin's hands and on the last hung in a glass case a wind instrument of the side-blown type which looked to Wexford to be made of solid gold. Under it was the inscription: 'Presented to Manuel Camargue by Aldo Cazzini, 1949'. Was it a flute and could it be of gold? He lifted the lid of a case which lay on a low table and saw inside a similar instrument but made of humbler metal, perhaps silver.

He was resolving to go downstairs again and send Muriel Hicks to find Mrs Arno, when he was aware of a movement in the air behind him and of a presence that was not wholly welcoming. He turned round. Natalie Arno stood framed in the embrasure of the further arch, watching him with an unfathomable expression in her eyes.

CHAPTER FOUR

Wexford was the first to speak.

'Good morning, Mrs Arno.'

She was absolutely still, one hand up to her cheek, the other resting against one of the columns which supported the arch. She was silent.

He introduced himself and said pleasantly, 'I hear you've had some sort of break-in. Is that right?'

Why did he feel so strongly that she was liberated by relief? Her face did not change and it was a second or two before she moved. Then, slowly, she came forward.

'It's good of you to come so quickly.' Her voice was as unlike Dinah Sternhold's as it was reasonably possible for one woman's voice to differ from another's. She had a faint American accent and in her tone there was an underlying hint of amusement. He was always to be aware of that in his dealings with her. 'I'm afraid I may be making a fuss about nothing. He only took a few spoons.' She made a comic grimace, pursing her lips as she drew out the long vowel sound. 'Let's go into the drawing room and I'll tell you about it.'

The cast of her countenance was that which one would immediately categorize as Spanish, full-fleshed yet strong, the nose straight if a fraction too long, the mouth full and flamboyantly curved, the eyes splendid, as near to midnight black as a white woman's eyes can ever be. Her black hair was strained tightly back from her face and knotted high on the back of her head, a style which most women's faces could scarcely take but which suited hers, exposing its fine bones. And her figure was no less arresting than her face. She was very slim but for a too-full bosom, and this was not at all disguised by her straight skirt and thin sweater. Such an appearance, the ideal of men's fantasies, gives a woman a slightly indecent look, particularly if she carries herself with a certain provocative air. Natalie Arno did not quite do this but when she moved as she now did, mounting the steps to the higher level, she walked very sinuously with a stressing of her narrow waist.

During his absence two people had come into the drawing room, a man and a woman. They were behaving in the rather aimless fashion of house guests who have perhaps just got up or at least just put in an appearance, and who are wondering where to find breakfast, newspapers and an occupation. It occurred to Wexford for the first time that it was rather odd, not to say presumptuous, of Natalie Arno to have taken possession of Sterries so immediately after her father's death, to have moved in and to have invited people to stay. Did his solicitors approve? Did they know?

'This is Chief Inspector Wexford who has come to catch our burglar,' she said. 'My friends, Mr and Mrs Zoffany.'

The man was one of those who had been in the circle round her after the inquest. He seemed about forty. His fair hair was thick and wavy and he had a Viking's fine golden beard, but his body had grown soft and podgy and a flap of belly hung over the belt of his too-tight and too-juvenile fawn cord jeans. His wife, in the kind of clothes which unmistakably mark the superannuated hippie, was as thin as he was stout. She was young still, younger probably than Camargue's daughter, but her face was worn and there were coarse, bright threads of grey in her dark curly hair.

Natalie Arno sat down in one of the jade armchairs. She sat with elegant slim legs crossed at the calves, her feet arched in their high-heeled shoes. Mrs Zoffany, on the other hand, flopped on to the floor and sat cross-legged, tucking her long patchwork skirt around her knees. The costume she wore, and which like so many of her contemporaries she pathetically refused to relinquish, would date her more ruthlessly than might any perm or pair of stockings on another woman. Yet not so long ago it had been the badge of an élite who hoped to alter the world. Sitting there, she looked as if she might be at one of the pop concerts of her youth, waiting for the entertainment to begin. Her head was lifted expectantly, her eyes on Natalie's face.

'I'll tell you what there is to tell,' Natalie began, 'and I'm afraid that's not much. It must have been around five this morning I thought I heard the sound of glass breaking. I've been sleeping in Papa's room. Jane and Ivan are in one of the spare rooms in the other wing. You didn't hear anything, did you, Jane?'

Jane Zoffany shook her head vehemently. 'I only wish I had. I might have been able to *help.*'

'I didn't go down. To tell you the truth I was just a little scared.' Natalie smiled deprecatingly. She didn't look as if she had ever been scared in her life. Wexford wondered why he had at first felt her presence as hostile. She was entirely charming. 'But I did look out of the window. And just outside the window — on that side all the rooms are more or less on the ground floor, you know — there was a van parked. I put the light on and took a note of the registration number. I've got it here somewhere. What did I do with it?'

Jane Zoffany jumped up. 'I'll look for it, shall I? You put it down somewhere in here. I remember, I was still in my dressing gown . . .' She began hunting about the room, her scarves and the fringe of her shawl catching on ornaments.

Natalie smiled, and in that smile Wexford thought he detected patronage. 'I didn't quite know what to do,' she said. 'Papa didn't have a phone extension put in his room. Just as I was wondering I heard the van start up and move off. I felt brave enough to go down to the dining room then, and sure enough there was a pane gone from one of the casements.'

'A pity you didn't phone us then. We might have got him.'

'I know.' She said it ruefully, amusedly, with a soft sigh of a laugh. 'But there were only those half-dozen silver spoons missing and two five-pound notes out of my purse. I'd left my purse on the sideboard.'

'But would *you* know exactly what was missing, Mrs Arno?'

'Right. I wouldn't really. But Mrs Hicks has been round with me this morning and she can't find anything else gone.'

'It's rather curious, isn't it? This house seems to me full of very valuable objects. There's a Kandinsky downstairs and a Boudin, I think.' He pointed. 'And those are signed Hockney prints. That yellow porcelain . . .'

She looked surprised at his knowledge. 'Yes, but . . .' Her

cheeks had slightly flushed. 'Would you think me very forward if I said I had a theory?'

'Not at all. I'd like to hear it.'

'Well, first, I think he knew Papa used to sleep in that room and now poor Papa is gone he figured no one would be in there. And, secondly, I think he saw my light go on before he'd done any more than filch the spoons. He was just too scared to stop any longer. How does that sound?'

'Quite a possibility,' said Wexford. Was it his imagination that she had expected a more enthusiastic or flattering response? Jane Zoffany came up with the van registration number on a piece of paper torn from an exercise book. Natalie Arno didn't thank her for her pains. She rose, tensing her shoulders and throwing back her head to show off that amazing shape. Her waist could easily have been spanned by a pair of hands.

'Do you want to see the rest of the house?' she said. 'I'm sure he didn't come up to this level.'

Wexford would have loved to, but for what reason? 'We usually ask the householder to make a list of missing valuables in a case like this. It might be wise for me to go round with Mrs Hicks . . .'

'Of *course*.'

Throughout these exchanges Ivan Zoffany had not spoken. Wexford, without looking at him, had sensed a brooding concentration, the aggrieved attitude perhaps of a man not called on to participate in what might seem to be men's business. But now, as he turned his eyes in Zoffany's direction, he got a shock. The man was gazing at Natalie Arno, had probably been doing so for the past ten minutes, and his expression, hypnotic and fixed, was impenetrable. It might indicate contempt or envy or desire or simple hatred. Wexford was unable to analyse it but he felt a pang of pity for Zoffany's wife, for anyone who had to live with so much smouldering emotion.

Passing through the music room, Muriel Hicks took him first into the wing which had been private to Camargue. Here all was rather more austere than what he had so far seen. The bedroom, study-cum-sitting-room and bathroom were all carpeted in Camargue's favourite yellow — wasn't it in the Luscher

Test that you were judged the best-adjusted if you gave your favourite colour as yellow? — but the furnishings were sparse and there were blinds at the windows instead of curtains. A dress of Natalie's lay on the bed.

Muriel Hicks had not so far spoken beyond asking him to follow her. She was not an attractive woman. She had the bright pink complexion that sometimes goes with red-gold hair and piglet features. Wexford who, by initially marrying one, had surrounded himself with handsome women, wondered at Camargue who had a beautiful daughter yet had picked an ugly housekeeper and a nonentity for a second wife. Immediately he had thought that he regretted it with shame. For, turning round, he saw that Mrs Hicks was crying. She was standing with her hand on an armchair, on the seat of which lay a folded rug, and the tears were rolling down her round, red cheeks.

She was one of the few people he had ever come across who did not apologize for crying. She wiped her face, scrubbing at her eyes. 'I've lost the best employer,' she said, 'and the best friend anyone could have. And I've taken it hard, I can tell you.'

'Yes, it was a sad business.'

'If you'll look out of that window you'll see a house over to the left. That's ours. Really ours, I mean — he *gave* it to us. God knows what it's worth now. D'you know what he said? I'm not having you and Ted living in a tied cottage, he said. If you're good enough to come and work for me you deserve to have a house of your own to live in.'

It was a largish Victorian cottage and it had its own narrow driveway out into Ploughman's Lane. Sheila wouldn't have wanted it, he supposed, its not going with Sterries would make no difference to her. He put up a show for Mrs Hicks' benefit of scrutinizing the spot where Natalie Arno said the van had been.

'There weren't many like him,' said Muriel Hicks, closing the door behind Wexford as they left. It was a fitting epitaph, perhaps the best and surely the simplest Camargue would have.

Along the corridor, back through the music room, across the drawing room, now deserted, and into the other wing. Here was a large room full of books, a study or a library, and three bedrooms, all with bathrooms *en suite*. Their doors were all open

592

but in one of them, standing in front of a long glass and studying the effect of various ways of fastening the collar of a very old Persian lamb coat, was Jane Zoffany. She rushed, at the sight of Wexford, into a spate of apologies — very nearly saying sorry for existing at all — and scuttled from the room. Muriel Hicks' glassy stare followed her out.

'There's nothing missing from here,' she said in a depressed tone. 'Anyway, those people would have heard something.' There was a chance, he thought, that she might lose another kind of control and break into a tirade against Camargue's daughter and her friends. But she didn't. She took him silently into the second room and the third.

Why had Natalie Arno chosen to occupy her father's bedroom, austere, utilitarian and moreover the room of a lately dead man and a parent, rather than one of these luxurious rooms with fur rugs on the carpets and duckdown duvets on the beds? Was it to be removed from the Zoffanys? But they were her friends whom she had presumably invited. To revel in the triumph of possessing the place and all that went with it at last? To appreciate this to the full by sleeping in the inner sanctum, the very holy of holies? It occurred to him that by so doing she must have caused great pain to Mrs Hicks, and then he reminded himself that this sort of speculation was pointless, he wasn't investigating any crime more serious than petty larceny. And his true reason for being here was to make a preliminary survey for a possible buyer.

'Is anything much kept in that chest?' he asked Mrs Hicks. It was a big teak affair with brass handles, standing in the passage.

'Only blankets.'

'And that cupboard?'

She opened it. 'There's nothing missing.'

He went downstairs. Morgan and his van had gone. In the hall were Burden, Natalie Arno and the Zoffanys, the man who had been sweeping the path, and a woman in a dark brown fox fur who had evidently just arrived.

Everyone was dressed for the outdoors and for bitterly cold weather. It struck Wexford forcefully, as he descended the stairs towards them, that Natalie and her friends looked thoroughly disreputable compared with the other three. Burden was always well turned-out and in his new sheepskin he was more than that. The newcomer was smart, even elegant, creamy cashmere showing above the neckline of the fur, her hands in sleek gloves, and even Ted Hicks, in aran and anorak, had the look of a gentleman farmer. Beside them Natalie and the Zoffanys were a rag-bag crew, Zoffany's old overcoat as shabby as Wexford's own, his wife with layers of dipping skirts hanging out beneath the hem of the Persian lamb. Nothing could make Natalie less than striking. In a coat that appeared to be made from an old blanket and platform-soled boots so out of date and so worn that Wexford guessed she must have bought them in a second-hand shop, she looked raffish and down on her luck. They were hardly the kind of people, he said to himself with an inward chuckle, that one (or the neighbours) would expect to see issuing from a house in Ploughman's Lane.

That the woman in the fur was one of these neighbours Burden immediately explained. Mrs Murray-Burgess. She had seen the police cars and then she had encountered Mr Hicks in the lane. Yes, she lived next door, if next door it could be called when something like an acre separated Kingsfield House from Sterries, and she thought she might have some useful information.

They all trooped into the dining room where Hicks resumed his task of boarding up the broken window. Wexford asked Mrs Murray-Burgess the nature of her information.

She had seen a man in the Sterries grounds. No, not last night, a few days before. In fact, she had mentioned it to Mrs Hicks, not being acquainted with Mrs Arno. She gave Natalie a brief glance that seemed to indicate her desire for a continuation of this state of affairs. No, she couldn't recall precisely when it had been. Last night she had happened to be awake at five-thirty — she always awoke early — and had seen the lights of a vehicle turning out from Sterries into the lane. Wexford nodded. Could she identify this man were she to see him again?

'I'm sure I could,' said Mrs Murray-Burgess emphatically. 'And what's more, I *would*. All this sort of thing has got to be stopped before the country goes completely to the dogs. If I've got to get up in court and say that's the man! — well, I've got to and no two ways about it. It's time someone gave a lead.'

Natalie's face was impassive but in the depths of her eyes Wexford saw a spark of laughter. Almost anyone else in her position would now have addressed this wealthy and majestic neighbour, thanking her perhaps for her concern and public spirit. Most people would have suggested a meeting on more social terms, on do-bring-your-husband-in-for-a-drink lines. Many would have spoken of the dead and have mentioned the coming memorial service. Natalie behaved exactly as if Mrs Murray-Burgess were not there. She shook hands with Wexford, thanking him warmly while increasing the pressure of her fingers. Burden was as prettily thanked and given an alluring smile. They were ushered to the door, the Zoffanys following, everyone coming out into the crisp cold air and the bright sunlight. Mrs Murray-Burgess, left stranded in the dining room with Ted Hicks, emerged in offended bewilderment a moment or two later.

Wexford, no doubt impressing everyone with his frown and preoccupied air, was observing the extent of the double glazing and making rough calculations as to the size of the grounds. Getting at last into their car, he remarked to Burden — a propos of what the inspector had no idea — that sometimes these cogitations still amazed the troubled midnight and the noon's repose.

CHAPTER FIVE

The owner of the van was quickly traced through its registration number. He was a television engineer called Robert Clifford who said he had lent the van to a fellow-tenant of his in Finsbury Park, north London, a man of thirty-six called John Cooper. Cooper, who was unemployed, admitted the break-in after the spoons had been found in his possession. He said he had read in the papers about the death of Camargue and accounts of the arrangements at Sterries.

'It was an invite to do the place,' he said impudently. 'All that stuff about valuable paintings and china, and then that the housekeeper didn't sleep in the house. She didn't either, the first time I went.'

When had that been?

'Tuesday night,' said Cooper. He meant Tuesday the 29th, two days after Camargue's death. When he returned to break in. 'I didn't know which was the old man's room,' he said. 'How would I? The papers don't give you a plan of the bloody place.' He had parked the van outside that window simply because it seemed the most convenient spot and couldn't be seen from the road. 'It gave me a shock when the light came on.' He sounded aggrieved, as if he had been wantonly interrupted while about some legitimate task. His was a middle-class accent. Perhaps, like Burden's little villain, he was a pathological kleptomaniac with personality-scarring. Cooper appeared before the Kingsmarkham magistrates and was remanded in custody until the case could be heard at Myringham Crown Court.

Wexford was able to give Sheila a favourable report on Camargue's house, but she seemed to have lost interest in the place. (One's children had a way of behaving like this, he had noticed.) Andrew's house in Keats Grove was really very nice, and he did have the cottage in Dorset. If they lived in Sussex they would have to keep a flat in town as well. She couldn't go all the way back to Kingsmarkham after an evening performance, could she? The estate agents had found a buyer for her own flat in St John's Wood and they were getting an amazing price for it. Had Mother been to hear her banns called for the second time? Mother had.

The day of the memorial service was bright and sunny. Alpine weather, Wexford called it, the frozen snow sparkling, melting a little in the sun, only to freeze glass-hard again when the sun went down. Returning from his visit to Sewingbury Comprehensive School — where there was an alarming incidence of glue-sniffing among fourteen-year-olds — he passed St Peter's church as the mourners were leaving. The uniform men wear disguises them. Inside black overcoat and black Homburg might breathe equally Sir Manuel's accompanist or Sir Manuel's wine merchant. But he was pretty sure he had spotted James Galway, and he stood to gaze like any lion-hunting sightseer.

Sheila, making her escape with Dinah Sternhold to a hire car, was attracting as much attention as anyone — a warning, her father thought, of what they might expect in a fortnight's time. The Zoffanys were nowhere to be seen but Natalie Arno, holding the arm of an elderly wisp of a man, a man so frail-looking that it seemed wonderful the wind did not blow him about like a feather, was standing on the steps shaking hands with departing visitors. She wore a black coat and a large black hat, new clothes they appeared to be and suited to the occasion, and she stood erectly, her thin ankles pressed together. By the time Wexford was driven away by the cold, though several dozen people had shaken hands with her and passed on, four or five of the men as well as the elderly wisp remained with her. He smiled to himself, amused to see his prediction fulfilled.

By the end of the week Sheila had received confirmation from the estate agents that her flat was sold, or that negotiations to buy it had begun. This threw her into a dilemma. Should she sign the contract and then go merrily off on her Bermuda honeymoon, leaving the flat full of furniture? Or should she arrange to have the flat cleared and the furniture stored before she left? Persuaded by her prudent mother, she fixed on the Wednesday before her wedding for the removal and Wexford, who had the day off, promised to go with her to St John's Wood.

'We could go to Bermuda too,' said Dora to her husband.

'I know it was the custom for Victorian brides to take a friend with them on their honeymoon,' said Wexford, 'but surely even they didn't take their parents.'

'Darling, I don't mean at the same time. I mean we could go to Bermuda later on. When you get your holiday. We can afford it now we aren't paying for this wedding.'

'How about my new car? How about the new hall carpet? And I thought you'd decided life was insupportable without a freezer.'

'We couldn't have all those things anyway.'

'That's for sure,' said Wexford.

A wonderful holiday or a new car? A thousand pounds' worth of sunshine and warmth took priority now, he reflected as he was driven over to Myringham and the crown court. The snow was still lying and the bright weather had given place to freezing fog. But would he still feel like this when it was sunny here and spring again? Then the freezer and the carpet would seem the wiser option.

John Cooper was found guilty of breaking into and entering Sterries and of stealing six silver spoons, and, since he had previous convictions, sent to prison for six months. Wexford was rather surprised to hear that one of these convictions, though long in the past, was for robbery with violence. Mrs Murray-Burgess was in court and she flushed brick-red with satisfaction when the sentence was pronounced. Throughout the proceedings she had been eyeing the dark, rather handsome, slouching Cooper in the awed and fascinated way one looks at a bull or a caged tiger.

It occurred to Wexford to call in at Sterries on his way back and impart the news to Natalie Arno. He had promised to let her know the outcome. She would very likely be as delighted as her neighbour, and she could have her spoons back now.

A man who tried to be honest with himself, he wondered if this could be his sole motive for a visit to Ploughman's Lane. After all, it was a task Sergeant Martin or even Constable Loring could more properly have done. Was he, in common with those encircling men, attracted by Natalie? Could she have said of him too, like Cleopatra with her fishing rod, 'Aha, you're caught'? Honestly he asked himself — and said an honest, almost unqualified no. She amused him, she intrigued him, he suspected she would be entertaining to watch at certain manipulating ploys, but he was not attracted. There remained with him a nagging little memory of how, in the music room at Sterries, before he had ever spoken to her, he had sensed her presence behind him as unpleasing. She was good to look at, she was undoubtedly clever, she was full of charm, yet wasn't there about her something snake-like? And although this image might dissolve when confronted by the real Natalie, out of her company he must think of her sinuous movements as reptilian and her marvellous eyes when cast down as hooded.

So in going to Sterries he knew he was in little danger. No one need tie him to the mast. He would simply be calling on Natalie Arno for an obligatory talk, perhaps a cup of tea, and the opportunity to watch a powerful personality at work with the weak. If the Zoffanys were still there, of course. He would soon know.

It was three o'clock on the afternoon of a dull day. Not a light showed in the Sterries windows. Still, many people preferred to sit in the dusk rather than anticipate the night too soon. He rang the bell. He rang and rang again, was pleased to find himself not particularly disappointed that there was no one at home.

After a moment's thought he walked down the path to Sterries Cottage. Ted Hicks answered his ring. Yes, Mrs Arno was out. In fact, she had returned to London. Her friends had gone and then she had gone, leaving him and his wife to look after the house.

'Does she mean to come back?'

'I'm afraid I've no idea about that, sir. Mrs Arno didn't say.' Hicks spoke respectfully. Indeed, he had far more the air of an old-fashioned servant than his wife. Yet again Wexford felt, as he had felt with Muriel Hicks, that at any moment the discreet speaker might break into abuse, either heaping insults on Natalie or dismissing her with contempt. But nothing like this happened. Hicks compressed his lips and stared blankly at Wexford, though without meeting his eyes. 'Would you care to come in? I can give you Mrs Arno's London address.'

Why bother with it? He refused, thanked the man, asked almost as an afterthought if the house was to be sold.

'Very probably, sir.' Hicks, stiff, soldierly almost, unbent a little. 'This house will be. The wife and me, we couldn't stick it here now Sir Manuel's gone.'

It seemed likely that Natalie had taken her leave of Kingsmarkham and the town would not see her again. Perhaps she meant to settle in London or even return to America. He said something on these lines to Sheila as he drove her up to London on the following morning. But she had lost interest in Sterries and its future and was preoccupied with the morning paper which was carrying a feature about her and the forthcoming wedding. On the whole she seemed pleased with it, a reaction that astonished Wexford and Dora. They had been appalled by the description of her as the 'beautiful daughter of a country policeman' and the full-length photograph which showed her neither as Stewardess Curtis nor in one of her Royal Shakespeare Company roles, but reclining on a heap of cushions in little more than a pair of spangled stockings and a smallish fur.

'Dorset Stores It' was the slogan on the side of the removal van that had arrived early in Hamilton Terrace. Two men sat in its cab, glumly awaiting the appearance of the owner of the flat. Recognition of who that owner was mollified them, and on the way up in the lift the younger man asked Sheila if she would give him her autograph for his wife who hadn't missed a single instalment of *Runway* since the serial began.

The other man looked very old. Wexford was thinking he was too old to be of much use until he saw him lift Sheila's big bow-fronted chest of drawers and set it like a light pack on his shoulders. The younger man smiled at Wexford's astonishment.

'Pity you haven't got a piano,' he said. 'He comes from the most famous piano-lifting family in the country.'

Wexford had never before supposed that talents of that kind ran in families or even that one might enjoy a reputation for such a skill. He looked at the old man, who seemed getting on for Camargue's age, with new respect.

'Where are you taking all this stuff?'

A list was consulted. 'This piece and them chairs and that chest up to Keats Grove and ...'

'Yes, I mean what isn't going to Keats Grove.'

'Down the warehouse. That's our warehouse down Thornton Heath, Croydon way if you know it. The lady's not got so much she'll need more than one container.' He named the rental Sheila would have to pay per week for the storage of her tables and chairs.

'It's stacked up in this container, is it, and stored along with a hundred others? Suppose you said you wanted it stored for a year and then you changed your mind and wanted to get, say, one item out?'

'That'd be no problem, guv'nor. It's yours, isn't it? While you pay your rent you can do what you like about it, leave it alone if that's what you want like or inspect it once a week. Thanks very much, lady.' This last was addressed to Sheila who was dispensing cans of beer.

'Give us a hand, George,' said the old man.

He had picked up Sheila's four-poster on his own, held it several inches off the ground, then thought better of it. He and the man called George began dismantling it.

'You'd be amazed,' said George, 'the things that go on. We're like a very old-established firm and we've got stuff down the warehouse been stored since before the First War. . . .'

'The Great War,' said the old man.

'OK, then, the *Great* War. We've got stuff been stored since before 1914. The party as stored it's dead and gone and the rent's like gone up ten, twenty times, but the family wants it kept and they go on paying. Furniture that's been stored twenty years, that's common, that's nothing out of the way. We got one lady, she put her grand piano in store 1936 and she's dead now, but her daughter, she keeps the rent up. She comes along every so often and we open up her container for her and let her have a look her piano's OK.'

'See if you can shift that nut, George,' said the old man.

By two they were finished. Wexford took Sheila out to lunch, to a little French restaurant in Blenheim Terrace, a far cry from Mr Haq's. They shared a bottle of Domaine du Parc and as Wexford raised his glass and drank to her happiness he felt a rush of unaccustomed sentimentality. She was so very much his treasure. His heart swelled with pride when he saw people look at her, whisper together and then look again. For years now she had hardly been his, she had been something like public property, but after Saturday she would be Andrew's and lost to him for ever. . . . Suddenly he let out a bark of laughter at these maudlin indulgences.

'What's funny, Pop darling?'

'I was thinking about those removal men,' he lied.

He drove her up to Hampstead where she was staying the night and began the long haul back to Kingsmarkham. Not very experienced in London traffic, he had left Keats Grove at four and by the time he came to Waterloo Bridge found himself in the thick of the rush. It was after seven when he walked, cross and tired, into his house.

Dora came out to meet him in the hall. She kept her voice low. 'Reg, that friend of Sheila's who was going to marry Manuel Camargue is here. Dinah Whatever-it-is.'

'Didn't you tell her Sheila wouldn't be back tonight?'

Dora, though aware that she must move with the times, though aware that Sheila and Andrew had been more or less living together for the past year, nevertheless still made attempts to present to the world a picture of her daughter as an old-fashioned maiden bride. Her husband's accusing look — he disapproved of this kind of Mrs Grundy-ish concealment — made her blush and say hastily:

'She doesn't want Sheila, she wants you. She's been here an hour, she insisted on waiting. She says . . .' Dora cast up her eyes. 'She says she didn't know till this morning that you were a policeman!'

Wedding presents were still arriving. The house wasn't big enough for this sort of influx, and now the larger items were beginning to take over the hall. He nearly tripped over an object which, since it was swathed in corrugated cardboard and brown paper, might have been a plant stand, a lectern or a standard lamp, and cursing under his breath made his way into the living room.

This time the alsatian had been left behind. Dinah Stern-hold had been sitting by the hearth, gazing into the heart of the fire perhaps while preoccupied with her own thoughts. She jumped up when he came in and her round pale face grew pink.

'Oh, I'm so sorry to bother you, Mr Wexford. Believe me, I wouldn't be here if I didn't think it was absolutely — well, absolutely vital. I've delayed so long and I've felt so bad and now I can't sleep with the worry .... But it wasn't till this morning I found out you were a detective chief inspector.'

'You read it in the paper,' he said, smiling. ' "Beautiful daughter of a country policeman." '

'Sheila never told me, you see. Why should she? I never told her my father's a bank manager.'

Wexford sat down. 'Then what you have to tell me is something serious, I suppose. Shall we have a drink? I'm a bit tired and you look as if you need Dutch courage.'

On doctor's orders, he could allow himself nothing stronger than vermouth but she, to his surprise, asked for whisky. That she wasn't used to it he could tell by the way she shuddered as she took her first sip. She lifted to him those greyish-brown eyes that seemed full of soft light. He had thought that face plain but it was not, and for a moment he could intuit what Camargue had seen in her. If his looks had been spiritual and sensitive so, superlatively, were hers. The old musician and this young creature had shared, he sensed, an approach to life that was gentle, impulsive and joyous.

There was no joy now in her wan features. They seemed convulsed with doubt and perhaps with fear.

'I know I ought to tell someone about this,' she began again. 'As soon as — as Manuel was dead I knew I ought to tell someone. I thought of his solicitors but I imagined them listening to me and knowing I wasn't to — well, inherit, and thinking it was all sour grapes. . . . It seemed so — so wild to go to the police. But this morning when I read that in the paper — you see, I know you, you're Sheila's father, you won't . . . I'm afraid I'm not being very articulate. Perhaps you understand what I mean?'

'I understand you've been feeling diffident about giving some sort of information but I'm mystified as to what it is.'

'Oh, of course you are! The point is, I don't really believe it myself. I can't, it seems so — well, outlandish. But Manuel believed it, he was so sure, so I don't think I ought to keep it to myself and just let things go ahead, do you?'

'I think you'd better tell me straight away, Mrs Sternhold. Just tell me what it is and then we'll have the explanations afterwards.'

She set down her glass. She looked a little away from him, the firelight reddening the side of her face.

'Well, then. Manuel told me that Natalie Arno, or the woman who calls herself Natalie Arno, wasn't his daughter at all. He was absolutely convinced she was an impostor.'

CHAPTER SIX

He said nothing and his face showed nothing of what he felt. She was looking at him now, the doubt intensified, her hands lifted and clasped hard together under her chin. In the firelight the ruby on her finger burned and twinkled.

'There,' she said, 'that's it. It was something to — to hesitate about, wasn't it? But I don't really believe it. Oh, I don't mean he wasn't marvellous for his age and his mind absolutely sound. I don't mean that. But his sight was poor and he'd worked himself into such an emotional state over seeing her, it was nineteen years, and perhaps she wasn't very kind and — oh, I don't know! When he said she wasn't his daughter, she was an impostor, and he'd leave her nothing in his will, I. . . .'

Wexford interrupted her. 'Why don't you tell me about it from the beginning?'

'Where is the beginning? From the time she, or whoever she is. . . .'

'Tell me about it from the time of her return to this country in November.'

Dora put her head round the door. He knew she had come to ask him if he was ready for his dinner but she retreated without a word. Dinah Sternhold said:

'I think I'm keeping you from your meal.'

'It doesn't matter. Let's go back to November.'

'I only know that it was in November she came back. She didn't get in touch with Manuel until the middle of December — 12 December it was. She didn't say anything about our getting married, just could she come and see him and something about healing the breach. At first she wanted to come at Christmas but when Manuel wrote back that that would be fine and I should be there and my parents, she said no, the first time she wanted to see him alone. It sounds casual, putting it like that, Manuel writing back and inviting her, but in fact it wasn't a bit. Getting her first letter absolutely threw him. He was very

605

— well, excited about seeing her and rather confused and it was almost as if he was afraid. I suggested he phone her — she gave a phone number — but he couldn't bring himself to do that and it's true he was difficult on the phone if you didn't know him. His hearing was fine when he could *see* the speaker. Anyway, she suggested 10 January and we had the same excitement and nervousness all over again. I wasn't to be there or the Hickses, Muriel was to get the tea ready and leave him to make it and she was to get one of the spare rooms ready in case Natalie decided to stay.

'Well, two or three days before, it must have been about the 7th, a woman called Mrs Zoffany phoned. Muriel took the call. Manuel was asleep. This Mrs Zoffany said she was speaking on behalf of Natalie who couldn't come on the 10th because she had to go into hospital for a check-up and could she come on the 19th instead? Manuel got into a state when Muriel told him. I went over there in the evening and he was very depressed and nervous, saying Natalie didn't really want a reconciliation, whatever she may have intended at first, she was just trying to get out of seeing him. You can imagine. He went on about how he was going to die soon and at any rate that would be a blessing for me, not to be tied to an old man *et cetera*. All nonsense, of course, but natural, I think. He was *longing* to see her. It's a good thing I haven't got a jealous nature. Lots of women would have been jealous.'

Perhaps they would. Jealousy knows nothing of age discrepancies, suitability. Camargue, thought Wexford, had chosen for his second wife a surrogate daughter, assuming his true daughter would never reappear. No wonder, when she did, that emotions had run high. He said only:

'I take it that it was on the 19th she came?'

'Yes. In the afternoon, about three. She came by train from Victoria and then in a taxi from the station. Manuel asked the Hickses not to interrupt them and Ted even took Nancy away for the afternoon. Muriel left tea prepared on the table in the drawing room and there was some cold duck and stuff for supper in the fridge.'

'So that when she came Sir Manuel was quite alone?'

'Quite alone. What I'm going to tell you is what he told me

the next day, the Sunday, when Ted drove him over to my house in the morning.

'He told me he intended to be rather cool and distant with her at first.' Dinah Sternhold smiled a tender, reminiscent smile. 'I didn't have much faith in that,' she said. 'I knew him, you see. I knew it wasn't in him not to be warm and kind. And in fact, when he went down and opened the front door to her he said he forgot all about that resolve of his and just took her in his arms and held her. He was ashamed of that afterwards, poor Manuel, he was sick with himself for giving way.

'Well, they went upstairs and sat down and talked. That is, Manuel talked. He said he suddenly found he had so much to say to her. He talked on and on about his life since she went away, her mother's death, his retirement because of the arthritis in his hands, how he had built that house. She answered him, he said, but a lot of things she said he couldn't hear. Maybe she spoke low, but my voice is low and he could always hear me. However . . .'

'She has an American accent,' said Wexford.

'Perhaps that was it. The awful thing was, he said, that when he talked of the long time she'd been away he actually cried. I couldn't see it was important, but he was so ashamed of having cried. Still, he pulled himself together. He said they must have tea and he hoped she would stay the night and would she like to see over the house? He was always taking people over the house, I think it was something his generation did, and then . . .'

Wexford broke in, 'All this time he believed her to be his daughter?'

'Oh, yes! He was in no doubt. The way he said he found out — well, it's so crazy. . . . Anyway, he actually told her he was going to make a new will after his marriage, and although he intended to leave me the house and its contents, everything else was to go to her, including what remained of her mother's fortune. It was a lot of money, something in the region of a million, I think.

'He showed her the bedroom that was to be hers, though she did say at this point that she couldn't stay, and then they went back and into the music room. Oh, I don't suppose you've ever been in the house, have you?'

'As a matter of fact, I have,' said Wexford.

She gave him a faintly puzzled glance. 'Yes. Well, you'll know then that there are alcoves all round the music room and in one of the alcoves is a flute made of gold. It was given to Manuel by a sort of patron and fan of his, an American of Italian origin called Aldo Cazzini, and it's a real instrument, it's perfectly *playable*, though in fact Manuel had never used it.

'He and Natalie went in there and Natalie took one look in the alcove and said, 'You still have Cazzini's golden flute,' and it was at this point, he said, that he knew. He knew for certain she wasn't Natalie.'

Wexford said, 'I don't follow you. Surely recognizing the flute would be confirmation of her identity rather than proof she was an impostor?'

'It was the way she pronounced it. It ought to be pronounced Catzini and this woman pronounced it Cassini. Or so he said. Now the real Natalie grew up speaking English, French and Spanish with equal ease. She learnt German at school and when she was fifteen Manuel had her taught Italian because he intended her to be a musician and he thought some Italian essential for a musician. The real Natalie would never have mispronounced an Italian name. She would no more have done that, he said — these are his own words — than a Frenchman would pronounce Camargue to rhyme with Montague. So as soon as he heard her pronunciation of Cazzini he knew she couldn't be Natalie.'

Wexford could almost have laughed. He shook his head in dismissal. 'There must have been more to it.'

'There was. He said the shock was terrible. He didn't say anything for a moment. He looked hard at her, he studied her, and then he could *see* she wasn't his daughter. Nineteen years is a long time but she couldn't have changed that much and in that way. Her features were different, the colour of her eyes was different. He went back with her into the drawing room and then he said, 'You are not my daughter, are you?''

'He actually asked her, did he?'

'He asked her and — you understand, Mr Wexford, that I'm telling you what he said — I feel a traitor to him, doubting

608

him, as if he were senile or mad — he wasn't, he was wonderful, but. . . .'

'He was old,' said Wexford. A foolish, fond old man, fourscore years. . . . 'He was overwrought.'

'Oh, yes, exactly! But the point is he said he asked her and she admitted it.'

Wexford leaned forward, frowning a little, his eyes on Dinah Sternhold's flushed, intent face.

'Are you telling me this woman admitted to Sir Manuel that she wasn't Natalie Arno? Why didn't you say so before?'

'Because I don't believe it. I think that when he said she admitted she wasn't Natalie and seemed ashamed and embarrassed, I think he was — well, dreaming. You see, he told her to go. He was trembling, he was terribly distressed. It wasn't in him to shout at anyone or be violent, you understand, he just told her not to say any more but to go. He heard her close the front door and then he did something he absolutely never did. He had some brandy. He never touched spirits in the normal way, a glass of wine sometimes or a sherry, that was all. But he had some brandy to steady him, he said, and then he went to lie down because his heart was racing — and he fell asleep.'

'It was next day when you saw him?'

She nodded. 'Next day at about eleven. I think that while he was asleep he dreamt that bit about her admitting she wasn't Natalie. I told him so. I didn't humour him — ours wasn't that kind of relationship. I told him I thought he was mistaken. I told him all sorts of things that I believed and believe now — that eye colour fades and features change and one can forget a language as one can forget anything else. He wouldn't have any of it. He was so sweet and good and a genius — but he was terribly impulsive and stubborn as well.

'Anyway, he started saying he was going to cut her out of his will. She was a fraud and an impostor who was attempting to get hold of a considerable property by false pretences. She was to have nothing, therefore, and I was to have the lot. Perhaps you won't believe me if I say I did my best to dissuade him from that?'

Wexford slightly inclined his head. 'Why not?'

'It would have been in my own interest to agree with him. However, I did try to dissuade him and he was sweet to me as he always was but he wouldn't listen. He wrote to her, telling her what he intended to do, and then he wrote to his solicitors, asking one of the partners to come up to Sterries on February 4th — that would have been two days after our wedding.'

'Who are these solicitors?'

'Symonds, O'Brien and Ames,' she said, 'in the High Street here.'

Kingsmarkham's principal firm of solicitors. They had recently moved their premises into the new Kingsbrook Precinct. It was often Wexford's lot to have dealings with them.

'He invited Mr Ames to lunch with us,' Dinah Sternhold said, 'and afterwards he was to draw up a new will for Manuel. It must have been on the 22nd or the 23rd that he wrote to Natalie and on the 27th — he was drowned.' Her voice shook a little.

Wexford waited. He said gently, 'He had no intention of coming to us and he wasn't going to confide in his solicitor?'

She did not answer him directly. 'I think I did right,' she said. 'I prevented that. I couldn't dissuade him from the decision to disinherit her but I did manage to stop him going to the police. I told him he would make a — well, a scandal, and he would have hated that. What I meant to do was this. Let him make a new will if he liked. Wills can be unmade and remade. I knew Natalie probably disliked me and was jealous but I thought I'd try to approach her myself a month or so after we were married, say, and arrange another meeting. I thought that somehow we'd all meet and it would come right. It would turn out to have been some misunderstanding like in a play, like in one of those old comedies of mistaken identity.'

Wexford was silent. Then he said, 'Would you like to tell me about it all over again, Mrs Sternhold?'

'What I've just told?'

He nodded. 'Please.'

'But why?'

To test your veracity. He didn't say that aloud. If she were intelligent enough she would know without his saying, and her flush told him that she did.

Without digressions this time, she repeated her story. He listened concentratedly. When she had finished he said rather sharply:

'Did Sir Manuel tell anyone else about this?'

'Not so far as I know. Well, no, I'm sure he didn't.' Her face was pale again and composed. She asked him, 'What will you do?'

'I don't know.'

'But you'll do something to find out. You'll prove she *is* Natalie Arno?'

Or that she is not? He didn't say it, and before he had framed an alternative reply she had jumped up and was taking her leave of him in that polite yet child-like way she had.

'It was very good and patient of you to listen to me, Mr Wexford. I'm sure you understand why I had to come. Will you give my love to Sheila, please, and say I'll be thinking of her Saturday? She did ask me to come but of course that wouldn't be possible. I'm afraid I've taken up a great deal of your time . . .'

He walked with her out to the Volkswagen which she had parked round the corner of the street on an ice-free patch. She looked back once as the drove away and raised her hand to him. How many times, in telling her story, had she said she didn't believe it? He had often observed how people will say they are sure of something when they truly mean they are unsure, how a man will hotly declare that he doesn't believe a word of it when he believes only too easily. If Dinah Sternhold had not believed, would she have come to him at all?

He asked himself if he believed and if so what was he going to do about it?

Nothing till after the wedding. . . .

CHAPTER SEVEN

The success or failure of a wedding, as Wexford remarked, is no augury of the marriage itself. This wedding might be said to have failed. In the first place, the thaw set in the evening before and by Saturday morning it was raining hard. All day long it rained tempestuously. The expected crowd of well-wishers come to see their favourite married, a youthful joyous crowd of confetti-hurlers, became in fact a huddle of pensioners under umbrellas, indifferently lingering on after the Over-Sixties meeting in St Peter's Hall. But the press was there, made spiteful by rain and mud, awaiting opportunities. And these were many: a bridesmaid's diaphanous skirt blown almost over her head by a gust of wind, a small but dismaying accident when the bride's brother-in-law's car went into the back of a press photographer's car, and later the failure of the Olive and Dove management to provide luncheon places for some ten of the guests.

The Sunday papers made the most of it. Their pictures might have been left to speak for themselves, for the captions, snide or sneering, only added insult to injury. Dora wept.

'I suppose it's inevitable.' Wexford, as far as he could recall it and with a touch of paraphrase, quoted Shelley to her. 'They scatter their insults and their slanders without heed as to whether the poisoned shafts light on a heart made callous by many blows or one like yours composed of more penetrable stuff.'

'And is yours made callous by many blows?'

'No, but Sheila's is.'

He took the papers away from her and burnt them, hoping none would have found their way into the Burdens' bungalow where they were going to lunch. And when they arrived just after noon, escorted from their car by Burden with a large coloured golf umbrella, there was not a newspaper to be seen. Instead, on the coffee table, where the *Sunday Times* might have reposed, lay a book in a glossy jacket entitled *The Tichborne Swindle*.

In former days, during the lifetime of Burden's first wife and afterwards in his long widowerhood, no book apart from those strictly necessary for the children's school work was ever seen in that house. But when he re-married things changed. And it could not be altogether due to the fact that his wife's brother was a publisher, though this might have helped, that the inspector was becoming a reading man. It was even said, though Wexford refused to believe it, that Burden and Jenny read aloud to each other in the evenings, that they had got through Dickens and were currently embarking on the Waverley novels.

Wexford picked up the book. It had been, as he expected, published by Carlyon Brent, and was a reappraisal of the notorious nineteenth-century Tichborne case in which an Australian butcher attempted to gain possession of a great fortune by posing as heir to an English baronetcy. Shades of the tale he had been told by Dinah Sternhold. . . . The coincidence of finding the book there decided him. For a little while before lunch he and Burden were alone together.

'Have you read this yet?'

'I'm about half-way through.'

'Listen.' He repeated the account he had been given baldly and without digressions. 'There aren't really very many points of similarity,' he said. 'From what I remember of the Tichborne case the claimant didn't even look like the Tichborne heir. He was much bigger and fatter for one thing and obviously not of the same social class. Lady Tichborne was a hysterical woman who would have accepted practically anyone who said he was her son. You've almost got the reverse here. Natalie Arno looks very much like the young Natalie Camargue and, far from accepting her, Camargue seems to have rumbled her within half an hour.'

' "Rumbled" sounds as if you think there might be something in this tale.'

'I'm not going to stomp up and down raving that I don't believe a word of it, if that's what you mean. I just don't know. But I'll tell you one thing. I expected you to have shouted you didn't believe it long before now.'

Burden gave one of his thin, rather complacent little smiles.

In his domestic circle he behaved, much as he had during his first marriage, as if nobody but he had ever quite discovered the heights of marital felicity. Today he was wearing a new suit of smooth matt cloth the colour of a ginger nut. When happy he always seemed to grow thinner and he was very thin now. The smile was still on his mouth as he spoke. 'It's a funny old business altogether, isn't it? But I wouldn't say I don't believe it. It's fertile ground for that sort of con trick, after all. A nineteen-year absence, an old man on his own with poor sight, an old man who has a great deal of money . . . By the way, how do you know this woman looks like the young Natalie?'

'Dinah Sternhold sent me this.' Wexford handed him a snapshot. 'Camargue was showing her a family photograph album, apparently, and he left it behind in her house.'

The picture showed a dark, Spanish-looking girl, rather plump, full-faced and smiling. She was wearing a summer dress in the style known at the time when the photograph was taken as 'the sack' on account of its shapelessness and lack of a defined waist. Her black hair was short and she had a fringe.

'That could be her. Why not?'

'A whitely wanton with a velvet brow,' said Wexford, 'and two pitchballs stuck in her face for eyes. Camargue said the eyes of the woman he saw were different from his daughter's and Dinah told him that eyes fade. I've never heard of eyes or anything else fading to black, have you?'

Burden refilled their glasses. 'If Camargue's sight was poor I think you can simply discount that sort of thing. I mean, you can't work on the premise that she's not Natalie Camargue because she looks different or he thought she did. The pronouncing of that name wrong, that's something else again, that's really weird.'

Wexford, hesitating for his figure's sake between potato crisps, peanuts or nothing at all, looked up in surprise. 'You think so?'

The thin smile came again. 'Oh, I know you reckon on me being a real philistine but I've got kids, remember. I've watched them getting an education if I've never had much myself. Now my Pat, she had a Frenchwoman teaching them French from when she was eleven, and when she speaks a French word she pronounces the R like the French, sort of rolls it in her throat. The point I'm making is, it happens naturally now, Pat couldn't pronounce a French word with an R in it any other way and *she never will.*'

'Mm hmm.' While pondering Wexford had absentmindedly sneaked two crisps. He held his hands firmly together in his lap. 'There's always the possibility Camargue *heard* the name incorrectly because of defective hearing while it was, in fact, pronounced in the proper way. What I'm sure of is that Dinah is telling the truth. I tested her and she told the same story almost word for word the second time as she has the first, dates, times, everything.'

'Pass over those crisp things, will you? I don't see what motive she'd have for inventing it, anyway. Even if Natalie were out of the way she wouldn't inherit.'

'No. Incidentally, we must find out who would. Dinah could have had spite for a motive, you know. If Natalie is the real Natalie no one of course could hope to prove she is not, and no doubt she could very quickly prove she *is*, but an inquiry would look bad for her, the mud would stick. If there were publicity about it and there very likely would be, there would be some people who would always believe her to be an impostor and many others who would feel a doubt.'

Burden nodded. 'And there must inevitably be an inquiry now, don't you think?'

'Tomorrow I shall have to pass on what I know to Symonds, O'Brien and Ames,' said Wexford, and he went on thoughtfully, 'It would be deception under the '68 Theft Act. Section Fifteen, I believe.' And he quoted with some small hesitations, 'A person who by any deception dishonestly obtains property belonging to another, with the intention of permanently depriving the other of it, shall on conviction on indictment be liable to imprisonment for a term not exceeding ten years.'

'No one's obtained anything yet. It'll take a bit of time for the will to be proved.' Burden gave his friend and superior officer a dubious and somewhat wary look. 'I don't want to speak out of turn and no offence meant,' he said, 'but this could be the kind of thing you get — well, you get obsessional about.'

Wexford's indignant retort was cut off in mid-sentence by the entry of Jenny and Dora to announce lunch.

Kingsmarkham's principal firm of solicitors had moved their offices when the new Kingsbrook shopping precinct was built, deserting the medieval caverns they had occupied for fifty years for the top floor above the British Home Stores. Here all was light, space and purity of line. The offices had that rather disconcerting quality, to be constantly met with nowadays, of looking cold and feeling warm. It was much the same in the police station.

Wexford knew Kenneth Ames well by sight, though he couldn't recall ever having spoken to him before. He was a thin, spare man with a boyish face. That is, his face like his figure had kept its youthful contours, though it was by now seamed all over with fine lines as if a web had been laid upon the skin. He wore a pale grey suit that seemed too lightweight for the time of year. His manner was both chatty and distant which gave the impression, perhaps a false one, that his mind was not on what he was saying or listening to.

This made repeating Dinah Sternhold's account a rather uneasy task. Mr Ames sat with his elbows on the arms of an uncomfortable-looking metal chair and the tips of his fingers pressed together. He stared out of the window at St Peter's spire. As the story progressed he pushed his lips and gradually his whole jaw forward until the lower part of his face grew muzzle-like. This doggy expression he held for a moment or two after Wexford had finished. Then he said:

'I don't think I'd place too much credence on all that, Mr Wexford. I don't think I would. It sounds to me as if Sir Manuel rather got a bee in his belfry, you know, and this young lady, Mrs — er, Steinhalt, is it? — Mrs Steinhall maybe gilded the gingerbread.' Mr Ames paused and coughed slightly after delivering these confused metaphors. He studied his short clean fingernails with interest. 'Once Sir Manuel was married he'd have had to make a new will. There was nothing out of the way in that. We have no reason to believe he meant to disinherit Mrs Arno.' The muzzle face returned as Mr Ames glared at his fingernails and enclosed them suddenly in his fists as if they offended him. 'In point of fact,' he said briskly, 'Sir Manuel invited me to lunch to discuss a new will and to meet his bride, Mrs — er, Sternhill, but unfortunately his death intervened. You know, Mr Wexford, if Sir Manuel had really believed he'd been visited by an impostor, don't you think he'd have said something to us? There was over a week between the visit and his death and during that week he wrote to me and phoned me. No, if this extraordinary tale were true I fancy he'd have said something to his solicitors.'

'He seems to have said nothing to anyone except Mrs Sternhold.'

An elastic smile replaced the muzzle look. 'Ah, yes. People like to make trouble. I can't imagine why. You may have noticed?'

'Yes,' said Wexford. 'By the way, in the event of Mrs Arno not inheriting, who would?'

'Oh dear, oh dear, I don't think there's much risk of Mrs Arno not inheriting, do you, really?'

Wexford shrugged. 'Just the same, who would?'

'Sir Manuel had — has, I suppose I should say if one may use the present tense in connection with the dead — Sir Manuel has a niece in France, his dead sister's daughter. A Mademoiselle Thérèse Something. Latour? Lacroix? No doubt I can find the name for you if you really want it.'

'As you say, there may be no chance of her inheriting. Am I to take it then that Symonds, O'Brien and Ames intend to do nothing about this story of Mrs Sternhold's?'

'I don't follow you, Mr Wexford.' Mr Ames was once more contemplating the church spire which was now veiled in fine driving rain.

'You intend to accept Mrs Arno as Sir Manuel's heir without investigation?'

The solicitor turned round. 'Good heavens, no, Mr Wexford. What can have given you that idea?' He became almost animated, almost involved. 'Naturally, in view of what you've told us we shall make the most thorough and exhaustive inquiries. No doubt, you will too?'

'Oh, yes.'

'A certain pooling of our findings would be desirable, don't you agree? It's quite unthinkable that a considerable property such as Sir Manuel left could pass to an heir about whose provenance there might be the faintest doubt.' Mr Ames half closed his eyes. He seemed to gather himself together in order to drift once more into remoteness. 'It's only,' he said with an air of extreme preoccupation, 'that it doesn't really do, you know, to place too much credence on these things.'

As the receiver was lifted the deep baying of a dog was the first sound he heard. Then the soft gentle voice gave the Forby number.

'Mrs Sternhold, do you happen to know if Sir Manuel had kept any samples of Mrs Arno's handwriting from *before* she went away to America?'

'I don't know. I don't think so.' Her tone sounded dubious, cautious, as if she regretted having told him so much. Perhaps she did, but it was too late now. 'They'd be inside Sterries, anyway.' She didn't add what Wexford was thinking, that if Camargue had kept them and if Natalie was an impostor, they would by now have been destroyed.

'Then perhaps you can help me in another way. I gather Sir Manuel had no relatives in this country. Who is there I can call on who knew Mrs Arno when she was Natalie Camargue?'

Burden's Burberry was already hanging on the palm tree hatstand when Wexford walked into the Pearl of Africa. And Burden was already seated under the plastic fronds, about to start on his antipasto Ankole.

'I don't believe they have shrimps in Uganda,' said Wexford, sitting down opposite him.

'Mr Haq says they come out of Lake Victoria. What are you going to have?'

'Oh, God. Avocado with Victorian shrimps, I suppose, and maybe an omelette. Mike, I've been on to the California police through Interpol, asking them to give us whatever they can about the background of Natalie Arno, but if she's never been in trouble, and we've no reason to think she has, it won't be much. And I've had another talk with Dinah. The first — well, the only really — Mrs Camargue had a sister who's still alive and in London. Ever heard of a composer called Philip Cory? He was an old pal of Camargue's. Either or both of them ought to be able to tell us if this is the real Natalie.'

Burden said thoughtfully, 'All this raises something else, doesn't it? Or, rather, what we've been told about Camargue's will does. And in that area it makes no difference whether Natalie is Natalie or someone else.'

'What does it raise?'

'You know what I mean.'

Wexford did. That Burden too had seen it scarcely surprised him. A year or two before the inspector had often seemed obtuse. But happiness makes so much difference to a person, Wexford thought. It doesn't just make them happy, it makes them more intelligent, more aware, more alert, while unhappiness deadens, dulls and stupefies. Burden had seen what he had seen because he was happy, and happiness was making a better policeman of him.

'Oh, I know what you mean. Perhaps it was rather too readily assumed that Camargue died a natural death.'

'I wouldn't say that. It's just that then there was no reason to suspect foul play, nothing and no one suspicious seen in the neighbourhood, no known enemies, no unusual bruising on the body. A highly distinguished but rather frail old man happened to go too near a lake on a cold night in deep snow.'

'And if we had known what we know now? We can take it for granted that Natalie's aim — whether she is Camargue's daughter or an impostor — her aim in coming to her father was to secure his property or the major part of it for herself. She came to him and, whether he actually saw through her and denounced her or thought he saw through her and dreamed he denounced her, he at any rate apparently wrote to her and told her she was to be disinherited.'

'She could either attempt to dissuade him,' said Burden, 'or take steps of another sort.'

'Her loss wouldn't have been immediate. Camargue was getting married and had therefore to make a new will after his marriage. She might count on his not wishing to make a new will at once and then another after his marriage. She had two weeks in which to act.'

'There's a point too that, whereas she might have dissuaded him from cutting her out, she couldn't have dissuaded him from leaving Sterries to Dinah. But there don't seem to have been any efforts at dissuasion, do there? Dinah doesn't know of any or she'd have told you, nor did Natalie come to Sterries again.'

'Except perhaps,' said Wexford, 'on the night of Sunday, 27 January.'

Burden's answer was checked by the arrival of Mr Haq, bowing over the table.

'How are you doing, my dear?'

'Fine, thanks.' Any less hearty reply would have summoned forth a stream of abject apology and the cook from the kitchen as well as causing very real pain to Mr Haq.

'I can recommend the mousse Maherere.'

Mr Haq, if his advice was rejected, was capable of going off into an explanation of how this dish was composed of coffee beans freshly plucked in the plantations of Toro and of cream from the milk of the taper-horned Sanga cattle. To prevent this, and though knowing its actual provenance to be Sainsbury's instant dessert, Burden ordered it. Wexford always had the excuse of his shaky and occasional diet. A bowl of pale brown froth appeared, served by Mr Haq's own hands.

Quietly Wexford repeated his last remark.

'The night of 27 January?' echoed Burden. 'The night of Camargue's death? If he was murdered, and I reckon we both think he was, if he was pushed into that water and left to drown, Natalie didn't do it.'

'How d'you know that?'

'Well, in a funny sort of way,' Burden said almost apologetically, 'she told me so.'

'It was while we were up at Sterries about that burglary. I was in the dining room talking to Hicks when Natalie and the Zoffany couple came downstairs. She may have known I was within earshot but I don't think she did. She and Mrs Z. were talking and Natalie was saying she supposed she would have to get Sotheby's or someone to value Camargue's china for her. On the other hand, there had been that man she and Mrs Z. had met that someone had said was an expert on Chinese

620

porcelain and she'd like to get hold of his name and phone number. Zoffany said what man did she mean and Natalie said he wouldn't know, he hadn't been there, it had been at so-and-so's party *last Sunday evening.*'

'A bit too glib, wasn't it?'

'Glib or not, if Natalie was at a party there'll be at least a dozen people to say she was, as well as Mrs Z. And if Camargue was murdered *we will never prove it.* If we'd guessed it at the time it would have been bad enough with snow lying everywhere, with snow falling to obliterate all possible evidence. No weapon but bare hands. Camargue cremated. We haven't a hope in hell of proving it.'

'You're over-pessimistic,' said Wexford, and he quoted softly, 'If a man will begin with certainties, he shall end in doubts, but if he will be content to begin with doubts he shall end in certainties.'

CHAPTER EIGHT

A shop that is not regularly open and manned seems to announce this fact to the world even when the 'open' sign hangs on its door and an assistant can be seen pottering inside. An indefinable air of neglect, of lack of interest, of precarious existence and threatened permanent closure hangs over it. So it was with the Zodiac, nestling in deep Victoriana, tucked behind a neo-Gothic square, on the borders of Islington and Hackney.

Its window was stacked full of paperback science fiction, but some of the books had tumbled down, and those which lay with their covers exposed had their gaudy and bizarre designs veiled in dust. Above the shop was a single storey — for this was a district of squat buildings and wide streets — and behind it a humping of rooms, shapelessly huddled and with odd little scraps of roof, gables protruding, seemingly superfluous doors and even a cowled chimney. Wexford pushed open the shop door and walked in. There was a sour, inky, musty smell, inseparable from secondhand books. These lined the shop like wallpaper, an asymmetrical pattern of red and green and yellow and black spines. They were all science fiction, *The Trillion Project, Nergal of Chaldea, Neuropodium, Course for Umbrial, The Triton Occultation*. He was replacing on the shelf a book whose cover bore a picture of what appeared to be a Boeing 747 coated in fish scales and with antennae, when Ivan Zoffany came in from a door at the back.

Recognition was not mutual. Zoffany showed intense surprise when Wexford said who he was, but it seemed like surprise alone and not fear.

'I'd like a few words with you.'

'Right. It's a mystery to me what about but I'm easy. I may as well close up for lunch anyway.'

It was ten past twelve. Could they hope to make any sort of living out of this place? Did they try? The 'open' sign was turned round and Zoffany led Wexford into the room from which he had come. By a window which gave on to a paved yard and scrap of garden and where the light was best, Jane Zoffany, in antique gown, shawl and beads, sat sewing. She appeared to be turning up or letting down the hem of a skirt and Wexford, whose memory was highly retentive about this sort of thing, recognized it as the skirt Natalie had been wearing on the day they were summoned after the burglary.

'What can we do for you?'

Zoffany had the bluff, insincere manner of the man who has a great deal to hide. Experience had taught Wexford that what such a nature is hiding is far more often some emotional disturbance or failure of nerve than guilty knowledge. He could hardly have indulged in greater self-deception than when he had said he was easy. There was something in Zoffany's eyes and the droop of his mouth when he was not forcing it into a grin that spoke of frightful inner suffering. And it was more apparent here, on his home ground, than it had been at Sterries.

'How long have you known Mrs Arno?'

Instinctively, Jane Zoffany glanced towards the ceiling. And at that moment a light footstep sounded overhead. Zoffany didn't look up.

'Oh, I'd say a couple of years, give or take a little.'

'You knew her before she came to this country then?'

'Met her when my poor sister died. Mrs Arno and my sister used to share a house in Los Angeles. Perhaps you didn't know that? Tina, my sister, she died the summer before last, and I had to go over and see to things. Grisly business but someone had to. There wasn't anyone else, barring my mother, and you can't expect an old lady of seventy — I say, what's all this in aid of?'

Wexford ignored the question as he usually ignored such questions until the time was ripe to answer them. 'Your sister and Mrs Arno shared a house?'

'Well, Tina had a flat in her house.'

'A room actually, Ivan,' said Jane Zoffany.

'A room in her house. Look, could you tell me why you want . . . ?'

'She must have been quite a young woman. What did she die of?'

'Cancer. She had cancer in her twenties while she was still married. Then she got divorced, but she didn't keep his name, she went back to her maiden name. She was thirty-nine if you want to know. The cancer came back suddenly, it was all over her, carcinomatosis, they called it. She was dead in three weeks from the onset.'

Wexford thought he spoke callously and with a curious kind of resentment. There was also an impression that he talked for the sake of talking, perhaps to avoid an embarrassing matter.

'I hadn't seen her for sixteen or seventeen years,' he said, 'but when she went like that someone had to go over. I can't think what you want with all this.'

It was on the tip of Wexford's tongue to retort that he had not asked for it. He said mildly, 'When you arrived you met Mrs Arno? Stayed in her house perhaps?'

Zoffany nodded, uneasy again.

'You got on well and became friends. After you came home you corresponded with her and when you heard she was coming back here and needed somewhere to live, you and your wife offered her the upstairs flat.'

'That's quite correct,' said Jane Zoffany. She gave a strange little skittish laugh. 'I'd always admired her from afar, you see. Just to think of my own sister-in-law living in Manuel Camargue's own daughter's house! I used to worship him when I was young. And Natalie and I are very close now. It was a really good idea. I'm sure Natalie has been a true friend to me.' She re-threaded her needle, holding the eye up against the yellowed and none-too-clean net curtain. 'Please, why are you asking all these questions?'

'A suggestion has been made that Mrs Arno is not in fact the late Sir Manuel Camargue's daughter but an impostor.'

He was interested by the effect of these words on his hearers. One of them expected this statement and was not surprised by it, the other was either flabbergasted or was a superb actor. Ivan Zoffany seemed stricken dumb with astonishment. Then he asked Wexford to repeat what he had said.

'That is the most incredible nonsense,' Zoffany said with a loaded pause between the words. 'Who has suggested it? Who would put about a story like that? Now just you listen to me. . . .' Wagging a finger, he began lecturing Wexford on the subject of Natalie Arno's virtues and misfortunes. 'One of the most charming, delightful girls you could wish to meet, and as if she hasn't had enough to put up with. . . .'

Wexford cut him short again. 'It's her identity, not her charm, that's in dispute.' He was intrigued by the behaviour of Jane Zoffany who was sitting hunched up, looking anywhere but at him, and who appeared to be very frightened indeed. She had stopped sewing because her hands would have shaken once she moved each out of the other's grasp.

He went back into the shop. Natalie Arno was standing by the counter on the top of which now lay an open magazine. She was looking at this and laughing with glee rather than amusement. When she saw Wexford she showed no surprise, but smiled, holding her head a little on one side.

'Good morning, Mr — er, Wexford, isn't it? And how are you today?' It was an Americanism delivered with an American lilt and one that seemed to require no reply. 'When you close the shop, Ivan,' she said, 'you should also remember to lock the door. All sorts of undesirables could come in.'

Zoffany said with gallantry, but stammering a little, 'That certainly doesn't include you, Natalie!'

'I'm not sure the chief inspector would agree with you.' She gave Wexford a sidelong smile. She knew. Symonds, O'Brien and Ames had lost no time in telling her. Jane Zoffany was afraid but she was not. Her black eyes sparkled. Rather ostentatiously, she closed the magazine she had been looking at, revealing the cover which showed it to belong to the medium hard genre of pornography. Plainly, this was Zoffany's under-the-counter solace that she had lighted on. He flushed, seized it rather too quickly from under her hands and thrust it between some catalogues in a pile. Natalie's face became pensive and innocent. She put up her hands to her hair and her full breasts in the sweater rose with the movement, which seemed to have been made quite artlessly, simply to tuck in a tortoiseshell pin.

'Did you want to interrogate me, Mr Wexford?'

'Not yet,' he said. 'At present I'll be content if you'll give me the name and address of the people whose party you and Mrs Zoffany went to on the evening of 27 January.'

She told him, without hesitation or surprise.

'Thank you, Mrs Arno.'

At the door of the room where Jane Zoffany was she paused, looked at him and giggled. 'You can call me Mrs X, if you like. Feel free.'

A housekeeper in a dark dress that was very nearly a uniform admitted him to the house in a cul-de-sac off Kensington Church Street. She was a pretty, dark-haired woman in her thirties who doubtless looked on her job as a career and played her part so well that he felt she *was* playing, was acting with some skill the role of a deferential servant. In a way she reminded him of Ted Hicks.

'Mrs Mountnessing hopes you won't mind going upstairs, Chief Inspector. Mrs Mountnessing is taking her coffee after luncheon in the little sitting room.'

It was a far cry from the house in De Beauvoir Square to which Natalie had sent him, a latter-day Bohemia where there had been Indian bedspreads draping the walls and a smell of marijuana for anyone who cared to sniff for it. Here the wall decorations were hunting prints, ascending parallel to the line of the staircase whose treads were carpeted in thick soft olive-green. The first-floor hall was wide, milk chocolate with white cornice and mouldings, the same green carpet, a *Hortus siccus* in a copper trough on a console table, a couple of fat-seated, round-backed chairs upholstered in golden-brown velvet, a twinkling chandelier and a brown table lamp with a cream satin shade. There are several thousand such interiors in the Royal Borough of Kensington and Chelsea. A panelled door was pushed open and Wexford found himself in the presence of Natalie Arno's Aunt Gladys, Mrs Rupert Mountnessing, the sister of Kathleen Camargue.

His first impression was of someone cruelly encaged and literally gasping for breath. It was a fleeting image. Mrs Mountnessing was just a fat woman in a too-tight corset which compressed her body from thighs to chest into the shape of a sausage and thrust a shelf of bosom up to buttress her double chin. This constrained flesh was sheathed in biscuit-coloured wool and upon the shelf rested three strands of pearls. Her face had become a cluster of pouches rather than a nest of wrinkles. It was thickly painted and surmounted by an intricate white-gold coiffure that was as smooth and stiff as a wig. The only area of Mrs Mountnessing which kept some hint of youth was her legs. And these were still excellent: slender, smooth, not varicosed, the ankles slim, the tapering feet shod in classic court shoes of beige glacé kid. They reminded him of Natalie's legs, they were exactly like. Did that mean anything? Very little. There are only a few types of leg, after all. One never said 'She has her aunt's legs' as one might say a woman had her father's nose or her grandmother's eyes.

The room was as beige and gold as its owner. On a low table was a coffee cup, coffee pot, sugar basin and cream jug in ivory china with a Greek key design on it in gold. Mrs Mountnessing rose when he came in and held out a hand much be-ringed, the old woman's claw-like nails filed to points and painted dark red.

'Bring another cup, will you, Miranda?'

It was the voice of an elderly child, petulant, permanently aggrieved. Wexford thought that the voice and the puckered face told of a lifetime of hurts, real or imagined. Rupert Mountnessing was presumably dead and gone long ago, and Dinah Sternhold had told him there had been no children. Would Natalie, real or false, hope for an inheritance here? Almost the first words uttered by Mrs Mountnessing told him that, if so, she hoped in vain.

'You said on the phone you wanted to talk to me about my niece. But I know nothing about my niece in recent years and I don't — I don't want to. I should have explained that to you, I realize that now. I shouldn't have let you come all this way when I've nothing at all to tell you.' Her eyes blinked more often or more obviously than most people's. The effect was to give the impression she fought off tears. 'Thank you, Miranda.' She took the coffee cup and listened, subsiding back into her chair as he told her the reason for his visit.

'Anastasia,' she said.

The Tichborne Claimant had been recalled, now the Tsar's

youngest daughter. Wexford did not relish the reminder, for wasn't it a fact that Anastasia's grandmother, the one person who could positively have identified her, had refused ever to see the claimant, and that as a result of that refusal no positive identification had ever been made?

'We hope it won't come to that,' he said. 'You seem to be her nearest relative, Mrs Mountnessing. Will you agree to see her in my presence and tell me if she is who she says she is?'

Her reaction, the look on her face, reminded him of certain people he had in the past asked to come and identify, not a living person, but a corpse in the mortuary. She put a hand up to each cheek. 'Oh no, I couldn't do that. I'm sorry, but it's impossible. I couldn't ever see Natalie again.'

He accepted it. She had forewarned him with her mention of Anastasia. If he insisted on her going with him the chances were she would make a positive identification simply to get the whole thing over as soon as possible. Briefly he wondered what it could have been that her niece, while still a young girl, had done to her, and then he joined her at the other end of the room where she stood contemplating a table that was used entirely as a stand for photographs in silver frames.

'That's my sister.'

A dark woman with dark eyes, but nevertheless intensely English. Perhaps there was something of the woman he knew as Natalie Arno in the broad brow and pointed chin.

'She had cancer. She was only forty-five when she died. It was a terrible blow to my poor brother-in-law. He sold their house in Pomfret and built that one in Kingsmarkham and called it Sterries. Sterries is the name of the village in Derbyshire where my parents had their country place. Kathleen and Manuel first met there.'

Camargue and his wife were together among the photographs on the table. Arm-in-arm, walking along some Mediterranean sea front; seated side by side on a low wall in an English garden; in a group with a tall woman so like Camargue that she had to be his sister, and with two small dark-haired smiling girls. A ray of sunlight, obliquely slanted at three on a winter's afternoon, fell upon the handsome moustached face of a man in the uniform of a colonel of the Grenadier Guards. Rupert Mountnessing, no doubt. A little bemused by so many faces, Wexford turned away.

'Did Sir Manuel go to the United States after your niece went to live there?'

'Not to see *her*. I think he went there on a tour — yes, I'm sure he did, though it must be ten or twelve years since he gave up playing. His arthritis crippled him, poor Manuel. We saw very little of each other in recent years, but I was fond of him, he was a sweet man. I would have gone to the memorial service but Miranda wouldn't let me. She didn't want me to risk bronchitis in that terrible cold.'

Mrs Mountnessing, it seemed, was willing to talk about any aspect of family life except her niece. She sat down again, blinking back non-existent tears, held ramrod stiff by her corset. Wexford persisted.

'He went on a tour. Did he make any private visits?'

'He may have done.' She said it in the way people do when they dodge the direct affirmative but don't want to lie.

'But he didn't visit his daughter while he was there?'

'California's three thousand miles from the east coast,' she said, 'it's as far again as from here.'

Wexford shook his head dismissively. 'I don't understand that for nineteen years Sir Manuel never saw his daughter. It's not as if he was a poor man or a man who never travelled. If he had been a vindictive man, a man to bear a grudge — but everyone tells me how nice he was, how kind, how good. I might say I'd had golden opinions from all sorts of people. Yet for nineteen years he never made an effort to see his only child and allegedly all because she ran away from college and married someone he didn't know.'

She said so quietly that Wexford hardly heard her, 'It wasn't like that.' Her voice gained a little strength but it was full of distress. 'He wrote to her — oh, ever so many times. When my sister was very ill, was in fact dying, he wrote to her and asked her to come home. I don't know if she answered but she didn't come. My sister died and she didn't come. Manuel made a new will and wrote to her, telling her he was leaving her everything because it was right she should have his money and her mother's. She didn't answer and he gave up writing.'

I wonder how you come to know that? he asked himself, looking at the crumpled profile, the chin that now trembled.

'I'm telling you all this,' said Mrs Mountnessing, 'to make you understand that my niece is cruel, cruel, a cruel unfeeling girl and violent too. She even struck her mother once. Did you know that?' The note in her voice grew hysterical and Wexford, watching the blinking eyes, the fingers clasping and unclasping in her lap, wished he had not mentioned the estrangement. 'She's a nymphomaniac too. Worse than that, it doesn't matter to her who the men are, her own relations, it's too horrible to talk about, it's too. . . .'

He interrupted her gently. He got up to go. 'Thank you for your help, Mrs Mountnessing. I can't see a sign of any of these propensities in the woman I know.'

Miranda showed him out. As he crossed to the head of the stairs he heard a very soft whimpering sound from the room he had left, the sound of an elderly child beginning to cry.

CHAPTER NINE

A birth certificate, a marriage certificate, an American driving licence complete with immediately recognizable photograph taken three years before, a United States passport complete with immediately recognizable photograph taken the previous September, and perhaps most convincing of all, a letter to his daughter from Camargue, dated 1963, in which he informed her that he intended to make her his sole heir. All these documents had been readily submitted to Symonds, O'Brien and Ames, who invited Wexford along to their offices in the precinct over the British Home Stores to view them.

Kenneth Ames, distant and chatty as ever, said he had personally seen Mrs Arno, interviewed her exhaustively and elicited from her a number of facts about the Camargue family and her own childhood which were currently being verified. Mrs Arno had offered to take a blood test but since this could only prove that she was *not* Camargue's daughter, not that she was, and since no one seemed to know what Camargue's blood group had been, it was an impracticable idea. Mr Ames said she seemed heartily amused by the whole business, a point of course in her favour. She had even produced samples of her handwriting from when she was at the Royal Academy of Music to be compared with her writing of the present day.

'Do you know what she said to him?' Wexford said afterwards, meeting Burden for a drink in the Olive and Dove. 'She's got a nerve. "It's a pity I didn't do anything criminal when I was a teenager," she said. "They'd have my fingerprints on record and that would solve everything".'

Burden didn't smile. 'If she's not Natalie Camargue, when could the change-over have taken place?'

'Provided we accept what Zoffany says, not recently. Say more than two years ago but after the death of Vernon Arno. According to Ames, he would seem to have died in a San Francisco hospital in 1971.'

'He must have been young still.' Burden echoed Wexford's words to Ivan Zoffany. 'What did he die of?'

'Leukaemia. No one's suggesting there was anything odd about his death, though there's a chance we'll know more when we hear from the California police. But, Mike, if there was substitution, if this is an assumed identity, it was assumed for some other reason. That is, it wasn't put on for the sake of inheriting from Carmargue.'

Burden gave a dubious nod. 'It would mean the true Natalie was dead.'

'She may be but there are other possibilities. The true Natalie may be incurably ill in some institution or have become insane or gone to live in some inaccessible place. And the impostor could be someone who needed an identity because keeping her own was dangerous, because, for instance, she was some kind of fugitive from justice. That Camargue was rich, that Camargue was old, that Natalie was to be his sole heir, all these facts might be *incidental*, might be a piece of luck for the impostor which she only later decided to take advantage of. The identity would have been taken on originally as a safety measure, even perhaps as the only possible lifeline, and I think it was taken on at a point where the minimum of deception would have been needed. Maybe at the time the move was made from San Francisco to Los Angeles or much later, at the time when Tina Zoffany died.'

Burden, who seemed not to have been concentrating particularly on any of this, said suddenly, looking up from his drink and fixing Wexford with his steel-coloured eyes:

'Why did she come to this country at all?'

'To make sure of the dibs,' said Wexford.

'No.' Burden shook his head. 'No, that wasn't the reason. Impostor or real, she was in no doubt about what you call the dibs. She'd had that letter from Camargue, promising her her inheritance. She need do nothing but wait. There was no need to re-establish herself in his eyes, no need to placate him. If she'd felt there was she'd have tried it before. After all, he was getting on for eighty.

'And it's no good saying she came back because he was getting married again. No one knew he was getting married till

632

10 December when his engagement was in the *Telegraph*. She came back to this country in November but she made no attempt to see Camargue until after she read about his engagement. She was here for three or four weeks before that. Doing what? Planning what?'

Admiration was not something Wexford had often felt for the inspector in the past. Sympathy, yes, affection and a definite need, for Burden had most encouragingly fulfilled the function of an Achates or a Boswell, if not quite a Watson. But admiration? Burden was showing unexpected deductive powers that were highly gratifying to witness, and Wexford wondered if they were the fruit of happiness or of reading aloud from great literature in the evenings.

'Go on,' he said.

'So why did she come back? Because she was sentimental for her own home, her ain countree, as you might say?' As Scott might say, thought Wexford. Burden went on, 'She's a bit young for those feelings. She's an American citizen, she was settled in California. If she is Natalie Camargue she'd lived there longer than here, she'd no relatives here but a father and an aunt she didn't get on with, and no friends unless you count those Zoffanys.

'If she's an impostor, coming back was a mad thing to do. Stay in America and when Camargue dies his solicitors will notify her of the death, and though she'll no doubt then have to come here and swear affidavits and that sort of thing, *no one will question who she is*. No one would have questioned it if she hadn't shown herself to Camargue.'

'But she had to do that,' Wexford objected. 'Her whole purpose surely in going to see him was to persuade him not to re-marry.'

'She didn't know that purpose would even exist when she left the United States in November. And if she'd stayed where she was she might never have known of Camargue's re-marriage until he eventually died. What would that announcement have merited in a California newspaper? The *Los Angeles Times*, for instance? A paragraph tucked away somewhere. "Former world-famous British flautist . . ." '

'They say flutist over there.'

'Flautist, flutist, what does it matter? Until we know *why* she came here I've got a feeling we're not going to get at the truth about this.'

'The truth about who she is, d'you mean?'

'The truth about Camargue's death.' And Burden said with a certain crushing triumph, 'You're getting an obsession about who this woman is. I knew you would, I said so. What interests me far more is the murder of Carmargue and who did it. Can't you see that in the context of the murder, who she is is an irrelevance?'

'No', said Wexford. 'Who she is is everything.'

The California police had nothing to tell Wexford about Natalie Arno. She was unknown to them, had never been in any trouble or associated with any trouble.

'The litigation in the Tichborne case,' said Burden gloomily, 'went on for three years and cost ninety thousand pounds. That was in 1874. Think what the equivalent of that would be today.'

'We haven't had any litigation yet,' said Wexford, 'or spent a single penny. Look on the bright side. Think of the claimant getting a fourteen-year sentence for perjury.'

In the meantime Kenneth Ames had interviewed two people who had known Camargue's daughter when she was an adolescent. Mavis Rolland had been at the Royal Academy of Music at the same time as Natalie Camargue and was now head of the music department at a girls' school on the South Coast. In her opinion there was no doubt that Natalie Arno was the former Natalie Camargue. She professed to find her not much changed except for her voice which she would not have recognized. On the other hand, Mary Woodhouse, a living-in maid who had worked for the Camargue family while they were in Pomfret, said she would have known the voice anywhere. In Ames's presence Mrs Woodhouse had talked to Natalie about Shaddough's Hall Farm where they had lived and Natalie had been able to recall events which Mrs Woodhouse said no impostor could have known.

Wexford wondered why Natalie had not proffered as witnesses for her support her aunt and that old family friend, Philip

Cory. It was possible, of course, that in the case of her aunt (if she really was Natalie Arno) the dislike was mutual and that, just as he had feared Mrs Mountnessing would recognize her as her niece to avoid protracting an interview, so Natalie feared to meet her aunt lest animosity should make her refuse that recognition. But Cory she had certainly seen since she returned home, and Cory had so surely believed in her as to cling to her arm in the excess of emotion he had no doubt felt at his old friend's obsequies. Was there some reason she didn't want Cory brought into this?

In the early years of broadcasting Philip Cory had achieved some success by writing incidental music for radio. But this is not the kind of thing which makes a man's name. If Cory had done this at all it was on the strength of his light opera *Aimée*, based on the story of the Empress Josephine's cousin, the French Sultana. After its London season it had been enthusiastically taken up by amateur operatic societies, largely because it was comparatively easy to sing, had a huge cast, and the costumes required for it could double for *Entführung* or even *Aladdin*. This was particularly the case in Cory's own locality, where he was looked upon as something of a pet bard. Driving out to the environs of Myringham where the composer lived, Wexford noted in the villages at least three posters announcing that *Aimée* was to be performed yet again. It was likely then to be a disappointed man he was on his way to see. Local fame is gratifying only at the beginning of a career, and it could not have afforded much solace to Cory to see that his more frivolous work was to be staged by the Myfleet and District Operatic Society (tickets £1.20, licensed bar opens seven-thirty) while his tone poem *April Fire* and his ballet music for the *Flowers of Evil* were forgotten.

Parents can of course (as Wexford knew personally) enjoy success vicariously. Philip Cory might be scarcely remembered outside village-hall audiences, but his son Blaise Cory was a celebrity as only a television personality can be. His twice-weekly show of soul-searching interviews, drumming up support for charities, and professing aid for almost anyone out of a job, a home or a marriage, vied for pride of place with *Runway* in the popularity ratings. The name was as much a household word as Frost or Parkinson; the bland, handsome, rather larger-than-life face instantly familiar.

'But he doesn't live here, does he?' said Burden whose *bête noire* Blaise Cory was.

'Not as far as I know.' Wexford tapped the driver on the shoulder. 'Those are the gates up ahead, I think. On the left.'

It had been necessary to keep an eye out, for Moidore Lodge, which was in deep country, was three miles from the nearest village and, Cory had told Wexford on the phone, was invisible from the road. The pillars that supported the gates and on which sat a pair of stone wolves or possibly alsatians — they very much resembled Nancy — were, however, unmistakable. The car turned in and, as the drive descended, entered an avenue of plane trees. And very strange and sinister they looked at this season, their trunks and limbs half covered in olive-green bark, half stripped to flesh colour, so that they appeared, or would have appeared to the fanciful, like shivering forms whose nakedness was revealed through rags. At the end of this double row of trees Moidore Lodge, three floors tall, narrow, and painted a curious shade of pale pea-green, glared formidably at visitors.

To ring the front-door bell it was necessary to climb half a dozen steps, though at the top of them there was no covered porch, nothing but a thin railing on each side. The wind blew sharply off the downs. Wexford, accustomed of late, as he remarked to Burden, to moving amongst those in the habit of being waited on, expected to be let in by a man or a maid or at least a cleaning woman, and was surprised when the door was opened by Cory himself.

He was no bigger than the impression of him Wexford had gained from that glimpse outside St Peter's, a little thin old man with copious white hair as silky as floss. Rather than appearing disappointed, he had a face that was both cheerful and peevish. He wore jeans and the kind of heavy navy-blue sweater that is called a guernsey, which gave him a look of youth, or the look perhaps of *a* youth who suffers from some terrible prematurely ageing disease. Before speaking, he looked them up and down closely. Indeed, they had passed through the over-heated, dusty, amazingly untidy and untended hall and were in the overheated, dusty rubbish heap of a living room before he spoke.

'Do you know,' he said, 'you are the first policemen I've ever actually had in my house. In any house I've ever lived in. Not the first I've ever *spoken* to, of course. I've *spoken* to them to ask the way and so forth. No doubt, I've lived a sheltered life.' Having done his best to make them feel like lepers or untouchables, Cory cracked his face into a nervous smile. 'The idea was distinctly strange to me. I've had to take two tranquillizers. As a matter of fact, my son is coming. I expect you've heard of my son.'

Burden's face was a mask of blankness. Wexford said, Who hadn't? and proceeded to enlighten Cory as to the purpose of their visit. The result of this was that the old man had to take another Valium. It took a further full ten minutes to convince him there was a serious doubt about Natalie Arno's identity.

'Oh dear,' said Cory, 'oh dear, oh dear, how dreadful. Little Natalie. And she was so kind and considerate to me at poor Manuel's memorial service. Who could possibly have imagined she wasn't Natalie at all?'

'Well, she may be,' said Wexford. 'We're hoping you can establish that one way or the other.'

Looking at the distracted little man on whom tranquillizers seemed to have no effect, Wexford couldn't help doubting if the truth could be established through his agency. 'You want me to come with you and ask her a lot of questions? How horribly embarrassing that will be.' Cory actually ran his fingers through his fluffy hair. Then he froze, listening, and looking for all the world like an alerted rabbit. 'A car!' he cried. 'That will be Blaise. And none too soon. I must say, really, he knew what he was about when he insisted on being here to support me.'

If the father was no larger than Wexford had anticipated, the son was much smaller. The screen is a great deceiver when it comes to height. Blaise Cory was a small, wide man with a big face and eyes that twinkled as merrily as those of Santa Claus or a friendly elf. He came expansively into the room, holding out both hands to Wexford.

'And how is Sheila? Away on her honeymoon? Isn't that marvellous?' Forewarned, astute, one who had to make it his business to know who was who, he had done his homework. 'You know, she's awfully like you. I almost think I should have known if I hadn't known, if you see what I mean.'

'They want me to go and look at poor Manuel's girl and tell them if she's really her,' said Cory dolefully.

His son put up his eyebrows, made a soundless whistle. 'You don't mean it? Is *that* what it's about?'

He seemed less surprised than his father or Mrs Mountnessing had been. But perhaps that was only because he daily encountered more surprising things than they did.

'Do you also know her, Mr Cory?' Wexford asked.

'Know her? We took our first violin lessons together. Well, that's an exaggeration. Let me say we, as tots, went to the same master.'

'You didn't keep it up, Blaise,' said Cory senior. 'You were never a *concentrating* boy. Now little Natalie was very good. I remember little Natalie playing so beautifully to me when she was fifteen or sixteen, it was Bach's Chaconne from the D minor Partita and she . . .'

Blaise interrupted him. 'My dear father, it is twelve-thirty, and though I seem to remember promising to take you out to lunch, a drink wouldn't come amiss. With the possible exception of Macbeth, you must be the world's worst host.' He chuckled irrepressibly at his own joke. 'Now surely you have something tucked away in one of these glory holes?'

Once more Cory put his hands through his hair. He began to trot about the room, opening cupboard doors and peering along cluttered shelves as if he were as much a stranger to the house as they were. 'It's because I've no one to look after me,' he said distractedly. 'I asked Natalie — or whoever she is, you know — I asked her if she didn't want those Hickses and if she didn't, would they come and work for me? She was rather non-committal, said she'd ask them, but I haven't heard another word. How do *you* manage?'

Wexford was saved from replying by a triumphant shout from Blaise Cory who had found a bottle of whisky and one of dry sherry. It was now impossible to refuse a drink especially as

Blaise Cory, with ferocious twinkles, declared that he knew for a fact policemen did drink on duty. The glasses were dusty and fingermarked, not to be too closely scrutinized. Nothing now remained but to fix a time with Philip Cory for visiting Natalie, and Wexford felt it would be wise, in spite of Burden's prejudice, to invite Blaise too.

'Ah, but I've already seen her. And frankly I wouldn't have the foggiest whether she was the late lamented Sir Manuel's daughter or not, I hadn't set eyes on her since we were teenagers. She said she was Natalie and that was good enough for me.'

'You were also at the memorial service?'

'Oh, no, no, no. Those morbid affairs give me the shivers. I'm a *life* person, Mr Wexford. No, I gave Natalie lunch. Oh, it must have been a good five or six weeks ago.'

'May I ask why you did that, Mr Cory?'

'Does one have to have a reason for taking attractive ladies out to lunch apart from the obvious one? No, I'm teasing you. It was actually Natalie who phoned me, recalled our former acquaintance and asked me if I could get a friend of hers a job, a man, she didn't say his name. I'm afraid it was all rather due to my programme. I don't know if a busy man like you ever has a moment to watch it? A poor thing, but mine own. I do make rather bold claims on it — not, however, without foundation *and* results — to aid people in finding — well, niches for themselves. This chap was apparently some sort of musician. Fancied himself on the box, I daresay. Anyway, I couldn't hold out much hope but I asked her to have lunch with me. Now I come to think of it, it was January 17th. I remember because that was the dear old dad's birthday.'

'I was seventy-four,' said Cory senior in the tone of one intending to astonish nobody, as indeed he had.

'And when you met her that day you had no doubt she was the Natalie Camargue you had once known?'

'Now wait a minute. When it came to it, I didn't meet her that day. She cancelled on account of some medical thing she had to have, a biopsy, I think she said. We made a fresh date for the following Tuesday. She kept that and I must say we had a delightful time, she was absolutely charming, full of fun. I was only sorry to have to say I hadn't anything cooking for this bloke of hers. But, you know, I couldn't actually tell you if she was *our* Natalie. I mean, it obviously never occurred to me.' He let his eyes light on Burden as being closer to his own age than the others. 'Would you recognize a lady you hadn't seen since you were nineteen?'

Burden responded with a cold smile which had no disconcerting effect on Blaise Cory.

'It 's all rather thrilling, isn't it? Quite a tonic it must be for the dear old dad.'

'No, it isn't,' said the composer. 'It's very upsetting indeed. I think I'll come back to London with you, Blaise, since I've got to be up there tomorrow. And I think I may stay awhile. I suppose you can put up with me for a couple of weeks?'

Blaise Cory put an arm round his father's shoulders and answered with merry affirmatives. Perhaps it was Wexford's imagination that the twinkle showed signs of strain.

The kind of coincidence that leads to one's coming across a hitherto unknown word three times in the same day or receiving a letter from an acquaintance one has dreamed of the night before was no doubt responsible for the poster in the window of the Kingsbrook Precinct travel agents. *Come to sunny California, land of perpetual spring.* . . . A picture of what might be Big Sur and next to it one of what might be Hearst Castle. Wexford paused and looked at it and wondered what the chief constable would say if he suggested being sent to the Golden West in quest of Natalie Arno's antecedents. He could just imagine Colonel Griswold's face.

Presently he turned away and went back to the police station. He had come from Symonds, O'Brien and Ames. Their handwriting expert had examined the writing of the eighteen-year-old Natalie Camargue and that of the thirty-seven-year-old Natalie Arno and expressed his opinion that, allowing for normal changes over a period of nearly two decades, the two samples had in all probability been made by the same person. Wexford had suggested the samples also be examined by an expert of police choosing. Without making any positive objection, Ames murmured that it would be unwise to spoil the ship with too many cooks.

Wexford thought he saw a better way.

'Mike,' he said, putting his head round the door of Burden's office, 'where can we get hold of a violin?'

CHAPTER TEN

Burden's wife was something of a paragon. She was a history teacher, she was well-read in English literature, she was an excellent cook and dressmaker and now it appeared she was musical too.

'You never told me Jenny played the violin,' said Wexford.

'As a matter of fact,' said Burden rather shyly, 'she used to be with the Pilgrim String Quartet.' This was a local ensemble that enjoyed a little more than local fame. 'I expect we could borrow her Hills if we were very careful with it.'

'Her *what?*'

'Her Hills. It's a well-known make of violin.'

'If you say so, Stradivarius.'

Burden brought the violin along in the morning. They were going to call for Philip Cory at his son's home and drive him to De Beauvoir Place. It was a bright sunny day, the first since the snow had gone.

Blaise Cory lived on Campden Hill, not far from Mrs Mountnessing, and work seemed to have claimed him, for his father was alone in the big penthouse flat. Although he popped a Valium pill into his mouth as soon as he saw them, a night in London had evidently done him good. He was sprightly, his cheeks pink, and he had dressed himself in a dark suit with a thin red stripe, a pink shirt and a burgundy silk tie, more as if he were going to a smart luncheon party than taking part in a criminal investigation.

In the car he was inclined to be talkative.

'I think I shall write to those Hickses personally. I've no reason to believe they're not well-disposed towards me. I understand they like the country and the thing about Moidore Lodge is, it's in the real country. Charming as poor Manuel's place is, I always used to think there was something Metroland-ish about it. One might as well be living in Hampstead Garden Suburb. Do you know, I thought it would be quite an ordeal facing little Natalie today, but actually I feel rather excited at the prospect. London is such a stimulus, don't you find? It seems to tone up one's whole system. And if she isn't Natalie, there's nothing to be embarrassed about.'

Wexford had no intention of going into the bookshop. The door to the upstairs flat was at the side of the building, a panelled door with a pane of glass in it, set under a porch with a steep tiled roof. As they walked up the path, Wexford leading and Burden bringing up the rear with the violin, the door opened, a woman came out and it immediately closed again. The woman was elderly and so tiny as to be almost a midget. She wore a black coat and a brightly coloured knitted hat and gloves. Cory said:

'Good gracious me! It's Mrs Woodhouse, isn't it?'

'That's right, sir, and you're Mr Cory.' She spoke with a Sussex burr. 'How have you been keeping? Mustn't grumble, that's what I always say. I see Mr Blaise on the telly last night, he's a real scream, just the same as ever. You living in London now, are you?'

'Oh dear, no,' said Cory. 'Down in the same old place.' His eyes widened suddenly as if with inspiration. 'I haven't anyone to look after me. I don't suppose . . .'

'I'm retired, sir, and never had so much to do. I don't have a moment for myself let alone other folks, So I'll say bye-bye now and nice to see you after all this time.'

She scuttled off in the direction of De Beauvoir Square, looking at her watch like the White Rabbit as she went.

'Who was that?' said Burden.

'She used to work for poor Manuel and Kathleen when they lived at Shaddough's Hall Farm. I can't think what she's doing up here.'

The door, though closed, had been left on the latch. Wexford pushed it open and they went up the steep staircase. Natalie had come out on to the landing and was waiting for them at the top. Wexford had thought about her so much, had indeed become so obsessive about her, that since last seeing her he had created an image of her in his mind that was seductive, sinister, Mata Hari-like, corrupt, guileful and serpentine. Before the reality this chimera showed itself briefly for the absurd delusion it was and then dissolved. For here, standing before them, was a charming and pretty woman to whom none of these pejorative expressions could possibly apply. Her black hair hung loose to her shoulders, held back by a velvet Alice band. She wore the skirt Jane Zoffany had been altering and with it a simple white shirt and dark blue cardigan. It was very near a school uniform and there was something of the schoolgirl about her as she brought her face down to Cory's and kissed him, saying with the slightest edge of reproach:

'It's good to see you, Uncle Philip. I only wish the circumstances were different.'

Cory drew his face away. He said in a kind of sharp chirp, 'One must do one's duty as a citizen.'

She laughed at that and patted his shoulder. They all went into a small and unpretentious living room from which a kitchen opened. It was all a far cry from Sterries. The furnishings looked if they had come down to the Zoffanys from defunct relatives who hadn't paid much for them when they were new. Nothing seemed to have been added by Natalie except a small shelf of paperbacks which could only be designated as non-Zoffany because none of them was science fiction.

There was an aroma of coffee and from the kitchen the sound, suggestive of some large hibernating creature snoring, that a percolator makes.

'Do sit down,' said Natalie, 'Make yourselves at home. Excuse me while I see to the coffee.' She seemed totally carefree and gave no sign of having noticed what Burden had brought into the flat. There's no art, thought Wexford, to find the mind's construction in the face.

The coffee, when it came, was good. 'The secret', said Natalie gaily, 'is to put enough in.' Uttering this cliché, she laughed. 'I'm afraid the British don't do that.'

She surely couldn't be enjoying herself like this if she was not Natalie, if there was any chance of her failing the test ahead of her. He glanced at Burden whose eyes were on her, who seemed to be studying her appearance and was recalling perhaps newspaper photographs or actual glimpses of Camargue. Having taken a sip of his coffee into which he ladled three spoonfuls of sugar, Cory started at once on his questioning. He would have made a good quizmaster. Perhaps it was from him that Blaise had inherited his talents.

'You and your parents went to live at Shaddough's Hall Farm when you were five. Can you remember what I gave you for your sixth birthday?'

She didn't hesitate. 'A kitten. It was a grey one, a British Blue.'

'Your cat had been run over and I gave you that one to replace it.'

'We called it Panther.'

Cory had forgotten that. But Wexford could see that now he remembered and was shaken. He asked less confidently: 'Where was the house?'

'On the Pomfret to Cheriton road. You'll have to do better than that, Uncle Philip. Anyone could have found out where Camargue lived.'

For answer he threw a question at her in French. Wexford wasn't up to understanding it but he gave Cory full marks for ingenuity. There was more to this old man than at first met the eye. She answered in fluent French and Cory addressed her in what Wexford took to be Spanish. This was something he was sure Symonds, O'Brien and Ames had not thought of. But what a sound test it was. Momentarily he held his breath, for she was not answering, her face had that puzzled foolish look people have when spoken to in a language they know less thoroughly than they have claimed.

Cory repeated what he had said. Burden cleared his throat and moved a little in his chair. Wexford held himself perfectly still, waiting, knowing that every second which passed made it more likely that she had been discovered and exposed. And then, as Cory was about to speak for the third time, she broke into a flood of fast Spanish so that Cory himself was taken aback, uncomprehending apparently, until she explained more slowly what it was that she had said.

Wexford drank his coffee and she, looking at him mischievously, refilled his cup. On Burden she bestowed one of her sparkling smiles. Her long hair fell forward, Cleopatra-like, in two heavy tresses to frame her face. It was a young face, Wexford thought, even possibly too young for the age she professed to be. And wasn't it also *too Spanish*? Natalie Camargue's mother had been English, typically English, her father half-French. Would their daughter look quite so much like one of Goya's women? None of the evidence, convincing though it was, was as yet conclusive. Why shouldn't an impostor speak Spanish? If the substitution had taken place in Los Angeles she might even be Mexican. Why not know about the kitten and its name if she had been a friend of the true Natalie and had set out to absorb her childhood history?

'What was the first instrument you learned to play?' Cory was asking.

'The recorder.'

'How old were you when you began the violin?'

'Eight.'

'Who was your first master?'

'I can't remember,' she said.

'When you were fifteen you were living at Shaddough's Hall Farm and you were on holiday from school. It was August. Your father had just come back from a tour of — America, I think.'

'Canada.'

'I do believe you're right.' Cory, having been determined almost from Wexford's first words on the subject to consider her an impostor, grew more and more astonished as the interrogation went on. 'You're right, it was. God bless my soul. Do you remember my coming to dinner with your parents? I and my wife? Can you remember that evening?'

'I think so. I hadn't seen you for about a year.'

'Before dinner I asked you to play something for me and you did and . . .'

She didn't even allow him to finish.

'I played Bach's Chaconne from the D minor Partita.'

Cory was stunned into silence. He stared at her and then turned on Wexford an affronted look.

'It was too difficult for me,' she said lightly. 'You clapped but I felt I'd made a mess of it.' The expressions on the three men's faces afforded her an amused satisfaction. 'That's proof enough, isn't it? Shall we all have a drink to celebrate my reinstatement?' She jumped up, took the tray and went into the kitchen, leaving the door open.

It was perhaps this open door and the sound of their hostess humming lightheartedly that stopped Cory from rounding on Wexford. Instead he raised his whiskery white eyebrows almost into his fluffy white hair and shook his head vigorously, a gesture that plainly said he felt he had been brought here on a wild-goose chase. If she wasn't Natalie, Wexford thought, there was no way she could have known about that piece of music. It was impossible to imagine circumstances in which the true Natalie would have spoken of such a thing to the false. If she had done so it would presuppose her having recounted every occasion on which she had played to a friend, listing every friend and every piece of music, since it could never have been foreseen that this particular piece would be inquired about. That Cory would ask this question, a question that had no doubt come into his mind because of his reference to the Bach Chaconne on the previous day, could only have been guessed at by those who had been present at the time, himself, Burden and Blaise.

So one could almost agree with her and acclaim her reinstated as Camargue's heir. She had passed the test no impostor could have passed. He looked at her wonderingly as she returned to the room, the contents of the tray now exchanged for a couple of bottles and an ice bucket. If she was, as she now seemed undoubtedly to be, Natalie Arno, how had Camargue possibly been deceived in the matter? This woman would never have mispronounced a word or a name in a foreign language known to her. And if Camargue had indeed accused her of doing so, it had been in her power to correct that misapprehension at once and to furnish him with absolute proof of who she was. For now Wexford had no doubt that if Camargue had asked her she would have recalled for him the minutest details of her infancy, of the family, of esoteric domestic customs which no one living but he and she could have known. But Camargue had been an old man, wandering in his wits as well as short-sighted and growing deaf. That tiresome woman Dinah Sternhold had wasted their time, repeating to him what was probably only one amongst several of a dotard's paranoid delusions.

Burden looked as if he was ready to leave. He had reached down to grasp once more the handle of the violin case.

'Would you play that piece of music for us now, Mrs Arno?' Wexford said.

If she had noticed the violin, as she surely must have done, she had presumably supposed it the property of Cory and unconnected with herself, for with his question her manner changed. She had put the tray down and had been about to lift her hands from it, but her hands remained where they were and slightly stiffened. Her face was unaltered, but she was no longer quite in command of the situation and she was no longer amused.

'No, I don't think I would,' she said.

'You've given up the violin?'

'No, I still play in an amateurish sort of way, but I'm out of practice.'

'We'll make allowances, Mrs Arno,' said Wexford. 'The inspector and I aren't competent to judge, anyway.' Burden gave him a look implying that *he* might be. 'If you'll play the violin so as to satisfy Mr Cory I will myself be satisfied that Sir Manuel had — made a mistake.'

She was silent. She sat still, looking down, considering. Then she put out her hand for the violin case and drew it towards her. But she seemed not quite to know how to open it, for she fumbled with the catch.

'Here, let me,' said Burden.

She got up and looked at the tray she had brought in. 'I forgot the glasses. Excuse me.'

Burden lifted out the violin carefully, then the bow. The sight of it restored Cory's temper and he touched one of the strings lightly with his finger. From the kitchen came a sudden tinkle of breaking glass, an exclamation, then a sound of water running.

'You may as well put that instrument away again,' said Wexford quietly.

She came in and her face was white. 'I broke a glass.' Wrapped round her left hand was a bunch of wet tissues, rapidly reddening, and as she scooped the sodden mass away, Wexford saw a long thin cut, bright red across three fingertips.

CHAPTER ELEVEN

It should have been the beginning, not the end. They should have been able to proceed with a prosecution for deception and an investigation of the murder of Sir Manuel Camargue. And Wexford, calling on Symonds, O'Brien and Ames with what he thought to be proof that Natalie Arno was not who she said she was, felt confident he had a case. She might speak French and Spanish, she might know the most abstruse details about the Camargues' family life, but she couldn't play the violin and that was the crux. She had not dared to refuse so she had deliberately cut her fingers on the tips where they must press the strings. Kenneth Ames listened to all this with a vagueness bordering on indifference which would have alarmed Wexford if he hadn't been used to the man's manner. He seemed reluctant to disclose the address of Mrs Mary Woodhouse but finally did so when pressed.

She lived with her son and daughter-in-law, both of whom were out at work, in a council flat on the Pomfret housing estate. While Wexford talked to her, explaining gently but at some length what he suspected, she at first sat still and attentive, but when the purpose of his visit became clear to her, she pushed her brows together and struck out her underlip and picked up the work on which she had been engaged before he arrived. This was some sort of bed cover, vast in size, of dead-white cotton crochet work. Mrs Woodhouse's crochet hook flashed in and out as she expended her anger through her fingers.

'I don't know what you're talking about, I don't know what you mean.' She repeated these sentences over and over whenever he paused for a reply. She was a small, sharp-featured old woman whose dark hair had faded to charcoal colour. 'I went to see Mrs Arno because she asked me. Why shouldn't I? I've got a sister living in Hackney that's been a bit off-colour. I've been stopping with her and what with Mrs Arno living like only a stone's throw away, it's only natural I'd go and see her, isn't it? I've known her since she was a kiddy, it was me brought her up as much as her mother.'

'How many times have you seen her, Mrs Woodhouse?'

'I don't know what you mean. Hundreds of times, thousands of times. If you mean been to her place like this past week, just the twice. The time you saw me and two days previous. I'd like to know what you're getting at.'

'Were some of those "hundreds of times" last November and December, Mrs Woodhouse? Did Mrs Arno go and see you when she first arrived in this country?'

'I'll tell you when I first saw her. Two weeks back. When that solicitor, that Mr Ames, come here and asked me the same sort of nonsense you're asking me. Only he knew when he was beaten.' The crochet hook jerked faster and the ball of yarn bounced on Mary Woodhouse's lap. 'Had I any doubt Mrs Arno was Miss Natalie Camargue?' She put a wealth of scorn into her voice. 'Of course I hadn't, not a shadow of doubt.'

'I expect Mrs Arno asked you a great many questions, didn't she? I expect she asked you to remind her of things in her childhood which had slipped her mind. The name of a grey kitten, for instance?'

'Panther,' said Mrs Woodhouse. 'That was his name. Why shouldn't I tell her? She'd forgotten, she was only a kiddy. I don't know what you mean, asking me things like that. Of course I've got a good memory, I was famous in the family for my memory. Mr Camargue — he was Mr Camargue then — he used to say, Mary, you're just like an elephant, and people'd look at me, me being so little and thin, and he'd say, You never forget a thing.'

'I expect you understand what conspiracy is, don't you, Mrs Woodhouse? You understand what is meant by a conspiracy to defraud someone of what is theirs by right of law? I don't think you would want to be involved in something of that kind, would you? Something which could get you into very serious trouble?'

She repeated her formula fiercely, one hand clutching the crochet hook, the other the ball of yarn. 'I don't know what you mean. I don't know what you're talking about.'

Mavis Rolland, the music teacher, was next on his list to be seen. He had the phone in his hand, he was about to dial the school number and arrange an appointment with her when Kenneth Ames was announced.

It was as warm in Wexford's office as it was in the Kingsbrook Precinct, but Ames removed neither his black, waisted overcoat nor his black-and-grey check worsted scarf. He took the chair Wexford offered him and fixed his eyes on the northern aspect of St Peter's spire just as he was in the habit of contemplating its southern elevation from his own window.

The purpose of his call, he said, was to inform the police that Symonds, O'Brien and Ames had decided to recognize Mrs Natalie Kathleen Camargue Arno as Sir Manuel Camargue's rightful heir.

In fact, said Ames, it was only their regard for truth and their horror of the possibility of fraud that had led them to investigate in the first place what amounted to malicious slander.

'We were obliged to look into it, of course, though it never does to place too much credence on that kind of mischief-making.'

'Camargue himself . . .' Wexford began.

'My dear chap, according to Mrs Steinbeck, according to *her*. I'm afraid you've been a bit led up the garden. Lost your sense of proportion too, if I may say so. Come now. You surely can't have expected my client to play you a pretty tune on that fiddle when she'd got a nasty cut on her hand.'

Wexford noted that Natalie Arno had become 'my client'. He was more surprised than he thought he could be by Ames's statement, he was shocked, and he sat in silence, digesting it, beginning to grasp its implications. Still staring skywards, Ames said chattily:

'There was never any real doubt, of course.' He delivered one of his strange confused metaphors. 'It was a case of making a mare's nest out of a molehill. But we do now have incontrovertible proof.'

'Oh yes?' Wexford's eyebrows went up.

'My client was able to produce her dentist, chappie who used to see to the Camargue family's teeth. Man called Williams from London, Wigmore Street, in point of fact. He'd still got his records and — well, my client's jaw and Miss Natalie Camargue's are indisputably one and the same. She hasn't even lost a tooth.'

Wexford made his appointment with Miss Rolland but was obliged to cancel it next day. For in the interim he had an unpleasant interview with the chief constable. Charles Griswold, with his uncanny resemblance to the late General de Gaulle, as heavily built, grave and intense a man as Ames was slight, shallow and *distrait*, stormed in upon him on the following morning.

'Leave it, Reg, forget it. Let it be as if you had never heard the name Camargue.'

'Because an impostor has seduced Ames into believing a pack of lies, sir?'

'*Seduced?*'

Wexford made an impatient gesture with his hand. 'I was speaking metaphorically, of course. *She is not Natalie Arno.* My firm belief is that ever since she came here she's been employing a former servant of the Camargue family to instruct her in matters of family history. As for the dentist, did Symonds, O'Brien and Ames check on him? Did they go to him or did he come to them? If this is a conspiracy in which a considerable number of people are involved. . . .'

'You know I haven't the least idea what you're talking about, don't you? All I'm saying is, if a reputable firm of solicitors such as Symonds, O'Brien and Ames will accept this woman and permit her to inherit a very significant property, we will accept her too. And we'll forget way-out notions of pushing old men into frozen lakes when we have not a shred of evidence that Camargue died anything but a natural death. Is that understood?'

'If you say so, it must be, sir.'

'It must,' said the chief constable.

Not the beginning but the end. Wexford had become obsessional about cases before, and the path these obsessions took had been blocked by just such obstacles and opposition. The feeling of frustration was a familiar one to him but it was none the less bitter for that. He stood by the window, cursing under his breath, gazing at the opaque pale sky. The weather had become raw and icy again, a white mist lifting only at midday and then hanging threateningly at tree height. Sheila was coming back today. He couldn't remember whether she was due in at ten in the morning or ten at night and he didn't want to know. That way he couldn't worry too precisely about what was happening to her aircraft in the fog, unable to land maybe, sent off to try Luton or Manchester, running short of fuel. . . . He told himself sternly, reminded himself, that air transport was the safest of all forms of travel, and let his thoughts turn back to Natalie Arno. Or whoever. Was he never to know now? Even if it were only for the satisfaction of his own curiosity, was he never to know who she was and how she had done it? The switch from one identity to another, the impersonation, the murder. . . .

After what Griswold had said, he dare not, for his very job's sake, risk another interview with Mary Woodhouse, keep his appointment with Mavis Rolland, attempt to break down the obduracy of Mrs Mountnessing or set about exposing that fake dentist, Williams. What could he do?

The way home had necessarily to be via the Kingsbrook Precinct, for Dora had asked him to pick up a brace of pheasants ordered at the poulterers there. Proximity to the premises of Symonds, O'Brien and Ames angered him afresh, and he wished he might for a split moment become a delinquent teenager in order to daub appropriate graffiti on their brass plate. Turning from it, he found himself looking once more into the window of the travel agents.

A helpful young man spread a handful of brochures in front of him. What had been Dora's favourites? Bermuda, Mexico, anywhere warm in the United States. They had discussed it endlessly without coming to a decision, knowing this might be the only holiday of such magnitude they would ever have. The poster he had seen in the window had its twin and various highly coloured siblings inside. He glanced up and it was the skyscraper-scape of San Francisco that met his eyes.

The fog had thickened while he was in there. It seemed to lay a cold wet finger on the skin of his face. He drove home very slowly, thinking once more about Sheila, but as he put his key into the front door lock the door was pulled open and there she was before him, browner than he had ever seen her, her hair bleached pale as ivory.

She put out her arms and hugged him. Dora and Andrew were in the living room.

'Heathrow's closed and we had to land at Gatwick,' said Sheila, 'so we thought we'd come and see you on our way. We've had such a fabulous time, Pop, I've been telling Mother, you just have to go.'

Wexford laughed. 'We are going to California,' he said.

Part Two

CHAPTER TWELVE

The will, published in the *Kingsmarkham Courier*, as well as in the national press, showed Sir Manuel Camargue to have left the sum of £1,146,000 net. This modest fortune became Natalie Arno's a little more than two months after Camargue's death.

'I shouldn't call a million pounds modest,' said Burden.

'It is when you consider all the people who will want their pickings,' Wexford said. 'All the conspirators. No wonder she's put the house up for sale.'

She had moved into Sterries, but immediately put the house on the market, the asking price being £110,000. For some weeks Kingsmarkham's principal estate agents, Thacker, Prince and Co., displayed in their window coloured photographs of its exterior, the music room, the drawing room and the garden, while less distinguishable shots of it appeared in the local press. But whether the house itself was too stark and simplistic in design for most people's taste or whether the price was too high, the fact was that it remained on sale throughout that period of the year when house-buying is at its peak.

'Funny to think that we know for sure she's no business to be there and no right to sell it and no right to what she gets for it,' said Burden, 'and there's not a damn thing we can do about it.'

But Wexford merely remarked that summer had set in with its usual severity and that he was looking forward to going somewhere warm for his holiday.

The Wexfords were not seasoned travellers and this would be the farthest away from home either had ever been. Wexford felt this need not affect the preparations they must make, but Dora had reached a point just below the panic threshold. All day she had been packing and unpacking and re-packing, confessing shamefacedly that she was a fool and then beginning to worry about the possibility of the house being broken into while they were away. It was useless for Wexford to point out that whether they were known to be in San Francisco or

Southend would make little difference to a prospective burglar. He could only assure her that the police would keep an eye on the house. If they couldn't do that for him, whom could they do it for? Sylvia had promised to go into the house every other day in their absence and he set off that evening to give her a spare key.

Wexford's elder daughter and her husband had in the past year moved to a newer house in north Kingsmarkham, and it was only a slightly longer way round to return from their home to his own by taking Ploughman's Lane. To go and look at the house Camargue had built, and on the night before he set out to prove Natalie Arno's claim to it fraudulent, seemed a fitting act. He drove into Ploughman's Lane by way of the side road which skirted the grounds of Kingsfield House. But if Sterries had been almost invisible from the roadway in January and February, it was now entirely hidden. The screen of hornbeams, limes and planes that had been skeletons when last he was there, were in full leaf and might have concealed an empty meadow rather than a house for all that could be seen of it.

It was still light at nearly nine. He was driving down the hill when he heard the sound of running feet behind him. In his rear mirror he saw a flying figure, a woman who was running down Ploughman's Lane as if pursued. It was Jane Zoffany.

There were no pursuers. Apart from her, the place was deserted, sylvan, silent, as such places mostly are even on summer nights. He pulled into the kerb and got out. She was enough in command of herself to swerve to avoid him but as she did so she saw who it was and immediately recognized him. She stopped and burst into tears, crying where she stood and pushing her knuckles into her eyes.

'Come and sit in the car,' said Wexford.

She sat in the passenger seat and cried into her hands, into the thin gauzy scarf which she wore swathed round her neck over a red and yellow printed dress of Indian make. Wexford gave her his handkerchief. She cried some more and laid her head back against the headrest, gulping, the tears running down her face. She had no handbag, no coat or jacket, though the dress was sleeveless, and on her stocklingless feet were Indian sandals with only a thong to attach them. Suddenly she began to speak, pausing only when sobs choked her voice.

'I thought she was wonderful. I thought he was the most wonderful, charming, gifted, *kind* person I'd ever met. And I thought she liked me, I thought she actually wanted my company. I never thought she'd really noticed my husband much, I mean except as my husband, that's all I thought he was to her, I thought it was *me*. . . . And now he says . . . oh God, what am I going to do? Where shall I go? What's going to become of me?'

Wexford was nonplussed. He could make little sense of what she said but guessed she was spilling all this misery out on to him only because he was there. Anyone willing to listen would have served her purpose. He thought too, and not for the first time, that there was something unhinged about her. You could see disturbance in her eyes as much when they were dry as when they were swollen and wet with tears. She put her hand on his arm.

'I did everything for her, I bent over backwards to make her feel at home, I ran errands for her, I even mended her clothes. She took all that from me and all the time she and Ivan had been — when he went out to California they had a relationship!'

He neither winced nor smiled at the incongruous word, relic of the already outdated jargon of her youth. 'Did she tell you that, Mrs Zoffany?' he asked gently.

'He told me. Ivan told me.' She wiped her face with the handkerchief. 'We came down here on Wednesday to stay, we meant to stay till — oh, Sunday or Monday. The shop's a dead loss anyway, no one ever comes in, it makes no difference whether we're there or not. She invited us and we came. I know why she did now. She doesn't want him but she wants him in love with her, she wants him on a string.' She shuddered and her voice broke again. 'He told me this evening, just now, half an hour ago. He said he'd been in love with her for two years, ever since he first saw her. He was longing for her to come and live here so that they could be together and then when she did come she kept fobbing him off and telling him to wait and now . . .'

'Why did he tell you all this?' Wexford interrupted.

She gulped, put out a helpless hand. 'He had to tell someone, he said, and there was no one but me. He overheard her talking to someone on the phone like he was her lover, telling him to come down once we'd gone but to be discreet. Ivan understood then. He's broken-hearted because she doesn't want him. He told his own wife that, that he doesn't know how he can go on living because another woman won't have him. I couldn't take it in at first, I couldn't believe it, then I started screaming. She came into our room and said what was the matter? I told her what he'd said and she said, "I'm sorry, darling, but I didn't know you then". She said that to *me*. "I didn't know you then," she said, "and it wasn't anything important anyway. It only happened three or four times, it was just that we were both lonely." As if that made it better!'

Wexford was silent. She was calmer now, though trembling. Soon she would begin regretting that she had poured out her heart to someone who was almost a stranger. She passed her hands over her face and dropped her shoulders with a long heavy sigh.

'Oh God. What am I going to do? Where shall I go? I can't stay with him, can I? When she said that to me I ran out of the house, I didn't even take my bag, I just ran and you were there and — oh God, I don't know what you must think of me talking to you like this. You must think I'm out of my head, crazy, mad. Ivan says I'm mad, "If you're going to carry on like that," he said, "a psychiatric ward's the best place for you." ' She gave him a sideways look. 'I've been in those places, that's why he said that. If only I had a friend I could go to but I've lost all my friends, in and out of hospital the way I've been. People don't want to know you any more when they think you've got something wrong with your mind. In my case it's only depression, it's a disease like any other, but they don't realize.' She gave a little whimpering cry. 'Natalie wasn't like that, she knew about my depression, she was *kind*. I thought she was, but all the time. . . . I've lost my only friend as well as my husband!'

Her mouth worked unsteadily from crying, her eyes were red. She looked like a hunted gypsy, the greying bushy hair hanging in shaggy bundles against her cheeks. And it was plain from her expression and her fixed imploring eyes that, because of his profession and his manner and his having caught her the way he had, she expected him to do something for her. Wreak vengeance on Natalie Arno, restore an errant husband or at least provide some dignified shelter for the night.

She began to speak rapidly, almost feverishly. 'I can't go back there, I can't face it. Ivan's going home, he said so, he said he'd go home tonight, but I can't be with him, I can't be alone with him, I couldn't bear it. I've got my sister in Wellridge but she won't want me, she's like the rest of them. . . . There must be somewhere I could go, you must know somewhere, if you could only. . . .'

There flashed into Wexford's mind the idea that he could take her home with him and get Dora to give her a bed for the night. The sheer nuisance this would be stopped him. They were going on holiday tomorrow, their flight went at one p.m, which meant leaving Kingsmarkham for Heathrow at ten. Suppose she refused to leave? Suppose Zoffany arrived? It just wasn't on.

She was still talking non-stop. 'So if I could possibly be with you there are lots of things I'd like to tell you. I feel if I could only get them off my chest I'd be that much better and they'd help you, they're things you'd want to know.'

'About Mrs Arno?' he said sharply.

'Well, not exactly about her, about *me*. I need someone to listen and be sympathetic, that does you more good than all the therapy and pills in the world, I can tell you. I can't be alone, don't you understand?'

Later he was to castigate himself for not giving in to that first generous impulse. If he had done he might have known the true facts that night and, more important, a life might have been saved. But as much as the unwillingness to be involved and to create trouble for himself, a feeling of caution prevented him. He was a policeman, the woman was a little mad. . . .

'The best thing will be for me to drive you back up the hill to Sterries, Mrs Zoffany. Let me. . . .'

'No!'

'You'll very probably find your husband is ready to leave and waiting for you. You and he would still be in time to catch the last train to Victoria. Mrs Zoffany, you have to realize he'll get over this, it's something that will very likely lose its force now he's brought it into the open. Why not try to . . . ?'

'No!'

'Come, let me take you back.'

For answer, she gathered up her skirts and draperies and half jumped, half tumbled out of the car. In some consternation, Wexford too got out to help her, but she had got to her feet and as he put out his arm she threw something at him, a crumpled ball. It was his handkerchief.

She stood for a little while a few yards from him, leaning against the high jasmine-hung wall of one of these sprawling gardens. She hung her head, her hands up to her chin, like a child who has been scolded. It was deep dusk now and growing cool. Suddenly she began to walk back the way she had come. She walked quite briskly up the hill, up over the crown of the hill, to be lost amid the soft, hanging, darkening green branches.

He waited a while, he hardly knew what for. A car passed him just as he started his own, going rather fast down the hill. It was a mustard-coloured Opel, and although it was much too dark to see at all clearly, the woman at the wheel looked very much like Natalie Arno. It was a measure, of course, of how much she occupied his thoughts.

He drove home to Dora who had packed for the last time and was watching Blaise Cory's programme on the television.

CHAPTER THIRTEEN

Wexford was driving on the wrong side of the road. Or that was how he put it to himself. It wasn't as bad as he had expected, the San Diego Freeway had so many lanes and traffic moved at a slower pace than at home. What was alarming and didn't seem to get any better was that he couldn't judge the space he had on the right-hand side so that Dora exclaimed, 'Oh, Reg, you were only about an inch from that car. I was sure you were going to scrape!'

The sky was a smooth hazy blue and it was very hot. Nine hours' flying had taken its toll of both of them. Stopped at the lights — traffic lights hung somewhere up in the sky here — Wexford glanced at his wife. She looked tired, she was bound to, but excited as well. For him it wasn't going to be much of a holiday, unless you agreed with those who say that a change is as good as a rest, and he was beginning to feel guilty about the amount of time he would have to spend apart from her. He had tried to explain that if it wasn't for this quest of his they wouldn't be coming here at all, and she had taken it with cheerful resignation. But did she understand quite what he meant? It was all very well her saying she was going to look up those long-lost friends of hers, the Newtons. Wexford thought he knew just how much they would do for a visitor, an invitation to dinner was what that would amount to.

He had just got used to the road, was even beginning to enjoy driving the little red automatic Chevette he had rented at the airport, when the palms of Santa Monica were before them and they were on Ocean Drive. He had promised Dora two days here, staying in luxury at the Miramar, before they set off for wherever his investigations might lead them.

Where was he going to begin? He had one meagre piece of information to go on. Ames had given it to him back in February and it was Natalie Arno's address in Los Angeles. The magnitude of his task was suddenly apparent as, once they had checked in and Dora had lain down in their room to sleep, he stood under the eucalyptus trees, looking at the Pacific. Everything seemed so big, a bigger sea, a bigger beach, a vaster sky than he had ever seen before. And as their plane had come in to land he had looked down and been daunted by the size of the sprawling, glittering, metallic-looking city spread out there below them. The secret of Natalie Arno had appeared enormous in Kingsmarkham; here in Los Angeles it was surely capable of hiding itself and becoming for ever lost in one of a hundred million crannies.

But one of these crannies he would explore in the morning. Tuscarora Avenue, where Natalie had lived for eight years after coming south from San Francisco, Tuscarora Avenue in a suburb called Opuntia. The fancy names suggested to Wexford that he might expect a certain slumminess, for at home Vale Road would be the site of residential elegance and Valhalla Grove of squalor.

The shops were still open. He walked up Wilshire Boulevard and bought himself a larger and more detailed street plan of Los Angeles than the car hire company had provided.

The next morning when he went out Dora was preparing to phone Rex and Nonie Newton. A year or two before she met Wexford Dora had been engaged to Rex Newton; a boy-and-girl affair it had been, they were both in their teens, and Rex had been supplanted by the young policeman. Married for thirty years now, Rex had retired early and emigrated with his American wife to California. Wexford hoped wistfully that they would be welcoming to Dora, that Nonie Newton would live up to the promises she had made in her last letter. But he could only hope for the best. By ten he was on his way to Opuntia.

The names had misled him. Everything here had an exotic name, the grand and tawdry alike. Opuntia wasn't shabby but paintbox bright with houses like Swiss chalets or miniature French chateaux set in garden plots as lush as jungles. He had previously only seen such flowers in florist's shops or the hothouses of public gardens, oleanders, bougainvilleas, the orange-and-blue bird-of-paradise flower, emblem of the City of the Angels. No wind stirred the fronds of the fan palms. The sky was blue, but white with smog at the horizon.

Tuscarora Avenue was packed so tightly with cars that two drivers could hardly pass each other. Wexford despaired of finding a niche for the Chevette up there, so he left it at the foot of the hill and walked. Though there were side streets called Mar Vista and Oceania Way, the sea wasn't visible, being blocked from view by huge apartment buildings which raised their penthouse tops out of a forest of palm and eucalyptus. 1121 Tuscarora, where Natalie Arno had lived, was a small squat house of pink stucco. It and its neighbours, a chocolate-coloured mini-castle and a baby hacienda painted lemon, reminded Wexford of the confections on the sweets trolley at the Miramar the previous night. He hesitated for a moment, imagining Natalie there, the light and the primary colours suiting her better than the pallor and chill of Kingsmarkham, and then he went up to the door of the nearest neighbour, the chocolate-fudge-iced 1123.

A man in shorts and a tee-shirt answered his ring. Wexford, who had no official standing in California, who had no right to be asking questions, had already decided to represent himself as on a quest for a lost relative. Though he had never before been to America, he knew enough of Americans to be pretty sure that this kind of thing, which might at home be received with suspicion, embarrassment and taciturnity, would here be greeted with warmth.

The householder, whose shirt campaigned in red printed letters for the Equal Rights Amendment, said he was called Leo Dobrowski and seemed to justify Wexford's belief. He asked him in, explained that his wife and children had gone to church, and within a few minutes Wexford found himself drinking coffee with Mr Dobrowski on a patio hung with the prussian-blue trumpets of morning glory.

But in pretending to a family connection with Tina Zoffany he had made a mistake. Leo Dobrowski knew all about Tina Zoffany and scarcely anything about Natalie Arno or any other occupants of 1121 Tuscarora. Hadn't Tina, in the two years she had lived next door, become Mrs Dobrowski's closest friend? It was a pleasure, though a melancholy one, for Mr Dobrowski at last to be able to talk about Tina to someone who *cared*. Her brother, he thought, had never cared, though he hoped he wasn't speaking out of turn in saying so. If Wexford was Tina's uncle, he would know what a sweet lovely person she had been and what a tragedy her early death was. Mrs Dobrowski herself had been made sick by the shock of it. If Wexford would care to wait until she came back from church he knew his wife had some lovely snapshots of Tina and could probably let him have some small keepsake of Tina's. Her brother had brought all her little odds and ends to them, wouldn't want the expense of sending them home, you could understand that.

'You sure picked the right place when you came to us,' said Mr Dobrowski. 'I guess there's not another family on Tuscarora knew Tina like we did. You have ESP or something?'

After that Wexford could scarcely refuse to meet the church-going wife. He promised to come back an hour later. Mr Dobrowski beamed his pleasure and the words on his tee-shirt — 'Equality of rights under the law shall not be denied or abridged by the United States or any state on account of sex' — expanded with his well-exercised muscles.

The occupants of 1125 — this time Wexford was a cousin of Natalie's and no nonsense about it — were new to the district and so were those who lived further down the hill in a redwood-and-stucco version of Anne Hathaway's cottage. He went to 1121 itself and picked up from the man he spoke to his first piece of real information, that the house had not been bought but was rented from Mrs Arno. Who was there in the neighbourhood, Wexford asked him, who might have known Mrs Arno when she lived here? Try 1122 on the opposite side, he was advised. In an ever-changing population, the people at 1122, the Romeros, had been in residence longest.

Natalie's cousin once more, he tried at 1122.

'You English?' said Mrs Donna Romero, a woman who looked even more Spanish than Natalie and whose jet-black hair was wound on to pink plastic rollers.

Wexford nodded.

'Natalie's English. She went home to her folks in London. That's all I know. Right now she's somewhere in London, England.'

'How long have you been living here?'

'I just love your accent,' said Mrs Romero. 'How long have

we been here? I guess it'd be four years, right? We came the summer Natalie went on that long vacation up the coast. Must've been the summer of '76. I guess I just thought the house was empty, no one living there, you know, you get a lot of that round here, and then one day my husband says to me, there's folks moved into 1121, and that was Natalie.'

'But she'd lived there before?'

'Oh, sure she lived there before but we didn't, did we?' Donna Romero said this triumphantly as if she had somehow caught him out. 'She had these roomers, you know? There was this guy she had, he was living here illegally. Well, I guess everyone knew it, but my husband being in the Police Department — well, he had to do what he had to do, you know?'

'You mean he had him deported?'

'That's what I mean.'

Wexford decided he had better make himself scarce before an encounter threatened with the policeman husband. He contented himself with merely asking when this deportation had taken place. Not so long ago, said Mrs Romero, maybe only last fall, as far as she could remember.

It was now noon and growing fiercely hot. Wexford reflected that whoever it was who had first described the climate of California as perpetual spring hadn't had much experience of an English April. He went back across the road.

The presence on the drive of 1123 of a four-year-old manoeuvring a yellow and red truck and a six-year-old riding a blue bicycle told him Mrs Dobrowski was back. She greeted him so enthusiastically and with such glistening if not quite tearful eyes that he felt a thrust of guilt when he thought of her conferring later with the man at 1121 and with Patrolman (Lieutenant? Captain?) Romero. But it was too late now to abandon the role of Tina's uncle. He was obliged to listen to a catalogue of Tina's virtues while Mrs Dobrowski, small and earnest and wearing a tee-shirt campaigning for the conservation of the sea otter, pressed Tina souvenirs on him, a brooch, a pair of antique nail scissors, and a curious object she said was a purse ashtray.

At last he succeeded in leading the conversation to Natalie by saying with perfect truth that he had seen her in London before he left. It was immediately clear that Mrs Dobrowski hadn't approved of Natalie. Her way of life had not been what Mrs Dobrowski was used to or expected from people in a nice neighbourhood. Turning a little pink, she said she came from a family of Baptists, and when you had children you had standards to maintain. Clearly she felt that she had said enough on the subject and reverted to Tina, her prowess as what she called a stenographer, the sad fact of her childlessness, the swift onset of the disease which had killed her. Wexford made a second effort.

'I've often wondered how Tina came to live here.'

'I guess Natalie needed the money after Rolf Ilbert moved out. Johnny was the one who told Tina Natalie had a room for rent.'

Wexford made a guess. 'Johnny was Natalie's — er, friend?'

Mrs Dobrowski gave him a grim smile. 'I've heard it called that. Johnny Fassbender was her lover.'

The name sounded German but here might not be. When Wexford asked if he were a local man Mrs Dobrowski said no, he was Swiss. She had often told Tina that one of them should report him to the authorities for living here without a residence permit, and eventually someone must have done so, for he was discovered and deported.

'That would have been last autumn,' Wexford said.

'Oh, ro. Whatever gave you that idea? It was all of three years ago. Tina was still alive.'

There was evidently a mystery here, but not perhaps one of pressing importance. It was Natalie's identity he was primarily concerned with, not her friendships. But Mrs Dobrowski seemed to feel that she had digressed too far for politeness and moved rapidly on to her visitor's precise relationship to Tina. Was he her true uncle or uncle only by marriage? Strangely, Tina had never mentioned him. But she had mentioned no one but the brother who came over when she died. She, Mrs Dobrowski, would have liked Ivan to have stayed at her house while he was in Los Angeles but hadn't known how to broach this as she had hardly exchanged a word with Natalie all the years they had lived there. Wexford pricked up his ears at that. No, it was true, she had never set foot inside 1121 or seen Natalie closer than across the yard.

Wexford noted that what she called the yard was, by Kingsmarkham standards, a large garden, dense with oleanders, peach trees and tall cacti. In order not to offend Mrs Dobrowski, he was obliged to carry off with him the brooch as a keepsake. Perhaps he could pass it on to the Zoffanys.

'It's been great meeting you,' said Mrs Dobrowski. 'I guess I can see a kind of look of Tina about you now. Around the eyes.' She gathered the four-year-old up in her arms and waved to Wexford from the porch. 'Say hello to Ivan for me.'

In the heat of the day he drove back to the Miramar and took Dora out to lunch in a seafood restaurant down by the boardwalk. He hardly knew how to tell her he was going to have to leave her alone for the afternoon as well. But he did tell her and she bore it well, only saying that she would make another attempt to phone the Newtons. In their room she dialled their number again while he consulted the directory, looking for Ilberts. There was no Rolf Ilbert in the Los Angeles phone book or in the slimmer Santa Monica directory, but in this latter he did find a Mrs Davina Lee Ilbert at a place called Paloma Canyon.

Dora had got through. He heard her say delightedly, 'Will you really come and pick me up? About four?' Considerably relieved, he touched her shoulder, got a wide smile from her, and then he ran out to the lift, free from guilt at least for the afternoon.

It was too far to walk, half-way to Malibu. He found Paloma Canyon without difficulty and encouraged the car up an impossibly steep slope. The road zig-zagged as on some alpine mountainside, opening up at each turn bigger and better views of the Pacific. But otherwise he might have been in Ploughman's Lane. All super residential areas the world over are the same, he thought, paraphrasing Tolstoy, it is only the slums that differ from each other. Paloma Canyon was Ploughman's Lane with palms. And with a bluer sky, daisy lawns and an architecture Spanish rather than Tudor.

She wasn't the wife but the ex-wife of the man called Rolf Ilbert. No, she didn't mind him asking, she would be only too glad if there was anything she could do to get back at Natalie

Arno. Would he mind coming around to the pool? They always spent their Sunday afternoons by the pool.

Wexford followed her along a path through a shrubbery of red and purple fuchsias taller than himself. She was a tall thin woman, very tanned and with bleached blonde hair, and she wore a sky-blue terry-cloth robe and flat sandals. He wondered what it must be like to live in a climate where you took it for granted you spent every Sunday afternoon round the pool. It was extremely hot, too hot to be down there on the beach, he supposed.

The pool, turquoise blue and rectangular with a fountain playing at the far end, was in a patio formed by the balconied wings of the lemon-coloured stucco house. Davina Lee Ilbert had evidently been lying in a rattan lounging chair, for there was a glass of something with ice in it and a pair of sunglasses on the table beside it. A girl of about sixteen in a bikini was sitting on the rim of the fountain and a boy a bit younger was swimming lengths. They both had dark curly hair and Wexford supposed they must resemble their father. The girl said 'Hi' to him and slipped into the water.

'You care for iced tea?' Mrs Ilbert asked him.

He had never tasted it but he accepted. While she was fetching it he sat down in one of the cane peacock chairs, looking over the parapet to the highway and the beaches below.

'You want to know where Rolf met her?' Davina Ilbert took off her robe and stretched out on the lounger, a woman of forty with a good if stringy figure who had the discretion to wear a one-piece swimsuit. 'It was in San Francisco in '76. Her husband had died and she was staying with friends in San Rafael. The guy was a journalist or something and they all went into the city for this writers' conference that was going on, a cocktail party, I guess it was. Rolf was there.'

'Your former husband is a writer?'

'Movie and TV scripts,' she said. 'You wouldn't have heard of him. Whoever heard of script writers? You have a serial called *Runway* on your TV?'

Wexford said nothing, nodded.

'Rolf's done some of that. You know the episodes set at Kennedy? That's his stuff. And he's made a mint from it, thank

God.' She made a little quick gesture at the balconies, the fountain, her own particular expanse of blue sky. 'It's Natalie you want to know about, right? Rolf brought her back to LA and bought that house on Tuscarora for her.'

The boy came out of the pool and shook himself like a dog. His sister said something to him and they both stared at Wexford, looking away when he met their eyes.

'He lived there with her?' he asked their mother.

'He kind of divided his time between me and her.' She drank from the tall glass. 'I was really dumb in those days, I trusted him. It took me five years to find out and when I did I flipped. I went over to Tuscarora and beat her up. No kidding.'

Wexford said impassively, 'That would have been in 1976?'

'Right. Spring of '76. Rolf came back and found her all bruised and with two black eyes and he got scared and took her on a trip up the coast to get away from me. It was summer, I don't suppose she minded. She was up there two, three months? He'd go up and join her when he could but he never really lived with her again.' She gave a sort of tough chuckle. 'I'd thrown him out too. All he had was a hotel room in Marina del Rey.'

The sun was moving round. Wexford shifted into the shade and the boy and girl walked slowly away into the house. A humming bird, no larger than an insect, was hovering on the red velvet threshold of a trumpet flower. Wexford had never seen one before. He said:

'You said "up the coast". Do you know where?'

She shrugged. 'They didn't tell me their plans. But it'd be somewhere north of San Simeon and south of Monterey, maybe around Big Sur. It could have been a motel, but Rolf was generous, he'd have rented a house for her.' She changed her tone abruptly. 'Is she in trouble? I mean, real trouble?'

'Not at the moment,' said Wexford. 'She's just inherited a very nice house and a million from her father.'

'Dollars?'

'Pounds.'

'Jesus, and they say cheating never pays.'

'Mrs Ilbert, forgive me, but you said your former husband and Mrs Arno never lived together again after the summer of '76. Why was that? Did he simply get tired of her?'

She gave her dry bitter laugh. '*She* got tired of him. She met someone else. Rolf was still crazy about her. He told me so, he told me all about it.'

Wexford recalled Jane Zoffany. Husbands seemed to make a practice of confiding in their wives their passion for Natalie Arno. 'She met someone while she was away on this long holiday?'

'That's what Rolf told me. She met this guy and took him back to the house on Tuscarora — it was hers, you see, she could do what she wanted — and Rolf never saw her again.'

'*He never saw her again?*'

'That's what he said. She wouldn't see him or speak to him. I guess it was because he still hadn't divorced me and married her, but I don't know. Rolf went crazy. He found out this guy she was with was living here illegally and he got him deported.'

Wexford nodded. 'He was a Swiss called Fassbender.'

'Oh, no. Where d'you get that from? I don't recall his name but it wasn't what you said. He was English. Rolf had him deported to England.'

'Did *you* ever see her again?'

'Me? No, why would I?'

'Thank you, Mrs Ilbert. You've been very frank and I'm grateful.'

'You're welcome. I guess I still feel pretty hostile towards her for what she did to me and my kids. It wouldn't give me any grief to hear she'd lost that house and that million.'

Wexford drove down the steep hill, noticing attached to a house wall something he hadn't seen on the way up. A printed notice that said 'No Solicitors'. He chuckled. He knew very well that this was an American equivalent of the 'nice' suburb's injunction to hawkers or people delivering circulars, but it still made him laugh. He would have liked to prise it off the wall and take it home for Symonds, O'Brien and Ames.

Dora was out when he got back to the Miramar and there was a note for him telling him not to wait for dinner if she wasn't back by seven-thirty. Rex Newton, whom he had rather disliked in the days when they had been acquaintances, he now blessed. And tomorrow he would devote the whole day exclusively to Dora.

CHAPTER FOURTEEN

From the map it didn't look as if there was much in the way of
habitation in the vicinity of Big Sur, and Wexford's idea that
Natalie Arno's trail might therefore easily be followed was
confirmed by an elderly lady in the hotel lobby. This was a Mrs
Lewis from Denver, Colorado, who had spent, it appeared, at
least twenty holidays in California. There was hardly a house,
hotel or restaurant, according to Mrs Lewis, between San
Simeon in the south and Carmel in the north. The coast was
protected, Wexford concluded, it was conserved by whatever
the American equivalent might be of the National Trust.

The Miramar's enormous lobby had carpet sculpture on
the walls. Although it was probably the grandest hotel Wexford
had ever stayed in, the bar was so dark as to imply raffishness
or at least that it would be wiser not to see what one was
drinking. In his case this was white wine, the pleasant, innocuous, rather weak chablis which must be produced here by the
millions of gallons considering the number of people he had
seen swilling it down. What had become of the whisky sours and
dry martinis of his reading? He sat alone — Dora and Mrs
Lewis were swapping family snaps and anecdotes — reflecting
that he should try to see Rolf Ilbert before he began the drive
northwards. Ilbert was surely by now over Natalie and would
have no objection to telling him the name of the place where
she had stayed in the summer of 1976. Wexford finished his
second glass of wine and walked down past the sculptured
carpet palms to phone Davina Ilbert, but there was no reply.

In the morning, when he tried her number again, she told
him her ex-husband was in London. He had been in London
for two months, researching for a television series about American girls who had married into the English aristocracy. Wexford
realized he would just have to trace Natalie on what he had.
They drove off at lunchtime and stopped for the night at a
motel in Santa Maria. It was on the tip of Wexford's tongue to
grumble to Dora that there was nothing to do in Santa Maria,

miles from the coast and with Route 101 passing through it. But then it occurred to him that a visitor might say exactly that about Kingsmarkham. Perhaps there was only ever something obvious to do in the centre of cities or by the sea. Elsewhere there was ample to do if you lived there and nothing if you didn't. He would have occupation soon enough and then his guilt about Dora would come back.

Over dinner he confided his theory to her.

'If you look at the facts you'll see that there was a distinct change of personality in 1976. The woman who went away with Ilbert had a different character from the woman who came back to Los Angeles. Think about it for a minute. Camargue's daughter had led a very sheltered, cared-for sort of life, she'd never been out in the world on her own. First there was a secure home with her parents, then elopement with and marriage to Arno, and when Arno died, Ilbert. She was always under the protection of some man. But what of the woman who appears *after* the summer of '76? She lets off rooms in her house to bring in an income. She doesn't form long steady relationships but has casual love affairs — with the Swiss Fassbender, with the English man who was deported, with Zoffany. She can't sell the house Ilbert bought for her so she lets it out and comes to England. Not to creep under her father's wing as Natalie Camargue might have done, but to shift for herself in a place of her own.'

'But surely it was a terrible risk to go to Natalie's own house and live there as Natalie? The neighbours would have known at once, and then there'd be her friends . . .'

'Good fences make good neighbours,' said Wexford. 'There's a lot of space between those houses, it's a shifting population, and if my idea is right Natalie Camargue was a shy, reserved sort of woman. Her neighbours never saw much of her. As to friends — if a friend of Natalie's phoned she had only to say Natalie was still away. If a friend comes to the house she has only to say that she herself is a friend who happens to be staying there for the time being. Mrs Ilbert says Ilbert never saw her after she came back. Now if the real Natalie came back it's almost impossible Ilbert never saw her. Never was alone with her maybe, never touched her, but never saw her? No, it was the impostor who fobbed him off every time he called with excuses, with apologies, and at last with direct refusals, allegedly on the part of the real Natalie, ever to see him again.'

'But, Reg, how could the impostor know so much about the real Natalie's past?'

He took her up quickly. 'You spent most of last evening talking to Mrs Lewis. How much do you know about her from, say, two hours' conversation?'

Dora giggled. 'Well, she lives in a flat, not a house. She's a widow. She's got two sons and a daughter. One of the sons is a realtor, I don't know what that is.'

'Estate agent.'

'Estate agent, and the other's a vet. Her daughter's called Janette and she's married to a doctor and they've got twin girls and they live in a place called Bismarck. Mrs Lewis has got a four-wheel-drive Chevrolet for the mountain roads and a holiday house, a log cabin, in the Rockies and ...'

'Enough! You found all that out in two hours and you're saying the new Natalie couldn't have formed a complete dossier of the old Natalie in — what? Five or six weeks? And when she came to England she had a second mentor in Mary Wood-house.'

'All right, perhaps she could have.' Dora hesitated. He had had a feeling for some hours that she wanted to impart — or even break — something to him. 'Darling,' she said suddenly, 'You won't mind, will you? I told Rex and Nonie we'd be staying at the Redwood Hotel in Carmel and it so happens, I mean, it's a complete coincidence, that they'll be staying with Nonie's daughter in Monterey at the same time. If we had lunch with them once or twice — or I did — well, you won't mind, will you?'

'I think it's a wonderful idea.'

'Only you didn't used to like Rex, and I can't honestly say he's changed.'

'It's such a stupid name,' Wexford said unreasonably. 'Stupid for a man, I mean. It's all right for a dog.'

Dora couldn't help laughing. 'Oh, come. It only just misses being the same as yours.'

'A miss is as good as a mile. What d'you think of my theory then?'

'Well — what became of the old Natalie?'
'I think it's probable she murdered her.'

The road came back to the sea again after San Luis Obispo. It was like Cornwall, Wexford thought, the Cornish coast gigantically magnified both in size and in extent. Each time you came to a bend in the road another bay opened before you, vaster, grander, more majestically beautiful than the last. At San Simeon Dora wanted to see Hearst Castle, so Wexford drove her up there and left her to take the guided tour. He went down on the beach where shade was provided by eucalyptus trees. Low down over the water he saw a pelican in ponderous yet graceful flight. The sun shone with an arrogant, assured permanence, fitting for the finest climate on earth.

There wasn't much to San Simeon, a car park, a restaurant, a few houses. And if Mrs Lewis was to be believed, the population would be even sparser as he drove north. The Hearst Castle tour lasted a long time and they made no more progress that day, but as they set off next morning Wexford began to feel something like dismay. It was true that if you were used to living in densely peopled areas you might find the coast here sparsely populated, but it wasn't by any means *unpopulated*. Little clusters of houses — you could hardly call them villages — with a motel or two, a store, a petrol station, a restaurant, occurred more often then he had been led to believe. And when they came to Big Sur and the road wandered inland through the redwood forest, there were habitations and places to stay almost in plenty.

They reached the Redwood Hotel at about eight that night. Simply driving through Carmel had been enough to lower Wexford's spirits. It looked a lively place, a considerable seaside resort, and it was full of hotels. Another phone call to Davina Ilbert elicited only that she had no idea of Ilbert's London address. Wexford realized that there was nothing for it but to try all the hotels in Carmel, armed with his photograph of Natalie.

All he derived from that was the discovery that Americans are more inclined to be helpful than English people, and if this is because they are a nation of salesmen just as the English are a nation of small shopkeepers, it does little to detract from the overall pleasant impression. Hotel receptionists exhorted him on his departure to have a good day, and then when he was still at it after sundown, to have a nice evening. By that time he had been inside every hotel, motel and lobby of apartments-for-rent in Carmel, Carmel Highlands, Carmel Woods and Carmel Point, and he had been inside them in vain.

Rex Newton and his American wife were sitting in the hotel bar with Dora when he got back. Newton's skin had gone very brown and his hair very white, but otherwise he was much the same. His wife, in Wexford's opinion, looked twenty years older than Dora, though she was in fact younger. It appeared that the Newtons were to dine with them, and Newton walked into the dining room with one arm round his wife's waist and the other round Dora's. Dora had given them to understand he was there on official police business — what else could she have said? — and Newton spent most of his time at the table holding forth on the American legal system, American police, the geography and geology of California and the rival merits of various hotels. His wife was a meek quiet little woman. They were going to take Dora to Muir Woods, the redwood forest north of San Francisco, on the following day.

'If he knows so much,' Wexford grumbled later, 'he might have warned you there are more hotels up here than in the West End of London.'

'I'm sorry, darling. I didn't ask him. He does rather talk the hind leg off a donkey, doesn't he?'

Wexford didn't know why he suddenly liked Rex Newton very much and felt even happier that Dora was having such a good time with him.

For his own part, he spent the next day and the next making excursions down the coast the way they had come, visiting every possible place to stay. In each he got the same response — or worse, that the motel had changed hands or changed management and that there were no records for 1976 available. He was learning that in California change is a very important aspect of life and that Californians, like the Athenians of old, are attracted by any new thing.

Nonie Newton was confined to bed in her daughter's house with a migraine. Wexford cut short his inquiries in Monterey to get back to Dora, who would have been deserted by her friends. The least he could do for her was take her on the beach for the afternoon. He asked himself if he hadn't mismanaged everything. The trip wasn't succeeding either as an investigation or as a holiday. Dora was out when he got back, there was no note for him, and he spent the rest of the day missing his wife and reproaching himself. Rex Newton brought her back at ten and, in spite of Nonie's illness, sat in the bar for half an hour, holding forth on the climate of California, seismology and the San Andreas Fault. Wexford couldn't wait for him to be gone to unburden his soul to Dora.

'You could always phone Sheila,' she said when they were alone.

'Sure I could,' he said. 'I could phone Sylvia and talk to the kids. I could phone your sister and my nephew Howard and old Mike. It would cost a great deal of money and they'd all no doubt say hard cheese very kindly, but where would it get me?'

'To Ilbert,' she said simply.

He looked at her.

'Rolf Ilbert. You said he does part of the script for *Runway*. He's in London. Even if he's not working on *Runway* now, even if she's never met him, Sheila's in a position to find out where he is, she could easily do it.'

'So she could,' he said slowly. 'Why didn't I think of that?'

It was eleven o'clock on the Pacific coast but seven in London, and he was lucky to find her up. Her voice sounded as if she were in the next room. He knew exactly what her voice in the next room would sound like because his hotel neighbours had had *Runway* on for the past half-hour.

'I don't know him, Pop darling, but I'm sure I can find him. Nothing easier. I'll shop around some likely agents. Where shall I ring you back?'

'Don't call us,' said her father. 'We'll call you. God knows where we'll be.'

'How's Mother?'

'Carrying on alarmingly with her old flame.'

He would have laughed as he said that if Dora had shown the least sign of laughing.

*

Because it wasn't his nature to wait about and do nothing he spent all the next day covering what remained of the Monterey Peninsula. Something in him wanted to say, forget it, make a holiday of the rest of it, but it was too late for that. Instead of relaxing, he would only have tormented himself with that constantly recurring question, where had she stayed? It was awkward phoning Sheila because of the time difference. All the lines were occupied when he tried at eight in the morning, tea time for her, and again at noon, her early evening. When at last he heard the ringing there was no answer. Next day, or the day after at the latest, they would have to start south and leave behind all the possible places where Natalie Arno might have changed her identity. They had only had a fortnight and eleven days of it were gone.

As he was making another attempt to phone Sheila from the hotel lobby, Rex Newton walked in with Dora. He sat down, drank a glass of chablis, and held forth on Californian vineyards, migraine, the feverfew diet and the gluten-free diet. After half an hour he went, kissing Dora — on the cheek but very near the mouth — and reminding her of a promise to spend their last night in America staying at the Newtons' house. And also their last day.

'I suppose I'm included in that,' Wexford said in a rather nasty tone. Newton was still not quite out of earshot.

She was cool. 'Of course, darling.'

His investigation was over, failed, fruitless. He had rather hoped to have the last two days alone with his wife. But what a nerve he had and how he was punished for it!

'I'm hoist with my own petard, aren't I?' he said and went off to bed.

The Newtons were flying back that morning. It would be a long weary drive for Wexford. He and Dora set off at nine.

The first of the *Danaus* butterflies to float across the windscreen made them both gasp. Dora had seen one only once before, Wexford never. The Milkweed, the Great American Butterfly, the Monarch, is a rare visitor to the cold British Isles. They watched that one specimen drift out over the sea, seeming to lose itself in the blue meeting the blue, and then a cloud of its fellows were upon them, thick as autumnal leaves that strow the brooks in Vallombrosa. And like leaves too, scarlet leaves veined in black, they floated rather than flew across the span of California One, down from the cliffs of daisies, out to the ocean. The air was red with them. All the way down from Big Sur they came, wings of cinnabar velvet, butterflies in flocks like birds made of petals.

'The Spanish for butterfly is *mariposa*,' said Dora. 'Rex told me. Don't you think it's a beautiful name?'

Wexford said nothing. Even if he managed to get hold of Sheila now, even if she had an address or a phone number for him, would he have time to drive back perhaps a hundred miles along this route? Not when he had to be in Burbank or wherever those Newtons lived by nightfall. A red butterfly came to grief on his windscreen, smashed, fluttered, died.

They stopped for a late lunch not far north of San Luis Obispo. He tried in vain to get through to Sheila again and then Dora said she would try. She came back from the phone with a little smile on her lips. She looked young and tanned and happy, but she hadn't been able to reach Sheila. Wexford wondered why she should look like that if she hadn't been talking to anyone. The Newtons would have been back in their home for hours by now. He felt that worst kind of misery, that which afflicts us as the result entirely of our own folly.

The road that returned from inland to the coast wound down through yellow hills. Yuccas pushed their way up through the sun-bleached grass and the rounded mountains were crowned with olives. The hills folded and dipped and rose and parted to reveal more hills, all the same, all ochreish in colour, until through the last dip the blue ocean appeared again. Dora was occupied with her map and guide book.

There was a little seaside town ahead. A sign by the roadside said: Santa Xavierita, height above sea level 50.2 metres, population 482. Dora said:

'According to the book there's a motel here called the Mariposa. Shall we try it?'

'What for?' said Wexford crossly. 'Half an hour's kip? We have to be two hundred miles south of here by eight and it's five now.'

'We don't have to. Our plane doesn't go till tomorrow night. We could stay at the Mariposa, I think we're meant to, it was a sign.'

He nearly stopped the car. He chuckled. He had known her thirty-five years but he didn't know her yet. 'You phoned Newton back there?' he said but in a very different tone from the one he would have used if he had asked that question ten minutes before. 'You phoned Newton and said we couldn't make it?'

She said demurely, 'I think Nonie was quite relieved really.'

'I don't deserve it,' said Wexford.

Santa Xavierita had a wide straggly street with a dozen side turnings at right angles to it, as many petrol stations, a monster market, a clutch of restaurants and among a dozen motels, the Mariposa. Wexford found himself being shown, not to a room, but to a little house rather like a bungalow at home in Ramsgate or Worthing. It stood in a garden, one of a score of green oases in this corner of Santa Xavierita, and up against its front door was a pink and white geranium as big as a tree.

He walked back between sprinklers playing on the grass to the hotel reception desk and phoned Sheila on a collect call. In London it was two in the morning, but by now he was unscrupulous. Sheila had got Ilbert's address. She had had it for two days and couldn't understand why her father hadn't phoned. Ilbert was staying at Durrant's Hotel in George Street by Spanish Place. Wexford wrote down the number. He looked round for someone to inform that he intended to make a call to London.

There was no sign of the little spry man called Sessamy who had checked them in. No doubt he was somewhere about, watering the geraniums and fuchsias and the heliotrope that smelt of cherries. Wexford went back to find Dora and tell her the news, such as it was. She was in the kitchen of their bungalow, arranging in a glass bowl, piling like an Arcimboldo still life, the fruit they had bought.

'Reg,' she said, turning round, a nectarine in her hand, 'Reg, Mrs Sessamy who owns this place, she's English. And she says we're the first English people to stay here since — a Mrs Arno in 1976.'

CHAPTER FIFTEEN

'Tell me about it,' Wexford said.

'I don't know anything about it. I don't know any more than I've told you. Your Natalie Arno stayed here in 1976. After we've eaten we're to go and have coffee with Mrs Sessamy and she'll enlighten you.'

'Will she now? And how did you account for my curiosity? What did you tell her about me?'

'The truth. The idea of you being a real English policeman almost made her cry. She was a GI bride, I think, she's about the right age. I honestly think she expects you to turn up in a blue uniform and say 'ere, 'ere, what's all this about? and she'd love it!'

He laughed. It was rare for him to praise his wife, almost unknown for him to call her by an endearment. That wasn't his way, she knew it and wouldn't have wanted it. It would have bracketed her with those he loved on the next level down. He put his hand on her arm.

'If something comes of all this,' he said, 'and one of us gets sent back here at the government's expense, can I come too?'

There was, of all things, a Lebanese restaurant in the main street of Santa Xavierita. They walked there and ate delicate scented versions of humous and kebab and honey cake. The sun had long gone, sunk almost with a fizzle into that blue sea, and now the moon was rising. The moonlight painted the little town white as with frost. It was no longer very warm. In the gardens, which showed as dark little havens of lushness in aridity, the sprinklers still rotated and sprayed.

Wexford marvelled at his wife and, with hindsight, at his own ignorant presumption. Instead of allowing herself to be a passive encumbrance, she had made him absurdly jealous and had hoodwinked him properly. By some sixth sense or some gift of serendipity, she had done in an instant what had eluded him for nearly a fortnight — found Natalie Arno's hideout. And like

682

Trollope's Archdeacon of his wife, he wondered at and admired the greatness of that lady's mind.

The Sessamys lived in a white-painted frame building, half their home and half the offices of the motel. Their living room was old-fashioned in an unfamiliar way, furnished with pieces from a thirties culture more overblown and Hollywood-influenced than that which Wexford himself had known. On a settee, upholstered in snow-white grainy plastic, a settee that rather resembled some monstrous dessert, a cream-coated log perhaps, rolled in coconut, sat the fattest woman Wexford had ever seen. He and Dora had come in by way of the open French windows, as she had been instructed, and Mrs Sessamy struggled to get to her feet. Like a great fish floundering to raise itself over the rim of the keeper net, she went on struggling until her guests were seated. Only then did she allow herself to subside again. She gave a big noisy sigh.

'It's such a pleasure to see you! You don't know how I've been looking forward to it ever since Mrs Wexford here said who you was. A real bobby! I turned on the waterworks, didn't I, Tom?'

Nearly forty years' domicile in the United States had not robbed her of a particle of her old accent or given her a hint of new. She was a Londoner who still spoke the cockney of Bow or Limehouse.

'Bethnal Green,' she said as if Wexford had asked. 'I've never been back. My people all moved out to one of them new towns, Harlow. Been there, of course. Like every other year mostly we go, don't we, Tom?'

Her husband made no reply. He was a little brown monkey of a man with a face like a nut. He suggested they have a drink and displayed a selection of bottles ranged behind a small bar. There was no sign of the promised coffee. When Dora had apologetically refused bourbon, rye, chablis, Hawaiian cocktail, Perrier, grape juice and gin, Mrs Sessamy announced that they would have tea. Tom would make it, the way she had taught him.

'It's such a pleasure to see you,' she said again, sinking comfortably back into white plastic. 'The English who come here, mostly they stop up at the Ramada or the Howard Johnson. But you picked the old Mariposa.'

'Because of the butterflies,' said Dora.

'Come again?'

'*Mariposa* — well, it means butterfly, doesn't it?'

'It does?' said Tom Sessamy, waiting for the kettle to boil. 'You hear that, Edie? How about that then?'

It seemed the policy of the Sessamys to question each other frequently but never to answer. Mrs Sessamy folded plump hands in her enormous lap. She was wearing green trousers and a tent-like green and pink flowered smock. In her broad moon face, in the greyish-fair hair, could still be seen traces of the pretty girl who had married an American soldier and left Bethnal Green for ever.

'Mrs Wexford said you wanted to know about that girl who lived here — well, stopped here. Though she must have been here three months. We thought she'd go on renting the chalet for ever, didn't we, Tom? We thought we'd got a real sinecure.'

'I'd heard it was up around Big Sur she stayed,' said Wexford.

'So it was at first. She couldn't stick it, not enough life for her, and it was too far to drive to Frisco. You can get up to San Luis in twenty minutes from here by car. She had her own car and he used to come up in a big Lincoln Continental.'

'Ilbert?'

'That's right, that was the name. I will say for her she never pretended, she never called herself Mrs Ilbert. Couldn't have cared less what people thought.'

Tom Sessamy came in with the tea. Wexford who, while in California, had drunk from a pot made with one teabag, had seen tea made by heating up liquid out of a bottle or by pouring warm water on to a powder, noted that Tom had been well taught by his wife.

'I never did fancy them bags,' said Edith Sessamy. 'You can get tea loose here if you try.'

'Hafta go to the specialty shop over to San Luis,' said Tom.

Mrs Sessamy put cream and sugar into her cup. 'What more d'you want to know about her?' she said to Wexford.

He showed her the photograph. 'Is that her?'

She put on glasses with pink frames and rhinestone decoration. Mrs Sessamy had become Californian in all ways but for her tea and her speech. 'Yes,' she said, 'yes, I reckon that's her.' Her voice was full of doubt.

'I guess that's her,' said Tom. 'It's kinda hard to say. She kinda wore her hair loose. She got this terrific tan and wore her hair loose. Right, Edie?'

Edith Sessamy didn't seem too pleased by her husband's enthusiastic description of Natalie Arno. She said rather sharply, 'One man wasn't enough for her. She was two-timing that Ilbert the minute he was off to L.A. For instance, there used to be a young fella hung about here, kipped down on the beach, I reckon you'd have called him a beachcomber in olden times.'

'Kinda hippie,' said Tom.

'She carried on with him. I say he slept on the beach, that summer I reckoned he slept most nights in Natalie's chalet. Then there was an English chap, but it wasn't long before she left she met him, was it, Tom?'

'Played the guitar at the Maison Suisse over to San Luis.'

'Why did she leave?' Wexford asked.

'Now that I can't tell you. We weren't here when she left. We were at home, we were in England.'

'Visiting with her sister over to Harlow,' said Tom.

'She was living here like she'd stay for the rest of her life when we left. That'd have been the end of July, I reckon. Tom's cousin from Ventura, she come up to run the place like she always does when we're off on our holidays. She kept in touch, I reckon we got a letter once a week. I remember her writing us about that woman who got drowned here, don't you, Tom? But she never mentioned that girl leaving. Why should she? There was guests coming and going all the time.'

'You weren't curious yourselves?'

Edith Sessamy heaved up her huge shoulders and dropped them again. 'So if we were? There wasn't much we could do about it, six thousand miles away. She wasn't going to tell Tom's cousin why she upped and went, was she? When we come back we heard that's what she'd done, a moonlight flit like. Ilbert come up the next day but the bird was flown. She went off in her car, Tom's cousin said, and she'd got a young chap with her, and she left that poor mug Ilbert to pay the bill.'

Wexford woke up very early the next morning. The sun was perhaps the brightest and the clearest he had ever seen and the little town looked as if it had been washed clean in the night. Yet Edith Sessamy had told him that apart from a few showers the previous December they had had no rain for a year. He bathed and dressed and went out. Dora was still fast asleep. He walked down the narrow straight road bordered with fan palms, feather dusters on long tapering handles, that led to Santa Xavierita state beach.

The sky was an inverted pan of speckless blue enamel, the sea rippling blue silk. Along the silver sand a young man in yellow tee-shirt and red shorts was jogging. Another, in swimming trunks, was doing gymnastic exercises, sit-ups, press-ups, toe-touching. There was no one in the water. In the middle of the beach was a chair raised up high on stilts for the use of the lifeguard who would sit on it and halloo through his trumpet at over-venturesome swimmers.

Wexford's thoughts reverted to the night before. There was a question he ought to have asked, that he had simply overlooked at the time, because of the crushing disappointment he had felt at the paucity of Edith Sessamy's information. Disappointment had made him fail to select from that mass of useless matter the one significant sentence. He recalled it now, picking it out as the expert might pick out the uncut diamond from a handful of gravel.

Two hours later, as early as he decently could, he was waiting in the motel's reception area by the counter. Ringing the bell summoned Tom Sessamy in shortie dressing gown which left exposed hairless white legs and long white feet in sandals of plaited straw.

'Hi, Reg, you wanna check out?'

'I wanted to ask you and your wife a few more questions first if you'll bear with me.'

'Edie, are ya decent? Reg's here ta pick your brains.'

Mrs Sessamy was rather more decent than her husband in an all-enveloping pink kimono printed with birds of paradise.

She sat on the white sofa drinking more strong black tea, and on her lap on a tray were fried eggs and fried bacon and hash browns and English muffins and grape jelly.

'It's been such a pleasure meeting you and Dora, I can't tell you.' She had told him at least six times already, but the repetition was somehow warming and pleasant to hear. Wexford returned the compliment with a few words about how much they had enjoyed themselves.

'You wanna cup of Edie's tea?' said Tom.

Wexford accepted. 'You said last night a woman was drowned here. While you were away. D'you know any more than that? Who she was? How it happened?'

'Not a thing. Only what I said, a woman was drowned. Well, it was a young woman, a girl really, I do know that, and I reckon I heard she was on holiday here from the East somewhere.'

'You hafta talk to the cops over to San Luis,' said Tom.

'Wait a minute, though — George Janveer was lifeguard here then, wasn't he, Tom? I reckon you could talk to George.'

'Why don't I call George right now?' said Tom.

He was dissuaded from this by his wife since it was only just after eight. They would phone George at nine. Wexford wasn't pressed for time, was he? No, he wasn't, not really, he had all day. He had a 200-mile drive ahead of him, of course, but that was nothing here. Edith Sessamy said she knew what he meant, it was nothing here.

He walked slowly back. At last a clear pattern was emerging from the confusion. The pieces fluttered and dropped into a design as the coloured fragments do when you shake a kaleidoscope. Camargue too had been drowned, he thought.

Just after nine he went back and paid his bill. Tom said apologetically that he had phoned George Janveer's home and talked to Mrs Janveer who said George had gone to Grover City but she expected him back by eleven.

'Oughta've called him at eight like I said,' said Tom.

Wexford and Dora put the cases in the car and went to explore what they hadn't yet seen of Santa Xavierita. Wouldn't it be best, Wexford asked himself, to head straight for San Luis Obispo and call on the police there and see what facts he could get out of them? But suppose he couldn't get any? Suppose, before they imparted anything to him, they required proof of who he was and what he was doing there? He could prove his identity, of course, and present them with bona fides but it would all take time and he hadn't much left. He had to be at Los Angeles international airport by six in time for their flight home at seven. Better wait for Janveer who would know as much as the police did and would almost certainly talk to him.

Mrs Janveer was as thin as Edith Sessamy was fat. She was in her kitchen baking something she called devil's food and her overweight black labrador was sitting at her feet, hoping to lick out the bowl.

It was after eleven and her husband still hadn't come back from Grover City. Maybe he had met a friend and they had got drinking. Mrs Janveer did not say this in a shrewish or condemnatory way or even as if there were anything to be defensive about. She said it in exactly the same tone, casual, indifferent, even slightly complacent, she would have used to say he had met the mayor or gone to a meeting of the Lions.

Wexford was driven to ask her if she remembered anything about the drowned woman. Mrs Janveer put the tin of chocolate cake mixture into the oven. The dog's tail began to thump the floor. No, she couldn't say she remembered much about it at all, except the woman's first name had been Theresa, she recalled that because it was hers too, and after the drowning some of her relations had come out to Santa Xavierita, from Boston, she thought it was, and stayed at the Ramada Inn. She put the mixing bowl under the tap and her hand to the tap. The dog let out a piteous squeal. Mrs Janveer shrugged, looking upset, and slapped the bowl down in front of the dog with a cross exclamation.

Wexford waited until half-past eleven. Janveer still hadn't come. 'Considering what I know now,' he said to Dora, 'they're bound to send me back here. It's only time I need.'

'It's a shame, darling, it's such bad luck.'

He drove quickly out of the town, heading for the Pacific Highway.

CHAPTER SIXTEEN

The difference between California and Kingsmarkham was a matter of colour as well as temperature. The one was blue and gold, the sun burning the grass to its own colour; the other was grey and green, the lush green of foliage watered daily by those massy clouds. Wexford went to work, not yet used to seeing grass verges instead of daisy lawns, shivering a little because the temperature was precisely what Tom Sessamy had told him it could fall to in Santa Xavierita in December.

Burden was waiting for him in his office. He had on a lightweight silky suit in a shade of taupe and a beige silk shirt. No one could possibly have taken him for a policeman or even a policeman in disguise. Wexford, who had been considering telling him at once what he had found out in California, now decided not to and instead asked him to close the window.

'I opened it because it's such a muggy stuffy sort of day,' said Burden. 'Not cold, are you?'

'Yes, I am. Very cold.'

'Jet lag. Did you have a good time?'

Wexford grunted. He wished he had the nerve to start the central heating. It probably wouldn't start, though, not in July. For all he knew, the chief constable had to come over himself on 1 November and personally press a button on the boiler. 'I don't suppose there've been any developments while I was away?' he said.

Burden sat down. 'Well, yes, there have. That's what I'm doing in here. I thought I ought to tell you first thing. Jane Zoffany has disappeared.'

Zoffany had not reported her missing until she had been gone a week. His story, said Burden, was that he and his wife had been staying at Sterries with their friend Natalie Arno, and on the evening of Friday, 27 June his wife had gone out alone for a walk and had never come back. Zoffany, when pressed, admitted that immediately prior to this he and his wife had quarrelled over an affair he had had with another woman. She had said she was going to leave him, she could never live with him again, and had left the house. Zoffany himself had left soon after, taking the 10.05 p.m. train to Victoria. He believed his wife would have gone home by an earlier train.

However, when he got to De Beauvoir Place she wasn't there. Nor did she appear the next day. He concluded she had gone to her sister in Horsham. This had apparently happened once before after a quarrel. But Friday 4 July had been Jane Zoffany's birthday, her thirty-fifth, and a birthday card came for her from her sister. Zoffany then knew he had been wrong and he went to his local police station.

Where no one had shown much interest, Burden said. Why should they? That a young woman should temporarily leave her husband after a quarrel over his infidelity was hardly noteworthy. It happened all the time. And of course she wouldn't tell him where she had gone, that was the last thing she had wanted him to know. Burden only got to hear of it when Zoffany also reported his wife's disappearance to the Kingsmarkham police. He seemed genuinely worried. It would not be putting it too strongly to say he was distraught.

'Guilt,' said Wexford, and as he pronounced the word he felt it himself. It was even possible he was the last person — the last but one — to have seen Jane Zoffany alive. And he had let her go. Because he was off on holiday, because he didn't want to inconvenience Dora or upset arrangements. Of course she hadn't taken refuge with her sister or some friend. She had had no handbag, no money. He had let her go, overwrought as she was, to walk away into the dusk of Ploughman's Lane — to go back to Sterries and Natalie Arno.

'I had a feeling we ought to take it a bit more seriously,' Burden said. 'I mean, I wasn't really alarmed but I couldn't help thinking about poor old Camargue. We've got our own ideas about what kind of a death that was, haven't we? I talked to Zoffany myself, I got him to give me the names of people she could possibly have gone to. There weren't many and we checked on them all.'

'And what about Natalie? Have you talked to her?'

'I thought I'd leave that to you.'

'We'll have to drag the lake,' said Wexford, 'and dig up the garden if necessary. But I'll talk to her first.'

The effect of her inherited wealth was now displayed. A new hatchback Opel, mustard-coloured, automatic transmission, stood on the gravel circle outside the front door. Looking at her, staring almost, Wexford remembered the skirt Jane Zoffany had mended, the old blanket coat. Natalie wore a dress of some thin clinging jersey material in bright egg-yellow with a tight bodice and full skirt. Around her small neat waist was tied a belt of yellow with red, blue and purple stripes. It was startling and effective and very fashionable. Her hair hung loose in a glossy black bell. There was a white gold watch on one wrist and a bracelet of woven white gold threads on the other. The mysterious lady from Boston, he thought, and he wondered how you felt when you knew your relatives, parents maybe, and your friends thought you were dead and grieved for you while in fact you were alive and living in the lap of luxury.

'But Mr Wexford,' she said with her faint accent — a New England accent? 'But, Mr Wexford, Jane never came back here that night.' She smiled in the way a model does when her mouth and not her eyes are to show in the toothpaste ad. 'Her things are still in the room she and Ivan used. Would you like to see?'

He nodded. He followed her down to the spare rooms. On the carved teak chest stood a Chinese bowl full of Peace roses. They went into the room where he had once before seen Jane Zoffany standing before the long mirror and fastening the collar of a Persian lamb coat. Her suitcase lay open on the top of a chest of drawers. There was a folded nightdress inside it, a pair of sandals placed heel to toe and a paperback edition of Daphne du Maurier's *Rebecca*. On the black-backed hairbrush on the dressing table and the box of talcum powder lay a fine scattering of dust.

'Has Mrs Hicks left you?'

'In the spirit if not the flesh yet, Mr Wexford. She and Ted are going to Uncle Philip.' She added, as if in explanation to someone who could not be expected to know intimate family usage, 'Philip Cory, that is. He was just crazy to have them and it's made him so happy. Meanwhile this place is rather neglected while they get ready to leave. They've sold their house and I think I've sold this one at last. Well, practically sold it. Contracts have been exchanged.' She chatted on, straightening the lemon floral duvet, opening a window, for all the world as if he too were a prospective purchaser rather than a policeman investigating an ominous disappearance. 'I'm having some of the furniture put in store and the rest will go to the flat I've bought in London. Then I'm thinking of going off on vacation somewhere.'

He glanced into the adjoining bathroom. It had evidently been cleaned before Muriel Hicks withdrew her services. The yellow bath and basin were immaculate and fresh honey-coloured towels hung on the rail. Without waiting for permission, he made his way into the next room, the one Natalie had rejected in favour of using Camargue's very private and personal territory.

There were no immediately obvious signs that this room had ever been occupied since Camargue's death. In fact, it seemed likely that the last people to have slept here were Dinah Sternhold's parents when they stayed with Camargue at Christmas. But Wexford, peering quickly, pinched from the frill that edged one of the green and blue flowered pillows, a hair. It was black but it was not from Natalie's head, being wavy and no more than three inches long.

This bathroom too lacked the pristine neatness and cleanliness of the other. A man no more than ordinarily observant might have noticed nothing, but Wexford was almost certain that one of the blue towels had been used. On the basin, under the cold tap, was a small patch of tide mark. He turned as Natalie came up softly behind him. She was not the kind of person one much fancied creeping up on one, and he thought, as he had done when he first met her, of a snake.

'That night,' he said, 'Mrs Zoffany ran out of the house and then afterwards her husband left. How long afterwards?'

'Twenty minutes, twenty-five. Shall we say twenty-two and a half minutes, Mr Wexford, to be on the safe side?'

He gave no sign that he had noticed the implicit mockery. 'He walked to the station, did he?'

'I gave him a lift in my car.'

Of course. Now he remembered that he had seen them. 'And after that you never saw Mrs Zoffany again?'

'Never.' She looked innocently at Wexford, her black eyes very large and clear, the lashes lifted and motionless. 'It's the most extraordinary thing I ever came across in my life.'

Considering what he knew of her life, Wexford doubted this statement. 'I should like your consent to our dragging the lake,' he said.

'That's just a polite way of saying you're going to drag it anyway, isn't it?'

'Pretty well,' he said. 'It'll save time if you give your permission.'

Out of the lake came a quantity of blanket weed, sour green and sour smelling; two car tyres, a bicycle lamp, half a dozen cans and a broken wrought-iron gate as well as a lot of miscellaneous rubbish of the nuts and bolts and nails variety. They also found Sir Manuel Camargue's missing glove, but there was no trace of Jane Zoffany. Wexford wondered if he had chosen the lake as the first possible place to search because of the other drownings associated with Natalie Arno.

It was, of course, stretching a point to touch the garden at all. But the temptation to tell the men to dig up the flowerbed between the lake and the circular forecourt was very great. It was, after all, no more than three or four yards from the edge of the lake and the soil in it looked suspiciously freshly turned and the bedding plants as if they had been there no more than a day or two. Who would put out bedding plants in July? They dug. They dug to about three feet down and then even Wexford had to admit no body was buried there. Ted Hicks, who had been watching them for hours, now said that he had dug the bed over a week ago and planted out a dozen biennials. Asked why he hadn't said so before, he said he hadn't thought it his place to interfere. By then it was too late to do any more, nine on a typical English July evening, twilight, greyish, damp and cool.

Wexford's phone was ringing when he got in. The chief constable. Mrs Arno had complained that he was digging up the grounds of her house without her permission and without a warrant.

'True,' said Wexford, because it was and it seemed easier to confess than to get involved in the ramifications of explaining. A scalding lecture exploded at him from the mouthpiece. Once again he was overstepping the bounds of his duty and his rights, once again he was allowing an obsession to warp his judgement. And this time the obsession looked as if it were taking the form of a vindictive campaign against Mrs Arno.

Had her voice on the phone achieved this? Or had she been to Griswold in person, in the yellow dress, holding him with her glowing black eyes, moving her long pretty hands in feigned distress? For the second time he promised to persecute Natalie Arno no more, in fact to act as if he had never heard her name.

What changed the chief constable's mind must have been the systematic searching of the Zodiac. Two neighbours of Ivan Zoffany went independently to the police, one to complain that Zoffany had been lighting bonfires in his garden by night, the other to state that she had actually seen Jane in the vicinity of De Beauvoir Place on the night of Sunday, 29 June.

The house and the shop were searched without result. Zoffany admitted to the bonfires, saying that he intended to move away and take up some other line of work, and it was his stock of science-fiction paperbacks he had been burning. Wexford applied for a warrant to search the inside of Sterries and secured one three days after the dragging of the lake.

CHAPTER SEVENTEEN

The house was empty. Not only deserted by its owner but half-emptied of its furnishings. Wexford remembered that Natalie Arno had said she would be going away on holiday and also that she intended having some of the furniture put in store. Mrs Murray-Burgess, that inveterate observer of unusual vehicles, told Burden when he called at Kingsfield House that she had seen a removal van turn out of the Sterries drive into Plough-man's Lane at about three on Tuesday afternoon. It was now Thursday, 17 July.

With Wexford and Burden were a couple of men, detective constables, called Archbold and Bennett. They were prepared not only to search but to dismantle parts of the house if need be. They began in the double garage, examining the cupboards at the end of it and the outhouse tacked on to its rear. Since Sterries Cottage was also empty and had been since the previous day, Wexford intended it to be searched as well. Archbold, who had had considerable practice at this sort of thing, picked the locks on both front doors.

The cottage was bare of furniture and carpets. Like most English houses, old or new, it was provided with inadequate cupboard space. Its walls were of brick but were not cavity walls, and at some recent period, perhaps when Sir Manuel and the Hickses had first come, the floors at ground level had been relaid with tiles on a concrete base. No possibility of hiding a body there and nowhere upstairs either. They turned their attention to the bigger house.

Here, at first, there seemed even less likelihood of being able safely to conceal the body of a full-grown woman. It was for no more than form's sake that they cleared out the cloaks cupboard inside the front door, the kitchen broom cupboard and the small room off the kitchen which housed the central-heating boiler and a stock of soap powders and other cleansers. From the first floor a great many pieces had gone, including the pale green settee and armchairs, the piano and all the furniture from Camargue's bedroom and sitting room. Everywhere there seemed to be blank spaces or marks of discolouration on the walls where this or that piece had stood. The Chinese vase of Peace roses, wilted now, had been stuck on the floor up against a window.

Bennett, tapping walls, discovered a hollow space between the right-hand side of the hanging cupboard and the outside wall in Camargue's bedroom. And outside there were signs that it had been the intention on someone's part to use this space as a cupboard for garden tools or perhaps to contain a dustbin, for an arch had been built into which to fit a door and this arch subsequently filled in with bricks of a slightly lighter colour.

From the inside of the hanging cupboard Bennett set about unscrewing the panel at its right-hand end. Wexford wondered if he were getting squeamish in his old age. It was with something amounting to nausea that he stood there anticipating the body falling slowly forward as the panel came away, crumpling into Bennett's arms, the tall thin body of Jane Zoffany with a gauzy scarf and a red and yellow dress of Indian cotton for a winding sheet. Burden sat on the bed, rubbing away fastidiously at a small powder or plaster mark that had appeared on the hem of his light fawn trousers.

The last screw was out and the panel fell, Bennett catching it and resting it against the wall. There was nothing inside the cavity but a spider which swung across its webs. A little bright light and fresh air came in by way of a ventilator brick. Wexford let out his breath in a sigh. It was time to take a break for lunch.

Mr Haq, all smiles and gratified to see Wexford back, remarked that he was happy to be living in a country where they paid policemen salaries on which they could afford to have holidays in California. With perfect sincerity, he said this made him feel more secure. Burden ordered for both of them, steak Soroti, an innocuous beef stew with carrots and onions. When Mr Haq and his son were out of earshot he said he often suspected that the Pearl of Africa's cook hailed from Bradford. Wexford said nothing.

'It's no good,' said Burden, 'we aren't going to find anything in that place. You may as well resign yourself. You're too much of an optimist sometimes for your own good.'

'D'you think I want the poor woman to be dead?' Wexford retorted. 'Optimist, indeed.' And he quoted rather crossly, 'The optimist proclaims that we live in the best of all possible worlds. The pessimist fears this is true.'

'You want Natalie Arno to be guilty of something and you don't much care what,' said Burden. 'Why should she murder her?'

'Because Jane Zoffany knew who she really is. Either that or she found out how the murder of Camargue was done and who did it. There's a conspiracy here, Mike, involving a number of conspirators and Jane Zoffany was one of them. But there's no more honour among conspirators than there is among thieves, and when she discovered how Natalie had betrayed her she saw no reason to be discreet any longer.' He told Burden what had happened when he encountered Jane Zoffany in Ploughman's Lane on 27 June. 'She had something to tell me, she would have told me then only I didn't realize, I didn't give her a word of encouragement. Instead she went back to Sterries and no doubt had the temerity to threaten Natalie. It was a silly thing to do. But she was a silly woman, hysterical and unstable.'

The steak Soroti came. Wexford ate in silence. It was true enough that he wanted Natalie Arno to have done something, or rather that he now saw that charging her with something was almost within his grasp. Who would know where she had gone on holiday? Zoffany? Philip Cory? Would anyone know? They had the ice cream eau-de-Nil to follow but Wexford left half of his.

'Let's get back there,' he said.

It had begun to rain. The white walls of Sterries were streaked with water. Under a lowering sky of grey and purple cloud the house had the shabby faded look which belongs particularly to English houses built to a design intended for the Mediterranean. There were lights on in the upper rooms.

Archbold and Bennett were working on the drawing room, Bennett having so thoroughly investigated the chimney as to clamber half-way up inside it. Should they take up the floor? Wexford said no, he didn't think so. No one could hope to conceal a body for long by burying it under the floor in a house which was about to change hands. Though, as Wexford now

697

told himself, it wasn't necessarily or exclusively a body they were looking for. By six o'clock they were by no means finished but Wexford told them to leave the rest of the house till next day. It was still raining, though slightly now, little more than a drizzle. Wexford made his way down the path between the conifers to check that they had closed and locked the door of Sterries Cottage.

In the wet gloom the alsatian's face looking out of a ground-floor window and almost on a level with his own made him jump. It evoked strange ideas, that there had been a time shift and it was six months ago and Camargue still lived. Then again, from the way some kind of white cloth seemed to surround the dog's head . . .

'Now I know how Red Riding Hood felt,' said Wexford to Dinah Sternhold.

She was wearing a white raincoat with its collar turned up and she had been standing behind the dog, surveying the empty room. A damp cotton scarf was tied under her chin. She smiled. The sadness that had seemed characteristic of her had left her face now. It seemed fuller, the cheeks pink with rain and perhaps with running.

'They've gone,' she said, 'and the door was open. It was a bit of a shock.'

'They're working for Philip Cory now.'

She shrugged. 'Oh well, I suppose there was no reason they should bother to tell me. I'd got into the habit of bringing Nancy over every few weeks just for them to see her. Ted loves Nancy.' She took her hand from the dog's collar and Nancy bounded up to Wexford as if they were old friends. 'Sheila said you'd been to California.'

'For our summer holiday.'

'Not entirely, Mr Wexford, was it? You went to find out if what Manuel thought was true. But you haven't found out, have you?'

He said nothing, and she went on quickly, perhaps thinking she had gone too far or been indiscreet. 'I often think how strange it is she could get the solicitors to believe in her and Manuel's old friends to believe in her and the police and people who'd known the Camargues for years, yet Manuel who wanted to believe, who was pretty well geared up to believe anything, saw her on that one occasion and didn't believe in her for more than half an hour.' She shrugged her shoulders again and gave a short little laugh. Then she said politely as was her way, 'I'm so sorry, I'm keeping you. Did you want to lock up?' She took hold of the dog again and walked her out into the rain. 'Has she sold the house?' Her voice suddenly sounded thin and strained.

Wexford nodded. 'So she says.'

'I shall never come here again.'

He watched her walk away down the narrow lane which led from the cottage to the road. Raindrops glistened on the alsatian's fur. Water slid off the flat branches of the conifers and dripped on to the grass. Uncut for more than a week, it was already shaggy, giving the place an unkempt look. Wexford walked back to the car.

Burden was watching Dinah Sternhold shoving Nancy on to the rear seat of the Volkswagen. 'It's a funny thing,' he said. 'Jenny's got a friend, a Frenchwoman, comes from Alsace. But you can't call her an Alsatian, can you? That word always means a dog.'

'You couldn't call anyone a Dalmatian either,' said Wexford.

Burden laughed. 'Americans call alsatians German Shepherds.'

'We ought to. That's their proper name and I believe the Kennel Club have brought it in again. When they were brought here from Germany after the First World War there was a lot of anti-German feeling — hence we used the euphemism "alsatian". About as daft as refusing to play Beethoven and Bach at concerts because they were German.'

'Jenny and I are going to German classes,' said Burden rather awkwardly.

'What on earth for?'

'Jenny says education should go on all one's life.'

Next morning it was heavy and sultry, the sun covered by a thick yellow mist. Sterries awaited them, full of secrets. Before he left news had come in for Wexford through Interpol that the woman who drowned in Santa Xavierita in July 1976 was Theresa or Tessa Lanchester, aged thirty, unmarried, a paralegal secretary from Boston, Massachusetts. The body had been recovered after having been in the sea some five days and identified a further four days later by Theresa Lanchester's aunt, her parents both being dead. Driving up to Sterries, Wexford thought about being sent back to California. He wouldn't mind a few days in Boston, come to that.

Archbold and Bennett got to work on the spare bedrooms but without positive result and after lunch they set about the study and the two bathrooms.

In the yellow bathroom they took up the honey-coloured carpet, leaving exposed the white vinyl tiles beneath. It was obvious that none of these tiles had been disturbed since they were first laid. The carpet was replaced and then the same procedure gone through in the blue bathroom. Here there was a shower cabinet as well as a bath. Archbold unhooked and spread out the blue and green striped shower curtain. This was made of semi-transparent nylon with a narrow machine-made hem at the bottom. Archbold, who was young and had excellent sight, noticed that the machine stitches for most of the seam's length were pale blue but in the extreme right-hand corner, for about an inch, they were not blue but brown. He told Wexford.

Wexford, who had been sitting on a window-sill in the study, thinking, watching the cloud shadows move across the meadows, went into the blue bathroom and looked at the curtain and knelt down. And about a quarter of an inch from the floor, on the panelled side of the bath, which had been covered for nearly half an inch by the carpet pile, were two minute reddish-brown spots.

'Take up the floor tiles,' said Wexford.

Would they find enough blood to make a test feasible? It appeared so after two of the tiles had been lifted and the edge of the one which had been alongside the bath panelling showed a thick dark encrustation.

CHAPTER EIGHTEEN

'You might tell me where we're going.'

'Why? You're a real ignoramus when it comes to London.' Wexford spoke irritably. He was nervous because he might be wrong. The chief constable had said he was and had frowned and shaken his head and talked about infringements of rights and intrusions of privacy. If he was wrong he was going to look such a fool. He said to Burden, 'If I said we were going to Thornton Heath, would that mean anything to you?'

Burden said nothing. He looked huffily out of the window. The car was passing through Croydon, through industrial complexes, estates of small red terraced houses, shopping centres, big spreadeagled roundabouts with many exits. Soon after Thornton Heath station Wexford's driver turned down a long bleak road that was bounded by a tall wire fence on one side and a row of sad thin poplars on the other. Thank God there were such neighbours about as Mrs Murray-Burgess, thought Wexford. A woman endowed with a memory and a gimlet eye as well as a social conscience.

'An enormous removal van,' she had said, 'a real pantechnicon, and polluting what's left of our country air with clouds of the filthiest black diesel fumes. Of course I can tell you the name of the firm. I sat down and wrote to their managing director at once to complain. William Dorset and Company. I expect you've seen that slogan of theirs, "Dorset Stores It", it's on all their vans.'

The company had branches in north and south London, in Brighton, Guildford, and in Kingsmarkham, which was no doubt why both Sheila and Natalie Arno had employed them. Kingsmarkham people moving house or storing furniture mostly did use Dorset's.

Here and there along the road was the occasional factory as well as the kind of long, low, virtually windowless building whose possible nature or use it is hard for the passer-by to guess at. Perhaps all such buildings, Wexford thought as they turned into the entrance drive to one of them, served the same purpose as this one.

It was built of grey brick and roofed with red sheet iron. What windows it had were high up under the roof. In the concrete bays in front of the iron double doors stood two monster vans, dark red and lettered 'Dorset Stores It' in yellow.

'They're expecting us,' Wexford said. 'I reckon that's the office over there, don't you?'

It was an annexe built out on the far side. Someone came out before they reached the door. Wexford recognized him as the younger of the two men who had moved Sheila's furniture, the one whose wife had not missed a single episode of *Runway*. He looked at Wexford as if he thought he had seen him somewhere before but knew just the same that he was mistaken.

'Come in, will you, please? Mr Rochford's here, our deputy managing director. He reckoned he ought to be here himself.'

Wexford's heart did not exactly sink but it floundered a little. He would so much rather have been alone, without even Burden. Of course he could have stopped all these people coming with him, he had the power to do that, but he wouldn't. Besides, two witnesses would be better than one and four better than two. He followed the man who said his name was George Prince into the office. Rochford, a man of Prince's age and in the kind of suit which, while perfectly clean and respectable, looks as if it has been worn in the past for emergency manual labour and could be put to such use again if the need arose, sat in a small armchair with an unopened folder on his knees. He jumped up and the folder fell on the floor. Wexford shook hands with him and showed him the warrant.

Although he already knew the purpose of the visit, he turned white and looked nauseous.

'This is a serious matter,' he said miserably, 'a very serious matter.'

'It is.'

'I find it hard to believe. I imagine there's a chance you're wrong.'

'A very good chance, sir.'

'Because,' said Rochford hopefully and extremely elliptically, 'in summertime and after — well, I mean, there's been nothing of that sort, has there, George?'

Not yet, thought Wexford. 'Perhaps we might terminate this suspense,' he said, attempting a smile, 'by going and having a look?'

'Oh yes, yes, by all means. This way, through here. Perhaps you'll lead the way, George. I hope you're wrong, Mr Wexford, I only hope you're wrong.'

The interior of the warehouse was cavernous and dim. The roof, supported by girders of red iron, was some thirty feet high. Up there sparrows flitted about and perched on these man-made branches. The sunlight was greenish, filtering through the tinted panes of high, metal-framed windows. George Prince pressed a switch and strip lighting came on, setting the sparrows in flight again. It was chilly inside the warehouse, though the outdoor temperature had that morning edged just into the seventies.

The place had the air of a soulless and shabby township erected on a grid plan. A town of caravans, placed symmetrically a yard or two apart and with streets crossing each other at right angles to give access to them. It might have been a camp for refugees or the rejected spill-over of some newly constituted state, or the idea of such a place in grim fiction or cinema, a settlement in a northern desert without a tree or a blade of grass. Wexford felt the fantasy and shook it off, for there were no people, no inhabitants of this container camp but himself and Burden and George Prince and Rochford padding softly up the broadest aisle.

Of these rectangular houses, these metal cuboids ranked in rows, iron red, factory green, camouflage khaki, the one they were making for stood at the end of the topmost lane to debouch from the main aisle. It stood up against the cream-washed wall under a window. Prince produced a key and was about to insert it into the lock on the container door when Rochford put out a hand to restrain him and asked to see the warrant again. Patiently, Wexford handed it to him. They stood there, waiting while he read it once more. Wexford had fancied for minutes now that he could smell something sweetish and foetid but this became marked the nearer he got to Rochford and it was only the stuff the man put on his hair or his underarms. Rochford said:

'Mrs N. Arno, 27a De Beauvoir Place, London, N1. We didn't move it from there, did we, George? Somewhere in Sussex, didn't you say?'

'Kingsmarkham, sir. It was our Kingsmarkham branch done it.'

'Ah, yes. And it was put into store indefinitely at the rate of £5.50 per week starting from 15 July?'

Wexford said gently, 'Can we open up now, sir, please?'

'Oh, certainly, certainly. Get it over, eh?'

Get it over.... George Prince unlocked the door and Wexford braced himself for the shock of the foul air that must escape. But there was nothing, only a curious staleness. The door swung silently open on oiled hinges. The place might be sinister and evocative of all manner of disagreeable things, but it was well-kept and well-run for all that.

The inside of the container presented a microcosm of Sterries, a drop of the essence of Sir Manuel Camargue. His desk was there and the austere furnishings from the bedroom and sitting room in his private wing, the record player too and the lyre-backed chairs from the music room and the piano. If you closed your eyes you could fancy hearing the first movement from the Flute and Harp Concerto. You could smell and hear Camargue and nothing else. Wexford turned away to face the furniture from the spare bedrooms, a green velvet ottoman in a holland cover, two embroidered footstools, sheathed in plastic, a pair of golden Afghan rugs rolled up in hessian, and under a bag full of quilts and cushions, the carved teak chest, banded now with two stout leather straps.

The four men looked at it. Burden humped the quilt bag off on to the ottoman and knelt down to undo the buckles on the straps. There was a rattly intake of breath from Rochford. The straps fell away and Burden tried the iron clasps. They were locked. He looked inquiringly at Prince who hesitated and then muttered something about having to go back to the office to check in his book where the keys were.

Wexford lost his temper. 'You knew what we'd come for. Couldn't you have checked where the keys were before we came all the way down here? If they can't be found I'll have to have it broken open.'

'Look here. . . .' Rochford was almost choking. 'Your warrant doesn't say anything about breaking. What's Mrs Arno going to say when she finds her property's been damaged? I can't take the responsibility for that sort of. . . .'

'Then you'd better find the keys.'

Prince scratched his head. 'I reckon she said they were in that desk. In one of the pigeonholes in that desk.'

They opened the desk. It was entirely empty. Burden unrolled both rugs, emptied the quilt bag, pulled out the drawers of the bedside cabinet from Camargue's bedroom.

'You say you've got a note of where they are in some book of yours?' said Wexford.

'The note says there in the desk,' said Prince.

'Right. We break the chest open.'

'They're down here,' said Burden. He pulled out his hand from the cleft between the ottoman's arm and seat cushion and waved at them a pair of identical keys on a ring.

Wexford fitted one key into the lock on the right-hand side, turned it, and then unlocked the left-hand side. The clasps opened and he raised the lid. The chest seemed to be full of black heavy-duty polythene sheeting. He grasped a fold of it and pulled.

The heavy thing that was contained in this cold glossy slippery shroud lurched against the wooden wall and seemed to roll over. Wexford began to unwrap the black stuff and then a horrible thing happened. Slowly, languidly, as if it still retained life, a yellowish-white waxen arm and thin hand rose from the chest and loomed trembling over it. It hung in the air for a moment before it subsided. Wexford stepped back with a grunt. The icy thing had brushed his cheek with fingers of marble.

Rochford let out a cry and stumbled out of the container. There was a sound of retching. But George Prince was made of tougher stuff and he came nearer to the chest with awe. With Burden's help, Wexford lifted the body on to the floor and stripped away its covering. Its throat had been cut and the wound wadded with a bloody towel, but this had not kept blood off the yellow dress, which was splashed and stained with red all over like some bizarre map of islands.

Wexford looked into the face, knowing he had been wrong, feeling as much surprise as the others, and then he looked at Burden.

Burden shook his head, appalled and mystified, and together they turned slowly back to gaze into the black dead eyes of Natalie Arno.

CHAPTER NINETEEN

'*Cui bono?*' said Kenneth Ames. 'Who benefits?' He made a church steeple of his fingers and looked out at St Peter's spire. 'Well, my dear chap, the same lady who would have benefited had you been right in your preposterous assumption that poor Mrs Arno was not Mrs Arno. Or to cut a tall story short, Sir Manuel's niece in France.'

'You never did tell me her name,' said Wexford.

He did not then. 'It's an extraordinary thing. Poor Mrs Arno simply followed in her father's footmarks. It's no more than a week ago she asked me if she should make a will and I naturally advised her to do so. But, as was true in the case of Sir Manuel, she died before a will was drawn up. She too had been going to get married, you know, but she changed her mind.'

'No, I didn't know.'

Ames made his doggy face. 'So, as I say, the beneficiary will be this French lady, there being no other living relatives whatsoever. I've got her name somewhere.' He hunted in a drawer full of folders. 'Ah, yes. A Mademoiselle Thérèse Lerèmy. Do you want her precise address?'

The transformation of Moidore Lodge was apparent long before the house was reached. The drive was swept, the signboard bearing the name of the house had been re-painted black and white, and Wexford could have sworn the bronze wolves (or alsatians) had received a polish.

Blaise Cory's Porsche was parked up in front of the house and it was he, not Muriel Hicks, who opened the door. They send for him like other people might send for their solicitor, thought Wexford. He stepped into a hall from which all dust and clutter had been removed, which even seemed lighter and airier. Blaise confided, looking once or twice over his shoulder:

'Having these good people has made all the difference to the dear old dad. I do hope you're not here to do anything which might — well, in short, which might put a spanner in the works.'

'I hardly think so, Mr Cory. I have a question or two to ask Mrs Hicks, that's all.'

'Ah, that's what you people always say.' He gave the short, breathy, fruity laugh with which, on his show, he was in the habit of receiving the more outrageous of the statements made by his interviewees. 'I believe she's about the house, plying her highly useful equipment.'

The sound of a vacuum cleaner immediately began overhead as if on cue, and Wexford would have chosen to go straight upstairs but he found himself instead ushered into Philip Cory's living room.

Ted Hicks was cleaning the huge Victorian french windows, the old man, once more attired in his boy's jeans and guernsey, watching him with fascinated approval. Hicks stopped work the moment Wexford came in and took up his semi-attention stance.

'Good morning, sir!'

'Welcome, Chief Inspector, welcome.' Cory spread out his meagre hands expansively. 'A pleasure to see you, I'm sure. It's so delightful for me to have visitors and not be ashamed of the old place, not to mention being able to find things. Now, for instance, if you or Blaise were to require a drink I shouldn't have to poke about looking for bottles. Hicks here would bring them in a jiffy, wouldn't you, Hicks?'

'I certainly would, sir.'

'So you have only to say the word.'

It being not yet ten in the morning, Wexford was not inclined to utter any drink-summoning word but asked if he might have a talk in private with Mrs Hicks.

'I saw in the newspaper about poor little Natalie,' said Cory. 'Blaise thought it would upset me. Blaise was always a very *sensitive* boy. But I said to him, how can I be upset when I don't know if she was Natalie or not?'

Wexford went upstairs, Hicks leading the way. Moidore Lodge was a very large house. Several rooms had been set aside to make a dwelling for the Hickses without noticeably depleting the Cory living space. Muriel Hicks, who had been cleaning

Cory's own bedroom with its vast four-poster, came into her own rooms, drying her newly washed hands on a towel. She had put on weight since last he saw her and her pale red hair had grown longer and bushier. But her brusque and taciturn manner was unchanged.

'Mrs Arno was going away on her holidays. She says to me to see to the moving when the men came next day. It wasn't convenient, we were leaving ourselves and I'd got things to do, but that was all the same to her, I daresay.' Her husband flashed her an admonitory look, implying that respect should be accorded to *all* employers, or else perhaps that she must in no way hint at ill of the dead. Her pink face flushed rosily. 'Well, she said that was the only day Dorset's could do it, so it was no use arguing. She'd had a chap there staying the weekend. . . .'

'A *gentleman*,' said Hicks.

'All right, Ted, a gentleman. I thought he'd gone by the Sunday, and maybe he had, but he was back the Monday afternoon.'

'You saw him?'

'I *heard* him. I went in about six to check up with her what was going and what was staying, and I heard them talking upstairs. They heard me come in and they started talking French so I wouldn't understand, and she laughed and said in English, 'Oh, your funny Swiss accent!' By the time I got upstairs he'd hid himself.'

'Did you hear his name, Mrs Hicks?'

She shook her head. 'Never heard his name and never saw him. She was a funny one, she didn't mind me knowing he was there and what he was to her like, but she never wanted me nor anyone to actually see him. I took it for granted they both went off on their holidays that same evening. She said she was going, she told me, and the car was gone.'

'What happened next day?'

'The men came from Dorset's nine in the morning. I let them in and told them what to take and what not to. She'd left everything labelled. When they'd gone I had a good clear-up. There was a lot of blood about in the blue bathroom, but I never gave it a thought, reckoned one of them had cut theirselves.' Wexford remembered the deliberate cutting of Natalie's fingertips in the bathroom in De Beauvoir Place and he almost shuddered. Muriel Hicks was more stolid about it than he. 'I had a bit of a job getting it off the carpet,' she said. 'I saw in the paper they found her at Dorset's warehouse. Was she . . . ? I mean, was *it* in that chest?'

He nodded.

She said indifferently, 'The men did say it was a dead weight.'

Blaise Cory walked out to the car with him. It was warm today, the sky a serene blue, the leaves of the plane trees fluttering in a light frisky breeze. Blaise said suddenly and without his usual affected geniality:

'Do you know Mrs Mountnessing, Camargue's sister-in-law?'

'I've seen her once.'

'There was a bit of a scandal in the family. I was only seventeen or eighteen at the time and Natalie and I — well, it wasn't an affair or anything, we were like brother and sister. We were close, she used to tell me things. The general made a pass at her and the old girl caught them kissing.'

'The general?' said Wexford.

Blaise made one of his terrible jokes. 'Must have been caviare to him.' He gave a yelp of laughter. 'Sorry. I mean old Roo Mountnessing, General Mountnessing. Mrs M told her sister and made a great fuss, put all the blame on poor little Nat, called her incestuous and a lot of crap like that. As if everyone didn't know the old boy was a satyr. Camargue was away on a tour of Australia at the time or he'd have intervened. Mrs Camargue and her sister tried to lock Nat up, keep her a sort of prisoner. She got out and hit her mother. She hit her in the chest, quite hard, I think. I suppose they had a sort of brawl over Natalie trying to get out of the house.'

'And?'

'Well, when Mrs Camargue got cancer Mrs Mountnessing said it had been brought on by the blow. I've heard it said that can happen. The doctors said no but Mrs M. wouldn't listen to that and she more or less got Camargue to believe it too. I've always thought that's why Natalie went off with Vernon Arno, she couldn't stand things at home.'

'So that was the cause of the breach,' said Wexford. 'Camargue blamed her for her mother's death.'

Blaise shook his head. 'I don't think he did. He was just confused by Mrs M. and crazy with grief over his wife dying. The dear old dad says Camargue tried over and over again to make things right between himself and Nat, wrote again and again, offered to go out there or pay her fare home. I suppose it wasn't so much him blaming her for her mother's death as her blaming herself. It was guilt kept her away.'

Wexford looked down at the little stocky man.

'Did she tell you all this when you had lunch with her, Mr Cory?'

'Good heavens, no. We didn't talk about that. I'm a *present* person, Chief Inspector, I live in the moment. And so did she. Curious,' he said reflectively, 'that rumour which went around back in the winter that she was some sort of impostor.'

'Yes,' said Wexford.

It was not a long drive from Moidore Lodge to the village on the borders of St Leonard's Forest. It was called Bayeux Green, between Horsham and Wellridge, and the house Wexford was looking for bore the name Bayeux Villa. Well, it was not all that far from Hastings, there was another village nearby called Doomsday Green, and very likely the name had something to do with the tapestry.

He found the house without having to ask. It was in the centre of the village, a narrow, detached, late nineteenth-century house, built of small pale grey bricks and with only a small railed-in area separating it from the pavement. The front door was newer and inserted in it was a picture in stained glass of a Norman soldier in chain mail. Wexford rang the bell and got no answer. He stepped to one side and looked in at the window. There was no sign of recent habitation. The occupants, at this time of the year, were very likely away on holiday. It seemed strange that they had made no arrangements for the care of their houseplants. Tradescantias, peperomias, a cissus that climbed to the ceiling on carefully spaced strings, a Joseph's coat, a variegated ivy, all hung down leaves that were limp and parched.

He walked around the house, looking in more windows,

711

and he had a sensation of being watched, though he could see no one. The two little lawns looked as if they had not been cut for a month and there were weeds coming up in the rosebed. After he had rung the bell again he went to the nearest neighbour, a cottage separated from Bayeux Villa by a greengrocer's and a pair of garages.

It was a comfort to be himself once more, to have resumed his old standing. The woman looked at his warrant card.

'They went off on holiday — oh, it'd be three weeks ago. When I come to think of it, they must be due back today or tomorrow. They've got a caravan down in Devon, they always take three weeks.'

'Don't they have friends to come in and keep an eye on the place?'

She said quickly, 'Don't tell me it's been broken into.'

He reassured her. 'Nobody's watered the plants.'

'But the sister's there. She said to me on the Saturday, my sister'll be staying while we're away.'

This time he caught her off guard. He came up to the kitchen window and their eyes met. She had been on the watch for him too, creeping about the house, looking out for him. She was still wearing the red and yellow dress of Indian cotton, she had been shut up in there for three weeks, and it hung on her. Her face looked sullen, though not frightened. She opened the back door and let him in.

'Good morning, Mrs Zoffany,' he said. 'It's a relief to find you well and unharmed.'

'Who would harm me?'

'Suppose you tell me that. Suppose you tell me all about it.'

She said nothing. He wondered what she had done all by herself in this house since 27 July. Not eaten much, that was obvious. Presumably, she had not been out. Nor even opened a window. It was insufferably hot and stuffy and a strong smell of sweat and general unwashedness emanated from Jane Zoffany as he followed her into the room full of dying plants. She sat down and looked at him in wary silence.

'If you won't tell me,' he said, 'shall I tell you? After you left me on that Friday evening you went back to Sterries and found the house empty. Mrs Arno had driven your husband to the station. As a matter of fact, her car passed me as I was driving down the hill.' She continued to eye him uneasily. Her eyes had more madness in them than when he had last seen her. 'You took your handbag but you left your suitcase; didn't want to be lumbered with it, I daresay. There's a bus goes to Horsham from outside St Peter's. You'd have had time to catch the last one, or else maybe you had a hire car.'

She said stonily, 'I haven't money for hire cars. I didn't know about the bus, but it came and I got on.'

'When you got here you found your sister and her husband were leaving for their summer holiday the next day. No doubt they were glad to have someone here to keep an eye on the place while they were gone. Then a week later you got yourself a birthday card. . . .'

'No.' She shook her head vehemently. 'I only posted it. My sister had bought a card for me and written in it and done the envelope and everything. She said, here, you'd better have this now, save the postage. I went out at night and posted it.' She gave a watery vague smile. 'I liked hiding, I enjoyed it.'

He could understand that. The virtue for her would be twofold. To some extent she would lose her identity, that troubling self, she would have hidden here from herself as successfully as she had hidden from others. And there would be the satisfaction of becoming for a brief while important, of causing anxiety, for once of stimulating emotions.

'What I don't see,' he said, 'is how you managed when the police came here making inquiries.'

She giggled. 'That was funny. They took me for my sister.'

'I see.'

'They just took it for granted I was my sister and they kept on talking about Mrs Zoffany. Did I have any idea where Mrs Zoffany might be? When had I last seen her? I said no and I didn't know and they had to believe me. It was funny, it was a bit like . . .' She put her fingers over her mouth and looked at him over the top of them.

'I shall have to tell your husband where you are. He's been very worried about you.'

'Has he? Has he *really*?'

Had she, during her semi-incarceration, watched television,

heard a radio, seen a newspaper? Presumably not, since she had not mentioned Natalie's death. He wouldn't either. She was safe enough here, he thought, with the sister coming back. Zoffany himself would no doubt come down before that. Would they perhaps get her back into a mental hospital between them? He had no faith that the kind of treatment she might get would do her good. He wanted to tell her to have a bath, eat a meal, open the windows, but he knew she would take no advice, would hardly hear it.

'I thought you'd be very angry with me.'

He treated that no more seriously than if the younger of his grandsons had said it to him. 'You and I are going to have to have a talk, Mrs Zoffany. When you've settled down at home again and I've got more time. Just at present I'm very busy and I have to go abroad again.'

She nodded. She no longer looked sullen. He let himself out into Bayeux Green's little high street, and when he glanced back he saw her gaunt face at the window, the eyes following him. In spite of what he had said, he might never see her again, he might never need to, for in one of those flashes of illumination that he had despaired of ever coming in this case, he saw the truth. She had told him. In a little giggly confidence she had told him everything there still remained for him to know.

In the late afternoon he drove out to the home of the chief constable, Hightrees Farm, Millerton. Mrs Griswold exemplified the reverse of the Victorian ideal for children; she was heard but not seen. Some said she had been bludgeoned into passivity by forty years with the colonel. Her footsteps could sometimes be heard overhead, her voice whispering into the telephone. Colonel Griswold himself opened the front door, something which Wexford always found disconcerting. It was plunging in at the deep end.

'I want to go to the South of France, sir.'

'I daresay,' said Griswold. 'I shall have to settle for a cottage in north Wales myself.'

In a neutral voice Wexford reminded him that he had already had his holiday. The chief constable said yes, he remembered, and Wexford had been somewhere very exotic, hadn't he? He had wondered once or twice how that sort of thing would go down with the public when the police started screaming for wage increases.

'I want to go to the South of France,' Wexford said more firmly, 'and I know it's irregular but I would like to take Mike Burden with me. It's a little place *inland* —' Griswold's lips seemed silently to be forming the syllables St Tropez, '— and there's a woman there who will inherit Camargue's money and property. She's Camargue's niece and her name is Thérèse Lerèmy.'

'A French citizen?'

'Yes, sir, but . . .'

'I don't want you going about putting people's backs up, Reg. Particularly foreign backs. I mean, don't think you can go over there and arrest this woman on some of your thin suspicions and. . . .'

But before Wexford had even begun to deny that this was his intention he knew from the moody truculent look which had replaced obduracy in Grisworld's face that he was going to relent.

CHAPTER TWENTY

From the city of the angels to the bay of the angels. As soon as they got there the taxi driver took them along the Promenade des Anglais, though it was out of their way, but he said they had to see it, they couldn't come to Nice and just see the airport. While Wexford gazed out over the Baie des Anges, Burden spoke from his newly acquired store of culture. Jenny had a reproduction of a picture of this by a painter called Dufy, but it all looked a bit different now.

It was still only late morning. They had come on the early London to Paris flight and changed planes at Roissy-Charles de Gaulle. Now their drive took them through hills crowned with orange and olive trees. Saint Jean-de-l'Éclaircie lay a few miles to the north of Grasse, near the river Loup. A bell began to chime noon as they passed through an ivy-hung archway in the walls into the ancient town. They drove past the ochre-stone cathedral into the Place aux Eaux Vives where a fountain was playing and where stood Picasso's statue 'Woman with a Lamb', presented to the town by the artist (according to Wexford's guide book) when he lived and worked there for some months after the war. The guide book also said that there was a Fragonard in the cathedral, some incomparable Sevres porcelain in the museum, the Fondation Yeuse, and a mile outside the town the well-preserved remains of a Roman amphitheatre. The taxi driver said that if you went up into the cathedral belfry you could see Corsica on the horizon.

Wexford had engaged rooms for one night — on the advice of his travel agent in the Kingsbrook Precinct — at the Hotel de la Rose Blanche in the *place*. Its vestibule was cool and dim, stone-walled, stone-flagged, and with that indefinable atmosphere that is a combination of complacency and gleeful anticipation and which signifies that the food is going to be good. The chef's in his kitchen, all's right with the world.

Kenneth Ames had known nothing more about Mademoiselle

Lerèmy than her name, her address and her relationship to Camargue. It was also known that her parents were dead and she herself unmarried. Recalling the photograph of the two little girls shown him by Mrs Mountnessing, Wexford concluded she must be near the age of Camargue's daughter. He looked her up in the phone book, dialled the number apprehensively because of his scanty French, but got no reply.

They lunched off seafood, bread that was nearly all crisp crust, and a bottle of Monbazillac. Wexford said in an abstracted sort of voice that he felt homesick already, the hors d'oeuvres reminded him of Mr Haq and antipasto Ankole. He got no reply when he attempted once more to phone Thérèse Lerèmy, so there seemed nothing for it but to explore the town.

It was too hot to climb the belfry. On 24 July Saint-Jean-de-l'Éclaircie was probably at its hottest. The square was deserted, the narrow steep alleys that threaded the perimeter just inside the walls held only the stray tourist, and the morning market which had filled the Place de la Croix had packed up and gone. They went into the cathedral of St Jean Baptiste, dark, cool, baroque. A nun was walking in the aisle, eyes cast down, and an old man knelt at prayer. They looked with proper awe at Fragonard's 'Les Pains et Les Poissons', a large hazy canvas of an elegant Christ and an adoring multitude, and then they returned to the bright white sunshine and hard black shadows of the *place*.

'I suppose she's out at work,' said Wexford. 'A single woman would be bound to work. It looks as if we'll have to hang things out a few hours.'

'It's no hardship,' said Burden. 'I promised Jenny I wouldn't miss the museum.'

Wexford shrugged. 'O.K.'

The collection was housed in a sienna-red stucco building with Fondation Yeuse lettered on a black marble plaque. Wexford had expected it to be deserted inside but in fact they met other tourists in the rooms and on the winding marble staircase. As well as the Sevres, Burden had been instructed to look at some ancient jewellery discovered in the Condamine, and Wexford, hearing English spoken, asked for directions from the woman who had been speaking correctly but haltingly to an

717

American visitor. She seemed to be a curator, for she wore on one of the lapels of her dark red, near-uniform dress an oval badge inscribed Fondation Yeuse. He forced himself not to stare — and then wondered how many thousands before him had forced themselves not to stare. The lower part of her face was pitted densely and deeply with the scars of what looked like smallpox but was almost certainly acne. In her careful stumbling English she instructed him where to find the jewellery. He and Burden went upstairs again where the American woman had arrived before them. The sun penetrating drawn Venetian blinds shone on her flawless ivory skin. She had hands like Natalie Arno's, long and slender, display stands for rings as heavy and roughly made as those on the linen under the glass.

'We may as well get on up there,' said Wexford after they had bought a *flacon* of Grasse perfume for Dora and a glazed stoneware jar in a Picasso design for Jenny. 'Get on up there and have a look at the place.'

The two local taxis, which were to be found between the fountain and the hotel de la Rose Blanche, were not much in demand at this hour. Their driver spoke no English but as soon as Wexford mentioned the Maison du Cirque he understood and nodded assent.

On the north-eastern side of the town, outside the walls, was an estate of depressing pale grey flats and brown wooden houses with scarlet switchback roofs. It was as bad as home. Worse? ventured Burden. But the estate was soon left behind and the road ran through lemon groves. The driver persisted in talking to them in fast, fluent, incomprehensible French. Wexford managed to pick out two facts from all this, one that Saint-Jean-de-l'Éclaircie held a lemon festival each February, and the other that on the far side of the hill was the amphitheatre.

They came upon the house standing alone at a bend in the road. It was flat-fronted, unprepossessing but undoubtedly large. At every window were wooden shutters from which most of the paint had flaked away. Big gardens, neglected now, stretched distantly towards olive and citrus groves, separated from them by crumbling stone walls.

'Mariana in the moated grange,' said Wexford. 'We may as well go to the circus while we're waiting for her.'

The driver took them back. The great circular plain which was the base of the amphitheatre was strangely green as if watered by a hidden spring. The tiers of seating, still defined, still unmistakable, rose in their parallel arcs to the hillside, the pines, the crystalline blue of the sky. Wexford sat down where some prefect or consul might once have sat.

'I hope we're in time,' he said. 'I hope we can get to her before any real harm has been done. The woman has been dead nine days. He's been here, say, eight. . . .'

'If he's here. The idea of him being here is all based on your ESP. We don't know if he's here and, come to that, we don't know who he is or what he looks like or what name he'll be using.'

'It's not as bad as that,' said Wexford. 'He would naturally come here. This place, that girl, would draw him like magnets. He won't want to lose the money now, Mike.'

'No, not after plotting for years to get it. How long d'you reckon we're going to be here?'

Wexford shrugged. The air was scented with the herbs that grew on the hillsides, sage and thyme and rosemary and bay, and the sun was still very warm. 'However long it may be,' he said enigmatically, 'to me it would be too short.' He looked at his watch. 'Martin should have seen Williams by now and done a spot of checking up for me at Guy's Hospital.'

'Guy's Hospital?'

'In the course of this case we haven't remembered as often as we should that Natalie Arno went into hospital a little while before Camargue died. She had a biopsy.'

'Yes, what *is* that?'

'It means to look at living tissue. It usually describes the kind of examination that is done to determine whether certain cells are cancerous or not.'

Once this subject would have been a highly emotive one for Burden, an area to be avoided by all his sensitive acquaintances. His first wife had died of cancer. But time and his second marriage had changed things. He responded not with pain but only with an edge of embarrassment to his voice.

'But she didn't have cancer.'

'Oh, no.'

He sat down in the tier below Wexford. 'I'd like to tell you what I think happened, see if we agree.' On the grass beside him the shadow of Wexford's head nodded. 'Well, then. Tessa Lanchester went on holiday to that place in California, Santa – what was it?'

'Santa Xavierita.'

'And while she was there she met a man who played the guitar or whatever in a restaurant in the local town. He was living in America illegally and was very likely up to a good many other illegal activities as well. He was a con man. He had already met Natalie Arno and found out from her who her father was and what her expectations were. He introduced Tessa to Natalie and the two women became friends.

'He persuaded Tessa not to go back home to Boston but to remain longer in Santa Xavierita learning all she could about Natalie's life and past. Then he took Natalie out swimming by night and drowned her and that same night left with Tessa for Los Angeles in Natalie's car with Natalie's luggage and the key to Natalie's house. From then on Tessa became Natalie. The changes Natalie's body had undergone after five days in the sea made a true identification impossible and, since Tessa was missing, the corpse was identified as that of Tessa.

'Tessa and her accomplice then set about their plan to inherit Camargue's property, though this was somewhat frustrated by Ilbert's intervening and the subsequent deportation. Tessa tried in vain to sell Natalie's house. I think at this time she rather cooled off the plan. Otherwise I don't know how to account for a delay of more than three years between making the plan and putting it into practice. I think she cooled off. She settled into her new identity, made new friends and, as we know, had two further love affairs. Then one of these lovers, Ivan Zoffany, wrote from London in the autumn of 1979 to say he had heard from his sister-in-law who lived near Wellridge that Camargue was about to re-marry. That alerted her and fetched her to England. There she was once more able to join forces with the man who had first put her up to the idea. They had the support and help of Zoffany and his wife. How am I doing so far?'

Wexford raised his eyebrows. 'How did they get Williams and Mavis Rolland into this? Bribery?'

'Of course. It would have to be a heavy bribe. Williams's professional integrity presumably has a high price. I daresay Mrs Woodhouse could be bought cheaply enough.'

'I never took you for a snob before, Mike.'

'It's not snobbery,' said Burden hotly. 'It's simply that the poorer you are the more easily you're tempted. Shall I go on?'

The shadow nodded.

'They hesitated a while before the confrontation. Tessa was naturally nervous about this very important encounter. Also she'd been ill and had to have hospital treatment. When she finally went down to Sterries she blundered, not in having failed to do her homework — she knew every fact about the Camargue household she could be expected to, she knew them like she knew her own family in Boston — but over the pronunciation of an Italian name. Spanish she knew — many Americans do — French she knew, but it never occurred to her she would have to pronounce Italian.

'The rest we know. Camargue told her she would be cut out of his will, so on the following Sunday she made a sound alibi for herself by going to a party with Jane Zoffany. *He* went down to Sterries, waited for Camargue in the garden and drowned him in the lake.'

Wexford said nothing.

'Well?'

As befitted a person of authority sitting in the gallery of an amphitheatre, Wexford turned down his thumbs. 'The last bit's more or less right, the drowning bit.' He got up. 'Shall we go?'

Burden was still muttering that it had to be that way, that all else was impossible, when they arrived back at the Maison du Cirque. Ahead of them a bright green Citroen 2 CV had just turned into the drive.

The woman who got out of it, who came inquiringly towards them, was the curator of the Fondation Yeuse.

CHAPTER TWENTY-ONE

The sun shone cruelly on that pitted skin. She had done her best to hide it with heavy make-up, but there would never be any hiding it. And now as she approached these two strangers she put one hand up, half covering a cheek. Close to, she had a look of Camargue, all the less attractive traits of the Camargue physiognomy were in her face, too-high forehead, too-long nose, too-fleshy mouth, and added to them that acne-scarred skin. She was sallow and her hair was very dark. But she was one of those plain people whose smiles transform them. She smiled uncertainly at them, and the change of expression made her look kind and sweet-tempered.

Wexford introduced them. He explained that he had seen her earlier that day. Her surprise at being called upon by two English policemen seemed unfeigned. She was astonished but not apparently nervous.

'This is some matter concerning the *musée* — the museum?' she asked in her heavily accented English.

'No, mademoiselle,' said Wexford, 'I must confess I'd never heard of the Fondation Yeuse till this morning. You've worked there long?'

'Since I leave the university — that is, eighteen years. M. Raoul Yeuse, the Paris art dealer, he is, was, the brother of my father's sister. He has founded the museum, you understand? Excuse me, monsieur, I fear my English is very bad.'

'It is we who should apologize for having no French. May we go into the house, Mademoiselle Lerèmy? I have something to tell you.'

Did she know already? The announcement of the discovery of the body at Dorset's would have scarcely appeared in the French newspapers until three days ago. And when it appeared would it have merited more than a paragraph on an inside page? A murder, in England, of an obscure woman? The dark eyes of Camargue's niece looked merely innocent and inquiring. She led them into a large high-ceilinged room and opened latticed glass doors on to a terrace. From the back of the Maison du Cirque you could see the green rim of the amphitheatre and smell the scented hillsides. But the house itself was shabby and neglected and far too big. It had been built for a family and that family's servants in days when perhaps money came easily and went a long way.

Now that they were indoors and seated she had become rather pale. 'This is not bad news, I hope, monsieur?' She looked from one to the other of them with a rising anxiety that Wexford thought he understood. He let Burden answer her.

'Serious news,' said Burden. 'But not personally distressing to you, Miss Lerèmy. You hardly knew your cousin Natalie Camargue, did you?'

She shook her head. 'She was married. I have not heard her husband's name. When last I am seeing her she is sixteen, I seventeen. It is many years . . .'

'I'm afraid she's dead. To put it bluntly, she was murdered and so was your uncle. We're here to investigate these crimes. It seems the same person killed them both. For gain. For money.'

Both hands went up to her cheeks. She recoiled a little.

'But this is terrible!'

Wexford had decided not to tell her of the good fortune this terrible news would bring her. Kenneth Ames could do that. If what he thought was true she would be in need of consolation. He must now broach the subject of this belief of his. Strange that this time he could be so near hoping he was wrong . . .

Her distress seemed real. Her features were contorted into a frown of dismay, her tall curved forehead all wrinkles. 'I am so sorry, this is so very bad.'

'Mademoiselle Lerèmy . . .'

'When I am a little girl I see him many many times, monsieur. I stay with them in Sussex. Natalie is, was, nice, I think, always laughing, always very gay, have much sense of *humeur*. The world has become a very bad place, monsieur, when such things as this happen.' She paused, bit her lip. 'Excuse me, I must not say "sir" so much, is it not so? This I am learning to understand . . .' She hesitated and hazarded, 'Lately? Recently?'

Her words brought him the thrill of knowing he was right — and sickened him too. Must he ask her? Burden was looking at him.

The telephone rang.

'Please excuse me,' she said.

The phone was in the room where they were, up beside the windows. She picked up the receiver rather too fast and the effect on her of the voice of her caller was pitiful to see. She flushed deeply and it was somehow apparent that this was a flush of intense fearful pleasure as well as embarrassment.

She said softly, 'Ah, Jean... We see each other again tonight? Of course it is all right, it is fine, very good.' She made an effort, for their benefit or her caller's, to establish formality. 'It will be a great pleasure to see you again.'

He was here all right then, he was talking to her. But where was he? She had her back to them now. 'When you have finished your work, yes. *Entends*, Jean, I will fetch — pick up — pick you up. Ten o'clock?' Suddenly she changed into rapid French. Wexford could not understand a word but he understood *her*. She had been speaking English to a French speaker so that her English hearers would know she had a boy friend, a lover. For all her scarred face, her plainness, her age, her obscure job in this backwater, she had a lover to tell the world about.

She put the phone down after a murmured word or two, a ripple of excited laughter. Wexford was on his feet, signalling with a nod to Burden.

'You do not wish to ask me questions concerning my uncle and my *cousine* Natalie, monsieur?'

'It is no longer necessary, mademoiselle.'

The taxi driver had gone to sleep. Wexford woke him with a prod in his chest.

'La Rose Blanche, *s'il vous plaît*.'

The sun was going down. There were long violet shadows and the air was sweet and soft.

'He's a fast worker if ever there was one,' said Burden.

'The material he is working on could hardly be more receptive and malleable.'

'Pardon? Oh, yes, I see what you mean. Poor girl. It's a

terrible handicap having all that pitting on her face, did you notice? D'you think he knew about that? Before he came here, I mean? The real Natalie might have known — you usually get that sort of acne in your teens — but Tessa Lanchester wouldn't have. Unless she picked it up when she was gathering all the rest of her info in Santa Xavierita.'

'Mrs Woodhouse might have known,' said Wexford. 'At any rate, he knew she was unmarried and an heiress and no doubt that she worked in the museum here. It was easy enough for him to scrape up an acquaintance.'

'Bit more than an acquaintance,' said Burden grimly.

'Let's hope it hasn't progressed far yet. Certainly his intention is to marry her.'

'Presumably his intention was to marry that other woman, but at the last she wouldn't have him and for that he killed her.' Burden seemed gratified to get from Wexford a nod of approval. 'Once he'd done that he'd realize who the next heir was and come here as fast as he could. But there's something here doesn't make sense. In putting her body in that chest he seems to have meant to keep it concealed for months, possibly even years, but the paradox there is that until the body was found death wouldn't be presumed and Thérèse Lerèmy wouldn't get anything.'

Wexford looked slyly at him. 'Suppose he intended by some means or other to prove, as only he could, that it was Natalie Arno and not Tessa Lanchester who drowned at Santa Xavierita in 1976? If that were proved Thérèse would become the heir at once and in fact *would have been* the rightful possessor of Sterries and Camargue's money for the past six months.'

'You really think that was it?'

'No, I don't. It would have been too bold and too risky and fraught with problems. I think this was what was in his mind. He didn't want the body found at once because if he then started courting Thérèse even someone as desperate as she might suspect he was after her money. But he wanted it found at some time in the not too distant future or his conquest of Thérèse would bring him no profit at all. What better than that the presence of a corpse in that warehouse should make itself apparent after, say, six months? And if it didn't he could always send the police an anonymous letter.'

'That's true,' said Burden. 'And there was very little to connect him with it, after all. If you hadn't been to California we shouldn't have known of his existence.'

Wexford laughed shortly. 'Yes, there was some profit in it.' They walked into the hotel. Outside Burden's room where they would have separated prior to dressing, or at least sprucing up, for dinner, Burden said, 'Come in here a minute. I want to ask you something.' Wexford sat on the bed. From the window you could see, not the square and the fountain but a mazy mosaic of little roofs against the backdrop of the city walls. 'I'd like to know what we're going to charge those others with. I mean, Williams and Zoffany and Mary Woodhouse. Conspiracy, I suppose – but not conspiracy to murder?'

Wexford pondered. He smiled a little ruefully. 'We're not going to charge them with anything.'

'You mean their evidence will be more valuable as prosecution witnesses?'

'Not really. I shouldn't think any of them would be a scrap of use as witnesses of any kind. They didn't witness anything and they haven't done anything. They all seem to me to be perfectly blameless, apart from a spot — and I'd guess a very small spot — of adultery on the part of Zoffany.' Wexford paused. 'That reconstruction of the case you gave me while we were at the amphitheatre, didn't it strike you there was something unreal about it?'

'Sort of illogical, d'you mean? Maybe, bits of it. Surely that's because they were so devious that there are aspects which aren't clear and never will be?'

Wexford shook his head. 'Unreal. One can't equate it with what one knows of human nature. Take, for instance, their foresight and their patience. They kill Natalie in the summer of 1976 and Tessa impersonates her. Fair enough. Why not go straight to England, make sure Natalie is the beneficiary under Camargue's will and then kill Camargue?'

'I know there's a stumbling block. I said so.'

'It's more than a stumbling block, Mike, it's a bloody great barrier across the path. Think what you — and I — believed they did. Went back to Los Angeles, ran the risk of being suspected by the neighbours, exposed by Ilbert — returned to and settled in what of all cities in the world was the most dangerous to them. And for what?'

'Surely she stayed there to sell the house?'

'Yet she never succeeded in selling it, did she? No, a delay of three-and-a-half years between the killing of Natalie and the killing of Camargue was too much for me to swallow. I can come up with just one feeble reason for it — that they were waiting for Camargue to die a natural death. But, as I say, that's a feeble reason. He might easily have lived another ten years.' Wexford looked at his watch. 'I'll leave you to your shaving and showering or whatever. A wash and brush-up will do me. Laquin won't be here before seven.'

They met again in the bar where they each had a Stella Artois. Wexford said:

'Your suggestion is that Tessa came to England finally because, through Zoffany's sister-in-law, she heard that Camargue intended to marry again. Doesn't it seem a bit thin that Jane Zoffany's sister should come to know this merely because she lives in a village near the Kathleen Camargue School?'

'Not if she was set by the others to watch Camargue.'

Wexford shrugged. 'The others, yes. There would be five of them, our protagonist and her boy friend, the Zoffanys and Jane Zoffany's sister. Five conspirators working for the acquisition of Camargue's money. Right?'

'Yes, for a start,' said Burden. 'There were finally more like eight or nine.'

'Mary Woodhouse to give Tessa some advanced coaching, Mavis Rolland to identify her as an old school chum, and Williams the dentist.' Wexford gave a little shake of the head. 'I've said I was amazed at their foresight and their patience, Mike, but that was nothing to the trouble they took. That staggered me. All these subsidiary conspirators were persuaded to lie, to cheat or to sell their professional integrity. Tessa studied old samples of Natalie's handwriting, had casts made of her jaw, took lessons to perfect her college French and Spanish — though she neglected to polish up her Italian — while one of the others made a survey of the lie of the land round Sterries and of Camargue's habits. Prior to this Zoffany's sister-in-law was sending a secret agent's regular dispatches out to Los

Angeles. Oh, and let's not forget — Jane Zoffany was suborning her neighbours into providing a fake alibi. And all this machinery was set in motion and relentlessly kept in motion for the sake of acquiring a not very large house in an acre of ground and an *unknown sum of money* that, when the time came, would have to be split between eight people.

'I've kept thinking of that and I couldn't believe in it. I couldn't understand why those two had chosen Camargue as their prey. Why not pick on some tycoon? Why not some American oil millionaire? Why an old musician who wasn't and never had been in the tycoon class?'

Burden supplied a hesitant answer. 'Because his daughter fell into their hands, one supposes. Anyway, there's no alternative. We know there was a conspiracy, we know there was an elaborate plan, and one surely simply comments that it's impossible fully to understand people's motivations.'

'But isn't there an alternative? You said I was obsessed, Mike. I think more than anything I became obsessed by the complexity of this case, by the deviousness of the protagonist, by the subtlety of the web she had woven. It was only when I saw how wrong I'd been in these respects that things began to clear for me.'

'I don't follow you.'

Wexford drank his beer. He said rather slowly, 'It was only then that I began to see that this case wasn't complicated, there was no deviousness, there was no plotting, no planning ahead, no conspiracy whatsoever, and that even the two murders happened so spontaneously as really to be unpremeditated.' He rose suddenly, pushing back his chair. Commissaire Mario Laquin of the Compagnies Republicaines de Securité of Grasse had come in and was scanning the room. Wexford raised a hand. He said absently to Burden as the commissaire came towards their table, 'The complexity was in our own minds, Mike. The case itself was simple and straightforward, and almost everything that took place was the result of accident or of chance.'

It was a piece of luck for Wexford that Laquin had been transferred to Grasse from Marseilles some six months before, for they had once or twice worked on cases together and since then the two policemen and their wives had met when M. and Mme Laquin were in London on holiday. It nevertheless came as something of a shock to be clasped in the commissaire's arms and kissed on both cheeks. Burden stood by, trying to give his dry smile but succeeding only in looking astonished.

Laquin spoke English that was almost flawless. 'You pick some charming places to come for your investigations, my dear Reg. A little bird tells me you have already had two weeks in California. I should be so lucky. Last year when I was in pursuit of Honorat L'Eponge, where does he lead me to but Dusseldorf, I ask you!'

'Have a drink,' said Wexford. 'It's good to see you. I haven't a clue where this chap of ours is. Nor do I know what name he's going under while here.'

'Or even what he looks like,' said Burden for good measure. He seemed cheered by the presence of Laquin whom he had perhaps expected to speak with a Peter Sellers accent.

'I know what he looks like,' said Wexford. 'I've seen him.'

Burden glanced at him in surprise. Wexford took no notice of him and ordered their drinks.

'You'll dine with us, of course?' he said to Laquin.

'It will be a pleasure. The food here is excellent.'

Wexford grinned wryly. 'Yes, it doesn't look as though we'll be here to enjoy it tomorrow. I reckon we're going to have to take him at the Maison du Cirque, in that wretched girl's house.'

'Reg, she has known him no time at all, a mere week at most.'

'Even so quickly can one catch the plague. . . . You're right, of course.'

'A blessing for her we're going to rid her of him, if you ask me,' said Burden. 'A couple of years and he'd have put her out of the way as well.'

'She implied he was working here . . .'

'Since Britain came in the European Economic Community, Reg, there is no longer need for your countrymen to have work permits or to register. Therefore to trace his whereabouts would be a long and laborious business. And since we know that later on tonight he will be at the Maison du Cirque . . .'

'Sure, yes, I know. I'm being sentimental, Mario, I'm a fool.' Wexford gave a grim little laugh. 'But not such a fool as to warn her and have him hop off on the next plane into Switzerland.'

After *bouillabaisse* and a fine *cassoulet* with brie to follow and a small armagnac each, it was still only nine. Ten-thirty was the time fixed on by Wexford and Laquin for their visit to the house by the amphitheatre. Laquin suggested they go to a place he knew on the other side of the Place aux Eaux Vives where there was sometimes flamenco dancing.

In the evening there was some modest floodlighting in the square. Apparently these were truly living waters and the fountain was fed by a natural spring. While they dined tiers of seating had been put up for the music festival of Saint Jean-de-l'Éclaircie, due to begin on the following day. A little warm breeze rustled through the plane and chestnut leaves above their heads.

The flamenco place was called La Mancha. As they passed down the stairs and into a kind of open, deeply sunken courtyard or cistern, a waiter told Laquin there would be no dancing tonight. The walls were made of yellow stone over which hung a deep purple bougainvillea. Instead of the dancers a thin girl in black came out and sang in the manner of Piaf. Laquin and Burden were drinking wine but Wexford took nothing. He felt bored and restless. Nine-thirty. They went up the stairs again and down an alley into the cobbled open space in front of the cathedral.

The moon had come up, a big golden moon flattened like a tangerine. Laquin had sat down at a table in a pavement cafe and was ordering coffee for all three men. From here you could see the city walls, part Roman, part medieval, their rough stones silvered by the light from that yellow moon.

Some teenagers went by. They were on their way, Laquin said, to the discotheque in the Place de la Croix. Wexford wondered if Camargue had ever, years ago, sat on this spot where they were. And that dead woman, when she was a child . . .? It was getting on for ten. Somewhere in St Jean she would be meeting him now in the little green Citroen. The yellow hatchback Opel was presumably left in the long-term car park at Heathrow. He felt a tautening of tension and at the same time relief when Laquin got to his feet and said in his colloquial way that they should be making tracks.

Up through the narrow winding defile once more, flattening themselves tolerantly against stone walls to let more boys and girls pass them. Wexford heard the music long before they emerged into the Place aux Eaux Vives. A Mozart serenade. The serenade from *Don Giovanni*, he thought it was, that should properly be played on a mandolin.

Round the last turn in the alley and out into the wide open square. A group of young girls, also no doubt on their way to the discotheque, were clustered around the highest tier of the festival seating. They clustered around a man who sat on the top, playing a guitar, and they did so in the yearning, worshipping fashion of muses or nymphs on the plinth of some statue of a celebrated musician. The man sat aloft, his tune changed now to a Latin American rhythm, not looking at the girls, looking across the square, his gaze roving as if he expected at any moment the person he waited for to come.

'That's him,' said Wexford.

Laquin said, 'Are you sure?'

'Absolutely. I've only seen him once before but I'd know him anywhere.'

'I know him too,' said Burden incredulously. 'I've seen him before. I can't for the life of me think where, but I've seen him.'

'Let's get it over.'

The little green 2CV was turning into the *place* and the guitarist had seen it. He drew his hand across the strings with a flourish and jumped down from his perch, nearly knocking one of the girls over. He didn't look back at her, he made no apology, he was waving to the car.

And then he saw the three policemen, recognizing them immediately for what they were. His arm fell to his side. He was a tall thin man in his late thirties, very dark with black curly hair. Wexford steadfastly refused to look over his shoulder to see her running from the car. He said:

'John Fassbender, it is my duty to warn you that anything you say will be taken down and may be used in evidence . . .'

CHAPTER TWENTY-TWO

They were in the Pearl of Africa, having what Wexford called a celebration lunch. No one could possibly feel much in the way of pity for Fassbender, so why not celebrate his arrest? Burden said it ought to be called an elucidation lunch because there were still a lot of things he didn't understand and wanted explained. Outside it was pouring with rain again. Wexford asked Mr Haq for a bottle of wine, *good* moselle or a riesling, none of your living waters from Lake Victoria. They had got into sybaritic habits during their day in France. Mr Haq bustled off to what he called his cellar through the fronds of polyethylene Spanish moss.

'Did you mean what you said about there having been no conspiracy?'

'Of course I did,' Wexford said, 'and if we'd had a moment after that I'd have told you something else, something I realized before we ever went to France. The woman we knew as Natalie Arno, the woman Fassbender murdered, was never Tessa Lanchester. Tessa Lanchester was drowned in Santa Xavierita in 1976 and we've no reason to believe either Natalie or Fassbender even met her. The woman who came to London in November of last year came solely because Fassbender was in London. She was in love with Fassbender and since he had twice been deported from the United States he could hardly return there.'

'How could he have been deported twice?' asked Burden.

'I wondered that until the possibility of dual nationality occurred to me and then everything about Fassbender became simple. I'd been asking myself if she had two boy-friends, an Englishman and a Swiss. There was a good deal of confusion in people's minds over him. He was Swiss. He was English. He spoke French. He spoke French with a Swiss accent. He was deported to London. He was deported to Geneva. Well, I'll come back to him in a minute. Suffice it to say that it was after he had been deported a second time that she followed him to London.'

He stopped. Mr Haq, beaming, teeth flashing and spilling, was bringing the wine, a quite respectable-looking white medoc. He poured Wexford a trial half-glassful. Wexford sipped it, looking serious. He had sometimes said, though, that he would rather damage his liver than upset Mr Haq by sending back a bottle. Anyway, the only fault with this wine was that it was at a temperature of around twenty-five degrees Celsius.

'Excellent,' he said to Mr Haq's gratification, and just stopped himself from adding, 'Nice and warm.' He continued to Burden as Mr Haq trotted off, 'She had a brief affair with Zoffany during Fassbender's first absence. I imagine this was due to nothing more than loneliness and that she put it out of her head once Zoffany had departed. But he kept up a correspondence with her and when she needed a home in London he offered her a flat. Didn't I tell you it was simple and straightforward?

'Once there, she saw that Zoffany was in love with her and hoped to take up their relationship (to use Jane Zoffany's word) where it had ended a year and a half before. She wasn't having that, she didn't care for Zoffany at all in that way. But it made things awkward. If she had Fassbender to live with her there, would Zoffany be made so jealous and angry as to throw her out? She couldn't live with Fassbender, he was living in one room. The wisest thing obviously was to keep Fassbender discreetly in the background until such time as he got a job and made some money and they could afford to snap their fingers at Zoffany and live together. We know that Fassbender was in need of work and that she tried to get him a job through Blaise Cory. The point I'm making is that Zoffany never knew of Fassbender's existence until he overheard Natalie talking on the phone to him *last month*.

'I suspect, though I don't know for certain, that there was no urgency on her part to approach Camargue. Probably she gave very little thought to Camargue. It was the announcement of his engagement that brought her to get in touch with him — perhaps reminded her of his existence. But there was no complex planning about that approach, no care taken with the handwriting or the style of the letter, no vetting of it by, say, Mrs Woodhouse. . . .'

Young Haq came with their starter of prawns Pakwach. This was a shocking pink confection into which Burden manfully plunged his spoon before saying, 'There must have been. It may be that the identity of the woman we found in that chest will never be known, but we know very well she was an impostor and a fraudulent claimant.'

'Her identity is known,' said Wexford. 'She was Natalie Arno, Natalie Camargue, Camargue's only child.'

Pouring more wine for them, Mr Haq burst into a flowery laudation of various offerings among the entrées. There was caneton Kioga, wild duck breasts marinated in a succulent sauce of wine, cream and basil, or T-bone Toro, tender steaks *flambés*. Burden's expression was incredulous, faintly dismayed. Fortunately, his snapped 'Bring us some of that damned duck,' was lost on Mr Haq who responded only to Wexford's gentler request for two portions of caneton.

'I don't understand you,' Burden said coldly when Mr Haq had gone. 'Are you saying that the woman Camargue refused to recognize, the woman who deliberately cut her hand to avoid having to play the violin, whose antecedents you went rooting out all over America — that woman was Camargue's daughter all the time? We were wrong. Ames was right, Williams and Mavis Rolland and Mary Woodhouse and Philip Cory were right, but we were wrong. Camargue was wrong. Camargue was a senile half-blind old man who happened to make a mistake. Is that it?'

'I didn't say that,' said Wexford. 'I only said that Natalie Arno was Natalie Arno. Camargue made no mistake, though it would be true to say he misunderstood.' He sighed. 'We were such fools, Mike — you, me, Ames, Dinah Sternhold. Not one of us saw the simple truth, that though the woman who visited Camargue was not his daughter, she was not his daughter, if I may so put it, for just one day.'

'You see,' he went on, 'an illusion was created, as if by a clever trick. Only it was a trick we played upon ourselves. We were the conjurors and we held the mirrors. Dinah Sternhold told me Camargue said the woman who went to see him wasn't his daughter. I jumped to the conclusion — you did, Dinah did, we all did — that therefore the woman *we* knew as Natalie Arno wasn't his daughter. It never occurred to us he could be right and yet she might still be his daughter. It never occurred to us that the woman he saw might not be the woman who claimed to be his heir and lived in his house and inherited his money.'

'It wasn't Natalie who went there that day but it was Natalie before and always Natalie after that?' Burden made the face people do when they realize they have been conned by a stratagem unworthy of their calibre. 'Is that what you're saying?'

'Of course it is.' Wexford grinned and gave a rueful shake of the head. 'I may as well say here and now that Natalie wasn't the arch-villainess I took her for. She was cruel and devious and spiteful only in my imagination. Mind you, I'm not saying she was an angel of light. She may not have killed her father or plotted his death, but she connived at it afterwards and she had no scruples about taking an inheritance thus gained. Nor did she have any scruples about appropriating other women's husbands either on a temporary or a permanent basis. She was no paragon of virtue but she was no Messalina either. Why did I ever think she was? Largely, I'm ashamed to say, because Dinah Sternhold told me so.

'Now Dinah Sternhold is a very nice girl. If she blackened Natalie's character to me before I'd even met her, I'm sure it was unconscious. The thing with Dinah, you see, is that odd though it undoubtedly seems, she was genuinely in love with that old man. He was old enough to be her grandfather but she was as much in love with him as if he'd been fifty years younger. Have you ever noticed that it's only those who suffer most painfully from jealousy that say, "I haven't a jealous nature"? Dinah said that to me. She was deeply jealous of Natalie and perhaps with justification. For in marrying her, wasn't Camargue looking to replace his lost daughter? How then must she have felt when that lost daughter turned up? Dinah was jealous and in her jealousy, all unconsciously, without malice, she painted Natalie as a scheming adventuress and so angled the tale of the visit to Camargue to make her appear at once as a fraudulent claimant.'

'I'd like to hear your version of that visit.'

Wexford nodded. The duck had arrived, modestly veiled in a thick brown sauce. Wexford took a sip of his wine instead of a long draught, having decided with some soul-searching that it would hardly do to send for a second bottle. He sampled the duck, which wasn't too bad, and said after a few moments:

'The first appointment Natalie made with her father she couldn't keep. In the meantime something very disquieting had happened to her. She discovered a growth in one of her breasts.'

'How d'you know that?'

'A minute scar where the biopsy was done showed at the post-mortem,' said Wexford. 'Natalie went to her doctor and was sent to Guy's Hospital, the appointment being on the day she had arranged to go down to Sterries. She didn't want to talk to her father on the phone — I think we can call that a perfectly natural shrinking in the circumstances — so she got Jane Zoffany to do it. Shall I say here that Natalie was a congenital slave-owner and Jane Zoffany a born slave?

'Well, Jane made the call and a new date for the 19th. Natalie went to the hospital where they were unable to tell her whether the growth was malignant or not. She must come into their Hedley Atkins Unit in New Cross for a biopsy under anaesthetic.

'Now we're all of us afraid of cancer but Natalie maybe had more reason than most of us. She had seen her young husband die of leukaemia, a form of cancer, her friend Tina too, but most traumatic for her, her mother had died of it and died, it had been implied, through her daughter's actions. Moreover, at the time she had only been a few years older than Natalie then was. Small wonder if she was terrified.

'Then — due no doubt to some aberration on the part of the Post Office — the letter telling her she was to go into the Hedley Atkins Unit on 17 January didn't arrive till the morning before. This meant she couldn't go to Kingsmarkham on the 19th. I imagine she was past caring. All that mattered to her now was that she shouldn't have cancer, shouldn't have her beautiful figure spoilt, shouldn't live in dread of a recurrence or an early death. Jane Zoffany could deal with her father for her, phone or write or send a telegram.'

From staring down at his empty plate, Burden now lifted

his eyes and sat bolt upright. 'It was Jane Zoffany who came down here that day?'

Wexford nodded. 'Who else?'

'She too is thin and dark and about the right age. . . . But why? Why pose as Natalie? For whatever possible purpose?'

'It wasn't deliberate,' Wexford said a shade testily. 'Haven't I said scarcely anything in this case was deliberate, planned or premeditated? It was just typical silly muddled Jane Zoffany behaviour. And what months it took me to guess it! I suppose I had an inkling of the truth, that wet day in the garden at Sterries, when Dinah said how strange it was Natalie could get the solicitors and Camargue's old friends to believe in her, yet Camargue who wanted to believe, who was longing to believe, saw her *on that one occasion* and didn't believe in her for more than half an hour. And when Jane Zoffany said how the police had taken her for her own sister and then stuck her hand up over her mouth — I knew then, I didn't need to be told any more.'

'But she did tell you more?'

'Sure. When I talked to her last night. She filled in the gaps.'

'Why did she go down to Sterries at all?' asked Burden.

'Two reasons. She wanted to see the old man for herself — she'd been an admirer of his — and she didn't want his feelings hurt. She knew that if she phoned and told him Natalie had yet again to keep a hospital appointment he'd think she was making excuses not to see him and he'd be bitterly hurt. For nineteen years his daughter had stayed away from him and now that she had come back and they were on the brink of a reunion, he was to be fobbed off with a phone call — and a second phone call at that. So she decided to go down and see him herself. But not, of course, with any idea of posing as Natalie, nothing of that sort entered her head. It's just that she's a rather silly muddled creature who isn't always quite mentally stable.'

'You mean,' said Burden, 'that she came down here simply because it seemed kinder and more polite to call in person? She came to explain why Natalie couldn't come and — well, sort of assure him of Natalie's affection for him? Something like that?'

'Something very much like that. And also to get a look at

the man who had been acclaimed the world's greatest flautist.' Wexford caught Mr Haq's eye for their coffee. 'Now Camargue,' he said, 'was the first person to cast a doubt on Natalie's identity, it was Camargue who started all this, yet it was Camargue himself who took Jane Zoffany for his daughter because it was *his daughter that he expected to see.*

'He had waited for nineteen years — eventually without much hope. Hope had reawakened in the past five weeks and he was keyed up to a pitch of very high tension. He opened the door to her and put his arms round her and kissed her before she could speak. Did she try to tell him then that he had made a mistake? He was deaf. He was carried away with emotion. She has told me she was so confused and aghast that she played along with him while trying to decide what to do. She says she was embarrassed, she was afraid to disillusion him.

'She humoured him by speaking of the Cazzini gold flute — which Natalie had possibly mentioned to her but which was in any case clearly labelled — and having no knowledge of Italian, she mispronounced the name. We know what happened then. Camargue accused her of imposture. But it was no dream of Camargue's, no senile fantasy, that his visitor confessed. Jane Zoffany freely admitted what she had been longing to admit for the past half-hour — but it did her no good. Camargue was convinced by then this was a deception plotted to secure Natalie's inheritance and he turned her out of the house.

'And that, Mike, was all this so-called imposture ever amounted to, half an hour's misunderstanding between a well-meaning neurotic and a "foolish, fond old man." '

While Burden experimented yet again with ice cream eau-de-Nil, Wexford contented himself with coffee.

'Natalie,' he said, 'came out of hospital on January 20th and she was so elated that the biopsy had shown the growth to be benign that instead of being angry she was simply amused by Jane's activities. As I've said, she had a very lively sense of fun. I think it must have tickled her to imagine the pair of them at cross-purposes, the wretched Jane Zoffany confessing and the irate Camargue throwing her out. What did it matter, anyway?

She hadn't got cancer, she was fit and well and on top of the world and she could easily put that nonsense with her father right again. Let her only see if she could get a job out of Blaise Cory for her Johnny and then she'd see her father and patch things up.

'Before she could get around to that Camargue had written to her, informing her she should inherit nothing under the new will he intended to make.'

'Which led her,' said Burden, 'to plan on killing him first.'

'No, no, I've told you. There was no planning. Even after that letter I'm sure Natalie was confident she could make things smooth with her father. Perhaps she even thought, as Dinah says *she* did, that this could best be effected after the marriage. Natalie was not too concerned. She was amused. The mistake she made was in telling Fassbender. Probably for the first time Fassbender realized just how potentially wealthy a woman his girl friend actually was.'

'Why do you say for the first time?'

'If he'd known it before,' Wexford retorted, 'why hadn't he married her while they were both in California? That would have been a way of ensuring he didn't get deported. She was an American citizen. In those days, no doubt, she would have been willing enough to marry him, so if they didn't it must have been because he couldn't see there was anything in it for him. But now he did. Now he could see there was a very pleasant little sinecure here for the rest of their lives if only she wasn't so carefree and idle as to cast it all away.

'That Sunday Natalie went to a party with Jane Zoffany. She went because she liked parties, she liked enjoying herself, her whole life had been blithely dedicated to enjoying herself. There was no question of establishing an alibi. Nor, I'm sure, did she know Fassbender had taken himself off down to Kingsmarkham to spy out the land and have a look at the house and the affluence Natalie was apparently so indifferent to. It was on the impulse of the moment, in a sudden frenzy of — literally — taking things at the flood, that he seized Camargue and forced him into the water under the ice.'

For a moment they were both silent. Then Burden said:

'He told her what he'd done?'

A curious look came into Wexford's face. 'I suppose so. At any rate, she knew. By the time of the inquest she knew. How much she cared I don't know. She hadn't seen her father for nineteen years, but still he was her father. She didn't care enough to shop Fassbender, that's for sure. Indeed, you might say she cared so little that she was prepared to take considerable risks to *defend* Fassbender. No doubt, she liked what she got out of it. Life had been a bit precarious in the past four years, hadn't it? Once rid of Ilbert, it was a hand-to-mouth affair, and one imagines that while she was in De Beauvoir Place she was living solely on the rent from her house in Los Angeles. But now she had Sterries and the money and everything was fine. I'd like to think it was his murdering her father that began the process of going off Fassbender for Natalie, but we've no evidence of that.'

'What I don't understand is, since she *was* Natalie Arno, why did she play around half pretending she wasn't? It was a hell of a risk she was taking. She might have lost everything.'

'There wasn't any risk,' said Wexford. 'There wasn't the slightest risk. If she wasn't Natalie there might be many ways of apparently proving she was. But since she was Natalie it could never possibly be proved that she was not.'

'But why? Why do it?'

Burden had never had much sense of humour. And lately, perhaps since his marriage, Wexford thought, this limited faculty had become quiescent. 'For fun, Mike,' he said, 'for fun. Don't you think she got enormous fun out of it? After all, by that time she believed there was no question of our associating Camargue's death with foul play. What harm could she do herself or Fassbender by just ever so slightly hinting she might be the impostor Dinah Sternhold said she was? And it must have been fun, I can see that. It must have been hilarious dumbfounding us by answering Cory's questions and then really giving me hope by nicking her fingers with a bit of glass.

'I said we were fools. I reckon I was an arch fool. Did I really believe an impostor would have had her instructor with her on the very morning she knew we were coming? Did I really believe in such an enormous coincidence as Mary Woodhouse leaving that flat by chance the moment we entered it? What fun

Natalie must have got out of asking her old nanny or whatever she was to come round for a cup of coffee and then shooing her out when our car stopped outside. Oh, yes, it was all great fun, and as soon as it had gone far enough she had only to call in her dentist and prove beyond the shadow of a doubt who she was. For Williams is genuinely her dentist, a blameless person of integrity who happens to keep all his records and happens to have been in practice a long time.' Wexford caught Mr Haq's eye. 'D'you want any more coffee?'

'Don't think so,' said Burden.

'I may as well get the bill then.' Mr Haq glided over through the jungle. 'Once,' Wexford said, 'she had proved herself Natalie Arno to the satisfaction of Symonds, O'Brien and Ames, everything was plain sailing. The first thing to do was sell Sterries because it wouldn't do to have Fassbender show his face much around Kingsmarkham. But I think she was already beginning to go off Fassbender. Perhaps she saw that though he hadn't been prepared to marry her in America, even for the reward of legal residence there, he was anxious to do so now she was rich. Perhaps, after all, she simply decided there was no point in marrying. She hadn't done much of it, had she? Once only and she'd been a widow for nine years. And what would be the point of marrying when she now had plenty of money of her own and was happily independent? Still, this sort of speculation is useless. Suffice it to say that she had intended to marry Fassbender but she changed her mind. They quarrelled about it on the very eve of their going away on holiday together, and in his rage at being baulked of possession of the money he had killed for, had been to prison for, he attacked her and cut her throat.

'The body he put into that chest, which he locked, knowing it would be removed by Dorset's on the following day. Then off he went in the yellow Opel to Heathrow to use one of the two air tickets they had bought for their holiday in the South of France.'

Wexford paid the bill. It was modest, as always. By rights he ought, months ago, to have run Mr Haq in for offences under the Trade Descriptions Act. He would never do that now. They walked out into the High Street where the sun had unaccountably begun to shine. The pavements were drying up, the heavy grey clouds rushing at a great rate away to the horizon. At too great a rate, though, for more than temporary disappearance.

The Kingsbrook tumbled under the old stone bridge like a river in winter spate. Burden leaned over the parapet. 'You knew Fassbender when we came upon him in that place in France,' he said. 'I've been meaning to ask you how you did. You hadn't seen him in America, had you?'

'Of course I hadn't. He wasn't in America while I was. He'd been back here for over a year by then.'

'Then where had you seen him?'

'Here. Back at the very start of this case. Back in January just after Camargue died. He was at Sterries too, Mike. Can't you remember?'

'You saw him too,' Wexford went on. 'You said when we spotted him, "I've seen him somewhere before."'

Burden made a gesture of dismissal. 'Yes, I know I did. But I was mistaken. I couldn't have seen him, I was mixing him up with someone else. One wouldn't forget that name.'

Instead of replying, Wexford said, 'Fassbender's father was a Swiss who lived here without ever becoming naturalized. I don't know what his mother was or is, it hardly matters. John Fassbender was born here and has dual nationality, Swiss and British, not at all an uncommon thing. Ilbert had him deported to this country in 1976 but of course there was nothing to stop him going back into America again on his Swiss passport. When Romero shopped him three years later he was sent back to Switzerland but he soon returned here. Presumably, he liked it better here. Maybe he just preferred the inside of our prisons – he'd seen enough of them.'

'He's got a record, has he?'

Wexford laughed. 'Don't happen to have your German dictionary on you, do you?'

'Of course I don't carry dictionaries about with me.'

'Pity. I don't know why we've walked all the way up here. We'd better take shelter, it's going to rain again heavens hard.'

He hustled Burden down the steps into the Kingsbrook Precinct. A large drop of rain splashed against the brass plate of Symonds, O'Brien and Ames, a score more against the travel

742

agency's window, blurring the poster that still invited customers to sunny California.

'In here,' said Wexford and pushed open the door of the bookshop. The dictionaries section was down at the back on the left-hand side. Wexford took down a tome in a green-and-yellow jacket. 'I want you to look up a word. It won't be much use to you in your studies, I'm afraid, but if you want to know where you saw Fassbender before you'll have to find out what his name means.'

Burden put the book down on the counter and started on the Fs. He looked up. 'Spelt Fassbinder, a barrel maker, a maker of casks . . .'

'Well?'

'A cooper. . . .' He hesitated, then said slowly, 'John Cooper, thirty-six, Selden Road, Finsbury Park. He broke into Sterries the night after the inquest on Camargue.'

Wexford took the dictionary away from him and replaced it on the shelf. 'His father called himself Cooper during the war — Fassbender wasn't generally acceptable then, on the lines of Beethoven and German Shepherds, one supposes. Fassbender held his British passport in the name of Cooper and his Swiss as Fassbender.

'That burglary was the only bit of planning he and Natalie did and that was done on the spur of the moment. It was a desperate measure taken in what they saw as a desperate situation. What alerted Natalie, of course, was Mrs Murray-Burgess telling Muriel Hicks she'd seen a suspicious-looking character in the Sterries grounds and that without a doubt she'd know him again. The only thing was, she couldn't quite remember which night. Natalie and Fassbender knew which night, of course. They knew it was the night Camargue drowned. So they faked up a burglary. Natalie slept in her late father's room, not to keep away from the amorous marauding Zoffany, still less to wound the feelings of Muriel Hicks, but to be in a room where she could credibly have heard breaking glass and seen the van's number.

'She had to have seen that to facilitate our rapidly getting our hands on Fassbender. Then Mrs Murray-Burgess could do her worst — it was a burglar she had seen and not a killer. In the event, he served four months. He came out in June, with two months' remission for good conduct.'

'I only saw him once,' said Burden. 'I saw him down the station here when we charged him.'

'With nicking six silver spoons,' said Wexford. 'Come on, the rain's stopped.'

They went outside. Once more a bright sun had appeared, turning the puddles into blinding mirrors.

Burden said doubtfully, 'It was a bit of a long shot, wasn't it? I mean, weren't they — well, over-reacting? They were supposing in the first place that Mrs Murray-Burgess would come to us and secondly that if she did we'd connect the presence of a man in the Sterries garden on an unspecified night with an old man's accidental death.'

'There was more to it than that,' said Wexford with a grin. 'She'd seen me, you see.'

'Seen you? What d'you mean?'

'At the inquest. You said at the time people would think things and you were right. Someone must have told Natalie who I was, and that was enough. I only went there because our heating had broken down, I was looking for somewhere to get warm, but she didn't know that. She thought I was there because at that early stage we suspected foul play.'

Burden started to laugh.

'Come,' said Wexford, 'let us shut up the box and the puppets, for our play is played out.'

And in the uncertain sunshine they walked up the street to the police station.